THE
BOURNE
IDENTITY

ROBERT LUDLUM

BANTAM BOOKS
TORONTO · NEW YORK · LONDON

*This low-priced Bantam Book
has been completely reset in a type face
designed for easy reading, and was printed
from new plates. It contains the complete
text of the original hard-cover edition.*
NOT ONE WORD HAS BEEN OMITTED.

THE BOURNE IDENTITY

*A Bantam Book/published by arrangement with
The Robertmary Company*

PRINTING HISTORY
*Richard Marek edition published March 1980
6 printings through March 1980
Bantam export edition/June 1980*

*Acknowledgment and thanks are made for
permission to reprint articles from:
The Associated Press, © 1975 by The Associated Press.
The New York Times, © 1975 by The New York Times Company.*

ISBN 0-553-17030-9

Bantam Books are published by Bantam Books, Inc. Its trademark, consisting of the words "Bantam Books" and the por-
trayal of a bantam, is Registered in U. S. Patent and Trademark
Office and in other countries. Marca Registrada. Bantam
Books, Inc., 666 Fifth Avenue, New York, New York 10019.

PRINTED IN THE UNITED STATES OF AMERICA

0 9 8 7 6 5 4 3 2 1

For Glynis
A very special light we all adore.
With our love and deep respect.

PREFACE

The New York Times
Friday, July 11, 1975
FRONT PAGE

DIPLOMATS SAID TO BE LINKED WITH FUGITIVE TERRORIST KNOWN AS CARLOS

PARIS, July 10—France expelled three high-ranking Cuban diplomats today in connection with the worldwide search for a man called Carlos, who is believed to be an important link in an international terrorist network.

The suspect, whose real name is thought to be Ilich Ramirez Sanchez, is being sought in the killing of two French counterintelligence agents and a Lebanese informer at a Latin Quarter apartment on June 27.

The three killings have led the police here and in Britain to what they feel is the trail of a major network of international terrorist agents. In the search for Carlos after the killings, French and British policemen discovered large arms caches that linked Carlos to major terrorism in West Germany and led them to suspect a connection between many terrorist acts throughout Europe.

Reported Seen in London

Since then Carlos has been reported seen in London and in Beirut, Lebanon. . . .

Associated Press
Monday, July 7, 1975
syndicated dispatch

A DRAGNET FOR ASSASSIN

LONDON (AP)—Guns and girls, grenades and good suits, a fat billfold, airline tickets to romantic places and nice apartments in a half dozen world capitals. This is the portrait emerging of a jet age assassin being sought in an international manhunt.

The hunt began when the man answered his doorbell in Paris and shot dead two French intelligence agents and a Lebanese informer. It has put four women into custody in two capitals, accused of offenses in his wake. The assassin himself has vanished—perhaps in Lebanon, the French police believe.

In the past few days in London, those acquainted with him have described him to reporters as good looking, courteous, well educated, wealthy and fashionably dressed.

But his associates are men and women who have been called the most dangerous in the world. He is said to be linked with the Japanese Red Army, the Organization for the Armed Arab Struggle, the West German Baader-Meinhof gang, the Quebec Liberation Front, the Turkish Popular Liberation Front, separatists in France and Spain, and the Provisional wing of the Irish Republican Army.

When the assassin traveled—to Paris, to the Hague,

to West Berlin—bombs went off, guns cracked and there were kidnappings.

A breakthrough occurred in Paris when a Lebanese terrorist broke under questioning and led two intelligence men to the assassin's door in Paris on June 27. He shot all three to death and escaped. Police found his guns and notebooks containing "death lists" of prominent people.

Yesterday the London Observer said police were hunting for the son of a Venezuelan Communist lawyer for questioning in the triple slaying. Scotland Yard said, "We are not denying the report," but added there was no charge against him and he was wanted only for questioning.

The Observer identified the hunted man as Ilich Ramirez Sanchez, of Caracas. It said his name was on one of the four passports found by French police when they raided the Paris apartment where the slayings took place.

The newspaper said Ilich was named after Vladimir Ilych Lenin, founder of the Soviet state, and was educated in Moscow and speaks fluent Russian.

In Caracas, a spokesman for the Venezuelan Communist Party said Ilich is the son of a 70-year-old Marxist lawyer living 450 miles west of Caracas, but "neither father nor son belong to our party."

He told reporters he did not know where Ilich was now.

BOOK I

BOOK I

— 1 —

The trawler plunged into the angry swells of the dark, furious sea like an awkward animal trying desperately to break out of an impenetrable swamp. The waves rose to goliathan heights, crashing into the hull with the power of raw tonnage; the white sprays caught in the night sky cascaded downward over the deck under the force of the night wind. Everywhere there were the sounds of inanimate pain, wood straining against wood, ropes twisting, stretched to the breaking point. The animal was dying.

Two abrupt explosions pierced the sounds of the sea and the wind and the vessel's pain. They came from the dimly lit cabin that rose and fell with its host body. A man lunged out of the door grasping the railing with one hand, holding his stomach with the other.

A second man followed, the pursuit cautious, his intent violent. He stood bracing himself in the cabin door; he raised a gun and fired again. And again.

The man at the railing whipped both his hands up to his head, arching backward under the impact of the fourth bullet. The trawler's bow dipped suddenly into the valley of two giant waves, lifting the wounded man off his feet; he twisted to his left unable to take his hands away from his head. The boat surged upward, bow and midships more out of the water than in it, sweeping the figure in the doorway back into the cabin, a fifth gunshot fired wildly. The wounded man screamed, his hands now lashing out at anything he could grasp, his eyes blinded by blood and the unceasing spray of the sea. There was nothing he could grab, so he grabbed at nothing; his legs buckled as his body lurched forward. The boat rolled violently leeward and the man whose skull was ripped open plunged over the side into the madness of the darkness below.

He felt rushing cold water envelop him, swallowing him, sucking him under, and twisting him in circles, then propelling him up to the surface—only to gasp a single breath of air. A gasp and he was under again.

And there was heat, a strange moist heat at his temple that seared through the freezing water that kept swallowing him, a fire where no fire should burn. There was ice, too; an icelike throbbing in his stomach and his legs and his chest, oddly warmed by the cold sea around him. He felt these things, acknowledging his own panic as he felt them. He could see his own body turning and twisting, arms and feet working frantically against the pressures of the whirlpool. He could feel, think, see, perceive panic and struggle—yet strangely there was peace. It was the calm of the observer, the uninvolved observer, separated from the events, knowing of them but not essentially involved.

Then another form of panic spread through him, surging through the heat and the ice and the uninvolved recognition. He could not submit to peace! Not yet! It would happen any second now; he was not sure what it was, but it would happen. He had to *be* there!

He kicked furiously, clawing at the heavy walls of water above, his chest burning. He broke surface, thrashing to stay on top of the black swells. Climb up! *Climb up!*

A monstrous rolling wave accommodated; he was on the crest, surrounded by pockets of foam and darkness. Nothing. Turn! *Turn!*

It happened. The explosion was massive; he could hear it through the clashing waters and the wind, the sight and the sound somehow his doorway to peace. The sky lit up like a fiery diadem and within that crown of fire, objects of all shapes and sizes were blown through the light into the outer shadows.

He had won. Whatever it was, he had won.

Suddenly he was plummeting downward again, into an abyss again. He could feel the rushing waters crash over his shoulders, cooling the white-hot heat at his temple, warming the ice-cold incisions in his stomach and his legs and. . . .

His chest. His chest was in agony! He had been struck—the blow crushing, the impact sudden and intolerable. It happened again! *Let me alone. Give me peace.*

And again!

And he clawed again, and kicked again . . . until he felt it. A thick, oily object that moved only with the movements of the sea. He could not tell what it was, but it was there and he could feel it, hold it.

Hold it! It will ride you to peace. To the silence of darkness . . . and peace.

The rays of the early sun broke through the mists of the eastern sky, lending glitter to the calm waters of the Mediterranean. The skipper of the small fishing boat, his eyes bloodshot, his hands marked with rope burns, sat on the stern gunnel smoking a Gauloise, grateful for the sight of the smooth sea. He glanced over at the open wheelhouse; his younger brother was easing the throttle forward to make better time, the single other crewman checking a net several feet away. They were laughing at something and that was good; there had been nothing to laugh about last night. Where had the storm come from? The weather reports from Marseilles had indicated nothing; if they had he would have stayed in the shelter of the coastline. He wanted to reach the fishing grounds eighty kilometers south of La Seyne-sur-Mer by daybreak, but not at the expense of costly repairs, and what repairs were not costly these days?

Or at the expense of his life, and there were moments last night when that was a distinct consideration.

"*Tu es fatigué, hein, mon frère?*" his brother shouted, grinning at him. "*Va te coucher maintenant. Laisse-moi faire.*"

"*D'accord,*" the brother answered, throwing his cigarette over the side and sliding down to the deck on top of a net. "A little sleep won't hurt."

It was good to have a brother at the wheel. A member of

the family should always be the pilot on a family boat; the eyes were sharper. Even a brother who spoke with the smooth tongue of a literate man as opposed to his own coarse words. Crazy! One year at the university and his brother wished to start a *compagnie*. With a single boat that had seen better days many years ago. Crazy. What good did his books do last night? When his *compagnie* was about to capsize.

He closed his eyes, letting his hands soak in the rolling water on the deck. The salt of the sea would be good for the rope burns. Burns received while lashing equipment that did not care to stay put in the storm.

"Look! Over there!"

It was his brother; apparently sleep was to be denied by sharp family eyes.

"What is it?" he yelled.

"Port bow! There's a man in the water! He's holding on to something! A piece of debris, a plank of some sort."

The skipper took the wheel, angling the boat to the right of the figure in the water, cutting the engines to reduce the wake. The man looked as though the slightest motion would send him sliding off the fragment of wood he clung to; his hands were white, gripped around the edge like claws, but the rest of his body was limp—as limp as a man fully drowned, passed from this world.

"Loop the ropes!" yelled the skipper to his brother and the crewman. "Submerge them around his legs. Easy now! Move them up to his waist. Pull gently."

"His hands won't let go of the plank!"

"Reach down! Pry them up! It may be the death lock."

"No. He's alive . . . but barely, I think. His lips move, but there's no sound. His eyes also, though I doubt he sees us."

"The hands are free!"

"Lift him up. Grab his shoulders and pull him over. *Easy*, now!"

"Mother of God, look at his head!" yelled the crewman. "It's split open."

"He must have crashed it against the plank in the storm," said the brother.

"No," disagreed the skipper, staring at the wound. "It's a clean slice, razorlike. Caused by a bullet; he was shot."

"You can't be sure of that."

"In more than one place," added the skipper, his eyes roving over the body. "We'll head for Ile de Port Noir; it's the nearest island. There's a doctor on the waterfront."

"The Englishman?"

"He practices."

"When he can," said the skipper's brother. "When the wine lets him. He has more success with his patients' animals than with his patients."

"It won't matter. This will be a corpse by the time we get there. If by chance he lives, I'll bill him for the extra petrol and whatever catch we miss. Get the kit; we'll bind his head for all the good it will do."

"Look!" cried the crewman. "Look at his eyes."

"What about them?" asked the brother.

"A moment ago they were gray—as gray as steel cables. Now they're blue!"

"The sun's brighter," said the skipper, shrugging. "Or it's playing tricks with your own eyes. No matter, there's no color in the grave."

Intermittent whistles of fishing boats clashed with the incessant screeching of the gulls; together they formed the universal sounds of the waterfront. It was late afternoon, the sun a fireball in the west, the air still and too damp, too hot. Above the piers and facing the harbor was a cobblestone street and several blemished white houses, separated by overgrown grass shooting up from dried earth and sand. What remained of the verandas were patched latticework and crumbling stucco supported by hastily implanted pilings. The residences had seen better days a number of decades ago when the residents mistakenly believed Ile de Port Noir might become another Mediterranean playground. It never did.

All the houses had paths to the street, but the last house in the row had a path obviously more trampled than the others. It belonged to an Englishman who had come to Port Noir eight years before under circumstances no one understood or cared to; he was a doctor and the waterfront had need of a doctor. Hooks, needles and knives were at once means of livelihood as well as instruments of incapacitation. If one saw *le docteur* on a good day, the sutures were not too bad. On the other hand, if the stench of wine or whiskey was too pronounced, one took one's chances.

Tant pis! He was better than no one.

But not today; no one used the path today. It was Sunday and it was common knowledge that on any Saturday night the doctor was roaring drunk in the village, ending the evening with whatever whore was available. Of course, it was also granted that during the past few Saturdays the doctor's routine had altered; he had not been seen in the village. But nothing ever changed that much; bottles of scotch were sent to the doctor on a regular basis. He was simply staying in his house; he had been doing so since the fishing boat from La Ciotat had brought in the unknown man who was more corpse than man.

Dr. Geoffrey Washburn awoke with a start, his chin settled into his collarbone causing the odor of his mouth to invade his nostrils; it was not pleasant. He blinked, orienting himself, and glanced at the open bedroom door. Had his nap been interrupted by another incoherent monologue from his patient? No; there was no sound. Even the gulls outside were mercifully quiet; it was Ile de Port Noir's holy day, no boats coming in to taunt the birds with their catches.

Washburn looked at the empty glass and the half-empty bottle of whiskey on the table beside his chair. It was an improvement. On a normal Sunday both would be empty by now, the pain of the previous night having been spiraled out by the scotch. He smiled to himself, once again blessing an older sister in Coventry who made the scotch possible with her monthly stipend. She was a good girl, Bess was, and God knew she could afford a hell of a lot more than she sent him, but he was grateful she did what she did. And one day she would stop, the money would stop, and then the oblivions would be achieved with the cheapest wine until there was no pain at all. Ever.

He had come to accept that eventuality . . . until three weeks and five days ago when the half-dead stranger had been dragged from the sea and brought to his door by fishermen who did not care to identify themselves. Their errand was one of mercy, not involvement. God would understand; the man had been shot.

What the fishermen had not known was that far more than bullets had invaded the man's body. And mind.

The doctor pushed his gaunt frame out of the chair and walked unsteadily to the window overlooking the harbor.

[12]

He lowered the blind, closing his eyes to block out the sun, then squinted between the slats to observe the activity in the street below, specifically the reason for the clatter. It was a horse-drawn cart, a fisherman's family out for a Sunday drive. Where the hell else could one see such a sight? And then he remembered the carriages and the finely groomed geldings that threaded through London's Regent Park with tourists during the summer months; he laughed out loud at the comparison. But his laughter was short-lived, replaced by something unthinkable three weeks ago. He had given up all hope of seeing England again. It was possible that might be changed now. The stranger could change it.

Unless his prognosis was wrong, it would happen any day, any hour or minute. The wounds to the legs, stomach, and chest were deep and severe, quite possibly fatal were it not for the fact the bullets had remained where they had lodged, self-cauterized and continuously cleansed by the sea. Extracting them was nowhere near as dangerous as it might have been, the tissue primed, softened, sterilized, ready for an immediate knife. The cranial wound was the real problem; not only was the penetration subcutaneous, but it appeared to have bruised the thalamus and hippocampus fibrous regions. Had the bullet entered millimeters away on either side the vital functions would have ceased; they had not been impeded, and Washburn had made a decision. He went dry for thirty-six hours, eating as much starch and drinking as much water as was humanly possible. Then he performed the most delicate piece of work he had attempted since his dismissal from Macleans Hospital in London. Millimeter by agonizing millimeter he had brush-washed the fibrous areas, then stretched and sutured the skin over the cranial wound, knowing that the slightest error with brush, needle, or clamp would cause the patient's death.

He had not wanted this unknown patient to die for any number of reasons. But especially one.

When it was over and the vital signs had remained constant, Dr. Geoffrey Washburn went back to his chemical and psychological appendage. His bottle. He had gotten drunk and he had remained drunk, but he had not gone over the edge. He knew exactly where he was and what he was doing at all times. Definitely an improvement.

Any day now, any hour perhaps, the stranger would focus his eyes and intelligible words would emerge from his lips.

Even any moment.

The words came first. They floated in the air as the early morning breeze off the sea cooled the room.

"Who's there? Who's in this room?"

Washburn sat up in the cot, moved his legs quietly over the side, and rose slowly to his feet. It was important to make no jarring note, no sudden noise or physical movement that might frighten the patient into a psychological regression. The next few minutes would be as delicate as the surgical procedures he had performed; the doctor in him was prepared for the moment.

"A friend," he said softly.

"Friend?"

"You speak English. I thought you would. American or Canadian is what I suspected. Your dental work didn't come from the UK or Paris. How do you feel?"

"I'm not sure."

"It will take awhile. Do you need to relieve your bowels?"

"What?"

"Take a crapper, old man. That's what the pan's for beside you. The white one on your left. When we make it in time, of course."

"I'm sorry."

"Don't be. Perfectly normal function. I'm a doctor, *your* doctor. My name is Geoffrey Washburn. What's yours?"

"What?"

"I asked you what your name was."

The stranger moved his head and stared at the white wall streaked with shafts of morning light. Then he turned back, his blue eyes leveled at the doctor. "I don't know."

"Oh, my God."

"I've told you over and over again. It will take time. The more you fight it, the more you crucify yourself, the worse it will be."

"You're drunk."

"Generally. It's not pertinent. But I can give you clues, if you'll listen."

"I've listened."

"No, you don't; you turn away. You lie in your cocoon and pull the cover over your mind. Hear me again."

"I'm listening."

"In your coma—your prolonged coma—you spoke in three different languages. English, French and some god-damned twangy thing I presume is Oriental. That means you're multilingual; you're at home in various parts of the world. Think geographically. What's most comfortable for you?"

"Obviously English."

"We've agreed to that. So what's most *un*comfortable?"

"I don't know."

"Your eyes are round, not sloped. I'd say obviously the Oriental."

"Obviously."

"Then why do you speak it? Now, think in terms of association. I've written down words; listen to them. I'll say them phonetically. *Ma—kwa. Tam—kwan. Kee—sah.* Say the first thing that comes to mind."

"Nothing."

"Good show."

"What the hell do you want?"

"Something. Anything."

"You're drunk."

"We've agreed to that. Consistently. I also saved your bloody life. Drunk or not, I *am* a doctor. I was once a very good one."

"What happened?"

"The patient questions the doctor?"

"Why not?"

Washburn paused, looking out the window at the water-front. "I was drunk," he said. "They said I killed two patients on the operating table because I was drunk. I could have gotten away with one. Not two. They see a pattern very quickly, God bless them. Don't ever give a man like me a knife and cloak it in respectability."

"Was it necessary?"

"Was what necessary?"

"The bottle."

"Yes, damn you," said Washburn softly, turning from the window. "It was and it is. And the patient is not permitted to make judgments where the physician is concerned."

"Sorry."

"You also have an annoying habit of apologizing. It's an overworked protestation and not at all natural. I don't for a minute believe you're an apologetic person."

"Then you know something I don't know."

"About you, yes. A great deal. And very little of it makes sense."

The man sat forward in the chair. His open shirt fell away from his taut frame, exposing the bandages on his chest and stomach. He folded his hands in front of him, the veins in his slender, muscular arms pronounced. "Other than the things we've talked about?"

"Yes."

"Things I said while in coma?"

"No, not really. We've discussed most of that gibberish. The languages, your knowledge of geography—cities I've never or barely heard of—your obsession for avoiding the use of names, names you want to say but won't; your propensity for confrontation—attack, recoil, hide, run—all rather violent, I might add. I frequently strapped your arms down, to protect the wounds. But we've covered all that. There are other things."

"What do you mean? What are they? Why haven't you told me?"

"Because they're physical. The outer shell, as it were. I wasn't sure you were ready to hear. I'm not sure now."

The man leaned back in the chair, dark eyebrows below the dark brown hair joined in irritation. "Now it's the physician's judgment that isn't called for. I'm ready. What are you talking about?"

"Shall we begin with that rather acceptable looking head of yours? The face, in particular."

"What about it?"

"It's not the one you were born with."

"What do you mean?"

"Under a thick glass, surgery always leaves its mark. You've been altered, old man."

"Altered?"

"You have a pronounced chin; I daresay there was a cleft in it. It's been removed. Your upper left cheekbone—your cheekbones are also pronounced, conceivably Slavic generations ago—has minute traces of a surgical scar. I would venture to say a mole was eliminated. Your nose is an English nose, at one time slightly more prominent than it is now. It was thinned ever so subtly. Your very sharp features have been softened, the character submerged. Do you understand what I'm saying?"

"No."

"You're a reasonably attractive man but your face is more distinguished by the category it falls into than by the face itself."

"Category?"

"Yes. You're the prototype of the white Anglo-Saxon people see every day on the better cricket fields, or the tennis court. Or the bar at Mirabel's. Those faces become almost indistinguishable from one another, don't they? The features properly in place, the teeth straight, the ears flat against the head—nothing out of balance, everything in position and just a little bit soft."

"Soft?"

"Well, 'spoiled' is perhaps a better word. Definitely self-assured, even arrogant, used to having your own way."

"I'm still not sure what you're trying to say."

"Try this then. Change the color of your hair, you change the face. Yes, there are traces of discoloration, brittleness, dye. Wear glasses and a mustache, you're a different man. I'd guess you were in your middle to late thirties, but you could be ten years older, or five younger." Washburn paused, watching the man's reactions, as if wondering whether or not to proceed. "And speaking of glasses, do you remember those exercises, the tests we ran a week ago?"

"Of course."

"Your eyesight's perfectly normal; you have no need of glasses."

"I didn't think I did."

"Then why is there evidence of prolonged use of contact lenses about your retinas and lids?"

"I don't know. It doesn't make sense."

"May I suggest a possible explanation?"

"I'd like to hear it."

"You may not." The doctor returned to the window and peered absently outside. "Certain types of contact lenses are designed to change the color of the eyes. And certain types of eyes lend themselves more readily than others to the device. Usually those that have a gray or bluish hue; yours are a cross. Hazel-gray in one light, blue in another. Nature favored you in this regard; no altering was either possible or required."

"Required for what?"

"For changing your appearance. Very professionally, I'd say. Visas, passport, driver's licenses—switched at will. Hair: brown, blond, auburn. Eyes—can't tamper with the eyes—green, gray, blue? The possibilities are far-ranging, wouldn't you say? All within that recognizable category in which the faces are blurred with repetition."

The man got out of the chair with difficulty, pushing himself up with his arms, holding his breath as he rose. "It's also possible that you're reaching. You could be way out of line."

"The traces are there, the markings. That's evidence."

"Interpreted by you, with a heavy dose of cynicism thrown in. Suppose I had an accident and was patched up? That would explain the surgery."

"Not the kind you had. Dyed hair and the removal of clefts and moles aren't part of a restoration process."

"You don't *know* that!" said the unknown man angrily. "There are different kinds of accidents, different procedures. You weren't there; you can't be certain."

"Good! Get furious with me. You don't do it half often enough. And while you're mad, *think*. What were you? What *are* you?"

"A salesman . . . an executive with an international company, specializing in the Far East. That could be it. Or a teacher . . . of languages. In a university somewhere. That's possible, too."

"Fine. Choose one. Now!"

"I . . . I *can't*." The man's eyes were on the edge of helplessness.

"Because you don't believe either one."

The man shook his head. "No. Do you?"

"No," said Washburn. "For a specific reason. Those occupations are relatively sedentary and you have the body of a man who's been subjected to physical stress. Oh, I don't mean a trained athlete or anything like that; you're no jock, as they say. But your muscle tone's firm, your arms and hands used to strain and quite strong. Under other circumstances, I might judge you to be a laborer, accustomed to carrying heavy objects, or a fisherman, conditioned by hauling in nets all day long. But your range of knowledge, I daresay your intellect, rules out such things."

"Why do I get the idea that you're leading up to something? Something else."

"Because we've worked together, closely and under pressure, for several weeks now. You spot a pattern."

"I'm right then?"

"Yes. I had to see how you'd accept what I've just told you. The previous surgery, the hair, the contact lenses."

"Did I pass?"

"With infuriating equilibrium. It's time now; there's no point in putting it off any longer. Frankly, I haven't the patience. Come with me." Washburn preceded the man through the living room to the door in the rear wall that led to the dispensary. Inside, he went to the corner and picked up an antiquated projector, the shell of its thick round lens rusted and cracked. "I had this brought in with the supplies from Marseilles," he said, placing it on the small desk and inserting the plug into the wall socket. "It's hardly the best equipment, but it serves the purpose. Pull the blinds, will you?"

The man with no name or memory went to the window and lowered the blind; the room was dark. Washburn snapped on the projector's light; a bright square appeared on the white wall. He then inserted a small piece of celluloid behind the lens.

The square was abruptly filled with magnified letters.

GEMEINSCHAFT BANK
BAHNHOFSTRASSE. ZURICH.
ZERO—SEVEN—SEVENTEEN—TWELVE—ZERO—
FOURTEEN—TWENTY-SIX—ZERO

"What is it?" asked the nameless man.

"Look at it. Study it. *Think*."

"It's a bank account of some kind."

"Exactly. The printed letterhead and address is the bank, the handwritten numbers take the place of a name, but insofar as they *are* written out, they constitute the signature of the account holder. Standard procedure."

"Where did you get it?"

"From you. This is a very small negative, my guess would be half the size of a thirty-five millimeter film. It was implanted—surgically implanted—beneath the skin above your right hip. The numbers are in your handwriting; it's your signature. With it you can open a vault in Zurich."

—— 2 ——

They chose the name Jean-Pierre. It neither startled nor offended anyone, a name as common to Port Noir as any other.

And books came from Marseilles, six of them in varying sizes and thicknesses, four in English, two in French. They were medical texts, volumes that dealt with injuries to the head and mind. There were cross-sections of the brain, hundreds of unfamiliar words to absorb and try to understand. *Lobus occipitalis* and *temporalis,* the *cortex* and the connecting fibers of the *corpus callosum;* the *limbic system*—specifically the *hippocampus* and *mammillary bodies* that together with the *fornix* were indispensable to memory and recall. Damaged, there was amnesia.

There were psychological studies of emotional stress that produced *stagnate hysteria* and *mental aphasia,* conditions which also resulted in partial or total loss of memory. Amnesia.

Amnesia.

"There are no rules," said the dark-haired man, rubbing his eyes in the inadequate light of the table lamp. "It's a geometric puzzle; it can happen in any combination of ways. Physically or psychologically—or a little of both. It can be permanent or temporary, all or part. No *rules!*"

"Agreed," said Washburn, sipping his whiskey in a chair across the room. "But I think we're getting closer to what happened. What I *think* happened."

"Which was?" asked the man apprehensively.

"You just said it: 'a little of both.' Although the word 'little' should be changed to 'massive.' Massive shocks."

"Massive shocks to what?"

"The physical *and* the psychological. They were related, interwoven—two strands of experience, or stimulae, that became knotted."

"How much sauce have you had?"

"Less than you think; it's irrelevant." The doctor picked up a clipboard filled with pages. "This is your history—your new history—begun the day you were brought here. Let me summarize. The physical wounds tell us that the situation in which you found yourself was packed with psychological stress, the subsequent hysteria brought on by at least nine hours in the water, which served to solidify the psychological damage. The darkness, the violent movement, the lungs barely getting air; these were the instruments of hysteria. Everything that preceded it—the hysteria—had to be erased so you could cope, survive. Are you with me?"

"I think so. The head was protecting itself."

"Not the head, the mind. Make the distinction; it's important. We'll get back to the head, but we'll give it a label. The brain."

"All right. Mind, not head . . . which is really the brain."

"Good." Washburn flipped his thumb through the pages on the clipboard. "These are filled with several hundred observations. There are the normal medicinal inserts—dosage, time, reaction, that sort of thing—but in the main they deal with *you*, the man himself. The words you use, the words you react to; the phrases you employ—when I can write them down—both rationally and when you talk in your sleep and when you were in coma. Even the way you walk, the way you talk or tense your body when startled or seeing something that interests you. You appear to be a mass of contradictions; there's a subsurface violence almost always in control, but very much alive. There's also a pensiveness that seems painful for you, yet you rarely

[21]

give vent to the anger that pain must provoke."

"You're provoking it now," interrupted the man. "We've gone over the words and the phrases time and time again—"

"And we'll continue to do so," broke in Washburn, "as long as there's progress."

"I wasn't aware any progress had been made."

"Not in terms of an identity or an occupation. But we *are* finding out what's most comfortable for you, what you deal with best. It's a little frightening."

"In what way?"

"Let me give you an example." The doctor put the clipboard down and got out of the chair. He walked to a primitive cupboard against the wall, opened a drawer, and took out a large automatic handgun. The man with no memory tensed in his chair; Washburn was aware of the reaction. "I've never used this, not sure I'd know how to, but I do live on the waterfront." He smiled, then suddenly, without warning, threw it to the man. The weapon was caught in midair, the catch clean, swift, and confident. "Break it down; I believe that's the phrase."

"What?"

"Break it down. *Now.*"

The man looked at the gun. And then, in silence, his hands and fingers moved expertly over the weapon. In less than thirty seconds it was completely dismantled. He looked up at the doctor.

"See what I mean?" said Washburn. "Among your skills is an extraordinary knowledge of firearms."

"Army?" asked the man, his voice intense, once more apprehensive.

"Extremely unlikely," replied the doctor. "When you first came out of coma, I mentioned your dental work. I assure you it's not military. And, of course, the surgery, I'd say, would totally rule out any military association."

"Then what?"

"Let's not dwell on it now; let's go back to what happened. We were dealing with the mind, remember? The psychological stress, the hysteria. Not the physical brain, but the mental pressures. Am I being clear?"

"Go on."

"As the shock recedes, so do the pressures, until there's no fundamental need to protect the psyche. As this process takes place, your skills and talents will come back to you.

[22]

You'll remember certain behavior patterns; you may live them out quite naturally, your surface reactions instinctive. But there's a gap and everything in those pages tell me it's irreversible." Washburn stopped and went back to his chair and his glass. He sat down and drank, closing his eyes in weariness.

"Go *on*," whispered the man.

The doctor opened his eyes, leveling them at his patient. "We return to the head, which we've labeled the brain. The *physical* brain with its millions upon millions of cells and interacting components. You've read the books; the fornix and the limbic system, the hippocampus fibers and the thalamus; the callosum and especially the lobotomic surgical techniques. The slightest alteration can cause dramatic changes. That's what happened to you. The damage was *physical*. It's as though blocks were rearranged, the *physical* structure no longer what it was." Again Washburn stopped.

"*And*," pressed the man.

"The recessed psychological pressures will allow—*are* allowing—your skills and talents to come back to you. But I don't think you'll ever be able to relate them to anything in your past."

"Why? Why not?"

"Because the physical conduits that permit and transmit those memories have been altered. Physically rearranged to the point where they no longer function as they once did. For all intents and purposes, they've been destroyed."

The man sat motionless. "The answer's in Zurich," he said.

"Not yet. You're not ready; you're not strong enough."

"I will be."

"Yes, you will."

The weeks passed; the verbal exercises continued as the pages grew and the man's strength returned. It was midmorning of the nineteenth week, the day bright, the Mediterranean calm and glistening. As was the man's habit he had run for the past hour along the waterfront and up into the hills; he had stretched the distance to something over twelve miles daily, the pace increasing daily, the rests less frequent. He sat in the chair by the bedroom window, breathing heavily, sweat drenching his undershirt. He had come in through the back door, entering the bedroom from

[23]

the dark hallway that passed the living room. It was simply easier; the living room served as Washburn's waiting area and there were still a few patients with cuts and gashes to be repaired. They were sitting in chairs looking frightened, wondering what *le docteur*'s condition would be that morning. Actually, it wasn't bad. Geoffrey Washburn still drank like a mad Cossack, but these days he stayed on his horse. It was as if a reserve of hope had been found in the recesses of his own destructive fatalism. And the man with no memory understood; that hope was tied to a bank in Zurich's Bahnhofstrasse. Why did the street come so easily to mind?

The bedroom door opened and the doctor burst in, grinning, his white coat stained with his patient's blood.

"I did it!" he said, more triumph in his words than clarification. "I should open my own hiring hall and live on commissions. It'd be steadier."

"What are you talking about?"

"As we agreed, it's what you need. You've *got* to function on the outside, and as of two minutes ago Monsieur Jean-Pierre No-Name is gainfully employed! At least for a week."

"How did you do that? I thought there weren't any openings."

"What was about to be opened was Claude Lamouche's infected leg. I explained that my supply of local anesthetic was very, *very* limited. We negotiated; you were the bartered coin."

"A week?"

"If you're any good, he may keep you on." Washburn paused. "Although that's not terribly important, is it?"

"I'm not sure any of this is. A month ago, maybe, but not now. I told you. I'm ready to leave. I'd think you'd want me to. I have an appointment in Zurich."

"And I'd prefer you function the very best you can at that appointment. My interests are extremely selfish, no remissions permitted."

"I'm ready."

"On the surface, yes. But take my word for it, it's vital that you spend prolonged periods of time on the water, some of it at night. Not under controlled conditions, not as a passenger, but subjected to reasonably harsh conditions— the harsher the better, in fact."

"Another test?"

"Every single one I can devise in this primitive Menningers of Port Noir. If I could conjure up a storm and a minor shipwreck for you, I would. On the other hand, Lamouche is something of a storm himself; he's a difficult man. The swelling in his leg will go down and he'll resent you. So will others; you'll have to replace someone."

"Thanks a lot."

"Don't mention it. We're combining two stresses. At least one or two nights on the water, if Lamouche keeps to schedule—that's the hostile environment which contributed to your hysteria—and exposure to resentment and suspicion from men around you—symbolic of the initial stress situation."

"Thanks again. Suppose they decide to throw me overboard? That'd be your ultimate test, I suppose, but I don't know how much good it would do if I drowned."

"Oh, there'll be nothing like that," said Washburn, scoffing.

"I'm glad you're so confident. I wish I were."

"You can be. You have the protection of my presence. I may not be Christiaan Barnard or Michael De Bakey, but I'm all these people have. They need me; they won't risk losing me."

"But you want to leave. I'm your passport out."

"In ways unfathomable, my dear patient. Come on, now. Lamouche wants you down at the dock so you can familiarize yourself with his equipment. You'll be starting out at four o'clock tomorrow morning. Consider how beneficial a week at sea will be. Think of it as a cruise."

There had never been a cruise like it. The skipper of the filthy, oil-soaked fishing boat was a foul-mouthed rendering of an insignificant Captain Bligh; the crew a quartet of misfits who were undoubtedly the only men in Port Noir willing to put up with Claude Lamouche. The regular fifth member was a brother of the chief netman, a fact impressed on the man called Jean-Pierre within minutes after leaving the harbor at four o'clock in the morning.

"You take food from my brother's table!" whispered the netman angrily between rapid puffs on an immobile cigarette. "From the stomachs of his children!"

"It's only for a week," protested Jean-Pierre. It would have been easier—far easier—to offer to reimburse the unemployed brother from Washburn's monthly stipend, but the doctor and his patient had agreed to refrain from such compromises.

"I hope you're good with the nets!"

He was not.

There were moments during the next seventy-two hours when the man called Jean-Pierre thought the alternative of financial appeasement was warranted. The harassment never stopped, even at night—especially at night. It was as though eyes were trained on him as he lay on the infested deck mattress, waiting for him to reach the brink of sleep.

"You! Take the watch! The mate is sick. You fill in."

"Get up! Philippe is writing his memoirs! He can't be disturbed."

"On your feet! You tore a net this afternoon. We won't pay for your stupidity. We've all agreed. Fix it now!"

The nets.

If two men were required for one flank, his two arms took the place of four. If he worked beside one man, there were abrupt hauls and releases that left him with the full weight, a sudden blow from an adjacent shoulder sending him crashing into the gunnel and nearly over the side.

And Lamouche. A limping maniac who measured each kilometer of water by the fish he had lost. His voice was a grating, static-prone bullhorn. He addressed no one without an obscenity preceding his name, a habit the patient found increasingly maddening. But Lamouche did not touch Washburn's patient; he was merely sending the doctor a message: *Don't ever do this to me again. Not where my boat and my fish are concerned.*

Lamouche's schedule called for a return to Port Noir at sundown on the third day, the fish to be unloaded, the crew given until four the next morning to sleep, fornicate, get drunk, or, with luck, all three. As they came within sight of land, it happened.

The nets were being doused and folded at midships by the netman and his first assistant. The unwelcomed crewman they cursed as "Jean-Pierre Sangsue" ("the Leech") scrubbed down the deck with a long-handled brush. The two remaining crew heaved buckets of sea water in front of the brush, more often than not drenching the Leech with truer aim than the deck.

A bucketful was thrown too high, momentarily blinding Washburn's patient, causing him to lose his balance. The heavy brush with its metal-like bristles flew out of his hands, its head upended, the sharp bristles making contact with the kneeling netman's thigh.

"*Merde alors!*"

"*Désolé,*" said the offender casually, shaking the water from his eyes.

"The hell you say!" shouted the netman.

"I said I was sorry," replied the man called Jean-Pierre. "Tell your friends to wet the deck, not me."

"My friends don't make me the object of their stupidity!"

"They were the cause of mine just now."

The netman grabbed the handle of the brush, got to his feet, and held it out like a bayonet. "You want to play, Leech?"

"Come on, give it to me."

"With pleasure, Leech. Here!" The netman shoved the brush forward, downward, the bristles scraping the patient's chest and stomach, penetrating the cloth of his shirt.

Whether it was the contact with the scars that covered his previous wounds, or the frustration and anger resulting from three days of harassment, the man would never know. He only knew he had to respond. And his response was as alarming to him as anything he could imagine.

He gripped the handle with his right hand, jamming it back into the netman's stomach, pulling it forward at the instant of impact; simultaneously, he shot his left foot high off the deck, ramming it into the man's throat.

"*Tao!*" The guttural whisper came from his lips involuntarily; he did not know what it meant.

Before he could understand, he had pivoted, his right foot now surging forward like a battering ram, crashing into the netman's left kidney.

"*Che-sah!*" he whispered.

The netman recoiled, then lunged toward him in pain and fury, his hands outstretched like claws. "Pig!"

The patient crouched, shooting his right hand up to grip the netman's left forearm, yanking it downward, then rising, pushing his victim's arm up, twisting it at its highest arc clockwise, yanking again, finally releasing it while jamming his heel into the small of the netman's back. The Frenchman sprawled forward over the nets, his head smashing into the wall of the gunnel.

"*Mee-sah!*" Again he did not know the meaning of his silent cry.

A crewman grabbed his neck from the rear. The patient

[27]

crashed his left fist into the pelvic area behind him, then bent forward, gripping the elbow to the right of his throat. He lurched to his left; his assailant was lifted off the ground, his legs spiraling in the air as he was thrown across the deck, his face and neck impaled between the wheels of a winch.

The two remaining men were on him, fists and knees pummeling him, as the captain of the fishing boat repeatedly screamed his warnings.

"*Le docteur! Rappelons le docteur! Va doucement!*"

The words were as misplaced as the captain's appraisal of what he saw. The patient gripped the wrist of one man, bending it downward, twisting it counterclockwise in one violent movement; the man roared in agony. The wrist was broken.

Washburn's patient viced the fingers of his hands together, swinging his arms upward like a sledgehammer, catching the crewman with the broken wrist at the midpoint of his throat. The man somersaulted off his feet and collapsed on the deck.

"*Kwa-sah!*" The whisper echoed in the patient's ears!

The fourth man backed away, staring at the maniac who simply looked at him.

It was over. Three of Lamouche's crew were unconscious, severely punished for what they had done. It was doubtful that any would be capable of coming down to the docks at four o'clock in the morning.

Lamouche's words were uttered in equal parts, astonishment and contempt. "Where you come from I don't know, but you will get off this boat."

The man with no memory understood the unintentional irony of the captain's words. *I don't know where I came from, either.*

"You can't stay here now," said Geoffrey Washburn, coming into the darkened bedroom. "I honestly believed I could prevent any serious assault on you. But I can't protect you when you've done the damage."

"It was provoked."

"To the extent it was inflicted? A broken wrist and lacerations requiring sutures on a man's throat and face, and another's skull. A severe concussion, and an undetermined injury to a kidney? To say nothing of a blow to the groin that's caused a swelling of the testicles? I believe the word is overkill."

"It would have been just plain 'kill,' and I would have been the dead man, if it'd happened any other way." The patient paused, but spoke again before the doctor could interrupt. "I think we should talk. Several things happened; other words came to me. We should talk."

"We should, but we can't. There isn't time. You've got to leave now. I've made arrangements."

"Now?"

"Yes. I told them you went into the village, probably to get drunk. The families will go looking for you. Every able-bodied brother, cousin, and in-law. They'll have knives, hooks, perhaps a gun or two. When they can't find you, they'll come back here. They won't stop until they *do* find you."

"Because of a fight I didn't start?"

"Because you've injured three men who will lose at least a month's wages between them. And something else that's infinitely more important."

"What's that?"

"The insult. An off-islander proved himself more than a match for not one, but three respected fishermen of Port Noir."

"Respected?"

"In the physical sense. Lamouche's crew is considered the roughest on the waterfront."

"That's ridiculous."

"Not to them. It's their honor. . . . Now hurry—get your things together. There's a boat in from Marseilles; the captain's agreed to stow you, and drop you a half-mile offshore north of La Ciotat."

The man with no memory held his breath. "Then it's time," he said quietly.

"It's time," replied Washburn. "I think I know what's going through your mind. A sense of helplessness, of drifting without a rudder to put you on a course. I've been your rudder, and I won't be with you; there's nothing I can do about that. But believe me when I tell you, you are *not* helpless. You *will* find your way."

"To Zurich," added the patient.

"To Zurich," agreed the doctor. "Here. I've wrapped some things together for you in this oilcloth. Strap it around your waist."

"What is it?"

"All the money I have, some two thousand francs. It's not much, but it will help you get started. And my passport, for whatever good it will do. We're about the same age and it's eight years old; people change. Don't let anyone study it. It's merely an official paper."

"What will you do?"

"I won't ever need it if I don't hear from you."

"You're a decent man."

"I think you are, too. . . . As I've known you. But then I didn't know you before. So I can't vouch for that man. I wish I could, but there's no way I can."

The man leaned against the railing, watching the lights of Ile de Port Noir recede in the distance. The fishing boat was heading into darkness, as he had plunged into darkness nearly five months ago.

As he was plunging into another darkness now.

— 3 —

There were no lights on the coast of France; only the wash of the dying moon outlined the rocky shore. They were two hundred yards from land, the fishing boat bobbing gently in the crosscurrents of the inlet. The captain pointed over the side.

"There's a small stretch of beach between those two clusters of rock. It's not much, but you'll reach it if you swim to the right. We can drift in another thirty, forty feet, no more than that. Only a minute or two."

"You're doing more than I expected. I thank you for that."

"No need to. I pay my debts."

"And I'm one?"

"Very much so. The doctor in Port Noir sewed up three of my crew after that madness five months ago. You weren't the only one brought in, you know."

"The storm? You know me?"

"You were chalk white on the table, but I don't know you and I don't want to know you. I had no money then, no catch; the doctor said I could pay when my circumstances were better. You're my payment."

"I need papers," said the man, sensing a source of help. "I need a passport altered."

"Why speak to me?" asked the captain. "I said I would put a package over the side north of La Ciotat. That's all I said."

"You wouldn't have said that if you weren't capable of other things."

"I will *not* take you into Marseilles. I will *not* risk the patrol boats. The Sûreté has squadrons all over the harbor; the narcotics teams are maniacs. You pay *them* or you pay twenty years in a cell."

"Which means I can get papers in Marseilles. And you can help me."

"I did not say that."

"Yes, you did. I need a service and that service can be found in a place where you won't take me—still the service is there. You said it."

"Said what?"

"That you'll talk to me in Marseilles—if I can get there without you. Just tell me where."

The skipper of the fishing boat studied the patient's face; the decision was not made lightly, but it was made. "There's a café on rue Sarrasin, south of Old Harbor—Le Bouc de Mer. I'll be there tonight between nine and eleven. You'll need money, some of it in advance."

"How much?"

"That's between you and the man you speak with."

"I've got to have an idea."

"It's cheaper if you have a document to work with; otherwise one has to be stolen."

"I told you. I've got one."

The captain shrugged. "Fifteen hundred, two thousand francs. Are we wasting time?"

The patient thought of the oilcloth packet strapped to his waist. Bankruptcy lay in Marseilles, but so did an altered passport, a passport to Zurich. "I'll handle it," he said, not knowing why he sounded so confident. "Tonight, then."

The captain peered at the dimly lit shoreline. "This is as far as we can drift. You're on your own now. Remember, if we don't meet in Marseilles, you've never seen me and I've never seen you. None of my crew has seen you, either."

"I'll be there. Le Bouc de Mer, rue Sarrasin, south of Old Harbor."

"In God's hands," said the skipper, signaling a crewman

at the wheel; the engines rumbled beneath the boat. "By the way, the clientele at Le Bouc are not used to the Parisian dialect. I'd rough it up if I were you."

"Thanks for the advice," said the patient as he swung his legs over the gunnel and lowered himself into the water. He held his knapsack above the surface, legs scissoring to stay afloat. "See you tonight," he added in a louder voice, looking up at the black hull of the fishing boat.

There was no one there; the captain had left the railing. The only sounds were the slapping of the waves against the wood and the muffled acceleration of the engines.

You're on your own now.

He shivered and spun in the cold water, angling his body toward the shore, remembering to sidestroke to his right, to head for a cluster of rocks on the right. If the captain knew what he was talking about, the current would take him into the unseen beach.

It did; he could feel the undertow pulling his bare feet into the sand, making the last thirty yards the most difficult to cross. But the canvas knapsack was relatively dry, still held above the breaking waves.

Minutes later he was sitting on a dune of wild grass, the tall reeds bending with the offshore breezes, the first rays of morning intruding on the night sky. The sun would be up in an hour; he would have to move with it.

He opened the knapsack and took out a pair of boots and heavy socks along with rolled-up trousers and a coarse denim shirt. Somewhere in his past he had learned to pack with an economy of space; the knapsack contained far more than an observer might think. Where had he learned that? Why? The questions never stopped.

He got up and took off the British walking shorts he had accepted from Washburn. He stretched them across the reeds of grass to dry; he could discard nothing. He removed his undershirt and did the same.

Standing there naked on the dune, he felt an odd sense of exhilaration mingled with a hollow pain in the middle of his stomach. The pain was fear, he knew that. He understood the exhilaration, too.

He had passed his first test. He had trusted an instinct— perhaps a compulsion—and had known what to say and how to respond. An hour ago he was without an immediate destination, knowing only that Zurich was his objective, but knowing, too, that there were borders to cross, official eyes to satisfy. The eight-year-old passport was so obviously not his own that even the dullest immigration clerk would spot the fact. And even if he managed to cross into Switzerland with it, he had to get out; with each move the odds of his being detained were multiplied. He could not permit that. Not now; not until he knew more. The answers were in Zurich, he had to travel freely, and he had honed in on a captain of a fishing boat to make that possible.

You are not *helpless. You* will *find your way.*

Before the day was over he would make a connection to have Washburn's passport altered by a professional, transformed into a license to travel. It was the first concrete step, but before it was taken there was the consideration of money. The two thousand francs the doctor had given him were inadequate; they might not even be enough for the passport itself. What good was a license to travel without the means to do so? Money. He had to get money. He had to think about that.

He shook out the clothes he had taken from the knapsack, put them on, and shoved his feet into the boots. Then he lay down on the sand, staring at the sky, which progressively grew brighter. The day was being born, and so was he.

He walked the narrow stone streets of La Ciotat, going into the shops as much to converse with the clerks as anything else. It was an odd sensation to be part of the human traffic, not an unknown derelict, dragged from the sea. He remembered the captain's advice and gutturalized his French, allowing him to be accepted as an unremarkable stranger passing through town.

Money.

There was a section of La Ciotat that apparently catered to a wealthy clientele. The shops were cleaner and the merchandise more expensive, the fish fresher and the meat several cuts above that in the main shopping area. Even the vegetables glistened; many exotic, imported from North Africa and the Mid East. The area held a touch of Paris or Nice set down on the fringes of a routinely middle-class coastal community. A small café, its entrance at the end of a flagstone path, stood separated from the shops on either side by a manicured lawn.

Money.

He walked into a butcher shop, aware that the owner's appraisal of him was not positive, nor the glance friendly. The man was waiting on a middle-aged couple, who from their speech and manner were domestics at an outlying estate. They were precise, curt, and demanding.

"The veal last week was barely passable," said the woman. "Do better this time, or I'll be forced to order from Marseilles."

"And the other evening," added the man, "the marquis mentioned to me that the chops of lamb were much too thin. I repeat, a full inch and a quarter."

The owner sighed and shrugged, uttering obsequious phrases of apology and assurance. The woman turned to her escort, her voice no less commanding than it was to the butcher.

"Wait for the packages and put them in the car. I'll be at the grocer's; meet me there."

"Of course, my dear."

The woman left, a pigeon in search of further seeds of conflict. The moment she was out the door her husband turned to the shopowner, his demeanor entirely different. Gone was the arrogance; a grin appeared.

"Just your average day, eh, Marcel?" he said, taking a pack of cigarettes from his pocket.

"Seen better, seen worse. Were the chops really too thin?"

"My God, no. When was *he* last able to tell? But she feels better if I complain, you know that."

"Where is the Marquis of the Dungheap now?"

"Drunk next door, waiting for the whore from Toulon. I'll come down later this afternoon, pick him up, and sneak him past the marquise into the stables. He won't be able to drive his car by then. He uses Jean-Pierre's room above the kitchen, you know."

"I've heard."

At the mention of the name Jean-Pierre, Washburn's patient turned from the display case of poultry. It was an automatic reflex, but the movement only served to remind the butcher of his presence.

"What is it? What do you want?"

It was time to degutturalize his French. "You were recommended by friends in Nice," said the patient, his accent more befitting the Quai d'Orsay than Le Bouc de Mer.

"Oh?" The shopowner made an immediate reappraisal.

Among his clientele, especially the younger ones, there were those who preferred to dress in opposition to their status. The common Basque shirt was even fashionable these days. "You're new here, sir?"

"My boat's in for repairs; we won't be able to reach Marseilles this afternoon."

"May I be of service?"

The patient laughed. "You may be to the chef; I wouldn't dare presume. He'll be around later and I do have some influence."

The butcher and his friend laughed. "I would think so, sir," said the shopowner.

"I'll need a dozen ducklings and, say, eighteen chateaubriands."

"Of course."

"Good. I'll send our master of the galley directly to you." The patient turned to the middle-aged man. "By the way, I couldn't help overhearing . . . no, please don't be concerned. The marquis wouldn't be that jackass d'Ambois, would he? I think someone told me he lived around here."

"Oh no, sir," replied the servant. "I don't know the Marquis d'Ambois. I was referring to the Marquis de Chamford. A fine gentleman, sir, but he has problems. A difficult marriage, sir. Very difficult; it's no secret."

"Chamford? Yes, I think we've met. Rather short fellow, isn't he?"

"No, sir. Quite tall, actually. About your size, I'd say."

"Really?"

The patient learned the various entrances and inside staircases of the two-story café quickly—a produce delivery man from Roquevaire unsure of his new route. There were two sets of steps that led to the second floor, one from the kitchen, the other just beyond the front entrance in the small foyer; this was the staircase used by patrons going to the upstairs washrooms. There was also a window through which an interested party outside could see anyone who used this particular staircase, and the patient was sure that if he waited long enough he would see two people doing so. They would undoubtedly go up separately, neither heading for a washroom but, instead, to a bedroom above the kitchen. The patient wondered which of the expensive automobiles parked on the quiet street belonged to the Marquis de Chamford. Whichever, the middle-aged manservant in the butcher shop did not have to be concerned; his employer would not be driving it.

Money.

The woman arrived shortly before one o'clock. She was a windswept blonde, her large breasts stretching the blue silk of her blouse, her long legs tanned, striding gracefully above spiked heels, thighs and fluid hips outlined beneath the tight-fitting white skirt. Chamford might have problems but he also had taste.

Twenty minutes later he could see the white skirt through the window; the girl was heading upstairs. Less than sixty seconds later another figure filled the window-frame; dark trousers and a blazer beneath a white face cautiously lurched up the staircase. The patient counted off the minutes; he hoped the Marquis de Chamford owned a watch.

Carrying his canvas knapsack as unobtrusively as possible by the straps, the patient walked down the flagstone path to the entrance of the restaurant. Inside, he turned left in the foyer, excusing himself past an elderly man trudging up the staircase, reached the second floor and turned left again down a long corridor that led toward the rear of the building, above the kitchen. He passed the washrooms and came to a closed door at the end of the narrow hallway where he stood motionless, his back pressed into the wall. He turned his head and waited for the elderly man to reach the washroom door and push it open while unzipping his trousers.

The patient—instinctively, without thinking, really—raised the soft knapsack and placed it against the center of the door panel. He held it securely in place with his outstretched arms, stepped back, and in one swift movement, crashed his left shoulder into the canvas, dropping his right hand as the door sprang open, gripping the edge before the door could smash into a wall. No one below in the restaurant could have heard the muted forced entry.

"*Nom de Dieu!*" she shrieked. "*Qui est-cel . . .*"

"*Silence!*"

The Marquis de Chamford spun off the naked body of the blond woman, sprawling over the edge of the bed onto the floor. He was a sight from a comic opera, still wearing his starched shirt, the tie knotted in place, and on his feet black silk, knee-length socks; but that was all he wore. The woman grabbed the covers, doing her best to lessen the indelicacy of the moment.

The patient issued his commands swiftly. "Don't raise your voices. No one will be hurt if you do exactly as I say."

"My wife hired you!" cried Chamford, his words slurred, his eyes barely in focus. "I'll pay you more!"

"That's a beginning," answered Dr. Washburn's patient. "Take off your shirt and tie. Also the socks." He saw the glistening gold band around the marquis' wrist. "And the watch."

Several minutes later the transformation was complete. The marquis' clothes were not a perfect fit, but no one could deny the quality of the cloth or the original tailoring. Too, the watch was a Girard Perregaux, and Chamford's billfold contained over thirteen thousand francs. The car keys were also impressive; they were set in monogrammed heads of sterling silver.

"For the love of God, give me your clothes!" said the marquis, the implausibility of his predicament penetrating the haze of alcohol.

"I'm sorry, but I can't do that," replied the intruder, gathering up both his own clothes and those of the blond woman.

"You can't take *mine!*" she yelled.

"I told you to keep your voice down."

"All right, all *right,*" she continued, "but you *can't* . . ."

"Yes, I can." The patient looked around the room; there was a telephone on a desk by a window. He crossed to it and yanked the cord out of the socket. "Now no one will disturb you," he added, picking up the knapsack.

"You won't go free, you know!" snapped Chamford. "You won't get away with this! The police will find you!"

"The police?" asked the intruder. "Do you really think you should call the police? A formal report will have to be made, the circumstances described. I'm not so sure that's such a good idea. I think you'd be better off waiting for that fellow to pick you up later this afternoon. I heard him say he was going to get you past the marquise into the stables. All things considered, I honestly believe that's what you should do. I'm sure you can come up with a better story than what really happened here. I won't contradict you."

The unknown thief left the room, closing the damaged door behind him.

You are not *helpless. You* will *find your way.*

So far he had and it was a little frightening. What had Washburn said? That his skills and talents would come back . . . *but I don't think you'll ever be able to relate them to anything in your past.* The past. What kind of past was it that produced the skills he had displayed during the past twenty-four hours? Where had he learned to maim and cripple with lunging feet, and fingers entwined into hammers? How did he know precisely where to deliver the blows? Who had taught him to play upon the criminal mind, provoking and evoking a reluctant commitment? How did he zero in so quickly on mere implications, convinced beyond doubt that his instincts were right? Where had he learned to discern instant extortion in a casual conversation overheard in a butcher shop? More to the point, perhaps, was the simple decision to carry out the crime. My God, how *could* he?

The more you fight it, the more you crucify yourself, the worse it will be.

He concentrated on the road and on the mahogany dashboard of the Marquis de Chamford's Jaguar. The array of instruments was not familiar; his past did not include extensive experience with such cars. He supposed that told him something.

In less than an hour he crossed a bridge over a wide canal and knew he had reached Marseilles. Small square houses of stone, angling like blocks up from the water; narrow streets and walls everywhere—the outskirts of the old harbor. He knew it all, and yet he did not know it. High in the distance, silhouetted on one of the surrounding hills, were the outlines of a cathedral, a statue of the Virgin seen clearly atop its steeple. Notre-Dame-de-la-Garde. The name came to him; he had seen it before—and yet he had not seen it.

Oh, Christ! *Stop it!*

Within minutes he was in the pulsing center of the city, driving along the crowded Canebière, with its proliferation of expensive shops, the rays of the afternoon sun bouncing off expanses of tinted glass on either side, and on either side enormous sidewalk cafés. He turned left, toward the harbor, passing warehouses and small factories and fenced-off lots that contained automobiles prepared for transport north to the showrooms of Saint-Etienne, Lyons and Paris. And to points south across the Mediterranean.

Instinct. Follow instinct. For nothing could be disregarded. Every resource had an immediate use; there was value in a rock if it could be thrown, or a vehicle if someone wanted it. He chose a lot where the cars were both new and used, but all expensive; he parked at the curb and got out. Beyond the fence was a small cavern of a garage, mechanics in overalls laconically wandering about carrying tools. He walked casually around inside until he spotted a man in a thin, pin-striped suit whom instinct told him to approach.

It took less than ten minutes, explanations kept to a minimum, a Jaguar's disappearance to North Africa guaranteed with the filing of engine numbers.

The silver monogrammed keys were exchanged for six thousand francs, roughly one-fifth the value of Chamford's automobile. Then Dr. Washburn's patient found a taxi, and asked to be taken to a pawnbroker—but not an establishment that asked too many questions. The message was clear; this was Marseilles. And a half hour later the gold Girard Perregaux was no longer on his wrist, having been replaced by a Seiko chronograph and eight hundred francs. Everything had a value in relationship to its practicality; the chronograph was shockproof.

The next stop was a medium-sized department store in the southeast section of La Canebière. Clothes were chosen off the racks and shelves, paid for and worn out of the fitting rooms, an ill-fitting dark blazer and trousers left behind.

From a display on the floor, he selected a soft leather suitcase, additional garments placed inside with the knapsack. The patient glanced at his new watch; it was nearly five o'clock, time to find a comfortable hotel. He had not really slept for several days; he needed to rest before his appointment in the rue Sarrasin, at a café called Le Bouc de Mer, where arrangements could be made for a more important appointment in Zurich.

He lay back on the bed and stared at the ceiling, the wash of the streetlamps below causing irregular patterns of light to dance across the smooth white surface. Night had come rapidly to Marseilles, and with its arrival a certain sense of freedom came to the patient. It was as if the darkness were a gigantic blanket, blocking out the harsh glare of daylight that revealed too much too quickly. He was learning something else about himself: he was more comfortable in the night. Like a half-starved cat, he would forage better in the darkness. Yet there was a contradiction, and he recognized that, too. During the months in Ile de Port Noir, he had craved the sunlight, hungered for it, waited for it each dawn, wishing only for the darkness to go away.

Things were happening to him; he was changing.

Things *had* happened. Events that gave a certain lie to the concept of foraging more successfully at night. Twelve hours ago he was on a fishing boat in the Mediterranean, an objective in mind and two thousand francs strapped to his waist. Two thousand francs, something less than five hundred American dollars according to the daily rate of exchange posted in the hotel lobby. Now he was outfitted with several sets of acceptable clothing and lying on a bed in a reasonably expensive hotel with something over twenty-three thousand francs in a Louis Vuitton billfold belonging to the Marquis de Chamford. Twenty-three-thousand francs . . . nearly six thousand American dollars.

Where had he come from that he was able to do the things he did?

Stop it!

The rue Sarrasin was so ancient that in another city it might have been designated as a landmark thoroughfare, a wide brick alley connecting streets built centuries later. But this was Marseilles; ancient coexisted with old, both uncomfortable with the new. The rue Sarrasin was no more than two hundred feet long, frozen in time between the stone walls of waterfront buildings, devoid of streetlights, trapping the mists that rolled off the harbor. It was a back-street conducive to brief meetings between men who did not care for their conferences to be observed.

The only light and sound came from Le Bouc de Mer. The café was situated roughly in the center of the wide alley, its premises once a nineteenth-century office building. A number of cubicles had been taken down to allow for a large barroom and tables; an equal number were left standing for less public appointments. These were the waterfront's answer to those private rooms found at restaurants along La Canebière, and, as befitting their status, there were curtains, but no doors.

The patient made his way between the crowded tables, cutting his way through the layers of smoke, excusing himself past lurching fishermen and drunken soldiers and red-faced whores looking for beds to rest in as well as new francs. He peered into a succession of cubicles, a crewman looking for his companions—until he found the captain of the fishing boat. There was another man at the table. Thin, pale faced, narrow eyes peering up like a curious ferret's.

"Sit down," said the dour skipper. "I thought you'd be here before this."

"You said between nine and eleven. It's quarter to eleven."

"You stretch the time, you can pay for the whiskey."

"Be glad to. Order something decent if they've got it."

The thin, pale-faced man smiled. Things were going to be all right.

They were. The passport in question was, naturally, one of the most difficult in the world to tamper with, but with great care, equipment, and artistry, it could be done.

"How much?"

"These skills—and equipment—do not come cheap. Twenty-five hundred francs."

"When can I have it?"

"The care, the artistry, they take time. Three or four days. And that's putting the artist under great pressure; he'll scream at me."

"There's an additional one thousand francs if I can have it tomorrow."

"By ten in the morning," said the pale-faced man quickly. "I'll take the abuse."

"And the thousand," interrupted the scowling captain. "What did you bring out of Port Noir? Diamonds?"

"Talent," answered the patient, meaning it but not understanding it.

"I'll need a photograph," said the connection.

"I stopped at an arcade and had this made," replied the patient, taking a small square photograph out of his shirt pocket. "With all that expensive equipment I'm sure you can sharpen it up."

"Nice clothes," said the captain, passing the print to the pale-faced man.

"Well tailored," agreed the patient.

The location of the morning rendezvous was agreed upon, the drinks paid for, and the captain slipped five hundred francs under the table. The conference was over; the buyer left the cubicle and started across the crowded, raucous, smoke-layered barroom toward the door.

It happened so rapidly, so suddenly, so completely unexpectedly, there was no time to think. Only *react*.

The collision was abrupt, casual, but the eyes that stared at him were not casual; they seemed to burst out of their sockets, widening in disbelief, on the edge of hysteria.

"No! Oh my God, no! It *cannot*—" The man spun in the crowd; the patient lurched forward, clamping his hand down on the man's shoulder.

"Wait a minute!"

The man spun again, thrusting the V of his outstretched thumb and fingers up into the patient's wrist, forcing the hand away. "*You!* You're *dead!* You could not have *lived!*"

"I lived. What do you *know?*"

The face was now contorted, a mass of twisted fury, the eyes squinting, the mouth open, sucking air, baring yellow teeth that took on the appearance of animals' teeth. Suddenly the man pulled out a knife, the snap of its recessed blade heard through the surrounding din. The arm shot forward, the blade an extension of the hand that gripped it, both surging in toward the patient's stomach. "I know I'll finish it!" whispered the man.

The patient swung his right forearm down, a pendulum sweeping aside all objects in front of it. He pivoted, lashing his left foot up, his heel plunging into his attacker's pelvic bone.

"*Che-sah.*" The echo in his ears was deafening.

The man lurched backward into a trio of drinkers as the knife fell to the floor. The weapon was seen; shouts followed, men converged, fists and hands separating the combatants.

"Get out of here!"

"Take your argument somewhere else!"

"We don't want the police in here, you drunken bastards!"

The angry coarse dialects of Marseilles rose over the cacophonous sounds of Le Bouc de Mer. The patient was hemmed in; he watched as his would-be killer threaded his way through the crowd, holding his groin, forcing a path to the entrance. The heavy door swung open; the man raced into the darkness of rue Sarrasin.

Someone who thought he was dead—wanted him dead—knew he was alive.

— 4 —

The economy class section of Air France's Caravelle to Zurich was filled to capacity, the narrow seats made more uncomfortable by the turbulence that buffeted the plane. A baby was screaming in its mother's arms; other children whimpered, swallowing cries of fear as parents smiled with tentative reassurances they did not feel. Most of the remaining passengers were silent, a few drinking their whiskey more rapidly than obviously was normal. Fewer still were forcing laughter from tight throats, false bravados that emphasized their insecurity rather than disguising it. A terrible flight was many things to many people, but none escape the essential thoughts of terror. When man encased himself in a metal tube thirty thousand feet above the ground, he was vulnerable. With one elongated, screaming dive he could be plummeting downward into the earth. And there were fundamental questions that accompanied the essential terror. What thoughts would go through one's mind at such a time? How would one react?

The patient tried to find out; it was important to him. He sat next to the window, his eyes on the aircraft's wing, watching the broad expanse of metal bend and vibrate under the brutalizing impact of the winds. The currents were clashing against one another, pounding the manmade tube into a kind of submission, warning the microscopic pretenders that they were no match for the vast infirmities of nature. One ounce of pressure beyond the flex tolerance and the wing would crack, the lift-sustaining limb torn from its tubular body, shredded into the winds; one burst of rivets and there would be an explosion, the screaming plunge to follow.

What would he do? What would he think? Other than the uncontrollable fear of dying and oblivion, would there be anything else? That's what he had to concentrate on; that was the *projection* Washburn kept emphasizing in Port Noir. The doctor's words came back to him.

Whenever you observe a stress situation—and you have the time—do your damndest to project yourself into it. Associate as freely as you can; let words and images fill your mind. In them you may find clues.

The patient continued to stare out the window, consciously trying to raise his unconscious, fixing his eyes on the natural violence beyond the glass, distilling the movement, silently doing his "damndest" to let his reactions give rise to words and images.

They came—slowly. There was the darkness again, and the sound of rushing wind, ear-shattering, continuous, growing in volume until he thought his head would burst. His head. . . . The winds were lashing the left side of his head and face, burning his skin, forcing him to raise his left shoulder for protection. . . . Left shoulder. Left *arm*. His arm was raised, the gloved fingers of his left hand gripping a straight edge of metal, his right holding a . . . a strap; he was holding on to a strap, waiting for something. A signal . . . a flashing light or a tap on the shoulder, or both. A signal. It *came*. He plunged. Into the darkness, into the void, his body tumbling, twisting, swept away into the night sky. He had . . . parachuted!

"Etes-vous malade?"

His insane reverie was broken; the nervous passenger next to him had touched his left arm—which was raised, the fingers of his hand spread, as if resisting, rigid in their locked position. Across his chest his right forearm was pressed into the cloth of his jacket, his right hand gripping the lapel, bunching the fabric. And on his forehead were

[46]

rivulets of sweat; it had happened. The something-else had come briefly—insanely—into focus.

"*Pardon,*" he said, lowering his arms. "*Un mauvais rêve,*" he added meaninglessly.

There was a break in the weather; the Caravelle stabilized. The smiles on the harried stewardesses' faces became genuine again; full service was resumed as embarrassed passengers glanced at one another.

The patient observed his surroundings but reached no conclusions. He was consumed by the images and the sounds that had been so clearly defined in his mind's eye and ear. He had hurled himself from a plane . . . at night . . . signals and metal and straps intrinsic to his leap. He *had* parachuted. *Where? Why?*

Stop crucifying yourself!

If for no other reason than to take his thoughts away from the madness, he reached into his breast pocket, pulled out the altered passport, and opened it. As might be expected, the name *Washburn* had been retained; it was common enough and its owner had explained that there were no flags out for it. The *Geoffrey R.,* however, had been changed to *George P.,* the eliminations and spaceline blockage expertly accomplished. The photographic insertion was expert, too; it no longer resembled a cheap print from a machine in an amusement arcade.

The identification numbers, of course, were entirely different, guaranteed not to cause an alarm in an immigration computer. At least, up until the moment the bearer submitted the passport for its first inspection; from that time on it was the buyer's responsibility. One paid as much for this guarantee as he did for the artistry and the equipment, for it required connections within Interpol and the immigration clearing houses. Customs officials, computer specialists, and clerks throughout the European border networks were paid on a regular basis for this vital information; they rarely made mistakes. If and when they did, the loss of an eye or an arm was not out of the question—such were the brokers of false papers.

George P. Washburn. He was not comfortable with the name; the owner of the unaltered original had instructed him too well in the basics of projection and association. *George P.* was a sidestep from *Geoffrey R.,* a man who had been eaten away by a compulsion that had its roots in escape—escape from identity. That was the last thing the patient wanted; he wanted more than his *life* to know who he was.

Or did he?

No matter. The answer was in Zurich. In Zurich there was . . .

"*Mesdames et messieurs. Nous commençons notre descente pour l'aéroport de Zurich.*"

He knew the name of the hotel: Carillon du Lac. He had given it to the taxi driver without thinking. Had he read it somewhere? Had the name been one of those listed in the Welcome-to-Zurich folders placed in the elasticized pockets in front of his seat in the plane?

No. He knew the lobby; the heavy, dark, polished wood was familiar . . . somehow. And the huge plateglass windows that looked out over Lake Zurich. He had been here *before;* he had stood where he was standing now—in front of the marble-topped counter—a long time ago.

It was all confirmed by the words spoken by the clerk behind the desk. They had the impact of an explosion.

"It's good to see you again, sir. It's been quite a while since your last visit."

Has it? How long? Why don't you call me by my name? For God's sake. I don't know you! I don't know me! Help me! Please, help me!

"I guess it has," he said. "Do me a favor, will you? I sprained my hand; it's difficult to write. Could you fill in the registration and I'll do my damndest to sign it?" The patient held his breath. Suppose the polite man behind the counter asked him to repeat his name, or the spelling of his name?

"Of course." The clerk turned the card around and wrote. "Would you care to see the hotel doctor?"

"Later, perhaps. Not now." The clerk continued writing, then lifted up the card, reversing it for the guest's signature.

Mr. J. Bourne. New York, N.Y. U.S.A.

He stared at it, transfixed, mesmerized by the letters. He had a name—part of a name. And a country as well as a city of residence.

J. Bourne. John? James? Joseph? What did the *J* stand for?

"Is something wrong, Herr Bourne?" asked the clerk.

"Wrong? No, not at all." He picked up the pen, remembering to feign discomfort. Would he be expected to write

[48]

out a first name? No; he would sign exactly as the clerk had printed.

Mr. J. Bourne.

He wrote the name as naturally as he could, letting his mind fall free, allowing whatever thoughts or images that might be triggered come through. None did; he was merely signing an unfamiliar name. He felt nothing.

"You had me worried, mein Herr," said the clerk. "I thought perhaps I'd made a mistake. It's been a busy week, a busier day. But then, I was quite certain."

And if he had? Made a mistake? Mr. J. Bourne of New York City, U.S.A., did not care to think about the possibility. "It never occurred to me to question your memory . . . Herr Stossel," replied the patient, glancing up at the On-Duty sign on the left wall of the counter; the man behind the desk was the Carillon du Lac's assistant manager.

"You're most kind." The assistant manager leaned forward. "I assume you'll require the usual conditions of your stay with us?"

"Some may have changed," said J. Bourne. "How did you understand them before?"

"Whoever telephones or inquires at the desk is to be told you're out of the hotel, whereupon you're to be informed immediately. The only exception is your firm in New York. The Treadstone Seventy-One Corporation, if I remember correctly."

Another name! One he could trace with an overseas call. Fragmentary shapes were falling into place. The exhilaration began to return.

"That'll do. I won't forget your efficiency."

"This is Zurich," replied the polite man, shrugging. "You've always been exceedingly generous, Herr Bourne. *Page—hierher, bitte!*"

As the patient followed the page into the elevator, several things were clearer. He had a name and he understood why that name came so quickly to the Carillon du Lac's assistant manager. He had a country and a city and a firm that employed him—*had* employed him, at any rate. And whenever he came to Zurich, certain precautions were implemented to protect him from unexpected, or unwanted, visitors. That was what he could not understand. One either protected oneself thoroughly or one did not bother to protect oneself at all. Where was any real advantage in a screening process that was so loose, so vulnerable to penetration? It struck him as second-rate, without value, as if a small child were playing hide-and-seek. *Where am I? Try and find me. I'll say something out loud and give you a hint.*

It was not professional, and if he had learned anything about himself during the past forty-eight hours it was that he *was* a professional. Of what he had no idea, but the status was not debatable.

The voice of the New York operator faded sporadically over the line. Her conclusion, however, was irritatingly clear. And final.

"There's no listing for any such company, sir. I've checked the latest directories as well as the private telephones and there's no Treadstone Corporation—and nothing even resembling Treadstone with numbers following the name."

"Perhaps they were dropped to shorten . . ."

"There's *no* firm or company with that name, sir. I repeat, if you have a first or second name, or the type of business the firm's engaged in, I might be of further help."

"I don't. Only the name, Treadstone Seventy-One, New York City."

"It's an odd name, sir. I'm sure if there were a listing it would be a simple matter to find it. I'm sorry."

"Thanks very much for your trouble," said J. Bourne, replacing the phone. It was pointless to go on; the name was a code of some sort, words relayed by a caller that gained him access to a hotel guest not so readily accessible. And the words could be used by anyone regardless of where he had placed the call; therefore the location of New York might well be meaningless. According to an operator five thousand miles away it was.

The patient walked to the bureau where he had placed the Louis Vuitton billfold and the Seiko chronograph. He put the billfold in his pocket and the watch on his wrist; he looked in the mirror and spoke quietly.

"You are J. Bourne, citizen of the United States, resident of New York City, and it's entirely possible that the numbers 'zero-seven—seventeen-twelve—zero-fourteen—twenty-six-zero' are the most important things in your life."

The sun was bright, filtering through the trees along the elegant Bahnhofstrasse, bouncing off the windows of the shops, and creating blocks of shadows where the great banks intruded on its rays. It was a street where solidity and money, security and arrogance, determination and a touch of frivolity all coexisted; and Dr. Washburn's patient had walked along its pavements before.

He strolled into the Burkli Platz, the square that overlooked the Zurichsee, with its numerous quays along the waterfront, bordered by gardens that in the heat of summer became circles of bursting flowers. He could picture them in his mind's eye; images were coming to him. But no thoughts, no memories.

He doubled back into the Bahnhofstrasse, instinctively knowing that the Gemeinschaft Bank was a nearby building of off-white stone; it had been on the opposite side of the street on which he had just walked; he had passed it deliberately. He approached the heavy glass doors and pushed the center plate forward. The right-hand door swung open easily and he was standing on a floor of brown marble; he had stood on it before, but the image was not as strong as others. He had the uncomfortable feeling that the Gemeinschaft was to be avoided.

It was not to be avoided now.

"Bonjour, monsieur. Vous désirez . . .?" The man asking the question was dressed in a cutaway, the red *boutonnière* his symbol of authority. The use of French was explained by the client's clothes; even the subordinate gnomes of Zurich were observant.

"I have personal and confidential business to discuss," replied J. Bourne in English, once again mildly startled by the words he spoke so naturally. The reason for the English was twofold: he wanted to watch the gnome's expression at his error, and he wanted no possible misinterpretation of anything said during the next hour.

"Pardon, sir," said the man, his eyebrows arched slightly, studying the client's topcoat. "The elevator to your left, second floor. The receptionist will assist you."

The receptionist referred to was a middle-aged man with close-cropped hair and tortoise-shell glasses; his expression was set, his eyes rigidly curious. "Do you currently have personal and confidential business with us, sir?" he asked, repeating the new arrival's words.

"I do."

"Your signature, please," said the official, holding out a

[51]

sheet of Gemeinschaft stationery with two blank lines centered in the middle of the page.

The client understood; no name was required. *The handwritten numbers take the place of a name . . . they constitute the signature of the account holder. Standard procedure.* Washburn.

The patient wrote out the numbers, relaxing his hand so the writing would be free. He handed the stationery back to the receptionist, who studied it, rose from the chair, and gestured to a row of narrow doors with frosted glass panels. "If you'll wait in the fourth room, sir, someone will be with you shortly."

"The fourth room?"

"The fourth door from the left. It will lock automatically."

"Is that necessary?"

The receptionist glanced at him, startled. "It is in line with your own request, sir," he said politely, an undertone of surprise beneath his courtesy. "This is a three-zero account. It's customary at the Gemeinschaft for holders of such accounts to telephone in advance so that a private entrance can be made available."

"I know that," lied Washburn's patient with a casualness he did not feel. "It's just that I'm in a hurry."

"I'll convey that to Verifications, sir."

"Verifications?" Mr. J. Bourne of New York City, U.S.A., could not help himself; the word had the sound of an alarm.

"Signature Verifications, sir." The man adjusted his glasses; the movement covered his taking a step nearer his desk, his lower hand inches from a console. "I suggest you wait in Room Four, sir." The suggestion was not a request; it was an order, the command in the praetorian's eyes.

"Why not? Just tell them to hurry, will you?" The patient crossed to the fourth door, opened it and walked inside. The door closed automatically; he could hear the click of the lock. J. Bourne looked at the frosted panel; it was no simple pane of glass, for there was a network of thin wires webbed beneath the surface. Undoubtedly if cracked, an alarm would be triggered; he was in a cell, waiting to be summoned.

The rest of the small room was paneled and furnished tastefully, two leather armchairs next to one another, across from a miniature couch flanked by antique tables.

At the opposite end was a second door, startling in its contrast; it was made of gray steel. Up-to-date magazines and newspapers in three languages were on the tables. The patient sat down and picked up the Paris edition of the *Herald-Tribune*. He read the printed words but absorbed nothing. The summons would come any moment now; his mind was consumed by thoughts of maneuver. Maneuver without memory, only by instinct.

Finally, the steel door opened, revealing a tall, slender man with aquiline features and meticulously groomed gray hair. His face was patrician, eager to serve an equal who needed his expertise. He extended his hand, his English refined, mellifluous under his Swiss intonation.

"So very pleased to meet you. Forgive the delay; it was rather humorous, in fact."

"In what way?"

"I'm afraid you rather startled Herr Koenig. It's not often a three-zero account arrives without prior notice. He's quite set in his ways, you know; the unusual ruins his day. On the other hand, it generally makes mine more pleasant. I'm Walther Apfel. Please, come in."

The bank officer released the patient's hand and gestured toward the steel door. The room beyond was a V-shaped extension of the cell. Dark paneling, heavy comfortable furniture and a wide desk that stood in front of a wider window overlooking the Bahnhofstrasse.

"I'm sorry I upset him," said J. Bourne. "It's just that I have very little time."

"Yes, he relayed that." Apfel walked around the desk, nodding at the leather armchair in front. "Do sit down. One or two formalities and we can discuss the business at hand." Both men sat; the instant they did so the bank officer picked up a white clipboard and leaned across his desk, handing it to the Gemeinschaft client. Secured in place was another sheet of stationery, but instead of two blank lines there were ten, starting below the letterhead and extending to within an inch of the bottom border. "Your signature, please. A minimum of five will be sufficient."

"I don't understand. I just did this."

"And very successfully. Verification confirmed it."

"Then why again?"

"A signature can be practiced to the point where a single rendition is acceptable. However, successive repetitions will result in flaws if it's not authentic. A graphological scanner will pick them up instantly; but then I'm sure that's no concern of yours." Apfel smiled as he placed a pen at the edge of the desk. "Nor of mine, frankly, but Koenig insists."

"He's a cautious man," said the patient, taking the pen and starting to write. He had begun the fourth set when the banker stopped him.

"That will do; the rest really is a waste of time." Apfel held out his hand for the clipboard. "Verifications said you weren't even a borderline case. Upon receipt of this, the account will be delivered." He inserted the sheet of paper into the slot of a metal case on the right side of his desk and pressed a button; a shaft of bright light flared and then went out. "This transmits the signatures directly to the scanner," continued the banker. "Which, of course, is programmed. Again, frankly, it's all a bit foolish. No one forewarned of our precautions would consent to the additional signatures if he were an imposter."

"Why not? As long as he'd gone this far, why not chance it?"

"There is only one entrance to this office, conversely one exit. I'm sure you heard the lock snap shut in the waiting room."

"And saw the wire mesh in the glass," added the patient.

"Then you understand. A certified imposter would be trapped."

"Suppose he had a gun?"

"You don't."

"No one searched me."

"The elevator did. From four different angles. If you had been armed, the machinery would have stopped between the first and second floors."

"You're all cautious."

"We try to be of service." The telephone rang. Apfel answered. "Yes? . . . Come in." The banker glanced at his client. "Your account file's here."

"That was quick."

"Herr Koenig signed for it several minutes ago; he was merely waiting for the scanner release." Apfel opened a drawer and took out a ring of keys. "I'm sure he's disappointed. He was quite certain something was amiss."

The steel door opened and the receptionist entered carrying a black metal container, which he placed on the

[54]

desk next to a tray that held a bottle of Perrier and two glasses.

"Are you enjoying your stay in Zurich?" asked the banker, obviously to fill in the silence.

"Very much so. My room overlooks the lake. It's a nice view, very peaceful, quiet."

"Splendid," said Apfel, pouring a glass of Perrier for his client. Herr Koenig left; the door was closed and the banker returned to business.

"Your account, sir," he said, selecting a key from the ring. "May I unlock the case or would you prefer doing so yourself?"

"Go ahead. Open it."

The banker looked up. "I said unlock, not open. That's not my privilege, nor would I care for the responsibility."

"Why not?"

"In the event your identity is listed, it's not my position to be aware of it."

"Suppose I wanted business transacted? Money transferred, sent to someone else?"

"It could be accomplished with your numerical signature on a withdrawal form."

"Or sent to another bank—outside of Switzerland? For me."

"Then a name would be required. Under those circumstances an identity would be both my responsibility and my privilege."

"Open it."

The bank officer did so. Dr. Washburn's patient held his breath, a sharp pain forming in the pit of his stomach. Apfel took out a sheaf of statements held together by an outsized paperclip. His banker's eyes strayed to the righthand column of the top pages, his banker's expression unchanged, but not totally. His lower lip stretched ever so slightly, creasing the corner of his mouth; he leaned forward and handed the pages to their owner.

Beneath the Gemeinschaft letterhead the typewritten words were in English, the obvious language of the client:

Account: Zero—Seven—Seventeen—Twelve—
Zero—Fourteen—Twenty-six—Zero
Name: Restricted to Legal Instructions and Owner
Access: Sealed Under Separate Cover
Current Funds on Deposit: 7,500,000 Francs

The patient exhaled slowly, staring at the figure. Whatever he *thought* he was prepared for, nothing prepared him for this. It was as frightening as anything he had experienced during the past five months. Roughly calculated the amount was over five million American dollars.

$5,000,000!

How? Why?

Controlling the start of a tremble in his hand, he leafed through the statements of entry. They were numerous, the sums extraordinary, none less than 300,000 francs, the deposits spaced every five to eight weeks apart, going back twenty-three months. He reached the bottom statement, the first. It was a transfer from a bank in Singapore and the largest single entry. Two million, seven hundred thousand Malaysian dollars converted into 5,175,000 Swiss francs.

Beneath the statement he could feel the outline of a separate envelope, far shorter than the page itself. He lifted up the paper; the envelope was rimmed with a black border, typewritten words on the front.

Identity: *Owner Access*
Legal Restrictions: *Access—Registered Officer, Treadstone Seventy-One Corporation, Bearer Will Produce Written Instructions From Owner. Subject To Verifications.*

"I'd like to check this," said the client.

"It's your property," replied Apfel. "I can assure you it has remained intact."

The patient removed the envelope and turned it over. A Gemeinschaft seal was pressed over the borders of the flap; none of the raised letters had been disturbed. He tore the flap open, took out the card, and read:

Owner: *Jason Charles Bourne*
Address: *Unlisted*
Citizenship: *U.S.A.*

Jason Charles Bourne.
Jason.

The J was for Jason! His name was *Jason Bourne*. The *Bourne* had meant nothing, the *J*. Bourne still meaningless, but in the combination Jason *and* Bourne, obscure tumblers locked into place. He could accept it; he *did* accept it. He was Jason Charles Bourne, American. Yet he could feel his chest pounding; the vibration in his ears was deafening, the pain in his stomach more acute. *What was it? Why did he have the feeling that he was plunging into the darkness again, into the black waters again?*

"Is something wrong?" asked Walther Apfel.

Is something wrong, Herr Bourne?

"No. Everything's fine. My name's Bourne. Jason Bourne."

Was he shouting? Whispering? He could not tell.

"My privilege to know you, Mr. Bourne. Your identity will remain confidential. You have the word of an officer of the Bank Gemeinschaft."

"Thank you. Now, I'm afraid I've got to transfer a great deal of this money and I'll need your help."

"Again, my privilege. Whatever assistance or advice I can render, I shall be happy to do so."

Bourne reached for the glass of Perrier.

The steel door of Apfel's office closed behind him; within seconds he would walk out of the tasteful anteroom cell, into the reception room and over to the elevators. Within minutes he would be on the Bahnhofstrasse with a name, a great deal of money, and little else but fear and confusion.

He had done it. Dr. Geoffrey Washburn had been paid far in excess of the value of the life he had saved. A teletype transfer in the amount of 1,500,000 Swiss francs had been sent to a bank in Marseilles, deposited to a coded account that would find its way to Ile de Port Noir's only doctor, without Washburn's name ever being used or revealed. All Washburn had to do was to get to Marseilles, recite the codes, and the money was his. Bourne smiled to himself, picturing the expression on Washburn's face when the account was turned over to him. The eccentric, alcoholic doctor would have been overjoyed with ten or fifteen thousand pounds; he had more than a million dollars. It would either ensure his recovery or his destruction; that was his choice, his problem.

A second transfer of 4,500,000 francs was sent to a bank in Paris on the rue Madeleine, deposited in the name of Jason C. Bourne. The transfer was expedited by the Gemeinschaft's twice-weekly pouch to Paris, signature cards in triplicate sent with the documents. Herr Koenig had assured both his superior and the client that the papers would reach Paris in three days.

The final transaction was minor by comparison. One hundred thousand francs in large bills were brought to Apfel's office, the withdrawal slip signed in the account holder's numerical signature.

Remaining on deposit in the Gemeinschaft Bank were 1,400,000 Swiss francs, a not inconsequential sum by any standard.

How? Why? From where?

The entire business had taken an hour and twenty minutes, only one discordant note intruding on the smooth proceedings. In character, it had been delivered by Koenig, his expression a mixture of solemnity and minor triumph. He had rung Apfel, was admitted, and had brought a small, black-bordered envelope to his superior.

"*Une fiche*," he had said in French.

The banker had opened the envelope, removed a card, studied the contents, and had returned both to Koenig. "Procedures will be followed," he had said.

Koenig had left.

"Did that concern me?" Bourne had asked.

"Only in terms of releasing such large amounts. Merely house policy." The banker had smiled reassuringly.

The lock clicked. Bourne opened the frosted glass door and walked out into Herr Koenig's personal fiefdom. Two other men had arrived, seated at opposite ends of the reception room. Since they were not in separate cells behind opaque glass windows, Bourne presumed that neither had a three-zero account. He wondered if they had signed names or written out a series of numbers, but he stopped wondering the instant he reached the elevator and pressed the button.

Out of the corner of his eye he perceived movement; Koenig had shifted his head, nodding at both men. They rose as the elevator door opened. Bourne turned; the man on the right had taken a small radio out of his overcoat pocket; he spoke into it—briefly, quickly.

The man on the left had his right hand concealed beneath the cloth of his raincoat. When he pulled it out he was holding a gun, a black .38 caliber automatic pistol with a perforated cylinder attached to the barrel. A silencer.

Both men converged on Bourne as he backed into the deserted elevator.

The madness began.

— 5 —

The elevator doors started to close; the man with the hand-held radio was already inside, the shoulders of his armed companion angling between the moving panels, the weapon aimed at Bourne's head.

Jason leaned to his right—a sudden gesture of fear—then abruptly, without warning, swept his left foot off the floor, pivoting, his heel plunging into the armed man's hand, sending the gun upward, reeling the man backward out of the enclosure. Two muted gunshots preceded the closing of the doors, the bullets embedding themselves in the thick wood of the ceiling. Bourne completed his pivot, his shoulder crashing into the second man's stomach, his right hand surging into the chest, his left pinning the hand with the radio. He hurled the man into the wall. The radio flew across the elevator; as it fell, words came out of its speaker.

"Henri? Ça va? Qu'es-ce qui se passe?"

The image of another Frenchman came to Jason's mind. A man on the edge of hysteria, disbelief in his eyes; a would-be killer who had raced out of Le Bouc de Mer into the shadows of the rue Sarrasin less than twenty-four hours ago. *That* man had wasted no time sending his message to Zurich; the one they thought was dead was alive. Very much alive. *Kill him!*

Bourne grabbed the Frenchman in front of him now, his left arm around the man's throat, his right hand tearing at the man's left ear. "How *many?*" he asked in French. "How many are there down there? Where *are* they?"

"Find out, *pig!*"

The elevator was halfway to the first floor lobby.

Jason angled the man's face down, ripping the ear half out of its roots, smashing the man's head into the wall. The Frenchman screamed, sinking to the floor. Bourne rammed his knee into the man's chest; he could feel the holster. He yanked the overcoat open, reached in, and pulled out a short-barreled revolver. For an instant it occurred to him that someone had deactivated the scanning machinery in the elevator. *Koenig.* He would remember; there'd be no amnesia where Herr Koenig was concerned. He jammed the gun into the Frenchman's open mouth.

"Tell me or I'll blow the back of your skull off!" The man expunged a throated wail; the weapon was withdrawn, the barrel now pressed into his cheek.

"Two. One by the elevators, one outside on the pavement, by the car."

"What *kind* of car?"

"Peugeot."

"Color?" The elevator was slowing down, coming to a stop.

"Brown."

"The man in the lobby. What's he wearing?"

"I don't know . . ."

Jason cracked the gun across the man's temple. "You'd better remember!"

"A black coat!"

The elevator stopped; Bourne pulled the Frenchman to his feet; the doors opened. To the left, a man in a dark raincoat, and wearing an odd-looking pair of gold-rimmed spectacles, stepped forward. The eyes beyond the lenses recognized the circumstances; blood was trickling down across the Frenchman's cheek. He raised his unseen hand, concealed by the wide pocket of his raincoat, another silenced automatic leveled at the target from Marseilles.

Jason propelled the Frenchman in front of him through the doors. Three rapid *spits* were heard; the Frenchman shouted, his arms raised in a final, guttural protest. He arched his back and fell to the marble floor. A woman to the right of the man with the gold-rimmed spectacles screamed, joined by several men who called to no one and everyone for *Hilfe!* for the *Polizei!*

Bourne knew he could not use the revolver he had taken from the Frenchman. It had no silencer; the sound of a gunshot would mark him. He shoved it into his topcoat pocket, sidestepped the screaming woman and grabbed the uniformed shoulders of the elevator starter, whipping the bewildered man around, throwing him into the figure of the killer in the dark raincoat.

The panic in the lobby mounted as Jason ran toward the glass doors of the entrance. The *boutonnièred* greeter who had mistaken his language an hour and a half ago was shouting into a wall telephone, a uniformed guard at his side, weapon drawn, barricading the exit, eyes riveted on the chaos, riveted suddenly on *him*. Getting out was instantly a problem. Bourne avoided the guard's eyes, directing his words to the guard's associate on the telephone.

"The man wearing gold-rimmed glasses!" he shouted. "He's the one! I saw him!"

"*What?* Who are you?"

"I'm a friend of Walther Apfel! *Listen* to me! The man wearing gold-rimmed glasses, in a black raincoat. Over there!"

Bureaucratic mentality had not changed in several millenniums. At the mention of a superior officer's name, one followed orders.

"Herr Apfel!" The Gemeinschaft greeter turned to the guard. "You heard him! The man wearing glasses. Gold-rimmed glasses!"

"Yes, sir!" The guard raced forward.

Jason edged past the greeter to the glass doors. He shoved the door on the right open, glancing behind him, knowing he had to run again but not knowing if a man outside on the pavement, waiting by a brown Peugeot, would recognize him and fire a bullet into his head.

The guard had run past a man in a black raincoat, a man walking more slowly than the panicked figures around him, a man wearing no glasses at all. He accelerated his pace toward the entrance, toward Bourne.

Out on the sidewalk, the growing chaos was Jason's protection. Word had gone out of the bank; wailing sirens grew louder as police cars raced up the Bahnhofstrasse. He walked several yards to the right, flanked by pedestrians, then suddenly ran, wedging his way into a curious crowd taking refuge in a storefront, his attention on the automobiles at the curb. He saw the Peugeot, saw the man standing beside it, his hand ominously in his overcoat pocket. In less than fifteen seconds, the driver of the Peugeot was joined by the man in the black raincoat, now replacing his gold-rimmed glasses, adjusting his eyes to his restored vision. The two men conferred rapidly, their eyes scanning the Bahnhofstrasse.

Bourne understood their confusion. He had walked with an absence of panic out of the Gemeinschaft's glass doors into the crowd. He had been prepared to run, but he had *not* run, for fear of being stopped until he was reasonably clear of the entrance. No one else had been permitted to do so—and the driver of the Peugeot had not made the connection. He had *not* recognized the target identified and marked for execution in Marseilles.

The first police car reached the scene as the man in the gold-rimmed spectacles removed his raincoat, shoving it through the open window of the Peugeot. He nodded to the driver, who climbed in behind the wheel and started the engine. The killer took off his delicate glasses and did the most unexpected thing Jason could imagine. He walked rapidly back toward the glass doors of the bank, joining the police who were racing inside.

Bourne watched as the Peugeot swung away from the curb and sped off down the Bahnhofstrasse. The crowd in the storefront began to disperse, many edging their way toward the glass doors, craning their necks around one another, rising on the balls of their feet, peering inside. A police officer came out, waving the curious back, demanding that a path be cleared to the curb. As he shouted, an ambulance careened around the northwest corner, its horn joining the sharp, piercing notes from its roof, warning all to get out of its way; the driver nosed his outsized vehicle to a stop in the space created by the departed Peugeot. Jason could watch no longer. He had to get to the Carillon du Lac, gather his things, and get out of Zurich, out of Switzerland. To Paris.

Why Paris? Why had he insisted that the funds be transferred to *Paris?* It had not occurred to him before he sat in Walther Apfel's office, stunned by the extraordinary figures presented him. They had been beyond anything in his imagination—so much so that he could only react numbly, instinctively. And instinct had evoked the city of Paris. As though it were somehow vital. *Why?*

Again, no time . . . He saw the ambulance crew carry a stretcher through the doors of the bank. On it was a body, the head covered, signifying death. The significance was not lost on Bourne; save for skills he could not relate to anything he understood, he was the dead man on that stretcher.

He saw an empty taxi at the corner and ran toward it. He had to get out of Zurich; a message had been sent from Marseilles, yet the dead man was alive. Jason Bourne was alive. Kill him. Kill Jason Bourne!

God in heaven, *why?*

He was hoping to see the Carillon du Lac's assistant manager behind the front desk, but he was not there. Then he realized that a short note to the man—what was his name—Stossel? Yes, Stossel—would be sufficient. An explanation for his sudden departure was not required and five hundred francs would easily take care of the few hours he had accepted from the Carillon du Lac—and the favor he would ask of Herr Stossel.

In his room, he threw his shaving equipment into his unpacked suitcase, checked the pistol he had taken from the Frenchman, leaving it in his topcoat pocket, and sat down at the desk; he wrote out the note for Herr Stossel, Ass't. Mgr. In it he included a sentence that came easily—almost too easily.

. . . I may be in contact with you shortly relative to messages I expect will have been sent to me. I trust it will be convenient for you to keep an eye out for them, and accept them on my behalf.

If any communication came from the elusive Treadstone Seventy-One, he wanted to know about it. This was Zurich; he would.

He put a five hundred franc note between the folded stationery and sealed the envelope. Then he picked up his suitcase, walked out of the room, and went down the hallway to the bank of elevators. There were four; he touched a button and looked behind him, remembering the Gemeinschaft. There was no one there; a bell pinged and the red light above the third elevator flashed on. He had caught a descending machine. Fine. He had to get to the airport just as fast as he could; he had to get out of Zurich, out of Switzerland. A message had been delivered.

The elevator doors opened. Two men stood on either side of an auburn-haired woman; they interrupted their conversation, nodded at the newcomer—noting the suitcase and moving to the side—then resumed talking as the doors closed. They were in their mid-thirties and spoke French softly, rapidly, the woman glancing alternately at both men, alternately smiling and looking pensive. Decisions of no great import were being made. Laughter intermingled with semi-serious interrogation.

"You'll be going home then after the summations tomorrow?" asked the man on the left.

"I'm not sure. I'm waiting for word from Ottawa," the woman replied. "I have relations in Lyon; it would be good to see them."

"It's impossible," said the man on the right, "for the steering committee to find ten people willing to summarize this Godforsaken conference in a single day. We'll all be here another week."

"Brussels will not approve," said the first man grinning. "The hotel's too expensive."

"Then by all means move to another," said the second with a leer at the woman. "We've been waiting for you to do just that, haven't we?"

"You're a lunatic," said the woman. "You're both lunatics, and that's *my* summation."

"You're not, Marie," interjected the first. "A lunatic, I mean. Your presentation yesterday was brilliant."

"It was nothing of the sort," she said. "It was routine and quite dull."

"No, no!" disagreed the second. "It was superb; it had to be. I didn't understand a word. But then I have other talents."

"Lunatic . . ."

The elevator was braking; the first man spoke again. "Let's sit in the back row of the hall. We're late anyway and Bertinelli is speaking—to little effect, I suggest. His theories of enforced cyclical fluctuations went out with the finances of the Borgias."

"Before then," said the auburn-haired woman, laughing. "Caesar's taxes." She paused, then added, "If not the Punic wars."

"The back row then," said the second man, offering his arm to the woman. "We can sleep. He uses a slide projector; it'll be dark."

"No, you two go ahead, I'll join you in a few minutes. I really must send off some cables and I don't trust the telephone operators to get them right."

The doors opened and the threesome walked out of the elevator. The two men started diagonally across the lobby together, the woman toward the front desk. Bourne fell in step behind her, absently reading a sign on a triangular stand several feet away.

WELCOME TO:
MEMBERS OF THE SIXTH WORLD
ECONOMIC CONFERENCE

TODAY'S SCHEDULE:

1:00 P.M.: THE HON. JAMES FRAZIER,
M.P. UNITED KINGDOM.
SUITE 12

6:00 P.M.: DR. EUGENIO BERTINELLI,
UNIV. OF MILAN, ITALY.
SUITE 7

9:00 P.M.: CHAIRMAN'S FAREWELL DINNER.
HOSPITALITY SUITE

"Room 507. The operator said there was a cablegram for me."

English. The auburn-haired woman now beside him at the counter spoke English. But then she had said she was "waiting for word from Ottawa." A Canadian.

The desk clerk checked the slots and returned with the cable. "Dr. St. Jacques?" he asked, holding out the envelope.

"Yes. Thanks very much."

The woman turned away, opening the cable, as the clerk moved in front of Bourne. "Yes, sir?"

"I'd like to leave this note for Herr Stossel." He placed the Carillon du Lac envelope on the counter.

"Herr Stossel will not return until six o'clock in the morning, sir. In the afternoons, he leaves at four. Might I be of service?"

"No, thanks. Just make sure he gets it, please." Then Jason remembered: this was Zurich. "It's nothing urgent," he added, "but I need an answer. I'll check with him in the morning."

"Of course, sir."

Bourne picked up his suitcase and started across the lobby toward the hotel's entrance, a row of wide glass doors that led to a circular drive fronting the lake. He could see several taxis waiting in line under the floodlights of the canopy; the sun had gone down; it was night in Zurich. Still, there were flights to all points of Europe until well past midnight. . . .

He stopped walking, his breath suspended, a form of paralysis sweeping over him. His eyes did not believe what else he saw beyond the glass doors. A brown Peugeot pulled up in the circular drive in front of the first taxi. Its door opened and a man stepped out—a killer in a black raincoat, wearing thin, gold-rimmed spectacles. Then from the other door another figure emerged, but it was not the driver who had been at the curb on the Bahnhofstrasse, waiting for a target he did not recognize. Instead, it was another killer, in another raincoat, its wide pockets recessed for powerful weapons. It was the man who had sat in the reception room on the second floor of the Gemeinschaft Bank, the same man who had pulled a .38 caliber pistol from a holster beneath his coat. A pistol with a perforated cylinder on its barrel that silenced two bullets meant for the skull of the quarry he had followed into an elevator.

How? How could they have found him? . . . Then he remembered and felt sick. It had been so innocuous, so casual!

Are you enjoying your stay in Zurich? Walther Apfel had asked while they were waiting for a minion to leave and be alone again.

Very much. My room overlooks the lake. It's a nice view, very peaceful, quiet.

Koenig! Koenig had heard him say his room looked over the lake. How many hotels had rooms overlooking the lake? Especially hotels a man with a three-zero account might frequent. Two? Three? . . . From unremembered memory names came to him: *Carillon du Lac, Baur au Lac, Eden au Lac.* Were there others? No further names came. How easy it must have been to narrow them down! How easy it had been for him to say the words. How stupid!

[66]

No time. Too late. He could see through the row of glass doors; so, too, could the killers. The second man had spotted him. Words were exchanged over the hood of the Peugeot, gold-rimmed spectacles adjusted, hands placed in outsized pockets, unseen weapons gripped. The two men converged on the entrance, separating at the last moment, one on either end of the row of clear glass panels. The flanks were covered, the trap set; he could not race outside.

Did they think they could walk into a crowded hotel lobby and simply *kill* a man?

Of course they could, The crowds and the noise were their cover. Two, three, four muted gunshots fired at close range would be as effective as an ambush in a crowded square in daylight, escape easily found in the resulting chaos.

He could not let them get near him! He backed away, thoughts racing through his mind, outrage paramount. How *dared* they? What made them think he would not run for protection, scream for the police? And then the answer was clear, as numbing as the question itself. The killers knew with certainty that which he could only surmise: he could not seek that kind of protection—he could not seek the police. For Jason Bourne, all the authorities had to be avoided. . . . Why? Were they seeking *him?*

Jesus Christ, why?

The two opposing doors were opened by outstretched hands, other hands hidden, around steel. Bourne turned; there were elevators, doorways, corridors—a roof and cellars; there had to be a dozen ways out of the hotel.

Or were there? Did the killers now threading their way through the crowds know something else he could only surmise? Did the Carillon du Lac have only two or three exits? Easily covered by men outside, easily used as traps themselves to cut down the lone figure of a running man.

A lone man; a lone man was an obvious target. But suppose he were not alone? Suppose someone was with him? Two people were not one, but for one alone an extra person was camouflage—especially in crowds, especially at night, and it *was* night. Determined killers avoided taking the wrong life, not from compassion but for practicality; in any ensuing panic the real target might escape.

He felt the weight of the gun in his pocket, but there was not much comfort in knowing it was there. As at the bank, to use it—to even display it—was to mark him. Still, it was there. He started back toward the center of the lobby, then turned to his right where there was a greater concentration of people. It was the pre-evening hour during an international conference, a thousand tentative plans being made, rank and courtesan separated by glances of approval and rebuke, odd groupings everywhere.

There was a marble counter against the wall, a clerk behind it checking pages of yellow paper with a pencil held like a paintbrush. *Cablegrams*. In front of the counter were two people, an obese elderly man and a woman in a dark red dress, the rich color of the silk complementing her long, titian hair. . . . Auburn hair. It was the woman in the elevator who had joked about Caesar's taxes and the Punic wars, the doctor who had stood beside him at the hotel desk, asking for the cable she knew was there.

Bourne looked behind him. The killers were using the crowds well, excusing themselves politely but firmly through, one on the right, one on the left, closing in like two prongs of a pincer attack. As long as they kept him in sight, they could force him to keep running blindly, without direction, not knowing which path he took might lead to a dead end where he could run no longer. And then the muted spits would come, pockets blackened by powder burns. . . .

Kept him in sight?

The back row then. . . . *We can sleep. He uses a slide projector; it'll be dark.*

Jason turned again and looked at the auburn-haired woman. She had completed her cable and was thanking the clerk, removing a pair of tinted, horn-rimmed glasses from her face, placing them into her purse. She was not more than eight feet away.

Bertinelli is speaking, to little effect, I suggest.

There was no time for anything but instinctive decisions. Bourne shifted his suitcase to his left hand, walked rapidly over to the woman at the marble counter, and touched her elbow, gently, with as little alarm as possible.

"Doctor? . . ."

"I beg your pardon?"

"You *are* Doctor? . . ." He released her, a bewildered man.

"St. Jacques," she completed, using the French pronunciation of Saint. "You're the one in the elevator."

"I didn't realize it was you," he said. "I was told you'd know where this Bertinelli is speaking."

"It's right on the board. Suite Seven."

"I'm afraid I don't know where it is. Would you mind showing me? I'm late and I've got to take notes on his talk."

"On Bertinelli? Why? Are you with a Marxist newspaper?"

"A neutral pool," said Jason, wondering where the phrases came from. "I'm covering for a number of people. They don't think he's worth it."

"Perhaps not, but he should be heard. There are a few brutal truths in what he says."

"I lost, so I've got to find him. Maybe you can point him out."

"I'm afraid not. I'll show you the room, but I've a phone call to make." She snapped her purse shut.

"Please. *Hurry!*"

"What?" She looked at him, not kindly.

"Sorry, but I *am* in a hurry." He glanced to his right; the two men were no more than twenty feet away.

"You're also rude," said the St. Jacques woman coldly.

"*Please.*" He restrained his desire to propel her forward, away from the moving trap that was closing in.

"It's this way." She started across the floor toward a wide corridor carved out of the left rear wall. The crowds were thinner, prominence less apparent in the back regions of the lobby. They reached what looked like a velvet-covered tunnel of deep red, doors on opposite sides, lighted signs above them identifying Conference Room One, Conference Room Two. At the end of the hallway were double doors, the gold letters to the right proclaiming them to be the entrance to Suite Seven.

"There you are," said Marie St. Jacques. "Be careful when you go in; it's probably dark. Bertinelli lectures with slides."

"Like a movie," commented Bourne, looking behind him at the crowds at the far end of the corridor. He was there; the man with gold-rimmed spectacles was excusing himself past an animated trio in the lobby. He was walking into the hallway, his companion right behind him.

". . . a considerable difference. He sits below the stage and pontificates." The St. Jacques woman had said something and was now leaving him.

"What did you say? A stage?"

"Well, a raised platform. For exhibits usually."

"They have to be brought in," he said.

"What does?"

"Exhibits. Is there an exit in there? Another door?"

"I have no idea, and I really must make my call. Enjoy the *professore*." She turned away.

He dropped the suitcase and took her arm. At the touch, she glared at him. "Take your hand off me, please."

"I don't want to frighten you, but I have no choice." He spoke quietly, his eyes over her shoulder; the killers had slowed their pace, the trap sure, about to close. "You have to come with me."

"Don't be ridiculous!"

He viced the grip around her arm, moving her in front of him. Then he pulled the gun out of his pocket, making sure her body concealed it from the men thirty feet away. "I don't want to use this. I don't want to hurt you, but I'll do both if I have to."

"My God . . ."

"Be quiet. Just do as I say and you'll be fine. I have to get out of this hotel and you're going to help me. Once I'm out, I'll let you go. But not until then. Come on. We're going in there."

"You *can't* . . ."

"Yes, I can." He pushed the barrel of the gun into her stomach, into the dark silk that creased under the force of his thrust. She was terrified into silence, into submission. "Let's go."

He stepped to her left, his hand still gripping her arm, the pistol held across his chest inches from her own. Her eyes were riveted on it, her lips parted, her breath erratic. Bourne opened the door, propelling her through it in front of him. He could hear a single word shouted from the corridor.

"Schnell!"

They were in darkness, but it was brief; a shaft of white light shot across the room, over the rows of chairs, illuminating the heads of the audience. The projection on the faraway screen on the stage was that of a graph, the grids marked numerically, a heavy black line starting at the left, extending in a jagged pattern through the lines to the right. A heavily accented voice was speaking, amplified by a loudspeaker.

"You will note that during the years of seventy and seventy-one, when specific restraints in production were self-imposed—I repeat, *self*-imposed—by these leaders of industry, the resulting economic recession was far less severe than in—slide twelve, please—the so-called paternalistic regulation of the marketplace by government interventionists. The next slide, please."

The room went dark again. There was a problem with the projector; no second shaft of light replaced the first.

"Slide twelve, please!"

Jason pushed the woman forward, in front of the figures standing by the back wall, behind the last row of chairs. He tried to judge the size of the lecture hall, looking for a red light that could mean escape. He saw it! A faint reddish glow in the distance. On the stage, behind the screen. There were no other exits, no other doors but the entrance to Suite Seven. He had to reach it; he had to get them to that exit. On that stage.

"*Marie—par ici!*" The whisper came from their left, from a seat in the back row.

"*Non, chérie. Reste avec moi.*" The second whisper was delivered by the shadowed figure of a man standing directly in front of Marie St. Jacques. He had stepped away from the wall, intercepting her. "*On nous a séparé. I'l n'y a plus de chaises.*"

Bourne pressed the gun firmly into the woman's rib cage, its message unmistakable. She whispered without breathing, Jason grateful that her face could not be seen clearly. "Please, let us by," she said in French. "*Please.*"

"What's this? Is he your cablegram, my dear?"

"An old friend," whispered Bourne.

A shout rose over the increasingly louder hum from the audience. "May I please have *slide twelve! Per favore!*"

"We have to see someone at the end of the row," continued Jason, looking behind him. The right-hand door of the entrance opened; in the middle of a shadowed face, a pair of gold-rimmed glasses reflected the dim light of the corridor. Bourne edged the girl past her bewildered friend, forcing him back into the wall, whispering an apology.

"Sorry, but we're in a hurry!"

"You're damn rude, too!"

"Yes, I know."

"Slide *twelve! Ma che infamia!*"

The beam of light shot out from the projector; it vibrated

[71]

under the nervous hand of the operator. Another graph appeared on the screen as Jason and the woman reached the far wall, the start of the narrow aisle that led down the length of the hall to the stage. He pushed her into the corner, pressing his body against hers, his face against her face.

"I'll scream," she whispered.

"I'll shoot," he said. He peered around the figures leaning against the wall; the killers were both inside, both squinting, shifting their heads like alarmed rodents, trying to spot their target among the rows of faces.

The voice of the lecturer rose like the ringing of a cracked bell, his diatribe brief but strident. "*Ecco!* For the skeptics I address here this evening—and that is most of you—here is statistical proof! Identical in substance to a hundred other analyses I have prepared. Leave the marketplace to those who live there. Minor excesses can always be found. They are a small price to pay for the general good."

There was a scattering of applause, the approval of a definite minority. Bertinelli resumed a normal tone and droned on, his long pointer stabbing at the screen, emphasizing the obvious—his obvious. Jason leaned back again; the gold spectacles glistened in the harsh glare of the projector's side light, the killer who wore them touching his companion's arm, nodding to his left, ordering his subordinate to continue the search on the left side of the room; he would take the right. He began, the gold rims growing brighter as he sidestepped his way in front of those standing, studying each face. He would reach the corner, reach *them*, in a matter of seconds. Stopping the killer with a gunshot was all that was left; and if someone along the row of those standing moved, or if the woman he had pressed against the wall went into panic and shoved him . . . or if he missed the killer for any number of reasons, he was trapped. And even if he hit the man, there was another killer across the room, certainly a marksman.

"Slide *thirteen*, if you please."

That was *it. Now!*

The shaft of light went out. In the blackout, Bourne pulled the woman from the wall, spun her in her place, his face against hers. "If you make a sound, I'll kill you!"

"I believe you," she whispered, terrified. "You're a maniac."

"Let's go!" He pushed her down the narrow aisle that

led to the stage fifty feet away. The projector's light went on again; he grabbed the girl's neck, forcing her down into a kneeling position as he, too, knelt down behind her. They were concealed from the killers by the rows of bodies sitting in the chairs. He pressed her flesh with his fingers; it was his signal to keep moving, crawling . . . slowly, keeping down, but *moving*. She understood; she started forward on her knees, trembling.

"The conclusions of this phase are irrefutable," cried the lecturer. "The profit motive is inseparable from productivity incentive, but the adversary roles can never be equal. As Socrates understood, the inequality of values is constant. Gold simply is not brass or iron; who among you can deny it? Slide fourteen, if you please!"

The darkness again. *Now.*

He yanked the woman up, pushing her forward, toward the stage. They were within three feet of the edge.

"*Cosa succede?* What is the matter, please? Slide *fourteen!*"

It had happened! The projector was jammed again; the darkness was extended again. And there on the stage in front of them, above them, was the red glow of the exit sign. Jason gripped the girl's arm viciously. "Get up on that stage and run to the exit! I'm right behind you; you stop or cry out, I'll shoot."

"For God's sake, let me go!"

"Not yet." He meant it; there was another exit somewhere, men waiting outside for the target from Marseilles. "Go on! *Now.*"

The St. Jacques woman got to her feet and ran to the stage. Bourne lifted her off the floor, over the edge, leaping up as he did so, pulling her to her feet again.

The blinding light of the projector shot out, flooding the screen, washing the stage. Cries of surprise and derision came from the audience at the sight of two figures, the shouts of the indignant Bertinelli heard over the din.

"*È insoffribile! Ci sono comunisti qui!*"

And there were other sounds—three—lethal, sharp, sudden. Cracks of a muted weapon—weapons; wood splintered on the molding of the proscenium arch. Jason hammered the girl down and lunged toward the shadows of the narrow wing space, pulling her behind him.

"*Da ist er! Da oben!*"

"*Schnell! Der projektor!*"

A scream came from the center aisle of the hall as the light of the projector swung to the right, spilling into the wings—but not completely. Its beam was intercepted by receding upright flats that masked the offstage area; *light, shadow, light, shadow*. And at the end of the flats, at the rear of the stage, was the exit. A high, wide metal door with a crashbar against it.

Glass shattered; the red light exploded, a marksman's bullet blew out the sign above the door. It did not matter; he could see the gleaming brass of the crashbar clearly.

The lecture hall had broken out in pandemonium. Bourne grabbed the woman by the cloth of her blouse, yanking her beyond the flats toward the door. For an instant she resisted; he slapped her across the face and dragged her beside him until the crashbar was above their heads.

Bullets spat into the wall to their right; the killers were racing down the aisles for accurate sightlines. They would reach them in seconds, and in seconds other bullets, or a single bullet, would find its mark. There were enough shells left, he knew that. He had no idea how or why he knew, but he *knew*. By sound he could visualize the weapons, extract the clips, count the shells.

He smashed his forearm into the crashbar of the exit door. It flew open and he lunged through the opening, dragging the kicking St. Jacques woman with him.

"Stop it!" she screamed. "I won't go any farther! You're insane! Those were gunshots!"

Jason slammed the large metal door shut with his foot. "Get up!"

"No!"

He lashed the back of his hand across her face. "Sorry, but you're coming with me. Get up! Once we're outside, you have my word. I'll let you go." But where was he going now? They were in another tunnel, but there was no carpet, no polished doors with lighted signs above them. They were in some sort of deserted loading area; the floor was concrete, and there were two pipe-framed freight dollies next to him against the wall. He had been right: exhibits used on the stage of Suite Seven had to be trucked in, the exit door high enough and wide enough to accommodate large displays.

The *door!* He had to block the door! Marie St. Jacques was on her feet; he held her as he grabbed the first dolly, pulling it by its frame in front of the exit door, slamming it with his shoulder and knee until it was lodged against the metal. He looked down; beneath the thick wooden base were footlocks on the wheels. He jammed his heel down on the front lever lock, and then the back one.

The girl spun, trying to break his grip as he stretched his leg to the end of the dolly; he slid his hand down her arm, gripped her wrist, and twisted it inward. She screamed, tears in her eyes, her lips trembling. He pulled her alongside him, forcing her to the left, breaking into a run, assuming the direction was toward the rear of the Carillon du Lac, hoping he'd find the exit. For there and only there he might need the woman; a brief few seconds when a couple emerged, not a lone man running.

There was a series of loud crashes; the killers were trying to force the stage door open, but the locked freight dolly was too heavy a barrier.

He yanked the girl along the cement floor; she tried to pull away, kicking again, twisting her body again from one side to the other; she was over the edge of hysteria. He had no choice; he gripped her elbow, his thumb on the inner flesh, and pressed as hard as he could. She gasped, the pain sudden and excruciating; she sobbed, expelling breath, allowing him to propel her forward.

They reached a cement staircase, the four steps edged in steel, leading to a pair of metal doors below. It was the loading dock; beyond the doors was the Carillon du Lac's rear parking area. He was almost there. It was only a question of appearances now.

"Listen to me," he said to the rigid, frightened woman. "Do you want me to let you go?"

"Oh God, yes! *Please!*"

"Then you do exactly as I say. We're going to walk down these steps and out that door like two perfectly normal people at the end of a normal day's work. You're going to link your arm in mine and we're going to walk slowly, talking quietly, to the cars at the far end of the parking lot. And we're both going to laugh—not loudly, just casually—as if we were remembering funny things that happened during the day. Have you got that?"

"Nothing funny at all has happened to me during the past fifteen minutes," she answered in a barely audible monotone.

"Pretend that it has. I may be trapped; if I am I don't care. Do you understand?"

"I think my wrist is broken."

"It's not."

"My left arm, my shoulder. I can't move them; they're throbbing."

"A nerve ending was depressed; it'll pass in a matter of minutes. You'll be fine."

"You're an animal."

"I want to live," he said. "Come on. Remember, when I open the door, look at me and smile, tilt your head back, laugh a little."

"It will be the most difficult thing I've ever done."

"It's easier than dying."

She put her injured hand under his arm and they walked down the short flight of steps to the platform door. He opened it and they went outside, his hand in his topcoat pocket gripping the Frenchman's pistol, his eyes scanning the loading dock. There was a single bulb encased in wire mesh above the door, its spill defining the concrete steps to the left that led to the pavement below; he led his hostage toward them.

She performed as he had ordered, the effect macabre. As they walked down the steps, her face was turned to his, her terrified features caught in the light. Her generous lips were parted, stretched over her white teeth in a false, tense smile; her wide eyes were two dark orbs, reflecting primordial fear, her tear-stained skin taut and pale, marred by the reddish splotches where he had hit her. He was looking at a face of chiseled stone, a mask framed by dark red hair that cascaded over her shoulders, swept back by the night breezes—moving, the only living thing about the mask.

Choked laughter came from her throat, the veins in her long neck pronounced. She was not far from collapsing, but he could not think about that. He had to concentrate on the space around them, at whatever movement—however slight—he might discern in the shadows of the large parking lot. It was obvious that these back, unlit regions were used by the Carillon du Lac's employees; it was nearly 6:30, the night shift well immersed in its duties. Everything was still, a smooth black field broken up by rows of silent automobiles, ranks of huge insects, the dull glass of the headlamps, a hundred eyes staring at nothing.

A scratch. Metal had scraped against metal. It came

from the right, from one of the cars in a nearby row. Which *row*? Which *car*? He tilted his head back as if responding to a joke made by his companion, letting his eyes roam across the windows of the cars nearest to them. Nothing.

Something? It was there but it was so small, barely seen . . . so bewildering. A tiny circle of green, an infinitesimal glow of green light. It moved . . . as they moved.

Green. Small . . . *light*? Suddenly, from somewhere in a forgotten past the image of crosshairs burst across his eyes. His eyes were looking at two thin intersecting lines! *Crosshairs!* A scope . . . an infrared scope of a rifle.

How did the killers know? Any number of answers. A hand-held radio had been used at the Gemeinschaft; one could be in use now. He wore a topcoat; his hostage wore a thin silk dress and the night was cool. No woman would go out like that.

He swung to his left, crouching, lunging into Marie St. Jacques, his shoulder crashing into her stomach, sending her reeling back toward the steps. The muffled cracks came in staccato repetition; stone and asphalt exploded all around them. He dove to his right, rolling over and over again the instant he made contact with the pavement, yanking the pistol from his topcoat pocket. Then he sprang again, now straight forward, his left hand steadying his right wrist, the gun centered, aimed at the window with the rifle. He fired three shots.

A scream came from the dark open space of the stationary car; it was drawn out into a cry, then a gasp, and then nothing. Bourne lay motionless, waiting, listening, watching, prepared to fire again. Silence. He started to get up . . . but he could not. Something had happened. He could barely move. Then the pain spread through his chest, the pounding so violent he bent over, supporting himself with both hands, shaking his head, trying to focus his eyes, trying to reject the agony. His left shoulder, his lower chest —below the ribs . . . his left thigh—above the knee, below the hip; the locations of his previous wounds, where dozens of stitches had been removed over a month ago. He had damaged the weakened areas, stretching tendons and muscles not yet fully restored. Oh, Christ! He had to get up; he had to reach the would-be killer's car, pull the killer from it, and get away.

He whipped his head up, grimacing with the pain, and

looked over at Marie St. Jacques. She was getting slowly to her feet, first on one knee, then on one foot, supporting herself on the outside wall of the hotel. In a moment she would be standing, then running. Away.

He could not let her go! She would race screaming into the Carillon du Lac; men would come, some to take him . . . some to kill him. He had to stop her!

He let his body fall forward and started rolling to his left, spinning like a wildly out-of-control mannikin, until he was within four feet of the wall, four feet from her. He raised his gun, aiming at her head.

"Help me up," he said, hearing the strain in his voice.

"What?"

"You heard me! Help me *up*."

"You said I could go! You gave me your word!"

"I have to take it back."

"No, *please*."

"This gun is aimed directly at your face, Doctor. You come here and help me get up or I'll blow it off."

He pulled the dead man from the car and ordered her to get behind the wheel. Then he opened the rear door and crawled into the back seat out of sight.

"Drive," he said. "Drive where I tell you."

— 6 —

Whenever you're in a stress situation yourself—and there's time, of course—do exactly as you would do when you project yourself into one you're observing. Let your mind fall free, let whatever thoughts and images that surface come cleanly. Try not to exercise any mental discipline. Be a sponge; concentrate on everything and nothing. Specifics may come to you, certain repressed conduits electrically prodded into functioning.

Bourne thought of Washburn's words as he adjusted his body into the corner of the seat, trying to restore some control. He massaged his chest, gently rubbing the bruised muscles around his previous wound; the pain was still there, but not as acute as it had been minutes ago.

"You can't just tell me to drive!" cried the St. Jacques woman. "I don't know where I'm going!"

"Neither do I," said Jason. He had told her to stay on the lakeshore drive; it was dark and he had to have time to think. If only to be a sponge.

"People will be *looking* for me," she exclaimed.

"They're looking for me, too."

"You've taken me against my will. You struck me. Repeatedly." She spoke more softly now, imposing a control on herself. "That's kidnapping, assault . . . those are serious crimes. You're out of the hotel; that's what you said you wanted. Let me go and I won't say anything. I promise you!"

"You mean you'll give me your word?"

"Yes!"

"I gave you mine and took it back. So could you."

"You're different. I *won't*. No one's trying to kill me! Oh God! *Please!*"

"Keep driving."

One thing was clear to him. The killers had seen him drop his suitcase and leave it behind in his race for escape. That suitcase told them the obvious: he was getting out of Zurich, undoubtedly out of Switzerland. The airport and the train station would be watched. And the car he had taken from the man he had killed—who had tried to kill him—would be the object of a search.

He could not go to the airport or to the train station; he had to get rid of the car and find another. Yet he was not without resources. He was carrying 100,000 Swiss francs, and more than 16,000 French francs, the Swiss currency in his passport case, the French in the billfold he had stolen from the Marquis de Chamford. It was more than enough to buy him secretly to Paris.

Why Paris? It was as though the city were a magnet, pulling him to her without explanation.

You are not helpless. You will find your way. . . . Follow your instincts, reasonably, of course.

To Paris.

"Have you been to Zurich before?" he asked his hostage.

"Never."

"You wouldn't lie to me, would you?"

"I've no *reason* to! *Please*. Let me stop. Let me *go!*"

"How long have you been here?"

"A week. The conference was for a week."

"Then you've had time to get around, do some sightseeing."

"I barely left the hotel. There wasn't time."

"The schedule I saw on the board didn't seem very crowded. Only two lectures for the entire day."

"They were guest speakers; there were never more than two a day. The majority of our work was done in conference . . . small conferences. Ten to fifteen people from different countries, different interests."

"You're from Canada?"

"I work for the Canadian government Treasury Board, Department of National Revenue."

"The 'doctor's' not medical then."

"Economics. McGill University. Pembroke College, Oxford."

"I'm impressed."

Suddenly, with controlled stridency, she added, "My superiors expect me to be in contact with them. *Tonight*. If they don't hear from me, they'll be alarmed. They'll make inquiries; they'll call the Zurich police."

"I see," he said. "That's something to think about, isn't it?" It occurred to Bourne that throughout the shock and the violence of the last half hour, the St. Jacques woman had not let her purse out of her hand. He leaned forward, wincing as he did so, the pain in his chest suddenly acute again. "Give me your purse."

"What?" She moved her hand quickly from the wheel, grabbing the purse in a futile attempt to keep it from him.

He thrust his right hand over the seat, his fingers grasping the leather. "Just drive, Doctor," he said as he lifted the purse off the seat and leaned back again.

"You have no *right* . . ." She stopped, the foolishness of her remark apparent.

"I know that," he replied, opening the purse, turning on the sedan's reading lamp, moving the handbag into its spill. As befitted the owner, the purse was well organized. Passport, wallet, a change purse, keys, and assorted notes and messages in the rear pockets. He looked for a specific message; it was in a yellow envelope given her by the clerk at the Carillon du Lac's front desk. He found it, lifted the flap, and took out the folded paper. It was a cablegram from Ottawa.

DAILY REPORTS FIRST RATE. LEAVE GRANTED. WILL MEET YOU AT AIRPORT WEDNESDAY 26. CALL OR CABLE FLIGHT. IN LYON DO NOT MISS BELLE MEUNIERE. CUISINE SUPERB. LOVE PETER

Jason put the cable back in the purse. He saw a small book of matches, the cover a glossy white, scroll writing on the front. He picked it out and read the name. Kronenhalle. A restaurant . . . A restaurant. Something bothered him; he did not know what it was, but it was there. Something about a restaurant. He kept the matches, closed the purse, and leaned forward, dropping it on the front seat. "That's all I wanted to see," he said, settling back into the corner, staring at the matches. "I seem to remember your saying something about 'word from Ottawa.' You got it; the twenty-sixth is over a week away."

"Please . . ."

The supplication was a cry for help; he heard it for what it was but could not respond. For the next hour or so he needed this woman, needed her as a lame man needed a crutch, or more aptly, as one who could not function behind a wheel needed a driver. But not in this car.

"Turn around," he ordered. "Head back to the Carillon."

"To the . . . hotel?"

"Yes," he said, his eyes on the matches, turning them over and over in his hand under the light of the reading lamp. "We need another car."

"We? No, you *can't!* I won't go any—" Again she stopped before the statement was made, before the thought was completed. Another thought had obviously struck her; she was abruptly silent as she swung the wheel until the sedan was facing the opposite direction on the dark lakeshore road. She pressed the accelerator down with such force that the car bolted; the tires spun under the sudden burst of speed. She depressed the pedal instantly, gripping the wheel, trying to control herself.

Bourne looked up from the matches at the back of her head, at the long dark red hair that shone in the light. He took the gun from his pocket and once more leaned forward directly behind her. He raised the weapon, moving his hand over her shoulder, turning the barrel and pressing it against her cheek.

"Understand me clearly. You're going to do exactly as I tell you. You're going to be right at my side and this gun will be in my pocket. It will be aimed at your stomach, just as it's aimed at your head right now. As you've seen, I'm running for my life, and I won't hesitate to pull the trigger. I want you to understand."

"I understand." Her reply was a whisper. She breathed through her parted lips, her terror complete. Jason removed the barrel of the gun from her cheek; he was satisfied.

Satisfied and revolted.

Let your mind fall free. . . . The matches. What was it about the matches? But it was not the matches, it was the restaurant—not the Kronenhalle, but a restaurant. Heavy beams, candlelight, black . . . triangles on the outside. White stone and black triangles. Three? . . . Three black triangles.

Someone was there . . . at a restaurant with three triangles in front. The image was so clear, so vivid . . . so disturbing. What was it? Did such a place even exist?

Specifics may come to you . . . certain repressed conduits . . . prodded into functioning.

Was it happening now? *Oh, Christ, I can't stand it!*

He could see the lights of the Carillon du Lac several hundred yards down the road. He had not fully thought out his moves, but was operating on two assumptions. The first was that the killers had not remained on the premises. On the other hand, Bourne was not about to walk into a trap of his own making. He knew two of the killers; he would not recognize others if they had been left behind.

The main parking area was beyond the circular drive, on the left side of the hotel. "Slow down," Jason ordered. "Turn into the first drive on the left."

"It's an exit," protested the woman, her voice strained. "We're going the wrong way."

"No one's coming out. Go on! Drive into the parking lot, past the lights."

The scene at the hotel's canopied entrance explained why no one paid attention to them. There were four police cars lined up in the circular drive, their roof lights revolving, conveying the aura of emergency. He could see uniformed police, tuxedoed hotel clerks at their sides, among the crowds of excited hotel guests; they were asking questions as well as answering them, checking off names of those leaving in automobiles.

Marie St. Jacques drove across the parking area beyond the floodlights and into an open space on the right. She turned off the engine and sat motionless, staring straight ahead.

"Be very careful," said Bourne, rolling down his window. "And move slowly. Open your door and get out, then stand by mine and help me. Remember, the window's open and the gun's in my hand. You're only two or three feet in front of me; there's no way I could miss if I fired."

She did as she was told, a terrified automaton. Jason supported himself on the frame of the window and pulled himself to the pavement. He shifted his weight from one foot to another; mobility was returning. He could walk. Not well, and with a limp, but he could walk.

"What are you going to do?" asked the St. Jacques woman, as if she were afraid to hear his answer.

"Wait. Sooner or later someone will drive a car back here and park it. No matter what happened in there, it's still dinnertime. Reservations were made, parties arranged, a lot of it business; those people won't change their plans."

"And when a car does come, how will you take it?" She paused, then answered her own question. "Oh, my God, you're going to kill whoever's driving it."

He gripped her arm, her frightened chalk-white face inches away. He had to control her by fear, but not to the point where she might slip into hysterics. "If I have to I will, but I don't think it'll be necessary. Parking attendants bring the cars back here. Keys are usually left on the dashboard or under the seats. It's just easier."

Headlight beams shot out from the fork in the circular drive; a small coupé entered the lot, accelerating once into it, the mark of an attendant driver. The car came directly toward them, alarming Bourne until he saw the empty space nearby. But they were in the path of the headlights; they had been seen.

Reservations for the dining room. . . . A restaurant. Jason made his decision; he would use the moment.

The attendant got out of the coupé and placed the keys under the seat. As he walked to the rear of the car, he nodded at them, not without curiosity. Bourne spoke in French.

"Hey, young fellow! Maybe you can help us."

"Sir?" The attendant approached them haltingly, cautiously, the events in the hotel obviously on his mind.

"I'm not feeling so well, too much of your excellent Swiss wine."

"It will happen, sir." The young man smiled, relieved.

"My wife thought it would be a good idea to get some air before we left for town."

"A good idea, sir."

"Is everything still crazy inside? I didn't think the police officer would let us out until he saw that I might be sick all over his uniform."

"Crazy, sir. They're everywhere. . . . We've been told not to discuss it."

"Of course. But we've got a problem. An associate flew in this afternoon and we agreed to meet at a restaurant, only I've forgotten the name. I've been there but I just can't remember where it is or what it's called. I do remember that on the front there were three odd shapes . . . a design of some sort, I think. Triangles. I believe."

"That's the Drei Alpenhäuser, sir. The . . . Three Chalets. It's in a sidestreet off the Falkenstrasse."

"Yes, of course, that's it! And to get there from here we . . ." Bourne trailed off the words, a man with too much wine trying to concentrate.

"Just turn left out of the exit, sir. Stay on the Uto Quai for about one hundred meters, until you reach a large pier, then turn right. It will take you into the Falkenstrasse. Once you pass Seefeld, you can't miss the street or the restaurant. There's a sign on the corner."

"Thank you. Will you be here a few hours from now, when we return?"

"I'm on duty until two this morning, sir."

"Good. I'll look for you and express my gratitude more concretely."

"Thank you, sir. May I get your car for you?"

"You've done enough, thanks. A little more walking is required." The attendant saluted and started for the front of the hotel. Jason led Marie St. Jacques toward the coupé, limping beside her. "Hurry up. The keys are under the seat."

"If they stop us, what will you do? That attendant will see the car go out; he'll know you've stolen it."

"I doubt it. Not if we leave right away, the minute he's back in that crowd."

"Suppose he *does?*"

"Then I hope you're a fast driver," said Bourne pushing her toward the door. "Get in." The attendant had turned the corner and suddenly hurried his pace. Jason took out the gun and limped rapidly around the hood of the coupé, supporting himself on it while pointing the pistol at the windshield. He opened the passenger door and climbed in beside her. "Goddamn it—I said get the *keys!*"

"All right . . . I can't *think.*"

"Try harder!"

"Oh, *God* . . ." She reached below the seat, stabbing her hand around the carpet until she found the small leather case.

"Start the motor, but wait until I tell you to back out." He watched for headlight beams to shine into the area from the circular drive; it would be a reason for the attendant to have suddenly broken into a near run; a car to be parked. They did not come; the reason could be something else. Two unknown people in the parking lot. "Go ahead. Quickly. I want to get out of here." She threw the gear into reverse; seconds later they approached the exit into the lakeshore drive. "Slow down," he commanded. A taxi was swinging into the curve in front of them.

Bourne held his breath and looked through the opposite window at the Carillon du Lac's entrance; the scene under the canopy explained the attendant's sudden decision to hurry. An argument had broken out between the police and a group of hotel guests. A line had formed, names checked off for those leaving the hotel, the resulting delays angering the innocent.

"Let's go," said Jason, wincing again, the pain shooting through his chest. "We're clear."

It was a numbing sensation, eerie and uncanny. The three triangles were as he had pictured them: thick dark wood raised in bas-relief on white stone. Three equal triangles, abstract renditions of chalet roofs in a valley of snow so deep the lower stories were obscured. Above the three points was the restaurant's name in Germanic letters: DREI ALPENHAUSER. Below the baseline of the center triangles was the entrance, double doors that together formed a cathedral arch, the hardware massive rings of iron common to an Alpine château.

The surrounding buildings on both sides of the narrow brick street were restored structures of a Zurich and a Europe long past. It was not a street for automobiles; instead one pictured elaborate coaches drawn by horses, drivers sitting high in mufflers and top hats, and gas lamps everywhere. It was a street filled with the sights and sounds of forgotten memories, thought the man who had no memory to forget.

Yet he *had* had one, vivid and disturbing. Three dark

triangles, heavy beams and candlelight. He had been right; it was a memory of Zurich. But in another life.

"We're here," said the woman.

"I know."

"Tell me what to do!" she cried. "We're going past it."

"Go to the next corner and turn left. Go around the block, then drive back through here."

"Why?"

"I wish I knew."

"What?"

"Because I said so." *Someone was there . . . at that restaurant. Why didn't other images come? Another image. A face.*

They drove down the street past the restaurant twice more. Two separate couples and a foursome went inside; a single man came out, heading for the Falkenstrasse. To judge from the cars parked on the curb, there was a medium-sized crowd at the Drei Alpenhäuser. It would grow in number as the next two hours passed, most of Zurich preferring its evening meal nearer ten-thirty than eight. There was no point in delaying any longer; nothing further came to Bourne. He could only sit and watch and hope something *would* come. *Something.* For something had; a book of matches had evoked an image of reality. Within that reality there was a truth he had to discover.

"Pull over to your right, in front of the last car. We'll walk back."

Silently, without comment or protest, the St. Jacques woman did as she was told. Jason looked at her; her reaction was too docile, inconsistent with her previous behavior. He understood. A lesson had to be taught. Regardless of what might happen inside the Drei Alpenhäuser, he needed her for a final contribution. She had to drive him out of Zurich.

The car came to a stop, tires scraping the curb. She turned off the motor and began to remove the keys, her movement slow, too slow. He reached over and held her wrist; she stared at him in the shadows without breathing. He slid his fingers over her hand until he felt the key case.

"I'll take those," he said.

"Naturally," she replied, her left hand unnaturally at her side, poised by the panel of the door.

"Now get out and stand by the hood," he continued. "Don't do anything foolish."

"Why should I? You'd kill me."

"Good." He reached for the handle of the door, exaggerating the difficulty. The back of his head was to her; he snapped the handle down.

The rustle of fabric was sudden, the rush of air more sudden still; her door crashed open, the woman half out into the street. But Bourne was ready; a lesson had to be taught. He spun around, his left arm an uncoiling spring, his hand a claw, gripping the silk of her dress between her shoulder blades. He pulled her back into the seat, and, grabbing her by the hair, yanked her head toward him until her neck was stretched, her face against his.

"I won't do it again!" she cried, tears welling at her eyes. "I swear to you I won't!"

He reached across and pulled the door shut, then looked at her closely, trying to understand something in himself. Thirty minutes ago in another car he had experienced a degree of nausea when he had pressed the barrel of the gun into her cheek, threatening to take her life if she disobeyed him. There was no such revulsion now; with one overt action she had crossed over into another territory. She had become an enemy, a threat; he could kill her if he had to, kill her without emotion because it was the practical thing to do.

"*Say* something!" she whispered. Her body went into a brief spasm, her breasts pressing against the dark silk of her dress, rising and falling with the agitated movement. She gripped her own wrist in an attempt to control herself; she partially succeeded. She spoke again, the whisper replaced by a monotone. "I said I wouldn't do it again and I won't."

"You'll try," he replied quietly. "There'll come a moment when you think you can make it, and you'll try. Believe me when I tell you you can't, but if you try again I will have to kill you. I don't want to do that, there's no reason for it, no reason at all. Unless you become a threat to me, and in running away before I let you go you do just that. I can't allow it."

He had spoken the truth as he understood the truth. The simplicity of the decision was as astonishing to him as the decision itself. Killing was a practical matter, nothing else.

"You say you'll let me go," she said. "When?"

"When I'm safe," he answered. "When it doesn't make any difference what you say or do."

"When will that be?"

"An hour or so from now. When we're out of Zurich and I'm on my way to someplace else. You won't know where or how."

"Why should I believe you?"

"I don't care whether you do or not." He released her. "Pull yourself together. Dry your eyes and comb your hair. We're going inside."

"What's in there?"

"I wish I knew," he said, glancing through the rear window at the door of the Drei Alpenhäuser.

"You said that before."

He looked at her, at the wide brown eyes that were searching his. Searching in fear, in bewilderment. "I know. Hurry up."

There were thick beams running across the high Alpine ceiling, tables and chairs of heavy wood, deep booths and candlelight everywhere. An accordion player moved through the crowd, muted strains of Bavarian music coming from his instrument.

He had seen the large room before, the beams and the candlelight printed somewhere in his mind, the sounds recorded also. He had come here in another life. They stood in the shallow foyer in front of the maître d's station; the tuxedoed man greeted them.

"Haben Sie einen Tisch schon reserviert, mein Herr?"

"If you mean reservations, I'm afraid not. But you were highly recommended. I hope you can fit us in. A booth, if possible."

"Certainly, sir. It's the early sitting; we're not yet crowded. This way, please."

They were taken to a booth in the nearest corner, a flickering candle in the center of the table. Bourne's limp and the fact that he held on to the woman, dictated the closest available location. Jason nodded to Marie St. Jacques; she sat down and he slid into the booth opposite her.

"Move against the wall," he said, after the maître d' had left. "Remember, the gun's in my pocket and all I have to do is raise my foot and you're trapped."

"I said I wouldn't try."

"I hope you don't. Order a drink; there's no time to eat."

"I couldn't eat." She gripped her wrist again, her hands visibly trembling. "Why isn't there time? What are you waiting for?"

[89]

"I don't know."

"Why do you keep *saying* that? 'I don't know.' 'I wish I knew.' Why did you come here?"

"Because I've been here before."

"That's no answer!"

"There's no reason for me to give you one."

A waiter approached. The St. Jacques woman asked for wine; Bourne ordered scotch, needing the stronger drink. He looked around the restaurant, trying to concentrate *on everything and nothing*. A sponge. But there was only nothing. No images filled his mind; no thoughts intruded on his absence of thought. *Nothing.*

And then he saw the face across the room. It was a large face set in a large head, above an obese body pressed against the wall of an end booth, next to a closed door. The fat man stayed in the shadows of his observation point as if they were his protection, the unlit section of the floor his sanctuary. His eyes were riveted on Jason, equal parts fear and disbelief in his stare. Bourne did not know the face, but the face knew him. The man brought his fingers to his lips and wiped the corners of his mouth, then shifted his eyes, taking in each diner at every table. Only then did he begin what was obviously a painful journey around the room toward their booth.

"A man's coming over here," Jason said over the flame of the candle. "A fat man, and he's afraid. Don't say anything. No matter what he says, keep your mouth shut. And don't look at him; raise your hand, rest your head on your elbow casually. Look at the wall, not him."

The woman frowned, bringing her right hand to her face; her fingers trembled. Her lips formed a question, but no words came. Jason answered the unspoken.

"For your own good," he said. "There's no point in his being able to identify you."

The fat man edged around the corner of the booth. Bourne blew out the candle, throwing the table into relative darkness. The man stared him down and spoke in a low, strained voice.

"*Du lieber Gott!* Why did you *come* here? What have I done that you should do this to me?"

"I enjoy the food, you know that."

"Have you no *feelings?* I have a family, a wife and children. I did only as I was told. I gave you the envelope; I did not look inside, I know nothing!"

"But you were paid, weren't you?" asked Jason instinctively.

"Yes, but I said nothing. We never met, I never described you. I spoke to no one!"

"Then why are you afraid? I'm just an ordinary patron about to order dinner."

"I beg you. Leave."

"Now I'm angry. You'd better tell me why."

The fat man brought his hand to his face, his fingers again wiping the moisture that had formed around his mouth. He angled his head, glancing at the door, then turned back to Bourne. "Others may have spoken, others may know who you are. I've had my share of trouble with the police, they would come directly to me."

The St. Jacques woman lost control; she looked at Jason, the words escaping. "The police. . . . They were the *police*."

Bourne glared at her, then turned back to the nervous fat man. "Are you saying the police would harm your wife and children?"

"Not in themselves—as you well know. But their interest would lead others to me. To my family. How many are there that look for you, mein Herr? And what *are* they that do? You need no answer from me; they stop at nothing— the death of a wife or a child is nothing. *Please.* On my life. I've said nothing. *Leave.*"

"You're exaggerating." Jason brought the drink to his lips, a prelude to dismissal.

"In the name of Christ, don't *do* this!" The man leaned over, gripping the edge of the table. "You wish proof of my silence, I give it to you. Word was spread throughout the *Verbrecherwelt*. Anyone with any information whatsoever should call a number set up by the Zurich police. Everything would be kept in the strictest confidence; they would not lie in the *Verbrecherwelt* about that. Rewards were ample, the police in several countries sending funds through Interpol. Past misunderstandings might be seen in new judicial lights." The conspirator stood up, wiping his mouth again, his large bulk hovering above the wood. "A man like myself could profit from a kinder relationship with the police. Yet I did nothing. In spite of the guarantee of confidentiality, I did nothing at all!"

"Did anyone else? Tell me the truth; I'll know if you're lying."

"I know only Chernak. He's the only one I've ever spoken with who admits having even seen you. But you know that; the envelope was passed through him to me. He'd never say anything."

"Where's Chernak now?"

"Where he always is. In his flat on the Löwenstrasse."

"I've never been there. What's the number?"

"You've never been? . . ." The fat man paused, his lips pressed together, alarm in his eyes. "Are you testing me?"

"Answer the question."

"Number 37. You know it as well as I do."

"Then I'm testing you. Who gave the envelope to Chernak?"

The man stood motionless, his dubious integrity challenged. "I have no way of knowing. Nor would I ever inquire."

"You weren't even curious?"

"Of course not. A goat does not willingly enter the wolf's cave."

"Goats are surefooted; they've got an accurate sense of smell."

"And they are cautious, mein Herr. Because the wolf is faster, infinitely more aggressive. There would be only one chase. The goat's last."

"What was in the envelope?"

"I told you, I did not open it."

"But you know what was in it."

"Money, I presume."

"You *presume?*"

"Very well. Money. A great deal of money. If there was any discrepancy, it had nothing to do with me. Now *please,* I *beg* you. Get *out* of here!"

"One last question."

"*Anything.* Just leave!"

"What was the money for?"

The obese man stared down at Bourne, his breathing audible, sweat glistening on his chin. "You put me on the rack, mein Herr, but I will not turn away from you. Call it the courage of an insignificant goat who has survived. Every day I read the newspapers. In three languages. Six months ago a man was killed. His death was reported on the front page of each of those papers."

— 7 —

They circled the block, emerging on the Falkenstrasse, then
turned right on the Limmat Quai toward the cathedral of
Grossmünster. The Löwenstrasse was across the river, on
the west side of the city. The quickest way to reach it was
to cross the Münster Bridge to the Bahnhofstrasse, then to
the Nüschelerstrasse; the streets intersected, according to a
couple who had been about to enter the Drei Alpenhäuser.

Marie St. Jacques was silent, holding onto the wheel as
she had gripped the straps of her handbag during the madness at the Carillon, somehow her connection with sanity.
Bourne glanced at her and understood.

. . . *a man was killed, his death reported on the front*
pages of each of those papers.

Jason Bourne had been paid to kill, and the police in
several countries had sent funds through Interpol to con-
vert reluctant informers, to broaden the base of his capture.
Which meant that other men had been killed. . . .

How many are there that look for you, mein Herr? And
what are they that do? . . . They stop at nothing—the
death of a wife or a child is nothing!

Not the police. Others.

The twin bell towers of the Grossmünster church rose in the night sky, floodlights creating eerie shadows. Jason stared at the ancient structure; as so much else he knew it but did not know it. He had seen it before, yet he was seeing it now for the first time.

I know only Chernak. . . . The envelope was passed through him to me. . . . Löwenstrasse. Number 37. You know it as well as I do.

Did he? Would he?

They drove over the bridge into the traffic of the newer city. The streets were crowded, automobiles and pedestrians vying for supremacy at every intersection, the red and green signals erratic and interminable. Bourne tried to concentrate on nothing . . . and everything. The outlines of the truth were being presented to him, shape by enigmatic shape, each more startling than the last. He was not at all sure he was capable—*mentally* capable—of absorbing a great deal more.

"Halt! Die Dame da! Die Scheinwerfer sind aus und Sie haben links signaliziert. Das ist eine Einbahnstrasse!"

Jason looked up, a hollow pain knotting his stomach. A patrol car was beside them, a policeman shouting through his open window. Everything was suddenly clear . . . clear and infuriating. The St. Jacques woman had seen the police car in the sideview mirror; she had extinguished the headlights and slipped her hand down to the directional signal, flipping it for a left turn. A left turn into a one-way street whose arrows at the intersection clearly defined the traffic heading right. And turning left by bolting in front of the police car would result in several violations: the absence of headlights, perhaps even a premeditated collision; they would be stopped, the woman free to scream.

Bourne snapped the headlights on, then leaned across the girl, one hand disengaging the directional signal, the other gripping her arm where he had gripped it before.

"I'll kill you, Doctor," he said quietly, then shouted through the window at the police officer. "Sorry! We're a little confused! Tourists! We want the next block!"

The policeman was barely two feet away from Marie St. Jacques, his eyes on her face, evidently puzzled by her lack of reaction.

The light changed. "Ease forward. Don't do anything stupid," said Jason. He waved at the police officer through the glass. "Sorry again!" he yelled. The policeman

[94]

shrugged, turning to his partner to resume a previous conversation.

"I *was* confused," said the girl, her soft voice trembling. "There's so much traffic. . . . Oh, God, you've broken my arm! . . . You *bastard.*"

Bourne released her, disturbed by her anger; he preferred fear. "You don't expect me to believe you, do you?"

"My arm?"

"Your confusion."

"You said we were going to turn left soon; that's all I was thinking about."

"Next time look at the traffic." He moved away from her but did not take his eyes off her face.

"You *are* an animal," she whispered, briefly closing her eyes, opening them in fear; it had come back.

They reached the Löwenstrasse, a wide avenue where low buildings of brick and heavy wood stood sandwiched between modern examples of smooth concrete and glass. The character of nineteenth-century flats competed against the utilitarianism of contemporary neuterness; they did not lose. Jason watched the numbers; they were descending from the middle eighties, with each block the old houses more in evidence than the high-rise apartments, until the street had returned in time to that other era. There was a row of neat four-story flats, roofs and windows framed in wood, stone steps and railings leading up to recessed doorways washed in the light of carriage lamps. Bourne recognized the unremembered; the fact that he did so was not startling, but something else was. The row of houses evoked another image, a very strong image of another row of flats, similar in outlines, but oddly different. Weathered, older, nowhere near as neat or scrubbed . . . cracked windows, broken steps, incomplete railings—jagged ends of rusted iron. Further away, in another part of . . . Zurich, yes they *were* in Zurich. In a small district rarely if ever visited by those who did not live there, a part of the city that was left behind, but not gracefully.

"Steppdeckstrasse," he said to himself, concentrating on the image in his mind. He could see a doorway, the paint a faded red, as dark as the red silk dress worn by the woman beside him. "A boardinghouse . . . in the Steppdeckstrasse."

"What?" Marie St. Jacques was startled. The words he

uttered alarmed her; she had obviously related them to herself and was terrified.

"Nothing." He took his eyes off the dress and looked out the window. "There's Number 37," he said, pointing to the fifth house in the row. "Stop the car."

He got out first, ordering her to slide across the seat and follow. He tested his legs and took the keys from her.

"You can walk," she said. "If you can walk, you can *drive*."

"I probably can."

"Then let me go! I've done everything you've wanted."

"And then some," he added.

"I won't say anything, can't you *understand* that? You're the last person on earth I ever want to see again . . . or have anything to *do* with. I don't want to be a witness, or get involved with the police, or statements, or *anything!* I don't want to be a part of what you're a part of! I'm frightened to death . . . that's your protection, don't you see? Let me go, *please*."

"I can't."

"You don't believe me."

"That's not relevant. I need you."

"For what?"

"For something very stupid. I don't have a driver's license. You can't rent a car without a driver's license and I've got to rent a car."

"You've got *this* car."

"It's good for maybe another hour. Someone's going to walk out of the Carillon du Lac and want it. The description will be radioed to every police car in Zurich."

She looked at him, dead fear in the glaze of her eyes. "I don't want to go up there with you. I heard what that man said in the restaurant. If I hear any more you'll kill me."

"What you heard makes no more sense to me than it does to you. Perhaps less. Come on." He took her by the arm, and put his free hand on the railing so he could climb the steps with a minimum of pain.

She stared at him, bewilderment and fear converged in her look.

The name M. Chernak was under the second mail slot, a bell beneath the letters. He did not ring it, but pressed the adjacent four buttons. Within seconds a cacophony of voices sprang out of the small, dotted speakers, asking in Schweizerdeutsch who was there. But someone did not answer; he merely pressed a buzzer which released the lock. Jason opened the door, pushing Marie St. Jacques in front of him.

He moved her against the wall and waited. From above came the sounds of doors opening, footsteps walking toward the staircase.

"*Wer ist da?*"

"Johann?"

"*Wo bist du denn?*"

Silence. Followed by words of irritation. Footsteps were heard again; doors closed.

M. Chernak was on the second floor, Flat 2C. Bourne took the girl's arm, limped with her to the staircase, and started the climb. She was right, of course. It would be far better if he were alone, but there was nothing he could do about that; he did need her.

He had studied road maps during the weeks in Port Noir. Lucerne was no more than an hour away, Bern two and a half or three. He could head for either one, dropping her off in some deserted spot along the way, and then disappear. It was simply a matter of timing; he had the resources to buy a hundred connections. He needed only a conduit out of Zurich and she was it.

But before he left Zurich he had to know; he had to talk to a man named . . .

M. Chernak. The name was to the right of the doorbell. He sidestepped away from the door, pulling the woman with him.

"Do you speak German?" Jason asked.

"No."

"Don't lie."

"I'm not."

Bourne thought, glancing up and down the short hallway. Then: "Ring the bell. If the door opens just stand there. If someone answers from inside, say you have a message—an urgent message—from a friend at the Drei Alpenhäuser."

"Suppose he—or she—says to slide it under the door?" Jason looked at her. "Very good."

"I just don't want any more violence. I don't want to *know* anything or *see* anything. I just want to—"

"I know," he interrupted. "Go back to Caesar's taxes and the Punic wars. If he—or she—says something like that, explain in a couple of words that the message is verbal

[97]

and can only be delivered to the man who was described to you."

"If he asks for that description?" said Marie St. Jacques icily, analysis momentarily pre-empting fear.

"You've got a good mind, Doctor," he said.

"I'm precise. I'm frightened; I told you that. What do I do?"

"Say to hell with them, someone else can deliver it. Then start to walk away."

She moved to the door and rang the bell. There was an odd sound from within. A scratching, growing louder, constant. Then it stopped and a deep voice was heard through the wood.

"*Ja?*"

"I'm afraid I don't speak German."

"*Englisch.* What is it? Who are you?"

"I have an urgent message from a friend at the Drei Alpenhäuser."

"Shove it under the door."

"I can't do that. It isn't written down. I have to deliver it personally to the man who was described to me."

"Well, that shouldn't be difficult," said the voice. The lock clicked and the door opened.

Bourne stepped away from the wall, into the doorframe.

"You're *insane!*" cried a man with two stumps for legs, propped up in a wheelchair. "Get *out!* Get away from here!"

"I'm tired of hearing that," said Jason, pulling the girl inside and closing the door.

It took no pressure to convince Marie St. Jacques to remain in a small, windowless bedroom while they talked; she did so willingly. The legless Chernak was close to panic, his ravaged face chalk white, his unkempt gray hair matted about his neck and forehead.

"What do you *want* from me?" he asked. "You swore the last transaction was our final one! I can do no more, I cannot take the risk. Messengers have been here. No matter how cautious, how many times removed from your sources, they have *been here!* If one leaves an address in the wrong surroundings, I'm a dead man!"

"You've done pretty well for the risks you've taken," said Bourne, standing in front of the wheelchair, his mind racing, wondering if there was a word or a phrase that could trigger a flow of information. Then he remembered the envelope. *If there was any discrepancy, it had nothing to do with me.* A fat man at the Drei Alpenhäuser.

"Minor compared to the magnitude of those risks." Chernak shook his head; his upper chest heaved; the stumps that fell over the chair moved obscenely back and forth. "I was content before you came into my life, mein Herr, for I *was* minor. An old soldier who made his way to Zurich—blown up, a cripple, worthless except for certain facts stored away that former comrades paid meagerly to keep suppressed. It was a decent life, not much, but enough. Then *you* found me. . . ."

"I'm touched," broke in Jason. "Let's talk about the envelope—the envelope you passed to our mutual friend at Drei Alpenhäuser. Who gave it to you?"

"A messenger. Who else?"

"Where did it come from?"

"How would *I* know? It arrived in a box, just like the others. I unpacked it and sent it on. It was *you* who wished it so. You said you could not come here any longer."

"But you opened it." A statement.

"Never!"

"Suppose I told you there was money missing."

"Then it was not paid; it was not in the envelope!" The legless man's voice rose. "However, I don't believe you. If that were so, you would not have accepted the assignment. But you did accept that assignment. So why are you here now?"

Because I have to know. Because I'm going out of my mind. I see things and I hear things I do not understand. I'm a skilled, resourceful . . . vegetable! Help me!

Bourne moved away from the chair; he walked aimlessly toward a bookcase where there were several upright photographs recessed against the wall. They explained the man behind him. Groups of German soldiers, some with shepherd dogs, posing outside of barracks and by fences . . . and in front of a high-wire gate with part of a name showing. DACH—

Dachau.

The man behind him. He was moving! Jason turned; the legless Chernak had his hand in the canvas bag strapped to his chair; his eyes were on fire, his ravaged face contorted. The hand came out swiftly, in it a short-barreled revolver, and before Bourne could reach his own, Chernak fired. The shots came rapidly, the icelike pain filling his left shoulder, then head—oh *God!* He dove to his right, spinning on the rug, shoving a heavy floor lamp toward the cripple, spinning again until he was at the far side of the wheelchair. He crouched and lunged, crashing his right shoulder into Chernak's back, sending the legless man out of the chair as he reached into his pocket for the gun.

"They'll pay for your corpse!" screamed the deformed man, writhing on the floor, trying to steady his slumped body long enough to level his weapon. "You won't put me in a coffin! I'll see you there! Carlos will pay! By Christ, he'll pay!"

Jason sprang to the left and fired. Chernak's head snapped back, his throat erupting in blood. He was dead.

A cry came from the door of the bedroom. It grew in depth, low and hollow, an elongated wail, fear and revulsion weaved into the chord. A woman's cry . . . of course it was a woman! His hostage, his conduit out of Zurich! Oh, *Jesus,* he could not focus his eyes! His temple was in agony!

He found his vision, refusing to acknowledge the pain. He saw a bathroom, the door open, towels and a sink and a . . . mirrored cabinet. He ran in, pulled the mirror back with such force that it jumped its hinges, crashing to the floor, shattered. *Shelves.* Rolls of gauze and tape and . . . they were all he could grab. He had to get out . . . *gunshots*; gunshots were alarms. He had to get out, take his hostage, and get away! The bedroom, the *bedroom.* Where *was* it?

The cry, the wail . . . follow the cry! He reached the door and kicked it open. The woman . . . his hostage—what the hell was her *name?*—was pressed against the wall, tears streaming down her face, her lips parted. He rushed in and grabbed her by the wrist, dragging her out.

"My *God,* you killed him!" she cried. "An old man with no—"

"Shut up!" He pushed her toward the door, opened it, and shoved her into the hallway. He could see blurred figures in open spaces, by railings, inside rooms. They began running, disappearing; he heard doors slam, people shout. He took the woman's arm with his left hand; the grip caused shooting pains in his shoulder. He propelled her to the staircase and forced her to descend with him, using her for support, his right hand holding the gun.

They reached the lobby and the heavy door. "Open it!" he ordered; she did. They passed the row of mailboxes to the outside entrance. He released her briefly, opening the door himself, peering out into the street, listening for sirens. There were none. "Come on!" he said, pulling her out to the stone steps and down to the pavement. He reached into his pocket, wincing, and took out the car keys. "Get in!"

Inside the car he unraveled the gauze, bunching it against the side of his head, blotting the trickle of blood. From deep inside his consciousness, there was a strange feeling of relief. The wound was a graze; the fact that it had been his head had sent him into panic, but the bullet had not entered his skull. It had *not* entered; there would be no return to the agonies of Port Noir.

"Goddamn it, start the car! Get *out* of here!"

"Where? You didn't say where." The woman was not screaming; instead she was calm. Unreasonably calm. Looking at him . . . was she looking at him?

He was feeling dizzy again, losing focus again. "Steppdeckstrasse. . . ." He heard the word as he spoke it, not sure the voice was his. But he could picture the doorway. Faded dark red paint, cracked glass . . . rusted iron. "Steppdeckstrasse," he repeated.

What was wrong? Why wasn't the motor going? Why didn't the car move forward? Didn't she *hear* him?

His eyes were closed; he opened them. The gun. It was on his lap; he had set it down to press the bandage . . . she was hitting it, *hitting* it! The weapon crashed to the floor; he reached down and she pushed him, sending his head against the window. Her door opened and she leaped out into the street and began running. She was running away! His hostage, his conduit was racing up the Löwenstrasse!

He could not stay in the car; he dared not try to drive it. It was a steel trap, marking him. He put the gun in his pocket with the roll of tape and grabbed the gauze, clutching it in his left hand, ready to press it against his temple at the first recurrence of blood. He got out and limped as fast as he could down the pavement.

Somewhere there was a corner, somewhere a taxi. *Steppdeckstrasse.*

Marie St. Jacques kept running in the middle of the wide, deserted avenue, in and out of the spills of the street-lamps, waving her arms at the automobiles in the Löwen-strasse. They sped by her. She turned in the wash of head-lights behind her, holding up her hands, pleading for attention; the cars accelerated and passed her by. This was Zurich, and the Löwenstrasse at night was too wide, too dark, too near the deserted park and the river Sihl.

The men in one automobile, however, were aware of her. Its headlights were off, the driver inside having seen the woman in the distance. He spoke to his companion in Schweizerdeutsch.

"It could be her. This Chernak lives only a block or so down the street."

"Stop and let her come closer. She's supposed to be wearing a silk . . . it's *her!*"

"Let's make certain before we radio the others."

Both men got out of the car, the passenger moving discreetly around the trunk to join the driver. They wore conservative business suits, their faces pleasant, but serious, businesslike. The panicked woman approached; they walked rapidly into the middle of the street. The driver called out.

"Was ist passiert, Fräulein?"

"Help me!" she screamed. "I . . . I don't speak German. *Nicht sprechen.* Call the police! The . . . *Polizei!*"

The driver's companion spoke with authority, calming her with his voice. "We are with the police," he said in English. "Zurich Sicherheitpolizei. We weren't sure, miss. You *are* the woman from the Carillon du Lac?"

"Yes!" she cried. "He wouldn't let me go! He kept hitting me, threatening me with his gun! It was horrible!"

"Where is he now?"

"He's hurt. He was shot. I ran from the car . . . he was in the car when I ran!" She pointed down the Löwen-strasse. "Over there. Two blocks, I think—in the middle of the block. A coupé, a gray coupé! He has a gun."

"So do we, miss," said the driver. "Come along, get in the back of the car. You'll be perfectly safe; we'll be very careful. Quickly, now."

They approached the gray coupé, coasting, headlights extinguished. There was no one inside. There were, however, people talking excitedly on the pavement and up the stone steps of Number 37. The driver's associate turned and spoke to the frightened woman pressed into the corner of the rear seat.

"This is the residence of a man named Chernak. Did he mention him? Did he say anything about going in to see him?"

"He *did* go; he made me come with him! He *killed* him! He killed that crippled old man!"

"*Der Sender—schnell*," said the associate to the driver, as he grabbed a microphone from the dashboard. "*Wir sind zwei Strassen von da.*" The car bolted forward; the woman gripped the front seat.

"What are you doing? A man was killed back there!"

"And we must find the killer," said the driver. "As you say, he was wounded; he may still be in the area. This is an unmarked vehicle and we could spot him. We'll wait, of course, to make sure the inspection team arrives, but our duties are quite separate." The car slowed down, sliding into the curb several hundred yards from Number 37 Löwenstrasse.

The associate had spoken into the microphone while the driver had explained their official position. There was static from the dashboard speaker, then the words "*Wir kommen binnen zwanzig Minuten. Wartet.*"

"Our superior will be here shortly," the associate said. "We're to wait for him. He wishes to speak with you."

Marie St. Jacques leaned back in the seat, closing her eyes, expelling her breath. "Oh, God—I wish I had a drink!"

The driver laughed, nodded to his companion. The associate took out a pint bottle from the glove compartment and held it up, smiling at the woman. "We're not very chic, miss. We have no glasses or cups, but we do have brandy. For medical emergencies, of course. I think this is one now. Please, our compliments."

She smiled back and accepted the bottle. "You're two very nice people, and you'll never know how grateful I am. If you ever come to Canada, I'll cook you the best French meal in the province of Ontario."

"Thank you, miss," said the driver.

Bourne studied the bandage on his shoulder, squinting at the dull reflection in the dirty, streaked mirror, adjusting his eyes to the dim light of the filthy room. He had been right about the Steppdeckstrasse, the image of the faded red doorway accurate, down to the cracked windowpanes and rusted iron railings. No questions had been asked when he rented the room, in spite of the fact that he was obviously hurt. However, a statement had been made by the building manager when Bourne paid him.

"For something more substantial a doctor can be found who keeps his mouth shut."

"I'll let you know."

The wound was not that severe; the tape would hold it until he found a doctor somewhat more reliable than one who practiced surreptitiously in the Steppdeckstrasse.

If a stress situation results in injury, be aware of the fact that the damage may be as much psychological as physical. You may have a very real revulsion to pain and bodily harm. Don't take risks, but if there's time, give yourself a chance to adjust. Don't panic. . . .

He had panicked; areas of his body had frozen. Although the penetration in his shoulder and the graze at his temple were real and painful, neither was serious enough to immobilize him. He could not move as fast as he might wish or with the strength he knew he had, but he could move deliberately. Messages were sent and received, brain to muscle and limb; he could function.

He would function better after a rest. He had no conduit now; he had to be up long before daybreak and find another way out of Zurich. The building manager on the first floor liked money; he would wake up the slovenly landlord in an hour or so.

He lowered himself onto the sagging bed and lay back on the pillow, staring at the naked lightbulb in the ceiling, trying not to hear the words so he could rest. They came anyway, filling his ears like the pounding of kettledrums.

A man was killed. . . .

But you did accept that assignment. . . .

He turned to the wall, shutting his eyes, blocking out the words. Then other words came and he sat up, sweat breaking out on his forehead.

They'll pay for your corpse! . . . Carlos will pay! By Christ, he'll pay!

Carlos.

A large sedan pulled up in front of the coupé and parked at the curb. Behind them, at 37 Löwenstrasse, the patrol cars had arrived fifteen minutes ago, the ambulance less than five. Crowds from surrounding flats lined the pavement near the staircase, but the excitement was muted now. A death had occurred, a man killed at night in this quiet section of the Löwenstrasse. Anxiety was uppermost; what had happened at Number 37 could happen at 32 or 40 or 53. The world was going mad, and Zurich was going with it.

"Our superior has arrived, miss. May we take you to him, please?" The associate got out of the car and opened the door for Marie St. Jacques.

"Certainly." She stepped out on the pavement and felt the man's hand on her arm; it was so much gentler than the hard grip of the animal who had held the barrel of a gun to her cheek. She shuddered at the memory. They approached the rear of the sedan and she climbed inside. She sat back in the seat and looked at the man beside her. She gasped, suddenly paralyzed, unable to breathe, the man beside her evoking a memory of terror.

The light from the streetlamps was reflected off the thin gold rims of his spectacles.

"*You!* . . . You were at the hotel! You were one of them!"

The man nodded wearily; his fatigue apparent. "That's right. We're a special branch of the Zurich police. And before we speak further, I must make it clear to you that at no time during the events of the Carillon du Lac were you in any danger of being harmed by us. We're trained marksmen; no shots were fired that could have struck you. A number were withheld because you were too close to the man in our sights."

Her shock eased, the man's quiet authority reassuring. "Thank you for that."

"It's a minor talent," said the official. "Now, as I understand, you last saw him in the front seat of the car back there."

"Yes. He was wounded."

"How seriously?"

"Enough to be incoherent. He held some kind of bandage to his head, and there was blood on his shoulder—on the cloth of his coat, I mean. Who is he?"

"Names are meaningless; he goes by many. But as you've seen, he's a killer. A brutal killer, and he must be found before he kills again. We've been hunting him for several years. Many police from many countries. We have the opportunity now none of them has had. We know he's in Zurich, and he's wounded. He would not stay in this area, but how far can he go? Did he mention how he expected to get out of the city?"

"He was going to rent a car. In my name, I gather. He doesn't have a driver's license."

"He was lying. He travels with all manner of false papers. You were an expendable hostage. Now, from the beginning, tell me everything he said to you. Where you went, whom he met, whatever comes to mind."

"There's a restaurant, Drei Alpenhäuser, and a large fat man who was frightened to death. . . ." Marie St. Jacques recounted everything she could remember. From time to time the police official interrupted, questioning her about a phrase, or reaction, or a sudden decision on the part of the killer. Intermittently he removed his gold spectacles, wiping them absently, gripping the frames as if the pressure controlled his irritation. The interrogation lasted nearly twenty-five minutes; then the official made his decision. He spoke to his driver.

"Drei Alpenhäuser. *Schnell!*" He turned to Marie St. Jacques. "We'll confront that man with his own words. *His* incoherence was quite intentional. He knows far more than he said at the table."

"Incoherence. . . ." She said the word softly, remembering her own use of it. "Steppdeck— Steppdeck*strasse*. Cracked windows, rooms."

"What?"

" 'A boardinghouse in the Steppdeckstrasse.' That's what he said. Everything was happening so fast, but he *said* it. And just before I jumped out of the car, he said it again. *Steppdeckstrasse.*"

The driver spoke. "*Ich kenne diese Strasse. Früher gab es Textilfabriken da.*"

"I don't understand," said Marie St. Jacques.

"It's a rundown section that has not kept up with the times," replied the official. "The old fabric mills used to be there. A haven for the less fortunate . . . and others. *Los!*" he ordered.

They drove off.

8

A crack. Outside the room. Snaplike, echoing off into a sharp coda, the sound penetrating, diminishing in the distance. Bourne opened his eyes.

The staircase. The staircase in the filthy hallway outside his room. Someone had been walking up the steps and had stopped, aware of the noise his weight had caused on the warped, cracked wood. A normal boarder at the Steppdeckstrasse rooming house would have no such concerns.

Silence.

Crack. Now closer. A risk was taken, timing paramount, speed the cover. Jason spun off the bed, grabbing the gun that was by his head, and lunged to the wall by the door. He crouched, hearing the footsteps—one man—the runner, no longer concerned with sound, only with reaching his destination. Bourne had no doubt what it was; he was right.

The door crashed open; he smashed it back, then threw his full weight into the wood, pinning the intruder against the doorframe, pummeling the man's stomach, chest, and arm into the recessed edge of the wall. He pulled the door back and lashed the toe of his right foot into the throat below him, reaching down with his left hand, grabbing blond hair and yanking the figure inside. The man's hand went limp; the gun in it fell to the floor, a long-barreled revolver with a silencer attached.

Jason closed the door and listened for sounds on the staircase. There were none. He looked down at the unconscious man. Thief? Killer? What was he?

Police? Had the manager of the boardinghouse decided to overlook the code of the Steppdeckstrasse in search of a reward? Bourne rolled the intruder over and took out a billfold. Second nature made him remove the money, knowing it was ludicrous to do so; he had a small fortune on him. He looked at the various credit cards and the driver's license; he smiled, but then his smile disappeared. There was nothing funny; the names on the cards were different ones, the name on the license matching none. The unconscious man was no police officer.

He was a professional, come to kill a wounded man in the Steppdeckstrasse. Someone had hired him. Who? Who could possibly know he was there?

The woman? Had he mentioned the Steppdeckstrasse when he had seen the row of neat houses, looking for Number 37? No, it was not she; he may have said something, but she would not have understood. And if she had, there'd be no professional killer in his room; instead, the rundown boardinghouse would be surrounded by police.

The image of a large fat man perspiring above a table came to Bourne. That same man had wiped the sweat from his protruding lips and had spoken of the courage of an insignificant goat—who had survived. Was this an example of his survival technique? Had he known about the Steppdeckstrasse? Was he aware of the habits of the patron whose sight terrified him? Had he *been* to the filthy rooming house? Delivered an envelope there?

Jason pressed his hand to his forehead and shut his eyes. *Why can't I remember? When will the mists clear? Will they ever clear?*

Don't crucify yourself. . . .

Bourne opened his eyes, fixing them on the blond man. For the briefest of moments he nearly burst out laughing; he had been presented with his exit visa from Zurich, and instead of recognizing it, he was wasting time tormenting himself. He put the billfold in his pocket, wedging it behind the Marquis de Chamford's, picked up the gun and shoved it into his belt, then dragged the unconscious figure over to the bed.

A minute later the man was strapped to the sagging mattress, gagged by a torn sheet wrapped around his face. He would remain where he was for hours, and in hours Jason would be out of Zurich, compliments of a perspiring fat man.

He had slept in his clothes. There was nothing to gather up or carry except his topcoat. He put it on, and tested his leg, somewhat after the fact, he reflected. In the heat of the past few minutes he had been unaware of the pain; it was there, as the limp was there, but neither immobilized him. The shoulder was not in as good shape. A slow paralysis was spreading; he had to get to a doctor. His head . . . he did not want to think about his head.

He walked out into the dimly lit hallway, pulled the door closed, and stood motionless, listening. There was a burst of laughter from above; he pressed his back against the wall, gun poised. The laughter trailed off; it was a drunk's laughter—incoherent, pointless.

He limped to the staircase, held on to the railing, and started down. He was on the third floor of the four-story building, having insisted on the highest room when the phrase *high ground* had come to him instinctively. *Why had it come to him? What did it mean in terms of renting a filthy room for a single night? Sanctuary?*

Stop it!

He reached the second floor landing, creaks in the wooden staircase accompanying each step. If the manager came out of his flat below to satisfy his curiosity, it would be the last thing he satisfied for several hours.

A noise. A scratch. Soft fabric moving briefly across an abrasive surface. Cloth against wood. Someone was concealed in the short stretch of hallway between the end of one staircase and the beginning of another. Without breaking the rhythm of his walk, he peered into the shadows; there were three recessed doorways in the right wall, identical to the floor above. In one of them . . .

He took a step closer. Not the first; it was empty. And it would not be the last, the bordering wall forming a cul-de-sac, no room to move. It had to be the second, yes, the second doorway. From it a man could rush forward, to his left or right, or throwing a shoulder into an unsuspecting victim, send his target over the railing, plunging down the staircase.

Bourne angled to his right, shifting the gun to his left hand and reaching into his belt for the weapon with a silencer. Two feet from the recessed door, he heaved the automatic in his left hand into the shadows as he pivoted against the wall.

"*Was ist? . . .*" An arm appeared; Jason fired once, blowing the hand apart. "*Ahh!*" The figure lurched out in shock, incapable of aiming his weapon. Bourne fired again, hitting the man in the thigh; he collapsed on the floor, writhing, cringing. Jason took a step forward and knelt, his knee pressing into the man's chest, his gun at the man's head. He spoke in a whisper.

"Is there anyone else down there?"

"*Nein!*" said the man, wincing in pain. "*Zwei . . .* two of us only. We were paid."

"By whom?"

"You know."

"A man named Carlos?"

"I will not answer that. Kill me first."

"How did you know I was here?"

"Chernak."

"He's dead."

"Now. Not yesterday. Word reached Zurich: you were alive. We checked everyone . . . everywhere. Chernak knew."

Bourne gambled. "You're lying!" He pushed the gun into the man's throat. "I never told Chernak about the Steppdeckstrasse."

The man winced again, his neck arched. "Perhaps you did not have to. The Nazi pig had informers everywhere. Why should the Steppdeckstrasse be any different? He could describe you. Who else could?"

"A man at the Drei Alpenhäuser."

"We never heard of any such man."

"Who's 'we?' "

The man swallowed, his lips stretched in pain. "Businessmen . . . only businessmen."

"And your service is killing."

"You're a strange one to talk. But, *nein.* You were to be taken, not killed."

"Where?"

"We would be told by radio. Car frequency."

[110]

"Terrific," said Jason flatly. "You're not only second-rate, you're accommodating. Where's your car?"

"Outside."

"Give me the keys." The radio would identify it.

The man tried to resist; he pushed Bourne's knee away and started to roll into the wall. "*Nein!*"

"You haven't got a choice." Jason brought the handle of the pistol down on the man's skull. The Swiss collapsed.

Bourne found the keys—there were three in a leather case—took the man's gun and put it into his pocket. It was a smaller weapon than the one he held in his hand and had no silencer, lending a degree of credence to the claim that he was to be taken, not killed. The blond man upstairs had been acting as the point, and therefore needed the protection of a silenced gunshot should wounding be required. But an unmuffled report could lead to complications; the Swiss on the second floor was a backup, his weapon to be used as a visible threat.

Then why was he on the second floor? Why hadn't he followed his colleague? On the staircase? Something was odd, but there was no accounting for tactics, nor the time to consider them. There was a car outside on the street and he had the keys for it.

Nothing could be disregarded. The third gun.

He got up painfully and found the revolver he had taken from the Frenchman in the elevator at the Gemeinschaft Bank. He pulled up his left trouser leg and inserted the gun under the elasticized fabric of his sock. It was secure.

He paused to get his breath and his balance, then crossed to the staircase, aware that the pain in his left shoulder was suddenly more acute, the paralysis spreading more rapidly. Messages from brain to limb were less clear. He hoped to God he could drive.

He reached the fifth step and abruptly stopped, listening as he had listened barely a minute ago for sounds of concealment. There was nothing; the wounded man may have been tactically deficient, but he had told the truth. Jason hurried down the staircase. He would drive out of Zurich—somehow—and find a doctor—somewhere.

He spotted the car easily. It was different from the other shabby automobiles on the street. An outsized, well-kept sedan, and he could see the bulge of an antenna base riveted into the trunk. He walked to the driver's side and ran his hand around the panel and left front fender; there was no alarm device.

He unlocked the door, then opened it, holding his breath in case he was wrong about the alarm; he was not. He climbed in behind the wheel, adjusting his position until he was as comfortable as he could be, grateful that the car had an automatic shift. The large weapon in his belt inhibited him. He placed it on the seat beside him, then reached for the ignition, assuming the key that had unlocked the door was the proper one.

It was not. He tried the one next to it, but it, too, would not fit. For the trunk, he assumed. It was the third key.

Or was it? He kept stabbing at the opening. The key would not enter; he tried the second again; it was blocked. Then the first. None of the keys would fit into the ignition! Or were the messages from brain to limb to fingers too garbled, his coordination too inadequate! Goddamn it! Try again!

A powerful light came from his left, burning his eyes, blinding him. He grabbed for the gun, but a second beam shot out from the right; the door was yanked open and a heavy flashlight crashed down on his hand, another hand taking the weapon from the seat.

"Get out!" The order came from his left, the barrel of a gun pressed into his neck.

He climbed out, a thousand coruscating circles of white in his eyes. As vision slowly came back to him, the first thing he saw was the outline of two circles. Gold circles; the spectacles of the killer who had hunted him throughout the night. The man spoke.

"They say in the laws of physics that every action has an equal and opposite reaction. The behavior of certain men under certain conditions is similarly predictable. For a man like you one sets up a gauntlet, each combatant told what to say if he falls. If he does not fall, you are taken. If he does, you are misled, lulled into a false sense of progress."

"It's a high degree of risk," said Jason. "For those in the gauntlet."

"They're paid well. And there's something else—no guarantee, of course, but it's there. The enigmatic Bourne does not kill indiscriminately. Not out of compassion, naturally, but for a far more practical reason. Men remember when they've been spared; he infiltrates the armies of others. Refined guerrilla tactics applied to a sophisticated battleground. I commend you."

"You're a horse's ass." It was all Jason could think to say. "But both your men are alive, if that's what you want to know."

Another figure came into view, led from the shadows of the building by a short, stocky man. It was the woman; it was Marie St. Jacques.

"That's him," she said softly, her look unwavering.

"Oh, my God. . . ." Bourne shook his head in disbelief. "How was it done, Doctor?" he asked her, raising his voice. "Was someone watching my room at the Carillon? Was the elevator timed, the others shut down? You're very convincing. And I thought you were going to crash into a police car."

"As it turned out," she replied, "it wasn't necessary. These are the police."

Jason looked at the killer in front of him; the man was adjusting his gold spectacles. "I commend you," he said.

"A minor talent," answered the killer. "The conditions were right. You provided them."

"What happens now? The man inside said I was to be taken, not killed."

"You forget. He was told what to say." The Swiss paused. "So this is what you look like. Many of us have wondered during the past two or three years. How much speculation there's been! How many contradictions! He's tall, you know; no, he's of medium height. He's blond; no, he has dark black hair. Very light blue eyes, of course; no, quite clearly they are brown. His features are sharp; no, they're really quite ordinary, can't pick him out in a crowd. But nothing was ordinary. It was all extraordinary."

Your features have been softened, the character submerged. Change your hair, you change your face. . . . Certain types of contact lenses are designed to alter the color of the eyes. . . . Wear glasses, you're a different man. Visas, passports . . . switched at will.

The design was there. Everything fit. Not all the answers, but more of the truth than he wanted to hear.

"I'd like to get this over with," said Marie St. Jacques, stepping forward. "I'll sign whatever I have to sign—at your office, I imagine. But then I really must get back to the hotel. I don't have to tell you what I've been through tonight."

The Swiss glanced at her through his gold-rimmed glasses. The stocky man who had led her out of the shadows took her arm. She stared at both men, then down at the hand that held her.

Then at Bourne. Her breathing stopped, a terrible realization becoming clear. Her eyes grew wide.

"Let her go," said Jason. "She's on her way back to Canada. You'll never see her again."

"Be practical, Bourne. She's seen *us*. We two are professionals; there are rules." The man flicked his gun up under Jason's chin, the barrel pressed once more into Bourne's throat. He ran his left hand about his victim's clothes, felt the weapon in Jason's pocket and took it out. "I thought as much," he said, and turned to the stocky man. "Take her in the other car. The Limmat."

Bourne froze. Marie St. Jacques was to be killed, her body thrown into the Limmat River.

"Wait a minute!" Jason stepped forward; the gun was jammed into his neck, forcing him back into the hood of the car. "You're being stupid! She works for the Canadian government. They'll be all over Zurich."

"Why should that concern you? You won't be here."

"Because it's a waste!" cried Bourne. "We're professionals, remember?"

"You bore me." The killer turned to the stocky man. *"Geh! Schnell. Guisan Quai!"*

"Scream your goddamn head off!" shouted Jason. "Start yelling! Don't stop!"

She tried, the scream cut short by a paralyzing blow to her throat. She fell to the pavement as her would-be executioner dragged her toward a small nondescript black sedan.

"That was stupid," said the killer, peering through his gold-rimmed spectacles into Bourne's face. "You only hasten the inevitable. On the other hand, it will be simpler now. I can free a man to tend to our wounded. Everything's so military, isn't it? It really is a battlefield." He turned to the man with the flashlight. "Signal Johann to go inside. We'll come back for them."

The flashlight was switched on and off twice. A fourth man, who had opened the door of the small sedan for the condemned woman, nodded. Marie St. Jacques was thrown into the rear seat, the door slammed shut. The man named Johann started for the concrete steps, nodding now at the executioner.

Jason felt sick as the engine of the small sedan was gunned and the car bolted away from the curb into the Steppdeckstrasse, the twisted chrome bumper disappearing into the shadows of the street. Inside that car was a woman he had never seen in his life . . . before three hours ago. And he had killed her. "You don't lack for soldiers," he said.

"If there were a hundred men I could trust, I'd pay them willingly. As they say, your reputation precedes you."

"Suppose *I* paid you. You were at the bank; you know I've got funds."

"Probably millions, but I wouldn't touch a franc note."

"Why? Are you afraid?"

"Most assuredly. Wealth is relative to the amount of time one has to enjoy it. I wouldn't have five minutes." The killer turned to his subordinate. "Put him inside. Strip him. I want photographs taken of him naked—before and after he leaves us. You'll find a great deal of money on him; I want him holding it. I'll drive." He looked again at Bourne. "Carlos will get the first print. And I have no doubt that I'll be able to sell the others quite profitably on the open market. Magazines pay outrageous prices."

"Why should 'Carlos' believe you? Why should *anyone* believe you? You said it: no one knows what I look like."

"I'll be covered," said the Swiss. "Sufficient unto the day. Two Zurich bankers will step forward identifying you as one Jason Bourne. The same Jason Bourne who met the excessively rigid standards set by Swiss law for the release of a numbered account. It will be enough." He spoke to the gunman. "*Hurry!* I have cables to send. Debts to collect."

A powerful arm shot over Bourne's shoulder, vicing his throat in a hammerlock. The barrel of a gun was jolted into his spine, pain spreading throughout his chest as he was dragged inside the sedan. The man holding him was a professional; even without his wounds it would have been impossible to break the grip. The gunman's expertise, however, did not satisfy the bespectacled leader of the hunt. He climbed behind the wheel and issued another command.

"Break his fingers," he said.

The armlock briefly choked off Jason's air as the barrel of the gun crashed down repeatedly on his hand—*hands*. Instinctively, Bourne had swung his left hand over his right, protecting it. As the blood burst from the back of his left, he twisted his fingers, letting it flow between them until both hands were covered. He choked his screams; the grip lessened; he shouted.

"My hands! They're broken!"

"*Gut.*"

But they were not broken; the left was damaged to the point where it was useless; not the right. He moved his fingers in the shadows; his hand was intact.

The car sped down the Steppdeckstrasse and swung into a sidestreet, heading south. Jason collapsed back in the seat, gasping. The gunman tore at his clothes, ripping his shirt, yanking at his belt. In seconds his upper body would be naked; passport, papers, cards, money no longer his, all the items intrinsic to his escape from Zurich taken from him. It was now or it was not to be. He screamed.

"My *leg!* My goddamned leg!" He lurched forward, his right hand working furiously in the dark, fumbling under the cloth of his trouser leg. He felt it. The handle of the automatic.

"*Nein!*" roared the professional in the front. "Watch him!" He knew; it was instinctive knowledge.

It was also too late. Bourne held the gun in the darkness of the floor; the powerful soldier pushed him back. He fell with the blow, the revolver, now at his waist, pointed directly at his attacker's chest.

He fired twice; the man arched backward. Jason fired again, his aim sure, the heart punctured; the man fell over into the recessed jump seat.

"Put it down!" yelled Bourne, swinging the revolver over the rounded edge of the front seat, pressing the barrel into the base of the driver's skull. "Drop it!"

His breathing erratic, the killer let the gun fall. "We will talk," he said, gripping the wheel. "We are professionals. We will talk." The large automobile lurched forward, gathering speed, the driver increasing pressure on the accelerator.

"Slow down!"

"What is your answer?" The car went faster. Ahead were the headlights of traffic; they were leaving the Steppdeckstrasse district, entering the busier city streets. "You want to get out of Zurich, I can get you out. Without me, you can't. All I have to do is spin the wheel, crash into the pavement. I have nothing whatsoever to lose, Herr Bourne.

There are police everywhere up ahead. I don't think you want the police."

"We'll talk," lied Jason. Everything was timing, split-second timing. There were now two killers in a speeding enclosure that was in itself a trap. Neither killer was to be trusted; both knew it. One had to make use of that extra half-second the other would not take. Professionals. "Put on the brakes," said Bourne.

"Drop your gun on the seat next to mine."

Jason released the weapon. It fell on top of the killer's, the ring of heavy metal proof of contact. "Done."

The killer took his foot off the accelerator, transferring it to the brake. He applied the pressure slowly, then in short stabs so that the large automobile pitched back and forth. The jabs on the pedal would become more pronounced; Bourne understood this. It was part of the driver's strategy, balance a factor of life and death.

The arrow on the speedometer swung left: *30 kilometers, 18 kilometers, 9 kilometers*. They had nearly stopped; it was the moment for the extra half-second of effort—balance a factor, life in balance.

Jason grabbed the man by the neck, clawing at his throat, yanking him up off the seat. Then he raised his bloody left hand and thrust it forward, smearing the area of the killer's eyes. He released the throat. surging his right hand down toward the guns on the seat. Bourne gripped a handle, shoving the killer's hand away; the man screamed, his vision blurred, the gun out of reach. Jason lunged across the man's chest, pushing him down against the door, elbowing the killer's throat with his left arm, grabbing the wheel with his bloody palm. He looked up through the windshield and turned the wheel to the right, heading the car toward a pyramid of trash on the pavement.

The automobile plowed into the mound of debris—a huge, somnambulant insect crawling into garbage, its appearance belying the violence taking place inside its shell.

The man beneath him lunged up, rolling on the seat. Bourne held the automatic in his hand, his fingers jabbing for the open space of the trigger. He found it. He bent his wrist and fired.

His would-be executioner went limp, a dark red hole in his forehead.

In the street, men came running toward what must have looked like a dangerously careless accident. Jason shoved the dead body across the seat and climbed over behind the wheel. He pushed the gearshift into reverse; the sedan backed awkwardly out of the debris, over the curb and into the street. He rolled down his window, calling out to the would-be rescuers as they approached.

"Sorry! Everything's fine! Just a little too much to drink!"

The small band of concerned citizens broke up quickly, a few making gestures of admonition, others running back to their escorts and companions. Bourne breathed deeply, trying to control the involuntary trembling that seized his entire body. He pulled the gear into drive; the car started forward. He tried to picture the streets of Zurich from a memory that would not serve him.

He knew vaguely where he was—where he had been—and more important, he knew more clearly where the Guisan Quai was in relationship to the Limmat.

Geh! Schnell. Guisan Quai!

Marie St. Jacques was to be killed on the Guisan Quai, her body thrown into the river. There was only one stretch where the Guisan and the Limmat met: it was at the mouth of Lake Zurich, at the base of the western shore. Somewhere in an empty parking lot or a deserted garden overlooking the water, a short, stocky man was about to carry out an execution ordered by a dead man. Perhaps by now the gun had been fired, or a knife plunged into its mark; there was no way to know, but Jason knew he had to find out. Whoever and whatever he was, he could not walk away blindly.

The professional in him, however, demanded that he swerve into the dark wide alley ahead. There were two dead men in the car; they were a risk and a burden he could not tolerate. The precious seconds it would take to remove them could avoid the danger of a traffic policeman looking through the windows and seeing death.

Thirty-two seconds was his guess; it had taken less than a minute to pull his would-be executioners from the car. He looked at them as he limped around the hood to the door. They were curled up obscenely next to one another against a filthy brick wall. In darkness.

He climbed behind the wheel and backed out of the alley.

Geh! Schnell. Guisan Quai!

— 9 —

He reached an intersection, the traffic light red. *Lights.* On the left, several blocks east, he could see lights arching gently into the night sky. A bridge! The Limmat! The signal turned green; he swung the sedan to the left.

He was back on the Bahnhofstrasse; the start of the Guisan Quai was only minutes away. The wide avenue curved around the water's edge, riverbank and lakefront merging. Moments later, on his left was the silhouetted outline of a park, in summer a stroller's haven, now dark, devoid of tourists and Zurichers. He passed an entrance for vehicles; there was a heavy chain across the white pavement, suspended between two stone posts. He came to a second, another chain prohibiting access. But it was not the same; something was different, something odd. He stopped the car and looked closer, reaching across the seat for the flashlight he had taken from his would-be executioner. He snapped it on and shot the beam over the heavy chain. What was it? What was different?

It was not the chain. It was *beneath* the chain. On the white pavement kept spotless by maintenance crews. There were tire marks, at odds with the surrounding cleanliness.

They would not be noticed during the summer months; they were now. It was as if the filth of the Steppdeckstrasse had traveled too well.

Bourne switched off the flashlight and dropped it on the seat. The pain in his battered left hand suddenly fused with the agony in his shoulder and his arm; he had to push all pain out of his mind; he had to curtail the bleeding as best he could. His shirt had been ripped; he reached inside and ripped it further, pulling out a strip of cloth which he proceeded to wrap around his left hand, knotting it with teeth and fingers. He was as ready as he would ever be.

He picked up the gun—his would-be executioner's gun—and checked the clip: full. He waited until two cars had passed him, then extinguished the headlights and made a U-turn, parking next to the chain. He got out, instinctively testing his leg on the pavement, then favoring it as he limped to the nearest post and lifted the hook off the iron circle protruding from the stone. He lowered the chain, making as little noise as possible, and returned to the car.

He pulled at the gearshift, gently pressed the accelerator, then released it. He was now coasting into the wide expanse of the unlit parking area, made darker by the abrupt end of the white entrance road and the start of a field of black asphalt. Beyond, two-hundred-odd yards in the distance, was the straight dark line of the seawall, a wall that contained no sea but, instead, the currents of the Limmat as they poured into the waters of Lake Zurich. Farther away were the lights of the boats, bobbing in stately splendor. Beyond these were the stationary lights of the Old City, the blurred floodlights of darkened piers. Jason's eyes took everything in, for the distance was his backdrop; he was looking for shapes in front of it.

To the right. The *right*. A dark outline darker than the wall, an intrusion of black on lesser black—obscure, faint, barely discernible, but there. A hundred yards away . . . now ninety, eighty-five; he cut off the engine and brought the car to a stop. He sat motionless by the open window, staring into the darkness, trying to see more clearly. He heard the wind coming off the water; it covered any sound the car had made.

Sound. A cry. Low, throated . . . delivered in fear. A harsh slap followed, then another, and another. A scream was formed, then swallowed, broken, echoing off into silence.

Bourne got out of the car silently, the gun in his right hand, the flashlight awkward in the bloody fingers of his left. He walked toward the obscure black shape, each step, each limp a study in silence.

What he saw first was what he had seen last when the small sedan had disappeared in the shadows of the Steppdeckstrasse. The shining metal of the twisted chrome bumper; it glistened now in the night light.

Four slaps in rapid succession, flesh against flesh, blows maniacally administered, received with muted screams of terror. Cries terminated, gasps permitted, thrashing movement part of it all. Inside the car!

Jason crouched as best he could, sidestepping around the trunk toward the right rear window. He rose slowly, then suddenly, using sound as a weapon of shock, shouted as he switched on the powerful flashlight.

"You move, you're dead!"

What he saw inside filled him with revulsion and fury. Marie St. Jacques' clothes were torn away, shredded into strips. Hands were poised like claws on her half-naked body, kneading her breasts, separating her legs. The executioner's organ protruded from the cloth of his trousers; he was inflicting the final indignity before he carried out the sentence of death.

"Get *out*, you *son of a bitch*!"

There was a massive shattering of glass; the man raping Marie St. Jacques saw the obvious. Bourne could not fire the gun for fear of killing the woman; he had spun off her, crashing the heel of his shoe into the window of the small car. Glass flew out, sharp fragments blanketing Jason's face. He closed his eyes, limping backward to avoid the spray.

The door swung open; a blinding spit of light accompanied the explosion. Hot, searing pain spread through Bourne's right side. The fabric of his coat was blown away, blood matting what remained of his shirt. He squeezed the trigger, only vaguely able to see the figure rolling on the ground; he fired again, the bullet detonating the surface of the asphalt. The executioner had rolled and lurched out of sight . . . into the darker blackness, unseen.

Jason knew he could not stay where he was; to do so was his own execution. He raced, dragging his leg, to the cover of the open door.

"Stay inside!" he yelled to Marie St. Jacques; the woman

had started to move in panic. "Goddamn it! Stay in there!"

A gunshot; the bullet imbedded in the metal of the door. A running figure was silhouetted above the wall. Bourne fired twice, grateful for an expulsion of breath in the distance. He had wounded the man; he had not killed him. But the executioner would function less well than he had sixty seconds ago.

Lights. Dim lights . . . squared, frames. What was it? What were they? He looked to the left and saw what he could not possibly have seen before. A small brick structure, some kind of dwelling by the seawall. Lights had been turned on inside. A watchman's station; someone inside had heard the gunshots.

"Was ist los? Wer ist da?" The shouts came from the figure of a man—a bent-over, old man—standing in a lighted doorway. Then the beam of a flashlight pierced the blacker darkness. Bourne followed it with his eyes, hoping it would shine on the executioner.

It did. He was crouched by the wall. Jason stood up and fired; at the sound of his gun, the beam swung over to him. *He* was the target; two shots came from the darkness, a bullet ricocheting off a metal strip in the window. Steel punctured his neck; blood erupted.

Racing footsteps. The executioner was running toward the source of the light.

"Nein!"

He had reached it; the figure in the doorway was lashed by an arm that was both his leash and his cage. The beam went out; in the light of the windows Jason could see the killer pulling the watchman away, using the old man as a shield, dragging him back into darkness.

Bourne watched until he could see no more, his gun raised helplessly over the hood. As he was helpless, his body draining.

There was a final shot, followed by a guttural cry and, once again, racing footsteps. The executioner had carried out a sentence of death, not with the condemned woman, but with an old man. He was running; he had made his escape.

Bourne could run no longer; the pain had finally immobilized him, his vision too blurred, his sense of survival exhausted. He lowered himself to the pavement. There was nothing; he simply did not care.

Whatever he was, let it be. Let it be.

The St. Jacques woman crawled out of the car, holding her clothes, every move made in shock. She stared at Jason, disbelief, horror and confusion coming together in her eyes.

"Go on," he whispered, hoping she could hear him. "There's a car back there, the keys are in it. Get out of here. He may bring others, I don't know."

"You came for me," she said, her voice echoing through a tunnel of bewilderment.

"Get out! Get in that car and go like hell, Doctor. If anyone tries to stop you, run him down. Reach the police . . . real ones, with uniforms, you damn fool." His throat was so hot, his stomach so cold. Fire and ice; he'd felt them before. Together. Where was it?

"You saved my life," she continued in that hollow tone, the words floating in the air. "You came for me. You came *back* for me, and saved . . . my . . . life."

"Don't make it what it wasn't." *You are incidental, Doctor. You are a reflex, an instinct born of forgotten memories, conduits electrically prodded by stress. You see, I know the words . . . I don't care anymore. I hurt—oh my God, I hurt.*

"You were free. You could have kept going but you didn't. You came back for me."

He heard her through mists of pain. He saw her, and what he saw was unreasonable—as unreasonable as the pain. She was kneeling beside him, touching his face, touching his head. *Stop it! Do not touch my head! Leave me.*

"Why did you do that?" It was her voice, not his.

She was asking him a question. Didn't she understand? He could not answer her.

What was she doing? She had torn a piece of cloth and was wrapping it around his neck . . . and now another, this larger, part of her dress. She had loosened his belt and was pushing the soft smooth cloth down into the boiling hot skin on his right hip.

"It wasn't *you*." He found words and used them quickly. He wanted the peace of darkness—as he had wanted it before but could not remember when. He could find it if she left him. "That man . . . he'd seen me. He could identify me. It was him. I wanted *him*. Now get out!"

"So could half a dozen others," she replied, another note in her voice. "I don't believe you."

[123]

"Believe me!"

She was standing above him now. Then she was not there. She was gone. She had left him. The peace would come quickly now; he would be swallowed up in the dark crashing waters and the pain would be washed away. He leaned back against the car and let himself drift with the currents of his mind.

A noise intruded. A motor, rolling and disruptive. He did not care for it; it interfered with the freedom of his own particular sea. Then a hand was on his arm. Then another, gently pulling him up.

"Come on," said the voice, "help me."

"Let go of me!" The command was shouted; he had shouted it. But the command was not obeyed. He was appalled; commands should be obeyed. Yet not always; something told him that. The wind was there again, but not a wind in Zurich. In some other place, high in the night sky. And a signal came, a light flashed on, and he leaped up, whipped by furious new currents.

"All right. You're all right," said the maddening voice that would not pay attention to his commands. "Lift your foot up. *Lift* it! . . . That's right. You did it. Now, inside the car. Ease yourself back . . . slowly. That's right."

He was falling . . . falling in the pitch black sky. And then the falling stopped, everything stopped, and there was stillness; he could hear his own breathing. And footsteps, he could hear footsteps . . . and the sound of a door closing, followed by the rolling, disruptive noise beneath him, in front of him, somewhere.

Motion, swaying in circles. Balance was gone and he was falling again, only to be stopped again, another body against his body, a hand holding him, lowering him. His face felt cool; and then he felt nothing. He was drifting again, currents gentler now, darkness complete.

There were voices above him, in the distance, but not so far away. Shapes came slowly into focus, lit by the spill of table lamps. He was in a fairly large room, and on a bed, a narrow bed, blankets covering him. Across the room were two people, a man in an overcoat and a woman . . . dressed in a dark red skirt beneath a white blouse. Dark red, as the hair was. . . .

The St. Jacques woman? It *was* she, standing by a door

talking to a man holding a leather bag in his left hand. They were speaking French.

"Rest, mainly," the man was saying. "If you're not accessible to me, anyone can remove the sutures. They can be taken out in a week, I'd guess."

"Thank you, Doctor."

"Thank *you*. You've been most generous. I'll go now. Perhaps I'll hear from you, perhaps not."

The doctor opened the door and let himself out. When he was gone the woman reached down and slid the bolt in place. She turned and saw Bourne looking at her. She walked slowly, cautiously, toward the bed.

"Can you hear me?" she asked.

He nodded.

"You're hurt," she said, "quite badly; but if you stay quiet, it won't be necessary for you to get to a hospital. That was a doctor . . . obviously. I paid him out of the money I found on you; quite a bit more than might seem usual, but I was told he could be trusted. It was your idea, incidentally. While we were driving, you kept saying you had to find a doctor, one you could pay to keep quiet. You were right. It wasn't difficult."

"Where are we?" He could hear his voice; it was weak, but he could hear it.

"A village called Lenzburg, about twenty miles outside of Zurich. The doctor's from Wohlen; it's a nearby town. He'll see you in a week, if you're here."

"How? . . ." He tried to raise himself but the strength wasn't there. She touched his shoulder; it was an order to lie back down.

"I'll tell you what happened, and perhaps that will answer your questions. At least I hope so, because if it doesn't, I'm not sure I can." She stood motionless, looking down at him, her tone controlled. "An animal was raping me—after which he had orders to kill me. There was no way I was going to live. In the Steppdeckstrasse, you tried to stop them, and when you couldn't, you told me to scream, to keep screaming. It was all you could do, and by shouting to me, you risked being killed at that moment yourself. Later, you somehow got free—I don't know how, but I know you were hurt very badly doing so—and you came back to find me."

"Him," interrupted Jason, "I wanted *him*."

"You told me that, and I'll say what I said before. I

[125]

don't believe you. Not because you're a poor liar, but because it doesn't conform with the facts. I work with statistics, Mr. Washburn, or Mr. Bourne, or whatever your name is. I respect observable data and I can spot inaccuracies; I'm trained to do that. Two men went in that building to find you, and I heard you say they were both alive. They could identify you. And there's the owner of the Drei Alpenhäuser; he could too. Those are the facts, and you know them as well as I do. No, you came back to find me. You came back and saved my life."

"Go on," he said, his voice gaining strength. "What happened?"

"I made a decision. It was the most difficult decision I've ever made in my life. I think a person can only make a decision like that if he's nearly *lost* his life by an act of violence, his life saved by someone else. I decided to help you. Only for a while—for just a few hours, perhaps—but I would help you get away."

"Why didn't you go to the police?"

"I almost did, and I'm not sure I can tell you why I didn't. Maybe it was the rape, I don't know. I'm being honest with you. I've always been told it's the most horrible experience a woman can go through. I believe it now. And I heard the anger—the disgust—in your own voice when you shouted at him. I'll never forget that moment as long as I live, as much as I may want to."

"The police?" he repeated.

"That man at the Drei Alpenhäuser said the police were looking for you. That a telephone number had been set up in Zurich." She paused. "I couldn't give you to the police. Not then. Not after what you did."

"Knowing what I am?" he asked.

"I know only what I've heard, and what I've heard doesn't correspond with the injured man who came back for me and offered his life for mine."

"That's not very bright."

"That's the one thing I am, Mr. Bourne—I assume it's Bourne, it's what he called you. *Very* bright."

"I hit you. I threatened to kill you."

"If I'd been you, and men were trying to kill *me*, I probably would have done the same—if I were capable."

"So you drove out of Zurich?"

"Not at first, not for a half hour or so. I had to calm down, reach my decision. I'm methodical."

[126]

"I'm beginning to see that."

"I was a wreck, a mess; I needed clothes, hairbrush, makeup. I couldn't walk anywhere. I found a telephone booth down by the river, and there was no one around, so I got out of the car and called a colleague at the hotel—"

"The Frenchman? The Belgian?" interrupted Jason.

"No. They'd been at the Bertinelli lecture, and if they had recognized me up on the stage with you, I assumed they'd given my name to the police. Instead, I called a woman who's a member of our delegation; she loathes Bertinelli and was in her room. We've worked together for several years and we're friends. I told her that if she heard anything about me to disregard it, I was perfectly all right. As a matter of fact, if anyone asked about me, she was to say I was with a friend for the evening—for the night, if pressed. That I'd left the Bertinelli lecture early."

"Methodical," said Bourne.

"Yes." Marie allowed herself a tentative smile. "I asked her to go to my room—we're only two doors away from each other and the night maid knows we're friends. If no one was there she was to put some clothes and makeup in my suitcase and come back to her room. I'd call her in five minutes."

"She just accepted what you said?"

"I told you, we're friends. She knew I was all right, excited perhaps, but all right. And that I wanted her to do as I asked." Marie paused again. "She probably thought I was telling her the truth."

"Go ahead."

"I called her back and she had my things."

"Which means the two other delegates didn't give your name to the police. Your room would have been watched, sealed off."

"I don't know whether they did or not. But if they did, my friend was probably questioned quite a while ago. She'd simply say what I told her to say."

"She was at the Carillon, you were down at the river. How did you get your things?"

"It was quite simple. A little tacky, but simple. She spoke to the night maid, telling her I was avoiding one man at the hotel, seeing another outside. I needed my overnight case and could she suggest a way to get it to me. To an automobile . . . down at the river. An off-duty waiter brought it to me."

[127]

"Wasn't he surprised at the way you looked?"

"He didn't have much of a chance to see anything. I opened the trunk, stayed in the car, and told him to put it in the back. I left a ten-franc note on the spare tire."

"You're not methodical, you're remarkable."

"Methodical will do."

"How did you find the doctor?"

"Right here. The *concierge*, or whatever he's called in Switzerland. Remember, I'd wrapped you up as best I could, reduced the bleeding as much as possible. Like most people, I have a working knowledge of first aid; that meant I had to remove some of your clothing. I found the money and then I understood what you meant by finding a doctor you could pay. You have thousands and thousands of dollars on you; I know the rates of exchange."

"That's only the beginning."

"What?"

"Never mind." He tried to rise again; it was too difficult. "Aren't you afraid of me? Afraid of what you've done?"

"Of course I am. But I know what you did for me."

"You're more trusting than I'd be under the circumstances."

"Then perhaps you're not that aware of the circumstances. You're still very weak and I have the gun. Besides, you don't have any clothes."

"None?"

"Not even a pair of shorts. I've thrown everything away. You'd look a little foolish running down the street in a plastic money belt."

Bourne laughed through his pain, remembering La Ciotat and the Marquis de Chamford. "Methodical," he said.

"Very."

"What happens now?"

"I've written out the name of the doctor and paid a week's rent for the room. The *concierge* will bring you meals starting at noon today. I'll stay here until midmorning. It's nearly six o'clock; it should be light soon. Then I'll return to the hotel for the rest of my things and my airline tickets, and do my best to avoid any mention of you."

"Suppose you can't? Suppose you were identified?"

"I'll deny it. It was dark. The whole place was in panic."

"Now you're *not* being methodical. At least, not as methodical as the Zurich police would be. I've got a better way. Call your friend and tell her to pack the rest of your

[128]

clothes and settle your bill. Take as much money as you want from me and grab the first plane to Canada. It's easier to deny long-distance."

She looked at him in silence, then nodded. "That's very tempting."

"It's very logical."

She continued to stare at him a moment longer, the tension inside her building, conveyed by her eyes. She turned away and walked to the window, looking out at the earliest rays of the morning sun. He watched her, feeling the intensity, knowing its roots, seeing her face in the pale orange glow of dawn. There was nothing he could do; she had done what she felt she had to do because she had been released from terror. From a kind of terrible degradation no man could really understand. From death. And in doing what she did, she had broken all the rules. She whipped her head toward him, her eyes glaring.

"Who *are* you?"

"You heard what they said."

"I know what I saw! What I *feel!*"

"Don't try to justify what you did. You simply did it, that's all. Let it be."

Let it be. Oh, God, you could have let me be. And there would have been peace. But now you have given part of my life back to me, and I've got to struggle again, face it again.

Suddenly she was standing at the foot of the bed, the gun in her hand. She pointed it at him and her voice trembled. "Should I undo it then? Should I call the police and tell them to come and take you?"

"A few hours ago I would have said go ahead. I can't bring myself to say it now."

"Then who are you?"

"They say my name is Bourne. Jason Charles Bourne."

"What does that mean? 'They say'?"

He stared at the gun, at the dark circle of its barrel. There was nothing left but the truth—as he knew the truth.

"What does it mean?" he repeated. "You know almost as much as I do, Doctor."

"What?"

"You might as well hear it. Maybe it'll make you feel better. Or worse, I don't know. But you may as well, because I don't know what else to tell you."

She lowered the gun. "Tell me what?"

"My life began five months ago on a small island in the Mediterranean called Ile de Port Noir. . . ."

The sun had risen to the midpoint of the surrounding trees, its rays filtered by windblown branches, streaming through the windows and mottling the walls with irregular shapes of light. Bourne lay back on the pillow, exhausted. He had finished; there was nothing more to say.

Marie sat across the room in a leather armchair, her legs curled up under her, cigarettes and the gun on a table to her left. She had barely moved, her gaze fixed on his face; even when she smoked, her eyes never wavered, never left his. She was a technical analyst, evaluating data, filtering facts as the trees filtered the sunlight.

"You kept saying it," she said softly, spacing out her next words. " 'I don't know.' . . . 'I wish I knew.' You'd stare at something, and I was frightened. I'd ask you, what was it? What were you going to do? And you'd say it again, 'I wish I knew.' My God, what you've been through. . . . What you're *going* through."

"After what I've done to you, you can even think about what's happened to me?"

"They're two separate lines of occurrence," she said absently, frowning in thought.

"Separate—"

"Related in origin, developed independently; that's economics nonsense. . . . And then on the Löwenstrasse, just before we went up to Chernak's flat, I begged you not to make me go with you. I was convinced that if I heard any more you'd kill me. That's when you said the strangest thing of all. You said, 'What you heard makes no more sense to me than it does to you. Perhaps less. . . .' I thought you were insane."

"What I've got is a form of insanity. A sane person remembers. I don't."

"Why didn't you tell me Chernak tried to kill you?"

"There wasn't time and I didn't think it mattered."

"It didn't at that moment—to you. It did to me."

"Why?"

"Because I was holding on to an outside hope that you wouldn't fire your gun at someone who hadn't tried to kill you first."

"But he did. I was wounded."

"I didn't know the sequence; you didn't tell me."

"I don't understand."

Marie lit a cigarette. "It's hard to explain, but during all the time you kept me hostage, even when you hit me, and dragged me and pressed the gun into my stomach and held it against my head—God knows, I was terrified—but I thought I saw something in your eyes. Call it reluctance. It's the best I can come up with."

"It'll do. What's your point?"

"I'm not sure. Perhaps it goes back to something else you said in the booth at the Drei Alpenhäuser. That fat man was coming over and you told me to stay against the wall, cover my face with my hand. 'For your own good,' you said. 'There's no point in his being able to identify you.' "

"There wasn't."

" 'For your own good.' That's not the reasoning of a pathological killer. I think I held on to that—for my own sanity, maybe—that and the look in your eyes."

"I still don't get the point."

"The man with the gold-rimmed glasses who convinced me he was the police said you were a brutal killer who had to be stopped before he killed again. Had it not been for Chernak I wouldn't have believed him. On either point. The police don't behave like that; they don't use guns in dark, crowded places. And you were a man running for your life—*are* running for your life—but you're not a killer."

Bourne held up his hand. "Forgive me, but that strikes me as a judgment based on false gratitude. You say you have a respect for facts—then look at them. I repeat: you heard what they said—regardless of what you think you saw and feel—you heard the words. Boiled down, envelopes were filled with money and delivered to me to fulfill certain obligations. I'd say those obligations were pretty clear, and I accepted them. I had a numbered account at the Gemeinschaft Bank totaling about five million dollars. Where did I get it? Where does a man like me—with the obvious skills I have—get that kind of money?" Jason stared at the ceiling. The pain was returning, the sense of futility also. "Those are the facts, Dr. St. Jacques. It's time you left."

Marie rose from the chair and crushed out her cigarette. Then she picked up the gun and walked toward the bed. "You're very anxious to condemn yourself, aren't you?"

"I respect facts."

"Then if what you say is true, *I* have an obligation, too, don't I? As a law-abiding member of the social order I must call the Zurich police and tell them where you are." She raised the gun.

Bourne looked at her. "I thought—"

"Why not?" she broke in. "You're a condemned man who wants to get it over with, aren't you? You lie there talking with such finality—with, if you'll forgive me, not a little self-pity, expecting to appeal to my . . . what was it? False gratitude? Well, I think you'd better understand something. I'm not a fool; if I thought for a minute you're what they say you are, I wouldn't be here and neither would you. Facts that cannot be documented aren't facts at all. You don't have facts, you have *conclusions*, your own conclusions based on statements made by men you know are garbage."

"And an unexplained bank account with five million dollars in it. Don't forget that."

"How could I? I'm supposed to be a financial whiz. That account may not be explained in ways that you'd like, but there's a proviso attached that lends a considerable degree of legitimacy to it. It can be inspected—probably invaded—by any certified director of a corporation called something-or-other Seventy-One. That's hardly an affiliation for a hired killer."

"The corporation may be named; it isn't listed."

"In a telephone book? You *are* naive. But let's get back to you. Right now. Shall I really call the police?"

"You know my answer. I can't stop you, but I don't want you to."

Marie lowered the gun. "And I won't. For the same reason you don't want me to. I don't believe what they say you are any more than you do."

"Then what do you believe?"

"I told you, I'm not sure. All I really know is that seven hours ago I was underneath an animal, his mouth all over me, his hands clawing me . . . and I knew I was going to die. And then a man came back for me—a man who could have kept running—but who came back for me and offered to die in my place. I guess I believe in him."

"Suppose you're wrong?"

"Then I'll have made a terrible mistake."

"Thank you. Where's the money?"

"On the bureau. In your passport case and billfold. Also the name of the doctor and the receipt for the room."

"May I have the passport, please? That's the Swiss currency."

"I know." Marie brought them to him. "I gave the *concierge* three hundred francs for the room and two hundred for the name of the doctor. The doctor's services came to four hundred and fifty, to which I added another hundred and fifty for his cooperation. Altogether I paid out eleven hundred francs."

"You don't have to give me an accounting," he said.

"You should know. What are you going to do?"

"Give you money so you can get back to Canada."

"I mean afterwards."

"See how I feel later on. Probably pay the *concierge* to buy me some clothes. Ask him a few questions. I'll be all right." He took out a number of large bills and held them out for her.

"That's over fifty thousand francs."

"I've put you through a great deal."

Marie St. Jacques looked at the money, then down at the gun in her left hand. "I don't want your money," she said, placing the weapon on the bedside table.

"What do you mean?"

She turned and walked back to the armchair, turning again to look at him as she sat down. "I think I want to help you."

"Now wait a minute—"

"Please," she interrupted. "Please don't ask me any questions. Don't say anything for a while."

BOOK II

——— 10 ———

Neither of them knew when it happened, or, in truth, whether it had happened. Or, if it had, to what lengths either would go to preserve it, or deepen it. There was no essential drama, no conflicts to overcome or barriers to surmount. All that was required was communication, by words and looks, and, perhaps as vital as either of these, the frequent accompaniment of quiet laughter.

Their living arrangements in the room at the village inn were as clinical as they might have been in the hospital ward it replaced. During the daylight hours Marie took care of various practical matters such as clothes, meals, maps, and newspapers. On her own she had driven the stolen car ten miles south to the town of Reinach where she had abandoned it, taking a taxi back to Lenzburg. When she was out Bourne concentrated on rest and mobility. From somewhere in his forgotten past he understood that recovery depended upon both and he applied rigid discipline to both; he had been there before . . . before Port Noir.

When they were together they talked, at first awkwardly, the thrusts and parries of strangers thrown together and surviving the shock waves of cataclysm. They tried to insert normalcy where none could exist, but it was easier when they both accepted the essential abnormality: there was nothing to say not related to what had happened. And if there was, it would begin to appear only during those moments when the probing of what-had-happened was temporarily exhausted, the silences springboards to relief, to other words and thoughts.

It was during such moments that Jason learned the salient facts about the woman who had saved his life. He protested that she knew as much about him as he did, but he knew nothing about her. Where had *she* sprung from? Why was an attractive woman with dark red hair and skin obviously nurtured on a farm somewhere pretending to be a doctor of economics?

"Because she was sick of the farm," Marie replied.

"No kidding? A farm, really?"

"Well, a small ranch would be more like it. Small in comparison to the king-sized ones in Alberta. In my father's time, when a Canuck went west to buy land, there were unwritten restrictions. Don't compete in size with your betters. He often said that if he'd used the name St. James rather than St. Jacques, he'd be a far wealthier man today."

"He was a rancher?"

Marie had laughed. "No, he was an accountant who became a rancher by way of a Vickers bomber in the war. He was a pilot in the Royal Canadian Air Force. I guess once he saw all that sky, an accounting office seemed a little dull."

"That takes a lot of nerve."

"More than you know. He sold cattle he didn't own on land he didn't have before he bought the ranch. French to the core, people said."

"I think I'd like him."

"You would."

She had lived in Calgary with her parents and two brothers until she was eighteen, when she went to McGill University in Montreal and the beginnings of a life she had never contemplated. An indifferent student who preferred racing over the fields on the back of a horse to the structured boredom of a convent school in Alberta discovered the excitement of using her mind.

"It was really as simple as that," she told him. "I'd

looked at books as natural enemies, and suddenly, here I was in a place surrounded by people who were caught up in them, having a marvelous time. Everything was talk. Talk all day, talk all night—in classrooms and seminars, in crowded booths over pitchers of beer; I think it was the talk that turned me on. Does that make sense to you?"

"I can't remember, but I can understand," Bourne said. "I have no memories of college or friends like that, but I'm pretty sure I was there." He smiled. "Talking over pitchers of beer is a pretty strong impression."

She smiled back. "And I was pretty impressive in that department. A strapping girl from Calgary with two older brothers to compete with could drink more beer than half the university boys in Montreal."

"You must have been resented."

"No, just envied."

A new world had been presented to Marie St. Jacques; she never returned to her old one. Except for proscribed midterm holidays, prolonged trips to Calgary grew less and less frequent. Her circles in Montreal expanded, the summers taken up with jobs in and outside the university. She gravitated first to history, then reasoned that most of history was shaped by economic forces—power and significance had to be paid for—and so she tested the theories of economics. And was consumed.

She remained at McGill for five years, receiving her masters degree and a Canadian government fellowship to Oxford.

"That was a day, I can tell you. I thought my father would have apoplexy. He left his precious cattle to my brothers long enough to fly east to talk me out of it."

"Talk you out of it? Why? He was an accountant; you were going after a doctorate in economics."

"Don't make *that* mistake," Marie exclaimed. "Accountants and economists *are* natural enemies. One views trees, the other forests, and the visions are usually at odds, as they should be. Besides, my father's not simply Canadian, he's French-Canadian. I think he saw me as a traitor to Versailles. But he was mollified when I told him that a condition of the fellowship was a commitment to work for the government for a minimum of three years. He said I could 'serve the cause better from within.' *Vive Québec libre—vive la France!*"

They both laughed.

The three-year commitment to Ottawa was extended for all the logical reasons: whenever she thought of leaving, she was promoted a grade, given a large office and an expanded staff.

"Power corrupts, of course"—she smiled—"and no one knows it better than a ranking bureaucrat whom banks and corporations pursue for a recommendation. But I think Napoleon said it better. 'Give me enough medals and I'll win you any war.' So I stayed. I enjoy my work immensely. But then it's work I'm good at and that helps."

Jason watched her as she talked. Beneath the controlled exterior there was an exuberant, childlike quality about her. She was an enthusiast, reining in her enthusiasm whenever she felt it becoming too pronounced. Of course she was good at what she did; he suspected she never did anything with less than her fullest application. "I'm sure you are—good, I mean—but it doesn't leave much time for other things, does it?"

"What other things?"

"Oh, the usual. Husband, family, house with the picket fence."

"They may come one day; I don't rule them out."

"But they haven't."

"No. There were a couple of close calls, but no brass ring. Or diamond, either."

"Who's Peter?"

The smile faded. "I'd forgotten. You read the cable."

"I'm sorry."

"Don't be. We've covered that. . . . Peter? I adore Peter. We lived together for nearly two years, but it didn't work out."

"Apparently he doesn't hold any grudges."

"He'd better not!" She laughed again. "He's director of the section, hopes for a cabinet appointment soon. If he doesn't behave himself, I'll tell the Treasury Board what he doesn't know and he'll be back as an SX-Two."

"He said he was going to pick you up at the airport on the twenty-sixth. You'd better cable him."

"Yes, I know."

Her leaving was what they had not talked about; they had avoided the subject as though it were a distant eventuality. It was not related to what-had-happened; it was something that was going to be. Marie had said she wanted to help him; he had accepted, assuming she was driven by false gratitude into staying with him for a day or so—and he was grateful for that. But anything else was unthinkable.

Which was why they did not talk about it. Words and looks had passed between them, quiet laughter evoked, comfort established. At odd moments there were tentative rushes of warmth and they both understood and backed away. Anything else *was* unthinkable.

So they kept returning to the abnormality, to what-had-happened. To *him* more than to them, for he was the irrational reason for their being together . . . together in a room at a small village inn in Switzerland. Abnormality. It was not part of the reasonable, ordered world of Marie St. Jacques, and because it was not, her orderly, analytical mind was provoked. Unreasonable things were to be examined, unraveled, explained. She became relentless in her probing, as insistent as Geoffrey Washburn had been on the Ile de Port Noir, but without the doctor's patience. For she did not have the time; she knew it and it drove her to the edges of stridency.

"When you read the newspapers, what strikes you?"

"The mess. Seems it's universal."

"Be serious. What's familiar to you?"

"Most everything, but I can't tell you why."

"Give me an example."

"This morning. There was a story about an American arms shipment to Greece and the subsequent debate in the United Nations; the Soviets protested. I understand the significance, the Mediterranean power struggle, the Mid East spillover."

"Give me another."

"There was an article about East German interference with the Bonn government's liaison office in Warsaw. Eastern bloc, Western bloc; again I understood."

"You see the relationship, don't you? You're politically—*geo*-politically—receptive."

"Or I have a perfectly normal working knowledge of current events. I don't think I was ever a diplomat. The money at the Gemeinschaft would rule out any kind of government employment."

"I agree. Still, you're politically aware. What about maps? You asked me to buy you maps. What comes to mind when you look at them?"

"In some cases names trigger images, just as they did in

Zurich. Buildings, hotels, streets . . . sometimes faces. But never names. The faces don't have any."

"Still you've traveled a great deal."

"I guess I have."

"You *know* you have."

"All right, I've traveled."

"How did you travel?"

"What do you mean, how?"

"Was it usually by plane, or by car—not taxis but driving yourself?"

"Both, I think. Why?"

"Planes would mean greater distances more frequently. Did people meet you? Are there faces at airports, hotels?"

"Streets," he replied involuntarily.

"Streets? Why streets?"

"I don't know. Faces met me in the streets . . . and in quiet places. Dark places."

"Restaurants? Cafés?"

"Yes. And rooms."

"Hotel rooms?"

"Yes."

"Not offices? Business offices?"

"Sometimes. Not usually."

"All right. People met you. Faces. Men? Women? Both?"

"Men mostly. Some women, but mostly men."

"What did they talk about?"

"I don't know."

"Try to remember."

"I can't. There aren't any voices; there aren't any words."

"Were there schedules? You met with people, that means you had appointments. They expected to meet with you and you expected to meet with them. Who scheduled those appointments? Someone had to."

"Cables. Telephone calls."

"From whom? From where?"

"I don't know. They would reach me."

"At hotels?"

"Mostly, I imagine."

"You told me the assistant manager at the Carillon said you *did* receive messages."

"Then they came to hotels."

"Something-or-other Seventy-One?"

[142]

"Treadstone."

"Treadstone. That's your company, isn't it?"

"It doesn't mean anything. I couldn't find it."

"Concentrate!"

"I *am*. It wasn't listed. I called New York."

"You seem to think that's so unusual. It's not."

"*Why* not?"

"It could be a separate in-house division, or a blind subsidiary—a corporation set up to make purchases for a parent company whose name would push up a negotiating price. It's done every day."

"Whom are you trying to convince?"

"You. It's entirely possible that you're a roving negotiator for American financial interests. Everything points to it: funds set up for immediate capital, confidentiality open for corporate approval, which was never exercised. These facts, plus your own antenna for political shifts, point to a trusted purchasing agent, and quite probably a large shareholder or part owner of the parent company."

"You talk awfully fast."

"I've said nothing that isn't logical."

"There's a hole or two."

"Where?"

"That account didn't show any withdrawals. Only deposits. I wasn't buying, I was selling."

"You don't know that; you can't remember. Payments can be made with shortfall deposits."

"I don't even know what that means."

"A treasurer aware of certain tax strategies would. What's the other hole?"

"Men don't try to kill someone for buying something at a lower price. They may expose him; they don't kill him."

"They do if a gargantuan error has been made. Or if that person has been mistaken for someone else. What I'm trying to tell you is that you can't be what you're not! No matter what anyone says."

"You're that convinced."

"I'm that convinced. I've spent three days with you. We've talked, I've listened. A terrible error *has* been made. Or it's some kind of conspiracy."

"Involving what? *Against* what?"

"That's what you have to find out."

"Thanks."

"Tell me something. What comes to mind when you think of money?"

Stop it! Don't do this! Can't you understand? You're wrong. When I think of money I think of killing.

"I don't know," he said. "I'm tired. I want to sleep. Send your cable in the morning. Tell Peter you're flying back."

It was well past midnight, the beginning of the fourth day, and still sleep would not come. Bourne stared at the ceiling, at the dark wood that reflected the light of the table lamp across the room. The light remained on during the nights; Marie simply left it on, no explanation sought, none offered.

In the morning she would be gone and his own plans had to crystallize. He would stay at the inn for a few more days, call the doctor in Wohlen and arrange to have the stitches removed. After that, Paris. The money was in Paris, and so was something else; he knew it, he felt it. A final answer; it was in Paris.

You are not helpless. You will find your way.

What would he find? A man named Carlos? Who was Carlos and what was he to Jason Bourne?

He heard the rustle of cloth from the couch against the wall. He glanced over, startled to see that Marie was not asleep. Instead, she was looking at him, staring at him really.

"You're wrong, you know," she said.

"About what?"

"What you're thinking."

"You don't know what I'm thinking."

"Yes, I do. I've seen that look in your eyes, seeing things you're not sure are there, afraid that they may be."

"They have been," he replied. "Explain the Steppdeckstrasse. Explain a fat man at the Drei Alpenhäuser."

"I can't, but neither can you."

"They were there. I saw them and they were there."

"Find out why. You can't be what you're not, Jason. Find out."

"Paris," he said.

"Yes, Paris." Marie got up from the couch. She was in a soft yellow nightgown, nearly white, pearl buttons at the neck; it flowed as she walked toward the bed in her bare feet. She stood beside him, looking down, then raised both her hands and began unbuttoning the top of the gown. She

[144]

let it fall away, as she sat on the bed, her breasts above him. She leaned toward him, reaching for his face, cupping it, holding him gently, her eyes as so often during the past few days unwavering, fixed on his. "Thank you for my life," she whispered.

"Thank you for mine," he answered, feeling the longing he knew she felt, wondering if an ache accompanied hers, as it did his. He had no memory of a woman and, perhaps because he had none she was everything he could imagine; everything and much, much more. She repelled the darkness for him. She stopped the pain.

He had been afraid to tell her. And she was telling him now it was all right, if only for a while, for an hour or so. For the remainder of that night, she was giving him a memory because she too longed for release from the coiled springs of violence. Tension was suspended, comfort theirs for an hour or so. It was all he asked for, but God in heaven, how he *needed* her!

He reached for her breast and pulled her lips to his lips, her moisture arousing him, sweeping away the doubts.

She lifted the covers and came to him.

She lay in his arms, her head on his chest, careful to avoid the wound in his shoulder. She slid back gently, raising herself on her elbows. He looked at her; their eyes locked, and both smiled. She lifted her left hand, pressing her index finger over his lips, and spoke softly.

"I have something to say and I don't want you to interrupt. I'm not sending the cable to Peter. Not yet."

"Now, just a *minute*." He took her hand from his face.

"Please, don't interrupt me. I said 'not yet.' That doesn't mean I won't send it, but not for a while. I'm staying with you. I'm going to Paris with you."

He forced the words. "Suppose I don't want you to."

She leaned forward brushing her lips against his cheek. "That won't wash. The computer just rejected it."

"I wouldn't be so certain, if I were you."

"But you're not me. I'm me, and I know the way you held me, and tried to say so many things you couldn't say. Things I think we both wanted to say to each other for the past several days. I can't explain what's happened. Oh, I suppose it's there in some obscure psychological theory somewhere, two reasonably intelligent people thrown into hell together and crawling out . . . together. And maybe that's all it is. But it's there right now and I can't run away from it. I can't run away from you. Because you need me, and you gave me my life."

"What makes you think I need you?"

"I can do things for you that you can't do for yourself. It's all I've thought about for the past two hours." She raised herself further, naked beside him. "You're somehow involved with a great deal of money, but I don't think you know a debit from an asset. You may have before, but you don't now. I do. And there's something else. I have a ranking position with the Canadian government. I have clearance and access to all manner of inquiries. And protection. International finance is rotten and Canada has been raped. We've mounted our own protection and I'm part of it. It's why I was in Zurich. To observe and report alliances, not to discuss abstract theories."

"And the fact that you have this clearance, this access, can help me?"

"I think it can. And embassy protection, that may be the most important. But I give you my word that at the first sign of violence, I'll send the cable and get out. My own fears aside, I won't be a burden to you under those conditions."

"At the first sign," repeated Bourne, studying her. "And I determine when and where that is?"

"If you like. My experience is limited. I won't argue."

He continued to hold her eyes, the moment long, magnified by silence. Finally he asked, "Why are you doing this? You just said it. We're two reasonably intelligent people who crawled out of some kind of hell. That may be all we are. Is it worth it?"

She sat motionless. "I also said something else; maybe you've forgotten. Four nights ago a man who could have kept running came back for me and offered to die in my place. I believe in that man. More than he does, I think. That's really what I have to offer."

"I accept," he said, reaching for her. "I shouldn't, but I do. I need that belief very badly."

"You may interrupt now," she whispered, lowering the sheet, her body coming to his. "Make love to me, I have needs too."

Three more days and nights went by, filled by the warmth of their comfort, the excitement of discovery. They

[146]

lived with the intensity of two people aware that change would come. And when it came, it would come quickly; so there were things to talk about which could not be avoided any longer.

Cigarette smoke spiraled above the table joining the steam from the hot, bitter coffee. The *concierge,* an ebullient Swiss whose eyes took in more than his lips would reveal, had left several minutes before, having delivered the *petit déjeuner* and the Zurich newspapers, in both English and French. Jason and Marie sat across from each other; both had scanned the news.

"Anything in yours?" asked Bourne.

"That old man, the watchman at the Guisan Quai, was buried the day before yesterday. The police still have nothing concrete. 'Investigation in progress,' it says."

"It's a little more extensive here," said Jason, shifting his paper awkwardly in his bandaged left hand.

"How is it?" asked Marie, looking at the hand.

"Better. I've got more play in the fingers now."

"I know."

"You've got a dirty mind." He folded the paper. "Here it is. They repeat the things they said the other day. The shells and blood scrapings are being analyzed." Bourne looked up. "But they've added something. Remnants of clothing; it wasn't mentioned before."

"Is that a problem?"

"Not for me. My clothes were bought off a rack in Marseilles. What about your dress? Was it a special design or fabric?"

"You embarrass me; it wasn't. All my clothes are made by a woman in Ottawa."

"It couldn't be traced, then?"

"I don't see how. The silk came from a bolt an FS-Three in our section brought back from Hong Kong."

"Did you buy anything at the shops in the hotel? Something you might have had on you. A kerchief, a pin, anything like that?"

"No. I'm not much of a shopper that way."

"Good. And your friend wasn't asked any questions when she checked out?"

"Not by the desk, I told you that. Only by the two men you saw me with in the elevator."

"From the French and Belgian delegations."

"Yes. Everything was fine."

"Let's go over it again."

"There's nothing to go over. Paul—the one from Brussels—didn't see anything. He was knocked off his chair to the floor and stayed there. Claude—he tried to stop us, remember?—at first thought it was me on the stage, in the light, but before he could get to the police he was hurt in the crowd and taken to the infirmary—"

"And by the time he might have said something," interrupted Jason, recalling her words, "he wasn't sure."

"Yes. But I have an idea he knew my main purpose for being at the conference; my presentation didn't fool him. If he did, it would reinforce his decision to stay out of it."

Bourne picked up his coffee. "Let me have *that* again," he said. "You were looking for . . . alliances?"

"Well, hints of them, really. No one's going to come out and say there are financial interests in his country working with interests in that country so they can buy their way into Canadian raw materials or any other market. But you see who meets for drinks, who has dinner together. Or sometimes it's as dumb as a delegate from, say, Rome—whom you know is being paid by Agnelli—coming up and asking you how serious Ottawa is about the declaration laws."

"I'm still not sure I understand."

"You should. Your own country's very touchy about the subject. Who owns what? How many American banks are controlled by OPEC money? How much industry is owned by European and Japanese consortiums? How many hundreds of thousands of acres have been acquired by capital that's fled England and Italy and France? We all worry."

"We do?"

Marie laughed. "Of course. Nothing makes a man more nationalistic than to think his country's owned by foreigners. He can adjust in time to losing a war—that only means the enemy was stronger—but to lose his economy means the enemy was smarter. The period of occupation lasts longer, and so do the scars."

"You've given these things a lot of thought, haven't you?"

For a brief moment the look in Marie's eyes lost its edge of humor; she answered him seriously. "Yes, I have. I think they're important."

"Did you learn anything in Zurich?"

"Nothing startling," she said. "Money's flying all over; syndicates are trying to find internal investments where bureaucratic machineries look the other way."

"That cablegram from Peter said your daily reports were first rate. What did he mean?"

"I found a number of odd economic bedfellows who I think may be using Canadian figureheads to buy up Canadian properties. I'm not being elusive; it's just that they wouldn't mean anything to you."

"I'm not trying to pry," countered Jason, "but I think you put *me* in one of those beds. Not with respect to Canada, but in general."

"I don't rule you out; the structure's there. You could be part of a financial combine that's looking for all manner of illegal purchases. It's one thing I can put a quiet trace on, but I want to do it over a telephone. Not words written out in a cable."

"Now I *am* prying. What do you mean and how?"

"If there's a Treadstone Seventy-One behind a multinational corporate door somewhere, there are ways to find which company, which door. I want to call Peter from one of those public telephone stations in Paris. I'll tell him that I ran across the name Treadstone Seventy-One in Zurich and it's been bothering me. I'll ask him to make a CS—a covert search—and say that I'll call him back."

"And if he finds it?"

"If it's there, he'll find it."

"Then I get in touch with whoever's listed as the 'certified directors' and surface."

"Very cautiously," added Marie. "Through intermediaries. Myself, if you like."

"Why?"

"Because of what they've done. Or *not* done, really."

"Which is?"

"They haven't tried to reach you in nearly six months."

"You don't know that—*I* don't know that."

"The bank knows it. Millions of dollars left untouched, unaccounted for, and no one has bothered to find out why. That's what I can't understand. It's as though you were being abandoned. It's where the mistake could have been made."

Bourne leaned back in the chair, looking at his bandaged left hand, remembering the sight of the weapon smashing repeatedly downward in the shadows of a racing car in the

Steppdeckstrasse. He raised his eyes and looked at Marie. "What you're saying is that if I was abandoned, it's because that mistake is thought to be the truth by the directors at Treadstone."

"Possibly. They might think you've involved them in illegal transactions—with criminal elements—that could cost them millions more. Conceivably risking expropriation of entire companies by angry governments. Or that you joined forces with an international crime syndicate, probably not knowing it. Anything. It would account for their not going near the bank. They'd want no guilt by association."

"So, in a sense, no matter what your friend Peter learns, I'm still back at square one."

"*We're* back, but it's not square one, more like four-and-a-half to five on a scale of ten."

"Even if it were nine, nothing's really changed. Men want to kill me and I don't know why. Others could stop them but they won't. That man at the Drei Alpenhäuser said Interpol has its nets out for me, and if I walk into one I don't have any answers. I'm guilty as charged because I don't know what I'm guilty of. Having no memory isn't much of a defense, and it's possible that I have no defense, period."

"I refuse to believe that, and so must you."

"Thanks."

"I *mean* it, Jason. Stop it."

Stop it. How many times do I say that to myself? You are my love, the only woman I have ever known, and you believe in me. Why can't I believe in myself?

Bourne got up, as always testing his legs. Mobility was coming back to him, the wounds less severe than his imagination had permitted him to believe. He had made an appointment that night with the doctor in Wohlen to remove the stitches. Tomorrow, change would come.

"Paris," said Jason. "The answer's in Paris. I know it as surely as I saw the outline of those triangles in Zurich. I just don't know where to begin. It's crazy. I'm a man waiting for an image, for a word or a phrase—or a book of matches—to tell me something. To send me somewhere else."

"Why not wait until I hear from Peter? I can call him tomorrow; we can be in Paris tomorrow."

"Because it wouldn't make any difference, don't you see? No matter what he came up with, the one thing I need to know wouldn't be there. For the same reason Treadstone hasn't gone near the bank. *Me*. I have to know why men want to kill me, why someone named Carlos will pay . . . what was it . . . a fortune for my corpse."

It was as far as he got, interrupted by the crash at the table. Marie had dropped her cup and was staring at him, her face white, as if the blood had drained from her head. "What did you just say?" she asked.

"What? I said I have to know . . ."

"The *name*. You just said the name Carlos."

"That's right."

"In all the hours we've talked, the days we've been together, you never mentioned him."

Bourne looked at her, trying to remember. It was true; he had told her everything that had come to him, yet somehow he had omitted Carlos . . . almost purposely, as if blocking it out.

"I guess I didn't," he said. "You seem to know. Who's Carlos?"

"Are you trying to be funny? If you are, the joke's not very good."

"I'm not trying to be funny. I don't think there's anything to be funny about. Who's Carlos?"

"My God—you *don't* know!" she exclaimed, studying his eyes. "It's part of what was taken from you."

"Who is Carlos?"

"An assassin. He's called the assassin of Europe. A man hunted for twenty years, believed to have killed between fifty and sixty political and military figures. No one knows what he looks like . . . but it's said he operates out of Paris."

Bourne felt a wave of cold going through him.

The taxi to Wohlen was an English Ford belonging to the *concierge*'s son-in-law. Jason and Marie sat in the back seat, the dark countryside passing swiftly outside the windows. The stitches had been removed, replaced by soft bandages held by wide strips of tape.

"Get back to Canada," said Jason softly, breaking the silence between them.

"I will, I told you that. I've a few more days left. I want to see Paris."

"I don't want you in Paris. I'll call you in Ottawa. You

can make the Treadstone search yourself and give me the information over the phone."

"I thought you said it wouldn't make any difference. You had to know the *why;* the *who* was meaningless until you understood."

"I'll find a way. I just need one man; I'll find him."

"But you don't know where to begin. You're a man waiting for an image, for a phrase, or a book of matches. They may not be there."

"Something will be there."

"Something *is*, but you don't see it. I *do*. It's why you need me. I know the words, the methods. You don't."

Bourne looked at her in the rushing shadows. "I think you'd better be clearer."

"The banks, Jason. Treadstone's connections are in the banks. But not in the way that you might think."

The stooped old man in the threadbare overcoat, black beret in hand, walked down the far left aisle of the country church in the village of Arpajon, ten miles south of Paris. The bells of the evening Angelus echoed throughout the upper regions of stone and wood; the man held his place at the fifth row and waited for the ringing to stop. It was his signal; he accepted it, knowing that during the pealing of the bells another, younger man—as ruthless as any man alive—had circled the small church and studied everyone inside and outside. Had that man seen anything he did not expect to see, anyone he considered a threat to his person, there would be no questions asked, simply an execution. That was the way of Carlos, and only those who understood that their lives could be snuffed out because they themselves had been followed accepted money to act as the assassin's messenger. They were all like himself, old men from the old days, whose lives were running out, months remaining limited by age, or disease, or both.

Carlos permitted no risks whatsoever, the single consolation being that if one died in his service—or by his hand— money would find its way to old women, or the children of old women, or their children. It had to be said: there was a certain dignity to be found in working for Carlos. And there was no lack of generosity. This was what his small army of infirm old men understood; he gave a purpose to the ends of their lives.

The messenger clutched his beret and continued down the aisle to the row of confessional booths against the left wall. He walked to the fifth booth, parted the curtain, and stepped inside, adjusting his eyes to the light of a single candle that glowed from the other side of the translucent drape separating priest from sinner. He sat down on the small wooden bench and looked at the silhouette in the holy enclosure. It was as it always was, the hooded figure of a man in a monk's habit. The messenger tried not to imagine what that man looked like; it was not his place to speculate on such things.

"Angelus Domini," he said.

"Angelus Domini, child of God," whispered the hooded silhouette. "Are your days comfortable?"

"They draw to an end," replied the old man, making the proper response, "but they are made comfortable."

"Good. It's important to have a sense of security at your age," said Carlos. "But to business. Did you get the particulars from Zurich?"

"The owl is dead; so are two others, possibly a third. Another's hand was severely wounded; he cannot work. Cain disappeared. They think the woman is with him."

"An odd turn of events," said Carlos.

"There's more. The one ordered to kill her has not been heard from. He was to take her to the Guisan Quai; no one knows what happened."

"Except that a watchman was killed in her place. It's possible she was never a hostage at all, but instead, bait for a trap. A trap that snapped back on Cain. I want to think about that. In the meantime, here are my instructions. Are you ready?"

The old man reached into his pocket and took out the stub of a pencil and a scrap of paper. "Very well."

"Telephone Zurich. I want a man in Paris by tomorrow who has seen Cain, who can recognize him. Also, Zurich is to reach Koenig at the Gemeinschaft and tell him to send his tape to New York. He's to use the post office box in Village Station."

"Please," interrupted the aged messenger. "These old hands do not write as they once did."

"Forgive me," whispered Carlos. "I'm preoccupied and inconsiderate. I'm sorry."

"Not at all, not at all. Go ahead."

"Finally, I want our team to take rooms within a block of the bank on the rue Madeleine. This time the bank will be Cain's undoing. The pretender will be taken at the source of his misplaced pride. A bargain price, as despicable as he is . . . unless he's something else."

— 11 —

Bourne watched from a distance as Marie passed through customs and immigration in Bern's airport, looking for signs of interest or recognition from anyone in the crowd that stood around Air France's departure area. It was four o'clock in the afternoon, the busiest hour for flights to Paris, a time when privileged businessmen hurried back to the City of Light after dull company chores at the banks in Bern. Marie glanced over her shoulder as she walked through the gate; he nodded, waited until she had disappeared, then turned and started for the Swissair lounge. George B. Washburn had a reservation on the 4:30 plane to Orly.

They would meet later at the café Marie remembered from visits during her Oxford days. It was called Au Coin de Cluny, on the boulevard Saint-Michel, several blocks from the Sorbonne. If by any chance it was no longer there, Jason would find her around nine o'clock on the steps of the Cluny Museum.

Bourne would be late, nearby but late. The Sorbonne had one of the most extensive libraries in all Europe and somewhere in that library were back issues of newspapers.

University libraries were not subject to the working hours of government employees; students used them during the evenings. So would he as soon as he reached Paris. There was something he had to learn.

Every day I read the newspapers. In three languages. Six months ago a man was killed, his death reported on the front page of each of those newspapers. So said a fat man in Zurich.

He left his suitcase at the library checkroom and walked to the second floor, turning left toward the arch that led to the huge reading room. The Salle de Lecture was at this annex, the newspapers on spindles placed in racks, the issues going back precisely one year from the day's date.

He walked along the racks, counting back six months, lifting off the first ten weeks' worth of papers before that date a half a year ago. He carried them to the nearest vacant table and without sitting down flipped through from front page to front page, issue to issue.

Great men had died in their beds; while others had made pronouncements; the dollar had fallen, gold risen; strikes had crippled, and governments had vacillated between action and paralysis. But no man had been killed who warranted headlines; there was no such incident—no such assassination.

Jason returned to the racks and went back further. Two weeks, twelve weeks, twenty weeks. Nearly eight months. Nothing.

Then it struck him; he had gone *back* in time, not forward from that date six months ago. An error could be made in either direction; a few days or a week, even two. He returned the spindles to the racks and pulled out the papers from four and five months ago.

Airplanes had crashed and revolutions had erupted bloodily; holy men had spoken only to be rebuked by other holy men; poverty and disease had been found where everyone knew they could be found, but no man of consequence had been killed.

He started on the last spindle, the mists of doubt and guilt clearing with each turn of a page. Had a sweating fat man in Zurich lied? Was it all a lie? *All* lies? Was he somehow living a nightmare that could vanish with . . .

AMBASSADEUR LELAND ASSASSINÉ
À MARSEILLE!

The thick block letters of the headline exploded off the page, hurting his eyes. It was not imagined pain, not invented pain, but a sharp ache that penetrated his sockets and seared through his head. His breathing stopped, his eyes rigid on the name LELAND. He knew it; he could picture the face, actually *picture* it. Thick brows beneath a wide forehead, a blunt nose centered between high cheekbones and above curiously thin lips topped by a perfectly groomed gray mustache. He knew the face, he knew the man. And the man had been killed by a single shot from a high-powered rifle fired from a waterfront window. Ambassador Howard Leland had walked down a Marseilles pier at five o'clock in the afternoon. His head had been blown off.

Bourne did not have to read the second paragraph to know that Howard Leland had been Admiral H. R. Leland, United States Navy, until an interim appointment as director of Naval Intelligence preceded his ambassadorship to the Quai d'Orsay in Paris. Nor did he have to reach the body of the article where motives for the assassination were speculated upon to know them; he knew them. Leland's primary function in Paris was to dissuade the French government from authorizing massive arms sales—in particular fleets of Mirage jets—to Africa and the Middle East. To an astonishing degree he had succeeded, angering interested parties at all points in the Mediterranean. It was presumed that he had been killed for his interference; a punishment which served as a warning to others. Buyers and sellers of death were not to be hindered.

And the seller of death who had killed him would have been paid a great deal of money, far from the scene, all traces buried.

Zurich. A messenger to a legless man; another to a fat man in a crowded restaurant off the Falkenstrasse.

Zurich.

Marseilles.

Jason closed his eyes, the pain now intolerable. He had been picked up at sea five months ago, his port of origin assumed to have been Marseilles. And if Marseilles, the waterfront had been his escape route, a boat hired to take him into the vast expanse of the Mediterranean. Everything fitted too well, each piece of the puzzle sculpted into the next. How could he know the things he knew if he were not that seller of death from a window on the Marseilles waterfront?

He opened his eyes, pain inhibiting thought, but not all thought, one decision as clear as anything in his limited memory. There would be no rendezvous in Paris with Marie St. Jacques.

Perhaps one day he would write her a letter, saying the things he could not say now. If he was alive and could write a letter; he could not write one now. There could be no written words of thanks or love, no explanations at all; she would wait for him and he would not come to her. He had to put distance between them; she could not be involved with a seller of death. She had been wrong, his worst fears accurate.

Oh, God! He could picture Howard Leland's face, and there was no photograph on the page in front of him! The front page with the terrible headline that triggered so much, confirmed so many things. The date. *Thursday, August 26. Marseilles.* It was a day he would remember as long as he could remember for the rest of his convoluted life.

Thursday, August 26 . . .

Something was wrong. What was it? What *was* it? Thursday? . . . Thursday meant nothing to him. The twenty-sixth of August? . . . The twenty-*sixth?* It could not be the twenty-*sixth!* The twenty-sixth was wrong! He had heard it over and over again. Washburn's diary—his patient's journal. How often had Washburn gone back over every fact, every phrase, every day and point of progress? Too many times to count. Too many times not to remember!

You were brought to my door on the morning of Tuesday, August twenty-fourth, at precisely eight-twenty o'clock. Your condition was . . .

Tuesday, August 24.

August 24.

He was not in Marseilles on the twenty-sixth! He could not have fired a rifle from a window on the waterfront. He was not the seller of death in Marseilles; he had not killed Howard Leland!

Six months ago a man was killed . . . But it was not six months; it was *close* to six months but *not* six months. And he had not killed that man; he was half dead in an alcoholic's house on Ile de Port Noir.

The mists were clearing, the pain receding. A sense of elation filled him; he had found one concrete lie! If there was one there could be others!

Bourne looked at his watch; it was quarter past nine. Marie had left the café; she was waiting for him on the steps of the Cluny Museum. He replaced the spindles in their racks, then started toward the large cathedral door of the reading room, a man in a hurry.

He walked down the boulevard Saint-Michel, his pace accelerating with each stride. He had the distinct feeling that he knew what it was to have been given a reprieve from hanging and he wanted to share that rare experience. For a time he was out of the violent darkness, beyond the crashing waters; he had found a moment of sunlight—like the moments and the sunlight that had filled a room in a village inn—and he had to reach the one who had given them to him. Reach her and hold her and tell her there was hope.

He saw her on the steps, her arms folded against the icy wind that swept off the boulevard. At first she did not see him, her eyes searching the tree-lined street. She was restless, anxious, an impatient woman afraid she would not see what she wanted to see, frightened that it would not be there.

Ten minutes ago he would not have been.

She saw him. Her face became radiant, the smile emerged and it was filled with life. She rushed to him as he raced up the steps toward her. They came together and for a moment neither said anything, warm and alone on the Saint-Michel.

"I waited and *waited,*" she breathed finally. "I was so afraid, so worried. Did anything happen? Are you all right?"

"I'm fine. Better than I've been in a long time."

"What?"

He held her by the shoulders. " 'Six months ago a man was killed. . . .' Remember?"

The joy left her eyes. "Yes, I remember."

"I didn't kill him," said Bourne. "I couldn't have."

They found a small hotel off the crowded boulevard Montparnasse. The lobby and the rooms were threadbare, but there was a pretense to forgotten elegance that gave it an air of timelessness. It was a quiet resting place set down in the middle of a carnival, hanging on to its identity by accepting the times without joining them.

Jason closed the door, nodding to the white-haired bell captain whose indifference had turned to indulgence upon the receipt of a twenty-franc note.

"He thinks you're a provincial deacon flushed with a night's anticipation," said Marie. "I hope you noticed I went right to the bed."

"His name is Hervé, and he'll be very solicitous of our needs. He has no intention of sharing the wealth." He crossed to her and took her in his arms. "Thanks for my life," he said.

"Any time, my friend." She reached up and held his face in her hands. "But don't keep me waiting like that again. I nearly went crazy; all I could think of was that someone had recognized you . . . that something terrible had happened."

"You forget, no one knows what I look like."

"Don't count on that; it's not true. There were four men in the Steppdeckstrasse, including that bastard in the Guisan Quai. They're alive, Jason. They saw you."

"Not really. They saw a dark-haired man with bandages on his neck and head, who walked with a limp. Only two were near me: the man on the second floor and that pig in the Guisan. The first won't be leaving Zurich for a while; he can't walk and he hasn't much of a hand left. The second had the beam of the flashlight in his eyes; it wasn't in mine."

She released him, frowning, her alert mind questioning. "You can't be sure. They were there; they did see you."

Change your hair. . . . you change your face. Geoffrey Washburn, Ile de Port Noir.

"I repeat, they saw a dark-haired man in shadows. How good are you with a weak solution of peroxide?"

"I've never used it."

"Then I'll find a shop in the morning. The Montparnasse is the place for it. Blonds have more fun, isn't that what they say?"

She studied his face. "I'm trying to imagine what you'll look like."

"Different. Not much, but enough."

"You may be right. I hope to God you are." She kissed

his cheek, her prelude to discussion. "Now, tell me what happened. Where did you go? What did you learn about that . . . incident six months ago?"

"It wasn't six months ago, and because it wasn't, I couldn't have killed him." He told her everything, save for the few brief moments when he thought he would never see her again. He did not have to; she said it for him.

"If that date hadn't been so clear in your mind, you wouldn't have come to me, would you?"

He shook his head. "Probably not."

"I knew it. I felt it. For a minute, while I was walking from the café to the museum steps, I could hardly breathe. It was as though I were suffocating. Can you believe that?"

"I don't want to."

"Neither do I, but it happened."

They were sitting, she on the bed, he in the single armchair close by. He reached for her hand. "I'm still not sure I should be here. . . . I *knew* that man, I saw his face, I was in Marseilles forty-eight hours before he was killed!"

"But you didn't kill him."

"Then why was I there? Why do people think I did? Christ, it's insane!" He sprang up from the chair, pain back in his eyes. "But then I forgot. I'm not sane, am I? Because I've forgotten. . . . Years, a lifetime."

Marie spoke matter-of-factly, no compassion in her voice. "The answers will come to you. From one source or another, finally from yourself."

"That may not be possible. Washburn said it was like blocks rearranged, different tunnels . . . different windows." Jason walked to the window, bracing himself on the sill, looking down on the lights of Montparnasse. "The views aren't the same; they never will be. Somewhere out there are people I know, who know me. A couple of thousand miles away are other people I care about and don't care about. . . . Or, oh God, maybe a wife and children— I don't know. I keep spinning around in the wind, turning over and over and I can't get down to the ground. Every time I try I get thrown back up again."

"Into the sky?" asked Marie.

"Yes."

"You've jumped from a plane," she said, making a statement.

Bourne turned. "I never told you that."

"You talked about it in your sleep the other night. You

were sweating; your face was flushed and hot and I had to wipe it with a towel."

"Why didn't you say anything?"

"I did, in a way. I asked you if you were a pilot, or if flying bothered you. Especially at night."

"I didn't know what you were talking about. Why didn't you press me?"

"I was afraid to. You were very close to hysterics, and I'm not trained in things like that. I can help you try to remember, but I can't deal with your unconscious. I don't think anyone should but a doctor."

"A doctor? I was with a doctor for damn near six months."

"From what you've said about him, I think another opinion is called for."

"I don't!" he replied, confused by his own anger.

"Why not?" Marie got up from the bed. "You need help, my darling. A psychiatrist might—"

"*No!*" He shouted in spite of himself, furious with himself. "I won't do that. I can't."

"Please, tell me why?" she asked calmly, standing in front of him.

"I . . . I . . . can't do it."

"Just tell me why, that's all."

Bourne stared at her, then turned and looked out the window again, his hands on the sill again. "Because I'm afraid. Someone lied, and I was grateful for that more than I can tell you. But suppose there aren't any more lies, suppose the rest is true. What do I do then?"

"Are you saying you don't want to find out?"

"Not that way." He stood up and leaned against the window frame, his eyes still on the lights below. "Try to understand me," he said. "I have to know certain things . . . enough to make a decision . . . but maybe not everything. A part of me has to be able to walk away, disappear. I have to be able to say to myself, what was isn't any longer, and there's a possibility that it *never* was because I have no memory of it. What a person can't remember didn't exist . . . for him." He turned back to her. "What I'm trying to tell you is that maybe it's better this way."

"You want evidence, but not proof, is that what you're saying?"

"I want arrows pointing in one direction or the other, telling me whether to run or not to run."

"Telling *you*. What about *us?*"

"That'll come with the arrows, won't it? You know that."

"Then let's find them," she replied.

"Be careful. You may not be able to live with what's out there. I mean that."

"I can live with you. And I mean that." She reached up and touched his face. "Come on. It's barely five o'clock in Ontario, and I can still reach Peter at the office. He can start the Treadstone search . . . and give us the name of someone here at the embassy who can help us if we need him."

"You're going to tell Peter you're in Paris?"

"He'll know it anyway from the operator, but the call won't be traceable to this hotel. And don't worry, I'll keep everything 'in-house,' even casual. I came to Paris for a few days because my relatives in Lyon are simply too dull. He'll accept that."

"Would he know someone at the embassy here?"

"Peter makes it a point to know someone everywhere. It's one of his more useful but less attractive traits."

"Sounds like he will." Bourne got their coats. "After your call we'll have dinner. I think we could both use a drink."

"Let's go past the bank on rue Madeleine. I want to see something."

"What can you see at night?"

"A telephone booth. I hope there's one nearby."

There was. Diagonally across the street from the entrance.

The tall blond man wearing tortoise-shell glasses checked his watch under the afternoon sun on the rue Madeleine. The pavements were crowded, the traffic in the street unreasonable, as most traffic was in Paris. He entered the telephone booth and untangled the telephone, which had been hanging free of its cradle, the line knotted. It was a courteous sign to the next would-be user that the phone was out of commission; it reduced the chance that the booth would be occupied. It had worked.

He glanced at his watch again; the time span had begun. Marie inside the bank. She would call within the next few minutes. He took several coins from his pocket, put them on the ledge and leaned against the glass panel, his eyes on the bank across the street. A cloud diminished the sunlight and he could see his reflection in the glass. He approved of what he saw, recalling the startled reaction of a hairdresser in Montparnasse who had sequestered him in a curtained booth while performing the blond transformation. The cloud passed, the sunlight returned, and the telephone rang.

"It's you?" asked Marie St. Jacques.

"It's me," said Bourne.

"Make sure you get the name and the location of the office. And rough up your French. Mispronounce a few words so he knows you're American. Tell him you're not used to the telephones in Paris. Then do everything in sequence. I'll call you back in exactly five minutes."

"Clock's on."

"What?"

"Nothing. I mean, let's go."

"All right. . . . The clock is on. Good luck."

"Thanks." Jason depressed the lever, released it, and dialed the number he had memorized.

"La Banque de Valois. *Bonjour.*"

"I need assistance," said Bourne, continuing with the approximate words Marie had told him to use. "I recently transferred sizable funds from Switzerland on a pouch-courier basis. I'd like to know if they've cleared."

"That would be our Foreign Services Department, sir. I'll connect you."

A click, then another female voice. "Foreign Services." Jason repeated his request.

"May I have your name, please?"

"I'd prefer speaking with an officer of the bank before giving it."

There was a pause on the line. "Very well, sir. I'll switch you to the office of Vice-President d'Amacourt."

Monsieur d'Amacourt's secretary was less accommodating, the bank officer's screening process activated, as Marie had predicted. So Bourne once more used Marie's words. "I'm referring to a transfer from Zurich, from the Gemeinschaft Bank on the Bahnhofstrasse, and I'm talking in the area of seven figures. Monsieur d'Amacourt, if you please. I have very little time."

It was not a secretary's place to be the cause of further delay. A perplexed first vice-president got on the line.

"May I help you?"

"Are you d'Amacourt?" asked Jason.

"I am Antoine d'Amacourt, yes. And who, may I ask, is calling?"

"Good! I should have been given your name in Zurich. I'll make certain next time certainly," said Bourne, the redundancy intended, his accent American.

"I beg your pardon? Would you be more comfortable speaking English, monsieur?"

"Yes," replied Jason, doing so. "I'm having enough trouble with this damn phone." He looked at his watch; he had less than two minutes. "My name's Bourne, Jason Bourne, and eight days ago I transferred four and a half million francs from the Gemeinschaft Bank in Zurich. They assured me the transaction would be confidential."

"All transactions are confidential, sir."

"Fine. Good. What I want to know is, has everything cleared?"

"I should explain," continued the bank officer, "that confidentiality excludes blanket confirmations of such transactions to unknown parties over the telephone."

Marie had been right, the logic of her trap clearer to Jason.

"I would hope so, but as I told your secretary I'm in a hurry. I'm leaving Paris in a couple of hours and I have to put everything in order."

"Then I suggest you come to the bank."

"I know *that*," said Bourne, satisfied that the conversation was going precisely the way Marie foresaw it. "I just wanted everything ready when I got there. Where's your office?"

"On the main floor, monsieur. At the rear, beyond the gate, center door. A receptionist is there."

"And I'll be dealing only with you, right?"

"If you wish, although any officer—"

"Look, mister," exclaimed the ugly American, "we're talking about over four million francs!"

"Only with me, Monsieur Bourne."

"Fine. Good." Jason put his fingers on the cradle bar. He had fifteen seconds to go. "Look, it's 2:35 now—" He pressed down twice on the lever, interrupting the line but not disconnecting it. "Hello? Hello?"

"I am here, monsieur."

"Damn phones! Listen, I'll—" He pressed down again, now three times in rapid succession. "Hello? Hello?"

"Monsieur, please—if you'll give me your telephone number."

"Operator? Operator!?"

"Monsieur Bourne, please—"

"I can't hear you!" *Four seconds, three seconds, two seconds.* "Wait a minute. I'll call you back." He held the lever down, breaking the connection. Three more seconds elapsed and the phone rang; he picked it up. "His name's d'Amacourt, office on the main floor, rear, center door."

"I've got it," said Marie, hanging up.

Bourne dialed the bank again, inserted coins again. *"Je parlais avec Monsieur d'Amacourt quand on m'a coupé . . ."*

"Je regrette, monsieur."

"Monsieur Bourne?"

"D'Amacourt?"

"Yes—I'm so terribly sorry you're having such trouble. You were saying? About the time?"

"Oh, yeah. It's a little after 2:30. I'll get there by 3:00."

"I look forward to meeting you, monsieur."

Jason reknotted the phone, letting it hang free, then left the booth and walked quickly through crowds to the shade of a storefront canopy. He turned and waited, his eyes on the bank across the way, remembering another bank in Zurich and the sound of sirens on the Bahnhofstrasse. The next twenty minutes would tell if Marie was right or not. If she was, there would be no sirens on the rue Madeleine.

The slender woman in the wide-brimmed hat that partially covered the side of her face hung up the public phone on the wall to the right of the bank's entrance. She opened her purse, removed a compact and ostensibly checked her makeup, angling the small mirror first to the left, then to the right. Satisfied, she replaced the compact, closed her purse, and walked past the tellers' cages toward the rear of the main floor. She stopped at a counter in the center, picked up a chained ballpoint pen, and began writing aimless numbers on a form that had been left on the marble surface. Less than ten feet away was a small, brass-framed gate, flanked by a low wooden railing that extended the width of the lobby. Beyond the gate and the railing were the desks of the lesser executives and behind them the desks of the major secretaries—five in all—in front of five doors in the rear wall. Marie read the name printed in gold script on the center door.

It would happen any moment now—if it was going to happen, if she was right. And if she was, she had to know what Monsieur A.R. d'Amacourt looked like; he would be the man Jason could reach. Reach him and talk to him, but not in the bank.

It happened. There was a flurry of controlled activity. The secretary at the desk in front of d'Amacourt's office rushed inside with her notepad, emerged thirty seconds later, and picked up the phone. She dialed three digits—an inside call—and spoke, reading from her pad.

Two minutes passed; the door of d'Amacourt's office opened and the vice-president stood in the frame, an anxious executive concerned over an unwarranted delay. He was a middle-aged man with a face older than his age, but striving to look younger. His thinning dark hair was singed and brushed to obscure the bald spots; his eyes were encased in small rolls of flesh, attesting to long hours with good wine. Those same eyes were cold, darting eyes, evidence of a demanding man wary of his surroundings. He barked a question to his secretary; she twisted in her chair, doing her best to maintain her composure.

D'Amacourt went back inside his office without closing the door, the cage of an angry cat left open. Another minute passed; the secretary kept glancing to her right, looking at something—*for* something. When she saw it, she exhaled, closing her eyes in relief.

From the far left wall, a green light suddenly appeared above two panels of dark wood; an elevator was in use. Seconds later the door opened and an elderly elegant man walked out carrying a small black case not much larger than his hand. Marie stared at it, experiencing both satisfaction and fear; she had guessed right. The black case had been removed from a confidential file inside a guarded room and signed out by a man beyond reproach or temptation— the elderly figure making his way past the ranks of desks toward d'Amacourt's office.

The secretary rose from her chair, greeted the senior executive and escorted him into d'Amacourt's office. She came out immediately, closing the door behind her.

Marie looked at her watch, her eyes on the sweep-second hand. She wanted one more fragment of evidence, and it would be hers shortly if she could get beyond the gate, with a clear view of the secretary's desk. If it was going to happen, it would happen in moments, the duration brief.

She walked to the gate, opening her purse and smiling vacuously at the receptionist, who was speaking into her phone. She mouthed the name d'Amacourt with her lips to the bewildered receptionist, reached down and opened the gate. She moved quickly inside, a determined if not very bright client of the Valois Bank.

"*Pardon, madame*—" The receptionist held her hand over the telephone, rushing her words in French, "Can I help you?"

Again Marie pronounced the name with her lips—now a courteous client late for an appointment and not wishing to be a further burden to a busy employee. "Monsieur d'Amacourt. I'm afraid I'm late. I'll just go see his secretary." She continued up the aisle toward the secretary's desk.

"*Please,* madame," called out the receptionist. "I must announce—"

The hum of electric typewriters and subdued conversations drowned out her words. Marie approached the stern-faced secretary, who looked up, as bewildered as the receptionist.

"Yes? May I help you?"

"Monsieur d'Amacourt, please."

"I'm afraid he's in conference, madame. Do you have an appointment?"

"Oh, yes, of course," said Marie, opening her purse again.

The secretary looked at the typed schedule on her desk. "I'm afraid I don't have anyone listed for this time period."

"Oh, my word!" exclaimed the confused client of the Valois Bank. "I just noticed. It's for tomorrow, not today! I'm *so* sorry!"

She turned and walked rapidly back to the gate. She had seen what she wanted to see, the last fragment of evidence. A single button was lighted on d'Amacourt's telephone; he had bypassed his secretary and was making an outside call. The account belonging to Jason Bourne had specific, confidential instructions attached to it which were not to be revealed to the account holder.

Bourne looked at his watch in the shade of the canopy; it was 2:49. Marie would be back by the telephone at the front of the bank, a pair of eyes inside. The next few minutes would give them the answer; perhaps she already knew it.

He edged his way to the left side of the store window, keeping the bank's entrance in view. A clerk inside smiled at him, reminding him that all attention should be avoided. He pulled out a pack of cigarettes, lit one, and looked at his watch again. Eight minutes to three.

And then he saw them. *Him.* Three well-dressed men walking rapidly up rue Madeleine, talking to each other, their eyes, however, directed straight ahead. They passed the slower pedestrians in front of them, excusing themselves with a courtesy that was not entirely Parisian. Jason concentrated on the man in the middle. It was *him.* A man named Johann.

Signal Johann to go inside. We'll come back for them. A tall, gaunt man wearing gold-rimmed spectacles had said the words in the Steppdeckstrasse. *Johann.* They had sent him here from Zurich; he had seen Jason Bourne. And that told him something: there were no photographs.

The three men reached the entrance. Johann and the man on his right went inside; the third man stayed by the door. Bourne started back to the telephone booth; he would wait four minutes and place his last call to Antoine d'Amacourt.

He dropped his cigarette outside the booth, crushed it under his foot and opened the door.

"*Monsieur*—" A voice came from behind.

Jason spun around, holding his breath. A nondescript man with a stubble of a beard pointed at the booth.

"*Le téléphone—il ne marche pas. Regardez la corde.*"

"*Merci bien. Je vais essayer quand même.*"

The man shrugged and left. Bourne stepped inside; the four minutes were up. He took the coins from his pocket— enough for two calls—and dialed the first.

"La Banque de Valois. *Bonjour.*"

Ten seconds later d'Amacourt was on the phone, his voice strained. "It is you, Monsieur Bourne? I thought you to say you were on your way to my office."

"A change of plans, I'm afraid. I'll have to call you tomorrow." Suddenly, through the glass panel of the booth,

[169]

Jason saw a car swing into a space across the street in front of the bank. The third man who was standing by the entrance nodded to the driver.

"—I can do?" D'Amacourt had asked a question.

"I beg your pardon?"

"I asked if there was anything I can do. I have your account; everything is in readiness for you here."

I'm sure it is, Bourne thought; the ploy was worth a try. "Look, I have to get over to London this afternoon. I'm taking one of the shuttle flights, but I'll be back tomorrow. Keep everything with you, all right?"

"To London, monsieur?"

"I'll call you tomorrow. I have to find a cab to Orly." He hung up and watched the entrance of the bank. In less than half a minute, Johann and his companion came running out; they spoke to the third man, then all three climbed into the waiting automobile.

The killers' escape car was still in the hunt, on its way now to Orly Airport. Jason memorized the number on the license plate, then dialed his second call. If the pay phone in the bank was not in use, Marie would pick it up before the ring had barely started. She did.

"Yes?"

"See anything?"

"A great deal. D'Amacourt's your man."

12

They moved about the store, going from counter to counter. Marie, however, remained near the wide front window, keeping a perpetual eye on the entrance of the bank across rue Madeleine.

"I picked out two scarves for you," said Bourne.

"You shouldn't have. The prices are far too high."

"It's almost four o'clock. If he hasn't come out by now, he won't until the end of office hours."

"Probably not. If he were going to meet someone, he would have done so by now. But we had to know."

"Take my word for it, his friends are at Orly, running from shuttle to shuttle. There's no way they can tell whether I'm on one or not, because they don't know what name I'm using."

"They'll depend on the man from Zurich to recognize you."

"He's looking for a dark-haired man with a limp, not me. Come on, let's go into the bank. You can point out d'Amacourt."

"We can't do that," said Marie, shaking her head. "The

cameras on the ceilings have wide-angle lenses. If they ran the tapes they could spot you."

"A blond-haired man with glasses?"

"Or me. I was there; the receptionist or his secretary could identify me."

"You're saying it's a regular cabal in there. I doubt it."

"They could think up any number of reasons to run the tapes." Marie stopped; she clutched Jason's arm, her eyes on the bank beyond the window. "There he is! The one in the overcoat with the black velvet collar—d'Amacourt."

"Pulling at his sleeves?"

"Yes."

"I've got him. I'll see you back at the hotel."

"Be careful. Be *very* careful."

"Pay for the scarves; they're at the counter in the back."

Jason left the store, wincing in the sunlight beyond the canopy, looking for a break in the traffic so he could cross the street; there was none. D'Amacourt had turned right and was strolling casually; he was not a man in a rush to meet anyone. Instead, there was the air of a slightly squashed peacock about him.

Bourne reached the corner and crossed with the light, falling behind the banker. D'Amacourt stopped at a news-stand to buy an evening paper. Jason held his place in front of a sporting goods shop, then followed as the banker continued down the block.

Ahead was a café, windows dark, entrance heavy wood, thick hardware on the door. It took no imagination to picture the inside; it was a drinking place for men, and for women brought with men other men would not discuss. It was as good a spot as any for a quiet discussion with Antoine d'Amacourt. Jason walked faster, falling in stride beside the banker. He spoke in the awkward, Anglicized French he had used on the phone.

"*Bonjour, monsieur. Je . . . pense que vous . . . êtes Monsieur d'Amacourt.* I'd say I was right, wouldn't you?"

The banker stopped. His cold eyes were frightened, remembering. The peacock shriveled further into his tailored overcoat. "Bourne?" he whispered.

"Your friends must be very confused by now. I expect they're racing all over Orly Airport, wondering, perhaps, if you gave them the wrong information. Perhaps on purpose."

"*What?*" The frightened eyes bulged.

"Let's go inside here," said Jason, taking d'Amacourt's arm, his grip firm. "I think we should have a talk."

"I know absolutely nothing! I merely followed the demands of the account. I am not involved!'

"Sorry. When I first talked to you, you said you wouldn't confirm the sort of bank account I was talking about on the phone; you wouldn't discuss business with someone you didn't know. But twenty minutes later you said you had everything ready for me. That's confirmation, isn't it? Let's go inside."

The café was in some ways a miniature version of Zurich's Drei Alpenhäuser. The booths were deep, the partitions between them high, and the light dim. From there, however, the appearances veered; the café on rue Madeleine was totally French, carafes of wine replacing steins of beer. Bourne asked for a booth in the corner; the waiter accommodated.

"Have a drink," said Jason. "You're going to need it."

"You presume," replied the banker coldly. "I'll have a whiskey."

The drinks came quickly, the brief interim taken up with d'Amacourt nervously extracting a pack of cigarettes from under his form-fitting overcoat. Bourne struck a match, holding it close to the banker's face. Very close.

"*Merci*." D'Amacourt inhaled, removed his cigarette, and swallowed half the small glass of whiskey. "I'm not the man you should talk with," he said.

"Who is?"

"An owner of the bank, perhaps. I don't know, but certainly not me."

"Explain that."

"Arrangements were made. A privately held bank has more flexibility than a publicly owned institution with stockholders."

"How?"

"There's greater latitude, shall we say, with regard to the demands of certain clients and sister banks. Less scrutiny than might be applied to a company listed on the Bourse. The Gemeinschaft in Zurich is also a private institution."

"The demands were made by the Gemeinschaft?"

"Requests . . . demands . . . yes."

"Who owns the Valois?"

"Who? Many—a consortium. Ten or twelve men and their families."

"Then I have to talk to you, don't I? I mean, it'd be a little foolish my running all over Paris tracking them down."

"I'm only an executive. An employee." D'Amacourt swallowed the rest of his drink, crushed out his cigarette and reached for another. And the matches.

"What are the arrangements?"

"I could lose my position, monsieur!"

"You could lose your life," said Jason, disturbed that the words came so easily to him.

"I'm not as privileged as you think."

"Nor as ignorant as you'd like me to believe," said Bourne, his eyes wandering over the banker across the table. "Your type's everywhere, d'Amacourt. It's in your clothes, the way you wear your hair, even your walk; you strut too much. A man like you doesn't get to be the vice-president of the Valois Bank without asking questions; you cover yourself. You don't make a smelly move unless you can save your own ass. Now, tell me what those arrangements were. You're not important to me, am I being clear?"

D'Amacourt struck a match and held it beneath his cigarette while staring at Jason. "You don't have to threaten me, monsieur. You're a very rich man. Why not pay me?" The banker smiled nervously. "You're quite right, incidentally. I did ask a question or two. Paris is not Zurich. A man of my station must have words if not answers."

Bourne leaned back, revolving his glass, the clicking of the ice cubes obviously annoying d'Amacourt. "Name a reasonable price," he said finally, "and we'll discuss it."

"I'm a reasonable man. Let the decision be based on value, and let it be yours. Bankers the world over are compensated by grateful clients they have advised. I would like to think of you as a client."

"I'm sure you would." Bourne smiled, shaking his head at the man's sheer nerve. "So we slide from bribe to gratuity. Compensation for personal advice and service."

D'Amacourt shrugged. "I accept the definition and, if ever asked, would repeat your words."

"The arrangements?"

"Accompanying the transfer of our funds from Zurich was *une fiche confidentielle*—"

"*Une fiche?*" broke in Jason, recalling the moment in

[174]

Apfel's office at the Gemeinschaft when Koenig came in saying the words. "I heard it once before. What is it?"

"A dated term, actually. It comes from the middle nineteenth century when it was a common practice for the great banking houses—primarily the Rothschilds—to keep track of the international flow of money."

"Thank you. Now what is it specifically?"

"Separate sealed instructions to be opened and followed when the account in question is called up."

" 'Called up'?"

"Funds removed or deposited."

"Suppose I'd just gone to a teller, presented a bank book, and asked for money?"

"A double asterisk would have appeared on the transaction computer. You would have been sent to me."

"I was sent to you anyway. The operator gave me your office."

"Irrelevant chance. There are two other officers in the Foreign Services Department. Had you been connected to either one, the *fiche* would have dictated that you still be sent to me. I am the senior executive."

"I see." But Bourne was not sure that he did see. There was a gap in the sequence; a space needed filling. "Wait a minute. You didn't know anything about a *fiche* when you had the account brought to your office."

"Why did I ask for it?" interrupted d'Amacourt, anticipating the question. "Be reasonable, monsieur. Put yourself in my place. A man calls and identifies himself, then says he is 'talking about over four million francs.' Four *million*. Would you not be anxious to be of service? Bend a rule here and there?"

Looking at the seedily elegant banker, Jason realized it was the most unstartling thing he had said. "The instructions. What were they?"

"To begin with a telephone number—unlisted, of course. It was to be called, all information relayed."

"Do you remember the number?"

"I make it a point to commit such things to memory."

"I'll bet you do. What is it?"

"I must protect myself, monsieur. How else could you have gotten it? I pose the question . . . how do you say it? . . . rhetorically."

"Which means you have the answer. How *did* I get it? If it ever comes up."

"In Zurich. You paid a very high price for someone to break not only the strictest regulation on the Bahnhof-strasse, but also the laws of Switzerland."

"I've got just the man," said Bourne, the face of Koenig coming into focus. "He's already committed the crime."

"At the Gemeinschaft? Are you joking?"

"Not one bit. His name is Koenig; his desk is on the second floor."

"I'll remember that."

"I'm sure you will. The number?" D'Amacourt gave it to him. Jason wrote it on a paper napkin. "How do I know this is accurate?"

"You have a reasonable guarantee. I have not been paid."

"Good enough."

"And as long as value is intrinsic to our discussion, I should tell you that it is the second telephone number; the first was canceled."

"Explain that."

D'Amacourt leaned forward. "A photostat of the original *fiche* arrived with accounts-courier. It was sealed in a black case, accepted and signed for by the senior keeper-of-records. The card inside was validated by a partner of the Gemeinschaft, countersigned by the usual Swiss notary; the instructions were simple, quite clear. In all matters pertaining to the account of Jason C. Bourne, a transatlantic call to the United States was to be placed immediately, the details relayed. . . . Here the card was altered, the number in New York deleted, one in Paris inserted and initialed."

"New York?" interrupted Bourne. "How do you know it was New York?"

"The telephone area code was parenthetically included, spaced in front of the number itself; it remained intact. It was 212. As first vice-president, Foreign Services, I place such calls daily."

"The alteration was pretty sloppy."

"Possibly. It could have been made in haste, or not thoroughly understood. On the other hand, there was no way to delete the body of the instructions without renotarization. A minor risk considering the number of telephones in New York. At any rate, the substitution gave me the latitude to ask a question or two. Change is a banker's anathema." D'Amacourt sipped what remained of his drink.

"Care for another?" asked Jason.

"No, thank you. It would prolong our discussion."

"You're the one who stopped."

"I'm thinking, monsieur. Perhaps you should have in mind a vague figure before I proceed."

Bourne studied the man. "It could be five," he said.

"Five what?"

"Five figures."

"I shall proceed. I spoke to a woman—"

"A woman? How did you begin?"

"Truthfully. I was the vice-president of the Valois, and was following instructions from the Gemeinschaft in Zurich. What else was there to say?"

"Go on."

"I said I had been in communication with a man claiming to be Jason Bourne. She asked me how recently, to which I replied a few minutes. She was then most anxious to know the substance of our conversation. It was at this point that I voiced my own concerns. The *fiche* specifically stated that a call should be made to New York, not Paris. Naturally, she said it was *not* my concern, and that the change was authorized by signature, and did I care for Zurich to be informed that an officer of the Valois refused to follow the Gemeinschaft instructions?"

"Hold it," interrupted Jason. "Who was she?"

"I have no idea."

"You mean you were talking all this time and she didn't tell you? You didn't ask?"

"That is the nature of the *fiche*. If a name is proffered, well and good. If it is not, one does not inquire."

"You didn't hesitate to ask about the telephone number."

"Merely a device; I wanted information. You transferred four and a half million francs, a sizable amount, and were therefore a powerful client with, perhaps, *more* powerful strings attached to him. . . . One balks, then agrees, then balks again only to agree again; that is the way one learns things. Especially if the party one is talking with displays anxiety. I can assure you, she did."

"What did you learn?"

"That you should be considered a dangerous man."

"In what way?"

"The definition was left open. But the fact that the term was used was enough for me to ask why the Sûreté was not involved. Her reply was extremely interesting. 'He is beyond the Sûreté, beyond Interpol,' she said."

"What did that tell you?"

"That it was a highly complicated matter for any number of possibilities, all best left private. Since our talk began, however, it now tells me something else."

"What's that?"

"That you really should pay me well, for I must be extremely cautious. Those who look for you are also, perhaps, beyond the Sûreté, beyond Interpol."

"We'll get to that. You told this woman I was on my way to your office?"

"Within the quarter hour. She asked me to remain on the telephone for a few moments, that she would be right back. Obviously she made another call. She returned with her final instructions. You were to be detained in my office until a man came to my secretary inquiring about a matter from Zurich. And when you left you were to be identified by a nod or a gesture; there could be no error. The man came, of course, and, of course, you never arrived, so he waited by the tellers' cages with an associate. When you phoned and said you were on your way to London, I left my office to find the man. My secretary pointed him out and I told him. The rest you know."

"Didn't it strike you as odd that I had to be identified?"

"Not so odd as intemperate. A *fiche* is one thing—telephone calls, faceless communications—but to be involved directly, in the open, as it were, is something else again. I said as much to the woman."

"What did she say to you?"

D'Amacourt cleared his throat. "She made it clear that the party she represented—whose stature was, indeed, confirmed by the *fiche* itself—would remember my cooperation. You see, I withhold nothing. . . . Apparently they don't know what you look like."

"A man was at the bank who saw me in Zurich."

"Then his associates do not trust his eyesight. Or, perhaps, what he thinks he saw."

"Why do you say that?"

"Merely an observation, monsieur; the woman was insistent. You must understand, I strenuously objected to any overt participation; that is *not* the nature of the *fiche*. She said there was no photograph of you. An obvious lie, of course."

"Is it?"

"Naturally. All passports have photographs. Where is the

immigration officer who cannot be bought or duped? Ten seconds in a passport-control room, a photograph of a photograph; arrangements can be made. No, they committed a serious oversight."

"I guess they did."

"And you," continued d'Amacourt, "just told me something else. Yes, you really must pay me very well."

"What did I just tell you?"

"That your passport does not identify you as Jason Bourne. Who are you, monsieur?"

Jason did not at first answer; he revolved his glass again. "Someone who may pay you a lot of money," he said.

"Entirely sufficient. You are simply a client named Bourne. And I must be cautious."

"I want that telephone number in New York. Can you get it for me? There'd be a sizable bonus."

"I wish I could. I see no way."

"It might be raised from the *fiche* card. Under a low-power scope."

"When I said it was deleted, monsieur, I did not mean it was crossed out. It was *deleted*—it was *cut* out."

"Then someone has it in Zurich."

"Or it has been destroyed."

"Last question," said Jason, anxious now to leave. "It concerns you, incidentally. It's the only way you'll get paid."

"The question will be tolerated, of course. What is it?"

"If I showed up at the Valois without calling you, without telling you I was coming, would you be expected to make another telephone call?"

"Yes. One does not disregard the *fiche*; it emanates from powerful boardrooms. Dismissal would follow."

"Then how do *we* get *our* money?"

D'Amacourt pursed his lips. "There is a way. Withdrawal *in absentia*. Forms filled out, instructions by letter, identification confirmed and authenticated by an established firm of attorneys. I would be powerless to interfere."

"You'd still be expected to make the call, though."

"It's a matter of timing. Should an attorney with whom the Valois has had numerous dealings call me requesting that I prepare, say, a number of cashiers checks drawn upon a foreign transfer he has ascertained to have been cleared, I would do so. He would state that he was sending over the completed forms, the checks, of course, made out to 'Bearer,' not an uncommon practice in these days of excessive taxes. A messenger would arrive with the letter during the most hectic hours of activity, and my secretary—an esteemed, trusted employee of many years—would simply bring in the forms for my countersignature and the letter for my initialing."

"No doubt," interrupted Bourne, "along with a number of other papers you were to sign."

"Exactly. I would *then* place my call, probably watching the messenger leave with his briefcase as I did so."

"You wouldn't, by any remote chance, have in mind the name of a law firm in Paris, would you? Or a specific attorney?"

"As a matter of fact, one just occurred to me."

"How much will he cost?"

"Ten thousand francs."

"That's expensive."

"Not at all. He was a judge on the bench, an honored man."

"What about you? Let's refine it."

"As I said, I'm reasonable, and the decision should be yours. Since you mentioned five figures, let us be consistent with your words. Five figures, commencing with five. Fifty thousand francs."

"That's outrageous!"

"So is whatever you've done, Monsieur Bourne."

"*Une fiche confidentielle,*" said Marie, sitting in the chair by the window, the late afternoon sun bouncing off the ornate buildings of the boulevard Montparnasse outside. "So that's the device they've used."

"I can impress you—I know where it comes from." Jason poured a drink from the bottle on the bureau and carried it to the bed; he sat down, facing her. "Do you want to hear?"

"I don't have to," she answered, gazing out the window, preoccupied. "I know exactly where it comes from and what it means. It's a shock, that's all."

"Why? I thought you expected something like this."

"The results, yes, not the machinery. A *fiche* is an archaic stab at legitimacy, almost totally restricted to private banks on the Continent. American, Canadian, and UK laws forbid its use."

Bourne recalled d'Amacourt's words; he repeated them.

" 'It emanates from powerful boardrooms'—that's what he said."

"He was right." Marie looked over at him. "Don't you see? I knew that a flag was attached to your account. I assumed that someone had been bribed to forward information. That's not unusual; bankers aren't in the front ranks for canonization. But this is different. That account in Zurich was established—at the very beginning—with the *fiche* as part of its activity. Conceivably with your own knowledge."

"Treadstone Seventy-One," said Jason.

"Yes. The owners of the bank had to work in concert with Treadstone. And considering the latitude of your access, it's possible you were aware that they did."

"But someone *was* bribed. Koenig. He substituted one telephone number for another."

"He was well paid, I can assure you. He could face ten years in a Swiss prison."

"Ten? That's pretty stiff."

"So are the Swiss laws. He had to be paid a small fortune."

"Carlos," said Bourne. "Carlos . . . Why? What am I to him? I keep asking myself. I say the name over and over and over again! I don't *get* anything, nothing at all. Just a . . . a . . . I don't know. Nothing."

"But there's something, isn't there?" Marie sat forward. "What is it, Jason? What are you thinking of?"

"I'm not thinking . . . I don't know."

"Then you're feeling. Something. What is it?"

"I don't know. Fear, maybe . . . Anger, nerves. I don't know."

"Concentrate!"

"Goddamn it, do you think I'm *not*? Do you think I haven't? Have you any idea what it's like?" Bourne stiffened, annoyed at his own outburst. "Sorry."

"Don't be. Ever. These are the hints, the clues you have to look for—*we* have to look for. Your doctor friend in Port Noir was right; things come to you, provoked by other things. As you yourself said, a book of matches, a face, or the front of a restaurant. We've seen it happen. Now, it's a name, a name you avoided for nearly a week while you told me everything that had happened to you during the past five months, down to the smallest detail. Yet you never mentioned Carlos. You should have, but you didn't. It *does* mean something to you, can't you see that? It's stirring things inside of you; they want to come out."

"I know." Jason drank.

"Darling, there's a famous bookstore on the boulevard Saint-Germain that's run by a magazine freak. A whole floor is crammed with back issues of old magazines, thousands of them. He even catalogues subjects, indexes them like a librarian. I'd like to find out if Carlos is in that index. Will you do it?"

Bourne was aware of the sharp pain in his chest. It had nothing to do with his wounds; it was fear. She saw it and somehow understood; he felt it and could not understand. "There are back issues of newspapers at the Sorbonne," he said, glancing up at her. "One of them put me on cloud nine for a while. Until I thought about it."

"A lie was exposed. That was the important thing."

"But we're not looking for a lie now, are we?"

"No, we're looking for the truth. Don't be afraid of it, darling. I'm not."

Jason got up. "Okay. Saint-Germain's on the schedule. In the meantime, call that fellow at the embassy." Bourne reached into his pocket and took out the paper napkin with the telephone number on it; he had added the numbers of the license plate on the car that had raced away from the bank on rue Madeleine. "Here's the number d'Amacourt gave me, also the license of that car. See what he can do."

"All right." Marie took the napkin and went to the telephone. A small, spiral-hinged notebook was beside it; she flipped through the pages. "Here it is. His name is Dennis Corbelier. Peter said he'd call him by noon today, Paris time. And I could rely on him; he was as knowledgeable as any attaché in the embassy."

"Peter knows him, doesn't he? He's not just a name from a list."

"They were classmates at the University of Toronto. I can call him from here, can't I?"

"Sure. But don't say where you are."

Marie picked up the phone. "I'll tell him the same thing I told Peter. That I'm moving from one hotel to another but don't know which yet." She got an outside line, then dialed the number of the Canadian Embassy on the avenue Montaigne. Fifteen seconds later she was talking with Dennis Corbelier, attaché.

Marie got to the point of her call almost immediately. "I assume Peter told you I might need some help."

"More than that," replied Corbelier, "he explained that you were in Zurich. Can't say I understood everything he said, but I got the general idea. Seems there's a lot of maneuvering in the world of high finance these days."

"More than usual. The trouble is no one wants to say who's maneuvering whom. That's my problem."

"How can I help?"

"I have a license and a telephone number, both here in Paris. The telephone's unlisted; it could be awkward if I called."

"Give them to me." She did. "*A mari usque ad mari*," Corbelier said, reciting the national motto of their country. "We have several friends in splendid places. We trade off favors frequently, usually in the narcotics area, but we're all flexible. Why not have lunch with me tomorrow? I'll bring what I can."

"I'd like that, but tomorrow's no good. I'm spending the day with an old friend. Perhaps another time."

"Peter said I'd be an idiot not to insist. He says you're a terrific lady."

"He's a dear, and so are you. I'll call you tomorrow afternoon."

"Fine. I'll go to work on these."

"Talk to you tomorrow, and thanks again." Marie hung up and looked at her watch. "I'm to call Peter in three hours. Don't let me forget."

"You really think he'll have something so soon?"

"*He* does; he started last night by calling Washington. It's what Corbelier just said; we all trade off. This piece of information here for that one there, a name from our side for one of yours."

"Sounds vaguely like betrayal."

"The opposite. We're dealing in money, not missiles. Money that's illegally moving around, outflanking laws that are good for all our interests. Unless you want the sheiks of Araby owning Grumman Aircraft. *Then* we're talking about missiles . . . after they've left the launching pads."

"Strike my objection."

"We've got to see d'Amacourt's man first thing in the morning. Figure out what you want to withdraw."

"All of it."

"All?"

"That's right. If you were the directors of Treadstone, what would you do if you learned that six million francs were missing from a corporate account?"

"I see."

"D'Amacourt suggested a series of cashiers checks made out to the bearer."

"He said that? Checks?"

"Yes. Something wrong?"

"There certainly is. The numbers of those checks could be punched on a fraud tape and sent to banks everywhere. You have to *go* to a bank to redeem them; payments would be stopped."

"He's a winner, isn't he? He collects from both sides. What do we do?"

"Accept half of what he told you—the bearer part. But not checks. Bonds. Bearer bonds of various denominations. They're far more easily brokered."

"You've just earned dinner," said Jason, reaching down and touching her face.

"I tries to earn my keep, sir," she replied, holding his hand against her cheek. "First dinner, then Peter . . . and then a bookstore on Saint-Germain."

"A bookstore on Saint-Germain," repeated Bourne, the pain coming to his chest again. *What was it? Why was he so afraid?*

They left the restaurant on the boulevard Raspail and walked to the telephone complex on rue Vaugirard. There were glass booths against the walls and a huge circular counter in the center of the floor where clerks filled out slips, assigning booths to those placing calls.

"The traffic is very light, madame," said the clerk to Marie. "Your call should go through in a matter of minutes. Number twelve, please."

"Thank you. Booth twelve?"

"Yes, madame. Directly over there."

As they walked across the crowded floor to the booth, Jason held her arm. "I know why people use these places," he said. "They're a hundred and ten times quicker than a hotel phone."

"That's only one of the reasons."

They had barely reached the booth and lighted cigarettes when they heard the two short bursts of the bell inside.

Marie opened the door and went in, her spiral-hinged notebook and a pencil in her hand. She picked up the receiver.

Sixty seconds later Bourne watched in astonishment as she stared at the wall, the blood draining from her face, her skin chalk white. She began shouting and dropped her purse, the contents scattering over the floor of the small booth; the notebook was caught on the ledge, the pencil broken in the grip of her hand. He rushed inside; she was close to collapse.

"This is Marie St. Jacques in Paris, Lisa. Peter's expecting my call."

"Marie? Oh, my God . . ." The secretary's voice trailed off, replaced by other voices in the background. Excited voices, muted by a cupped hand over the phone. Then there was a rustle of movement, the phone being given to or taken by another.

"Marie, this is Alan," said the first assistant director of the section. "We're all in Peter's office."

"What's the matter, Alan? I don't have much time; may I speak to him, please?"

There was a moment of silence. "I wish I could make this easier for you, but I don't know how. Peter's dead, Marie."

"He's . . . what?"

"The police called a few minutes ago; they're on their way over."

"The police? What happened? Oh God, he's *dead?* What *happened?*"

"We're trying to piece it together. We're studying his phone log, but we're not supposed to touch anything on his desk."

"His desk . . . ?"

"Notes or memos, or anything like that."

"Alan! Tell me what happened!"

"That's just it—we don't know. He didn't tell any of us what he was doing. All we know is that he got two phone calls this morning from the States—one from Washington, the other from New York. Around noon he told Lisa he was going to the airport to meet someone flying up. He didn't say who. The police found him an hour ago in one of those tunnels used for freight. It was terrible; he was shot. In the throat . . . Marie? *Marie?*"

The old man with the hollow eyes and the stubble of a white beard limped into the dark confessional booth, blinking his eyes repeatedly, trying to focus on the hooded figure beyond the opaque curtain. Sight was not easy for this eighty-year-old messenger. But his mind was clear; that was all that mattered.

"Angelus Domini," he said.

"Angelus Domini, child of God," whispered the hooded silhouette. "Are your days comfortable?"

"They draw to an end, but they are made comfortable."

"Good . . . Zurich?"

"They found the man from the Guisan Quai. He was wounded; they traced him through a doctor known to the *Verbrecherwelt*. Under severe interrogation he admitted assaulting the woman. Cain came back for her; it was Cain who shot him."

"So it was an arrangement, the woman and Cain."

"The man from the Guisan Quai does not think so. He was one of the two who picked her up on the Löwenstrasse."

"He's also a fool. He killed the watchman?"

"He admits it and defends it. He had no choice in making his escape."

"He may not have to defend it; it could be the most intelligent thing he did. Does he have his gun?"

"Your people have it."

"Good. There is a prefect on the Zurich police. That gun must be given to him. Cain is elusive, the woman far less so. She has associates in Ottawa; they'll stay in touch. We trap her, we trace him. Is your pencil ready?"

"Yes, Carlos."

— 13 —

Bourne held her in the close confines of the glass booth, gently lowering her to the seat that protruded from the narrow wall. She was shaking, breathing in swallows and gasps, her eyes glazed, coming into focus as she looked at him.

"They killed him. They *killed* him! My God, what did I *do?* Peter!"

"You didn't do it! If anyone did it, I did. Not you. Get that through your head."

"Jason, I'm frightened. He was half a world away . . . and they killed him!"

"Treadstone?"

"Who else? There were two phone calls, Washington . . . New York. He went to the airport to meet someone and he was killed."

"How?"

"Oh, Jesus Christ . . ." Tears came to Marie's eyes. "He was shot. In the throat," she whispered.

Bourne suddenly felt a dull ache; he could not localize it, but it was there, cutting off air. "Carlos," he said, not knowing why he said it.

"What?" Marie stared up at him. "What did you say?"

"Carlos," he repeated softly. "A bullet in the throat. Carlos."

"What are you trying to say?"

"I don't know." He took her arm. "Let's get out of here. Are you all right? Can you walk?"

She nodded, closing her eyes briefly, breathing deeply. "Yes."

"We'll stop for a drink; we both need it. Then we'll find it."

"Find what?"

"A bookstore on Saint-Germain."

There were three back issues of magazines under the "Carlos" index. A three-year-old copy of the international edition of *Potomac Quarterly* and two Paris issues of *Le Globe*. They did not read the articles inside the store; instead they bought all three and took a taxi back to the hotel in Montparnasse. There they began reading, Marie on the bed, Jason in the chair by the window. Several minutes passed, and Marie bolted up.

"It's here," she said, fear in both her face and voice.

"Read it."

" 'A particularly brutal form of punishment is said to be inflicted by Carlos and/or his small band of soldiers. It is death by a gunshot in the throat, often leaving the victim to die in excruciating pain. It is reserved for those who break the code of silence or loyalty demanded by the assassin, or others who have refused to divulge information. . . .' " Marie stopped, incapable of reading further. She lay back and closed her eyes. "He wouldn't tell them and he was killed for it. Oh, my *God* . . ."

"He couldn't tell them what he didn't know," said Bourne.

"But *you* knew!" Marie sat up again, her eyes open. "You knew about a gunshot in the throat! You *said* it!"

"I said it. I knew it. That's all I can tell you."

"How?"

"I wish I could answer that. I can't."

"May I have a drink?"

"Certainly." Jason got up and went to the bureau. He poured two short glasses of whiskey and looked over at her. "Do you want me to call for some ice? Hervé's on; it'll be quick."

"No. It won't be quick enough." She slammed the magazine down on the bed and turned to him—on him, perhaps. "I'm going crazy!"

"Join the party of two."

"I want to believe you; I *do* believe you. But I . . . I . . ."

"You can't be sure," completed Bourne. "Any more than I can." He brought her the glass. "What do you want me to say? What can I say? Am I one of Carlos' soldiers? Did I break the code of silence or loyalty? Is that why I knew the method of execution?"

"Stop it!"

"I say that a lot to myself. 'Stop it.' Don't think; try to remember, but somewhere along the line put the brakes on. Don't go too far, too deep. One lie can be exposed, only to raise ten other questions intrinsic to that lie. Maybe it's like waking up after a long drunk, not sure whom you fought with or slept with, or . . . goddamn it . . . killed."

"No . . ." Marie drew out the word. "You are *you*. Don't take that away from me."

"I don't want to. I don't want to take it away from myself." Jason went back to the chair and sat down, his face turned to the window. "You found . . . a method of execution. I found something else. I knew it, just as I knew about Howard Leland. I didn't even have to read it."

"Read what?"

Bourne reached down and picked up the three-year-old issue of *Potomac Quarterly*. The magazine was folded open to a page on which there was a sketch of a bearded man, the lines rough, inconclusive, as if drawn from an obscure description. He held it out for her.

"Read it," he said. "It starts with the upper left, under the heading 'Myth or Monster.' Then I want to play a game."

"A game?"

"Yes. I've read only the first two paragraphs; you'll have to take my word for that."

"All right." Marie watched him, bewildered. She lowered the magazine into the light and read.

MYTH OR MONSTER

For over a decade, the name "Carlos" has been whispered in the back streets of such diverse cities as Paris,

Teheran, Beirut, London, Cairo, and Amsterdam. He is said to be the supreme terrorist in the sense that his commitment is to murder and assassination in themselves, with no apparent political ideology. Yet there is concrete evidence that he has undertaken profitable executions for such extremist radical groups as the PLO and Baader-Meinhof, both as teacher and profiteer. Indeed, it is through his infrequent gravitation to, and the internal conflicts within, such terrorist organizations that a clearer picture of "Carlos" is beginning to emerge. Informers are coming out of the bloodied spleens and they talk.

Whereas tales of his exploits give rise to images of a world filled with violence and conspiracy, high-explosives and higher intrigues, fast cars and faster women, the facts would seem to indicate at least as much Adam Smith as Ian Fleming. "Carlos" is reduced to human proportions and in the compression a truly frightening man comes into focus. The sadoromantic myth turns into a brilliant, blood-soaked monster who brokers assassination with the expertise of a market analyst, fully aware of wages, costs, distribution, and the divisions of underworld labor. It is a complicated business and "Carlos" is the master of its dollar value.

The portrait starts with a reputed name, as odd in its way as the owner's profession. Ilich Ramirez Sanchez. He is said to be a Venezuelan, the son of a fanatically devoted but not very prominent Marxist attorney (the Ilich is the father's salute to Vladimir Ilyich Lenin, and partially explains "Carlos' " forays into extremist terrorism) who sent the young boy to Russia for the major part of his education, which included espionage training at the Soviet compound in Novgorod. It is here that portrait fades briefly, rumor and speculation now the artists. According to these, one or another committee of the Kremlin that regularly monitors foreign students for future infiltration purposes saw what they had in Ilich Sanchez and wanted no part of him. He was a paranoid, who saw all solutions in terms of a well-placed bullet or bomb; the recommendation was to send the youth back to Caracas and disassociate any and all Soviet ties with the family. Thus rejected by Moscow, and deeply antithetical to western society, Sanchez went about building his own world, one in which he was the supreme leader. What better way to become the apolitical assassin whose services could be contracted for by the widest range of political and philosophical clients?

The portrait becomes clearer again. Fluent in numerous languages including his native Spanish as well as Russian, French, and English, Sanchez used his Soviet training as a springboard for refining his techniques. Months of concentrated study followed his expulsion from Moscow, some say under the tutelage of the Cubans, Che Guevera in particular. He mastered the science and handling of all manner of weaponry and explosives; there was no gun he could not break down and reassemble blindfolded, no explosive he could not analyze by smell and touch and know how to detonate in a dozen different ways. He was ready; he chose Paris as his base of operations and the word went out. A man was for hire who would kill where others dared not.

Once again the portrait dims as much for lack of birth records as anything else. Just how old is "Carlos"? How many targets can be attributed to him and how many are myth—self-proclaimed or otherwise? Correspondents based in Caracas have been unable to unearth any birth certificates anywhere in the country for an Ilich Ramirez Sanchez. On the other hand, there are thousands upon thousands of Sanchezes in Venezuela, hundreds with Ramirez attached; but none with an Ilich in front. Was it added later, or is the omission simply further proof of "Carlos'" thoroughness? The consensus is that the assassin is between thirty-five and forty years of age. No one really knows.

A GRASSY KNOLL IN DALLAS?

But one fact not disputed is that the profits from his first several kills enabled the assassin to set up an organization that might be envied by an operations analyst of General Motors. It is capitalism at its most efficient, loyalty and service extracted by equal parts fear and reward. The consequences of disloyalty are swift in coming—death—but so, too, are the benefits of service—generous bonuses and huge expense allowances. The organization seems to have hand-picked executives everywhere; and this well-founded rumor leads to the obvious question. Where did the profits initially come from? Who were the original kills?

The one most often speculated upon took place thirteen years ago in Dallas. No matter how many times the murder of John F. Kennedy is debated, no one has ever satisfactorily explained a burst of smoke from a grassy knoll three hundred yards away from the motorcade. The smoke was caught on camera; two open police radios on motorcycles recorded noise(s). Yet neither shell casings nor footprints were found. In fact, the only information about the so-called grassy knoll at that moment was considered so irrelevant that it was buried in the FBI-Dallas investigation and never included in the Warren Commission Report. It was provided by a bystander, K. M. Wright of North Dallas, who when questioned made the following statement:

"Hell, the only son of bitch near there was old Burlap Billy, and he was a couple of hundred yards away."

The "Billy" referred to was an aged Dallas tramp seen frequently panhandling in the tourist areas; the "Burlap" defined his penchant for wrapping his shoes in coarse cloth to play upon the sympathies of his marks. According to our correspondents, Wright's statement was never made public.

Yet six weeks ago a captured Lebanese terrorist broke under questioning in Tel Aviv. Pleading to be spared execution he claimed to possess extraordinary information about the assassin "Carlos." Israeli intelligence forwarded the report to Washington; our capitol correspondents obtained excerpts.

Statement: "Carlos was in Dallas in November 1963. He pretended to be Cuban and programmed Oswald. He was the back-up. It was his operation."

Question: "What proof do you have?"

Statement: "I heard him say it. He was on a small embankment of grass beyond a ledge. His rifle had a wire shell-trap attached."

Question: "It was never reported; why wasn't he seen?"

Statement: "He may have been, but no one would have known it. He was dressed as an old man, with a shabby overcoat, and his shoes were wrapped in canvas to avoid footprints."

A terrorist's information is certainly not proof, but neither should it always be disregarded. Especially when it concerns a master assassin, known to be a scholar of deception, who has made an admission that so astonishingly corroborates an unknown unpublished statement about a moment of national crisis never investigated. That, indeed, must be taken seriously. As so many others associated—even remotely— with the tragic events in Dallas, "Burlap Billy" was found dead several days later from an overdose of drugs. He was known to be an old man drunk consistently on cheap wine; he was never known to use narcotics. He could not afford them.

Was "Carlos" the man on the grassy knoll? What an extraordinary beginning for an extraordinary career! If Dallas really was his "operation" how many millions of dollars must have been funneled to him? Certainly more than enough to establish a network of informers and soldiers that is a corporate world unto itself.

The myth has too much substance; Carlos may well be a monster of flesh and too much blood.

Marie put down the magazine. "What's the game?"

"Are you finished?" Jason turned from the window.

"Yes."

"I gather a lot of statements were made. Theory, supposition, equations."

"Equations?"

"If something happened here, and there was an effect over there, a relationship existed."

"You mean connections," said Marie.

"All right, connections. It's all there, isn't it?"

"To a degree, you could say that. It's hardly a legal brief; there's a lot of speculation, rumor, and secondhand information."

"There *are* facts, however."

"Data."

"Good. Data. That's fine."

"What's the game?" Marie repeated.

"It's got a simple title. It's called 'Trap.'"

"Trap whom?"

"Me." Bourne sat forward. "I want you to ask me questions. Anything that's in there. A phrase, the name of a city, a rumor, a fragment of . . . data. Anything. Let's hear what my responses are. My blind responses."

"Darling, that's no proof of—"

"*Do* it!" ordered Jason.

"All right." Marie raised the issue of *Potomac Quarterly*. "Beirut," she said.

"Embassy," he answered. "CIA station head posing as an attaché. Gunned down in the street. Three hundred thousand dollars."

Marie looked at him. "I remember—" she began.

"I don't!" interrupted Jason. "Go on."

She returned his gaze, then went back to the magazine. "Baader-Meinhof."

"Stuttgart. Regensburg. Munich. Two kills and a kidnapping, Baader accreditation. Fees from—" Bourne stopped, then whispered in astonishment, "U. S. sources. Detroit . . . Wilmington, Delaware."

"Jason, what are—"

"Go *on. Please.*"

"The name, Sanchez."

"The *name* is Ilich Ramirez Sanchez," he replied. "He is . . . Carlos."

"Why the Ilich?"

Bourne paused, his eyes wandering. "I don't know."

"It's Russian, not Spanish. Was his mother Russian?"

"No . . . yes. His mother. It had to be his mother . . . I think. I'm not sure."

"Novgorod."

"Espionage compound. Communications, ciphers, frequency traffic. Sanchez is a graduate."

"Jason, you read that here!"

"I did not read it! Please. Keep going."

Marie's eyes swept back to the top of the article. "Teheran."

"Eight kills. Divided accreditation—Khomeini and PLO. Fee, two million. Source: Southwest Soviet sector."

"Paris," said Marie quickly.

"All contracts will be processed through Paris."

"What contracts?"

"*The* contracts . . . Kills."

[194]

"Whose kills? Whose contracts?"

"Sanchez . . . Carlos."

"Carlos? Then they're Carlos' contracts, *his* kills. They have nothing to do with you."

"Carlos' contracts," said Bourne, as if in a daze. "Nothing to do with . . . me," he repeated, barely above a whisper.

"You just said it, Jason. None of this has anything to do with you!"

"No! That's not true!" Bourne shouted, lunging up from the chair, holding his place, staring down at her. "*Our* contracts," he added quietly.

"You don't know what you're saying!"

"I'm responding! Blindly! It's why I had to come to Paris!" He spun around and walked to the window, gripping the frame. "That's what the game is all about," he continued. "We're not looking for a lie, we're looking for the truth, remember? Maybe we've found it; maybe the game revealed it."

"This is no valid test! It's a painful exercise in incidental recollection. If a magazine like *Potomac Quarterly* printed this, it would have been picked up by half the newspapers in the world. You could have read it anywhere."

"The fact is I retained it."

"Not entirely. You didn't know where the Ilich came from, that Carlos' father was a Communist attorney in Venezuela. They're salient points, I'd think. You didn't mention a thing about the Cubans. If you had, it would have led to the most shocking speculation written here. You didn't say a word about it."

"What are you talking about?"

"Dallas," she said. "November 1963."

"Kennedy," replied Bourne.

"That's it? Kennedy?"

"It happened then." Jason stood motionless.

"It did, but that's not what I'm looking for."

"I know," said Bourne, his voice once again flat, as if speaking in a vacuum. "A grassy knoll . . . Burlap Billy."

"You read this!"

"No."

"Then you heard it before, read it before."

"That's possible, but it's not relevant, is it?"

"Stop it, Jason!"

"Those words again. I wish I could."

"What are you trying to tell me? You're Carlos?"

"God, no. Carlos wants to kill me, and I don't speak Russian, I know that."

"Then *what?*"

"What I said at the beginning. The game. The game is called Trap-the Soldier."

"A soldier?"

"Yes. One who defected from Carlos. It's the only explanation, the only reason I know what I know. In all things."

"Why do you say defect?"

"Because he *does* want to kill me. He has to; he thinks I know as much about him as anyone alive."

Marie had been crouching on the bed; she swung her legs over the side, her hands at her sides. "That's a result of defecting. What about the cause? If it's true, then you did it, became . . . became—" She stopped.

"All things considered, it's a little late to look for a moral position," said Bourne, seeing the pain of acknowledgment on the face of the woman he loved. "I could think of several reasons, clichés. How about a falling out among thieves . . . killers."

"Meaningless!" cried Marie. "There's not a shred of evidence."

"There's buckets of it and you know it. I could have sold out to a higher bidder or stolen huge sums of money from the fees. Either would explain the account in Zurich." He stopped briefly, looking at the wall above the bed, feeling, not seeing. "Either would explain Howard Leland, Marseilles, Beirut, Stuttgart . . . Munich. Everything. All the unremembered facts that want to come out. And one especially. Why I avoided his name, why I never mentioned him. I'm frightened. I'm afraid of him."

The moment passed in silence; more was spoken of than fear. Marie nodded. "I'm sure you believe that," she said, "and in a way I wish it were true. But I don't think it is. You want to believe it because it supports what you just said. It gives you an answer . . . an identity. It may not be the identity you want, but God knows it's better than wandering blindly through that awful labyrinth you face every day. Anything would be, I guess." She paused. "And *I* wish it were true because then we wouldn't be here."

"What?"

"That's the inconsistency, darling. The number or sym-

[196]

bol that doesn't fit in your equation. If you *were* what you say you were, and afraid of Carlos—and heaven knows you should be—Paris would be the last place on earth you'd feel compelled to go to. We'd be somewhere else; you said it yourself. You'd run away; you'd take the money from Zurich and disappear. But you're not doing that; instead, you're walking right back into Carlos' den. That's not a man who's either afraid or guilty."

"There isn't anything else. I came to Paris to find out; it's as simple as that."

"Then run away. We'll have the money in the morning; there's nothing stopping you—us. That's simple, too." Marie watched him closely.

Jason looked at her, then turned away. He walked to the bureau and poured himself a drink. "There's still Treadstone to consider," he said defensively.

"Why any more than Carlos? There's your real equation. Carlos and Treadstone. A man I once loved very much was killed by Treadstone. All the more reason for us to run, to survive."

"I'd think you'd want the people who killed him exposed," said Bourne. "Make them pay for it."

"I do. Very much. But others can find them. I have priorities, and revenge isn't at the top of the list. *We* are. You and I. Or is that only my judgment? My feelings."

"You know better than that." He held the glass tighter in his hand and looked over at her. "I love you," he whispered.

"Then let's run!" she said, raising her voice almost mechanically, taking a step toward him. "Let's forget it all, *really* forget, and run as fast as we can, as far away as we can! Let's do it!"

"I . . . I," Jason stammered, the mists interfering, infuriating him. "There are . . . things."

"What things? We love each other, we've found each *other!* We can go anywhere, be anyone. There's nothing to stop us, is there?"

"Only you and me," he repeated softly, the mists now closing in, suffocating him. "I know. I know. But I've got to think. There's so much to learn, so much that has to come out."

"Why is it so important?"

"It . . . just is."

"Don't you know?"

"Yes . . . No, I'm not sure. Don't ask me now."

"If not now, when? When can I ask you? When will it pass? Or will it ever?!"

"Stop it!" he suddenly roared, slamming the glass down on the wooden tray. "I can't run! I won't! I've got to stay here! I've got to know!"

Marie rushed to him, putting her hands first on his shoulders, then on his face, wiping away the perspiration. "Now you've said it. Can you hear yourself, darling? You can't run because the closer you get, the more maddening it is for you. And if you did run, it would only get worse. You wouldn't have a life, you'd live a nightmare. I know that."

He reached for her face, touching it, looking at her. "Do you?"

"Of course. But you had to say it, not me." She held him, her head against his chest. "I had to force you to. The funny thing is that I *could* run. I could get on a plane with you tonight and go wherever you wanted, disappear, and not look back, happier than I've ever been in my life. But you couldn't do that. What is—or isn't—here in Paris would eat away at you until you couldn't stand it anymore. That's the crazy irony, my darling. I could live with it but you couldn't."

"You'd just disappear?" asked Jason. "What about your family, your job—all the people you know?"

"I'm neither a child nor a fool," she answered quickly. "I'd cover myself somehow, but I don't think I'd take it very seriously. I'd request an extended leave for medical and personal reasons. Emotional stress, a breakdown; I could always go back, the department would understand."

"Peter?"

"Yes." She was silent for a moment. "We went from one relationship to another, the second more important to both of us, I think. He was like an imperfect brother you want to succeed in spite of his flaws, because underneath there was such decency."

"I'm sorry. I'm truly sorry."

She looked up at him. "You have the same decency. When you do the kind of work I do decency becomes very important. It's not the meek who are inheriting the earth, Jason, it's the corrupters. And I have an idea that the distance between corruption and killing is a very short step."

"Treadstone Seventy-One?"

[198]

"Yes. We were both right. I do want them exposed, I want them to pay for what they've done. And you can't run away."

He brushed his lips against her cheek and then her hair and held her. "I should throw you out," he said. "I should tell you to get out of my life. I can't do it, but I know damned well I should."

"It wouldn't make any difference if you did. I wouldn't go, my love."

The attorney's suite of offices was on the boulevard de la Chapelle, the book-lined conference room more a stage setting than an office; everything was a prop, and in its place. Deals were made in that room, not contracts. As for the lawyer himself, a dignified white goatee and silver pince-nez above an aquiline nose could not conceal the essential graft in the man. He even insisted on conversing in poor English, for which, at a later date, he could claim to have been misunderstood.

Marie did most of the talking, Bourne deferring, client to adviser. She made her points succinctly, altering the cashiers checks to bearer bonds, payable in dollars, in denominations ranging from a maximum of twenty thousand dollars to a minimum of five. She instructed the lawyer to tell the bank that all series were to be broken up numerically in threes, the international guarantors changed with every fifth lot of certificates. Her objective was not lost on the attorney; she so complicated the issuing of the bonds that tracing them would be beyond the facilities of most banks or brokers. Nor would such banks or brokers take on the added trouble or expense; payments were guaranteed.

When the irritated, goateed lawyer had nearly concluded his telephone conversation with an equally disturbed Antoine d'Amacourt, Marie held up her hand.

"Pardon me, but Monsieur Bourne insists that Monsieur d'Amacourt also include two hundred thousand francs in cash, one hundred thousand to be included with the bonds and one hundred to be held by Monsieur d'Amacourt. He suggests that the second hundred thousand be divided as follows. Seventy-five thousand for Monsieur d'Amacourt and twenty-five thousand for yourself. He realizes that he is greatly in debt to both of you for your advice and the additional trouble he has caused you. Needless to say, no specific record of breakdown is required."

Irritation and disturbance vanished with her words, replaced by an obsequiousness not seen since the court of Versailles. The arrangements were made in accordance with the unusual—but completely understandable—demands of Monsieur Bourne and his esteemed adviser.

A leather attaché case was provided by Monsieur Bourne for the bonds and the money; it would be carried by an armed courier who would leave the bank at 2:30 in the afternoon and meet Monsieur Bourne at 3:00 on the Pont Neuf. The distinguished client would identify himself with a small piece of leather cut from the shell of the case and which, when fitted in place, would prove to be the missing fragment. Added to this would be the words: "Herr Koenig sends greeting from Zurich."

So much for the details. Except for one, which was made clear by Monsieur Bourne's adviser.

"We recognize that the demands of the *fiche* must be carried out to the letter, and fully expect Monsieur d'Amacourt to do so," said Marie St. Jacques. "However, we also recognize that the timing can be advantageous to Monsieur Bourne, and would expect no less than that advantage. Were he not to have it, I'm afraid that I, as a certified—if for the present, anonymous—member of the International Banking Commission, would feel compelled to report certain aberrations of banking and legal procedures as I have witnessed them. I'm sure that won't be necessary; we're all very well paid, *n'est-ce pas, monsieur?*"

"*C'est vrai, madame!* In banking and law . . . indeed, as in life itself . . . timing is everything. You have nothing to fear."

"I know," said Marie.

Bourne examined the grooves of the silencer, satisfied that he had removed the particles of dust and lint that had gathered with nonuse. He gave it a final, wrenching turn, depressed the magazine release and checked the clip. Six shells remained; he was ready. He shoved the weapon into his belt and buttoned his jacket.

Marie had not seen him with the gun. She was sitting on the bed, her back to him, talking on the telephone with the Canadian Embassy attaché, Dennis Corbelier. Cigarette smoke curled up from an ashtray next to her notebook; she was writing down Corbelier's information. When he had finished, she thanked him and hung up the phone. She remained motionless for two or three seconds, the pencil still in her hand.

"He doesn't know about Peter," she said, turning to Jason. "That's odd."

"Very," agreed Bourne. "I thought he'd be one of the first to know. You said they looked over Peter's telephone logs; he'd placed a call to Paris, to Corbelier. You'd think someone would have followed up on it."

"I hadn't even considered that. I was thinking about the newspapers, the wire services. Peter was . . . was found eighteen hours ago, and regardless of how casual I may have sounded, he was an important man in the Canadian government. His death would be news in itself, his murder infinitely more so. . . . It wasn't reported."

"Call Ottawa tonight. Find out why."

"I will."

"What did Corbelier tell you?"

"Oh, yes." Marie shifted her eyes to the notebook. "The license in rue Madeleine was meaningless, a car rented at De Gaulle Airport to a Jean-Pierre Larousse."

"John Smith," interrupted Jason.

"Exactly. He had better luck with the telephone number d'Amacourt gave you, but he can't see what it could possibly have to do with anything. Neither can I, as a matter of fact."

"It's that strange?"

"I think so. It's a private line belonging to a fashion house on Saint-Honoré. Les Classiques."

"A fashion house? You mean a studio?"

"I'm sure it's got one, but it's essentially an elegant dress shop. Like the House of Dior, or Givenchy. *Haute couture*. In the trade, Corbelier said, it's known as the House of René. That's Bergeron."

"Who?"

"René Bergeron, a designer. He's been around for years, always on the fringes of a major success. I know about him because my little lady back home copies his designs."

"Did you get the address?"

Marie nodded. "Why didn't Corbelier know about Peter? Why doesn't everybody?"

"Maybe you'll learn when you call. It's probably as simple as time zones; too late for the morning editions here in Paris. I'll pick up the afternoon paper." Bourne went to the closet for his topcoat, conscious of the hidden weight in his

[201]

belt. "I'm going back to the bank. I'll follow the courier to the Pont Neuf." He put on the coat, aware that Marie was not listening. "I meant to ask you, do these fellows wear uniforms?"

"Who?"

"Bank couriers."

"That would account for the newspapers, not the wire services."

"I beg your pardon?"

"The difference in time. The papers might not have picked it up, but the wire services would have known. And embassies have teletypes; they would have known about it. It wasn't reported, Jason."

"You'll call tonight," he said. "I'm going."

"You asked about the couriers. Do they wear uniforms?"

"I was curious."

"Most of the time, yes. They also drive armored vans, but I was specific about that. If a van was used it was to be parked a block from the bridge, the courier to proceed on foot."

"I heard you, but I wasn't sure what you meant. Why?"

"A bonded courier's bad enough, but he's necessary; bank insurance requires him. A van is simply too obvious; it could be followed too easily. You won't change your mind and let me go with you?"

"No."

"Believe me, nothing will go wrong; those two thieves wouldn't permit it."

"Then there's no reason for you to be there."

"You're maddening."

"I'm in a hurry."

"I know. And you move faster without me." Marie got up and came to him. "I do understand." She leaned into him, kissing him on the lips, suddenly aware of the weapon in his belt. She looked into his eyes. "You are worried, aren't you?"

"Just cautious." He smiled, touching her chin. "It's an awful lot of money. It may have to keep us for a long time."

"I like the sound of that."

"The money?"

"No. Us." Marie frowned. "A safety deposit box."

"You keep talking in non sequiturs."

"You can't leave negotiable certificates worth over a million dollars in a Paris hotel room. You've got to get a deposit box."

"We can do it tomorrow." He released her, turning for the door. "While I'm out, look up Les Classiques in the phone book and call the regular number. Find out how late it's open." He left quickly.

Bourne sat in the back seat of a stationary taxi, watching the front of the bank through the windshield. The driver was humming an unrecognizable tune, reading a newspaper, content with the fifty-franc note he had received in advance. The cab's motor, however, was running; the passenger had insisted upon that.

The armored van loomed in the right rear window, its radio antenna shooting up from the center of the roof like a tapered bowsprit. It parked in a space reserved for authorized vehicles directly in front of Jason's taxi. Two small red lights appeared above the circle of bulletproof glass in the rear door. The alarm system had been activated.

Bourne leaned forward, his eyes on the uniformed man who climbed out of the side door and threaded his way through the crowds on the pavement toward the entrance of the bank. He felt a sense of relief; the man was not one of the three well-dressed men who had come to the Valois yesterday.

Fifteen minutes later the courier emerged from the bank, the leather attaché case in his left hand, his right covering an unlatched holster. The jagged rip on the side of the case could be seen clearly. Jason felt the fragment of leather in his shirt pocket; if nothing else it was the primitive combination that made a life beyond Paris, beyond Carlos, possible. If there was such a life and he could accept it without the terrible labyrinth from which he could find no escape.

But it was more than that. In a manmade labyrinth one kept moving, running, careening off walls, the contact itself a form of progress, if only blind. His personal labyrinth had no walls, no defined corridors through which to race. Only space, and swirling mists in the darkness that he saw so clearly when he opened his eyes at night and felt the sweat pouring down his face. Why was it always space and darkness and high winds? Why was he always plummeting through the air at night? A parachute. Why? Then other words came to him; he had no idea where they were from, but they were there and he heard them.

What's left when your memory's gone? And your identity, Mr. Smith?

Stop it!

The armored van swung into the traffic on rue Madeleine. Bourne tapped the driver on the shoulder. "Follow that truck, but keep at least two cars between us," he said in French.

The driver turned, alarmed. "I think you have the wrong taxi, monsieur. Take back your money."

"I'm with the armored-car company, you imbecile. It's a special assignment."

"Regrets, monsieur. We will not lose it." The driver plunged diagonally forward into the combat of traffic.

The van took the quickest route to the Seine, going down sidestreets. Turning left on the Quai de la Rapée toward the Pont Neuf. Then, within what Jason judged to be three or four blocks of the bridge, it slowed down, hugging the curb as if the courier had decided he was too early for his appointment. But, if anything, Bourne thought, he was running late. It was six minutes to three, barely enough time for the man to park and walk the one prescribed block to the bridge. Then why had the van slowed down? Slowed down? No, it had stopped; it wasn't moving! Why?

The traffic? . . . Good God, of course—the traffic!

"Stop here," said Bourne to the driver. "Pull over to the curb. Quickly!"

"What is it, monsieur?"

"You're a very fortunate man," said Jason. "My company is willing to pay you an additional one hundred francs if you simply go to the front window of that van and say a few words to the driver."

"What, monsieur?"

"Frankly, we're testing him. He's new. Do you want the hundred?"

"I just go to the window and say a few words?"

"That's all. Five seconds at the most, then you can go back to your taxi and drive off."

"There's no trouble? I don't want trouble."

"My firm's among the most respectable in France. You've seen our trucks everywhere."

"I don't know . . ."

"Forget it!" Bourne reached for the door handle.

"What are the words?"

Jason held out the hundred francs. "Just these: 'Herr

Koenig. Greetings from Zurich.' Can you remember those?"

" 'Koenig. Greetings from Zurich.' What's so difficult?"

"You? Behind me?"

"That's right." They walked rapidly toward the van, hugging the right side of their small alley in the traffic as cars and trucks passed them in starts and stops on their left. The van was Carlos' trap, thought Bourne. The assassin had bought his way into the ranks of the armed couriers. A single name and a rendezvous revealed over a monitored radio frequency could bring an underpaid messenger a great deal of money. *Bourne. Pont Neuf.* So simple. This particular courier was less concerned with being prompt than in making sure the soldiers of Carlos reached the Pont Neuf in time. Paris traffic was notorious; anyone could be late. Jason stopped the taxi driver, holding in his hand four additional two-hundred franc notes; the man's eyes were riveted on them.

"Monsieur?"

"My company's going to be very generous. This man must be disciplined for gross infractions."

"What, monsieur?"

"After you say 'Herr Koenig. Greetings from Zurich,' simply add, 'The schedule's changed. There's a fare in my taxi who must see you.' Have you got that?"

The driver's eyes returned to the franc notes. "What's difficult?" He took the money.

They edged their way along the side of the van, Jason's back pressed against the wall of steel, his right hand concealed beneath his topcoat, gripping the gun in his belt. The driver approached the window and reached up, tapping the glass.

"You inside! Herr Koenig! Greetings from Zurich!" he yelled.

The window was rolled down, no more than an inch or two. "What is this?" a voice yelled back. "You're supposed to be at the Pont Neuf, monsieur!"

The driver was no idiot; he was also anxious to leave as rapidly as possible. "Not me, you jackass!" he shouted through the din of the surrounding, perilously close traffic. "I'm telling you what I was told to say! The schedule's been changed. There's a man back there who says he has to see you!"

"Tell him to hurry," said Jason, holding a final fifty-franc note in his hand, beyond sight of the window.

The driver glanced at the money, then back up at the courier. "Be quick about it! If you don't see him right away you'll lose your job!"

"Now, get out of here!" said Bourne. The driver turned and ran past Jason, grabbing the franc note as he raced back to his taxi.

Bourne held his place, suddenly alarmed by what he heard through the cacaphony of pounding horns and gunning engines in the crowded street. There were voices from inside the van, not one man shouting into a radio, but two shouting at each other. The courier was not alone; there was another man with him.

"Those were the words. You heard them."

"He was to come *up* to you. He was to show himself."

"Which he will *do*. And present the piece of leather, which must fit exactly! Do you expect him to do that in the middle of a street filled with traffic?"

"I don't like it!"

"You paid me to help you and your people find someone. Not to lose my job. I'm going!"

"It *must* be the Pont Neuf!"

"Kiss my ass!"

There was the sound of heavy footsteps on the metal floorboards. "I'm coming with you!"

The panel door opened; Jason spun behind it, his hand still under his coat. Below him a child's face was pressed against the glass of a car window, the eyes squinting, the young features contorted into an ugly mask, fright and insult the childish intent. The swelling sound of angry horns, blaring in counterpoint, filled the street; the traffic had come to a standstill.

The courier stepped off the metal ledge, the attaché case in his left hand. Bourne was ready; the instant the courier was on the street, he slammed the panel back into the body of the second man, crashing the heavy steel into a descending kneecap and an outstretched hand. The man screamed, reeling backward inside the van. Jason shouted at the courier, the jagged scrap of leather in his free hand.

"I'm Bourne! Here's your fragment! And you keep that gun in its holster or you won't just lose your job, you'll lose your life, you son of a bitch!"

"I meant no harm, monsieur! They wanted to find you!

[206]

They have no interest in your delivery, you have my word on it!"

The door crashed open; Jason slammed it again with his shoulder, then pulled it back to see the face of Carlos' soldier, his hand on the weapon in his belt.

What he saw was the barrel of a gun, the black orifice of its opening staring him in the eyes. He spun back, aware that the split-second delay in the gunshot that followed was caused by the burst of a shrill ringing that exploded out of the armored van. The alarm had been tripped, the sound deafening, riding over the dissonance in the street; the gunshot seemed muted by comparison, the eruption of asphalt below not heard.

Once more Jason hammered the panel. He heard the impact of metal against metal; he had made contact with the gun of Carlos' soldier. He pulled his own from his belt, dropped to his knees in the street, and pulled the door open.

He saw the face from Zurich, the killer they had called Johann, the man they had brought to Paris to recognize him. Bourne fired twice; the man arched backward, blood spreading across his forehead.

The courier! The attaché case!

Jason saw the man; he had ducked below the tailgate for protection, his weapon in his hand, screaming for help. Bourne leaped to his feet and lunged for the extended gun, gripping the barrel, twisting it out of the courier's hand. He grabbed the attaché case and shouted.

"No harm, right? Give me that, you bastard!" He threw the man's gun under the van, got up and plunged into the hysterical crowds on the pavement.

He ran wildly, blindly, the bodies in front of him the movable walls of his labyrinth. But there was an essential difference between this gauntlet and one he lived in every day. There was no darkness; the afternoon sun was bright, as blinding as his race through the labyrinth.

14

"Everything is here," said Marie. She had collated the certificates by denominations, the stacks and the franc notes on the desk. "I told you it would be."

"It almost wasn't."

"What?"

"The man they called Johann, the one from Zurich. He's dead. I killed him."

"Jason, what *happened?*"

He told her. "They counted on the Pont Neuf," he said. "My guess is that the backup car got caught in traffic, broke into the courier's radio frequency, and told them to delay. I'm sure of it."

"Oh God, they're everywhere!"

"But they don't know where *I* am," said Bourne, looking into the mirror above the bureau, studying his blond hair while putting on the tortoise-shell glasses. "And the last place they'd expect to find me at this moment—if they conceivably thought I knew about it—would be a fashion house on Saint-Honoré."

"Les Classiques?" asked Marie, astonished.

"That's right. Did you call it?"

"Yes, but that's insane!"

"Why?" Jason turned from the mirror. "Think about it. Twenty minutes ago their trap fell apart; there's got to be confusion, recriminations, accusations of incompetency, or worse. Right now, at this moment, they're more concerned with each other than with me; nobody wants a bullet in his throat. It won't last long; they'll regroup quickly, Carlos will make sure of that. But during the next hour or so, while they're trying to piece together what happened, the one place they won't look for me is a relay-drop they haven't the vaguest idea I'm aware of."

"Someone will recognize you!"

"Who? They brought in a man from Zurich to do that and he's dead. They're not sure what I look like."

"The courier. They'll take him; he saw you."

"For the next few hours he'll be busy with the police."

"D'Amacourt. The lawyer!"

"I suspect they're halfway to Normandy or Marseilles or, if they're lucky, out of the country."

"Suppose they're stopped, caught?"

"Suppose they are? Do you think Carlos would expose a drop where he gets messages? Not on your life. Or his."

"Jason, I'm frightened."

"So am I. But not of being recognized." Bourne returned to the mirror. "I could give a long dissertation about facial classifications, and softened features, but I won't."

"You're talking about the evidences of surgery. Port Noir. You told me."

"Not all of it." Bourne leaned against the bureau, staring at his face. "What color are my eyes?"

"What?"

"No, don't look at me. Now, tell me, what color are my eyes? Yours are brown with speckles of green; what about mine?"

"Blue . . . bluish. Or a kind of gray, really . . ." Marie stopped. "I'm not really sure. I suppose that's dreadful of me."

"It's perfectly natural. Basically they're hazel, but not all the time. Even I've noticed it. When I wear a blue shirt or tie, they become bluer; a brown coat or jacket, they're gray. When I'm naked, they're strangely nondescript."

"That's not so strange. I'm sure millions of people are the same."

[209]

"I'm sure they are. But how many of them wear contact lenses when their eyesight is normal?"

"Contact—"

"That's what I said," interrupted Jason. "Certain types of contact lenses are worn to change the color of the eyes. They're most effective when the eyes are hazel. When Washburn first examined me there was evidence of prolonged usage. It's one of the clues, isn't it?"

"It's whatever you want to make of it," said Marie. "If it's true."

"Why wouldn't it be?"

"Because the doctor was more often drunk than sober. You've told me that. He piled conjecture on top of conjecture, heaven knows how warped by alcohol. He was never specific. He couldn't be."

"He was about one thing. I'm a chameleon, designed to fit a flexible mold. I want to find out whose; maybe I can now. Thanks to you I've got an address. Someone there may know the truth. Just one man, that's all I need. One person I can confront, break if I have to . . ."

"I can't stop you, but for God's sake be careful. If they do recognize you, they'll kill you."

"Not there they won't; it'd be rotten for business. This is Paris."

"I don't think that's funny, Jason."

"Neither do I. I'm counting on it very seriously."

"What are you going to do? I mean, how?"

"I'll know better when I get there. See if anyone's running around looking nervous or anxious or waiting for a phone call as if his life depended on it."

"Then what?"

"I'll do the same as I did with d'Amacourt. Wait outside and follow whoever it is. I'm this close; I won't miss. And I'll be careful."

"Will you call me?"

"I'll try."

"I may go crazy waiting. Not knowing."

"Don't wait. Can you deposit the bonds somewhere?"

"The banks are closed."

"Use a large hotel; hotels have vaults."

"You have to have a room."

"Take one. At the Meurice or the George Cinq. Leave the case at the desk but come back here."

Marie nodded. "It would give me something to do."

"Then call Ottawa. Find out what happened."

"I will."

Bourne crossed to the bedside table and picked up a number of five-thousand franc notes. "A bribe would be easier," he said. "I don't think it'll happen, but it could."

"It could," agreed Marie, and then in the same breath continued. "Did you hear yourself? You just rattled off the names of two hotels."

"I heard." He turned and faced her. "I've been here before. Many times. I lived here, but not in those hotels. In out-of-the-way streets, I think. Not very easily found."

The moment passed in silence, the fear electric.

"I love you, Jason."

"I love you, too," said Bourne.

"Come back to me. No matter what happens, come back to me."

The lighting was soft and dramatic, pinpoint spotlights shining down from the dark brown ceiling, bathing manikins and expensively dressed clients in pools of flattering yellows. The jewelry and accessories counters were lined with black velvet, silks of bright red and green tastefully flowing above the midnight sheen, glistening eruptions of gold and silver caught in the recessed frame lights. The aisles curved graciously in semicircles, giving an illusion of space that was not there, for Les Classiques, though hardly small, was not a large emporium. It was, however, a beautifully appointed store on one of the most costly strips of real estate in Paris. Fitting rooms with doors of tinted glass were at the rear, beneath a balcony where the offices of management were located. A carpeted staircase rose on the right beside an elevated switchboard in front of which sat an oddly out-of-place middle-aged man dressed in a conservative business suit, operating the console, speaking into a mouthpiece that was an extension of his single earphone.

The clerks were mostly women, tall, slender, gaunt of face and body, living postmortems of former fashion models whose tastes and intelligence had carried them beyond their sisters in the trade, other practices no longer feasible. The few men in evidence were also slender; reedlike figures emphasized by form-fitting clothes, gestures rapid, stances balletically defiant.

Light romantic music floated out of the dark ceiling, quiet crescendos abstractly punctuated by the beams of the miniature spotlights. Jason wandered through the aisles, studying manikins, touching the fabric, making his own appraisals. They covered his essential bewilderment. Where was the confusion, the anxiety he expected to find at the core of Carlos' message center? He glanced up at the open office doors and the single corridor that bisected the small complex. Men and women walked casually about as they did on the main floor, every now and then stopping one another, exchanging pleasantries or scraps of relevantly irrelevant information. Gossip. Nowhere was there the slightest sense of urgency, no sign at all that a vital' trap had exploded in their faces, an imported killer—the only man in Paris who worked for Carlos and could identify the target—shot in the head, dead in the back of an armored van on the Quai de la Rapée.

It was incredible, if only because the whole atmosphere was the opposite of what he had anticipated. Not that he expected to find chaos, far from it; the soldiers of Carlos were too controlled for that. Still he had expected *something*. And here there were no strained faces, or darting eyes, no abrupt movements that signified alarm. Nothing whatsoever was unusual; the elegant world of *haute couture* continued to spin in its elegant orbit, unmindful of events that should have thrown its axis off balance.

Still, there was a private telephone somewhere and someone who not only spoke for Carlos but was also empowered to set in motion three killers on the hunt. A woman . . .

He saw her; it had to be her. Halfway down the carpeted staircase, a tall imperious woman with a face that age and cosmetics had rendered into a cold mask of itself. She was stopped by a reedlike male clerk who held out a salesbook for the woman's approval; she looked at it, then glanced down at the floor, at a nervous, middle-aged man by a nearby jewelry counter. The glance was brief but pointed, the message clear. *All right, mon ami, pick up your bauble but pay your bill soon. Otherwise you could be embarrassed next time. Or worse. I might call your wife.* In milliseconds the rebuke was over; a smile as false as it was broad cracked the mask, and with a nod and a flourish the woman took a pencil from the clerk and initialed the sales slip. She continued down the staircase, the clerk following, leaning forward in further conversation. It was obvious he was flattering her; she turned on the bottom step, touching her crown of streaked dark hair and tapped his wrist in a gesture of thanks.

There was little placidity in the woman's eyes. They were as aware as any pair of eyes Bourne had ever seen, except perhaps behind gold-rimmed glasses in Zurich.

Instinct. She was his objective; it remained how to reach her. The first moves of the pavane had to be subtle, neither too much nor too little, but warranting attention. She had to come to him.

The next few minutes astonished Jason—which was to say he astonished himself. The term was "role-playing," he understood that, but what shocked him was the ease with which he slid into a character far from himself—as he knew himself. Where minutes before he had made appraisals, he now made inspections, pulling garments from their individual racks, holding the fabrics up to the light. He peered closely at stitchings, examined buttons and buttonholes, brushing his fingers across collars, fluffing them up, then letting them fall. He was a judge of fine clothes, a schooled buyer who knew what he wanted and rapidly disregarded that which did not suit his tastes. The only items he did not examine were the price tags; obviously they held no interest for him.

The fact that they did not prodded the interest of the imperious woman who kept glancing over in his direction. A sales clerk, her concave body floating upright on the carpet, approached him; he smiled courteously, but said he preferred to browse by himself. Less than thirty seconds later he was behind three manikins, each dressed in the most expensive designs to be found in Les Classiques. He raised his eyebrows, his mouth set in silent approval as he squinted between the plastic figures at the woman beyond the counter. She whispered to the clerk who had spoken to him; the former model shook her head, shrugging.

Bourne stood arms akimbo, billowing his cheeks, his breath escaping slowly as his eyes shifted from one manikin to another; he was an uncertain man about to make up his mind. And a potential client in that situation, especially one who did not look at prices, needed assistance from the most knowledgeable person in the vicinity; he was irresistible. The regal woman touched her hair and gracefully negotiated the aisles toward him. The pavane had come to its first conclusion; the dancers bowed, preparing for the gavotte.

"I see you've gravitated to our better items, monsieur," said the woman in English, a presumption obviously based on the judgment of a practiced eye.

"I trust I have," replied Jason. "You've got an interesting collection here, but one does have to ferret, doesn't one?"

"The ever-present and inevitable scale of values, monsieur. However, all our designs are exclusive."

"*Cela va sans dire, madame.*"

"*Ah, vous parlez français?*"

"*Un peu.* Passably."

"You are American?"

"I'm rarely there," said Bourne. "You say these are made for you alone?"

"Oh, yes. Our designer is under exclusive contract; I'm sure you've heard of him. René Bergeron."

Jason frowned. "Yes. I have. Very respected, but he's never made a breakthrough, has he?"

"He will, monsieur. It's inevitable; his reputation grows each season. A number of years ago he worked for St. Laurent, then Givenchy. Some say he did far more than cut the patterns, if you know what I mean."

"It's not hard to follow."

"And how those cats try to push him in the background! It's disgraceful! Because he adores women; he flatters them and does not make them into little boys, *vous comprenez?*"

"*Je vous comprends parfaitement.*"

"He'll emerge worldwide one day soon and they'll not be able to touch the hems of his creations. Think of these as the works of an emerging master, monsieur."

"You're very convincing. I'll take these three. I assume they're in the size twelve range."

"Fourteen, monsieur. They will be fitted, of course."

"I'm afraid not, but I'm sure there are decent tailors in Cap-Ferrat."

"*Naturellement,*" conceded the woman quickly.

"Also . . ." Bourne hesitated, frowning again. "While I'm here, and to save time, select a few others for me along these lines. Different prints, different cuts, but related, if that makes sense."

"Very *good* sense, monsieur."

"Thanks, I appreciate it. I've had a long flight from the Bahamas and I'm exhausted."

"Would monsieur care to sit down then?"

"Frankly, monsieur would care for a drink."

"It can be arranged, of course. As to the method of payment, monsieur . . . ?"

"*Je paierai cash,* I think," said Jason, aware that the exchange of merchandise for hard currency would appeal to the overseer of Les Classiques. "Checks and accounts are like spoors in the forest, aren't they?"

"You are as wise as you are discriminating." The rigid smile cracked the mask again, the eyes in no way related. "About that drink, why not my office? It's quite private; you can relax and I shall bring you selections for your approval."

"Splendid."

"As to the price range, monsieur?"

"*Les meilleurs, madame.*"

"*Naturellement.*" A thin white hand was extended. "I am Jacqueline Lavier, managing partner of Les Classiques."

"Thank you." Bourne took the hand without offering a name. One might follow in less public surroundings, his expression said, but not at the moment. For the moment, money was his introduction. "Your office? Mine's several thousand miles from here."

"This way, monsieur." The rigid smile appeared once more, breaking the facial mask like a sheet of progressively cracked ice. Madame Lavier gestured toward the staircase. The world of *haute couture* continued, its orbit uninterrupted by failure and death on the Quai de la Rapée.

That lack of interruption was as disturbing to Jason as it was bewildering. He was convinced the woman walking beside him was the carrier of lethal commands that had been aborted by gunfire an hour ago, the orders having been issued by a faceless man who demanded obedience or death. Yet there was not the slightest indication that a strand of her perfectly groomed hair had been disturbed by nervous fingers, no pallor on the chiseled mask that might be taken for fear. Yet there was no one higher at Les Classiques, no one else who would have a private number in a very private office. Part of an equation was missing . . . but another had been disturbingly confirmed.

Himself. The chameleon. The charade had worked; he was in the enemy's camp, convinced beyond doubt that he had not been recognized. The whole episode had a *déjà vu* quality about it. He had done such things before, experienced the feelings of similar accomplishment before. He was a man running through an unfamiliar jungle, yet somehow instinctively knowing his way, sure of where the traps were and how to avoid them. The chameleon was an expert.

They reached the staircase and started up the steps. Below on the right, the conservatively dressed, middle-aged operator was speaking quietly into the extended mouthpiece, nodding his gray-haired head almost wearily, as if assuring the party on the line that *their* world was as serene as it should be.

Bourne stopped on the seventh step, the pause involuntary. The back of the man's head, the outline of the cheekbone, the sight of the thinning gray hair—the way it fell slightly over the ear; he had seen that man before! Somewhere. In the past, in the unremembered past, but remembered now in darkness . . . and with flashes of light. Explosions, mists; buffeting winds followed by silences filled with tension. What was it? Where was it? Why did the pain come to his eyes again? The gray-haired man began to turn in his swivel chair; Jason looked away before they made contact.

"I see monsieur is taken by our rather unique switchboard," said Madame Lavier. "It's a distinction we feel sets Les Classiques apart from the other shops on Saint-Honoré."

"How so?" asked Bourne, as they proceeded up the steps, the pain in his eyes causing him to blink.

"When a client calls Les Classiques, the telephone is not answered by a vacuous female, but instead by a cultured gentleman who has all our information at his fingertips."

"A nice touch."

"Other gentlemen think so," she added. "Especially when making telephone purchases they would prefer to keep confidential. There are no spoors in our forest, monsieur."

They reached Jacqueline Lavier's spacious office. It was the lair of an efficient executive, scores of papers in separate piles on the desk, an easel against the wall holding watercolor sketches, some boldly initialed, others left untouched, obviously unacceptable. The walls were filled with framed photographs of the Beautiful People, their beauty too often marred by gaping mouths and smiles as false as the one on the mask of the inhabitant of the office. There was a bitch quality in the perfumed air; these were the

[216]

quarters of an aging, pacing tigress, swift to attack any who threatened her possessions or the sating of her appetites. Yet she was disciplined; all things considered, an estimable liaison to Carlos.

Who was that man on the switchboard? Where had he seen him?

He was offered a drink from a selection of bottles; he chose brandy.

"Do sit down, monsieur. I shall enlist the help of René himself, if I can find him."

"That's very kind, but I'm sure whatever you choose will be satisfactory. I have an instinct about taste; yours is all through this office. I'm comfortable with it."

"You're too generous."

"Only when it's warranted," said Jason, still standing. "Actually, I'd like to look around at the photographs. I see a number of acquaintances, if not friends. A lot of these faces pass through the Bahamian banks with considerable frequency."

"I'm sure they do," agreed Lavier, in a tone that bespoke regard for such avenues of finance. "I shan't be long, monsieur."

Nor would she, thought Bourne, as Les Classiques' partner swept out of the office. Mme. Lavier was not about to allow a tired, wealthy mark too much time to think. She would return with the most expensive designs she could gather up as rapidly as possible. Therefore, if there was anything in the room that could shed light on Carlos' intermediary—or on the assassin's operation—it had to be found quickly. And, if it was there, it would be on or around the desk.

Jason circled behind the imperial chair in front of the wall, feigning amused interest in the photographs, but concentrating on the desk. There were invoices, receipts, and overdue bills, along with dunning letters of reprimand awaiting Lavier's signature. An address book lay open, four names on the page; he moved closer to see more clearly. Each was the name of a company, the individual contacts bracketed, his or her positions underlined. He wondered if he should memorize each company, each contact. He was about to do so when his eyes fell on the edge of an index card. It was only the edge; the rest was concealed under the telephone itself. And there was something else—dull, barely discernible. A strip of transparent tape, running along the edge of the card, holding it in place. The tape itself was relatively new, recently stuck over the heavy paper and the gleaming wood; it was clean, no smudges or coiled borders or signs of having been there very long.

Instinct.

Bourne picked up the telephone to move it aside. It rang, the bell vibrating through his hand, the shrill sound unnerving. He replaced it on the desk and stepped away as a man in shirtsleeves rushed through the open door from the corridor. He stopped, staring at Bourne, his eyes alarmed but noncommittal. The telephone rang a second time; the man walked rapidly to the desk and picked up the receiver.

"*Allô?*" There was silence as the intruder listened, head down, concentration on the caller. He was a tanned, muscular man of indeterminate age, the sun-drenched skin disguising the years. His face was taut, his lips thin, his close-cropped hair thick, dark brown, and disciplined. The sinews of his bare arms moved under the flesh as he transferred the phone from one hand to the other, speaking harshly. "*Pas ici. Sais pas. Téléphonez plus tard . . .*" He hung up and looked at Jason. "*Où est Jacqueline?*"

"A little slower, please," said Bourne, lying in English. "My French is limited."

"Sorry," replied the bronzed man. "I was looking for Madame Lavier."

"The owner?"

"The title will suffice. Where is she?"

"Depleting my funds." Jason smiled, raising his glass to his lips.

"Oh? And who are you, monsieur?"

"Who are *you?*"

The man studied Bourne. "René Bergeron."

"Oh, Lord!" exclaimed Jason. "She's looking for *you.* You're very *good,* Mr. Bergeron. She said I was to look upon your designs as the work of an emerging master." Bourne smiled again. "You're the reason I may have to wire the Bahamas for a great deal of money."

"You're most kind, monsieur. And I apologize for barging in."

"Better that you answered that phone than me. Berlitz considers me a failure."

"Buyers, suppliers, all screaming idiots. To whom, monsieur, do I have the honor of speaking?"

"Briggs," said Jason, having no idea where the name

came from, astonished that it came so quickly, so naturally. "Charles Briggs."

"A pleasure to know you." Bergeron extended his hand; the grip was firm. "You say Jacqueline was looking for me?"

"On my behalf, I'm afraid."

"I shall find her." The designer left quickly.

Bourne stepped to the desk, his eyes on the door, his hand on the telephone. He moved it to the side, exposing the index card. There were two telephone numbers, the first recognizable as a Zurich exchange, the second obviously Paris.

Instinct. He had been right, a strip of transparent tape the only sign he had needed. He stared at the numbers, memorizing them, then moved the telephone back in place and stepped away.

He had barely managed to clear the desk when Madame Lavier swept back into the room, a half dozen dresses over her arm. "I met René on the steps. He approves of my selections most enthusiastically. He also tells me your name is Briggs, monsieur."

"I would have told you myself," said Bourne, smiling back, countering the pout in Lavier's voice. "But I don't think you asked."

"'Spoors in the forest,' monsieur. Here, I bring you a feast!" She separated the dresses, placing them carefully over several chairs. "I truly believe these are among the finest creations René has brought us."

"Brought you? He doesn't work here then?"

"A figure of speech; his studio's at the end of the corridor, but it is a holy sacristy. Even I tremble when I enter."

"They're magnificent," continued Bourne, going from one to another. "But I don't want to overwhelm her, just pacify her," he added, pointing out three garments. "I'll take these."

"A fine selection, Monsieur Briggs!"

"Box them with the others, if you will."

"Of course. She is, indeed, a fortunate lady."

"A good companion, but a child. A spoiled child, I'm afraid. However, I've been away a lot and haven't paid much attention to her, so I guess I should make peace. It's one reason I sent her to Cap-Ferrat." He smiled, taking out his Louis Vuitton billfold. "*La facture, si'il vous plaît?*"

"I'll have one of the girls expedite everything." Madame

Lavier pressed a button on the intercom next to the telephone. Jason watched closely, prepared to comment on the call Bergeron had answered in the event the woman's eyes settled on a slightly out-of-place phone. "*Faites venir Janine—avec les robes. La facture aussi.*" She stood up. "Another brandy, Monsieur Briggs?"

"*Merci bien.*" Bourne extended his glass; she took it and walked to the bar. Jason knew the time had not yet arrived for what he had in mind; it would come soon—as soon as he parted with money—but not now. He could, however, continue building a foundation with the managing partner of Les Classiques. "That fellow Bergeron," he said. "You say he's under exclusive contract to you?"

Madame Lavier turned, the glass in her hand. "Oh, yes. We are a closely knit family here."

Bourne accepted the brandy, nodded his thanks, and sat down in an armchair in front of the desk. "That's a constructive arrangement," he said pointlessly.

The tall, gaunt clerk he had first spoken with came into the office, a salesbook in her hand. Instructions were given rapidly, figures entered, the garments gathered and separated as the salesbook exchanged hands. Lavier held it out for Jason's perusal. "*Voici la facture, monsieur,*" she said.

Bourne shook his head, dismissing inspection. "*Combien?*" he asked.

"*Vingt-mille, soixante francs, monsieur,*" answered the Les Classiques partner, watching his reaction with the expression of a very large, wary bird.

There was none. Jason merely removed five five-thousand-franc notes and handed them to her. She nodded and gave them in turn to the slender salesclerk, who walked cadaverously out of the office with the dresses.

"Everything will be packaged and brought up here with your change." Lavier went to her desk and sat down. "You're on your way to Ferrat, then. It should be lovely."

He had paid; the time had come. "A last night in Paris before I go back to kindergarten," said Jason, raising his glass in a toast of self-mockery.

"Yes, you mentioned that your friend is quite young."

"A child is what I said, and that's what she is. She's a good companion, but I think I prefer the company of more mature women."

"You must be very fond of her," contested Lavier, touching her perfectly coiffed hair, the flattery accepted.

"You buy her such lovely—and, frankly—very expensive things."

"A minor price considering what she might try to opt for."

"Really."

"She's my wife, my third to be exact, and there are appearances to be kept up in the Bahamas. But all that's neither here nor there; my life's quite in order."

"I'm sure it is, monsieur."

"Speaking of the Bahamas, a thought occurred to me a few minutes ago. It's why I asked you about Bergeron."

"What is that?"

"You may think I'm impetuous; I assure you I'm not. But when something strikes me, I like to explore it. Since Bergeron's yours exclusively, have you ever given any thought to opening a branch in the islands?"

"The Bahamas?"

"And points south. Into the Caribbean, perhaps."

"Monsieur, Saint-Honoré by itself is often more than we can handle. Untended farmland generally goes fallow, as they say."

"It wouldn't have to be tended; not in the way that you think. A concession here, one there, the designs exclusive, local ownership on a percentage-franchise basis. Just a boutique or two, spreading, of course, cautiously."

"That takes considerable capital, Monsieur Briggs."

"Key prices, initially. What you might call entrance fees. They're high but not prohibitive. In the finer hotels and clubs it usually depends on how well you know the managements."

"And you know them?"

"Extremely well. As I say, I'm just exploring, but I think the idea has merit. Your labels would have a certain distinction—Les Classiques, Paris, Grand Bahama . . . Caneel Bay, perhaps." Bourne swallowed the rest of his brandy. "But you probably think I'm crazy. Consider it just talk. . . . Although I've made a dollar or two on risks that simply struck me on the spur of the moment."

"Risks?" Jacqueline Lavier touched her hair again.

"I don't give ideas away, madame. I generally back them."

"Yes, I understand. As you say, the idea does have merit."

"I think so. Of course, I'd like to see what kind of agreement you have with Bergeron."

"It could be produced, monsieur."

"Tell you what," said Jason. "If you're free, let's talk about it over drinks and dinner. It's my only night in Paris."

"And you prefer the company of more mature women," concluded Jacqueline Lavier, the mask cracked into a smile again, the white ice breaking beneath eyes now more in concert.

"*C'est vrai, madame.*"

"It can be arranged," she said, reaching for the phone. The phone. Carlos.

He would break her, thought Bourne. *Kill her if he had to. He would learn the truth.*

Marie walked through the crowd toward the booth in the telephone complex on rue Vaugirard. She had taken a room at the Meurice, left the attaché case at the front desk, and had sat alone in the room for exactly twenty-two minutes. Until she could not stand it any longer. She had sat in a chair facing a blank wall, thinking about Jason, about the madness of the last eight days that had propelled her into an insanity beyond her understanding. Jason. Considerate, frightening, bewildered Jason Bourne. A man with so much violence in him, and yet oddly, so much compassion. And too terribly capable in dealing with a world ordinary men knew nothing about. Where had he sprung from, this love of hers? Who had taught him to find his way through the dark back streets of Paris, Marseilles, and Zurich . . . as far away as the Orient, perhaps? What was the Far East to him? How did he know the languages? What *were* the languages? Or language?

Tao.

Che-sah.

Tam Quan.

Another world, and she knew nothing of it. But she knew Jason Bourne, or the man called Jason Bourne, and she held on to the decency she knew was there. Oh, God, how she loved him so!

Ilich Ramirez Sanchez. Carlos. What was he to Jason Bourne?

Stop it! she had screamed at herself while in that room

alone. And then she had done what she had seen Jason do so many times: she had lunged up from the chair, as if the physical movement would clear the mists away—or allow her to break through them.

Canada. She had to reach Ottawa and find out why Peter's death—his murder—was being handled so secretly, so obscenely. It did not make sense; she objected with all her heart. For Peter, too, was a decent man, and he had been killed by indecent men. She would be told why or she would expose that death—that murder—herself. She would scream out loud to the world that she knew, and say, "Do something!"

And so she had left the Meurice, taken a cab to the rue Vaugirard, and placed the call to Ottawa. She waited now outside the booth, her anger mounting, an unlit cigarette creased between her fingers. When the bell rang, she could not take the time to crush it out.

It rang. She opened the glass door of the booth and went inside.

"Is this you, Alan?"

"Yes," was the curt reply.

"Alan, what the hell is going on? Peter was *murdered*, and there hasn't been a single word in any newspaper or on any broadcast! I don't think the embassy even knows! It's as though no one cared! What are you people *doing?*"

"What we're told to do. And so will you."

"What? That was *Peter!* He was your friend! Listen to me, Alan . . ."

"No!" The interruption was harsh. "*You* listen. Get out of Paris. Now! Take the next direct flight back here. If you have any problems, the embassy will clear them—but you're to talk only to the ambassador, is that understood?"

"No!" screamed Marie St. Jacques. "I don't understand! Peter was killed and nobody cares! All you're saying is bureaucratic bullshit! Don't get involved; for God's sake, don't *ever* get involved!"

"Stay out of it, Marie!"

"Stay out of *what?* That's what you're not telling me, isn't it? Well, you'd better . . ."

"I can't!" Alan lowered his voice. "I don't know. I'm only telling you what I was told to tell you."

"By whom?"

"You can't ask me that."

"I *am* asking!"

"Listen to me, Marie. I haven't been home for the past twenty-four hours. I've been waiting here for the last twelve for you to call. Try to understand me—I'm not *suggesting* you come back. Those are orders from your government."

"*Orders?* Without explanations?"

"That's the way it is. I'll say this much. They want you out of there; they want him isolated. . . . That's the way it is."

"Sorry, Alan—that's *not* the way it is. Goodbye." She slammed the receiver down, then instantly gripped her hands to stop the trembling. *Oh, my God, she loved him so . . . and they were trying to kill him. Jason, my Jason. They all want you killed. Why?*

The conservatively dressed man at the switchboard snapped the red toggle that blocked the lines, reducing all incoming calls to a busy signal. He did so once or twice an hour, if only to clear his mind and expunge the empty insanities he had been required to mouth during the past minutes. The necessity to cut off all conversation usually occurred to him after a particularly tedious one; he had just had it. The wife of a Deputy trying to conceal the outrageous price of a single purchase by breaking it up into several, thus not to be so apparent to her husband. Enough! He needed a few minutes to breathe.

The irony struck him. It was not that many years ago when others sat in front of switchboards for *him*. At his companies in Saigon and in the communications room of his vast plantation in the Mekong Delta. And here he was now in front of someone else's switchboard in the perfumed surroundings of Saint-Honoré. The English poet said it best: There were more preposterous vicissitudes in life than a single philosophy could conjure.

He heard laughter on the staircase and looked up. Jacqueline was leaving early, no doubt with one of her celebrated and fully bankrolled acquaintances. There was no question about it, Jacqueline had a talent for removing gold from a well-guarded mine, even diamonds from De Beers. He could not see the man with her; he was on the other side of Jacqueline, his head oddly turned away.

Then for an instant he did see him; their eyes made contact; it was brief and explosive. The gray-haired switchboard operator suddenly could not breathe; he was suspended in a moment of disbelief, staring at a face, a head, he had not seen in years. And then almost always in darkness, for they had worked at night . . . died at night.

Oh, my God—it was *him!* From the living—dying—nightmares thousands of miles away. It *was him!*

The gray-haired man rose from the switchboard as if in a trance. He pulled the mouthpiece-earphone off and let it drop to the floor. It clattered as the board lit up with incoming calls that made no connections, answered only with discordant hums. He stepped off the platform and sidestepped his way quickly toward the aisle to get a better look at Jacqueline Lavier and the ghost that was her escort. The ghost who was a killer—above all men he had ever known, a *killer.* They said it might happen but he had never believed them; he believed them now. It *was* the *man.*

He saw them both clearly. Saw *him.* They were walking down the center aisle toward the entrance. He had to stop them. Stop *her!* But to rush out and yell would mean death. A bullet in the head, instantaneous.

They reached the doors; *he* pulled them open, ushering her out to the pavement. The gray-haired man raced out from his hiding place, across the intersecting aisle and down to the front window. Out in the street *he* had flagged a taxi. He was opening the door, motioning for Jacqueline to get inside. Oh, God! She was going!

The middle-aged man turned and ran as fast as he could toward the staircase. He collided with two startled customers and a salesclerk, pushing all three violently out of his way. He raced up the steps, across the balcony and down the corridor, to the open studio door.

"René! René!" he shouted, bursting inside.

Bergeron looked up from his sketchboard, astonished. "What is it?"

"That man with Jacqueline! Who is he? How long has he been here?"

"Oh? Probably the American," said the designer. "His name's Briggs. A fatted calf; he's done very well by our grosses today."

"Where did they go?"

"I didn't know they went anywhere."

"She left with him!"

"Our Jacqueline retains her touch, no? And her good sense."

"Find them! Get her!"

"Why?"

"He *knows!* He'll kill her!"

"What?"

"It's him! I'd swear to it! That man is Cain!"

—— 15 ——

"The man is Cain," said Colonel Jack Manning bluntly, as
if he expected to be contradicted by at least three of the
four civilians at the Pentagon conference table. Each was
older than he, and each considered himself more experienced. None was prepared to acknowledge that the army
had obtained information where his own organization had
failed. There was a fourth civilian but his opinion did not
count. He was a member of the Congressional Oversight
Committee, and as such to be treated with deference, but
not seriously. "If we don't move *now*," continued Manning,
"even at the risk of exposing everything we've learned, he
could slip through the nets again. As of eleven days ago, he
was in Zurich. We're convinced he's still there. And, gentlemen, it *is* Cain."

"That's quite a statement," said the balding, birdlike aca-
demic from the National Security Council as he read the
summary page concerning Zurich given to each delegate at
the table. His name was Alfred Gillette, an expert in personnel screening and evaluation, and was considered by the
Pentagon to be bright, vindictive, and with friends in high
places.

"I find it extraordinary," added Peter Knowlton, an associate director of the Central Intelligence Agency, a man in his middle fifties who perpetuated the dress, the appearance, and the attitude of an Ivy Leaguer of thirty years ago. "Our sources have Cain in Brussels, *not* Zurich, at the same time—eleven days ago. Our sources are rarely in error."

"*That's* quite a statement," said the third civilian, the only one at that table Manning really respected. He was the oldest there, a man named David Abbott, a former Olympic swimmer whose intellect had matched his physical prowess. He was in his late sixties now, but his bearing was still erect, his mind as sharp as it had ever been, his age, however, betrayed by a face lined from the tensions of a lifetime he would never reveal. He knew what he was talking about, thought the colonel. Although he was currently a member of the omnipotent Forty Committee, he had been with the CIA since its origins in the OSS. The Silent Monk of Covert Operations had been the sobriquet given him by his colleagues in the intelligence community. "In my days at the Agency," continued Abbott, chuckling, "the sources were often as not in conflict as in agreement."

"We have different methods of verification," pressed the associate director. "No disrespect, Mr. Abbott, but our transmissions equipment is literally instantaneous."

"That's equipment, not verification. But I won't argue; it seems we have a disagreement. Brussels or Zurich."

"The case for Brussels is airtight," insisted Knowlton firmly.

"Let's hear it," said the balding Gillette, adjusting his glasses. "We can return to the Zurich summary; it's right in front of us. Also, *our* sources have some input to offer, although it's not in conflict with Brussels or Zurich. It happened some six months ago."

The silver-haired Abbott glanced over at Gillette. "Six months ago? I don't recall NSC having delivered anything about Cain six months ago."

"It wasn't totally confirmed," replied Gillette. "We try not to burden the committee with unsubstantiated data."

"That's also quite a statement," said Abbott, not needing to clarify.

"Congressman Walters," interrupted the colonel, looking at the man from Oversight, "do you have any questions before we go on?"

"Hell, yes," drawled the congressional watchdog from the state of Tennessee, his intelligent eyes roaming the faces, "but since I'm new at this, you go ahead so I'll know where to begin."

"Very well, sir," said Manning, nodding at the CIA's Knowlton. "What's this about Brussels eleven days ago?"

"A man was killed in the Place Fontainas—a covert dealer in diamonds between Moscow and the West. He operated through a branch of Russolmaz, the Soviet firm in Geneva that brokers all such purchases. We know it's one way Cain converts his funds."

"What ties the killing to Cain?" asked the dubious Gillette.

"Method, first. The weapon was a long needle, implanted in a crowded square at noontime with surgical precision. Cain's used it before."

"That's quite true," agreed Abbott. "There was a Rumanian in London somewhat over a year ago; another only weeks before him. Both were narrowed to Cain."

"Narrowed but not confirmed," objected Colonel Manning. "They were high-level political defectors; they could have been taken by the KGB."

"Or by Cain with far less risk to the Soviets," argued the CIA man.

"*Or* by Carlos," added Gillette, his voice rising. "Neither Carlos nor Cain is concerned about ideology; they're both for hire. Why is it every time there's a killing of consequence, we ascribe it to Cain?"

"Whenever we do," replied Knowlton, his condescension obvious, "it's because informed sources unknown to each other have reported the same information. Since the informants have no knowledge of each other, there could hardly be collusion."

"It's all too pat," said Gillette disagreeably.

"Back to Brussels," interrupted the colonel. "If it was Cain, why would he kill a broker from Russolmaz? He used him."

"A covert broker," corrected the CIA director. "And for any number of reasons, according to our informants. The man was a thief, and why not? Most of his clients were too; they couldn't very well file charges. He might have cheated Cain, and if he did, it'd be his last transaction. Or he could have been foolish enough to speculate on Cain's identity; even a hint of that would call for the needle. Or perhaps

Cain simply wanted to bury his current traces. Regardless, the circumstances plus the sources leave little doubt that it was Cain."

"There'll be a lot more when I clarify Zurich," said Manning. "May we proceed to the summary?"

"A moment, please." David Abbott spoke casually while lighting his pipe. "I believe our colleague from the Security Council mentioned the occurrence related to Cain that took place six months ago. Perhaps we should hear about it."

"Why?" asked Gillette, his eyes owl-like beyond the lenses of his rimless glasses. "The time factor removes it from having any bearing on Brussels or Zurich. I mentioned that, too."

"Yes, you did," agreed the once-formidable Monk of Covert Services. "I thought, however, any background might be helpful. As you also said, we can return to the summary; it's right in front of us. But if it's not relevant, let's get on with Zurich."

"Thank you, Mr. Abbott," said the colonel. "You'll note that eleven days ago, four men were killed in Zurich. One of them was a watchman in a parking area by the Limmat River; it can be presumed that he was not involved in Cain's activities, but caught in them. Two others were found in an alley on the west bank of the city, on the surface unrelated murders, except for the fourth victim. He's tied in with the dead men in the alley—all three part of the Zurich-Munich underworld—and is, without question, connected to Cain."

"That's Chernak," said Gillette, reading the summary. "At least I assume it's Chernak. I recognize the name and associate it with the Cain file somewhere."

"You should," replied Manning. "It first appeared in a G-Two report eighteen months ago and cropped up again a year later."

"Which would make it six months ago," interjected Abbott, softly, looking at Gillette.

"Yes, sir," continued the colonel. "If there was ever an example of what's called the scum-of-the-earth, it was Chernak. During the war he was a Czechoslovakian recruit at Dachau, a trilingual interrogator as brutal as any guard in the camp. He sent Poles, Slovaks and Jews to the showers after torture sessions in which he extracted—and manufactured—'incriminating' information Dachau's commandants wanted to hear. He went to any length to curry favor with his superiors, and the most sadistic cliques were hard pressed to match his exploits. What they didn't realize was that *he* was cataloguing *theirs*. After the war he escaped, got his legs blown off by an undetected land mine, and still managed to survive very nicely on his Dachau extortions. Cain found him and used him as a go-between for payments on his kills."

"Now just wait a minute!" objected Knowlton strenuously. "We've been over this Chernak business before. If you recall, it was the Agency that first uncovered him; we would have exposed him long ago if State hadn't interceded on behalf of several powerful anti-Soviet officials in the Bonn government. You assume Cain's used Chernak; you don't know it for certain any more than we do."

"We do now," said Manning. "Seven and a half months ago we received a tip about a man who ran a restaurant called the Drei Alpenhäuser; it was reported that he was an intermediary between Cain and Chernak. We kept him under surveillance for weeks, but nothing came of it; he was a minor figure in the Zurich underworld, that was all. We didn't stay with him long enough." The colonel paused, satisfied that all eyes were on him. "When we heard about Chernak's murder, we gambled. Five nights ago two of our men hid in the Drei Alpenhäuser after the restaurant closed. They cornered the owner and accused him of dealing with Chernak, working for Cain; they put on a hell of a show. You can imagine their shock when the man broke, literally fell to his knees begging to be protected. He admitted that Cain was in Zurich the night Chernak was killed; that, in fact, he had seen Cain that night and Chernak had come up in the conversation. Very negatively."

The military man paused again, the silence filled by a slow soft whistle from David Abbott, his pipe held in front of his crag-lined face. "Now, that *is* a statement," said the Monk quietly.

"Why wasn't the Agency informed of this tip you received seven months ago?" asked the CIA's Knowlton abrasively.

"It didn't prove out."

"In your hands; it might have been different in ours."

"That's possible. I admitted we didn't stay with him long enough. Manpower's limited; which of us can keep up a nonproductive surveillance indefinitely?"

"We might have shared it if we'd known."

"And we could have saved you the time it took to build the Brussels file, if we'd been told about that."

"Where did the tip come from?" asked Gillette, interrupting impatiently, his eyes on Manning.

"It was anonymous."

"You settled for that?" The birdlike expression on Gillette's face conveyed his astonishment.

"It's one reason the initial surveillance was limited."

"Yes, of course, but you mean you never dug for it?"

"Naturally we did," replied the colonel testily.

"Apparently without much enthusiasm," continued Gillette angrily. "Didn't it occur to you that someone over at Langley, or on the Council, might have helped, might have filled in a gap? I agree with Peter. We should have been informed."

"There's a reason why you weren't." Manning breathed deeply; in less military surroundings it might have been construed as a sigh. "The informant made it clear that if we brought in any other branch, he wouldn't make contact again. We felt we had to abide by that; we've done it before."

"What did you say?" Knowlton put down the page summary and stared at the Pentagon officer.

"It's nothing new, Peter. Each of us sets up his own sources, protects them."

"I'm aware of that. It's why you weren't told about Brussels. Both drones said to keep the army out."

Silence. Broken by the abrasive voice of the Security Council's Alfred Gillette. "How often is 'we've done it before,' Colonel?"

"What?" Manning looked at Gillette, but was aware that David Abbott was watching both of them closely.

"I'd like to know how many times you've been told to keep your sources to yourself. I refer to Cain, of course."

"Quite a few, I guess."

"You guess?"

"Most of the time."

"And you, Peter? What about the Agency?"

"We've been severely limited in terms of in-depth dissemination."

"For God's sake, what's *that* mean?" The interruption came from the least expected member of the conference; the congressman from Oversight. "Don't misunderstand me, I haven't begun yet. I just want to follow the language." He turned to the CIA man. "What the hell did you just say? In-depth *what?*"

"Dissemination, Congressman Walters; it's throughout Cain's file. We risked losing informants if we brought them to the attention of other intelligence units. I assure you, it's standard."

"It sounds like you were test-tubing a heifer."

"With about the same results," added Gillette. "No cross-pollinization to corrupt the strain. And, conversely, no cross-checking to look for patterns of inaccuracy."

"A nice turn of phrases," said Abbott, his craggy face wrinkled in appreciation, "but I'm not sure I understand you."

"I'd say it's pretty damned clear," replied the man from NSC, looking at Colonel Manning and Peter Knowlton. "The country's two most active intelligence branches have been fed information about Cain—for the past *three years*—and there's been no cross-pooling for origins of fraud. We've simply received all information as bona fide data, stored and accepted as valid."

"Well, I've been around a long time—perhaps too long, I concede—but there's nothing here I haven't heard before," said the Monk. "Sources are shrewd and defensive people; they guard their contacts jealously. None are in the business for charity, only for profit and survival."

"I'm afraid you're overlooking my point." Gillette removed his glasses. "I said before that I was alarmed so many recent assassinations have been attributed to Cain— attributed *here* to Cain—when it seems to me that the most accomplished assassin of our time—perhaps in history— has been relegated to a comparatively minor role. I think that's wrong. I think Carlos is the man we should be concentrating on. What's happened to *Carlos?*"

"I question your judgment, Alfred," said the Monk. "Carlos' time has passed, Cain's moved in. The old order changes; there's a new and, I suspect, far more deadly shark in the waters."

"I can't agree with that," said the man from National Security, his owl-eyes boring into the elder statesman of the intelligence community. "Forgive me, David, but it strikes me as if Carlos himself were manipulating this committee. To take the attention away from himself, making us concentrate on a subject of much less importance. We're spending all our energies going after a toothless sand shark while the hammerhead roams free."

"No one's forgetting Carlos," objected Manning. "He's simply not as active as Cain's been."

"Perhaps," said Gillette icily, "that's exactly what Carlos wants us to believe. And, by God, we believe it."

"Can you doubt it?" asked Abbott. "The record of Cain's accomplishments is staggering."

"Can I doubt it?" repeated Gillette. "That's the question, isn't it? But can any of us be sure? That's also a valid question. We now find out that both the Pentagon and the Central Intelligence Agency have been literally operating independently of each other, without even conferring as to the accuracy of their sources."

"A custom rarely breached in this town," said Abbott, amused.

Again the congressman from Oversight interrupted. "What are you trying to say, Mr. Gillette?"

"I'd like more information about the activities of one Ilich Ramirez Sanchez. That's—"

"Carlos," said the congressman. "I remember my reading. I see. Thank you. Go on, gentlemen."

Manning spoke quickly. "May we get back to Zurich, please. Our recommendation is to go after Cain now. We can spread the word in the *Verbrecherwelt*, pull in every informer we have, request the cooperation of the Zurich police. We can't afford to lose another day. The man in Zurich *is* Cain."

"Then what was Brussels?" The CIA's Knowlton asked the question as much of himself as anyone at the table. "The method was Cain's, the informants unequivocal. What was the purpose?"

"To feed you false information, obviously," said Gillette. "And before we make any dramatic moves in Zurich, I suggest that each of you comb the Cain files and recheck every source given you. Have your European stations pull in every informant who so miraculously appeared to offer information. I have an idea you might find something you didn't expect: the fine Latin hand of Ramirez Sanchez."

"Since you're so insistent on clarification, Alfred," interrupted Abbott, "why not tell us about the unconfirmed occurrence that took place six months ago. We seem to be in a quagmire here; it might be helpful."

For the first time during the conference, the abrasive

delegate from the National Security Council seemed to hesitate. "We received word around the middle of August from a reliable source in Aix-en-Provence that Cain was on his way to Marseilles."

"August?" exclaimed the colonel. "Marseilles? That was Leland! Ambassador Leland was shot in Marseilles. In August!"

"But Cain didn't fire that rifle. It was a Carlos kill; that *was* confirmed. Bore-markings matched with previous assassinations, three descriptions of an unknown dark-haired man on the third and fourth floors of the waterfront warehouse, carrying a satchel. There was never any doubt that Leland was murdered by Carlos."

"For Christ's sake," roared the officer. "That's after the fact, after the kill! No matter whose, there was a contract out on Leland—hadn't that occurred to you? If we'd known about Cain, we might have been able to cover Leland. He was military property! Goddamn it, he might be alive today!"

"Unlikely," replied Gillette calmly. "Leland wasn't the sort of man to live in a bunker. And given his life-style, a vague warning would have served no purpose. Besides, had our strategy held together, warning Leland would have been counterproductive."

"In what way?" asked the Monk harshly.

"It's your fuller explanation. Our source was to make contact with Cain during the hours of midnight and three in the morning in the rue Sarrasin on August 23. Leland wasn't due until the twenty-fifth. As I say, had it held together we would have taken Cain. It didn't; Cain never showed up."

"And your *source* insisted on cooperating solely with *you*," said Abbott. "To the exclusion of all others."

"Yes," nodded Gillette, trying but unable to conceal his embarrassment. "In our judgment, the risk to Leland had been eliminated—which in terms of Cain turned out to be the truth—and the odds for capture greater than they'd ever been. We'd finally found someone willing to come out and identify Cain. Would any of you have handled it any other way?"

Silence. This time broken by the drawl of the astute congressman from Tennessee.

"Jesus Christ Almighty . . . what a bunch of bullshitters."

Silence, terminated by the thoughtful voice of David Abbott.

"May I commend you, sir, on being the first honest man sent over from the Hill. The fact that you are not overwhelmed by the rarefied atmosphere of these highly classified surroundings is not lost on any of us. It's refreshing."

"I don't think the congressman fully grasps the sensitivity of—"

"Oh, shut up, Peter," said the Monk. "I think the congressman wants to say something."

"Just for a bit," said Walters. "I thought you were all over twenty-one; I mean, you *look* over twenty-one, and by then you're supposed to know better. You're supposed to be able to hold intelligent conversations, exchange information while respecting confidentiality, and look for common solutions. Instead, you sound like a bunch of kids jumping on a goddamn carousel, squabbling over who's going to get the cheap brass ring. It's a hell of a way to spend taxpayers' money."

"You're oversimplifying, Congressman," broke in Gillette. "You're talking about a utopian fact-finding apparatus. There's no such thing."

"I'm talking about reasonable men, sir. I'm a lawyer, and before I came up to this godforsaken circus, I dealt with ascending levels of confidentiality every day of my life. What's so damn new about them?"

"And what's your point?" asked the Monk.

"I want an explanation. For over eighteen months I've sat on the House Assassination Subcommittee. I've plowed through thousands of pages, filled with hundreds of names and twice as many theories. I don't think there's a suggested conspiracy or a suspected assassin I'm not aware of. I've lived with those names and those theories for damn near two years, until I didn't think there was anything left to learn."

"I'd say your credentials were very impressive," interrupted Abbott.

"I thought they might be; it's why I accepted the Oversight chair. I thought I could make a realistic contribution, but now I'm not so sure. I'm suddenly beginning to wonder what I *do* know."

"Why?" asked Manning apprehensively.

"Because I've been sitting here listening to the four of you describe an operation that's been going on for three years, involving networks of personnel and informants and major intelligence posts throughout Europe—all centered on an assassin whose 'list of accomplishments' is staggering. Am I substantively correct?"

"Go on," replied Abbott quietly, holding his pipe, his expression rapt. "What's your question?"

"Who is he? Who the hell is this Cain?"

—— 16 ——

The silence lasted precisely five seconds, during which time eyes roamed other eyes, several throats were cleared, and no one moved in his chair. It was as if a decision were being reached without discussion: evasion was to be avoided. Congressman Efrem Walters, out of the hills of Tennessee by way of the Yale Law Review, was not to be dismissed with facile circumlocution that dealt with the esoterica of clandestine manipulations. Bullshit was out.

David Abbott put his pipe down on the table, the quiet clatter his overture. "The less public exposure a man like Cain receives the better it is for everyone."

"That's no answer," said Walters. "But I assume it's the beginning of one."

"It is. He's a professional assassin—that is, a trained expert in wide-ranging methods of taking life. That expertise is for sale, neither politics nor personal motivation any concern to him whatsoever. He's in business solely to make a profit—and his profits escalate in direct ratio to his reputation."

The congressman nodded. "So by keeping as tight a lid

as you can on that reputation you're holding back free advertising."

"Exactly. There are a lot of maniacs in this world with too many real or imagined enemies who might easily gravitate to Cain if they knew of him. Unfortunately, more than we care to think about already have; to date thirty-eight killings can be directly attributed to Cain, and some twelve to fifteen are probables."

"That's his list of 'accomplishments'?"

"Yes. And we're losing the battle. With each new killing his reputation spreads."

"He was dormant for a while," said Knowlton of the CIA. "For a number of months recently we thought he might have been taken himself. There were several probables in which the killers themselves were eliminated; we thought he might have been one of them."

"Such as?" asked Walters.

"A banker in Madrid who funneled bribes for the Europolitan Corporation for government purchases in Africa. He was shot from a speeding car on the Paseo de la Castellana. A chauffeur-bodyguard gunned down both driver and killer; for a time we believed the killer was Cain."

"I remember the incident. Who might have paid for it?"

"Any number of companies," answered Gillette, "who wanted to sell gold-plated cars and indoor plumbing to instant dictators."

"What else? Who else?"

"Sheik Mustafa Kalig in Oman," said Colonel Manning. "He was reported killed in an abortive coup."

"Not so," continued the officer. "There was no attempted coup; G-Two informants confirmed that. Kalig was unpopular, but the other sheiks aren't fools. The coup story was a cover for an assassination that could tempt other professional killers. Three troublesome nonentities from the Officer Corps were executed to lend credence to the lie. For a while, we thought one of them was Cain; the timing corresponds to Cain's dormancy."

"Who would pay Cain for assassinating Kalig?"

"We asked ourselves that over and over again," said Manning. "The only possible answer came from a source who claimed to know, but there was no way to verify it. He said Cain did it to prove it could be done. By him. Oil sheiks travel with the tightest security in the world."

"There are several dozen other incidents," added Knowlton. "Probables that fall into the same pattern where highly protected figures were killed, and sources came forward to implicate Cain."

"I see." The congressman picked up the summary page for Zurich. "But from what I gather you don't know who he is."

"No two descriptions have been alike," interjected Abbott. "Cain's apparently a virtuoso at disguise."

"Yet people have seen him, talked to him. Your sources, the informants, this man in Zurich; none of them may come out in the open and testify, but surely you've interrogated them. You've got to have come up with a composite, with *something*."

"We've come up with a great deal," replied Abbott, "but a consistent description isn't part of it. For openers, Cain never lets himself be seen in daylight. He holds meetings at night, in dark rooms or alleyways. If he's ever met more than one person at a time—as Cain—we don't know about it. We've been told he never stands, he's always seated—in a dimly lit restaurant, or a corner chair, or parked car. Sometimes he wears heavy glasses, sometimes none at all; at one rendezvous he may have dark hair, on another white or red or covered by a hat."

"Language?"

"We're closer here," said the CIA director, anxious to put the Company's research on the table. "Fluent English and French, and several Oriental dialects."

"Dialects? What dialects? Doesn't a language come first?"

"Of course. It's root-Vietnamese."

"Viet—" Walters leaned forward. "Why do I get the idea that I'm coming to something you'd rather not tell me?"

"Because you're probably quite astute at cross-examination, counselor." Abbott struck a match and lit his pipe.

"Passably alert," agreed the congressman. "Now, what is it?"

"Cain," said Gillette, his eyes briefly, oddly, on David Abbott. "We know where he came from."

"Where?"

"Out of Southeast Asia," answered Manning, as if sustaining the pain of a knife wound. "As far as we can gather, he mastered the fringe dialects so to be understood in the hill country along the Cambodian and Laos border routes, as well as in rural North Vietnam. We accept the data; it fits."

"With what?"

"Operation Medusa." The colonel reached for a large, thick manila envelope on his left. He opened it and removed a single folder from among several inside; he placed it in front of him. "That's the Cain file," he said, nodding at the open envelope. "This is the Medusa material, the aspects of it that might in any way be relevant to Cain."

The Tennessean leaned back in his chair, the trace of a sardonic smile creasing his lips. "You know, gentlemen, you slay me with your pithy titles. Incidentally, that's a beaut; it's very sinister, very ominous. I think you fellows take a course in this kind of thing. Go on, Colonel. What's this Medusa?"

Manning glanced briefly at David Abbott, then spoke. "It was a clandestine outgrowth of the search-and-destroy concept, designed to function behind enemy lines during the Vietnam war. In the late sixties and early seventies, units of American, French, British, Australian and native volunteers were formed into teams to operate in territories occupied by the North Vietnamese. Their priorities were the disruption of enemy communications and supply lines, the pinpointing of prison camps and, not the least, the assassination of village leaders known to be cooperating with the Communists, as well as the enemy commanders whenever possible."

"It was a war-within-a-war," broke in Knowlton. "Unfortunately, racial appearances and languages made participation infinitely more dangerous than, say, the German and Dutch undergrounds, or the French Resistance in World War Two. Therefore, Occidental recruitment was not always as selective as it might have been."

"There were dozens of these teams," continued the colonel, "the personnel ranging from old-line navy chiefs who knew the coastlines to French plantation owners whose only hope for reparations lay in an American victory. There were British and Australian drifters who'd lived in Indochina for years, as well as highly motivated American army and civilian intelligence career officers. Also, inevitably, there was a sizable faction of hard-core criminals. In the main, smugglers—men who dealt in running guns, narcotics, gold and diamonds throughout the entire South China Sea area. They were walking encyclopedias when it came to night landings and jungle routes. Many we employed were runaways or fugitives from the States, a number well-educated, all resourceful. We needed their expertise."

"That's quite a cross-section of volunteers," interrupted the congressman. "Old-line navy and army; British and Australian drifters, French colonials, and platoons of thieves. How the hell did you get them to work together?"

"To each according to his greeds," said Gillette.

"Promises," amplified the colonel. "Guarantees of rank, promotions, pardons, outright bonuses of cash, and, in a number of cases, opportunities to steal funds from the operation itself. You see, they all had to be a little crazy; we understood that. We trained them secretly, using codes, methods of transport, entrapment and killing—even weapons Command Saigon knew nothing about. As Peter mentioned, the risks were incredible—capture resulting in torture and execution; the price was high and they paid it. Most people would have called them a collection of paranoiacs, but they were geniuses where disruption and assassination were concerned. Especially assassination."

"What was the price?"

"Operation Medusa sustained over ninety percent casualties. But there's a catch—among those who didn't come back were a number who never meant to."

"From that faction of thieves and fugitives?"

"Yes. Some stole considerable amounts of money from Medusa. We think Cain is one of those men."

"Why?"

"His *modus operandi*. He's used codes, traps, methods of killing and transport that were developed and specialized in the Medusa training."

"Then for Christ's sake," broke in Walters, "you've got a direct line to his identity. I don't care where they're buried—and I'm damn sure you don't want them made public—but I assume records were kept."

"They were, and we've extracted them all from the clandestine archives, inclusive of this material here." The officer tapped the file in front of him. "We've studied everything, put rosters under microscopes, fed facts into computers—everything we could think of. We're no further along than when we began."

"That's incredible," said the congressman. "Or incredibly incompetent."

"Not really," protested Manning. "Look at the man; look at what we've had to work with. After the war, Cain made his reputation throughout most of East Asia, from as far north as Tokyo down through the Philippines, Malaysia and Singapore, with side trips to Hong Kong, Cambodia, Laos and Calcutta. About two and a half years ago reports began filtering in to our Asian stations and embassies. There was an assassin for hire; his name was Cain. Highly professional, ruthless. These reports started growing with alarming frequency. It seemed that with every killing of note, Cain was involved. Sources would phone embassies in the middle of the night, or stop attachés in the streets, always with the same information. It was Cain, Cain was the one. A murder in Tokyo; a car blown up in Hong Kong; a narcotics caravan ambushed in the Triangle; a banker shot in Calcutta; an ambassador assassinated in Moulmein; a Russian technician or an American businessman killed in the streets of Shanghai itself. Cain was everywhere, his name whispered by dozens of trusted informants in every vital intelligence sector. Yet no one—not one single person in the entire east Pacific area—would come forward to give us an identification. Where were we to begin?"

"But by this time hadn't you established the fact that he'd been with Medusa?" asked the Tennessean.

"Yes. Firmly."

"Then with the individual Medusa dossiers, damn it!"

The colonel opened the folder he had removed from the Cain file. "These are the casualty lists. Among the white Occidentals who disappeared from Operation Medusa—and when I say disappeared, I mean vanished without a trace—are the following. Seventy-three Americans, forty-six French, thirty-nine and twenty-four Australians and British respectively, and an estimated fifty white male contacts recruited from neutrals in Hanoi and trained in the field—most of *them* we never knew. Over two hundred and thirty possibilities; how many are blind alleys? Who's alive? Who's dead? Even if we learned the name of every man who actually survived, who is he now? What is he? We're not even sure of Cain's nationality. We think he's American, but there's no proof."

"Cain's one of the side issues contained in our constant pressure on Hanoi to trace MIAs," explained Knowlton. "We keep recycling these names in with the division lists."

"And there's a catch with that, too," added the army

officer. "Hanoi's counterintelligence forces broke and executed scores of Medusa personnel. They were aware of the operation, and we never ruled out the possibility of infiltration. Hanoi knew the Medusans weren't combat troops; they wore no uniforms. Accountability was never required."

Walters held out his hand. "May I?" he said, nodding at the stapled pages.

"Certainly." The officer gave them to the congressman. "You understand of course that those names still remain classified, as does the Medusa Operation itself."

"Who made that decision?"

"It's an unbroken executive order from successive presidents based on the recommendation of the Joint Chiefs of Staff. It was supported by the Senate Armed Services Committee."

"That's considerable firepower, isn't it?"

"It was felt to be in the national interest," said the CIA man.

"In this case, I won't argue," agreed Walters. "The specter of such an operation wouldn't do much for the glory of Old Glory. We don't train assassins, much less field them." He flipped through the pages. "And somewhere here just happens to be an assassin we trained and fielded and now can't find."

"We believe that, yes," said the colonel.

"You say he made his reputation in Asia, but moved to Europe. When?"

"About a year ago."

"Why? Any ideas?"

"The obvious, I'd suggest," said Peter Knowlton. "He overextended himself. Something went wrong and he felt threatened. He was a white killer among Orientals, at best a dangerous concept; it was time for him to move on. God knows his reputation *was* made; there'd be no lack of employment in Europe."

David Abbott cleared his throat. "I'd like to offer another possibility based on something Alfred said a few minutes ago." The Monk paused and nodded deferentially at Gillette. "He said that we had been forced to concentrate on a 'toothless sand shark while the hammerhead roamed free,' I believe that was the phrase, although my sequence may be wrong."

"Yes," said the man from NSC. "I was referring to Carlos, of course. It's not Cain we should be after. It's Carlos."

"Of course. Carlos. The most elusive killer in modern history, a man many of us truly believe has been responsible—in one way or another—for the most tragic assassinations of our time. You were quite right, Alfred, and, in a way, I was wrong. We cannot afford to forget Carlos."

"Thank you," said Gillette. "I'm glad I made my point."

"You did. With me, at any rate. But you also made me think. Can you imagine the temptation for a man like Cain, operating in the steamy confines of an area rife with drifters and fugitives and regimes up to their necks in corruption? How he must have envied Carlos; how he must have been jealous of the faster, brighter, more luxurious world of Europe. How often did he say to himself, 'I'm better than Carlos.' No matter how cold these fellows are, their egos are immense. I suggest he went to Europe to find that better world . . . and to dethrone Carlos. The pretender, sir, wants to take the title. He wants to be champion."

Gillette stared at the Monk. "It's an interesting theory."

"And if I follow you," interjected the congressman from Oversight, "by tracking Cain we may come up with Carlos."

"Exactly."

"I'm not sure *I* follow," said the CIA director, annoyed. "Why?"

"Two stallions in a paddock," answered Walters. "They tangle."

"A champion does not give up the title willingly." Abbott reached for his pipe. "He fights viciously to retain it. As the congressman says, we continue to track Cain, but we must also watch for other spoors in the forest. And when and if we find Cain, perhaps we should hold back. Wait for Carlos to come after him."

"Then take both," added the military officer.

"Very enlightening," said Gillette.

The meeting was over, the members in various stages of leaving. David Abbott stood with the Pentagon colonel, who was gathering together the pages of the Medusa folder; he had picked up the casualty sheets, prepared to insert them.

"May I take a look?" asked Abbott. "We don't have a copy over at Forty."

"Those were our instructions," replied the officer, handing the stapled pages to the older man. "I thought they came from you. Only three copies. Here, at the Agency, and over at the Council."

"They did come from me." The silent Monk smiled benignly. "Too damn many civilians in my part of town."

The colonel turned away to answer a question posed by the congressman from Tennessee. David Abbott did not listen; instead his eyes sped rapidly down the columns of names; he was alarmed. A number had been crossed out, accounted for. Accountability was the one thing they could not allow. Ever. Where *was* it? He was the only man in that room who knew the name, and he could feel the pounding in his chest as he reached the last page. The name was there.

Bourne, Jason C.—Last known station: Tam Quan.
What in God's name *had happened?*

René Bergeron slammed down the telephone on his desk; his voice only slightly more controlled than his gesture. "We've tried every café, every restaurant and bistro she's ever frequented!"

"There's not a hotel in Paris that has him registered," said the gray-haired switchboard operator, seated at a second telephone by a drafting board. "It's been more than two hours now; she could be dead. If she's not, she might well wish she were."

"She can only tell him so much," mused Bergeron. "Less than we could; she knows nothing of the old men."

"She knows enough; she's called Parc Monceau."

"She's relayed messages; she's not certain to whom."

"She knows why."

"So does Cain, I can assure you. And he would make a grotesque error with Parc Monceau." The designer leaned forward, his powerful forearms tensing as he locked his hands together, his eyes on the gray-haired man. "Tell me, again, everything you remember. Why are you so sure he's Bourne?"

"I don't know that. I said he was Cain. If you've described his methods accurately, he's the man."

"Bourne *is* Cain. We found him through the Medusa records. It's why you were hired."

"Then he's Bourne, but it's not the name he used. Of course, there were a number of men in Medusa who would not permit their real names to be used. For them, false

[246]

identities were guaranteed; they had criminal records. He would be one of those men."

"Why him? Others disappeared. You disappeared."

"I could say because he was here in Saint-Honoré and that should be enough. But there's more, much more. I watched him function. I was assigned to a mission he commanded; it was not an experience to be forgotten, nor was he. That man could be—*would* be—your Cain."

"Tell me."

"We parachuted at night into a sector called Tam Quan, our objective to bring out an American named Webb who was being held by the Viet Cong. We didn't know it, but the odds against survival were monumental. Even the flight from Saigon was horrendous; gale-force winds at a thousand feet, the aircraft vibrating as if it would fall apart. Still, he ordered us to jump."

"And you did?"

"His gun was pointed at our heads. At each of us as we approached the hatchway. We might survive the elements, not a bullet in our skulls."

"How many were there of you?"

"Ten."

"You could have taken him."

"You didn't know him."

"Go on," said Bergeron, concentrating; immobile at the desk.

"Eight of us regrouped on the ground; two, we assumed, had not survived the jump. It was amazing that I did. I was the oldest and hardly a bull, but I knew the area; it was why I was sent." The gray-haired man paused, shaking his head at the memory. "Less than an hour later we realized it was a trap. We were running like lizards through the jungle. And during the nights he went out alone through the mortar explosions and the grenades. To kill. Always coming back before dawn to force us closer and closer to the base camp. I thought at the time, sheer suicide."

"Why did you do it? He had to give you a reason; you were Medusans, not soldiers."

"He said it was the only way to get out alive, and there was logic to that. We were far behind the lines; we needed the supplies we could find at the base camp—if we could take it. He said we had to take it; we had no choice. If any argued, he'd put a bullet in his head—we knew it. On the third night we took the camp and found the man named

Webb more dead than alive, but breathing. We also found the two missing members of our team, very much alive and stunned at what had happened. A white man and a Vietnamese; they'd been paid by the Cong to trap us—trap him, I suspect."

"Cain?"

"Yes. The Vietnamese saw us first and escaped. Cain shot the white man in the head. I understand he just walked up to him and blew his head off."

"He got you back? Through the lines?"

"Four of us, yes, and the man named Webb. Five men were killed. It was during that terrible journey back that I thought I understood why the rumors might be true—that he was the highest-paid recruit in Medusa."

"In what sense?"

"He was the coldest man I ever saw, the most dangerous, and utterly unpredictable. I thought at the time it was a strange war for him; he was a Savonarola, but without religious principle, only his own odd morality which was centered about himself. All men were his enemies—the leaders in particular—and he cared not one whit for either side." The middle-aged man paused again, his eyes on the drafting board, his mind obviously thousands of miles away and back in time. "Remember, Medusa was filled with diverse and desperate men. Many were paranoid in their hatred of Communists. Kill a Communist and Christ smiled—odd examples of Christian teaching. Others—such as myself—had fortunes stolen from us by the Viet Minh; the only path to restitution was if the Americans won the war. France had abandoned us at Dienbienphu. But there were dozens who saw that fortunes could be made from Medusa. Pouches often contained fifty to seventy-five thousand American dollars. A courier siphoning off half during ten, fifteen runs, could retire in Singapore or Kuala Lumpur or set up his own narcotics network in the Triangle. Beyond the exorbitant pay—and frequently the pardoning of past crimes—the opportunities were unlimited. It was in this group that I placed that very strange man. He was a modern-day pirate in the purest sense."

Bergeron unlocked his hands. "Wait a minute. You used the phrase, 'a mission he commanded.' There were military men in Medusa; are you sure he wasn't an American officer?"

"American, to be sure, but certainly not army."

"Why?"

"He hated all aspects of the military. His scorn for Command Saigon was in every decision he made; he considered the army fools and incompetents. At one point orders were radioed to us in Tam Quan. He broke off the transmission and told a regimental general to have sex with himself—he would not obey. An army officer would hardly do that."

"Unless he was about to abandon his profession," said the designer. "As Paris abandoned you, and you did the best you could, stealing from Medusa, setting up your own hardly patriotic activities—wherever you could."

"My country betrayed me before I betrayed her, René."

"Back to Cain. You say Bourne was not the name he used. What was it?"

"I don't recall. As I said, for many, surnames were not relevant. He was simply 'Delta' to me."

"Mekong?"

"No, the alphabet, I think."

"'Alpha, Bravo, Charlie . . . Delta,'" said Bergeron pensively in English. "But in many operations the code word 'Charlie' was replaced by 'Cain' because 'Charlie' had become synonymous with the Cong. 'Charlie' became 'Cain.'"

"Quite true. So Bourne dropped back a letter and assumed 'Cain.' He could have chosen 'Echo' or 'Foxtrot' or 'Zulu.' Twenty-odd others. What's the difference? What's your point?"

"He chose Cain deliberately. It was symbolic. He wanted it clear from the beginning."

"Wanted what clear?"

"That Cain would replace Carlos. *Think.* 'Carlos' is Spanish for Charles—Charlie. The code word 'Cain' was substituted for 'Charlie'—Carlos. It was his intention from the start. Cain would replace Carlos. And he wanted Carlos to know it."

"*Does* Carlos?"

"Of course. Word goes out in Amsterdam and Berlin, Geneva and Lisbon, London and right here in Paris. Cain is available; contracts can be made, his price lower than Carlos' fee. He erodes! He constantly erodes Carlos' stature."

"Two matadors in the same ring. There can only be one."

[249]

"It will be Carlos. We've trapped the puffed-up sparrow. He's somewhere within two hours of Saint-Honoré."

"But where?"

"No matter. We'll find him. After all, he found us. He'll come back; his ego will demand it. And then the eagle will sweep down and catch the sparrow. Carlos will kill him."

The old man adjusted his single crutch under his left arm, parted the black drape and stepped into the confessional booth. He was not well; the pallor of death was on his face, and he was glad the figure in the priest's habit beyond the transparent curtain could not see him clearly. The assassin might not give him further work if he looked too worn to carry it out; he needed work now. There were only weeks remaining and he had responsibilities. He spoke.

"Angelus Domini."

"Angelus Domini, child of God," came the whisper. "Are your days comfortable?"

"They draw to an end, but they are made comfortable."

"Yes. I think this will be your last job for me. It is of such importance, however, that your fee will be five times the usual. I hope it will be of help to you."

"Thank you, Carlos. You know, then."

"I know. This is what you must do for it, and the information must leave this world with you. There can be no room for error."

"I have always been accurate. I will go to my death being accurate now."

"Die in peace, old friend. It's easier. . . . You will go to the Vietnamese Embassy and ask for an attaché named Phan Loc. When you are alone, say the following words to him: 'Late March 1968 Medusa, the Tam Quan sector. Cain was there. Another also.' Have you got that?"

" 'Late March 1968 Medusa, the Tam Quan sector. Cain was there. Another also.' "

"He'll tell you when to return. It will be in a matter of hours."

─── 17 ───

"I think it's time we talked about a *fiche confidentielle* out of Zurich."

"My God!"

"I'm not the man you're looking for."

Bourne gripped the woman's hand, holding her in place, preventing her from running into the aisles of the crowded, elegant restaurant in Argenteuil, a few miles outside of Paris. The pavane was over, the gavotte finished. They were alone; the velvet booth a cage.

"Who *are* you?" The Lavier woman grimaced, trying to pull her hand away, the veins in the cosmeticized neck pronounced.

"A rich American who lives in the Bahamas. Don't you believe that?"

"I should have known," she said, "no charges, no check—only cash. You didn't even look at the bill."

"Or the prices before that. It's what brought you over to me."

"I was a fool. The rich always look at prices, if only for the pleasure of dismissing them." Lavier spoke while glanc-

[251]

ing around, looking for a space in the aisles, a waiter she might summon. Escape.

"Don't," said Jason, watching her eyes. "It'd be foolish. We'd both be better off if we talked."

The woman stared at him, the bridge of hostile silence accentuated by the hum of the large, dimly lit, candelabraed room and the intermittent eruptions of quiet laughter from the nearby tables. "I ask you again," she said. "Who are you?"

"My name isn't important. Settle for the one I gave you."

"Briggs? It's false."

"So's Larousse, and that's on the lease of a rented car that picked up three killers at the Valois Bank. They missed there. They also missed this afternoon at the Pont Neuf. He got away."

"Oh, God!" she cried, trying to break away.

"I said *don't!*" Bourne held her firmly, pulling her back.

"If I scream, monsieur?" The powdered mask was cracked with lines of venom now, the bright red lipstick defining the snarl of an aging, cornered rodent.

"I'll scream louder," replied Jason. "We'd both be thrown out, and once outside I don't think you'll be unmanageable. Why not talk? We might learn something from each other. After all, we're employees, not employers."

"I have nothing to say to you."

"Then I'll start. Maybe you'll change your mind." He lessened his grip cautiously. The tension remained on her white, powdered face, but it, too, was lessened as the pressure of his fingers was reduced. She was ready to listen. "You paid a price in Zurich. We paid, too. Obviously more than you did. We're after the same man; we know why *we* want him." He released her. "Why do you?"

She did not speak for nearly half a minute, instead, studying him in silence, her eyes angry yet frightened. Bourne knew he had phrased the question accurately; for Jacqueline Lavier not to talk to him would be a dangerous mistake. It could cost her her life if subsequent questions were raised.

"Who is 'we?' " she asked.

"A company that wants its money. A great deal of money. He has it."

"He did not earn it, then?"

Jason knew he had to be careful; he was expected to know far more than he did. "Let's say there's a dispute."

"How could there be? Either he did or he did not, there's hardly a middle ground."

"It's my turn," said Bourne. "You answered a question with a question and I didn't avoid you. Now, let's go back. Why do you want him? Why is the private telephone of one of the better shops in Saint-Honoré put on a *fiche* in Zurich?"

"It was an accommodation, monsieur."

"For whom?"

"Are you mad?"

"All right, I'll pass on that for now. We think we know anyway."

"Impossible!"

"Maybe, maybe not. So it was an accommodation . . . to kill a man?"

"I have nothing to say."

"Yet a minute ago when I mentioned the car, you tried to run. That's saying something."

"A perfectly natural reaction." Jacqueline Lavier touched the stem of her wineglass. "I arranged for the rental. I don't mind telling you that because there's no evidence that I did so. Beyond that I know nothing of what happened." Suddenly she gripped the glass, her mask of a face a mixture of controlled fury and fear. "Who *are* you people?"

"I told you. A company that wants its money back."

"You're interfering! Get out of Paris! Leave this alone!"

"Why should we? We're the injured party; we want the balance sheet corrected. We're entitled to that."

"You're entitled to nothing!" spat Mme. Lavier. "The error was yours and you'll pay for it!"

"Error?" He had to be *very* careful. It was here—right below the hard surface—the eyes of the truth could be seen beneath the ice. "Come off it. Theft isn't an error committed by the victim."

"The error was in your *choice,* monsieur. You chose the wrong man."

"He stole millions from Zurich," said Jason. "But you know that. He took millions, and if you think you're going to take them from him—which is the same as taking them from us—you're very much mistaken."

"We want no money!"

[253]

"I'm glad to know it. Who's 'we?' "

"I thought you said you knew."

"I said we had an idea. Enough to expose a man named Koenig in Zurich; d'Amacourt here in Paris. If we decide to do that, it could prove to be a major embarrassment, couldn't it?"

"Money? Embarrassment? These are *not issues*. You are consumed with stupidity, all of you! I'll say it again. Get out of Paris. Leave this alone. It is not your concern any longer."

"We don't think it's yours. Frankly, we don't think you're competent."

"*Competent?*" repeated Lavier, as if she did not believe what she had heard.

"That's right."

"Have you any idea what you're *saying?* Whom you're *talking* about?"

"It doesn't matter. Unless you back off, my recommendation is that we come out loud and clear. Mock up charges—not traceable to us, of course. Expose Zurich, the Valois. Call in the Sûreté, Interpol . . . anyone and anything to create a manhunt—a massive manhunt."

"You *are* mad. And a fool."

"Not at all. We have friends in very important positions; we'll get the information first. We'll be waiting at the right place at the right time. We'll take him."

"You *won't* take him. He'll disappear again! Can't you *see* that? He's in Paris and a network of people he cannot know are looking for him. He may have escaped once, twice; but not a third time! He's trapped now. We've trapped him!"

"We don't want you to trap him. That's not in our interests." It was almost the moment, thought Bourne. Almost, but not quite; her fear had to match her anger. She had to be detonated into revealing the truth. "Here's our ultimatum, and we're holding you responsible for conveying it—otherwise you'll join Koenig and d'Amacourt. Call off your hunt tonight. If you don't we'll move first thing in the morning; we'll start shouting. Les Classiques'll be the most popular store in Saint-Honoré, but I don't think it'll be the right people."

The powdered face cracked. "You wouldn't dare! How dare you? Who are you to say this?!"

He paused, then struck. "A group of people who don't care much for your Carlos."

The Lavier woman froze, her eyes wide, stretching the taut skin into scar tissue. "You *do* know," she whispered. "And you think you can oppose him? You think you're a match for Carlos?"

"In a word, yes."

"You're *insane*. You don't give ultimatums to Carlos."

"I just did."

"Then you're dead. You raise your voice to *anyone* and you won't last the day. He has men everywhere; they'll cut you down in the street."

"They might if they knew whom to cut down," said Jason. "You forget. No one does. But they know who you are. And Koenig, and d'Amacourt. The minute we expose you, you'd be eliminated. Carlos couldn't afford you any longer. But no one knows me."

"You forget, monsieur. I do."

"The least of my worries. Find me . . . after the damage is done and before the decision is made regarding your own future. It won't be long."

"This is madness. You come out of nowhere and talk like a madman. You cannot do this!"

"Are you suggesting a compromise?"

"It's conceivable," said Jacqueline Lavier. "Anything is possible."

"Are you in a position to negotiate it?"

"I'm in a position to convey it . . . far better than I can an ultimatum. Others will relay it to the one who decides."

"What you're saying is what I said a few minutes ago: we can talk."

"We can talk, monsieur," agreed Mme. Lavier, her eyes fighting for her life.

"Then let's start with the obvious."

"Which is?"

Now. The truth.

"What's Bourne to Carlos? Why does he want him?"

"What's *Bourne*—" The woman stopped, venom and fear replaced by an expression of absolute shock. "*You* can ask *that*?"

"I'll ask it again," said Jason, hearing the pounding echoes in his chest. "What's Bourne to Carlos?"

"He's Cain! You know it as well as we do. He was your error, your choice! You chose the wrong man!"

Cain. He heard the name and the echoes erupted into cracks of deafening thunder. And with each crack, pain jolted him, bolts searing one after another through his head, his mind and body recoiling under the onslaught of the name. Cain. Cain. The mists were there again. The darkness, the wind, the explosions.

Alpha, Bravo, Cain, Delta, Echo, Foxtrot. . . . Cain, Delta. Delta, Cain. Delta . . . Cain.

Cain is for *Charlie.*

Delta is for *Cain!*

"What is it? What's wrong with you?"

"Nothing." Bourne had slipped his right hand over his left wrist, gripping it, his fingers pressed into his flesh with such pressure he thought his skin might break. He had to do *something*; he had to stop the trembling, lessen the noise, repulse the pain. He had to *clear his mind.* The eyes of the truth were staring at him; he could not look away. He was there, he was home, and the cold made him shiver. "Go on," he said, imposing a control on his voice that resulted in a whisper; he could not help himself.

"Are you ill? You're very pale and you're—"

"I'm fine," he interrupted curtly. "I said, go *on.*"

"What's there to tell you?"

"Say it all. I want to hear it from you."

"Why? There's nothing you don't know. You chose Cain. You dismissed Carlos; you think you can dismiss him now. You were wrong then and you are wrong now."

I will kill you. I will grab your throat and choke the breath out of you. Tell me! For Christ's sake, tell me! At the end, there is only my beginning! I must know it.

"That doesn't matter," he said. "If you are looking for a compromise—if only to save your life—tell me why we should listen. Why is Carlos so adamant . . . so paranoid . . . about Bourne? Explain it to me as if I hadn't heard it before. If you don't, those names that shouldn't be mentioned will be spread all over Paris, and you'll be dead by the afternoon."

Lavier was rigid, her alabaster mask set. "Carlos will follow Cain to the ends of the earth and kill him."

"We know that. We want to know why."

"He has to. Look to yourself. To people like you."

"That's meaningless. You don't know who we are."

"I don't have to. I know what you've done."

"Spell it out!"

"I did. You picked Cain over Carlos—that was your error. You chose the wrong man. You paid the wrong assassin."

"The wrong . . . assassin."

"You were not the first, but you will be the last. The arrogant pretender will be killed here in Paris, whether there is a compromise or not."

"We picked the wrong assassin . . ." The words floated in the elegant, perfumed air of the restaurant. The deafening thunder receded, angry still but far away in the storm clouds; the mists were clearing, circles of vapor swirling around him. He began to see, and what he saw was the outlines of a monster. Not a myth, but a monster. Another monster. There were two.

"Can you doubt it?" asked the woman. "Don't interfere with Carlos. Let him take Cain; let him have his revenge." She paused, both hands slightly off the table; Mother Rat. "I promise nothing, but I *will* speak for you, for the loss your people have sustained. It's possible . . . only possible, you understand . . . that your contract might be honored by the one you should have chosen in the first place."

"The one we should have chosen. . . . Because we chose the wrong one."

"You see that, do you not, monsieur? Carlos should be *told* that you see it. Perhaps . . . only perhaps . . . he might have sympathy for your losses if he were convinced you saw your error."

"That's your compromise?" said Bourne flatly, struggling to find a line of thought.

"Anything is possible. No good can come from your threats, I can tell you that. For any of us, and I'm frank enough to include myself. There would be only pointless killing; and Cain would stand back laughing. You would lose not once, but twice."

"If that's true . . ." Jason swallowed, nearly choking as dry air filled the vacuum in his dry throat, "then I'll have to explain to my people why we . . . chose . . . the . . . wrong man." *Stop it! Finish the statement. Control yourself.* "Tell me everything you know about Cain."

"To what purpose?" Lavier put her fingers on the table, her bright red nail polish ten points of a weapon.

"If we chose the wrong man, then we had the wrong information."

"You heard he was the equal of Carlos, no? That his fees were more reasonable, his apparatus more contained, and because fewer intermediaries were involved there was no possibility of a contract being traced. Is this not so?"

"Maybe."

"Of course it's so. It's what everyone's been told and it's all a lie. Carlos' strength is in his far-reaching sources of information—*infallible* information. In his elaborate system of reaching the right person at precisely the right moment prior to a kill."

"Sounds like too many people. There were too many people in Zurich, too many here in Paris."

"All blind, monsieur. Every one."

"Blind?"

"To put it plainly, I've been part of the operation for a number of years, meeting in one way or another dozens who have played their minor roles—none is major. I have yet to meet a single person who has ever spoken to Carlos, much less has any idea who he is."

"That's Carlos. I want to know about Cain. What *you* know about Cain." *Stay controlled. You cannot turn away. Look at her. Look at her!*

"Where shall I begin?"

"With whatever comes to mind first. Where did he come from?" *Do not look away!*

"Southeast Asia, of course."

"Of course . . ." *Oh, God.*

"From the American Medusa, we know that . . ."

Medusa! The winds, the darkness, the flashes of light, the pain. . . . The pain ripped through his skull now; he was not where he was, but where he had been. A world away in distance and time. The pain. Oh, Jesus. The pain . . .

Tao!
Che-sah!
Tam Quan!
Alpha, Bravo, Cain . . . Delta.
Delta . . . Cain!
Cain is for Charlie.
Delta is for Cain.

"What is it?" The woman looked frightened; she was studying his face, her eyes roving, boring into his. "You're perspiring. Your hands are shaking. Are you having an attack?"

"It passes quickly." Jason pried his hand away from his wrist and reached for a napkin to wipe his forehead.

"It comes with the pressures, no?"

"With the pressures, yes. Go on. There isn't much time; people have to be reached, decisions made. Your life is probably one of them. Back to Cain. You say he came from the American . . . Medusa."

"Les mercenaires du diable," said Lavier. "It was the nickname given Medusa by the Indochina colonials—what was left of them. Quite appropriate, don't you think?"

"It doesn't make any difference what I think. Or what I know. I want to hear what *you* think, what *you* know about Cain."

"Your attack makes you rude."

"My impatience makes me impatient. You say we chose the wrong man; if we did we had the wrong information. *Les mercenaires du diable.* Are you implying that Cain is French?"

"Not at all, you test me poorly. I mentioned that only to indicate how deeply we penetrated Medusa."

" 'We' being the people who work for Carlos."

"You could say that."

"I will say that. If Cain's not French, what is he?"

"Undoubtedly American."

Oh, God! "Why?"

"Everything he does has the ring of American audacity. He pushes and shoves with little or no finesse, taking credit where none is his, claiming kills when he had nothing to do with them. He had studied Carlos' methods and connections like no other man alive. We're told he recites them with total recall to potential clients, more often than not putting himself in Carlos' place, convincing fools that it was *he,* not Carlos, who accepted and fulfilled the contracts." Lavier paused. "I've struck a chord, no? He did the same with you—your people—yes?"

"Perhaps." Jason reached for his own wrist again, as the statements came back to him. Statements made in response to clues in a dreadful game.

Stuttgart. Regensburg. Munich. Two kills and a kidnapping, Baader accreditation. Fees from U. S. sources. . . .

Teheran? Eight kills. Divided accreditation—Khomeini and PLO. Fee, two million. Southwest Soviet sector.

Paris . . . All contracts will be processed through Paris.

Whose contracts?

Sanchez . . . Carlos.

". . . always such a transparent device."

The Lavier woman had spoken; he had not heard her. "What did you say?"

"You were remembering, yes? He used the same device with you—your people. It's how he gets his assignments."

"Assignments?" Bourne tensed the muscles in his stomach until the pain brought him back to the table in the candelabraed dining room in Argenteuil. "He gets assignments, then," he said pointlessly.

"And carries them out with considerable expertise; no one denies him that. His record of kills is impressive. In many ways, he is second to Carlos—not his equal, but far above the ranks of *les guérilleros*. He's a man of immense skill, extremely inventive, a trained lethal weapon out of Medusa. But it is his arrogance, his lies at the expense of Carlos that will bring him down."

"And that makes him American? Or is it your bias? I have an idea you like American money, but that's about all they export that you do like." *Immense skill; extremely inventive; a trained lethal weapon. . . . Port Noir, La Ciotat, Marseilles, Zurich, Paris.*

"It is beyond prejudice, monsieur. The identification is positive."

"How did you get it?"

Lavier touched the stem of her wineglass, her red-tipped index finger curling around it. "A discontented man was bought in Washington."

"Washington?"

"The Americans also look for Cain—with an intensity approaching Carlos', I suspect. Medusa has never been made public, and Cain might prove to be an extraordinary embarrassment. This discontented man was in a position to give us a great deal of information, including the Medusa records. It was a simple matter to match the names with those in Zurich. Simple for Carlos, not for anyone else."

Too simple, thought Jason, not knowing why the thought struck him. "I see," he said.

"And you? How did you find him? Not Cain, of course, but Bourne."

Through the mists of anxiety, Jason recalled another statement. Not his, but one spoken by Marie. "Far simpler," he said. "We paid the money to him by means of a shortfall deposit into one account, the surplus diverted blindly into another. The numbers could be traced; it's a tax device."

"Cain permitted it?"

"He didn't know it. The numbers were paid for . . . as you paid for different numbers—telephone numbers—on a *fiche*."

"I commend you."

"It's not required, but everything you know about Cain is. All you've done so far is explain an identification. Now, go on. Everything you know about this man Bourne, everything you've been told." *Be careful. Take the tension from your voice. You are merely . . . evaluating data. Marie, you said that. Dear, dear Marie. Thank God you're not here.*

"What we know about him is incomplete. He's managed to remove most of the vital records, a lesson he undoubtedly learned from Carlos. But not all; we've pieced together a sketch. Before he was recruited into Medusa, he supposedly was a French-speaking businessman living in Singapore, representing a collective of American importers from New York to California. The truth is he had been dismissed by the collective, which then tried to have him extradited back to the States for prosecution; he had stolen hundreds of thousands from it. He was known in Singapore as a reclusive figure, very powerful in contraband operations, and extraordinarily ruthless."

"Before that," interrupted Jason, feeling again the perspiration breaking out on his hairline. "Before Singapore. Where did he *come* from?" *Be careful! The images! He could see the streets of Singapore. Prince Edward Road, Kim Chuan, Boon Tat Street, Maxwell, Cuscaden.*

"Those are the records no one can find. There are only rumors, and they are meaningless. For example, it was said that he was a defrocked Jesuit, gone mad; another speculation was that he had been a young, aggressive investment banker caught embezzling funds in concert with several Singapore banks. There's nothing concrete, nothing that can be traced. Before Singapore, nothing."

You're wrong, there was a great deal. But none of that is part of it. . . . There is a void, and it must be filled, and you can't help me. Perhaps no one can; perhaps no one should.

"So far, you haven't told me anything startling," said

Bourne, "nothing relative to the information I'm interested in."

"Then I don't know what you want! You ask me questions, press for details, and when I offer you answers you reject them as immaterial. What *do* you want?"

"What do you know about Cain's . . . work? Since you're looking for a compromise, give me a reason for it. If our information differs, it would be over what he's done, wouldn't it? When did he first come to your attention? Carlos' attention? *Quickly!*"

"Two years ago," said Mme. Lavier, disconcerted by Jason's impatience, annoyed, frightened. "Word came out of Asia of a white man offering a service astonishingly similar to the one provided by Carlos. He was swiftly becoming an industry. An ambassador was assassinated in Moulmein; two days later a highly regarded Japanese politician was killed in Tokyo prior to a debate in the Diet. A week after that a newspaper editor was blown out of his car in Hong Kong, and in less than forty-eight hours a banker was shot on a street in Calcutta. Behind each one, Cain. Always Cain." The woman stopped, appraising Bourne's reaction. He gave none. "Don't you see? He was *everywhere.* He raced from one kill to another, accepting contracts with such rapidity that he had to be indiscriminate. He was a man in an enormous hurry, building his reputation so quickly that he shocked even the most jaded professionals. And no one doubted that *he* was a professional, least of all Carlos. Instructions were sent: find out about this man, learn all you can. You see, Carlos understood what none of us did, and in less than twelve months he was proven correct. Reports came from informers in Manila, Osaka, Hong Kong and Tokyo. Cain was moving to Europe, they said; he would make Paris itself his base of operations. The challenge was clear, the gauntlet thrown. Cain was out to destroy Carlos. He would become the *new* Carlos, his services *the* services required by those who sought them. As *you* sought them, monsieur."

"Moulmein, Tokyo, Calcutta . . ." Jason heard the names coming from his lips, whispered from his throat. Again they were floating, suspended in the perfumed air, shadows of a past forgotten. "Manila, Hong Kong . . ." He stopped, trying to clear the mists, peering at the outlines of strange shapes that kept racing across his mind's eye.

"These places and many others," continued Lavier. "That was Cain's error, his error still. Carlos may be many things to many people, but among those who have benefited from his trust and generosity, there is loyalty. His informers and hirelings are not so readily for sale, although Cain has tried time and again. It is said that Carlos is swift to make harsh judgments, but, as they also say, better a Satan one knows than a successor one doesn't. What Cain did not realize—does not realize now—is that Carlos' network is a vast one. When Cain moved to Europe, he did not know that his activities were uncovered in Berlin, Lisbon, Amsterdam . . . as far away as Oman."

"Oman," said Bourne involuntarily. "Sheik Mustafa Kalig," he whispered, as if to himself.

"Never proven!" interjected the Lavier woman defiantly. "A deliberate smokescreen of confusion, the contract itself fiction. He took credit for an internal murder; no one could penetrate that security. A lie!"

"A lie," repeated Jason.

"So many lies," added Mme. Lavier contemptuously. "He's no fool, however; he lies quietly, dropping a hint here and there, knowing that they will be exaggerated in the telling into substance. He provokes Carlos at every turn, promoting himself at the expense of the man he would replace. But he's no match for Carlos; he takes contracts he cannot fulfill. You are only one example; we hear there have been several others. It's said that's why he stayed away for months, avoiding people like yourselves."

"Avoiding people . . ." Jason reached for his wrist; the trembling had begun again, the sound of distant thunder vibrating in far regions of his skull. "You're . . . sure of that?"

"Very much so. He wasn't dead; he was in hiding. Cain botched more than one assignment; it was inevitable. He accepted too many in too short a time. Yet whenever he did, he followed an abortive kill with a spectacular, unsolicited one, to uphold his stature. He would select a prominent figure and blow him away, the assassination a shock to everyone, and unmistakably Cain's. The ambassador traveling in Moulmein was an example; no one had called for his death. There were two others that we know of—a Russian commissar in Shanghai and more recently a banker in Madrid. . . ."

The words came from the bright red lips working feverishly in the lower part of the powdered mask facing him. He heard them; he had heard them before. He had *lived* them before. They were no longer shadows, but remembrances of that forgotten past. Images and reality were fused. She began no sentence he could not finish, nor could she mention a name or a city or an incident with which he was not instinctively familiar.

She was talking about . . . him.

Alpha, Bravo, Cain, Delta . . .

Cain is for Charlie, and Delta is for Cain.

Jason Bourne was the assassin called Cain.

There was a final question, his brief reprieve from darkness two nights ago at the Sorbonne. Marseilles. August 23.

"What happened in Marseilles?" he asked.

"Marseilles?" the Lavier woman recoiled. "How *could* you? What lies were you told? What *other* lies?"

"Just tell me what happened."

"You refer to Leland, of course. The ubiquitous ambassador whose death *was* called for—paid for, the contract accepted by Carlos."

"What if I told you that there are those who think Cain was responsible?"

"It's what he wanted *everyone* to think! It was the ultimate insult to Carlos—to steal the kill from him. Payment was irrelevant to Cain; he only wanted to show the world—our world—that he could get there first and do the job for which Carlos had been paid. But he didn't, you know. He had nothing to do with the Leland kill."

"He was there."

"He was trapped. At least, he never showed up. Some said he'd been killed, but since there was no corpse, Carlos didn't believe it."

"How was Cain supposedly killed?"

Madame Lavier retreated, shaking her head in short, rapid movements. "Two men on the waterfront tried to take credit, tried to get paid for it. One was never seen again; it can be presumed Cain killed him, if it *was* Cain. They were dock garbage."

"What was the trap?"

"The *alleged* trap, monsieur. They claimed to have gotten word that Cain was to meet someone in the rue Sarrasin a night or so before the assassination. They say they left appropriately obscure messages in the street and lured the man they were convinced was Cain down to the piers, to a fishing boat. Neither trawler nor skipper were seen again, so they may have been right—but as I say, there was no proof. Not even an adequate description of Cain to match against the man led away from the Sarrasin. At any rate, that's where it ends."

You're wrong. That's where it began. For me.

"I see," said Bourne, trying again to infuse naturalness into his voice. "Our information's different naturally. We made a choice on what we thought we knew."

"The *wrong* choice, monsieur. What I've told you is the truth."

"Yes, I know."

"Do we have our compromise, then?"

"Why not?"

"*Bien.*" Relieved, the woman lifted the wineglass to her lips. "You'll see, it will be better for everyone."

"It . . . doesn't really matter now." He could barely be heard, and he knew it. What did he say? What had he just said? Why did he say it? . . . The mists were closing in again, the thunder getting louder; the pain had returned to his temples. "I mean . . . I mean, as you say, it's better for everyone." He could feel—*see*—Lavier's eyes on him, studying him. "It's a reasonable solution."

"Of course it is. You are not feeling well?"

"I said it was nothing; it'll pass."

"I'm relieved. Now, would you excuse me for a moment?"

"No." Jason grabbed her arm.

"*Je vous prie, monsieur.* The powder room, that is all. If you care to, stand outside the door."

"We'll leave. You can stop on the way." Bourne signaled the waiter for a check.

"As you wish," she said, watching him.

He stood in the darkened corridor between the spills of light that came from recessed lamps in the ceiling. Across the way was the ladies' room, denoted by small, uncapitalized letters of gold that read FEMMES. Beautiful people—stunning women, handsome men—kept passing by; the orbit was similar to that of Les Classiques. Jacqueline Lavier was at home.

She had also been in the ladies' room for nearly ten minutes, a fact that would have disturbed Jason had he been able to concentrate on the time. He could not; he was on fire. Noise and pain consumed him, every nerve ending raw, exposed, the fibers swelling, terrified of puncture. He stared straight ahead, a history of dead men behind him. The past was in the eyes of truth; they had sought him out and he had seen them. Cain . . . *Cain* . . . *Cain.*

He shook his head and looked up at the black ceiling. He had to function; he could not allow himself to keep falling, plunging into the abyss filled with darkness and high wind. There were decisions to make. . . . No, they were made; it was a question now of implementing them.

Marie. Marie? Oh, God, my love, we've been so wrong!

He breathed deeply and glanced at his watch—the chronometer he had traded for a thin gold piece of jewelry belonging to a marquis in the south of France. *He is a man of immense skill, extremely inventive.* . . . There was no joy in that appraisal. He looked across at the ladies' room.

Where was Jacqueline Lavier? Why didn't she come out? What could she hope to accomplish remaining inside? He had had the presence of mind to ask the maître d' if there was a telephone there; the man had replied negatively, pointing to a booth by the entrance. The Lavier woman had been at his side; she heard the answer, understanding the inquiry.

There was a blinding flash of light. He lurched backward, recoiling into the wall, his hands in front of his eyes. The pain! Oh, Christ! His eyes were on fire!

And then he heard the words, spoken through the polite laughter of well-dressed men and women walking casually about the corridor.

"In memory of your dinner at Roget's, monsieur," said an animated hostess, holding a press camera by its vertical flashbar. "The photograph will be ready in a few minutes. Compliments of Roget."

Bourne remained rigid, knowing that he could not smash the camera, the fear of another realization sweeping over him. "Why me?" he asked.

"Your fiancée requested it, monsieur," replied the girl, nodding her head toward the ladies' room. "We talked inside. You are most fortunate; she is a lovely lady. She asked me to give you this." The hostess held out a folded note; Jason took it as she pranced away toward the restaurant entrance.

Your illness disturbs me, as I'm sure it does you, my new friend. You may be what you say you are, and then again you may not. I shall have the answer in a half hour or so. A telephone call was made by a sympathetic diner, and that photograph is on its way to Paris. You cannot stop it any more than you can stop those driving now to Argenteuil. If we, indeed, have our compromise, neither will disturb you—as your illness disturbs me—and we shall talk again when my associates arrive.

It is said that Cain is a chameleon, appearing in various guises, and most convincing. It is also said that he is prone to violence and to fits of temper. These are an illness, no?

He ran down the dark street in Argenteuil after the receding roof light of the taxi; it turned the corner and disappeared. He stopped, breathing heavily, looking in all directions for another; there were none. The doorman at Roget's had told him a cab would take ten to fifteen minutes to arrive; why had not monsieur requested one earlier? The trap was set and he had walked into it.

Up ahead! A light, another taxi! He broke into a run. He had to stop it; he had to get back to Paris. To Marie.

He was back in a labyrinth, racing blindly, knowing, finally, there was no escape. But the race would be made alone; that decision was irrevocable. There would be no discussion, no debate, no screaming back and forth—arguments based in love and uncertainty. For the certainty had been made clear. He knew who he was . . . what he had been; he was guilty as charged—as suspected.

An hour or two saying nothing. Just watching, talking quietly about anything but the truth. Loving. And then he would leave; she would never know when and he could never tell her why. He owed her that; it would hurt deeply for a while, but the ultimate pain would be far less than that caused by the stigma of Cain.

Cain!

Marie. Marie! What have I done?

"Taxi! Taxi!"

— 18 —

Get out of Paris! Now! Whatever you're doing, stop it and get out! . . . Those are orders from your government. They want you out of there. They want him isolated.

Marie crushed out her cigarette in the ashtray on the bedside table, her eyes falling on the three-year-old issue of *Potomac Quarterly*, her thoughts briefly on the terrible game Jason had forced her to play.

"I won't listen!" she said to herself out loud, startled at the sound of her own voice in the empty room. She walked to the window, the same window he had faced, looking out, frightened, trying to make her understand.

I have to know certain things . . . enough to make a decision . . . but maybe not everything. A part of me has to be able . . . to run, disappear. I have to be able to say to myself, what was isn't any longer, and there's a possibility that it never was because I have no memory of it. What a person can't remember didn't exist . . . for him.

"My darling, my darling. Don't let them do this to you!" Her spoken words did not startle now, for it was as though he were there in the room, listening, heeding his own

[268]

words, willing to run, disappear . . . with her. But at the core of her understanding she knew he could not do that; he could not settle for a half-truth, or three-quarters of a lie.

They want him isolated.

Who were *they?* The answer was in Canada and Canada was cut off, another trap.

Jason was right about Paris; she felt it, too. Whatever it was, was here. If they could find one person to lift the shroud and let him see for himself he was being manipulated, then other questions might be manageable, the answers no longer pushing him toward self-destruction. If he could be convinced that whatever unremembered crimes he had committed, he was a pawn for a much greater single crime, he might be able to walk away, disappear with her. Everything *was* relative. What the man she loved had to be able to say to himself was not that the past no longer existed, but that it had, and he could live with it, and put it to rest. That was the rationalization he needed, the conviction that whatever he had been was far less than his enemies wanted the world to believe, for they would not use him otherwise. He was the scapegoat, his death to take the place of another's. If he could only *see* that; if she could only convince him. And if she did not, she would lose him. They would take him; they would kill him.

They.

"Who *are* you?" she screamed at the window, at the lights of Paris outside. "*Where* are you?"

She could feel a cold wind against her face as surely as if the panes of glass had melted, the night air rushing inside. It was followed by a tightening in her throat, and for a moment she could not swallow . . . could not breathe. The moment passed and she breathed again. She was afraid; it had happened to her before, on their first night in Paris, when she had left the café to find him on the steps of the Cluny. She had been walking rapidly down the Saint-Michel when it happened: the cold wind, the swelling of the throat . . . at that moment she had not been able to breathe. Later she thought she knew why; at that moment also, several blocks away inside the Sorbonne, Jason had raced to a judgment that in minutes he would reverse—but he had reached it then. He had made up his mind he would not come to her.

"Stop it!" she cried. "It's crazy," she added, shaking her

head, looking at her watch. He had been gone over five hours; where was he? *Where was he?*

Bourne got out of the taxi in front of the seedily elegant hotel in Montparnasse. The next hour would be the most difficult of his briefly remembered life—a life that was a void before Port Noir, a nightmare since. The nightmare would continue, but he would live with it alone; he loved her too much to ask her to live it with him. He would find a way to disappear, taking with him the evidence that tied her to Cain. It was as simple as that; he would leave for a nonexistent rendezvous and not return. And sometime during the next hour he would write her a note:

It's over. I've found my arrows. Go back to Canada and say nothing for both our sakes. I know where to reach you.

The last was unfair—he would never reach her—but the small, feathered hope had to be there, if only to get her on a plane to Ottawa. In time—with time—their weeks together would fade into a darkly kept secret, a cache of brief riches to be uncovered and touched at odd quiet moments. And then no more, for life was lived for active memories; the dormant ones lost meaning. No one knew that better than he did.

He passed through the lobby, nodding at the *concierge,* who sat on his stool behind the marble counter, reading a newspaper. The man barely looked up, noting only that the intruder belonged.

The elevator rumbled and groaned its way up to the fifth floor. Jason breathed deeply and reached for the gate; above all he would avoid dramatics—no alarms raised by words or by looks. The chameleon had to merge with his quiet part of the forest, one in which no spoors could be found. He knew what to say; he had thought about it carefully as he had the note he would write.

"Most of the night walking around," he said, holding her, stroking her dark red hair, cradling her head against his shoulder . . . and aching, "chasing down cadaverous clerks, listening to animated nonsense, and drinking coffee disguised as sour mud. Les Classiques was a waste of time; it's a zoo. The monkeys and the peacocks put on a hell of a show, but I don't think anyone really knows anything. There's one outside possibility, but he could simply be a sharp Frenchman in search of an American mark."

"He?" asked Marie, her trembling diminished.

"A man who operated the switchboard," said Bourne, repelling images of blinding explosions and darkness and high winds as he pictured the face he did not know but knew so well. That man now was only a device; he pushed the images away. "I agreed to meet him around midnight at the Bastringue on rue Hautefeuille."

"What did he say?"

"Very little, but enough to interest me. I saw him watching me while I was asking questions. The place was fairly crowded, so I could move around pretty freely, talk to the clerks."

"Questions? What questions did you ask?"

"Anything I could think of. Mainly about the manager, or whatever she's called. Considering what happened this afternoon, if she were a direct relay to Carlos, she should have been close to hysterics. I saw her. She wasn't; she behaved as if nothing had happened except a good day in the shop."

"But she *was* a relay, as you call it. D'Amacourt explained that. The *fiche*."

"Indirect. She gets a phone call and is told what to say before making another call herself." Actually, Jason thought, the invented assessment was based on reality. Jacqueline Lavier was, indeed, an indirect relay.

"You couldn't just walk around asking questions without seeming suspicious," protested Marie.

"You can," answered Bourne, "if you're an American writer doing an article on the stores in Saint-Honoré for a national magazine."

"That's very good, Jason."

"It worked. No one wants to be left out."

"What did you learn?"

"Like most of those kinds of places, Les Classiques has its own clientele, all wealthy, most known to each other and with the usual marital intrigues and adulteries that go with the scene. Carlos knew what he was doing; it's a regular answering service over there, but not the kind listed in a phone book."

"People told you that?" asked Marie, holding his arms, watching his eyes.

"Not in so many words," he said, aware of the shadows of her disbelief. "The accent was always on this Bergeron's talent, but one thing leads to another. You can get the picture. Everyone seems to gravitate to that manager. From what I've gathered, she's a font of social information, although she probably couldn't tell me anything except that she did someone a favor—an accommodation—and that someone will turn out to be someone else who did another favor for another someone. The source could be untraceable, but it's all I've got."

"Why the meeting tonight at Bastringue?"

"He came over to me when I was leaving and said a very strange thing." Jason did not have to invent this part of the lie. He had read the words on a note in an elegant restaurant in Argenteuil less than an hour ago. "He said, 'You may be what you say are, and then again you may not.' That's when he suggested a drink later on, away from Saint-Honoré." Bourne saw her doubts receding. He had done it; she accepted the tapestry of lies. And why not? He was a man *of immense skill, extremely inventive*. The appraisal was not loathsome to him; he was Cain.

"He may be the one, Jason. You said you only needed one; he could be it!"

"We'll see." Bourne looked at his watch. The countdown to his departure had begun; he could not look back. "We've got almost two hours. Where did you leave the attaché case?"

"At the Meurice. I'm registered there."

"Let's pick it up and get some dinner. You haven't eaten, have you?"

"No . . ." Marie's expression was quizzical. "Why not leave the case where it is? It's perfectly safe; we wouldn't have to worry about it."

"We would if we had to get out of here in a hurry," he said almost brusquely, going to the bureau. *Everything was a question of degree now, traces of friction gradually slipping into speech, into looks, into touch. Nothing alarming, nothing based on false heroics; she would see through such tactics. Only enough so that later she would understand the truth when she read his words.* "*It's over. I've found my arrows. . . .*"

"What's the matter, darling?"

"Nothing." The chameleon smiled. "I'm just tired and probably a little discouraged."

"Good heavens, why? A man wants to meet you confidentially late at night, a man who operates a switchboard. He could lead you somewhere. And you're convinced you've narrowed Carlos' contact down to this woman; she's bound to be able to tell you *something*—whether she wants to or not. In a macabre way, I'd think you'd be elated."

"I'm not sure I can explain it," said Jason, now looking at her reflection in the mirror. "You'd have to understand what I found there."

"What you found?" A question.

"What I found." A statement. "It's a different world," continued Bourne, reaching for the bottle of scotch and a glass, "different people. It's soft and beautiful and frivolous, with lots of tiny spotlights and dark velvet. Nothing's taken seriously except gossip and indulgence. Any one of those giddy people—including that woman—could be a relay for Carlos and never know it, never even suspect it. A man like Carlos would use such people; anyone like him would, including *me*. . . . That's what I found. It's discouraging."

"And unreasonable. Whatever you believe, those people make very conscious decisions. That indulgence you talk of demands it; they think. And you know what *I* think? I think you *are* tired, and hungry, and need a drink or two. I wish you could put off tonight; you've been through enough for one day."

"I can't do that," he said sharply.

"All right, you can't," she answered defensively.

"Sorry, I'm edgy."

"Yes. I know." She started for the bathroom. "I'll freshen up and we can go. Pour yourself a stiff one, darling. Your teeth are showing."

"Marie?"

"Yes?"

"Try to understand. What I found there upset me. I thought it would be different. Easier."

"While you were looking, I was waiting, Jason. Not knowing. That wasn't easy either."

"I thought you were going to call Canada. Didn't you?"

She held her place for a moment. "No," she said. "It was too late."

The bathroom door closed; Bourne walked to the desk across the room. He opened the drawer, took out stationery, picked up the ballpoint pen and wrote the words:

It's over. I've found my arrows. Go back to Canada and say nothing for both our sakes. I know where to reach you.

He folded the stationery, inserted it into an envelope, holding the flap open as he reached for his billfold. He took out both the French and the Swiss bills, slipping them behind the folded note, and sealed the envelope. He wrote on the front: MARIE.

He wanted so desperately to add: *My love, my dearest love.*

He did not. He could not.

The bathroom door opened. He put the envelope in his jacket pocket. "That was quick," he said.

"Was it? I didn't think so. What are you doing?"

"I wanted a pen," he answered, picking up the ballpoint. "If that fellow has anything to tell me I want to be able to write it down."

Marie was by the bureau; she glanced at the dry, empty glass. "You didn't have your drink."

"I didn't use the glass."

"I see. Shall we go?"

They waited in the corridor for the rumbling elevator, the silence between them awkward, in a real sense unbearable. He reached for her hand. At the touch she gripped his, staring at him, her eyes telling him that her control was being tested and she did not know why. Quiet signals had been sent and received, not loud enough or abrasive enough to be alarms, but they were there and she had heard them. It was part of the countdown, rigid, irreversible, prelude to his departure.

Oh God, I love you so. You are next to me and we are touching and I am dying. But you cannot die with me. You must not. I am Cain.

"We'll be fine," he said.

The metal cage vibrated noisily into its recessed perch. Jason pulled the brass grille open, then suddenly swore under his breath.

"Oh, Christ, I forgot!"

"What?"

"My wallet. I left it in the bureau drawer this afternoon in case there was any trouble in Saint-Honoré. Wait for me in the lobby." He gently swung her through the gate, pressing the button with his free hand. "I'll be right down." He closed the grille; the brass latticework cutting off the sight of her startled eyes. He turned away and walked rapidly back toward the room.

Inside, he took the envelope out of his pocket and placed it against the base of the lamp on the bedside table. He stared down at it, the ache unendurable.

"Goodbye, my love," he whispered.

Bourne waited in the drizzle outside the Hotel Meurice on the rue de Rivoli, watching Marie through the glass doors of the entrance. She was at the front desk, having signed for the attaché case, which had been handed to her over the counter. She was now obviously asking a mildly astonished clerk for her bill, about to pay for a room that had been occupied less than six hours. Two minutes passed before the bill was presented. Reluctantly; it was no way for a guest at the Meurice to behave. Indeed, all Paris shunned such inhibited visitors.

Marie walked out on the pavement, joining him in the shadows and the mistlike drizzle to the left of the canopy. She gave him the attaché case, a forced smile on her lips, a slight breathless quality in her voice.

"That man didn't approve of me. I'm sure he's convinced I used the room for a series of quick tricks."

"What did you tell him?" asked Bourne.

"That my plans had changed, that's all."

"Good, the less said the better. Your name's on the registration card. Think up a reason why you were there."

"Think up? . . . *I* should think up a reason?" She studied his eyes, the smile gone.

"I mean we'll think up a reason. Naturally."

"Naturally."

"Let's go." They started walking toward the corner, the traffic noisy in the street, the drizzle in the air fuller, the mist denser, the promise of heavy rain imminent. He took her arm—not to guide her, not even out of courtesy—only to touch her, to hold a part of her. There was so little time.

I am Cain. I am death.

"Can we slow down?" asked Marie sharply.

"What?" Jason realized he had been practically running; for a few seconds he had been back in the labyrinth, racing through it, careening, feeling, and not feeling. He looked up ahead and found an answer. At the corner an empty cab had stopped by a garish newsstand, the driver shouting through an open window to the dealer. "I want to catch that taxi," said Bourne, without breaking stride. "It's going to rain like hell."

They reached the corner, both breathless as the empty cab pulled away, swinging left into rue de Rivoli. Jason looked up into the night sky, feeling the wet pounding on his face, unnerved. The rain had arrived. He looked at Marie in the gaudy lights of the newsstand; she was wincing in the sudden downpour. No. She was not wincing; she was staring at something . . . staring in disbelief, in shock. In horror. Without warning she screamed, her face contorted, the fingers of her right hand pressed against her mouth. Bourne grabbed her, pulling her head into the damp cloth of his topcoat; she would not stop screaming.

He turned, trying to find the cause of her hysterics. Then he saw it, and in that unbelievable split half-second he knew the countdown was aborted. He had committed the final crime; he could not leave her. Not now, not yet.

On the first ledge of the newsstand was an early-morning tabloid, black headlines electrifying under the circles of light:

SLAYER IN PARIS
WOMAN SOUGHT IN ZURICH KILLINGS
SUSPECT IN RUMORED THEFT OF MILLIONS

Under the screaming words was a photograph of Marie St. Jacques.

"Stop it!" whispered Jason, using his body to cover her face from the curious newsdealer, reaching into his pocket for coins. He threw the money on the counter, grabbed two papers, and propelled her down the dark, rainsoaked street.

They were both in the labyrinth now.

Bourne opened the door and led Marie inside. She stood motionless, looking at him, her face pale and frightened, her breathing erratic, an audible mixture of fear and anger.

"I'll get you a drink," said Jason, going to the bureau. As he poured, his eyes strayed to the mirror and he had an overpowering urge to smash the glass, so despicable was his own image to him. What the hell had he *done?* Oh God!

I am Cain. I am death.

He heard her gasp and spun around, too late to stop her,

too far away to lunge and tear the awful thing from her hand. Oh, Christ, he had forgotten! She had found the envelope on the bedside table, and was reading his note. Her single scream was a searing, terrible cry of pain.

"*Jasonnnn! . . .*"

"Please! No!" He raced from the bureau and grabbed her. "It doesn't matter! It doesn't count anymore!" He shouted helplessly, seeing the tears swelling in her eyes, streaking down her face. "*Listen* to me! That was before, not now."

"You were leaving! My God, you were *leaving* me!" Her eyes went blank, two blind circles of panic. "I knew it! I felt it!"

"I *made* you feel it!" he said, forcing her to look at him. "But it's over now. I won't leave you. Listen to me. I won't leave you!"

She screamed again. "I couldn't breathe! . . . It was so cold!"

He pulled her to him, enveloping her. "We have to begin again. Try to understand. It's different now—and I can't change what was—but I won't leave you. Not like this."

She pushed her hands against his chest, her tear-stained face angled back, begging, "Why, Jason? Why?"

"Later. Not now. Don't say anything for a while. Just hold me; let me hold you."

The minutes passed, hysteria ran its course and the outlines of reality came back into focus. Bourne led her to the chair; she caught the sleeve of her dress on the frayed lace. They both smiled, as he knelt beside her, holding her hand in silence.

"How about that drink?" he said finally.

"I think so," she replied, briefly tightening her grip on his hand as he got up from the floor. "You poured it quite a while ago."

"It won't go flat." He went to the bureau and returned with two glasses half filled with whiskey. She took hers. "Feeling better?" he asked.

"Calmer. Still confused . . . frightened, of course. Maybe angry, too, I'm not sure. I'm too afraid to think about that." She drank, closing her eyes, her head pressed back against the chair. "Why did you do it, Jason?"

"Because I thought I had to. That's the simple answer."

"And no answer at all. I deserve more than that."

"Yes, you do, and I'll give it to you. I have to now because you have to hear it; you have to understand. You have to protect yourself."

"Protect—"

He held up his hand, interrupting her. "It'll come later. All of it, if you like. But the first thing we have to do is know what happened—not to *me*, but to *you*. That's where we have to begin. Can you do it?"

"The newspaper?"

"Yes."

"God knows, I'm interested," she said, smiling weakly.

"Here." Jason went to the bed where he had dropped the two papers. "We'll both read it."

"No games?"

"No games."

They read the long article in silence, an article that told of death and intrigue in Zurich. Every now and then Marie gasped, shocked at what she was reading; at other times she shook her head in disbelief. Bourne said nothing. He saw the hand of Ilich Ramirez Sanchez. *Carlos will follow Cain to the ends of the earth. Carlos will kill him.* Marie St. Jacques was expendable, a baited decoy that would die in the trap that caught Cain.

I am Cain. I am death.

The article was, in fact, two articles—an odd mixture of fact and conjecture, speculations taking over where evidence came to an end. The first part indicated a Canadian government employee, a female economist, Marie St. Jacques. She was placed at the scene of three murders, her fingerprints confirmed by the Canadian government. In addition, police found a hotel key from the Carillon du Lac, apparently lost during the violence on the Guisan Quai. It was the key to Marie St. Jacques' room, given to her by the hotel clerk, who remembered her well—remembered what appeared to him to be a guest in a highly disturbed state of anxiety. The final piece of evidence was a handgun discovered not far from the Steppdeckstrasse, in an alley close by the scene of two other killings. Ballistics held it to be the murder weapon, and again there were fingerprints, again confirmed by the Canadian government. They belonged to the woman, Marie St. Jacques.

It was at this point that the article veered from fact. It spoke of rumors along the Bahnhofstrasse that a multimillion-dollar theft had taken place by means of a computer manipulation dealing with a numbered, confidential account belonging to an American corporation called Treadstone Seventy-One. The bank was also named; it was of course the Gemeinschaft. But everything else was clouded, obscure, more speculation than fact.

According to "unnamed sources," an American male holding the proper codes transferred millions to a bank in Paris, assigning the new account to specific individuals who were to assume rights of possession. The assignees were waiting in Paris, and upon clearance, withdrew the millions and disappeared. The success of the operation was traced to the American's obtaining the accurate codes to the Gemeinschaft account, a feat made possible by penetrating the bank's numerical sequence related to year, month and day of entry, standard procedure for confidential holdings. Such an analysis could only be made through the use of sophisticated computer techniques and a thorough knowledge of Swiss banking practices. When questioned, an officer of the bank, Herr Walther Apfel, acknowledged that there was an ongoing investigation into matters pertaining to the American company, but pursuant to Swiss law, "the bank would have no further comment—to anyone."

Here the connection to Marie St. Jacques was clarified. She was described as a government economist extensively schooled in international banking procedures, as well as a skilled computer programmer. She was suspected of being an accomplice, her expertise necessary to the massive theft. And there *was* a male suspect; she was reported to have been seen in his company at the Carillon du Lac.

Marie finished the article first and let the paper drop to the floor. At the sound, Bourne looked over from the edge of the bed. She was staring at the wall, a strange pensive serenity having come over her. It was the last reaction he expected. He finished reading quickly, feeling depressed and hopeless—for a moment, speechless. Then he found his voice and spoke.

"Lies," he said, "and they were made because of me, because of who and what I am. Smoke you out, they find me. I'm sorry, sorrier than I can ever tell you."

Marie shifted her eyes from the wall and looked at him. "It goes deeper than lies, Jason," she said. "There's too much truth for lies alone."

"Truth? The only truth is that you were in Zurich. You never touched a gun, you were never in an alley near the

[279]

Steppdeckstrasse, you didn't lose a hotel key and you never went near the Gemeinschaft."

"Agreed, but that's not the truth I'm talking about."

"Then what is?"

"The Gemeinschaft, Treadstone Seventy-One, Apfel. Those are true and the fact that any were mentioned—especially Apfel's acknowledgment—is incredible. Swiss bankers are cautious men. They don't ridicule the laws, not this way; the jail sentences are too severe. The statutes pertaining to banking confidentiality are among the most sacrosanct in Switzerland. Apfel could go to prison for years for saying what he did, for even alluding to such an account, much less confirming it by name. Unless he was ordered to say what he did by an authority powerful enough to contravene the laws." She stopped, her eyes straying to the wall again. "Why? Why was the Gemeinschaft or Treadstone or Apfel ever made part of the story?"

"I told you. They want me and they know we're together. Carlos knows we're together. Find you, he finds me."

"No, Jason, it goes beyond Carlos. You really *don't* understand the laws in Switzerland. Not even a Carlos could cause them to be flaunted this way." She looked at him, but her eyes did not see him; she was peering through her own mists. "This isn't one story, it's two. Both are constructed out of lies, the first connected to the second by tenuous speculation—public speculation—on a banking crisis that would never be made public, unless and until a thorough and private investigation proved the facts. And that second story—the patently false statement that millions were stolen from the Gemeinschaft—was tacked onto the equally false story that I'm wanted for killing three men in Zurich. It was added. Deliberately."

"Explain that, please."

"It's there, Jason. Believe me when I tell you that; it's right in front of us."

"What is?"

"Someone's trying to send us a message."

— 19 —

The army sedan sped south on Manhattan's East River Drive, headlights illuminating the swirling remnants of a late-winter snowfall. The major in the back seat dozed, his long body angled into the corner, his legs stretched out diagonally across the floor. In his lap was a briefcase, a thin nylon cord attached to the handle by a metal clamp, the cord itself strung through his right sleeve and down his inner tunic to his belt. The security device had been removed only twice in the past nine hours. Once during the major's departure from Zurich, and again with his arrival at Kennedy Airport. In both places, however, U. S. government personnel had been watching the customs clerks—more precisely, watching the briefcase. They were not told why, they were simply ordered to observe the inspections, and at the slightest deviation from normal procedures—which meant any undue interest in the briefcase—they were to intercede. With weapons, if necessary.

There was a sudden, quiet ringing; the major snapped his eyes open and brought his left hand up in front of his face. The sound was a wrist alarm; he pressed the button on his watch and squinted at the second radium dial of his

[281]

two-zoned instrument. The first was on Zurich time, the second, New York; the alarm had been set twenty-four hours ago, when the officer had received his cabled orders. The transmission would come within the next three minutes. That is, thought the major, it would come if Iron Ass was as precise as he expected his subordinates to be. The officer stretched, awkwardly balancing the briefcase, and leaned forward, speaking to the driver.

"Sergeant, turn on your scrambler to 1430 megahertz, will you please?"

"Yes, sir." The sergeant flipped two switches on the radio panel beneath the dashboard, then twisted the dial to the 1430 frequency. "There it is, Major."

"Thanks. Will the microphone reach back here?"

"I don't know. Never tried it, sir." The driver pulled the small plastic microphone from its cradle and stretched the spiral cord over the seat. "Guess it does," he concluded.

Static erupted from the speaker, the scrambling transmitter electronically scanning and jamming the frequency. The message would follow in seconds. It did.

"Treadstone? Treadstone, confirm, please."

"Treadstone receiving," said Major Gordon Webb. "You're clear. Go ahead."

"What's your position?"

"About a mile south of the Triborough, East River Drive," said the major.

"Your timing is acceptable," came the voice from the speaker.

"Glad to hear it. It makes my day . . . sir."

There was a brief pause, the major's comment not appreciated. "Proceed to 139 East Seventy-first. Confirm by repeat."

"One-three-niner East Seventy-first."

"Keep your vehicle out of the area. Approach on foot."

"Understood."

"Out."

"Out." Webb snapped the transmission button in place and handed the microphone back to the driver. "Forget that address, Sergeant. Your name's on a very short file now."

"Gotcha', Major. Nothing but static on that thing anyway. But since I don't know where it is and these wheels aren't supposed to go there, where do you want to be dropped off?"

Webb smiled. "No more than two blocks away. I'd go to sleep in the gutter if I had to walk any further than that."

"How about Lex and Seventy-second?"

"Is that two blocks?"

"No more than three."

"If it's three blocks you're a private."

"Then I couldn't pick you up later, Major. Privates aren't cleared for this duty."

"Whatever you say, Captain." Webb closed his eyes. After two years, he was about to see Treadstone Seventy-One for himself. He knew he should feel a sense of anticipation; he did not. He felt only a sense of weariness, of futility. *What had happened?*

The incessant hum of the tires on the pavement below was hypnotic, but the rhythm was broken by sharp intrusions where concrete and wheels were not compatible. The sounds evoked memories of long ago, of screeching jungle noises woven into a single tone. And then the night—that night— when blinding lights and staccato explosions were all around him, and below him, telling him he was about to die. But he did not die; a miracle wrought by a man had given his life back to him . . . and the years went on, that night, those days never to be forgotten. *What the hell had happened?*

"Here we are, Major."

Webb opened his eyes, his hand wiping the sweat that had formed on his forehead. He looked at his watch, gripped his briefcase and reached for the handle of the door.

"I'll be here between 2300 and 2330 hours, Sergeant. If you can't park, just cruise around and I'll find you."

"Yes, sir." The driver turned in his seat. "Could the major tell me if we're going to be driving any distance later?"

"Why? Have you got another fare?"

"Come on, sir. I'm assigned to you until you say otherwise, you know that. But these heavy-plated trucks use gas like the old-time Shermans. If we're going far I'd better fill it."

"Sorry." The major paused. "Okay. You'll have to find out where it is, anyway, because I don't know. We're going to a private airfield in Madison, New Jersey. I have to be there no later than one hundred hours."

"I've got a vague idea," said the driver. "At 2330, you're cutting it pretty close, sir."

"OK—2300, then. And thanks." Webb got out of the car, closed the door and waited until the brown sedan entered the flow of traffic on Seventy-second Street. He stepped off the curb and headed south to Seventy-first.

Four minutes later he stood in front of a well-kept brownstone, its muted, rich design in concert with those around it in the tree-lined street. It was a quiet street, a monied street—old money. It was the last place in Manhattan a person would suspect of housing one of the most sensitive intelligence operations in the country. And as of twenty minutes ago, Major Gordon Webb was one of only eight or ten people in the country who knew of its existence.

Treadstone Seventy-One.

He climbed the steps, aware that the pressure of his weight on the iron grids embedded in the stone beneath him triggered electronic devices that in turn activated cameras, producing his image on screens inside. Beyond this, he knew little, except that Treadstone Seventy-One never closed; it was operated and monitored twenty-four hours a day by a select few, identities unknown.

He reached the top step and rang the bell, an ordinary bell, but not for an ordinary door, the major could see that. The heavy wood was riveted to a steel plate behind it, the decorative iron designs in actuality the rivets, the large brass knob disguising a hotplate that caused a series of steel bolts to shoot across into steel receptacles at the touch of a human hand when the alarms were turned on. Webb glanced up at the windows. Each pane of glass, he knew, was an inch thick, capable of withstanding the impact of .30 caliber shells. Treadstone Seventy-One was a fortress.

The door opened and the major involuntarily smiled at the figure standing there, so totally out of place did she seem. She was a petite, elegant-looking, gray-haired woman with soft aristocratic features and a bearing that bespoke monied gentility. Her voice confirmed the appraisal; it was mid-Atlantic, refined in the better finishing schools, and at innumerable polo matches.

"How good of you to drop by, Major. Jeremy wrote us that you might. Do come in. It's such a pleasure to see you again."

"It's good to see you again, too," replied Webb, stepping into the tasteful foyer, finishing his statement when the

[284]

door was closed, "but I'm not sure where it was we met before."

The woman laughed. "Oh, we've had dinner ever so many times."

"With Jeremy?"

"Of course."

"Who's Jeremy?"

"A devoted nephew who's also your devoted friend. Such a nice young man; it's a pity he doesn't exist." She took his elbow as they walked down a long hallway. "It's all for the benefit of neighbors who might be strolling by. Come along now, they're waiting."

They passed an archway that led to a large living room; the major looked inside. There was a grand piano by the front windows, harp beside it; and everywhere—on the piano and on polished tables glistening under the spill of subdued lamps—were silver-framed photographs, mementos of a past filled with wealth and grace. Sailboats, men and women on the decks of ocean liners, several military portraits. And, yes, two candid shots of someone mounted for a polo match. It was a room that belonged in a brownstone on this street.

They reached the end of the hallway; there was a large mahogany door, bas-relief and iron ornamentation part of its design, part of its security. If there was an infrared camera, Webb could not detect the whereabouts of the lens. The gray-haired woman pressed an unseen bell; the major could hear a slight hum.

"Your friend is here, gentlemen. Stop playing poker and go to work. Snap to, Jesuit."

"Jesuit?" asked Webb, bewildered.

"An old joke," replied the woman. "It goes back to when you were probably playing marbles and snarling at little girls."

The door opened and the aged but still erect figure of David Abbott was revealed. "Glad to see you, Major," said the former Silent Monk of Covert Services, extending his hand.

"Good to be here, sir." Webb shook hands. Another elderly, imposing-looking man came up beside Abbott.

"A friend of Jeremy's, no doubt," said the man, his deep voice edged with humor. "Dreadfully sorry time preludes proper introductions, young fellow. Come along, Margaret.

There's a lovely fire upstairs." He turned to Abbott. "You'll let me know when you're leaving, David?"

"Usual time for me, I expect," replied the Monk. "I'll show these two how to ring you."

It was then that Webb realized there was a third man in the room; he was standing in the shadows at the far end, and the major recognized him instantly. He was Elliot Stevens, senior aide to the president of the United States—some said his alter ego. He was in his early forties, slender, wore glasses and had the bearing of unpretentious authority about him.

". . . it'll be fine." The imposing older man who had not found time to introduce himself had been speaking; Webb had not heard him, his attention on the White House aide. "I'll be waiting."

"Till next time," continued Abbott, shifting his eyes kindly to the gray-haired woman. "Thanks, Sister Meg. Keep your habit pressed. And down."

"You're still wicked, Jesuit."

The couple left, closing the door behind them. Webb stood for a moment, shaking his head and smiling. The man and woman of 139 East Seventy-first belonged to the room down the hall, just as that room belonged in the brownstone, all a part of the quiet, monied, tree-lined street. "You've known them a long time, haven't you?"

"A lifetime, you might say," replied Abbott. "He was a yachtsman we put to good use in the Adriatic runs for Donovan's operations in Yugoslavia. Mikhailovitch once said he sailed on sheer nerve, bending the worst weather to his will. And don't let Sister Meg's graciousness fool you. She was one of Intrepid's girls, a piranha with very sharp teeth."

"They're quite a story."

"It'll never be told," said Abbott, closing the subject. "I want you to meet Elliot Stevens. I don't think I have to tell you who he is. Webb, Stevens. Stevens, Webb."

"That sounds like a law firm," said Stevens amiably, walking across the room, hand extended. "Nice to know you, Webb. Have a good trip?"

"I would have preferred military transport. I hate those damned commercial airlines. I thought a customs agent at Kennedy was going to slice the lining of my suitcase."

"You look too respectable in that uniform," laughed the Monk. "You're obviously a smuggler."

"I'm still not sure I understand the uniform," said the major, carrying his briefcase to a long hatch table against the wall, and unclipping the nylon cord from his belt.

"I shouldn't have to tell you," answered Abbott, "that the tightest security is often found in being quite obvious on the surface. An army intelligence officer prowling around undercover in Zurich at this particular time could raise alarms."

"Then I don't understand, either," said the White House aide, coming up beside Webb at the table, watching the major's manipulations with the nylon cord and the lock. "Wouldn't an obvious presence raise even more shrill alarms? I thought the assumption of undercover was that discovery was less probable."

"Webb's trip to Zurich was a routine consulate check, predated on the G-Two schedules. No one fools anybody about those trips; they're what they are and nothing else. Ascertaining new sources, paying off informants. The Soviets do it all the time; they don't even bother to hide it. Neither do we, frankly."

"But that *wasn't* the purpose of this trip," said Stevens, beginning to understand. "So the obvious conceals the unobvious."

"That's it."

"Can I help?" The presidential aide seemed fascinated by the briefcase.

"Thanks," said Webb. "Just pull the cord through."

Stevens did so. "I always thought it was chains around the wrist," he said.

"Too many hands cut off," explained the major, smiling at the White House man's reaction. "There's a steel wire running through the nylon." He freed the briefcase and opened it on the table, looking around at the elegance of the furnished library-den. At the rear of the room was a pair of French doors that apparently led to an outside garden, an outline of a high stone wall seen dimly through the panes of thick glass. "So this is Treadstone Seventy-One. It isn't the way I pictured it."

"Pull the curtains again, will you please, Elliot?" Abbott said. The presidential aide walked to the French doors and did so. Abbott crossed to a bookcase, opened the cabinet beneath it, and reached inside. There was a quiet whir; the entire bookcase came out of the wall and slowly revolved to the left. On the other side was an electronic radio console, one of the most sophisticated Gordon Webb had seen. "Is this more what you had in mind?" asked the Monk.

"Jesus . . ." The major whistled as he studied the dials, calibrations, cable patches and scanning devices built into the panel. The Pentagon war rooms had far more elaborate equipment, but this was the miniaturized equal of most well-structured intelligence stations.

"I'd whistle, too," said Stevens, standing in front of the dense curtain. "But Mr. Abbott already gave me my personal sideshow. That's only the beginning. For more buttons and this place looks like a SAC base in Omaha."

"Those same buttons also transform this room back into a graceful East Side library." The old man reached inside the cabinet; in seconds the enormous console was replaced by bookshelves. He then walked to the adjacent bookcase, opened the cabinet beneath and once again put his hand inside. The whirring began; the bookcase slid out, and shortly in its place were three tall filing cabinets. The Monk took out a key and pulled out a file drawer. "I'm not showing off, Gordon. When we're finished, I want you to look through these. I'll show you the switch that'll send them back. If you have any problems, our host will take care of everything."

"What am I to look for?"

"We'll get to it; right now I want to hear about Zurich. What have you learned?"

"Excuse me, Mr. Abbott," interrupted Stevens. "If I'm slow, it's because all this is new to me. But I was thinking about something you said a minute ago about Major Webb's trip."

"What is it?"

"You said the trip was predated on the G-Two schedules."

"That's right."

"Why? The major's obvious presence was to confuse Zurich, not Washington. Or was it?"

The Monk smiled. "I can see why the president keeps you around. We've never doubted that Carlos has bought his way into a circle or two—or ten—in Washington. He finds the discontented men and offers them what they do not have. A Carlos could not exist without such people. You must remember, he doesn't merely sell death, he sells a nation's secrets. All too frequently to the Soviets, if only to prove to them how rash they were to expel him."

"The president would want to know that," said the aide. "It would explain several things."

"It's why you're here, isn't it?" said Abbott.

"I guess it is."

"And it's a good place to begin for Zurich," said Webb, taking his briefcase to an armchair in front of the filing cabinets. He sat down, spreading the folds inside the case at his feet, and took out several sheets of paper. "You may not doubt Carlos is in Washington, but I can confirm it."

"Where? Treadstone?"

"There's no clear proof of that, but it can't be ruled out. He found the *fiche*. He altered it."

"Good God, how?"

"The how I can only guess; the who I know."

"Who?"

"A man named Koenig. Until three days ago he was in charge of primary verifications at the Gemeinschaft Bank."

"Three days ago? Where is he now?"

"Dead. A freak automobile accident on a road he traveled every day of his life. Here's the police report; I had it translated." Abbott took the papers, and sat down in a nearby chair. Elliot Stevens remained standing; Webb continued. "There's something very interesting there. It doesn't tell us anything we don't know, but there's a lead I'd like to follow up."

"What is it?" asked the Monk, reading. "This describes the accident. The curve, speed of vehicle, apparent swerving to avoid a collision."

"It's at the end. It mentions the killing at the Gemeinschaft, the bolt that got us off our asses."

"It does?" Abbott turned the page.

"Look at it. Last couple of sentences. See what I mean?"

"Not exactly," replied Abbott, frowning. "This merely states that Koenig was employed by the Gemeinschaft where a recent homicide took place . . . and he had been a witness to the initial gunfire. That's all."

"I don't think it is 'all,'" said Webb. "I think there was more. Someone started to raise a question, but it was left hanging. I'd like to find out who has his red pencil on the Zurich police reports. He could be Carlos' man; we know he's got one there."

The Monk leaned back in the chair, his frown unrelieved. "Assuming you're right, why wasn't the entire reference deleted?"

"Too obvious. The killing *did* take place; Koenig *was* a witness; the investigating officer who wrote up the report might legitimately ask why."

"But if he had speculated on a connection wouldn't he be just as disturbed that the speculation was deleted?"

"Not necessarily. We're talking about a bank in Switzerland. Certain areas are officially inviolable unless there's proof."

"Not always. I understood you were very successful with the newspapers."

"*Un*officially. I appealed to prurient journalistic sensationalism, and—although it damn near killed him—got Walther Apfel to corroborate halfway."

"Interruption," said Elliot Stevens. "I think this is where the Oval Office has to come in. I assume by the newspapers you're referring to the Canadian woman."

"Not really. That story was already out; we couldn't stop it. Carlos is wired into the Zurich police; they issued that report. We simply enlarged on it and tied her to an equally false story about millions having been stolen from the Gemeinschaft." Webb paused and looked at Abbott. "That's something we have to talk about; it may not be false after all."

"I can't believe that," said the Monk.

"I don't *want* to believe it," replied the major. "Ever."

"Would you mind backing up?" asked the White House aide, sitting down opposite the army officer. "I have to get this very clear."

"Let me explain," broke in Abbott, seeing the bewilderment on Webb's face. "Elliot's here on orders from the president. It's the killing at the Ottawa airport."

"It's an unholy mess," said Stevens bluntly. "The prime minister damn near told the president to take our stations out of Nova Scotia. He's one angry Canadian."

"How did it come down?" asked Webb.

"Very badly. All they know is that a ranking economist at National Revenue's Treasury Board made discreet inquiries about an unlisted American corporation and got himself killed for it. To make matters worse, Canadian Intelligence was told to stay out of it; it was a highly sensitive U. S. operation."

"Who the hell did *that*?"

"I believe I've heard the name Iron Ass bandied about here and there," said the Monk.

"General Crawford? Stupid son of a bitch—stupid iron-assed son of a bitch!"

"Can you imagine?" interjected Stevens. "*Their* man gets killed and *we* have the gall to tell them to stay out."

"He was right, of course," corrected Abbott. "It had to be done swiftly, no room for misunderstanding. A clamp had to be put on instantly, the shock sufficiently outrageous to stop everything. It gave me time to reach MacKenzie Hawkins—Mac and I worked together in Burma; he's retired but they listen to him. They're cooperating now and that's the important thing, isn't it?"

"There are other considerations, Mr. Abbott," protested Stevens.

"They're on different levels, Elliot. We working stiffs aren't on them; we don't have to spend time over diplomatic posturing. I'll grant you those postures are necessary, but they don't concern us."

"They do concern the president, sir. They're part of his every working-stiff day. And that's why I have to go back with a very clear picture." Stevens paused, turning to Webb. "Now, please, let me have it again. Exactly what did you do and why? What part did we play regarding this Canadian woman?"

"Initially not a goddamn thing; that was Carlos' move. Someone very high up in the Zurich police is on Carlos' payroll. It was the Zurich police who mocked up the so-called evidence linking her to the three killings. And it's ludicrous; she's no killer."

"All right, all right," said the aide. "That was Carlos. Why did he do it?"

"To flush out Bourne. The St. Jacques woman and Bourne are together."

"Bourne being this assassin who calls himself Cain, correct?"

"Yes," said Webb. "Carlos has sworn to kill him. Cain's moved in on Carlos all over Europe and the Middle East, but there's no photograph of Cain, no one really knows what he looks like. So by circulating a picture of the woman—and let me tell you, it's in every damn newspaper over there—someone may spot her. If she's found, the chances are that Cain—Bourne—will be found too. Carlos will kill them both."

"All right. Again, that's Carlos. Now what did *you* do?"

"Just what I said. Reached the Gemeinschaft and convinced the bank into confirming the fact that the woman might—just might—be tied with a massive theft. It wasn't easy, but it was their man Koenig who'd been bribed, not one of our people. That's an internal matter; they wanted a lid on it. Then I called the papers and referred them to Walther Apfel. Mysterious woman, murder, millions stolen; the editors leaped at it."

"For Christ's sake, why?" shouted Stevens. "You used a citizen of another country for a U. S. intelligence strategy! A staff employee of a closely allied government. Are you out of your minds? You only exacerbated the situation, you sacrificed her!"

"You're wrong," said Webb. "We're trying to save her life. We've turned Carlos' weapon against him."

"How?"

The Monk raised his hand. "Before we answer we have to go back to another question," he said. "Because the answer to that may give you an indication of how restricted the information must remain. A moment ago I asked the major how Carlos' man could have found Bourne—found the *fiche* that identified Bourne as Cain. I think I know, but I want him to tell you."

Webb leaned forward. "The Medusa records," he said, quietly, reluctantly.

"Medusa . . . ?" Stevens' expression conveyed the fact that the Medusa had been the subject of early White House confidential briefings. "They're buried," he said.

"Correction," intruded Abbott. "There's an original and two copies, and they're in vaults at the Pentagon, the CIA and the National Security Council. Access to them is limited to a select group, each one among the highest-ranking members of his unit. Bourne came out of Medusa; a cross-checking of those names with the bank records would produce his name. Someone gave them to Carlos."

Stevens stared at the Monk. "Are you saying that Carlos is . . . wired into . . . men like that? It's an extraordinary charge."

"It's the only explanation," said Webb.

"By why would Bourne ever use his own name?"

"It was necessary," replied Abbott. "It was a vital part of the portrait. It had to be authentic; everything had to be authentic. Everything."

"Authentic?"

"Maybe you'll understand now," continued the major.

"By tying the St. Jacques woman into millions supposedly stolen from the Gemeinschaft Bank, we're telling Bourne to surface. He knows it's false."

"Bourne to *surface?*"

"The man called Jason Bourne," said Abbott, getting to his feet and walking slowly toward the drawn curtains, "is an American intelligence officer. There is no Cain, not the one Carlos believes. He's a lure, a trap for Carlos; that's who he is. Or was."

The silence was brief, broken by the White House man. "I think you'd better explain. The president has to know."

"I suppose so," mused Abbott, parting the curtains, looking absently outside. "It's an insoluble dilemma, really. Presidents change, different men with different temperaments and appetites sit in the Oval Office. However, a long-range intelligence strategy doesn't change, not one like this. Yet an offhand remark over a glass of whiskey in a postpresidential conversation, or an egotistical phrase in a memoir, can blow that same strategy right to hell. There isn't a day that we don't worry about those men who have survived the White House."

"*Please,*" interrupted Stevens. "I ask you to remember that I'm here on the orders of *this* president. Whether you approve or disapprove doesn't matter. He has the right by law to know; and in his name I insist on that right."

"Very well," said Abbott, still looking outside. "Three years ago we borrowed a page from the British. We created a man who never was. If you recall, prior to the Normandy invasion British Intelligence floated a corpse into the coast of Portugal, knowing that whatever documents were concealed on it would find their way to the German Embassy in Lisbon. A life was created for that dead body; a name, a naval officer's rank; schools, training, travel orders, driver's license, membership cards in exclusive London clubs and a half-dozen personal letters. Scattered throughout were hints, vaguely worded allusions, and a few very direct chronological and geographical references. They all pointed to the invasion taking place a hundred miles away from the beaches at Normandy, and six weeks off the target date in June. After panicked checks were made by German agents all over England—and, incidentally, controlled and monitored by MI Five—the High Command in Berlin bought the story and shifted a large part of their defenses. As many as were lost, thousands upon thousands of lives were saved by that man who never was." Abbott let the curtain fall into place and walked wearily back to his chair.

"I've heard the story," said the White House aide. "And?"

"Ours was a variation," said the Monk, sitting down wearily. "Create a living man, a quickly established legend, seemingly everywhere at once, racing all over Southeast Asia, outdoing Carlos at every turn, especially in the area of sheer numbers. Whenever there was a killing, or an unexplained death, or a prominent figure involved in a fatal accident, there was Cain. Reliable sources—paid informants known for accuracy—were fed his name; embassies, listening posts, entire intelligence networks were repeatedly funneled reports that concentrated on Cain's rapidly expanding activities. His 'kills' were mounting every month, sometimes it seemed weekly. He was everywhere . . . and he *was*. In all ways."

"You mean this Bourne was?"

"Yes. He spent months learning everything there was to learn about Carlos, studying every file we had, every known and suspected assassination with which Carlos was involved. He pored over Carlos' tactics, his methods of operation, everything. Much of *that* material has never seen the light of day, and probably never will. It's explosive— governments and international combines would be at each others' throats. There was literally nothing Bourne did not know—that could be *known*—about Carlos. And then he'd show himself, always with a different appearance, speaking any of several languages, talking about things to selected circles of hardened criminals that only a professional killer would talk about. Then he'd be gone, leaving behind bewildered and often frightened men and women. They had seen Cain; he existed, and he was ruthless. That was the image Bourne conveyed."

"He's been underground like this for *three years?*" asked Stevens.

"Yes. He moved to Europe, the most accomplished white assassin in Asia, graduate of the infamous Medusa, challenging Carlos in his own yard. And in the process he saved four men marked by Carlos, took credit for others Carlos had killed, mocked him at every opportunity . . . always trying to force him out in the open. He spent nearly three years living the most dangerous sort of lie a man can live, the kind of existence few men ever know. Most would have broken under it; and that possibility can never be ruled out."

"What kind of man is he?"

"A professional," answered Gordon Webb. "Someone who had the training and the capability, who understood that Carlos had to be found, stopped."

"But three *years* . . . ?"

"If that seems incredible," said Abbott, "you should know that he submitted to surgery. It was like a final break with the past, with the man he was in order to become a man he wasn't. I don't think there's any way a nation can repay a man like Bourne for what he's done. Perhaps the only way is to give him the chance to succeed—and by God I intend to do that." The Monk stopped for precisely two seconds, then added, "If it *is* Bourne."

It was as if Elliot Stevens had been struck by an unseen hammer. "What did you say?" he asked.

"I'm afraid I've held this to the end. I wanted you to understand the whole picture before I described the gap. It may *not* be a gap—we just don't know. Too many things have happened that make no sense to us, but we don't know. It's the reason why there can be absolutely no interference from other levels, no diplomatic sugar pills that might expose the strategy. We could condemn a man to death, a man who's given more than any of us. If he succeeds, he can go back to his own life, but only anonymously, only without his identity ever being revealed."

"I'm afraid you'll have to explain that," said the astonished presidential aide.

"Loyalty, Elliot. It's not restricted to what's commonly referred to as the 'good guys.' Carlos has built up an army of men and women who are devoted to him. They may not know him but they revere him. However, if he can take Carlos—or trap Carlos so we can take him—then vanish, he's home free."

"But you say he may *not* be Bourne!"

"I said we don't know. It *was* Bourne at the bank, the signatures were authentic. But is it Bourne now? The next few days will tell us."

"If he surfaces," added Webb.

"It's delicate," continued the old man. "There are so many variables. If it isn't Bourne—or if he's turned—it could explain the call to Ottawa, the killing at the airport. From what we can gather, the woman's expertise *was* used to withdraw the money in Paris. All Carlos had to do was make a few inquiries at the Canadian Treasury Board. The rest would be child's play for him. Kill her contact, panic her, cut her off, and use her to contain Bourne."

"Were you able to get word to her?" asked the major.

"I tried and failed. I had Mac Hawkins call a man who also worked closely with the St. Jacques woman, a man named Alan somebody-or-other. He instructed her to return to Canada immediately. She hung up on him."

"God*damn* it!" exploded Webb.

"Precisely. If we could have gotten her back, we might have learned so much. She's the key. Why is she with him? Why he with her? Nothing makes sense."

"Less so to me!" said Stevens, his bewilderment turning into anger. "If you want the president's cooperation—and I promise nothing—you'd better be clearer."

Abbott turned to him. "Some six months ago Bourne disappeared," he said. "Something happened; we're not sure what, but we can piece together a probability. He got word into Zurich that he was on his way to Marseilles. Later—too late—we understood. He'd learned that Carlos had accepted a contract on Howard Leland, and Bourne tried to stop it. Then nothing; he vanished. Had he been killed? Had he broken under the strain? Had he . . . given up?"

"I can't accept that," interrupted Webb angrily. "I won't accept it!"

"I know you won't," said the Monk. "It's why I want you to go through that file. You know his codes; they're all in there. See if you can spot any deviations in Zurich."

"Please!" broke in Stevens. "What do you *think*? You must have found something concrete, something on which to base a judgment. I need that, Mr. Abbott. The president needs it."

"I wish to heaven I had," replied the Monk. "What have we found? Everything and nothing. Almost three years of the most carefully constructed deception in our records. Every false act documented, every move defined and justified; each man and woman—informants, contacts, sources—given faces, voices, stories to tell. And every month, every week just a little bit closer to Carlos. Then nothing. Silence. Six months of a vacuum."

"Not now," countered the president's aide. "That silence was broken. By whom?"

"That's the basic question, isn't it?" said the old man, his voice tired. "Months of silence, then suddenly an explosion of unauthorized, incomprehensible activity. The account penetrated, the *fiche* altered, millions transferred—by all appearances, stolen. Above all, men killed and traps set for other men. But for whom, *by* whom?" The Monk shook his head wearily. "Who *is* the man out there?"

—— 20 ——

The limousine was parked between two streetlamps, diagonally across from the heavy ornamental doors of the brownstone. In the front seat sat a uniformed chauffeur; such a driver at the wheel of such a vehicle not an uncommon sight on the tree-lined street. What was unusual, however, was the fact that two other men remained in the shadows of the deep back seat, neither making any move to get out. Instead, they watched the entrance of the brownstone, confident that they could not be picked up by the infrared beam of a scanning camera.

One man adjusted his glasses, the eyes beyond his thick lenses owl-like, flatly suspicious of most of what they surveyed. Alfred Gillette, director of Personnel Screening and Evaluation for the National Security Council, spoke. "How gratifying to be there when arrogance collapses. How much more so to be the instrument."

"You really dislike him, don't you?" said Gillette's companion, a heavy-shouldered man in a black raincoat whose accent was derived from a Slavic language somewhere in Europe.

"I loathe him. He stands for everything I hate in Washington. The right schools, houses in Georgetown, farms in Virginia, quiet meetings at their clubs. They've got their tight little world and you don't break in—they run it all. The *bastards*. The superior, self-inflated *gentry* of Washington. They use other men's intellects, other men's work, wrapping it all into decisions bearing their imprimaturs. And if you're on the outside, you become part of that amorphous entity, a 'damn fine staff.' "

"You exaggerate," said the European, his eyes on the brownstone. "You haven't done badly down there. We never would have contacted you otherwise."

Gillette scowled. "If I haven't done badly, it's because I've become indispensable to too many like David Abbott. I have in my head a thousand facts they couldn't possibly recall. It's simply easier for them to place me where the questions are, where problems need solutions. Director of Personnel Screening and Evaluation! They created that title, that post, for me. Do you know why?"

"No, Alfred," replied the European, looking at his watch, "I don't know why."

"Because they don't have the patience to spend hours poring over thousands of résumés and dossiers. They'd rather be dining at Sans Souci, or preening in front of Senate committees, reading from pages prepared by others—by those unseen, unnamed 'damn fine staffs.' "

"You're a bitter man," said the European.

"More than you'll know. A lifetime doing the work those bastards should have done for themselves. And for what? A title and an occasional lunch where my brains are picked between the shrimp and the entrée! By men like the supremely arrogant David Abbott; they're nothing without people like me."

"Don't underestimate the Monk. Carlos doesn't."

"How could he? He doesn't know what to evaluate. Everything Abbott does is shrouded in secrecy; no one knows how many mistakes he's made. And if any come to light, men like me are blamed for them."

The European shifted his gaze from the window to Gillette. "You're very emotional, Alfred," he said coldly. "You must be careful about that."

The bureaucrat smiled. "It never gets in the way: I believe my contributions to Carlos bear that out. Let's say I'm preparing myself for a confrontation I wouldn't avoid for anything in the world."

"An honest statement," said the heavy-shouldered man. "What about you? You found me."

"I knew what to look for." The European returned to the window.

"I mean *you*. The work you do. For Carlos."

"I have no such complicated reasoning. I come out of a country where educated men are promoted at the whim of morons who recite Marxist litany by rote. Carlos, too, knew what to look for."

Gillette laughed, his flat eyes close to shining. "We're not so different after all. Change the bloodlines of our Eastern establishment for Marx and there's a distinct parallel."

"Perhaps," agreed the European, looking again at his watch. "It shouldn't be long now. Abbott always catches the midnight shuttle, his every hour accounted for in Washington."

"You're sure he'll come out alone?"

"He always does, and he certainly wouldn't be seen with Elliot Stevens. Webb and Stevens will also leave separately; twenty-minute intervals is standard for those called in."

"How did you find Treadstone?"

"It wasn't so difficult. You contributed, Alfred; you were part of a damn fine staff." The man laughed, his eyes on the brownstone. "Cain was out of Medusa, you told us that, and if Carlos' suspicions are accurate, that meant the Monk, *we* knew *that*; it tied him to Bourne. Carlos instructed us to keep Abbott under twenty-four-hour surveillance; something had gone wrong. When the gunshots in Zurich were heard in Washington, Abbott got careless. We followed him here. It was merely a question of persistence."

"That led you to Canada? To the man in Ottawa?"

"The man in Ottawa revealed himself by looking for Treadstone. When we learned who the girl was, we had the Treasury Board watched, her section watched. A call came from Paris; it was she, telling him to start a search. We don't know why, but we suspect Bourne may be trying to blow Treadstone apart. If he's turned, it's one way to get out and keep the money. It doesn't matter. Suddenly, this section head no one outside the Canadian government had ever heard of was transformed into a problem of the highest priority. Intelligence communiqués were burning the wires. It meant Carlos was right; *you* were right, Alfred. There is no Cain. He's an invention, a trap."

"From the beginning," insisted Gillette. "I told you that.

Three years of false reports, sources unverified. It was all there."

"From the beginning," mused the European. "Undoubtedly the Monk's finest creation . . . until something happened and the creation turned. Everything's turning; it's all coming apart at the seams."

"Stevens' being here confirms that. The president insists on knowing."

"He has to. There's a nagging suspicion in Ottawa that a section head at the Treasury Board was killed by American Intelligence." The European turned from the window and looked at the bureaucrat. "Remember, Alfred, we simply want to know what happened. I've given you the facts as we've learned them; they're irrefutable and Abbott cannot deny them. But they must be presented as having been obtained independently by your own sources. You're appalled. You demand an accounting; the entire intelligence community has been duped."

"It has!" exclaimed Gillette. "Duped and used. No one in Washington knows about Bourne, about Treadstone. They've excluded everyone; it *is* appalling. I don't have to pretend. Arrogant bastards!"

"Alfred," cautioned the European, holding up his hand in the shadows, "do remember whom you're working for. The threat cannot be based on emotion, but in cold professional outrage. He'll suspect you instantly; you must dispel those suspicions just as swiftly. *You* are the accuser, not he."

"I'll remember."

"Good." Headlight beams bounced through the glass. "Abbott's taxi is here. I'll take care of the driver." The European reached to his right and flipped a switch beneath the armrest. "I'll be in my car across the street, listening." He spoke to the chauffeur. "Abbott will be coming out any moment now. You know what to do."

The chauffeur nodded. Both men got out of the limousine simultaneously. The driver walked around the hood as if to escort a wealthy employer to the south side of the street. Gillette watched through the rear window; the two men stayed together for several seconds, then separated, the European heading for the approaching cab, his hand held up, a bill between his fingers. The taxi would be sent away; the caller's plans had changed. The chauffeur had raced to the north side of the street and was now concealed in the shadows of a staircase two doors away from Tread-stone Seventy-One.

Thirty seconds later Gillette's eyes were drawn to the door of the brownstone. Light spilled through as an impatient David Abbott came outside, looking up and down the street, glancing at his watch, obviously annoyed. The taxi was late and he had a plane to catch; precise schedules had to be followed. Abbott walked down the steps, turning left on the pavement, looking for the cab, expecting it. In seconds he would pass the chauffeur. He did, both men well out of camera range.

The interception was quick, the discussion rapid. In moments, a bewildered David Abbott climbed inside the limousine and the chauffeur walked away into the shadows.

"You!" said the Monk, anger and disgust in his voice. "Of all people, *you*."

"I don't think you're in any position to be disdainful . . . much less arrogant."

"What you've *done!* How *dare* you? Zurich. The Medusa records. It was you!"

"The Medusa records, yes. Zurich, yes. But it's not a question of what *I've* done; it's what you've done. We sent our own men to Zurich, telling them what to look for. We found it. His name is Bourne, isn't it? He's the man you call Cain. The man you invented."

Abbott kept himself in check. "How did you find this house?"

"Persistence. I had you followed."

"You had *me* followed? What the hell did you think you were *doing?*"

"Trying to set a record straight. A record you've warped and lied about, keeping the truth from the rest of us. What did you think *you* were doing?"

"Oh, my God, you damn fool!" Abbott inhaled deeply. "Why did you do it? Why didn't you come to me yourself?"

"Because you'd have done nothing. You've manipulated the entire intelligence community. Millions of dollars, untold thousands of man hours, embassies and stations fed lies and distortions about a killer that never existed. Oh, I recall your words—what a challenge to Carlos! What an irresistible *trap* is what it was! Only we were your pawns too, and as a responsible member of the Security Council, I resent it deeply. You're all alike. Who elected you God so

[302]

you could break the rules—no, not just the rules, the laws—and make us look like fools?"

"There was no other way," said the old man wearily, his face a drawn mass of crevices in the dim light. "How many know? Tell me the truth."

"I've contained it. I gave you that."

"It may not be enough. Oh, Christ!"

"It may not last, period," said the bureaucrat emphatically. "I want to know what happened."

"What happened?"

"To this grand strategy of yours. It seems to be . . . falling apart at the seams."

"Why do you say that?"

"It's perfectly obvious. You've lost Bourne; you can't find him. Your Cain has disappeared with a fortune banked for him in Zurich."

Abbott was silent for a moment. "Wait a minute. What put you on to it?"

"You," said Gillette quickly, the prudent man rising to the baited question. "I must say I admired your control when that ass from the Pentagon spoke so knowingly of Operation Medusa . . . sitting directly across from the man who created it."

"History." The old man's voice was strong now. "That wouldn't have told you anything."

"Let's say it was rather unusual for you not to *say* anything. I mean, who at that table knew more about Medusa than you? But you didn't say a word, and that started me thinking. So I objected strenuously to the attention being paid this assassin, Cain. You couldn't resist, David. You had to offer a very plausible reason to continue the search for Cain. You threw Carlos into the hunt."

"It was the truth," interrupted Abbott.

"Certainly it was; you knew when to use it and I knew when to spot it. Ingenious. A snake pulled out of Medusa's head, groomed for a mythical title. The contender jumps into the champion's ring to draw the champion out of his corner."

"It was sound, sound from the beginning."

"Why not? As I say, it was ingenious, even down to every move made by his own people against Cain. Who better to relay those moves to Cain but the one man on the Forty Committee who's given reports on every covert operations conference. You used us all!"

The Monk nodded. "Very well. To a point you're right, there've been degrees of abuse—in my opinion, totally justified—but it's not what you think. There are checks and balances; there always are, I wouldn't have it any other way. Treadstone is comprised of a small group of men among the most trustworthy in the government. They range from Army G-Two to the Senate, from the CIA to Naval Intelligence, and now, frankly, the White House. Should there be any true abuse, there's not one of them that would hesitate to put a stop to the operation. None has ever seen fit to do so, and I beg you not to do so either."

"Would I be made part of Treadstone?"

"You *are* part of it now."

"I see. What happened? Where is Bourne?"

"I wish to God we knew. We're not even sure it *is* Bourne."

"You're not even sure of *what?*"

"I see. What happened? Where is Bourne?"

"I wish to God we knew. We're not even sure it is Bourne."

"You're not even sure of what?"

The European reached for the switch on the dashboard and snapped it off. "That's it," he said. "That's what we had to know." He turned to the chauffeur beside him. "Quickly, now. Get beside the staircase. Remember, if one of them comes out, you have precisely three seconds before the door is closed. Work fast."

The uniformed man got out first; he walked up the pavement toward Treadstone Seventy-One. From one of the adjacent brownstones, a middle-aged couple were saying loud goodbyes to their hosts. The chauffeur slowed down, reached into his pocket for a cigarette and stopped to light it. He was now a bored driver, whiling away the hours of a tedious vigil. The European watched, then unbuttoned his raincoat and withdrew a long, thin revolver, its barrel enlarged by a silencer. He switched off the safety, shoved the weapon back into his holster, got out of the car and walked across the street toward the limousine. The mirrors had been angled properly; by staying in the blind spot there was no way either man inside could see him approach. The European paused briefly for the rear trunk, then swiftly, hand extended, lunged for the right front door, opened it and spun inside, leveling his weapon over the seat.

Alfred Gillette gasped, his left hand surging for the door handle; the European snapped the four-way lock. David Abbott remained immobile, staring at the invader.

"Good evening, Monk," said the European. "Another, whom I'm told often assumes a religious habit, sends you his congratulations. Not only for Cain, but for your household personnel at Treadstone. The Yachtsman, for instance. Once a superior agent."

Gillette found his voice; it was a mixture of a scream and a whisper. "What *is* this? Who *are* you?" he cried, feigning ignorance.

"Oh come now, old friend. That's not necessary," said the man with the gun. "I can see by the expression on Mr. Abbott's face that he realizes his initial doubts about you were accurate. One should always trust one's first instincts, shouldn't one, Monk? You were right, of course. We found another discontented man; your system reproduces them with alarming rapidity. He, indeed, gave us the Medusa files, and they did, indeed, lead us to Bourne."

"What are you doing?!" screamed Gillette. "What are you *saying!*"

"You're a bore, Alfred. But you were always part of a damn fine staff. It's too bad you didn't know which staff to stay with; your kind never do."

"You! . . ." Gillette rose bodily off the seat, his face contorted.

The European fired his weapon, the cough from the barrel echoing briefly in the soft interior of the limousine. The bureaucrat slumped over, his body crumbling to the floor against the door, owl-eyes wide in death.

"I don't think you mourn him," said the European.

"I don't," said the Monk.

"It *is* Bourne out there, you know. Cain turned; he broke. The long period of silence is over. The snake from Medusa's head decided to strike out on his own. Or perhaps he was bought. That's possible too, isn't it? Carlos buys many men, the one at your feet now, for example."

"You'll learn nothing from me. Don't try."

"There's nothing to learn. We know it all. Delta, Charlie . . . Cain. But the names aren't important any longer; they never were, really. All that remains is the final isolation—removing of the man-monk who makes the decisions. You. Bourne is trapped. He's finished."

"There are others who make decisions. He'll reach them."

"If he does, they'll kill him on sight. There's nothing more despicable than a man who's turned, but in order for a man to turn, there has to be irrefutable proof that he was yours to begin with. Carlos has the proof; he *was* yours, his origins as sensitive as anything in the Medusa files."

The old man frowned; he was frightened, not for his life, but for something infinitely more indispensable. "You're out of your mind," he said. "There is no proof."

"That was the flaw, *your* flaw. Carlos is thorough; his tentacles reach into all manner of hidden recesses. You needed a man from Medusa, someone who had lived and disappeared. You chose a man named Bourne because the circumstances of his disappearance had been obliterated, eliminated from every existing record—or so you believed. But you didn't consider Hanoi's own field personnel who had infiltrated Medusa; those records exist. On March 25, 1968, Jason Bourne was executed by an American Intelligence officer in the jungles of Tam Quan."

The Monk lunged forward; there was nothing left but a final gesture, a final defiance. The European fired.

The door of the brownstone opened. From the shadows beneath the staircase the chauffeur smiled. The White House aide was being escorted out by the old man who lived at Treadstone, the one they called the Yachtsman; the killer knew that meant the primary alarms were off. The three-second span was eliminated.

"So good of you to drop by," said the Yachtsman, shaking hands.

"Thank you very much, sir."

Those were the last words either man spoke. The chauffeur aimed above the walled brick railing, pulling the trigger twice, the muffled reports indistinguishable from the myriad of distant sounds of the city. The Yachtsman fell back inside; the White House aide clutched his upper chest, reeling into the door frame. The chauffeur spun around the brick railing and raced up the steps, catching Stevens' body as it plummeted down. With bull-like strength, the killer lifted the White House man off his feet, hurling him back through the door into the foyer beyond the Yachtsman. Then he turned to the interior border of the heavy, steel-plated door. He knew what to look for; he found it. Along the upper molding, disappearing into the wall, was a thick cable, stained the color of the doorframe. He closed the door part way, raised his gun and fired into the cable. The spit was followed by an eruption of static and sparks; the security cameras were blown out, screens everywhere now dark.

He opened the door to signal; it was not necessary. The European was walking rapidly across the quiet street. Within seconds he had climbed the steps and was inside, glancing around the foyer and the hallway—the door at the end of the hallway. Together both men lifted a rug from the foyer floor, the European closing the door on its edge, welding cloth and steel together so that a two-inch space remained, the security bolts still in place. No backup alarms could be raised.

They stood erect in silence; both knew that if the discovery was going to be made, it would be made quickly. It came with the sound of an upstairs door opening, followed by footsteps and words that floated down the staircase in a cultured female voice.

"Darling! I just noticed, the damn camera's on the fritz. Would you check it, please?" There was a pause; then the woman spoke again. "On second thought why not tell David?" Again the pause, again with precise timing. "Don't bother the Jesuit, darling. Tell David!"

Two footsteps. Silence. A rustle of cloth. The European studied the stairwell. A light went out. David. Jesuit . . . Monk!

"*Get her!*" he roared at the chauffeur, spinning around, his weapon leveled at the door at the end of the hallway.

The uniformed man raced up the staircase; there was a gunshot; it came from a powerful weapon—unmuffled, unsilenced. The European looked up; the chauffeur was holding his shoulder, his coat drenched with blood, his pistol held out, spitting repeatedly up the well of the stairs.

The door at the end of the hallway was yanked open, the major standing there in shock, a file folder in his hand. The European fired twice; Gordon Webb arched backward, his throat torn open, the papers in the folder flying out behind him. The man in the raincoat raced up the steps to the chauffeur; above, over the railing, was the gray-haired woman, dead, blood spilling out of her head and neck. "Are you all right? Can you move?" asked the European.

The chauffeur nodded. "The bitch blew half my shoulder off, but I can manage."

"You have to!" commanded his superior, ripping off his raincoat. "Put on my coat. I want the Monk in here! Quickly!"

"Jesus! . . ."

"*Carlos* wants the Monk in here!"

Awkwardly the wounded man put on the black raincoat and made his way down the staircase around the bodies of the Yachtsman and the White House aide. Carefully, in pain, he let himself out the door and down the front steps.

The European watched him, holding the door, making sure the man was sufficiently mobile for the task. He was; he was a bull whose every appetite was satisfied by Carlos. The chauffeur would carry David Abbott's corpse back into the brownstone, no doubt supporting it as though helping an aging drunk for the benefit of anyone in the street; and then he would somehow contain his bleeding long enough to drive Alfred Gillette's body across the river, burying him in a swamp. Carlos' men were capable of such things; they were all bulls. Discontented bulls who had found their own causes in a single man.

The European turned and started down the hallway; there was work to do. The final isolation of the man called Jason Bourne.

It was more than could be hoped for, the exposed files a gift beyond belief. Included were folders containing every code and method of communication ever used by the mythical Cain. Now not so mythical, thought the European as he gathered the papers together. The scene was set, the four corpses in position in the peaceful, elegant library. David Abbott was arched in a chair, his dead eyes in shock, Elliot Stevens at his feet; the Yachtsman was slumped over the hatch table, an overturned bottle of whiskey in his hand, while Gordon Webb sprawled on the floor, clutching his briefcase. Whatever violence had taken place, the setting indicated that it had been unexpected; conversations interrupted by abrupt gunfire.

The European walked around in suede gloves, appraising his artistry, and it *was* artistry. He had dismissed the chauffeur, wiped every door handle, every knob, every gleaming surface of wood. It was time for the final touch. He walked to a table where there were brandy glasses on a silver tray, picked one up and held it to the light; as he expected, it was spotless. He put it down and took out a small, flat, plastic case from his pocket. He opened it and removed a strip of transparent tape, holding it, too, up to the light. There they were, as clear as portraits—for they were portraits, as undeniable as any photograph.

They had been taken off a glass of Perrier, removed from an office at the Gemeinschaft Bank in Zurich. They were the fingerprints of Jason Bourne's right hand.

The European picked up the brandy glass and, with the patience of the artist he was, pressed the tape around the lower surface, then gently peeled it off. Again he held the glass up; the prints were seen in dull perfection against the light of the table lamp.

He carried the glass over to a corner of the parquet floor and dropped it. He knelt down, studied the fragments, removed several, and brushed the rest under the curtain.

They were enough.

"Later," said Bourne, throwing their suitcases on the bed. "We've got to get out of here."

Marie sat in the armchair. She had reread the newspaper article again, selecting phrases, repeating them. Her concentration was absolute; she was consumed, more and more confident of her analysis.

"I'm right, Jason. Someone *is* sending us a message."

"We'll talk about it later; we've stayed here too long as it is. That newspaper'll be all over this hotel in an hour, and the morning papers may be worse. It's no time for modesty; you stand out in a hotel lobby, and you've been seen in this one by too many people. Get your things."

Marie stood up, but made no other move. Instead, she held her place and forced him to look at her. "We'll talk about several things later," she said firmly. "You were leaving me, Jason, and I want to know why."

"I told you I'd tell you," he answered without evasion, "because you have to know and I mean that. But right now I want to get out of here. Get your things, goddamn it!"

She blinked, his sudden anger having its effect. "Yes, of course," she whispered.

They took the elevator down to the lobby. As the worn marble floor came into view, Bourne had the feeling they were in a cage, exposed and vulnerable; if the machine stopped, they would be taken. Then he understood why the feeling was so strong. Below on the left was the front desk, the *concierge* sitting behind it, a pile of newspapers on the counter to his right. They were copies of the same tabloid Jason had put in the attaché case Marie was now carrying. The *concierge* had taken one; he was reading it avidly; poking a toothpick between his teeth, oblivious to everything but the latest scandal.

"Walk straight through," said Jason. "Don't stop, just go right to the door. I'll meet you outside."

"Oh, my God," she whispered, seeing the *concierge*.

"I'll pay him as quickly as I can."

The sound of Marie's heels on the marble floor was a distraction Bourne did not want. The *concierge* looked up as Jason moved in front of him, blocking his view.

"It's been very pleasant," he said in French, "but I'm in a great hurry. I have to drive to Lyon tonight. Just round out the figure to the nearest five hundred francs. I haven't had time to leave gratuities."

The financial distraction accomplished its purpose. The *concierge* reached his totals quickly; he presented the bill. Jason paid it and bent down for the suitcases, glancing up at the sound of surprise that exploded from the *concierge*'s gaping mouth. The man was staring at the pile of newspapers on his right, his eyes on the photograph of Marie St. Jacques. He looked over at the glass doors of the entrance; Marie stood on the pavement. He shifted his astonished gaze to Bourne; the connection was made, the man inhibited by sudden fear.

Jason walked rapidly toward the glass doors, angling his shoulder to push them open, glancing back at the front desk. The *concierge* was reaching for a telephone.

"Let's go!" he cried to Marie. "Look for a cab!"

They found one on rue Lecourbe, five blocks from the hotel. Bourne feigned the role of an inexperienced American tourist, employing the inadequate French that had served him so well at the Valois Bank. He explained to the driver that he and his *petite amie* wanted to get out of central Paris for a day or so, someplace where they could be alone. Perhaps the driver could suggest several places and they would choose one.

The driver could and did. "There's a small inn outside Issy-les-Moulineaux, called La Maison Carrée," he said. "Another in Ivry sur Seine, you might like. It's very private, monsieur. Or perhaps the Auberge du Coin in Montrouge; it's very discreet."

"Let's take the first," said Jason. "It's the first that came to your mind. How long will it take?"

"No more than fifteen, twenty minutes, monsieur."

"Good." Bourne turned to Marie and spoke softly. "Change your hair."

"What?"

"Change your hair. Pull it up or push it back, I don't care, but change it. Move out of sight of his mirror. Hurry up!"

Several moments later Marie's long auburn hair was pulled severely back, away from her face and neck, fastened with the aid of a mirror and hairpins from her purse into a tight chignon. Jason looked at her in the dim light.

"Wipe off your lipstick. All of it."

She took out a tissue and did so. "All right?"

"Yes. Have you got an eyebrow pencil?"

"Of course."

"Thicken your eyebrows; just a little bit. Extend them about a quarter of an inch; curve the ends down just a touch."

Again she followed his instructions. "Now?" she asked.

"That's better," he replied, studying her. The changes were minor but the effect major. She had been subtly transformed from a softly elegant, striking woman into a harsher image. At the least, she was not on first sight the woman in the newspaper photograph and that was all that mattered.

"When we reach Moulineaux," he whispered, "get out quickly and stand up. Don't let the driver see you."

"It's a little late for that, isn't it?"

"Just do as I say."

Listen to me. I am a chameleon called Cain and I can teach you many things I do not care to teach you, but at the moment I must. I can change my color to accommodate any backdrop in the forest, I can shift with the wind by smelling it. I can find my way through the natural and the manmade jungles. Alpha, Bravo, Charlie, Delta. . . . Delta is for Charlie and Charlie is for Cain. I am Cain. I am death. And I must tell you who I am and lose you.

"My darling, what is it?"

"What?"

"You're looking at me; you're not breathing. Are you all right?"

"Sorry," he said, glancing away, breathing again. "I'm figuring out our moves. I'll know better what to do when we get there."

They arrived at the inn. There was a parking lot bordered by a post-and-rail fence on the right; several late diners came out of the lattice-framed entrance in front. Bourne leaned forward in the seat.

"Let us off inside the parking area, if you don't mind," he ordered, offering no explanation for the odd request.

"Certainly, monsieur," said the driver, nodding his head, then shrugging, his movements conveying the fact that his passengers were, indeed, a cautious couple. The rain had subsided, returning to a mistlike drizzle. The taxi drove off. Bourne and Marie remained in the shadows of the foliage at the side of the inn until it disappeared. Jason put the suitcases down on the wet ground. "Wait here," he said.

"Where are you going?"

"To phone for a taxi."

The second taxi took them into the Montrouge district. This driver was singularly unimpressed by the stern-faced couple who were obviously from the provinces, and probably seeking cheaper lodgings. When and if he picked up a newspaper and saw a photograph of a French-Canadiènne involved with murder and theft in Zurich, the woman in his back seat now would not come to mind.

The Auberge du Coin did not live up to its name. It was not a quaint village inn situated in a secluded nook of the countryside. Instead, it was a large, flat, two-story structure a quarter of a mile off the highway. If anything, it was reminiscent of motels the world over that blighted the outskirts of cities; commerciality guaranteeing the anonymity of their guests. It was not hard to imagine various appointments by the scores that were best left to erroneous registrations.

So they registered erroneously and were given a plastic room where every accessory worth over twenty francs was bolted into the floor or attached with headless screws to lacquered formica. There was, however, one positive feature to the place; an ice machine down the hall. They knew it worked because they could hear it. With the door closed.

"All right, now. Who would be sending us a message?"

asked Bourne, standing, revolving the glass of whiskey in his hand.

"If I knew, I'd get in touch with them," she said, sitting at the small desk, chair turned, legs crossed, watching him closely. "It could be connected with why you were running away."

"If it was, it was a trap."

"It was no trap. A man like Walther Apfel didn't do what he did to accommodate a trap."

"I wouldn't be so sure of that." Bourne walked to the single plastic armchair and sat down. "Koenig did; he marked me right there in the waiting room."

"He was a bribed foot-soldier, not an officer of the bank. He acted alone. Apfel couldn't."

Jason looked up. "What do you mean?"

"Apfel's statement had to be cleared by his superiors. It was made in the name of the bank."

"If you're so sure, let's call Zurich."

"They don't want that. Either they haven't the answer or they can't give it. Apfel's last words were that they would have no further comment. To anyone. That, too, was part of the message. We're to contact someone else."

Bourne drank; he needed the alcohol, for the moment was coming when he would begin the story of a killer named Cain. "Then we're back to whom?" he said. "Back to the trap."

"You think you know who it is, don't you?" Marie reached for her cigarettes on the desk. "It's why you were running, isn't it?"

"The answer to both questions is yes." *The moment had come. The message was sent by Carlos. I am Cain and you must leave me. I must lose you. But first there is Zurich and you have to understand.* "That article was planted to find me."

"I won't argue with that," she broke in, surprising him with the interruption. "I've had time to think; they know the evidence is false—so patently false it's ridiculous. The Zurich police fully expect me to get in touch with the Canadian Embassy now—" Marie stopped, the unlit cigarette in her hand. "My God, Jason, that's what they want us to do!"

"Who wants us to do?"

"Whoever's sending us the message. They know I have no choice but to call the embassy, get the protection of the

Canadian government. I didn't think of it because I've already *spoken* to the embassy, to what's his name—Dennis Corbelier—and he had absolutely nothing to tell me. He only did what I asked him to do; there was nothing else. But that was *yesterday,* not *today,* not *tonight.*" Marie started for the telephone on the bedside table.

Bourne rose quickly from the chair and intercepted her, holding her arm. "Don't" he said firmly.

"Why not?"

"Because you're wrong."

"I'm right, Jason! Let me prove it to you."

Bourne moved in front of her. "I think you'd better listen to what I have to say."

"No!" she cried, startling him. "I don't want to hear it. Not now!"

"An hour ago in Paris it was the only thing you wanted to hear. Hear it!"

"No! An hour ago I was dying. You'd made up your mind to run. Without me. And I know now it will happen over and over again until it stops for you. You hear words, you see images, and fragments of things come back to you that you can't understand, but because they're there you condemn yourself. You always *will* condemn yourself until someone proves to you that whatever you were . . . there are others using you, who will sacrifice you. But there's also someone else out there who wants to help you, help us. That's the message! I know I'm right. I want to prove it to you. *Let* me!"

Bourne held her arms in silence, looking at her face, her lovely face filled with pain and useless hope, her eyes pleading. The terrible ache was everywhere within him. Perhaps it was better this way; she would see for herself, and her fear would make her listen, make her understand. There was nothing for them any longer. *I am Cain . . .* "All right, you can make the call, but it's got to be done my way." He released her and went to the telephone; he dialed the Auberge du Coin's front desk. "This is room 341. I've just heard from friends in Paris; they're coming out to join us in a while. Do you have a room down the hall for them? Fine. Their name is Briggs, an American couple. I'll come down and pay in advance and you can let me have the key. Splendid. Thank you."

"What are you doing?"

"Proving something to you," he said. "Get me a dress," he continued. "The longest one you've got."

"What?"

"If you want to make your call, you'll do as I tell you."

"You're crazy."

"I've admitted that," he said, taking trousers and a shirt from his suitcase. "The dress, please."

Fifteen minutes later, Mr. and Mrs. Briggs' room, six doors away and across the hall from room 341, was in readiness. The clothes had been properly placed, selected lights left on, others not functioning because the bulbs had been removed.

Jason returned to their room; Marie was standing by the telephone. "We're set."

"What have you done?"

"What I wanted to do; what I had to do. You can make the call now."

"It's very late. Suppose he isn't there?"

"I think he will be. If not, they'll give you his home phone. His name was in the telephone logs in Ottawa; it had to be."

"I suppose it was."

"Then he will have been reached. Have you gone over what I told you to say?"

"Yes, but it doesn't matter; it's not relevant. I know I'm not wrong."

"We'll see. Just say the words I told you. I'll be right beside you listening. Go ahead."

She picked up the phone and dialed. Seven seconds after she reached the embassy switchboard, Dennis Corbelier was on the line. It was quarter past one in the morning.

"Christ almighty, where *are* you?"

"You were expecting me to call, then?"

"I was hoping to hell you would! This place is in an uproar. I've been waiting here since five o'clock this afternoon."

"So was Alan. In Ottawa."

"Alan who? What are you talking about? Where the hell *are* you?"

"First I want to know what you have to tell me."

"*Tell* you?"

"You have a message for me, Dennis. What is it?"

"What is *what?* What message?"

[316]

Marie's face went pale. "I didn't kill anyone in Zurich. I wouldn't . . ."

"Then for God's sake," interrupted the attaché, "get *in* here! We'll give you all the protection we can. No one can touch you here!"

"Dennis, listen to me! You've been waiting there for my call, haven't you?"

"Yes, of course."

"Someone told you to wait, isn't that true?"

A pause. When Corbelier spoke, his voice was subdued. "Yes, he did. They did."

"What did they tell you?"

"That you need our help. Very badly."

Marie resumed breathing. "And they want to help us?"

"By us," replied Corbelier, "you're saying he's with you, then?"

Bourne's face was next to hers, his head angled to hear Corbelier's words. He nodded.

"Yes," she answered. "We're together, but he's out for a few minutes. It's all lies; they told you that, didn't they?"

"All they said was that you had to be found, protected. They *do* want to help you: they want to send a car for you. One of ours. Diplomatic."

"Who are they?"

"I don't know them by name; I don't have to. I know their rank."

"Rank?"

"Specialists, FS-Five. You don't get much higher than that."

"You trust them?"

"My God, yes! They reached me through Ottawa. Their orders came from Ottawa."

"They're at the embassy now?"

"No, they're outposted." Corbelier paused, obviously exasperated. "Jesus Christ, Marie—where *are* you?"

Bourne nodded again, she spoke.

"We're at the Auberge du Coin in Montrouge. Under the name of Briggs."

"I'll get that car to you right away."

"No, Dennis!" protested Marie, watching Jason, his eyes telling her to follow his instructions. "Send one in the morning. First thing in the morning—four hours from now, if you like."

"I can't *do* that! For your own sake."

"You have to; you don't understand. He was trapped into doing something and he's frightened; he wants to run. If he knew I called you, he'd be running now. Give me time. I can convince him to turn himself in. Just a few more hours. He's confused, but underneath he knows I'm right." Marie said the words, looking at Bourne.

"What kind of a son of a bitch is he?"

"A terrified one," she answered. "One who's being manipulated. I need the time. Give it to me."

"Marie . . . ?" Corbelier stopped. "All right, first thing in the morning. Say . . . six o'clock. And, Marie, they want to help you. They *can* help you."

"I know. Good night."

"Good night."

Marie hung up.

"Now, we'll wait," Bourne said.

"I don't know what you're proving. Of course he'll call the FS-Fives, and of course they'll show up here. What do you expect? He as much as admitted what he was going to do, what he thinks he has to do."

"And these diplomatic FS-Fives are the ones sending us the message?"

"My guess is they'll take us to who is. Or if those sending it are too far away, they'll put us in touch with them. I've never been surer of anything in my professional life."

Bourne looked at her. "I hope you're right, because it's your whole life that concerns me. If the evidence against you in Zurich isn't part of any message, if it was put there by experts to find me—if the Zurich police *believe* it—then I'm that terrified man you spoke about to Corbelier. No one wants you to be right more than I do. But I don't think you are."

At three minutes past two, the lights in the motel corridor flickered and went out, leaving the long hallway in relative darkness, the spill from the stairwell the only source of illumination. Bourne stood by the door of their room, pistol in hand, the lights turned off, watching the corridor through a crack between the door's edge and the frame. Marie was behind him, peering over his shoulder; neither spoke.

The footsteps were muffled, but there. Distinct, deliberate, two sets of shoes cautiously climbing the staircase. In seconds, the figures of two men could be seen emerging out of the dim light. Marie gasped involuntarily; Jason reached over his shoulder, his hand gripping her mouth harshly. He understood; she had recognized one of the two men, a man she had seen only once before. In Zurich's Steppdeckstrasse, minutes before another had ordered her execution. It was the blond man they had sent up to Bourne's room, the expendable scout brought now to Paris to spot the target he had missed. In his left hand was a small pencil light, in his right a long-barreled gun, swollen by a silencer.

His companion was shorter, more compact, his walk not unlike an animal's tread, shoulders and waist moving fluidly with his legs. The lapels of his topcoat were pulled up, his head covered by a narrow-brimmed hat, shading his unseen face. Bourne stared at this man; there was something familiar about him, about the figure, the walk, the way he carried his head. What was it? What *was* it? He knew him.

But there was not time to think about it; the two men were approaching the door of the room reserved in the name of Mr. and Mrs. Briggs. The blond man held his pencil light on the numbers, then swept the beam down toward the knob and the lock.

What followed was mesmerizing in its efficiency. The stocky man held a ring of keys in his right hand, placing it under the beam of light, his fingers selecting a specific key. In his left hand he gripped a weapon, its shape in the spill revealing an outsized silencer for a heavy-calibered automatic, not unlike the powerful Sternlicht Luger favored by the Gestapo in World War Two. It could cut through webbed steel and concrete, its sound no more than a rheumatic cough, ideal for taking enemies of the state at night in quiet neighborhoods, nearby residents unaware of any disturbance, only of disappearance in the morning.

The shorter man inserted the key, turned it silently, then lowered the barrel of the gun to the lock. Three rapid coughs accompanied three flashes of light; the wood surrounding any bolts shattered. The door fell free; the two killers rushed inside.

There were two beats of silence, then an eruption of muffled gunfire, spits and white flashes from the darkness. The door was slammed shut; it would not stay closed, falling back as louder sounds of thrashing and collision came from within the room. Finally a light was found; it was snapped on briefly, then shot out in fury, a lamp sent crashing to the floor, glass shattering. A cry of frenzy exploded from the throat of an infuriated man.

The two killers rushed out, weapons leveled, prepared for a trap, bewildered that there was none. They reached the staircase and raced down as a door to the right of the invaded room opened. A blinking guest peered out, then shrugged and went back inside. Silence returned to the darkened hallway.

Bourne held his place, his arm around Marie St. Jacques. She was trembling, her head pressed into his chest, sobbing quietly, hysterically, in disbelief. He let the minutes pass, until the trembling subsided and deep breaths replaced the sobs. He could not wait any longer; she had to see for herself. See completely, the impression indelible; she had to finally understand. *I am Cain. I am death.*

"Come on," he whispered.

He led her out into the hallway, guiding her firmly toward the room that was now his ultimate proof. He pushed the broken door open and they walked inside.

She stood motionless, both repelled and hypnotized by the sight. In an open doorway on the right was the dim silhouette of a figure, the light behind it so muted only the outline could be seen, and only then when the eyes adjusted to the strange admixture of darkness and glow. It was the figure of a woman in a long gown, the fabric moving gently in the breeze of an open window.

Window. Straight ahead was a second figure, barely visible but there, its shape an obscure blot indistinctly outlined by the wash of light from the distant highway. Again, it seemed to move, brief, spastic flutterings of cloth—of arms.

"Oh, God," said Marie, frozen. "Turn on the lights, Jason."

"None of them work," he replied. "Only two table lamps; they found one." He walked across the room cautiously and reached the lamp he was looking for; it was on the floor against the wall. He knelt down and turned it on; Marie shuddered.

Strung across the bathroom door, held in place by threads torn from a curtain, was her long dress, rippling from an unseen source of wind. It was riddled with bullet holes.

Against the far window, Bourne's shirt and trousers had been tacked to the frame, the panes by both sleeves smashed, the breeze rushing in, causing the fabric to move up and down. The white cloth of the shirt was punctured in a half-dozen places, a diagonal line of bullets across the chest.

"There's your message," said Jason. "Now you know what it is. And now I think you'd better listen to what I have to say."

Marie did not answer him. Instead, she walked slowly to the dress, studying it as if not believing what she saw. Without warning, she suddenly spun around, her eyes glittering, the tears arrested. "No! It's wrong! Something's terribly wrong! Call the embassy."

"What?"

"Do as I say. Now!"

"Stop it, Marie. You've got to understand."

"No, goddamn you! *You've* got to understand! It wouldn't happen this way. It couldn't."

"It did."

"Call the embassy! Use that phone over there and call it now! Ask for Corbelier. *Quickly*, for God's sake! If I mean anything to you, do as I ask!"

Bourne could not deny her. Her intensity was killing both herself and him. "What do I tell him?" he asked, going to the telephone.

"Get him first! *That's* what I'm afraid of . . . oh, God, I'm frightened!"

"What's the number?"

She gave it to him; he dialed, holding on interminably for the switchboard to answer. When it finally did, the operator was in panic, her words rising and falling, at moments incomprehensible. In the background he could hear shouts, sharp commands voiced rapidly in English and in French. Within seconds he learned why.

Dennis Corbelier, Canadian attaché, had walked down the steps of the embassy on the avenue Montaigne at 1:40 in the morning and had been shot in the throat. He was dead.

"There's the other part of the message, Jason," whispered Marie, drained, staring at him. "And now I'll listen to anything you have to say. Because there *is* someone out there trying to reach you, trying to help you. A message *was* sent, but not to us, not to me. Only to you, and only you were to understand it."

——— 22 ———

One by one the four men arrived at the crowded Hilton Hotel on Sixteenth Street in Washington, D.C. Each went to a separate elevator, taking it two or three floors above or below his destination, walking the remaining flights to the correct level. There was no time to meet outside the limits of the District of Columbia; the crisis was unparalleled. These were the men of Treadstone Seventy-One—those that remained alive. The rest were dead, slaughtered in a massacre on a quiet, tree-lined street in New York.

Two of the faces were familiar to the public, one more than the other. The first belonged to the aging senator from Colorado, the second was Brigadier General I. A. Crawford—Irwin Arthur, freely translated as Iron Ass— acknowledged spokesman for Army Intelligence and defender of the G-2 data banks. The other two men were virtually unknown except within the corridors of their own operations. One was a middle-aged naval officer, attached to Information Control, 5th Naval District. The fourth and last man was a forty-six-year-old veteran of the Central Intelligence Agency, a slender, coiled spring of anger who walked with a cane. His foot had been blown off by a grenade in Southeast Asia; he had been a deep-cover agent with the Medusa operation at the time. His name was Alexander Conklin.

There was no conference table in the room; it was an ordinary double occupancy with the standard twin beds, a couch, two armchairs, and a coffee table. It was an unlikely spot to hold a meeting of such consequence; there were no spinning computers to light up dark screens with green letters, no electronic communications equipment that would reach consoles in London or Paris or Istanbul. It was a plain hotel room, devoid of everything but four minds that held the secrets of Treadstone Seventy-One.

The senator sat on one end of the couch, the naval officer at the other. Conklin lowered himself into an armchair, stretching his immobile limb out in front of him, the cane between his legs, while Brigadier General Crawford remained standing, his face flushed, the muscles of his jaw pulsing in anger.

"I've reached the president," said the senator, rubbing his forehead, the lack of sleep apparent in his bearing. "I had to; we're meeting tonight. Tell me everything you can, each of you. You begin, General. What in the name of God happened?"

"Major Webb was to meet his car at 2300 hours on the corner of Lexington and Seventy-second Street. The time was firm, but he didn't show up. By 2330 the driver became alarmed because of the distance to the airfield in New Jersey. The sergeant remembered the address— mainly because he'd been told to forget it—drove around and went to the door. The security bolts had been jammed and the door just swung open; all the alarms had been shorted out. There was blood on the foyer floor, the dead woman on the staircase. He walked down the hallway into the operations room and found the bodies."

"That man deserves a very quiet promotion," said the naval officer.

"Why do you say that?" asked the senator.

Crawford replied. "He had the presence of mind to call the Pentagon and insist on speaking with covert transmissions, domestic. He specified the scrambler frequency, the time and the place of reception, and said he had to speak with the sender. He didn't say a word to anyone until he got me on the phone."

"Put him in the War College, Irwin," said Conklin

grimly, holding his cane. "He's brighter than most of the clowns you've got over there."

"That's not only unnecessary, Conklin," admonished the senator, "but patently offensive. Go on, please, General."

Crawford exchanged looks with the CIA man. "I reached Colonel Paul McClaren in New York, ordered him over there, and told him to do absolutely nothing until I arrived. I then phoned Conklin and George here, and we flew up together."

"I called a Bureau print team in Manhattan," added Conklin. "One we've used before and can trust. I didn't tell them what we were looking for, but I told them to sweep the place and give what they found only to me." The CIA man stopped, lifting his cane in the direction of the naval officer. "Then George fed them thirty-seven names, all men whose prints we knew were in the FBI files. They came up with the one set we didn't expect, didn't want . . . didn't believe."

"Delta's," said the senator.

"Yes," concurred the naval officer. "The names I submitted were those of anyone—no matter how remote—who might have learned the address of Treadstone, including, incidentally, all of us. The room had been wiped clean; every surface; every knob, every glass—except one. It was a broken brandy glass, only a few fragments in the corner under a curtain, but it was enough. The prints were there: third and index fingers, right hand."

"You're absolutely positive?" asked the senator slowly.

"The prints can't lie, sir," said the officer. "They were there, moist brandy still on the fragments. Outside of this room, Delta's the only one who knows about Seventy-first Street."

"Can we be sure of that? The others may have said something."

"No possibility," interrupted the brigadier general. "Abbott would never have revealed it, and Elliot Stevens wasn't given the address until fifteen minutes before he got there, when he called from a phone booth. Beyond that, assuming the worst, he would hardly ask for his own execution."

"What about Major Webb?" pressed the senator.

"The major," replied Crawford, "was radioed the address solely by me after he landed at Kennedy Airport. As you know, it was a G-Two frequency and scrambled. I remind you, he also lost his life."

"Yes, of course." The aging senator shook his head. "It's unbelievable. *Why?*"

"I should like to bring up a painful subject," said Brigadier General Crawford. "At the outset I was not enthusiastic about the candidate. I understood David's reasoning and agreed he was qualified, but if you recall, he wasn't my choice."

"I wasn't aware we had that many choices," said the senator. "We had a man—a qualified man, as you agreed—who was willing to go in deep cover for an indeterminate length of time, risking his life every day, severing all ties with his past. How many such men exist?"

"We might have found a more balanced one," countered the brigadier. "I pointed that out at the time."

"You pointed out," corrected Conklin, "your own definition of a balanced man, which *I*, at the time, pointed out was a crock."

"We were both in Medusa, Conklin," said Crawford angrily yet reasonably. "You don't have exclusive insights. Delta's conduct in the field was continuously and overtly hostile to command. I was in a position to observe that pattern somewhat more clearly than you."

"Most of the time he had every right to be. If you'd spent more time in the field and less in Saigon you would have understood that. *I* understood it."

"It may surprise you," said the brigadier, holding his hand up in a gesture of truce, "but I'm not defending the gross stupidities often rampant in Saigon—no one could. I'm trying to describe a pattern of behavior that could lead to the night before last on Seventy-first Street."

The CIA man's eyes remained on Crawford; his hostility vanished as he nodded his head. "I know you are. Sorry. That's the crux of it, isn't it? It's not easy for me; I worked with Delta in half a dozen sectors, was stationed with him in Phnom Penh before Medusa was even a gleam in the Monk's eye. He was never the same after Phnom Penh; it's why he went into Medusa, why he was willing to become Cain."

The senator leaned forward on the couch. "I've heard it, but tell me again. The president has to know everything."

"His wife and two children were killed on a pier in the Mekong River, bombed and strafed by a stray aircraft—nobody knew which side's—the identity never uncovered. He hated that war, hated everybody in it. He snapped."

Conklin paused, looking at the brigadier. "And I think you're right, General. He snapped again. It was in him."

"What was?" asked the senator sharply.

"The explosion, I guess," said Conklin. "The dam burst. He'd gone beyond his limits and the hate took over. It's not hard; you have to be very careful. He killed those men, that woman, like a madman on a deliberate rampage. None of them expected it except perhaps the woman who was upstairs, and she probably heard the shouts. He's not Delta anymore. We created a myth called Cain, only it's not a myth any longer. It's really him."

"After so many months . . ." The senator leaned back, his voice trailing off. "Why did he come back? From where?"

"From Zurich," answered Crawford. "Webb was in Zurich, and I think he's the only one who could have brought him back. The 'why' we may never know unless he expected to catch all of us there."

"He doesn't know who we are," protested the senator. "His only contacts were the Yachtsman, his wife, and David Abbott."

"And Webb, of course," added the general.

"Of course," agreed the senator. "But not at Treadstone, not even him."

"It wouldn't matter," said Conklin, tapping the rug once with his cane. "He knows there's a board; Webb might have told him we'd all be there, reasonably expecting that we would. We've got a lot of questions—six months' worth, and now several million dollars. Delta would consider it the perfect solution. He could take us and disappear. No traces."

"Why are you so certain?"

"Because, one, he was *there*," replied the intelligence man, raising his voice. "We have his prints on a glass of brandy that wasn't even finished. And, two, it's a classic trap with a couple of hundred variations."

"Would you explain that?"

"You remain silent," broke in the general, watching Conklin, "until your enemy can't stand it any longer and exposes himself."

"And we've become the enemy? *His* enemy?"

"There's no question about it now," said the naval officer. "For whatever reasons, Delta's turned. It's happened before—thank heaven not very often. We know what to do."

The senator once more leaned forward on the couch. "What *will* you do?"

"His photograph has never been circulated," explained Crawford. "We'll circulate it now. To every station and listening post, every source and informant we have. He has to go somewhere, and he'll start with a place he knows, if only to buy another identity. He'll spend money; he'll be found. When he is, the orders will be clear."

"You'll bring him in at once?"

"We'll kill him," said Conklin simply. "You don't bring in a man like Delta, and you don't take the risk that another government will. Not with what he knows."

"I can't tell the president that. There are laws."

"Not for Delta," said the agent. "He's beyond the laws. He's beyond salvage."

"Beyond—"

"That's right, Senator," interrupted the general. "Beyond salvage. I think you know the meaning of the phrase. You'll have to make the decision whether or not to define it for the president. It might be better to—"

"You've got to explore *everything*," said the senator, cutting off the officer. "I spoke to Abbott last week. He told me a strategy was in progress to reach Delta. Zurich, the bank, the naming of Treadstone; it's all part of it, isn't it?"

"It is, and it's over," said Crawford. "If the evidence on Seventy-first Street isn't enough for you, that should be. Delta was given a clear signal to come in. He didn't. What more do you want?"

"I want to be absolutely certain."

"I want him dead." Conklin's words, though spoken softly, had the effect of a sudden, cold wind. "He not only broke all the rules we each set down for ourselves—no matter what—but he sunk into the pits. He reeks; he *is* Cain. We've used the name Delta so much—not even Bourne, but Delta—that I think we've forgotten. Gordon Webb was his brother. Find him. Kill him."

BOOK III

BOOK III

—— 23 ——

It was ten minutes to three in the morning when Bourne approached the Auberge du Coin's front desk, Marie continuing directly to the entrance. To Jason's relief, there were no newspapers on the counter, but the late night clerk behind it was in the same mold as his predecessor in the center of Paris. He was a balding, heavy-set man with half-closed eyes, leaning back in a chair, his arms folded in front of him, the weary depression of his interminable night hanging over him. But this night, thought Bourne, would be one he'd remember for a long time to come—beyond the damage to an upstairs room, which would not be discovered until morning. A relief night clerk in Montrouge had to have transportation.

"I've just called Rouen," said Jason, his hands on the counter, an angry man, furious with uncontrollable events in his personal world. "I have to leave at once and need to rent a car."

"Why not?" snorted the man, getting out of the chair. "What would you prefer, monsieur? A golden chariot or a magic carpet?"

"I beg your pardon?"

"We rent rooms, not automobiles."

"I *must* be in Rouen before morning."

"Impossible. Unless you find a taxi crazy enough at this hour to take you."

"I don't think you understand. I could sustain considerable losses and embarrassment if I'm not at my office by eight o'clock. I'm willing to pay generously."

"You have a problem, monsieur."

"Surely there's someone here who would be willing to lend me his car for, say . . . a thousand, fifteen hundred francs."

"A thousand . . . *fifteen hundred*, monsieur?" The clerk's half-closed eyes widened until his skin was taut. "In cash, monsieur?"

"Naturally. My companion would return it tomorrow evening."

"There's no rush, monsieur."

"I beg your pardon? Of course, there's really no reason why I couldn't hire a taxi. Confidentiality can be paid for."

"I wouldn't know where to *reach* one," interrupted the clerk in persuasive frenzy. "On the other hand, my Renault is not so new, perhaps, and perhaps, not the fastest machine on the road, but it is a serviceable car, even a worthy car."

The chameleon had changed his colors again, had been accepted again for someone he was not. But he knew now who he was and he understood.

Daybreak. But there was no warm room at a village inn, no wallpaper mottled by the early light streaking through a window, filtered by the weaving leaves outside. Rather, the first rays of the sun spread up from the east, crowning the French countryside, defining the fields and hills of Saint-Germain-en-Laye. They sat in the small car parked off the shoulder of a deserted back road, cigarette smoke curling out through the partially open windows.

He had begun that first narrative in Switzerland with the words *My life began six months ago on a small island in the Mediterranean called Ile de Port Noir. . . .*

He had begun this with a quiet declaration: *I'm known as Cain.*

He had told it all, leaving out nothing he could remember, including the terrible images that had exploded in his mind when he had heard the words spoken by Jacqueline

[332]

Lavier in the candlelabraed restaurant in Argenteuil. Names, incidents, cities . . . assassinations.

"Everything fit. There wasn't anything I didn't know, nothing that wasn't somewhere in the back of my head, trying to get out. It was the truth."

"It *was* the truth," repeated Marie.

He looked closely at her. "We were wrong, don't you see?"

"Perhaps. But also right. You were right, and I was right."

"About what?"

"You. I have to say it again, calmly and logically. You offered your life for mine before you knew me; that's not the decision of a man you've described. If that man existed, he doesn't any longer." Marie's eyes pleaded, while her voice remained controlled. "You said it, Jason. 'What a man can't remember doesn't exist. For him.' Maybe that's what you're faced with. Can you walk away from it?"

Bourne nodded; the dreadful moment had come. "Yes," he said. "But alone. Not with you."

Marie inhaled on her cigarette, watching him, her hand trembling. "I see. That's your decision, then?"

"It has to be."

"You will heroically disappear so I won't be tainted."

"I have to."

"Thank you very much, and who the hell do you think you are?"

"What?"

"Who the *hell* do you think you *are?*"

"I'm a man they call Cain. I'm wanted by governments—by the police—from Asia to Europe. Men in Washington want to kill me because of what they think I know about this Medusa; an assassin named Carlos wants me shot in the throat because of what I've done to him. Think about it for a moment. How long do you think I can keep running before someone in one of those armies out there finds me, traps me, *kills* me? Is that the way you want your life to end?"

"Good God, no!" shouted Marie, something obviously very much on her analytical mind. "I intend to rot in a Swiss prison for fifty years or be hanged for things I never did in Zurich!"

"There's a way to take care of Zurich. I've thought about it; I can do it."

"How?" She stabbed out her cigarette in the ashtray.

"For God's sake, what difference does it make? A confession. Turning myself in, I don't know yet, but I can *do* it! I can put your life back together. I *have* to put it back!"

"Not that way."

"Why not?"

Marie reached for his face, her voice now soft once more, the sudden stridency gone. "Because I've just proved my point again. Even the condemned man—so sure of his own guilt—should see it. The man called Cain would never do what you just offered to do. For anyone."

"I *am* Cain!"

"Even if I were forced to agree that you were, you're not now."

"The ultimate rehabilitation? A self-induced lobotomy? Total loss of recall? That happens to be the truth, but it won't stop anyone who's looking for me. It won't stop him—them—from pulling a trigger."

"That happens to be the worst, and I'm not ready to concede it."

"Then you're not looking at the facts."

"I'm looking at two facts you seem to have disregarded. I can't. I'll live with them for the rest of my life because I'm responsible. Two men were killed in the same brutal way because they stood between you and a message someone was trying to send you. Through me."

"You saw Corbelier's message. How many bullet holes were there? Ten, fifteen?"

"Then he was used! You heard him on the phone and so did I. He wasn't lying; he was trying to help us. If not you, certainly me."

"It's . . . possible."

"Anything's possible. I have no answers, Jason, only discrepancies, things that can't be explained—that *should* be explained. You haven't once, ever, displayed a need or a drive for what you say you might have been. And without those things a man like that couldn't be. Or you couldn't be *him*."

"I'm him."

"Listen to me. You're very dear to me, my darling, and that could blind me, I know it. But I also know something about myself. I'm no wide-eyed flower child; I've seen a share of this world, and I look very hard and very closely at those who attract me. Perhaps to confirm what I like to think are my values—and they *are* values. Mine, nobody else's." She stopped for a moment and moved away from him. "I've watched a man being tortured—by himself and by others—and he won't cry out. You may have silent screams, but you won't let them be anyone else's burden but your own. Instead, you probe and dig and try to understand. And that, my friend, is not the mind of a cold-blooded killer, any more than what you've done and want to do for me. I don't know what you were before, or what crimes you're guilty of, but they're not what you believe— what others want you to believe. Which brings me back to those values I spoke of. I know myself. I couldn't love the man you say you are. I love the man I know you are. You just confirmed it again. No killer would make the offer you just made. And that offer, sir, is respectfully rejected."

"You're a goddamn fool!" exploded Jason. "I can help you; you can't help me! Leave me *something* for Christ's sake!"

"I won't! Not that way . . ." Suddenly Marie broke off. Her lips parted. "I think I just did," she said, whispering.

"Did what?" asked Bourne angrily.

"Give us both something." She turned back to him. "I just said it; it's been there a long time. 'What others want you to believe . . .'"

"What the hell are you talking about?"

"Your crimes . . . what others want you to believe are your crimes."

"They're there. They're mine."

"Wait a minute. Suppose they were there but they *weren't* yours? Suppose the evidence was planted—as expertly as it was planted against me in Zurich—but it belongs to someone else. Jason—you don't *know* when you lost your memory."

"Port Noir."

"That's when you began to build one, not when you lost it. *Before* Port Noir; it could explain so much. It could explain *you*, the contradiction between you and the man people think you are."

"You're wrong. Nothing could explain the memories— the images—that come back to me."

"Maybe you just remember what you've been told," said Marie. "Over and over and over again. Until there was nothing else. Photographs, recordings, visual and aural stimulae."

"You're describing a walking, functioning vegetable who's been brainwashed. That's not me."

She looked at him, speaking gently. "I'm describing an intelligent, very ill man whose background conformed with what other men were looking for. Do you know how easily such a man might be found? They're in hospitals everywhere, in private sanitoriums, in military wards." She paused, then continued quickly. "That newspaper article told another truth. I'm reasonably proficient with computers; anyone doing what I do would be. If I were looking for a curve-example that incorporated isolated factors, I'd know how to do it. Conversely, someone looking for a man hospitalized for amnesia, whose background incorporated specific skills, languages, racial characteristics, the medical data banks could provide candidates. God knows, not many in your case; perhaps only a few, perhaps only one. But one man was all they were looking for, all they needed."

Bourne glanced at the countryside, trying to pry open the steel doors of his mind, trying to find a semblance of the hope she felt. "What you're saying is that I'm a reproduced illusion," he said, making the statement flatly.

"That's the end effect, but it's not what I'm saying. I'm saying it's possible you've been manipulated. Used. It would explain so much." She touched his hand. "You tell me there are times when things want to burst out of you— blow your head apart."

"Words—places, names—they trigger things."

"Jason, isn't it possible they trigger the false things? The things you've been told over and over again, but you can't relive. You can't see them clearly, because they're *not* you."

"I doubt it. I've seen what I can do. I've done them before."

"You could have done them for other reasons! . . . *Goddamn* you, I'm fighting for my life! For *both* our lives! . . . All right! You can *think*, you can *feel*. Think *now*, *feel* now! Look at me and tell me you've looked inside yourself, inside your thoughts and feelings, and you know without a doubt you're an assassin called Cain! If you can do that—*really* do that—then bring me to Zurich, take the blame for everything, and get out of my life! But if you can't, stay with me and let me help you. And love me, for God's sake. *Love* me, Jason."

[336]

Bourne took her hand, holding it firmly, as one might an angry, trembling child's. "It's not a question of feeling or thinking. I saw the account at the Gemeinschaft; the entries go back a long time. They correspond with all the things I've learned."

"But that account, those entries, could have been created yesterday, or last week, or six months ago. Everything you've heard and read about yourself could be part of a pattern designed by those who want you to take Cain's place. You're *not* Cain, but they want you to think you are, want others to think you are. But there's someone out there who knows you're not Cain and he's trying to tell you. I have my proof, too. My lover's alive, but two friends are dead because they got between you and the one who's sending you the message, who's trying to save your life. They were killed by the same people who want to sacrifice you to Carlos in place of Cain. You said before that everything fit. It didn't, Jason, but *this* does! It explains *you*."

"A hollow shell who doesn't even own the memories he thinks he has? With demons running around inside kicking hell out of the walls? It's not a pleasant prospect."

"Those aren't demons, my darling. They're parts of you—angry, furious, screaming to get out because they don't belong in the shell you've given them."

"And if I blow that shell apart, what'll I find?"

"Many things. Some good, some bad, a great deal that's been hurt. But Cain won't be there, I promise you that. I believe in you, my darling. Please don't give up."

He kept his distance, a glass wall between them. "And if we're wrong? Finally wrong? What then?"

"Leave me quickly. Or kill me. I don't care."

"I love you."

"I know. That's why I'm not afraid."

"I found two telephone numbers in Lavier's office. The first was for Zurich, the other here in Paris. With any luck, they can lead me to the one number I need."

"New York? Treadstone?"

"Yes. The answer's there. If I'm not Cain, someone at that number knows who I am."

They drove back to Paris on the assumption that they would be far less obvious among the crowds of the city than in an isolated country inn. A blond-haired man wearing tortoise-shell glasses, and a striking but stern-faced woman, devoid of makeup, and with her hair pulled back like an intense graduate student at the Sorbonne, were not out of place in Montmartre. They took a room at the Terrasse on the rue de Maistre, registering as a married couple from Brussels.

In the room, they stood for a moment, no words necessary for what each was seeing and feeling. They came together, touching, holding, closing out the abusive world that refused them peace, that kept them balancing on taut wires next to one another, high above a dark abyss; if either fell, it was the end for both.

Bourne could not change his color for the immediate moment. It would be false, and there was no room for artifice. "We need some rest," he said. "We've got to get some sleep. It's going to be a long day."

They made love. Gently, completely, each with the other in the warm, rhythmic comfort of the bed. And there was a moment, a foolish moment, when adjustment of an angle was breathlessly necessary and they laughed. It was a quiet laugh, at first even an embarrassed laugh, but the observation was there, the appraisal of foolishness intrinsic to something very deep between them. They held each other more fiercely when the moment passed, more and more intent on sweeping away the awful sounds and the terrible sights of a dark world that kept them spinning in its winds. They were suddenly breaking out of that world, plunging into a much better one where sunlight and blue water replaced the darkness. They raced toward it feverishly, furiously, and then they burst through and found it.

Spent, they fell asleep, their fingers entwined.

Bourne woke first, aware of the horns and the engines in the Paris traffic below in the streets. He looked at his watch; it was ten past one in the afternoon. They had slept nearly five hours, probably less than they needed, but it was enough. It *was* going to be a long day. Doing what, he was not sure; he only knew that there were two telephone numbers that had to lead him to a third. In New York.

He turned to Marie, breathing deeply beside him, her face—her striking, lovely face—angled down on the edge of the pillow, her lips parted, inches from his lips. He kissed her and she reached for him, her eyes still closed.

"You're a frog and I'll make you a prince," she said in a sleep-filled voice. "Or is it the other way around?"

"As expanding as it may be, that's not in my present frame of reference."

"Then you'll have to stay a frog. Hop around, little frog. Show off for me."

"No temptations. I only hop when I'm fed flies."

"Frogs eat flies? I guess they do. Shudder; that's awful."

"Come on, open your eyes. We've both got to start hopping. We've got to start hunting."

She blinked and looked at him. "Hunting for what?"

"For me," he said.

From a telephone booth on the rue Lafayette, a collect call was placed to a number in Zurich by a Mr. Briggs. Bourne reasoned that Jacqueline Lavier would have wasted no time sending out her alarms; one had to have been flashed to Zurich.

When he heard the ring in Switzerland, Jason stepped back and handed the phone to Marie. She knew what to say.

She had no chance to say it. The international operator in Zurich came on the line.

"We regret that the number you have called is no longer in service."

"It was the other day," broke in Marie. "This is an emergency, operator. Do you have another number?"

"The telephone is no longer in service, madame. There is no alternate number."

"I may have been given the wrong one. It's most urgent. Could you give me the name of the party who had this number?"

"I'm afraid that's not possible."

"I told you; it's an emergency! May I speak with your superior, please?"

"He would not be able to help you. This number is an unpublished listing. Good afternoon, madame."

The connection was broken. "It's been disconnected," she said.

"It took too goddamn long to find that out," replied Bourne, looking up and down the street. "Let's get out of here."

"You think they could have traced it here? In Paris? To a public phone?"

"Within three minutes an exchange can be determined, a

district pinpointed. In four, they can narrow the blocks down to half a dozen."

"How do you know that?"

"I wish I could tell you. Let's go."

"Jason. Why not wait out of sight? And watch?"

"Because I don't know what to watch for and they do. They've got a photograph to go by; they could station men all over the area."

"I don't look anything like the picture in the papers."

"Not you. Me. Let's go!"

They walked rapidly within the erratic ebb and flow of the crowds until they reached the boulevard Malesherbes ten blocks away, and another telephone booth, this with a different exchange from the first. This time there were no operators to go through; this was Paris. Marie stepped inside, coins in her hand and dialed; she was prepared.

But the words that came over the line so astonished her:

"*La résidence du Général Villiers. Bonjour? . . . Allô? Allô?*"

For a moment Marie was unable to speak. She simply stared at the telephone. "*Je m'excuse,*" she whispered. "*Une erreur.*" She hung up.

"What's the matter?" asked Bourne, opening the glass door. "What happened? Who was it?"

"It doesn't make sense," she said. "I just reached the house of one of the most respected and powerful men in France."

— 24 —

"André François Villiers," repeated Marie, lighting a cigarette. They had returned to their room at the Terrasse to sort things out, to absorb the astonishing information. "Graduate of Saint-Cyr, hero of the Second World War, a legend in the Resistance, and, until his break over Algeria, De Gaulle's heir-apparent. Jason, to connect such a man with Carlos is simply unbelievable."

"The connection's there. Believe it."

"It's almost too difficult. Villiers is old-line honor-of-France, a family traced back to the seventeenth century. Today he's one of the ranking deputies in the National Assembly—politically to the right of Charlemagne, to be sure—but very much a law-and-order army man. It's like linking Douglas MacArthur to a Mafia hit man. It doesn't make sense."

"Then let's look for some. What was the break with De Gaulle?"

"Algeria. In the early sixties, Villiers was part of the OAS—one of the Algerian colonels under Salan. They opposed the Evian agreements that gave independence to Algeria, believing it rightfully belonged to France."

"'The mad colonels of Algiers,'" said Bourne, as with so many words and phrases, not knowing where they came from or why he said them.

"That means something to you?"

"It must, but I don't know what it is."

Think," said Marie. "Why should the 'mad colonels' strike a chord with you? What's the first thing that comes to your mind? Quickly!"

Jason looked at her helplessly, then the words came. "Bombings . . . infiltrations. *Provocateurs.* You study them; you study the mechanisms."

"*Why?*"

"I don't know."

"Are decisions based on what you learn?"

"I guess so."

"What kind of decisions? You decide *what?*"

"Disruptions."

"What does that mean to you? Disruptions."

"I don't know! I can't think!"

"All right . . . all right. We'll go back to it some other time."

"There isn't time. Let's get back to Villiers. After Algeria, what?"

"There was a reconciliation of sorts with De Gaulle; Villiers was never directly implicated in the terrorism, and his military record demanded it. He returned to France—was welcomed, really—a fighter for a lost but respected cause. He resumed his command, rising to the rank of general, before going into politics."

"He's a working politician, then?"

"More a spokesman. An elder statesman. He's still an entrenched militarist, still fumes over France's reduced military stature."

"Howard Leland," said Jason. "There's your connection to Carlos."

"How? Why?"

"Leland was assassinated because he interfered with the Quai D'Orsay's arms buildups and exports. We don't need anything more."

"It seems incredible, a man like that . . ." Marie's voice trailed off; she was struck by recollection. "His son was murdered. It was a political thing, about five or six years ago."

"Tell me."

[342]

"His car was blown up on the rue du Bac. It was in all the papers everywhere. *He* was the working politician, like his father a conservative, opposing the socialists and Communists at every turn. He was a young member of parliament, an obstructionist where government expenditures were concerned, but actually quite popular. He was a charming aristocrat."

"Who killed him?"

"The speculation was Communist fanatics. He'd managed to block some legislation or other favorable to the extreme left wing. After he was murdered, the ranks fell apart and the legislation passed. Many think that's why Villiers left the army and stood for the National Assembly. That's what's so improbable, so contradictory. After all, his son *was* assassinated; you'd think the last person on earth he'd want to have anything to do with was a professional assassin."

"There's also something else. You said he was welcomed back to Paris because he was never *directly* implicated in the terrorism."

"If he was," interrupted Marie, "it was buried. They're more tolerant of passionate causes over here where country and the bed are concerned. And he was a legitimate hero, don't forget that."

"But once a terrorist, always a terrorist, don't you forget that."

"I can't agree. People change."

"Not about some things. No terrorist ever forgets how effective he's been; he lives on it."

"How would you know that?"

"I'm not sure I want to ask myself right now."

"Then don't."

"But I *am* sure about Villiers. I'm going to reach him." Bourne crossed to the bedside table and picked up the telephone book. "Let's see if he's listed or if that number's private. I'll need his address."

"You won't get near him. If he's Carlos' connection, he'll be guarded. They'll kill you on sight; they have your photograph, remember?"

"It won't help them. I won't be what they're looking for. Here it is. Villiers, A. F. Parc Monceau."

"I still can't believe it. Just knowing whom she was calling must have put the Lavier woman in shock."

"Or frightened her to the point where she'd do anything."

"Doesn't it strike you as odd that she'd be given that number?"

"Not under the circumstances. Carlos wants his drones to know he isn't kidding. He wants Cain."

Marie stood up. "Jason? What's a 'drone'?"

Bourne looked up at her. "I don't know . . . Someone who works blind for somebody else."

"Blind? Not seeing?"

"Not knowing. Thinking he's doing one thing when he's really doing something else."

"I don't understand."

"Let's say I tell you to watch for a car at a certain street corner. The car never shows up, but the fact that you're there tells someone else who's watching for you that something else has happened."

"Arithmetically, an untraceable message."

"Yes, I guess so."

"That's what happened in Zurich. Walther Apfel was a drone. He released that story about the theft not knowing what he was really saying."

"Which was?"

"It's a good guess that you were being told to reach someone you know very well."

"Treadstone Seventy-One," said Jason. "We're back to Villiers. Carlos found me in Zurich through the Gemeinschaft. That means he had to know about Treadstone; it's a good chance that Villiers does too. If he doesn't, there may be a way of getting him to find out for us."

"How?"

"His name. If he's everything you say he is, he thinks pretty highly of it. The honor-of-France coupled with a pig like Carlos might have an effect. I'll threaten to go to the police, to the papers."

"He'd simply deny it. He'd say it's outrageous."

"Let him. It isn't. That was his number in Lavier's office. Besides, any retraction will be on the same page as his obituary."

"You still have to get to him."

"I will. I'm part chameleon, remember?"

The tree-lined street in Parc Monceau seemed familiar somehow, but not in the sense that he had walked it before.

Instead, it was the atmosphere. Two rows of well-kept stone houses, doors and windows glistening, hardware shining, staircases washed clean, the lighted rooms beyond filled with hanging plants. It was a monied street in a wealthy section of the city, and he knew he had been exposed to one like it before, and that exposure *had* meant something.

It was 7:35 in the evening, the March night cold, the sky clear, and the chameleon dressed for the occasion. Bourne's blond hair was covered by a cap, his neck concealed beneath the collar of a jacket that spelled out the name of a messenger service across his back. Slung over his shoulder was a canvas strap attached to a nearly empty satchel; it was the end of this particular messenger's run. He had two or three stops to make, perhaps four or five, if he thought they were necessary; he would know momentarily. The envelopes were not really envelopes at all, but brochures advertising the pleasures of the Bateaux Mouche, picked up from a hotel lobby. He would select at random several houses near General Villiers' residence and deposit the brochures in mail slots. His eyes would record everything they saw, one thing sought above everything else. What kind of security arrangements did Villiers have? Who guarded the general and how many were there?

And because he had been convinced he would find either men in cars or other men walking their posts, he was startled to realize there was no one. André François Villiers, militarist, spokesman for his cause, and the prime connection to Carlos, had no external security arrangements whatsoever. If he was protected, that protection was solely within the house. Considering the enormity of his crime, Villiers was either arrogant to the point of carelessness or a damn fool.

Jason climbed the steps of an adjacent residence, Villiers' door no more than twenty feet away. He deposited the brochure in the slot, glancing up at the windows of Villiers' house, looking for a face, a figure. There was no one.

The door twenty feet away suddenly opened. Bourne crouched, thrusting his hand beneath his jacket for his gun, thinking *he* was a damn fool; someone more observant than he had spotted him. But the words he heard told him it wasn't so. A middle-aged couple—a uniformed maid and a dark-jacketed man—were talking in the doorway.

"Make sure the ashtrays are clean," said the woman.

"You know how he dislikes ashtrays that are stuffed full."

"He drove this afternoon," answered the man. "That means they're full now."

"Clean them in the garage; you've got time. He won't be down for another ten minutes. He doesn't have to be in Nanterre until eight-thirty."

The man nodded, pulling up the lapels of his jacket as he started down the steps. "Ten minutes," he said aimlessly.

The door closed and silence returned to the quiet street. Jason stood up, his hand on the railing, watching the man hurry down the sidewalk. He was not sure where Nanterre was, only that it was a suburb of Paris. And if Villiers was driving there himself, and if he was alone, there was no point in postponing confrontation.

Bourne shifted the strap on his shoulder and walked rapidly down the steps, turning left on the pavement. Ten minutes.

Jason watched through the windshield as the door opened and General of the Army André François Villiers came into view. He was a medium-sized, barrel-chested man in his late sixties, perhaps early seventies. He was hatless, with close-cropped gray hair and a meticulously groomed white chin beard. His bearing was unmistakably military, imposing his body on the surrounding space, entering it by breaking it, invisible walls collapsing as he moved.

Bourne stared at him, fascinated, wondering what insanities could have possibly driven such a man into the obscene world of Carlos. Whatever the reasons, they had to be powerful, for *he* was powerful. And that made him dangerous—for he was respected and had the ears of his government.

Villiers turned, speaking to the maid and glancing at his wristwatch. The woman nodded, closing the door, as the general walked briskly down the steps and around the hood of a large sedan to the driver's side. He opened the door and climbed in, then started the engine and rolled slowly out into the middle of the street. Jason waited until the sedan reached the corner and turned right; he eased the Renault away from the curb and accelerated, reaching the intersection in time to see Villiers turn right again a block east.

There was a certain irony in the coincidence, an omen if

one could believe in such things. The route General Villiers chose to the outlying suburb of Nanterre included a stretch of back road in the countryside nearly identical to the one in Saint-Germain-en-Laye, where twelve hours ago Marie had pleaded with Jason not to give up—his life or hers. There were stretches of pastureland, fields that fused into the gently rising hills, but instead of being crowned by early light, these were washed in the cold, white rays of the moon. It occurred to Bourne that this stretch of isolated road would be as good a spot as any on which to intercept the returning general.

It was not difficult for Jason to follow at distances up to a quarter of a mile, which was why he was surprised to realize he had practically caught up with the old soldier. Villiers had suddenly slowed down and was turning into a graveled drive cut out of the woods, the parking lot beyond illuminated by floodlights. A sign, hanging from two chains on a high-angle post, was caught in the spill: L'ARBALÈTE. The general was meeting someone for dinner at an out-of-the-way restaurant, not *in* the suburb of Nanterre, but close by. In the country.

Bourne drove past the entrance and pulled off the shoulder of the road, the right side of the car covered by foliage. He had to think things out. He had to control himself. There was a fire in his mind; it was growing, spreading. He was suddenly consumed by an extraordinary possibility.

Considering the shattering events—the enormity of the embarrassment experienced by Carlos last night at the motel in Montrouge, it was more than likely that André Villiers had been summoned to an out-of-the-way restaurant for an emergency meeting. Perhaps even with Carlos *himself*. If that was the case, the premises would be guarded, and a man whose photograph had been distributed to those guards would be shot the instant he was recognized. On the other hand, the chance to observe a nucleus belonging to Carlos—or Carlos himself—was an opportunity that might never come again. He had to get inside L'Arbalète. There was a compulsion within him to take the risk. *Any* risk. It was crazy! But then he was not sane. Sane as a man with a memory was sane. *Carlos. Find Carlos! God in heaven, why?*

He felt the gun in his belt; it was secure. He got out and put on his topcoat, covering the jacket with the lettering across the back. He picked up a narrow-brimmed hat from the seat, the cloth soft, angled down all sides; it would cover his hair. Then he tried to remember if he had been wearing the tortoise-shell glasses when the photograph was taken in Argenteuil. He had not; he had removed them at the table when successive bolts of pain had seared through his head, brought on by words that told him of a past too familiar, too frightening to face. He felt his shirt pocket; the glasses were there if he needed them. He pressed the door closed and started for the woods.

The glare of the restaurant floodlights filtered through the trees, growing brighter with each several yards, less foliage to block the light. Bourne reached the edge of the short patch of forest, the graveled parking lot in front of him. He was at the side of the rustic restaurant, a row of small windows running the length of the building, flickering candles beyond the glass illuminating the figures of the diners. Then his eyes were drawn to the second floor—although it did not extend the length of the building, but only halfway, the rear section an open terrace. The enclosed part, however, was similar to the first floor. A line of windows, a bit larger, perhaps, but still in a row, and again glowing with candles. Figures were milling about, but they were different from the diners below.

They were all men. Standing, not sitting; moving casually, glasses in hands, cigarette smoke spiraling over their heads. It was impossible to tell how many—more than ten, less than twenty, perhaps.

There *he* was, crossing from one group to another, the white chin beard a beacon, switching on and off as it was intermittently blocked by figures nearer the windows. General Villiers had, indeed, driven out to Nanterre for a meeting, and the odds favored a conference that dealt with the failures of the past forty-eight hours, failures that permitted a man named Cain to remain alive.

The odds. What were the odds? Where were the guards? How many, and where were their stations? Keeping behind the edge of the woods, Bourne sidestepped his way toward the front of the restaurant, bending branches silently, his feet over the underbrush. He stood motionless, watching for men concealed in the foliage or in the shadows of the building. He saw none and retraced his path, breaking new ground until he reached the rear of the restaurant.

A door opened, the spill of light harsh, and a man in a white jacket emerged. He stood for a moment, cupping his hands, lighting a cigarette. Bourne looked to the left, to the right, above to the terrace; no one appeared. A guard stationed in the area would have been alarmed by the sudden light ten feet below the conference. There were no guards outside. Protection found—as it had to be at Villiers' house in Parc Monceau—within the building itself.

Another man appeared in the doorway, also wearing a white jacket, but with the addition of a chef's hat. His voice was angry, his French laced with the guttural dialect of Gascony. "While you piss off, we sweat! The pastry cart is half empty. Fill it. *Now*, you bastard!"

The pastry man turned and shrugged; he crushed out his cigarette and went back inside, closing the door behind him. The light vanished, only the wash of the moon remained, but it was enough to illuminate the terrace. There was no one there, no guard patrolling the wide double doors that led to the inside room.

Carlos. Find Carlos. Trap Carlos. Cain is for Charlie, and Delta is for Cain.

Bourne judged the distance and the obstacles. He was no more than forty feet from the rear of the building, ten or twelve below the railing that bordered the terrace. There were two vents in the exterior wall, vapor escaping from both, and next to them a drainpipe that was within reach of the railing. If he could scale the pipe and manage to get a toehold in the lower vent, he would be able to grab a rung of the railing and pull himself up to the terrace. But he could do none of this wearing the topcoat. He took it off, placing it at his feet, the soft-brimmed hat on top, and covered both with underbrush. Then he stepped to the edge of the woods and raced as quietly as possible across the gravel to the drainpipe.

In the shadows he tugged at the fluted metal; it was strongly in place. He reached as high as he could, then sprang up, gripping the pipe, his feet pressed into the wall, peddling one on top of the other until his left foot was parallel to the first vent. Holding on, he slipped his foot into the recess and propelled himself further up the drain. He was within eighteen inches of the railings; one surge launched from the vent and he could reach the bottom rung.

The door crashed open beneath him, white light shooting across the gravel into the woods. A figure plummeted out, weaving to maintain its balance, followed by the white-hatted chef, who was screaming.

"You piss-ant! You're drunk, that's what you are! You've been drunk the whole shit-filled night! Pastries all over the dining room floor. Everything a mess. Get out, you'll not get a *sou!*"

The door was pulled shut, the sound of a bolt unmistakably final. Jason held on to the pipe, arms and ankles aching, rivulets of sweat breaking out on his forehead. The man below staggered backward, making obscene gestures repeatedly with his right hand for the benefit of the chef who was no longer there. His glazed eyes wandered up the wall, settling on Bourne's face. Jason held his breath as their eyes met; the man stared, then blinked and stared again. He shook his head, closing his lids, then opened them wide, taking in the sight he was not entirely sure was there. He backed away, lurching into a sideslip and a forward walk, obviously deciding that the apparition halfway up the wall was the result of his pressured labors. He weaved around the corner of the building, a man more at peace with himself for having rejected the foolishness that had assaulted his eyes.

Bourne breathed again, letting his body slump against the wall in relief. But it was only for a moment; the ache in his ankle had descended to his foot, a cramp forming. He lunged, grabbing the iron bar that was the base of the railing with his right hand, whipping his left up from the drainpipe, joining it. He pressed his knees into the shingles and pulled himself slowly up the wall until his head was over the edge of the terrace. It was deserted. He kicked his right leg up to the ledge, his right hand reaching for the wrought-iron top; balanced, he swung over the railing.

He was on a terrace used for dining in the spring and summer months, a tiled floor that could accommodate ten to fifteen tables. In the center of the wall separating the enclosed section from the terrace were the wide double doors he had seen from the woods. The figures inside were now motionless, standing still, and for an instant Jason wondered whether an alarm had been set off—whether they were waiting for him. He stood immobile, his hand on his gun; nothing happened. He approached the wall, staying in the shadows. Once there, he pressed his back against the wood and edged his way toward the first door until his fingers touched the frame. Slowly, he inched his head to the pane of glass level with his eyes and looked inside.

What he saw was both mesmerizing and not a little frightening. The men were in lines—three separate lines, four men to a line—facing André Villiers, who was addressing them. Thirteen men in all, twelve of them not merely standing, but standing at attention. They were old men, but not merely old men; they were old soldiers. None wore uniforms; instead in each lapel they wore ribbons, regimental colors above decorations for valor and rank. And if there was one all-pervasive note about the scene, it, too, was unmistakable. These were men used to command—used to power. It was in their faces, their eyes, in the way they listened—respect rendered, but not blindly, judgment ever present. Their bodies were old, but there was strength in that room. Immense strength. That was the frightening aspect. If these men belonged to Carlos, the assassin's resources were not only far-reaching, they were extraordinarily dangerous. For these were not ordinary men; they were seasoned professional soldiers. Unless he was grossly mistaken, thought Bourne, the depth of experience and range of influence in that room was staggering.

The mad colonels of Algiers—what was left of them? Men driven by memories of a France that no longer existed, a world that was no more, replaced by one they found weak and ineffectual. Such men could make a pact with Carlos, if only for the covert power it gave them. Strike. Attack. Dispatch. Decisions of life and death that were once a part of their fabric, brought back by a force that could serve causes they refused to admit were no longer viable. Once a terrorist, always a terrorist, and assassination was the raw core of terror.

The general was raising his voice; Jason tried to hear the words through the glass. They became clearer.

". . . our presence will be felt, our purpose understood. We are together in our stand, and that stand is immovable; we *shall* be heard! In memory of all those who have fallen—our brothers of the tunic and the cannon—who laid down their lives for the glory of France. We shall force our beloved country to remember, and in their names to remain strong, lackey to no one! Those who oppose us will know our anger. In this, too, we are united. We pray to Almighty God that those who have gone before us have found peace, for we are still in conflict. . . . Gentlemen: I give you Our Lady—our France!"

There was a unison of muttered approvals, the old soldiers remaining rigidly at attention. And then another voice was raised, the first five words sung singly, joined at the sixth by the rest of the group.

Allons enfants de la patrie,
Le jour de gloire est arrivé . . .

Bourne turned away, sickened by the sight and the sounds inside that room. Lay waste in the name of glory; the death of fallen comrades perforce demands further death. It is required; and if it means a pact with Carlos, so be it.

What disturbed him so? Why was he suddenly swept by feelings of anger and futility? What triggered the revulsion he felt so strongly? And then he knew. He hated a man like André Villiers, despised the men in that room. They were all old men who made war, stealing life from the young . . . and the very young.

Why were the mists closing in again? Why was the pain so acute? There was no time for questions, no strength to tolerate them. He had to push them out of his mind and concentrate on André François Villiers, warrior and warlord, whose causes belonged to yesterday but whose pact with an assassin called for death today.

He would trap the general. Break him. Learn everything he knew, and probably kill him. Men like Villiers robbed life from the young and the very young. They did not deserve to live. *I am in my labyrinth again, and the walls are imbedded with spikes. Oh, God, they hurt.*

Jason climbed over the railing in the darkness and lowered himself to the drainpipe, each muscle aching. Pain, too, had to be erased. He had to reach a deserted stretch of road in the moonlight and trap a broker of death.

— 25 —

Bourne waited in the Renault, two hundred yards east of the restaurant entrance, the motor running, prepared to race ahead the instant he saw Villiers drive out. Several others had already left, all in separate cars. Conspirators did not advertise their association, and these old men were conspirators in the truest sense. They had traded whatever honors they had earned for the lethal convenience of an assassin's gun and an assassin's organization. Age and bias had robbed them of reason, as they had spent their lives robbing life . . . from the young and the very young.

What was it? Why won't it leave me? Some terrible thing is deep inside me, trying to break out, trying I think to kill me. The fear and the guilt sweep through me . . . but of what and for what I do not know. Why should these withered old men provoke such feelings of fear and guilt . . . and loathing?

They were war. They were death. On the ground and from the skies. From the skies . . . from the skies. Help me, Marie. For God's sake, help me!

There it was. The headlights swung out of the drive, the long black chassis reflecting the wash of the floodlights. Jason kept his own lights off as he pulled out of the shadows. He accelerated down the road until he reached the first curve, where he switched on the headlights and pressed the pedal to the floor. The isolated stretch in the countryside was roughly two miles away; he had to get there quickly.

It was ten past eleven, and as three hours before the fields swept into the hills, both bathed in the light of the March moon, now in the center of the sky. He reached the area; it *was* feasible. The shoulder was wide, bordering a pasture, which meant that both automobiles could be pulled off the road. The immediate objective, however, was to get Villiers to stop. The general was old but not feeble; if the tactic were suspect, he would break over the grass and race away. Everything was timing, and a totally convincing moment of the unexpected.

Bourne swung the Renault around in a U-turn, waited until he saw the headlights in the distance, then suddenly accelerated, swinging the wheel violently back and forth. The automobile careened over the road—an out-of-control driver, incapable of finding a straight line, but nevertheless speeding.

Villiers had no choice; he slowed down as Jason came racing insanely toward him. Then abruptly, when the two cars were no more than twenty feet from colliding, Bourne spun the wheel to the left, braking as he did so, sliding into a skid, tires screeching. He came to a stop, the window open, and raised his voice in an undefined cry. Half shout, half scream; it could have been the vocal explosion of an ill man or a drunk man, but the one thing it was not was threatening. He slapped his hand on the frame of the window and was silent, crouching in the seat, his gun on his lap.

He heard the door of Villiers' sedan open and peered through the steering wheel. The old man was not visibly armed; he seemed to suspect nothing, relieved only that a collision had been avoided. The general walked through the beams of the headlights to the Renault's left window, his shouts anxious, his French the interrogating commands of Saint-Cyr.

"What's the meaning of this? What do you think you're doing? Are you all right?" His hands gripped the base of the window.

"Yes, but you're not," replied Bourne in English, raising the gun.

"What . . ." The old man gasped, standing erect. "Who are you and what is this?"

Jason got out of the Renault, his left hand extended above the barrel of the weapon. "I'm glad your English is fluent. Walk back to your car. Drive it off the road."

"And if I refuse?"

"I'll kill you right now. It wouldn't take much to provoke me."

"Do these words come from the Red Brigades? Or the Paris branch of the Baader-Meinhof?"

"Why? Could you countermand them if they did?"

"I spit at them! And you!"

"No one's ever doubted your courage, General. Walk to your car."

"It's not a matter of courage!" said Villiers without moving. "It's a question of logic. You'll accomplish nothing by killing me, less by kidnapping me. My orders are firm, fully understood by my staff and my family. The Israelis are absolutely right. There can be no negotiations with terrorists. Use your gun, garbage! Or get out of here!"

Jason studied the old soldier, suddenly, profoundly uncertain, but not about to be fooled. It would be in the furious eyes that stared at him. One name soaked in filth coupled with another name heaped with the honors of his nation would cause another kind of explosion; it would be in the eyes.

"Back at that restaurant, you said France shouldn't be a lackey to anyone. But a general of France became someone's lackey. General André Villiers, messenger for Carlos. Carlos' contact, Carlos' soldier, Carlos' lackey."

The furious eyes did grow wide, but not in any way Jason expected. Fury was suddenly joined by hatred, not shock, not hysteria, but deep, uncompromising abhorrence. The back of Villiers' hand shot up, arching from his waist, the crack against Bourne's face sharp, accurate, painful. It was followed by a forward slap, brutal, insulting, the force of the blow reeling Jason back on his feet. The old man moved in, blocked by the barrel of the gun, but unafraid, undeterred by its presence, consumed only with inflicting punishment. The blows came one after another, delivered by a man possessed.

"Pig!" screamed Villiers. "Filthy, destestable pig! Garbage!"

"I'll shoot! I'll kill you! Stop it!" But Bourne could not

pull the trigger. He was backed into the small car, his shoulders pressed against the roof. Still the old man attacked, his hands flying out, swinging up, crashing down.

"Kill me if you can—if you *dare!* Dirt! *Filth!*"

Jason threw the gun to the ground, raising his arms to fend off Villiers' assault. He lashed his left hand out, grabbing the old man's right wrist, then his left, gripping the left forearm that was slashing down like a broadsword. He twisted both violently, bending Villiers into him, forcing the old soldier to stand motionless, their faces inches from each other, the old man's chest heaving.

"Are you telling me you're *not* Carlos' man? Are you denying it?"

Villiers lunged forward, trying to break Bourne's grip, his barrel-like chest smashing into Jason. "I revile you! *Animal!*"

"*Goddamn* you—yes or no?"

The old man spat in Bourne's face, the fire in his eyes now clouded, tears welling. "Carlos killed my son," he said in a whisper. "He killed my only son on the rue du Bac. My son's life was blown up with five sticks of dynamite on the rue du Bac!"

Jason slowly reduced the pressure of his fingers. Breathing heavily, he spoke as calmly as he could.

"Drive your car into the field and stay there. We have to talk, General. Something's happened you don't know about, and we'd both better learn what it is."

"*Never!* Impossible! It could not happen!"

"It happened," said Bourne, sitting with Villiers in the front seat of the sedan.

"An incredible mistake has been made! You don't know what you're saying!"

"No mistake—and I do know what I'm saying because I found the number myself. It's not only the right number, it's a magnificent cover. Nobody in his right mind would connect you with Carlos, especially in light of your son's death. Is it common knowledge he was Carlos' kill?"

"I would prefer different language, monsieur."

"Sorry. I mean that."

"Common knowledge? Among the Sûreté, a qualified yes. Within military intelligence and Interpol, most certainly. I read the reports."

"What did they say?"

"It was presumed that Carlos did a favor for his friends from his radical days. Even to the point of allowing them to appear silently responsible for the act. It was politically motivated, you know. My son was a sacrifice, an example to others who opposed the fanatics."

"Fanatics?"

"The extremists were forming a false coalition with the socialists, making promises they had no intention of keeping. My son understood this, exposed it, and initiated legislation to block the alignment. He was killed for it."

"Is that why you retired from the army and stood for election?"

"With all my heart. It is customary for the son to carry on for the father . . ." The old man paused, the moonlight illuminating his haggard face. "In this matter, it was the father's legacy to carry on for the son. He was no soldier, nor I a politician, but I am no stranger to weapons and explosives. His causes were molded by me, his philosophy reflected my own, and he was killed for these things. My decision was clear to me. I would carry on our beliefs into the political arena and let his enemies contend with me. The soldier was prepared for them."

"More than one soldier, I gather."

"What do you mean?"

"Those men back there at the restaurant. They looked like they ran half the armies in France."

"They did, monsieur. They were once known as the angry young commanders of Saint-Cyr. The Republic was corrupt, the military incompetent, the Maginot a joke. Had they been heeded in their time, France would not have fallen. They became the leaders of the Resistance; they fought the Boche and Vichy all through Europe and Africa."

"What do they do now?"

"Most live on pensions, many obsessed with the past. They pray to the Virgin that it will never be repeated. In too many areas, however, they see it happening. The military is reduced to a sideshow, Communists and socialists in the Assembly forever eroding the strength of the services. The Moscow apparatus runs true to form; it does not change with the decades. A free society is ripe for infiltration, and once infiltrated the changes do not stop until that society is remade into another image. Conspiracy is everywhere; it cannot go unchallenged."

"Some might say that sounds pretty extreme itself."

"For what? Survival? Strength? Honor? Are these terms too anachronistic for you?"

"I don't think so. But I can imagine a lot of damage being done in their names."

"Our philosophies differ and I don't care to debate them. You asked me about my associates and I answered you. Now, please, this incredible misinformation of yours. It's appalling. You don't know what it's like to lose a son, to have a child killed."

The pain comes back to me and I don't know why. Pain and emptiness, a vacuum in the sky . . . from the sky. Death in and from the skies. Jesus, it hurts. It. What is it?

"I can sympathize," said Jason, his hands gripped to stop the sudden trembling. "But it fits."

"Not for an instant! As you said, no one in his right mind would connect me to Carlos, least of all the killer pig himself. It's a risk he would not take. It's unthinkable."

"Exactly. Which is why you're being used; it *is* unthinkable. You're the perfect relay for final instructions."

"Impossible! How?"

"Someone at your phone is in direct contact with Carlos. Codes are used, certain words spoken to get that person on the phone. Probably when you're not there, possibly when you are. Do you answer the telephone yourself?"

Villiers frowned. "Actually, I don't. Not that number. There are too many people to be avoided, and I have a private line."

"Who does answer it?"

"Generally the housekeeper, or her husband who serves as part butler, part chauffeur. He was my driver during my last years in the army. If not either of them, my wife, of course. Or my aide, who often works at my office at the house; he was my adjutant for twenty years."

"Who else?"

"There is no one else."

"Maids?"

"None permanent; if they're needed, they're hired for an occasion. There's more wealth in the Villiers name than in the banks."

"Cleaning woman?"

"Two. They come twice a week and not always the same two."

"You'd better take a closer look at your chauffeur and the adjutant."

"Preposterous! Their loyalty is beyond question."

"So was Brutus', and Caesar outranked you."

"You can't be serious."

"I'm goddamned serious. And you'd better believe it. Everything I've told you is the truth."

"But then you haven't really told me very much, have you? Your name, for instance."

"It's not necessary. Knowing it could only hurt you."

"In what way?"

"In the very remote chance that I'm wrong about the relay—and that possibility barely exists."

The old man nodded the way old men do when repeating words that have stunned them to the point of disbelief. His lined face moved up and down in the moonlight. "An unnamed man traps me on a road at night, holds me under a gun, and makes an obscene accusation—a charge so filthy, I wish to kill him—and he expects me to accept his word. The word of a man without a name, with no face I recognize, and no credentials offered other than the statement that Carlos is hunting him. Tell me why should I believe this man?"

"Because," answered Bourne. "He'd have no reason to come to you if *he* didn't believe it was the truth."

Villiers stared at Jason. "No, there's a better reason. A while ago, you gave me my life. You threw down your gun, you did not fire it. You could have. Easily. You chose, instead, to plead with me to talk."

"I don't think I pleaded."

"It was in your eyes, young man. It's always in the eyes. And often in the voice, but one must listen carefully. Supplication can be feigned, not anger. It is either real or it's a posture. Your anger was real . . . as was mine." The old man gestured toward the small Renault ten yards away in the field. "Follow me back to Parc Monceau. We'll talk further in my office. I'd swear on my life that you're wrong about both men, but then as you pointed out, Caesar was blinded by false devotion. And indeed he did outrank me."

"If I walk into that house and someone recognizes me, I'm dead. So are you."

"My aide left shortly past five o'clock this afternoon and the chauffeur, as you call him, retires no later than ten to watch his interminable television. You'll wait outside while

I go in and check. If things are normal, I'll summon you; if they're not, I'll come back out and drive away. Follow me again. I'll stop somewhere and we'll continue."

Jason watched closely as Villiers spoke. "Why do you want me to go back to Parc Monceau?"

"Where else? I believe in the shock of unexpected confrontation. One of those men is lying in bed watching television in a room on the third floor. And there's another reason. I want my wife to hear what you have to say. She's an old soldier's woman and she has antennae for things that often escape the officer in the field. I've come to rely on her perceptions; she may recognize a pattern of behavior once she hears you."

Bourne had to say the words. "I trapped you by pretending one thing; you can trap me by pretending another. How do I know Parc Monceau isn't a trap?"

The old man did not waver. "You have the word of a general officer of France, and that's all you have. If it's not good enough for you, take your weapon and get out."

"It's good enough," said Bourne. "Not because it's a general's word, but because it's the word of a man whose son was killed in the rue du Bac."

The drive back into Paris seemed far longer to Jason than the journey out. He was fighting images again, images that caused him to break out into sweat. And pain, starting at his temples, sweeping down through his chest, forming a knot in his stomach—sharp bolts pounding until he wanted to scream.

Death in the skies . . . from the skies. Not darkness, but blinding sunlight. No winds that batter my body into further darkness, but instead silence and the stench of jungle and. . . . riverbanks. Stillness followed by the screeching of birds and the screaming pitch of machines. Birds . . . machines . . . racing downward out of the sky in blinding sunlight. Explosions. Death. Of the young and the very young.

Stop it! Hold the wheel! Concentrate on the road but do not think! Thought is too painful and you don't know why.

They entered the tree-lined street in Parc Monceau. Villiers was a hundred feet ahead, facing a problem that had not existed several hours ago: there were many more automobiles in the street now, parking at a premium.

There was, however, one sizable space on the left, across

[360]

from the general's house; it could accommodate both their cars. Villiers thrust his hand out the window, gesturing for Jason to pull in behind him.

And then it happened. Jason's eyes were drawn by a light in a doorway, his focus suddenly rigid on the figures in the spill; the recognition of one so startling and so out of place he found himself reaching for the gun in his belt.

Had he been led into a trap after all? Had the word of a general officer of France been worthless?

Villiers was maneuvering his sedan into place. Bourne spun around in the seat, looking in all directions; there was no one coming toward him, no one closing in. It was *not* a trap. It was something else, part of what was happening about which the old soldier knew nothing.

For across the street and up the steps of Villiers' house stood a youngish woman—a striking woman—in the doorway. She was talking rapidly, with small anxious gestures, to a man standing on the top step, who kept nodding as if accepting instructions. That man was the gray-haired, distinguished-looking switchboard operator from Les Classiques. The man whose face Jason knew so well, yet did not know. The face that had triggered other images . . . images as violent and as painful as those which had ripped him apart during the past half hour in the Renault.

But there was a difference. This face brought back the darkness and torrential winds in the night sky, explosions coming one after another, sounds of a staccato gunfire echoing through the myriad tunnels of a jungle.

Bourne pulled his eyes away from the door and looked at Villiers through the windshield. The general had switched off his headlights and was about to get out of the car. Jason released the clutch and rolled forward until he made contact with the sedan's bumper. Villiers whipped around in his seat.

Bourne extinguished his own headlights and turned on the small inside roof light. He raised his hand—palm downward—then raised it twice again, telling the old soldier to stay where he was. Villiers nodded and Jason switched off the light.

He looked back over at the doorway. The man had taken a step down, stopped by a last command from the woman. Bourne could see her clearly now. She was in her middle to late thirties, with short dark hair, stylishly cut, framing a face that was bronzed by the sun. She was a tall woman, statuesque, actually, her figure tapered, the swell of her breasts accentuated by the sheer, close-fitting fabric of a long white dress that heightened the tan of her skin. If she was part of the house, Villiers had not mentioned her, which meant she was not. She was a visitor who knew when to come to the old man's home; it would fit the strategy of relay-removed-from-relay. And that meant she had a contact in Villiers' house. The old man had to know her, but how well? The answer obviously was not well enough.

The gray-haired switchboard operator gave a final nod, descended the steps and walked rapidly down the block. The door closed, the light of the carriage lamps shining on the deserted staircase and the glistening black door with the brass hardware.

Why did those steps and that door mean something to him? Images. Reality that was not real.

Bourne got out of the Renault, watching the windows, looking for the movement of a curtain; there was nothing. He walked quickly to Villiers' car; the front window was rolled down, the general's face turned up, his thick eyebrows arched in curiosity.

"What in heaven's name are you doing?" he asked.

"Over there, at your house," said Jason, crouching on the pavement. "You saw what I just saw."

"I believe so. And?"

"Who was the woman? Do you know her?"

"I would hope to God I did! She's my wife."

"Your *wife?*" Bourne's shock was on his face. "I thought you said . . . I thought you said she was an *old* woman. That you wanted her to listen to me because over the years you'd learned to respect her judgment. In the field, you said. That's what you *said.*"

"Not exactly. I said she was an *old soldier's* woman. And I do, indeed, respect her judgment. But she's my second wife—my very much younger second wife—but every bit as devoted as my first, who died eight years ago."

"Oh, my God . . ."

"Don't let the disparity of our ages concern you. She is proud and happy to be the second Madame Villiers. She's been a great help to me in the Assembly."

"I'm sorry," whispered Bourne. "Christ, I'm sorry."

"What about? You mistook her for someone else? People frequently do; she's a stunning girl. I'm quite proud of her." Villiers opened the door as Jason stood up on the

[362]

pavement. "You wait here," said the general, "I'll go inside and check; if everything's normal, I'll open the door and signal you. If it isn't I'll come back to the car and we'll drive away."

Bourne remained motionless in front of Villiers, preventing the old man from stepping forward. "General, I've got to ask you something. I'm not sure how, but I have to. I told you I found your number at a relay drop used by Carlos. I didn't tell you where, only that it was confirmed by someone who admitted passing messages to and from contacts of Carlos." Bourne took a breath, his eyes briefly on the door across the street. "Now I've got to ask you a question, and please think carefully before you answer. Does your wife buy clothes at a shop called Les Classiques?"

"In Saint-Honoré?"

"Yes."

"I happen to know she does not."

"Are you sure?"

"Very much so. Not only have I never seen a bill from there, but she's told me how much she dislikes its designs. My wife is very knowledgeable in matters of fashion."

"Oh, Jesus."

"What?"

"General, I can't go inside that house. No matter what you find, I can't go in there."

"Why not? What are you saying?"

"The man on the steps who was talking to your wife. He's from the drop; it's Les Classiques. He's a contact to Carlos."

The blood drained from André Villiers' face. He turned and stared across the tree-lined street at his house, at the glistening black door and the brass fittings that reflected the light of the carriage lamps.

The pockmarked beggar scratched the stubble of his beard, took off his threadbare beret and trudged through the bronze doors of the small church in Neuilly-sur-Seine.

He walked down the far right aisle under the disapproving glances of two priests. Both clerics were upset; this was a wealthy parish and, biblical compassion notwithstanding, wealth did have its privileges. One of them was to maintain a certain status of worshiper—for the benefit of other worshipers—and this elderly, disheveled derelict hardly fit the mold.

The beggar made a feeble attempt to genuflect, sat down in a pew in the second row, crossed himself and knelt forward, his head in prayer, his right hand pushing back the left sleeve of his overcoat. On his wrist was a watch somewhat in contradistinction to the rest of his apparel. It was an expensive digital, the numbers large and the readout bright. It was a possession he would never be foolish enough to part with, for it was a gift from Carlos. He had once been twenty-five minutes late for confession, upsetting his benefactor, and had no other excuse but the lack of an accurate timepiece. During their next appointment, Carlos had pushed it beneath the translucent scrim separating sinner from holy man.

It was the hour and the minute. The beggar rose and walked toward the second booth on the right. He parted the curtain and went inside.

"Angelus Domini."

"Angelus Domini, child of God." The whisper from behind the black cloth was harsh. "Are your days comfortable?"

"They are made comfortable . . ."

"Very well," interrupted the silhouette. "What did you bring me? My patience draws to an end. I pay thousands—hundreds of thousands—for incompetence and failure. What happened in Montrouge? Who was responsible for the lies that came from the embassy in the Montaigne? Who accepted them?"

"The Auberge du Coin was a trap, yet not one for killing. It is difficult to know exactly what it was. If the attaché named Corbelier repeated lies, our people are convinced he was not aware of it. He was duped by the woman."

"He was duped by Cain! Bourne traces each source, feeding each false information, thus exposing each and confirming the exposure. But why? To whom? We know what and who he is now, but he relays nothing to Washington. He refuses to surface."

"To suggest an answer," said the beggar, "I would have to go back many years, but it's possible he wants no interference from his superiors. American Intelligence has its share of vacillating autocrats, rarely communicating fully with each other. In the days of the cold war, money was made selling information three and four times over to the same stations. Perhaps Cain waits until he thinks there is only one course of action to be taken, no differing strategies to be argued by those above."

"Age hasn't dulled your sense of maneuver, old friend. It's why I called upon you."

"Or perhaps," continued the beggar, "he really has turned. It's happened."

"I don't think so, but it doesn't matter. Washington thinks he has. The Monk is dead, they're all dead at Treadstone. Cain is established as the killer."

"The Monk?" said the beggar. "A name from the past; he was active in Berlin, in Vienna. We knew him well, healthier for it from a distance. There's your answer, Carlos. It was always the Monk's style to reduce the numbers to as few as possible. He operated on the theory that his circles were infiltrated, compromised. He must have ordered Cain to report only to him. It would explain Washington's confusion, the months of silence."

"Would it explain ours? For months there was no word, no activity."

"A score of possibilities. Illness, exhaustion, brought back for new training. Even to spread confusion to the enemy. The Monk had a cathedralful of tricks."

"Yet before he died he said to an associate that he did *not* know what had happened. That he wasn't even certain the man *was* Cain."

"Who was the associate?"

"A man named Gillette. He was our man, but Abbott couldn't have known it."

"Another possible explanation. The Monk had an instinct about such men. It was said in Vienna that David Abbott would distrust Christ on the mountain and look for a bakery."

"It's possible. Your words are comforting; you look for things others do not look for."

"I've had far more experience; I was once a man of stature. Unfortunately I pissed away the money."

"You still do."

"A profligate—what can I tell you?"

"Obviously something else."

"You're perceptive, Carlos. We should have known each other in the old days."

"Now you're presumptuous."

"Always. You know that I know you can swat my life away at any moment you choose, so I must be of value.

[365]

And not merely with words that come from experience."

"What have you got to tell me?"

"This may not be of great value, but it is something. I put on respectable clothes and spent the day at the Auberge du Coin. There was a man, an obese man—questioned and dismissed by the Sûreté—whose eyes were too unsteady. And he perspired too much. I had a chat with him, showing him an official NATO identification I had made in the early fifties. It seems he negotiated the rental of an automobile at three o'clock yesterday morning. To a blond man in the company of a woman. The description fits the photograph from Argenteuil."

"A rental?"

"Supposedly. The car was to be returned within a day or so by the woman."

"It will never happen."

"Of course not, but it raises a question, doesn't it? Why would Cain go to the trouble of obtaining an automobile in such a fashion?"

"To get as far away as possible as rapidly as possible."

"In which case the information *has* no value," said the beggar. "But then there are so many ways to travel faster less conspicuously. And Bourne could hardly trust an avaricious night clerk; he might easily look for a reward from the Sûreté. Or anyone else."

"What's your point?"

"I suggest that Bourne could have obtained that car for the sole purpose of following someone here in Paris. No loitering in public where he might be spotted, no rented cars that could be traced, no frantic searches for elusive taxis. Instead, a simple exchange of license plates and a nondescript black Renault in the crowded streets. Where would one begin to look?"

The silhouette turned. "The Lavier woman," said the assassin softly. "And everyone else he suspects at Les Classiques. It's the only place he has to start. They'll be watched, and within days—hours perhaps—a nondescript black Renault will be seen and he'll be found. Do you have a full description of the car?"

"Down to three dents in the left rear fender."

"Good. Spread the word to the old men. Comb the streets, the garages, the parking lots. The one who finds it will never have to look for work again."

"Speaking of such matters . . ."

An envelope was slipped between the taut edge of the curtain and the blue felt of the frame. "If your theory proves right, consider this a token."

"I *am* right, Carlos."

"Why are you so convinced?"

"Because Cain does what you would do, what I would have done—in the old days. He must be respected."

"He must be killed," said the assassin. "There's symmetry in the timing. In a few days it will be the twenty-fifth of March. On March 25, 1968, Jason Bourne was executed in the jungles of Tam Quan. Now, years later—nearly to the day—another Jason Bourne is hunted, the Americans as anxious as we are to see him killed. I wonder which of us will pull the trigger this time."

"Does it matter?"

"*I* want him," whispered the silhouette. "He was never real, and that's his crime against me. Tell the old men that if any find him, get word to Parc Monceau but do nothing. Keep him in sight, but do *nothing!* I want him alive on the twenty-fifth of March. On March 25 I'll execute him myself and deliver his body to the Americans."

"The word will go out immediately."

"Angelus Domini, child of God."

"Angelus Domini," said the beggar.

26

The old soldier walked in silence beside the younger man down the moonlit path in the Bois de Boulogne. Neither spoke, for too much had already been said—admitted, challenged, denied and reaffirmed. Villiers had to reflect and analyze, to accept or violently reject what he had heard. His life would be far more bearable if he could strike back in anger, attack the lie and find his sanity again. But he could not do that with impunity; he was a soldier and to turn away was not in him.

There was too much truth in the younger man. It was in his eyes, in his voice, in his every gesture that asked for understanding. The man without a name was not lying. The ultimate treason was in Villiers' house. It explained so many things he had not dared to question before. An old man wanted to weep.

For the man without a memory there was little to change or invent; the chameleon was not called upon. His story was convincing because the most vital part was based in the truth. He had to find Carlos, learn what the assassin knew; there would be no life for him if he failed. Beyond this he would say nothing. There was no mention of Marie

St. Jacques, or the Ile de Port Noir, or a message being sent by person or persons unknown, or a walking hollow shell that might or might not be someone he was or was not—who could not even be sure that the fragments of memories he possessed were really his own. None of this was spoken of.

Instead, he recounted everything he knew about the assassin called Carlos. That knowledge was so vast that during the telling Villiers stared at him in astonishment, recognizing information he knew to be highly classified, shocked at new and startling data that was in concert with a dozen existing theories, but to his ears never before put forth with such clarity. Because of his son, the general had been given access to his country's most secret files on Carlos, and nothing in those records matched the younger man's array of facts.

"This woman you spoke with in Argenteuil, the one who calls my house, who admitted being a courier to you . . ."

"Her name is Lavier," Bourne interrupted.

The general paused. "Thank you. She saw through you; she had your photograph taken."

"Yes."

"They had no photograph before?"

"No."

"So as you hunt Carlos, he in turn hunts you. But you have no photograph; you only know two couriers, one of which was at my house."

"Yes."

"Speaking with my wife."

"Yes."

The old man turned away. The period of silence had begun.

They came to the end of the path, where there was a miniature lake. It was bordered with white gravel, benches spaced every ten to fifteen feet, circling the water like a guard of honor surrounding a grave of black marble. They walked to the second bench. Villiers broke his silence.

"I should like to sit down," he said. "With age there comes a paucity of stamina. It often embarrasses me."

"It shouldn't," said Bourne, sitting down beside him.

"It shouldn't," agreed the general, "but it does." He paused for a moment, adding quietly, "Frequently in the company of my wife."

"That's not necessary," said Jason.

"You mistake me." The old man turned to the younger. "I'm not referring to the bed. There are simply times when I find it necessary to curtail activities—leave a dinner party early, absent myself on weekends to the Mediterranean, or decline a few days on the slopes in Gstaad."

"I'm not sure I understand."

"My wife and I are often apart. In many ways we live quite separate lives, taking pleasure, of course, in each other's pursuits."

"I still don't understand."

"Must I embarrass myself further?" said Villiers. "When an old man finds a stunning young woman anxious to share his life, certain things are understood, others not so readily. There is, of course, financial security and in my case a degree of public exposure. Creature comforts, entry into the great houses, easy friendship with the celebrated; it's all very understandable. In exchange for these things, one brings a beautiful companion into his home, shows her off among his peers—a form of continuing virility, as it were. But there are always doubts." The old soldier stopped for several moments; what he had to say was not easy for him. "Will she take a lover?" he continued softly. "Does she long for a younger, firmer body, one more in tune with her own? If she does, one can accept it—even be relieved, I imagine—hoping to God she has the sense to be discreet. A cuckolded statesman loses his constituency faster than a sporadic drunk; it means he's fully lost his grip. There are other worries. Will she abuse his name? Publicly condemn an adversary whom one is trying to convince? These are the inclinations of the young; they are manageable, part of the risks in the exchange. But there is one underlying doubt that if proved justified cannot be tolerated. And that is if she is part of a design. From the beginning."

"You've felt it then?" asked Jason quietly.

"Feelings are not reality!" shot back the old soldier vehemently. "They have no place in observing the field."

"Then why are you telling me this?"

Villiers' head arched back, then fell forward, his eyes on the water. "There could be a simple explanation for what we both saw tonight. I pray there is, and I shall give her every opportunity to provide it." The old man paused again. "But in my heart I know there isn't. I knew it the moment you told me about Les Classiques. I looked across the street, at the door of my house, and suddenly a number of things fell painfully into place. For the past two hours I have played the devil's advocate; there is no point in continuing. There was my son before there was this woman."

"But you said you trusted her judgment. That she was a great help to you."

"True. You see, I wanted to trust her, desperately wanted to trust her. The easiest thing in the world is to convince yourself that you're right. As one grows old it is easier still."

"What fell into place for you?"

"The very help she gave me, the very trust I placed in her." Villiers turned and looked at Jason. "You have extraordinary knowledge about Carlos. I've studied those files as closely as any man alive, for I would give more than any man alive to see him caught and executed, I alone the firing squad. And as swollen as they are, those files do not approach what you know. Yet your concentration is solely on his kills, his methods of assassination. You've overlooked the other side of Carlos. He not only sells his gun, he sells a country's secrets."

"I know that," Bourne said. "It's not the side—"

"For example," continued the general, as if he had not heard Jason. "I have access to classified documents dealing with France's military and nuclear security. Perhaps five other men—all above suspicion—share that access. Yet with damning regularity we find that Moscow has learned this, Washington that, Peking something else."

"You discussed those things with your wife?" asked Bourne, surprised.

"Of course not. Whenever I bring such papers home, they are placed in a vault in my office. No one may enter that room except in my presence. There is only one other person who has a key, one other person who knows the whereabouts of the alarm switch. My wife."

"I'd think that would be as dangerous as discussing the material. Both could be forced from her."

"There was a reason. I'm at the age when the unexpected is a daily occurrence; I commend you to the obituary pages. If anything happened to me she is instructed to telephone the Conseiller Militaire, go down to my office, and stay by that vault until the security personnel arrive."

"Couldn't she simply stay by the door?"

"Men of my years have been known to pass away at

their desks." Villiers closed his eyes. "All along it was she. The one house, the one place, no one believed possible."

"Are you sure?"

"More than I dare admit to myself. She was the one who insisted on the marriage. I repeatedly brought up the disparity of our ages, but she would have none of it. It was the years together, she claimed, not those that separated our birth dates. She offered to sign an agreement renouncing any claims to the Villiers estate and, of course, I would have none of that, for it was proof of her commitment to me. The adage is quite right: The old fool is the complete fool. Yet there were always the doubts; they came with the trips, with the unexpected separations."

"Unexpected?"

"She has many interests, forever demanding her attention. A Franco-Swiss museum in Grenoble, a fine arts gallery in Amsterdam, a monument to the Resistance in Boulogne-sur-Mer, an idiotic oceanography conference in Marseilles. We had a heated argument over that one. I needed her in Paris; there were diplomatic functions I had to attend and wanted her with me. She would not stay. It was as though she were being ordered to be here and there and somewhere else at a given moment."

Grenoble—near the Swiss border, an hour from Zurich. Amsterdam. Boulogne-sur-Mer—on the Channel, an hour from London. Marseilles . . . Carlos.

"When was the conference in Marseilles?" asked Jason.

"Last August, I believe. Toward the latter part of the month."

"On August 26, at five o'clock in the afternoon, Ambassador Howard Leland was assassinated on the Marseilles waterfront."

"Yes, I know," said Villiers. "You spoke of it before. I mourn the passing of the man, not his judgments." The old soldier stopped; he looked at Bourne. "My *God*," he whispered. "She had to be with him. Carlos summoned her and she came to him. She *obeyed*."

"I never went this far," said Jason. "I swear to you I thought of her as a relay—a blind relay. I never went this far."

Suddenly, from the old man's throat came a scream—deep and filled with agony and hatred. He brought his hands to his face, his head arched back once again in the moonlight; and he wept.

Bourne did not move; there was nothing he could do. "I'm sorry," he said.

The general regained control. "And so am I," he replied finally. "I apologize."

"No need to."

"I think there is. We will discuss it no further. I shall do what has to be done."

"Which is?"

The soldier sat erect on the bench, his jaw firm. "You can ask that?"

"I have to ask it."

"Having done what she's done is no different from having killed the child of mine she did not bear. She pretended to hold his memory dear. Yet she was and is an accomplice to his murder. And all the while she committed a second treason against the nation I have served throughout my life."

"You're going to kill her?"

"I'm going to kill her. She will tell me the truth and she will die."

"She'll deny everything you say."

"I doubt it."

"That's crazy!"

"Young man, I've spent over half a century trapping and fighting the enemies of France, even when they were Frenchmen. The truth will be heard."

"What do you think she's going to do? Sit there and listen to you and calmly agree that she's guilty?"

"She'll do nothing calmly. But she'll agree; she'll proclaim it."

"Why would she?"

"Because when I accuse her she'll have the opportunity to kill me. When she makes the attempt, I will have my explanation, won't I?"

"You'd take that risk?"

"I must take it."

"Suppose she doesn't make the attempt, doesn't try to kill you?"

"That would be another explanation," Villiers said. "In that unlikely event, I should look to my flanks if I were you, monsieur." He shook his head. "It will not happen. We both know it, I far more clearly than you."

"Listen to me," insisted Jason. "You say there was your son first. Think of him! Go after the killer, not the accomplice. She's an enormous wound for you, but he's a greater wound. Get the man who killed your son! In the end, you'll get both. Don't confront her; not yet. Use what you know against Carlos. Hunt him with me. No one's ever been this close."

"You ask more than I can give," said the old man.

"Not if you think about your son. If you think of yourself, it is. But not if you think of the rue du Bac."

"You are excessively cruel, monsieur."

"I'm right and you know it."

A high cloud floated by in the night sky, briefly blocking the light of the moon. Darkness was complete; Jason shivered. The old soldier spoke, resignation in his voice.

"Yes, you are right," he said. "Excessively cruel and excessively right. It's the killer, not the whore, who must be stopped. How do we work together? Hunt together?"

Bourne closed his eyes briefly in relief. "Don't do anything. Carlos has to be looking for me all over Paris. I've killed his men, uncovered a drop, found a contact. I'm too close to him. Unless we're both mistaken, your telephone will get busier and busier. I'll make sure of it."

"How?"

"I'll intercept a half a dozen employees of Les Classiques. Several clerks, the Lavier woman, Bergeron maybe, and certainly the man at the switchboard. They'll talk. And so will I. That phone of yours will be busy as hell."

"But what of me? What do I do?"

"Stay home. Say you're not feeling well. And whenever that phone rings, stay near whoever else answers. Listen to the conversation, try to pick up codes, question the servants as to what was said to them. You could even listen in. If you hear something, fine, but you probably won't. Whoever's on the line will know you're there. Still, you'll frustrate the relay. And depending upon where your wife is—"

"The whore is," broke in the old soldier.

"—in Carlos' hierarchy, we might even force him to come out."

"Again, how?"

"His lines of communication will be disrupted. The secure, unthinkable relay will be interfered with. He'll demand a meeting with your wife."

"He would hardly announce the whereabouts."

"He has to tell *her*." Bourne paused, another thought

coming into focus. "If the disruption is severe enough, there'll be that one phone call, or that one person you don't know coming to the house, and shortly after, your wife will tell you she has to go somewhere. When it happens insist she leave a number where she can be reached. Be firm about it; you're not trying to stop her from going, but you *must* be able to reach her. Tell her anything—use the relationship *she* developed. Say it's a highly sensitive military matter you can't talk about until you get a clearance. Then you want to discuss it with her before you render a judgment. She might jump at it."

"What will it serve?"

"She'll be telling you where she is. Maybe where Carlos is. If not Carlos, certainly others closer to him. Then reach me. I'll give you a hotel and a room number. The name on the registry is meaningless, don't bother about it."

"Why don't you give me your real name?"

"Because if you ever mentioned it—consciously or unconsciously—you'd be dead."

"I'm not senile."

"No, you're not. But you're a man who's been hurt very badly. As badly as a person can be hurt, I think. *You* may risk your life; I won't."

"You're a strange man, monsieur."

"Yes. If I'm not there when you call, a woman will answer. She'll know where I am. We'll set up timing for messages."

"A woman?" the general drew back. "You've said nothing about a woman, or anyone else."

"There is no one else. Without her I wouldn't be alive. Carlos is hunting both of us; he's tried to kill both of us."

"Does she know about me?"

"Yes. She's the one who said it couldn't be true. That you couldn't be allied with Carlos. I thought you were."

"Perhaps I'll meet her."

"Not likely. Until Carlos is taken—if he *can* be taken—we can't be seen with you. Of all people, not you. Afterwards—if there is an afterwards—you may not want to be seen with us. With me. I'm being honest with you."

"I understand that and I respect it. In any event, thank this woman for me. Thank her for thinking I could be no part of Carlos."

Bourne nodded. "Can you be sure your private line isn't tapped?"

"Absolutely. It is swept on a regular basis; all the telephones restricted by the Conseiller are."

"Whenever you expect a call from me, answer the phone and clear your throat twice. I'll know it's you. If for any reason you can't talk, tell me to call your secretary in the morning. I'll call back in ten minutes. What's the number?"

Villiers gave it to him. "Your hotel?" asked the general.

"The Terrasse. Rue de Maistre, Montmartre. Room 420."

"When will you begin?"

"As soon as possible. Noon, today."

"Be like a wolfpack," said the old soldier, leaning forward, a commander instructing his officer corps. "Strike swiftly."

27

"She was *so* charming, I simply *must* do something for her," cried Marie in ebullient French into the telephone. "Also for the sweet young man; he was of such help. I tell you, the dress was a *succès fou!* I'm *so* grateful."

"From your descriptions, madame," replied the cultured male voice on the switchboard at Les Classiques, "I'm sure you mean Janine and Claude."

"Yes, of course. Janine and Claude, I remember now. I'll drop each a note with a token of my thanks. Would you by any chance know their last names? I mean, it seems so crass to address envelopes simply to 'Janine' and 'Claude.' Rather like sending missives to servants, don't you think? Could you ask Jacqueline?"

"It's not necessary, madame. I know them. And may I say that madame is as sensitive as she is generous. Janine Dolbert and Claude Oreale."

"Janine Dolbert and Claude Oreale," repeated Marie, looking at Jason. "Janine is married to that cute pianist, isn't she?"

"I don't believe Mademoiselle Dolbert is married to anyone."

"Of course. I'm thinking of someone else."

"If I may, madame, I didn't catch *your* name."

"How silly of me!" Marie thrust the phone away and raised her voice. "Darling, you're back, and so soon! That's marvelous. I'm talking to those lovely people at Les Classiques. . . . Yes, right away, my dear." She pulled the phone to her lips. "Thank you *so* much. You've been *very* kind." She hung up. "How'd I do?"

"If you ever decide to get out of economics," said Jason, poring through the Paris telephone book, "go into sales. I bought every word you said."

"Were the descriptions accurate?"

"To a cadaver and a very limp wrist. Nice touch, the pianist."

"It struck me that if she were married, the phone would be in her husband's name."

"It isn't," interrupted Bourne. "Here it is. Dolbert, Janine, rue Losserand." Jason wrote down the address. "Oreale, that's with an *O*, like the bird, isn't it? Not *Au*."

"I think so." Marie lit a cigarette. "You're really going to go to their homes?"

Bourne nodded. "If I picked them up in Saint-Honoré, Carlos will have it watched."

"What about the others? Lavier, Bergeron, whoever-he-is on the switchboard."

"Tomorrow. Today's for the groundswell."

"The what?"

"Get them all talking. Running around saying things that shouldn't be said. By closing time, word will be spread through the store by Dolbert and Oreale. I'll reach two others tonight; they'll call Lavier and the man at the switchboard. We'll have the first shock wave, and then the second. The general's phone will start ringing this afternoon. By morning the panic should be complete."

"Two questions," said Marie, getting up from the edge of the bed and coming toward him. "How are you going to get two clerks away from Les Classiques during store hours? And what people will you reach tonight?"

"Nobody lives in a deep freeze," replied Bourne, looking at his watch. "Especially in *haute couture*. It's 11:15 now; I'll get to Dolbert's apartment by noon and have the superintendent reach her at work. He'll tell her to come home right away. There's an urgent, very personal problem she'd better deal with."

"What problem?"

"I don't know, but who hasn't got one?"

"You'll do the same with Oreale?"

"Probably even more effective."

"You're outrageous, Jason."

"I'm deadly serious," said Bourne, his finger once again sliding down a column of names. "Here he is. Oreale, Claude Giselle. No comment. Rue Racine. I'll reach him by three; when I'm finished he'll head right back to Saint-Honoré and start screaming."

"What about the other two? Who are they?"

"I'll get names from either Oreale or Dolbert, or both. They won't know it, but they'll be giving me the second shock wave."

Jason stood in the shadows of the recessed doorway, in rue Losserand. He was fifteen feet from the entrance to Janine Dolbert's small apartment house where moments before a bewildered and suddenly richer *surintendant* had obliged a well-spoken stranger by calling Mademoiselle Dolbert at work and telling her that a gentleman in a chauffeured limousine had been around twice asking for her. He was back again; what should the *surintendant* do?

A small black taxi pulled up to the curb, and an agitated, cadaverous Janine Dolbert literally jumped out. Jason rushed from the doorway, intercepting her on the pavement, only feet from the entrance.

"That was quick," he said, touching her elbow. "So nice to see you again. You were very helpful the other day."

Janine Dolbert stared at him, her lips parted in recollection, then astonishment. "*You.* The American," she said in English. "Monsieur Briggs, isn't it? Are you the one who—"

"I told my chauffeur to take an hour off. I wanted to see you privately."

"Me? What could you possibly wish to see me about?"

"Don't you know? Then why did you race back here?"

The wide eyes beneath the short, bobbed hair were fixed on his, her pale face paler in the sunlight. "You're from the House of Azur, then?" she asked tentatively.

"I could be." Bourne applied a bit more pressure to her elbow. "And?"

"I've delivered what I promised. There will be nothing more, we agreed to that."

"Are you sure?"

"Don't be an idiot! You don't know Paris *couture*. Someone will get furious with someone else and make bitchy comments in your own studio. What strange deviations! And when the fall line comes out, with you parading half of Bergeron's designs before *he* does, how long do you think I can stay at Les Classiques? I'm Lavier's number two girl, one of the few who has access to her office. You'd better take care of me as you promised. In one of your Los Angeles shops."

"Let's take a walk," said Jason, gently propelling her. "You've got the wrong man, Janine. I've never heard of the House of Azur, and haven't the slightest interest in stolen designs—except where the knowledge can be useful."

"Oh, my God . . ."

"Keep walking." Bourne gripped her arm. "I said I wanted to talk to you."

"About what? What do you want from me? How did you get my name?" The words came rapidly now, the phrases overlapping. "I took an early lunch hour and must return at once; we're very busy today. Please—you're hurting my arm."

"Sorry."

"What I said; it was foolishness. A lie. On the floor, we've heard rumors; I was testing you. *That's* what I was doing, I was testing you!"

"You're very convincing. I'll accept that."

"I'm loyal to Les Classiques. I've always been loyal."

"It's a fine quality, Janine. I admire loyalty. I was saying that the other day to . . . what's his name? . . . that nice fellow on the switchboard. What *is* his name? I forget."

"Philippe," said the salesclerk, frightened, obsequious. "Philippe d'Anjou."

"That's it. Thank you." They reached a narrow, cobblestone alleyway between two buildings. Jason guided her into it. "Let's step in here for a moment, just so we're off the street. Don't worry, you won't be late. I'll only take a few minutes of your time." They walked ten paces into the narrow enclosure. Bourne stopped; Janine Dolbert pressed her back against the brick wall. "Cigarette?" he asked, taking a pack from his pocket.

"Thank you, yes."

He lighted it for her, noting that her hand trembled. "Relaxed now?"

"Yes. No, not really. What do you want, Monsieur Briggs?"

"To begin with, the name's not Briggs, but I think you should know that."

"I don't. Why should I?"

"I was sure Lavier's number one girl would have told you."

"Monique?"

"Use last names, please. Accuracy's important."

"Brielle, then," said Janine frowning curiously. "Does she know you?"

"Why not ask her?"

"As you wish. What *is* it, monsieur?"

Jason shook his head. "You really *don't* know, do you? Three-quarters of the employees at Les Classiques are working with us and one of the brightest wasn't even contacted. Of course it's possible someone thought you were a risk; it happens."

"What happens? What risk? Who *are* you?"

"There isn't time now. The others can fill you in. I'm here because we've never received a report from you, and yet you speak to prime customers all day long."

"You *must* be clearer, monsieur."

"Let's say I'm the spokesman for a group of people—American, French, English, Dutch—closing in on a killer who's murdered political and military leaders in each of our countries."

"Murdered? Military, political . . ." Janine's mouth gaped, the ash of her cigarette breaking off, spilling over her rigid hand. "What *is* this? What are you *talking* about? I've heard none of this!"

"I can only apologize," said Bourne softly, sincerely. "You should have been contacted several weeks ago. It was an error on the part of the man before me. I'm sorry; it must be a shock to you."

"It *is* a shock, monsieur," whispered the salesclerk, her concave body tensed, a bent, lacquered reed against the brick. "You speak of things beyond my understanding."

"But now *I* understand," interrupted Jason. "Not a word from you about anyone. Now it's clear."

"It's not to me."

"We're closing in on Carlos. The assassin known as Carlos."

"Carlos?" The cigarette fell from Dolbert's hand, the shock complete.

"He's one of your most frequent customers, all the evidence points to it. We've narrowed the probabilities down to eight men. The trap is set for sometime in the next several days, and we're taking every precaution."

"Precaution . . . ?"

"There's always the danger of hostages, we all know that. We anticipate gunfire, but it will be kept to a minimum. The basic problem will be Carlos himself. He's sworn never to be taken alive; he walks the streets wired up to explosives calculated to be in excess of a thousand-pound bomb. But we can handle that. Our marksmen will be on the scene; one clean shot to the head and it'll be all over."

"Une seule balle . . ."

Suddenly Bourne looked at his watch. "I've taken up enough of your time. You've got to get back to the shop and I have to get back to my post. Remember, if you see me outside, you don't know me. If I come into Les Classiques, treat me as you would any rich client. *Except* if you've spotted a customer you think may be our man; then don't waste time telling me. Again, I'm sorry about all this. It was a breakdown in communications, that's all. It happens."

"Une rupture . . .?"

Jason nodded, turned in place, and began walking rapidly out of the alleyway toward the street. He stopped and glanced back at Janine Dolbert. She was comatose against the wall; for her the elegant world of *haute couture* was spinning wildly out of orbit.

Philippe d'Anjou. The name meant nothing to him, but Bourne could not help himself. He kept repeating it silently trying to raise an image . . . as the face of the gray-haired switchboard operator gave rise to such violent images of darkness and flashes of light. *Philippe d'Anjou.* Nothing. Nothing at all. Yet there had been something, something that caused Jason's stomach to knot, the muscles taut and inflexible, a flat panel of hard flesh constricted . . . by the darkness.

He sat by the front window and the door of a coffee shop on the rue Racine, prepared to get up and leave the moment he saw the figure of Claude Oreale arrive at the doorway of the ancient building across the street. His room was on the fifth floor, in a flat he shared with two other men, reached only by climbing a worn, angular staircase. When he did arrive, Bourne was sure he would not be walking.

For Claude Oreale, who had been so effusive with Jacqueline Lavier on another staircase in Saint-Honoré, had been told by a toothless landlady over the phone to get his *sale gueule* back to rue Racine and put a stop to the screaming and smashing of furniture that was taking place in his fifth-floor flat. Either he would stop it or the gendarmes would be called; he had twenty minutes to show up.

He did so in fifteen. His slight frame, encased in a Pierre Cardin suit—rear flap fluttering in the headwind—could be seen racing up the sidewalk from the nearby Métro exit. He avoided collisions with the agility of an out-of-shape broken-field runner trained by the Ballets Russe. His thin neck was thrust forward several inches in front of his vested chest, his long dark hair a flowing mane parallel to the pavement. He reached the entrance and gripped the railing, leaping up the steps and plunging into the shadows of the foyer.

Jason walked rapidly out of the coffee shop and raced across the street. Inside, he ran to the ancient staircase then started up the cracked steps. From the fourth floor landing, he could hear the pounding on the door above.

"Ouvrez! Ouvrez! Vite, nom de Dieu!" Oreale stopped, the silence within perhaps more frightening than anything else.

Bourne climbed the remaining steps until he could see Oreale between the bars of the railing and the floor. The clerk's frail body was pressed into the door, his hands on either side, fingers spread, his ear against the wood, his face flushed. Jason shouted in guttural, bureaucratic French, as he rushed up into view. "Sûreté! Stay exactly where you are, young man. Let's not have any unpleasantness. We've been watching you and your friends. We know about the darkroom."

"No!" screamed Oreale. "It has nothing to do with me, I swear it! *Darkroom?*"

Bourne raised his hand. "Be quiet. Don't shout so!" He immediately followed his commands by leaning over the railing and looking below.

"You can't involve me!" continued the salesclerk. "I'm

not involved! I've told them over and over again to get rid of it all! One day they'll kill themselves. Drugs are for idiots! My God, it's quiet. I think they're dead!"

Jason stood up from the railing and approached Oreale, his palms raised. "I told you to shut up," he whispered harshly. "Get inside there and be quiet! This was all for the benefit of that old bitch downstairs."

The salesclerk was transfixed, his panic suspended in silent hysteria. "What?"

"You've got a key," said Bourne. "Open up and get inside."

"It's bolted," replied Oreale. "It's always bolted during these times."

"You damn fool, we had to *reach* you! We had to get you here without anyone knowing why. Open that door. Quickly!"

Like the terrified rabbit he was, Claude Oreale fumbled in his pocket and found the key. He unlocked the door and pushed it open as a man might entering a storage vault filled with mutilated corpses. Bourne propelled him through the doorframe, stepped inside and closed the door.

What could be seen of the flat belied the rest of the building. The fair-sized living room was filled with sleek, expensive furniture, dozens of red and yellow velvet pillows scattered about on couches, chairs and the floor. It was an erotic room, a luxurious sanctuary in the midst of debris.

"I've only got a few minutes," said Jason. "No time for anything but business."

"Business?" asked Oreale, his expression flat-out paralyzed. "This . . . this darkroom? *What* darkroom?"

"Forget it. You had something better going."

"What business?"

"We received word from Zurich and we want you to get it to your friend Lavier."

"Madame Jacqueline? My *friend?*"

"We can't trust the phones."

"What phones? The word? *What* word?"

"Carlos is right."

"Carlos? Carlos who?"

"The assassin."

Claude Oreale screamed. He brought his hand up to his mouth, bit the knuckle of his index finger and screamed. "What are you *saying?*"

"Be quiet!"

"Why are you saying it to *me?*"

"You're number five. We're counting on you."

"Five *what? For* what?"

"To help Carlos escape the net. They're closing in. Tomorrow, the next day, perhaps the day after that. He's to stay away; he's *got* to stay away. They'll surround the shop, marksmen every ten feet. The crossfire will be murderous; if he's in there it could be a massacre. Every one of you. Dead."

Oreale screamed again, his knuckle red. "Will you *stop* this! I don't know what you're talking about! You're a maniac and I won't hear another word—I haven't heard *anything*. Carlos, crossfire . . . massacres! God, I'm suffocating . . . I need air!"

"You'll get money. A lot of it, I imagine. Lavier will thank you. Also d'Anjou."

"D'Anjou? He loathes me! He calls me a peacock, insults me every chance he gets."

"It's his cover, of course. Actually, he's very fond of you—perhaps more than you know. He's number six."

"What are these *numbers?* Stop talking numbers!"

"How else can we distinguish between you, allocate assignments? We can't use names."

"Who can't?"

"All of us who work for Carlos."

The scream was ear-shattering, as the blood trickled from Oreale's finger. "I won't *listen!* I'm a couturier, an *artist!*"

"You're number five. You'll do exactly as we say or you'll never see this passion pit of yours again."

"Aunghunn!"

"Stop screaming! We appreciate you; we know you're all under a strain. Incidentally, we don't trust the bookkeeper."

"Trignon?"

"First names only. Obscurity's important."

"Pierre, then. He's hateful. He deducts for telephone calls."

"We think he's working for Interpol."

"Interpol?"

"If he is, you could all spend ten years in prison. *You'd* be eaten alive, Claude."

"Aunghunn!"

"Shut up! Just let Bergeron know what we think. Keep

your eyes on Trignon, especially during the next two days. If he leaves the store for any reason, watch out. It could mean the trap's closing." Bourne walked to the door, his hand in his pocket. "I've got to get back, and so do you. Tell numbers one through six everything I told you. It's vital the word be spread."

Oreale screamed again, hysterically again. "Numbers! Always *numbers!* What *number?* I'm an artist, not a number!"

"You won't have a face unless you get back there as fast as you got here. Reach Lavier, d'Anjou, Bergeron. As quickly as you can. Then the others."

"*What* others?"

"Ask number two."

"Two?"

"Dolbert. Janine Dolbert."

"*Janine.* Her, too?"

"That's right. She's two."

The salesclerk flung his arms wildly above him in helpless protest.

"This is madness! Nothing makes sense!"

"Your life does, Claude," said Jason simply. "Value it. I'll be waiting across the street. Leave here in exactly three minutes. And don't use the phone; just leave and get back to Les Classiques. If you're not out of here in three minutes I'll have to return." He took his hand out of his pocket. In it was his gun.

Oreale expunged a lungful of air, his face ashen as he stared at the weapon.

Bourne let himself out and closed the door.

The telephone rang on the bedside table. Marie looked at her watch; it was 8:15 and for a moment she felt a sharp jolt of fear. Jason had said he would call at 9:00. He had left La Terrasse after dark, around 7:00, to intercept a salesclerk named Monique Brielle. The schedule was precise, to be interrupted only by emergency. Had something happened?

"Is this room 420?" asked the deep male voice on the line.

Relief swept over Marie; the man was André Villiers. The general had called late in the afternoon to tell Jason that panic had spread through Les Classiques; his wife had been summoned to the phone no less than six times over the span of an hour and a half. Not once, however, had he been able to listen to anything of substance; whenever he had picked up the phone, serious conversation had been replaced by innocuous banter.

"Yes," said Marie. "This is 420."

"Forgive me, we did not speak before."

"I know who you are."

"I'm also aware of you. May I take the liberty of saying thank you."

"I understand. You're welcome."

"To substance. I'm telephoning from my office, and, of course, there's no extension for this line. Tell our mutual friend that the crisis has accelerated. My wife has taken to her room, claiming nausea, but apparently she's not too ill to be on the phone. On several occasions, as before, I picked up only to realize that they were alert for any interference. Each time I apologized rather gruffly, saying I expected calls. Frankly, I'm not at all sure my wife was convinced, but of course she's in no position to question me. I'll be blunt, mademoiselle. There is unspoken friction building between us, and beneath the surface, it is violent. May God give me strength."

"I can only ask you to remember the objective," broke in Marie. "Remember your son."

"Yes," said the old man quietly. "My son. And the whore who claims to revere his memory. I'm sorry."

"It's all right. I'll convey what you've told me to our friend. He'll be calling within the hour."

"Please," interrupted Villiers. "There's more. It's the reason I had to reach you. Twice while my wife was on the telephone the voices held meaning for me. The second I recognized; a face came to mind instantly. He's on a switchboard in Saint-Honoré."

"We know his name. What about the first?"

"It was strange. I did not know the voice, there was no face to go with it, but I understood why it was there. It was an odd voice, half whisper, half command, an echo of itself. It was the command that struck me. You see, that voice was not having a conversation with my wife; it had issued an order. It was altered the instant I got on the line, of course; a prearranged signal for a swift goodbye, but the residue remained. That residue, even the tone, is well known to any soldier; it is his means of emphasis. Am I being clear?"

"I think so," said Marie gently, aware that if the old man was implying what she thought he was, the strain on him had to be unbearable.

"Be assured of it, mademoiselle," said the general, "it was the killer pig." Villiers stopped, his breathing audible, the next words drawn out, a strong man close to weeping. "He was . . . *instructing* . . . *my* . . . *wife* . . ." The old soldier's voice cracked. "Forgive me the unforgiveable. I have no right to burden you."

"You have every right," said Marie, suddenly alarmed. "What's happening has to be terribly painful for you, made worse because you have no one to talk to."

"I am talking to you, mademoiselle. I shouldn't, but I am."

"I wish we could keep talking. I wish one of us could be with you. But that's not possible and I know you understand that. Please try to hold on. It's terribly important that no connection be made between you and our friend. It could cost you your life."

"I think perhaps I have lost it."

"*Ça, c'est absurde*," said Marie sharply, an intended slap in the old soldier's face. "*Vous êtes un soldat. Arrêtez ça immédiatement!*"

"*C'est l'institutrice qui corrige le mauvais élève. Vous avez bien raison.*"

"*On dit que vous êtes un géant. Je le crois.*" There was silence on the line; Marie held her breath. When Villiers spoke she breathed again.

"Our mutual friend is very fortunate. You are a remarkable woman."

"Not at all. I just want my friend to come back to me. There's nothing remarkable about that."

"Perhaps not. But I should also like to be your friend. You reminded a very old man of who and what he is. Or who and what he once was, and must try to be again. I thank you for a second time."

"You're welcome . . . my friend." Marie hung up, profoundly moved and equally disturbed. She was not convinced Villiers could face the next twenty-four hours, and if he could not, the assassin would know how deeply his apparatus had been penetrated. He would order every contact at Les Classiques to run from Paris and disappear. Or there would be a bloodbath in Saint-Honoré, achieving the same results.

If either happened, there would be no answers, no address in New York, no message deciphered, nor the sender found. The man she loved would be returned to his labyrinth. And he would leave her.

28

Bourne saw her at the corner, walking under the spill of the streetlight toward the small hotel that was her home. Monique Brielle, Jacqueline Lavier's number one girl, was a harder, more sinewy version of Janine Dolbert; he remembered seeing her at the shop. There was an assurance about her, her stride the stride of a confident woman, secure in the knowledge of her expertise. Very unflappable. Jason could understand why she was Lavier's number one. Their confrontation would be brief, the impact of the message startling, the threat inherent. It was time for the start of the second shock wave. He remained motionless and let her pass on the sidewalk, her heels clicking martially on the pavement. The street was not crowded, but neither was it deserted; there were perhaps a half dozen people on the block. It would be necessary to isolate her, then steer her out of earshot of any who might overhear the words, for they were words that no messenger would risk being heard. He caught up with her no more than thirty feet from the entrance to the small hotel; he slowed his pace to hers, staying at her side.

"Get in touch with Lavier right away," he said in French, staring straight ahead.

"Pardon? What did you say? Who are you, monsieur?"

"Don't stop! Keep walking. Past the entrance."

"You know where I *live?*"

"There's very little we don't know."

"And if I go straight inside? There's a doorman——"

"There's also Lavier," interrupted Bourne. "You'll lose your job and you won't be able to find another in Saint-Honoré. And I'm afraid that will be the least of your problems."

"Who *are* you?"

"Not your enemy." Jason looked at her. "Don't make me one."

"*You.* The American! Janine . . . Claude Oreale!"

"Carlos," completed Bourne.

"Carlos? What is this *madness?* All afternoon, nothing but Carlos! And *numbers!* Everyone has a number no one's heard of! And talk of traps and men with guns! It's crazy!"

"It's happening. Keep walking. Please. For your own sake."

She did, her stride less sure, her body stiffened, a rigid marionette uncertain of its strings. "Jacqueline spoke to us," she said, her voice intense. "She told us it was all insane, that it—*you*—were out to ruin Les Classiques. That one of the other houses must have paid you to ruin us."

"What did you expect her to say?"

"You are a hired provocateur. She told us the truth."

"Did she also tell you to keep your mouth shut? Not to say a word about any of this to anyone?"

"Of course."

"Above all," ran on Jason as if he had not heard her, "not to contact the police, which under the circumstances would be the most logical thing in the world to do. In some ways, the *only* thing to do."

"Yes, naturally . . ."

"Not naturally," contradicted Bourne. "Look, I'm just a relay, probably not much higher than you. I'm not here to convince you, I'm here to deliver a message. We ran a test on Dolbert; we fed her false information."

"Janine?" Monique Brielle's perplexity was compounded by mounting confusion. "The things she said were incredible! As incredible as Claude's hysterical screaming—the things *he* said. But what she said was the opposite of what he said."

"We know; it was done intentionally. She's been talking to Azur."

"The House of Azur?"

"Check her out tomorrow. Confront her."

"Confront her?"

"Just do it. It could be tied in."

"With what?"

"The trap. Azur could be working with Interpol."

"Interpol? Traps? This is the same craziness! Nobody knows what you're talking about!"

"Lavier knows. Get in touch with her right away." They approached the end of the block; Jason touched her arm. "I'll leave you here at the corner. Go back to your hotel and call Jacqueline. Tell her it's far more serious than we thought. Everything's falling apart. Worst of all, someone has turned. Not Dolbert, not one of the clerks, but someone more highly placed. Someone who knows everything."

"Turned? What does that mean?"

"There's a traitor in Les Classiques. Tell her to be careful. Of everyone. If she isn't, it could be the end for all of us." Bourne released her arm, then stepped off the curb and crossed the street. On the other side he spotted a recessed doorway and quickly stepped inside.

He inched his face to the edge and peered out, looking back at the corner. Monique Brielle was halfway down the block, rushing toward the entrance of her hotel. The first panic of the second shock wave had begun. It was time to call Marie.

"I'm worried, Jason. It's tearing him apart. He nearly broke down on the phone. What happens when he looks at her? What must he be feeling, thinking?"

"He'll handle it," said Bourne, watching the traffic on the Champs-Elysées from inside the glass telephone booth, wishing he felt more confident about André Villiers. "If he doesn't, I've killed him. I don't want it on my head, but that's what I'll have done. I should have shut my goddamn mouth and taken her myself."

"You couldn't have done that. You saw d'Anjou on the steps; you couldn't have gone inside."

"I could have thought of something. As we've agreed, I'm resourceful—more than I like to think about."

"But you are doing something! You're creating panic, forcing those who carry out Carlos' orders to show themselves. Someone's got to stop the panic, and even you said you didn't think Jacqueline Lavier was high enough. Jason, you'll see someone and you'll know. You'll get him! You will!"

"I hope so; Christ, I hope so! I know exactly what I'm doing, but every now and then . . ." Bourne stopped. He hated saying it, but he had to—he had to say it to her. "I get confused. It's as if I'm split down the middle, one part of me saying 'Save yourself,' the other part . . . God help me . . . telling me to 'Get Carlos.' "

"It's what you've been doing from the beginning, isn't it?" said Marie softly.

"I don't *care* about Carlos!" shouted Jason, wiping away the sweat that had broken out on his hairline, aware, too, that he was cold. "It's driving me crazy," he added, not sure whether he had said the words out loud or to himself.

"Darling, come back."

"What?" Bourne looked at the telephone, again not sure whether he had heard spoken words, or whether he had wanted to hear them, and so they were there. *It was happening again. Things were and they were not. The sky was dark outside, outside a telephone booth on the Champs-Elysées. It had once been bright, so bright, so blinding. And hot, not cold. With screeching birds and screaming streaks of metal . . .*

"Jason!"

"What?"

"Come back. Darling, *please* come back."

"Why?"

"You're tired. You need rest."

"I have to reach Trignon. Pierre Trignon. He's the book-keeper."

"Do it tomorrow. It can wait until tomorrow."

"No. Tomorrow's for the captains." *What was he saying? Captains. Troops. Figures colliding in panic. But it was the only way, the only way. The chameleon was a . . . provocateur.*

"Listen to me," said Marie, her voice insistent. "Something's happening to you. It's happened before; we both know that, my darling. And when it does, you have got to stop, we know that, too. Come back to the hotel. Please."

Bourne closed his eyes, the sweat was drying and the

sounds of the traffic outside the booth replaced the screeching in his ears. He could see the stars in the cold night sky, no more blinding sunlight, no more unbearable heat. It had passed, whatever it was.

"I'm all right. Really, I'm okay now. A couple of bad moments, that's all."

"Jason?" Marie spoke slowly, forcing him to listen. "What caused them?"

"I don't know."

"You just saw the Brielle woman. Did she say something to you? Something that made you think of something else?"

"I'm not sure. I was too busy figuring out what to say myself."

"*Think,* darling!"

Bourne closed his eyes, trying to remember. Had there been something? Something spoken casually or so rapidly that it was lost at the moment? "She called me a *provocateur,*" said Jason, not understanding why the word came back to him. "But then, that's what I am, aren't I? That's what I'm doing."

"Yes," agreed Marie.

"I've got to get going," continued Bourne. "Trignon's place is only a couple of blocks from here. I want to reach him before ten."

"Be careful." Marie spoke as if her thoughts were elsewhere.

"I will. I love you."

"I believe in you," said Marie St. Jacques.

The street was quiet, the block an odd mixture of shops and flats indigenous to the center of Paris, bustling with activity during the day, deserted at night.

Jason reached the small apartment house listed in the telephone directory as Pierre Trignon's residence. He climbed the steps and walked into the neat, dimly lit foyer. A row of brass mailboxes was on the right, each one above a small spoked circle through which a caller raised his voice loudly enough to identify himself. Jason ran his finger along the printed names below the slots: M. PIERRE TRIGNON—42. He pushed the tiny black button twice; ten seconds later there was a crackling of static.

"*Oui?*"

"*Monsieur Trignon, s'il vous plaît?*"

"Ici."

"Télégramme, monsieur. Je ne peux pas quitter ma bicyclette."

"Télégramme? Pour moi?"

Pierre Trignon was not a man who often received telegrams; it was in his astonished tone. The rest of his words were barely distinguishable, but a female voice in the background was in shock, equating a telegram with all manner of horrendous disasters.

Bourne waited outside the frosted glass door that led to the apartment house interior. In seconds he heard the rapid clatter of footsteps growing louder as someone—obviously Trignon—came rushing down the staircase. The door swung open, concealing Jason; a balding, heavy-set man, unnecessary suspenders creasing the flesh beneath a bulging white shirt, walked to the row of mailboxes, stopping at number 42.

"Monsieur Trignon?"

The heavy-set man spun around, his cherubic face set in an expression of helplessness. "A telegram! I have a telegram!" he cried. "Did you bring me a telegram?"

"I apologize for the ruse, Trignon, but it was for your own benefit. I didn't think you wanted to be questioned in front of your wife and family."

"Questioned?" exclaimed the bookkeeper, his thick, protruding lips curled, his eyes frightened. *"Me?* What about? What is this? Why are you here at my home? I'm a law-abiding citizen!"

"You work in Saint-Honoré? For a firm called Les Classiques?"

"I do. Who are you?"

"If you prefer, we can go down to my office," said Bourne.

"Who *are* you?"

"I'm a special investigator for the Bureau of Taxation and Records, Division of Fraud and Conspiracy. Come along—my official car is outside."

"Outside? Come along? I have no jacket, no coat! My wife. She's upstairs expecting me to bring back a telegram. A telegram!"

"You can send her one if you like. Come along now. I've been at this all day and I want to get it over with."

"Please, monsieur," protested Trignon. "I do not insist on going anywhere! You said you had questions. Ask your questions and let me go back upstairs. I have no wish to go to your office."

"It might take a few minutes," said Jason.

"I'll ring through to my wife and tell her it's a mistake. The telegram's for old Gravet; he lives here on the first floor and can barely read. She will understand."

Madame Trignon did not understand, but her shrill objections were stilled by a shriller Monsieur Trignon. "There, you see," said the bookkeeper, coming away from the mailslot, the strings of hair on his bald scalp matted with sweat. "There's no reason to go anywhere. What's a few minutes of a man's life? The television shows will be repeated in a month or two. Now, what in God's name *is* this, monsieur? My books are immaculate, totally immaculate! Of course I cannot be responsible for the accountant's work. That's a separate firm; *he's* a separate firm. Frankly, I've never liked him; he swears a great deal, if you know what I mean. But then, who am I to say?" Trignon's hands were held out palms up, his face pinched in an obsequious smile.

"To begin with," said Bourne, dismissing the protestations, "do not leave the city limits of Paris. If for any reason, personal or professional, you are called upon to do so, notify us. Frankly, it will not be permitted."

"Surely you're joking, monsieur!"

"Surely I'm not."

"I have no reason to leave Paris—nor the money to do so—but to say such a thing to me is unbelievable. What have I done?"

"The Bureau will subpoena your books in the morning. Be prepared."

"Subpoena? For what cause? Prepared for what?"

"Payments to so-called suppliers whose invoices are fraudulent. The merchandise was never received—was never meant to be received—the payments, instead, routed to a bank in Zurich."

"Zurich? I don't know what you're talking about! I've prepared no checks for Zurich."

"Not directly, we know that. But how easy it was for you to prepare them for nonexistent firms, the monies paid, then wired to Zurich."

"Every invoice is initialed by Madame Lavier! I pay *nothing* on my own!"

[396]

Jason paused, frowning. "Now it's you who are joking," he said.

"On my word! It's the house policy. Ask anyone! Les Classiques does not pay a *sou* unless authorized by Madame."

"What you're saying, then, is that you take your orders directly from her."

"But naturally!"

"Whom does she take orders from?"

Trignon grinned. "It is said from God, when not the other way around. Of course, that's a joke, monsieur."

"I trust you can be more serious. Who are the specific owners of Les Classiques?"

"It is a partnership, monsieur. Madame Lavier has many wealthy friends; they have invested in her abilities. And, of course, the talents of René Bergeron."

"Do these investors meet frequently? Do they suggest policy? Perhaps advocate certain firms with which to do business?"

"I wouldn't know, monsieur. Naturally, everyone has friends."

"We may have concentrated on the wrong people," interrupted Bourne. "It's quite possible that you and Madame Lavier—as the two directly involved with the day-to-day finances—are being used."

"Used for what?"

"To funnel money into Zurich. To the account of one of the most vicious killers in Europe."

Trignon convulsed, his large stomach quivering as he fell back against the wall. "In the name of God, what are you *saying*?"

"Prepare yourselves. Especially you. You prepared the checks, no one else."

"Only upon approval!"

"Did you ever check the merchandise against the invoices?"

"It's not my job!"

"So, in essence you issued payments for supplies you never saw."

"I never see anything! Only invoices that have been initialed. I pay only on those!"

"You'd better find every one. You and Madame Lavier had better start digging up every backup in your files. Because the two of you—especially you—will face the charges."

"Charges? What charges?"

"For a lack of a specific writ, let's call it accessory to multiple homicide."

"Multiple—"

"Assassination. The account in Zurich belongs to the assassin known as Carlos. You, Pierre Trignon, and your current employer, Madame Jacqueline Lavier, are directly implicated in financing the most sought-after killer in Europe. Ilich Ramirez Sanchez. Alias Carlos."

"Aughhhh! . . ." Trignon slid down to the foyer floor, his eyes in shock, his puffed features twisted out of shape. "All afternoon . . ." he whispered. "People running around, hysterical meetings in the aisles, looking at me strangely, passing my cubicle and turning their heads. Oh, my *God*."

"If I were you, I wouldn't waste a moment. Morning will be here soon, and with it possibly the most difficult day of your life." Jason walked to the outside door and stopped, his hand on the knob. "It's not my place to advise you, but if I were you, I'd reach Madame Lavier at once. Start preparing your joint defense—it may be all you have. A public execution is not out of the question."

The chameleon opened the door and stepped outside, the cold night air whipping across his face.

Get Carlos. Trap Carlos. Cain is for Charlie and Delta is for Cain.

False!

Find a number in New York. Find Treadstone. Find the meaning of a message. Find the sender.

Find Jason Bourne.

Sunlight burst through the stained-glass windows as the clean-shaven old man in the dated suit of clothes rushed down the aisle of the church in Neuilly-sur-Seine. The tall priest standing by the rack of novena candles watched him, struck by a feeling of familiarity. For a moment the cleric thought he had seen the man before, but could not place him. There had been a disheveled beggar yesterday, about the same size, the same . . . No, this old man's shoes were shined, his white hair combed neatly, and the suit of clothes, although from another decade, were of good quality.

"Angelus Domini," said the old man, as he parted the curtains of the confessional booth.

"Enough!" whispered the silhouetted figure behind the scrim. "What have you learned in Saint-Honoré?"

"Little of substance, but respect for his methods."

"Is there a pattern?"

"Random, it would appear. He selects people who know absolutely nothing and instigates chaos through them. I would suggest no further activity at Les Classiques."

"Naturally," agreed the silhouette. "But what's his purpose?"

"Beyond the chaos?" asked the old man. "I'd say it was to spread distrust among those who do know something. The Brielle woman used the words. She said the American told her to tell Lavier there was 'a traitor' inside, a patently false statement. Which of them would dare? Last night was insane, as you know. The bookkeeper, Trignon, went crazy. Waiting until two in the morning outside Lavier's house, literally assaulting her when she returned from Brielle's hotel, screaming and crying in the street."

"Lavier herself did not behave much better. She was barely in control when she called Parc Monceau; she was told not to call again. No one is to call there . . . ever again. _Ever_."

"We received the word. The few of us who know the number have forgotten it."

"Be sure you have." The silhouette moved suddenly; there was a ripple in the curtain. "Of _course_ to spread distrust! It follows chaos. There's no question about it now. He'll pick up the contacts, try to force information from them and when one fails, throw him to the Americans and go on to the next. But he'll make the approaches alone; it's part of his ego. He _is_ a madman. And obsessed."

"He may be both," countered the old man, "but he's also a professional. He'll make sure the names are delivered to his superiors in the event he does fail. So regardless of whether you take him or not, _they_ will be taken."

"They will be dead," said the assassin. "But not Bergeron. He's far too valuable. Tell him to head for Athens; he'll know where."

"Am I to assume I'm taking the place of Parc Monceau?"

"_That_ would be impossible. But for the time being you will relay my final decisions to whomever they concern."

"And the first person I reach is Bergeron. To Athens."

"Yes."

"So Lavier and the colonial, d'Anjou, are marked, then?"

"They are marked. Bait rarely survives, and they will not. You may also relay another message, to the two teams covering Lavier and d'Anjou. Tell them I'll be watching them—all the time. There can be no mistakes."

It was the old man's turn to pause, to bid silently for attention. "I've saved the best for last, Carlos. The Renault was found an hour and a half ago in a garage in Montmartre. It was brought in last night."

In the stillness the old man could hear the slow, deliberate breathing of the figure beyond the cloth. "I assume you've taken measures to have it watched—even now at the moment—and followed—even now at the moment."

The once-bespoken beggar laughed softly. "In accord with your last instructions, I took the liberty of hiring a friend, a friend with a sound automobile. He in turn has employed three acquaintances, and together they are on four six-hour shifts on the street outside the garage. They know nothing, of course, except that they are to follow the Renault at any hour of day or night."

"You do not disappoint me."

"I can't afford to. And since Parc Monceau was eliminated, I had no telephone number to give them but my own, which as you know, is a rundown café in the Quarter. The owner and I were friends in the old days, the better days. I could reach him every five minutes for messages and he would never object. I know where he got the money to pay for his business, and whom he had to kill to get it."

"You've behaved well, you have value."

"I also have a problem, Carlos. As none of us are to call Parc Monceau, how can I reach you? In the event I must. Say, for instance, the Renault."

"Yes, I'm aware of the problem. Are you aware of the burden you ask for?"

"I would much prefer not to have it. My only hope is that when this is over and Cain is dead, you will remember my contributions and rather than killing me, change the number."

"You *do* anticipate."

"In the old days it was my means of survival."

The assassin whispered seven figures. "You are the only

man alive who has this number. Naturally it is untraceable."

"Naturally. Who would expect an old beggar to have it?"

"Every hour brings you closer to a better standard of living. The net is closing; every hour brings him nearer to one of several traps. Cain will be caught, and an imposter's body will be thrown back to the bewildered strategists who created him. They counted on a monstrous ego and he gave it to them. At the end, he was only a puppet, an expendable puppet. Everyone knew it but him."

Bourne picked up the telephone. "Yes?"

"Room 420?"

"Go ahead, General."

"The telephone calls have stopped. She's no longer being contacted—not at least by telephone. Our couple was out and the phone rang twice. Both times she asked me to answer it. She really wasn't up to talking."

"Who called?"

"The chemists with a prescription and a journalist requesting an interview. She couldn't have known either."

"Did you get the impression she was trying to throw you off by having you take the calls?"

Villiers paused, his reply laced with anger. "It was there, the effect less than subtle insofar as she mentioned she might be having lunch out. She said she had a reservation at the George Cinq, and I could reach her there if she decides to go."

"If she does, I want to get there first."

"I'll let you know."

"You said she's not being contacted by phone. 'Not at least by telephone,' I think you said. Did you mean something by that?"

"Yes. Thirty minutes ago a woman came to the house. My wife was reluctant to see her but nevertheless did so. I only saw her face for a moment in the parlor, but it was enough. The woman was in panic."

"Describe her."

Villiers did.

"Jacqueline Lavier," said Jason.

"I thought it might be. From the looks of her, the wolfpack was eminently successful; it was obvious she had not slept. Before taking her into the library, my wife told me she was an old friend in a marriage crisis. A fatuous lie;

at her age there are no crises left in marriage, only acceptance and extraction."

"I can't understand her going to your house. It's too much of a risk. It doesn't make sense. Unless she did it on her own, knowing that no further calls were to be made."

"These things occurred to me," said the soldier. "So I felt the need of a little air, a stroll around the block. My aide accompanied me—a doddering old man taking his limited constitutional under the watchful eye of an escort. But my eyes, too, were watchful. Lavier was followed. Two men were seated in a car four houses away, the automobile equipped with a radio. Those men did not belong to the street. It was in their faces, in the way they watched my house."

"How do you know she didn't come with them?"

"We live on a quiet street. When Lavier arrived, I was in the sitting room having coffee, and heard her running up the steps. I went to the window in time to see a taxi drive away. She came in a taxi; she was followed."

"When did she leave?"

"She hasn't. And the men are still outside."

"What kind of car are they in?"

"Citroën. Gray. The first three letters of the license plate are *NYR*."

"Birds in the air, following a contact. Where do the birds come from?"

"I beg your pardon. What did you say?"

Jason shook his head. "I'm not sure. Never mind. I'm going to try to get out there before Lavier leaves. Do what you can to help me. Interrupt your wife, say you have to speak with her for a few minutes. Insist her 'old friend' stay; say anything, just make sure she doesn't leave."

"I will do my best."

Bourne hung up and looked at Marie, standing by the window across the room. "It's working. They're starting to distrust each other. Lavier went to Parc Monceau and she was followed. They're beginning to suspect their own."

" 'Birds in the air,' " said Marie. "What did you mean?"

"I don't know; it's not important. There isn't time."

"I think it *is* important, Jason."

"Not now." Bourne walked to the chair where he had dropped his topcoat and hat. He put them on quickly and went to the bureau, opened the drawer and took out the gun. He looked at it for a moment, remembering. The images were there, the past that was his whole yet not his whole at all. Zurich. The Bahnhofstrasse and the Carillon du Lac; the Drei Alpenhäuser and the Löwenstrasse; a filthy boardinghouse on the Steppdeckstrasse. The gun symbolized them all, for it had once nearly taken his life in Zurich.

But this was Paris. And everything started in Zurich was in motion.

Find Carlos. Trap Carlos. Cain is for Charlie and Delta is for Cain.

False! Goddamn you, false!

Find Treadstone. Find a message. Find a man.

—— 29 ——

Jason remained in the far corner of the back seat as the taxi entered Villiers' block in Parc Monceau. He scanned the cars lining the curb; there was no gray Citroën, no license with the letters NYR.

But there was Villiers. The old soldier was standing alone on the pavement, four doors away from his house.

Two men . . . in a car four houses away from my house.

Villiers was standing now where that car had stood; it was a signal.

"*Arrêtez, s'il vous plaît,*" said Bourne to the driver. "*Le vieux là-bas. Je veux parler avec lui.*" He rolled down the window and leaned forward. "*Monsieur?*"

"In English," replied Villiers, walking toward the taxi, an old man summoned by a stranger.

"What happened?" asked Jason.

"I could not detain them."

"Them?"

"My wife left with the Lavier woman. I was adamant, however. I told her to expect my call at the George Cinq.

It was a matter of the utmost importance and I required her counsel."

"What did she say?"

"That she wasn't sure she'd be at the George Cinq. That her friend insisted on seeing a priest in Neuilly-sur-Seine, at the Church of the Blessed Sacrament. She said she felt obliged to accompany her."

"Did you object?"

"Strenuously. And for the first time in our life together, she stated the thoughts in my own mind. She said, 'If it's your desire to check up on me, André, why not call the parish? I'm sure someone might recognize me and bring me to a telephone.' Was she testing me?"

Bourne tried to think. "Perhaps. Someone would see her there, she'd make sure of it. But bringing her to a phone might be something else again. When did they leave?"

"Less than five minutes ago. The two men in the Citroën followed them."

"Were they in your car?"

"No. My wife called a taxi."

"I'm going out there," said Jason.

"I thought you might," said Villiers. "I looked up the address of the church."

Bourne dropped a fifty-franc note over the back of the front seat. The driver grabbed it. "It's important to me to reach Neuilly-sur-Seine as fast as possible. The Church of the Blessed Sacrament. Do you know where it is?"

"But of course, monsieur. It is the most beautiful parish in the district."

"Get there quickly and there'll be another fifty francs."

"We shall fly on the wings of blessed angels, monsieur!"

They flew, the flight plan jeopardizing most of the traffic in their path.

"There are the spires of the Blessed Sacrament, monsieur," said the victorious driver, twelve minutes later, pointing at three soaring towers of stone through the windshield. "Another minute, perhaps two if the idiots who should be taken off the street will permit. . . ."

"Slow down," interrupted Bourne, his attention not on the spires of the church but on an automobile several cars ahead. They had taken a corner and he had seen it during the turn; it was a gray Citroën, two men in the front seat.

They came to a traffic light; the cars stopped. Jason

dropped the second fifty-franc note over the seat and opened the door. "I'll be right back. If the light changes, drive forward slowly and I'll jump in."

Bourne got out, keeping his body low, and rushed between the cars until he saw the letters. NYR; the numbers following were 768, but for the moment they were inconsequential. The taxi driver had earned his money.

The light changed and the row of automobiles lurched forward like one elongated insect pulling its shelled parts together. The taxi drew alongside; Jason opened the door and climbed in. "You do good work," he said to the driver.

"I'm not sure I know the work I am doing."

"An affair of the heart. One must catch the betrayer in the act."

"In *church*, monsieur? The world moves too swiftly for me."

"Not in traffic," said Bourne. They approached the final corner before the Church of the Blessed Sacrament. The Citroën made the turn, a single car between it and a taxi, the passengers indistinguishable. Something bothered Jason. The surveillance on the part of the two men was too open, far too obvious. It was as if Carlos' soldiers wanted someone in that taxi to know they were there.

Of course! Villiers' wife was in that cab. With Jacqueline Lavier. And the two men in the Citroën wanted Villiers' wife to know they were behind her.

"There is the Blessed Sacrament," said the driver, entering the street where the church rose in minor medieval splendor in the center of a manicured lawn, crisscrossed by stone paths and dotted with statuary. "What shall I do, monsieur?"

"Pull into that space," ordered Jason, gesturing at a break in the line of parked cars. The taxi with Villiers' wife and the Lavier woman stopped in front of a path guarded by a concrete saint. Villiers' stunning wife got out first, extending her hand for Jacqueline Lavier, who emerged, ashen, on the pavement. She wore large, orange-rimmed sunglasses and carried a white purse, but she was no longer elegant. Her crown of silver-streaked hair fell in straight, disassociated lines down the sides of her death-white mask of a face, and her stockings were torn. She was at least three hundred feet away, but Bourne felt he could almost hear the erratic gasping for breath that accompanied the hesitant movements of the once regal figure stepping forward in the sunlight.

The Citroën had proceeded beyond the taxi and was now pulling to the curb. Neither man got out, but a thin metal rod, reflecting the glare of the sun, began rising out of the trunk. The radio antenna was being activated, codes sent over a guarded frequency. Jason was mesmerized, not by the sight and the knowledge of what was being done, but by something else. Words came to him, from where he did not know, but they were there.

Delta to Almanac, Delta to Almanac. We will not respond. Repeat, negative, brother.

Almanac to Delta. You will respond as ordered. Abandon, abandon. That is final.

Delta to Almanac. You're final, brother. Go fuck yourself. Delta out, equipment damaged.

Suddenly the darkness was all around him, the sunlight gone. There were no soaring towers of a church reaching for the sky; instead there were black shapes of irregular foliage shivering beneath the light of iridescent clouds. Everything was moving, *everything was moving;* he had to move with the movement. To remain immobile was to die. *Move!* For Christ's sake, *move!*

And take them *out*. One by *one*. Crawl in closer; overcome the fear—the terrible fear—and reduce the numbers. That was all there was to it. Reduce the numbers. The Monk had made that clear. Knife, wire, knee, thumb; you know the points of damage. Of death.

Death is a statistic for the computers. For you it is survival.

The Monk.

The *Monk?*

The sunlight came again, blinding him for a moment, his foot on the pavement, his gaze on the gray Citroën a hundred yards away. But it was difficult to see; why was it so difficult? Haze, mist . . . not darkness now but impenetrable mist. He was hot; no, he was cold. Cold! He jerked his head up, suddenly aware of where he was and what he was doing. His face had been pressed against the window; his breath had fogged the glass.

"I'm getting out for a few minutes," said Bourne. "Stay here."

"All day, if you wish, monsieur."

Jason pulled up the lapels of his topcoat, pushed his hat

forward and put on the tortoise-shell glasses. He walked alongside a couple toward a religious sidewalk bazaar, breaking away to stand behind a mother and child at the counter. He had a clear view of the Citroën, the taxi which had been summoned to Parc Monceau was no longer there, dismissed by Villiers' wife. It was a curious decision on her part, thought Bourne; cabs were not that available.

Three minutes later the reason was clear . . . and disturbing. Villiers' wife came striding out of the church, walking rapidly, her tall, statuesque figure drawing admiring glances from strollers. She went directly to the Citroën, spoke to the men in front, then opened the rear door.

The purse. A *white* purse! Villiers' wife was carrying the purse that only minutes before had been clutched in the hands of Jacqueline Lavier. She climbed into the Citroën's back seat and pulled the door shut. The sedan's motor was switched on and gunned, prelude to a quick and sudden departure. As the car rolled away, the shiny metal rod that was the vehicle's antenna became shorter and shorter, retracting into its base.

Where was Jacqueline Lavier? Why had she given her purse to Villiers' wife? Bourne started to move, then stopped, instinct warning him. A trap? If Lavier was followed, those following her might also be trailed—and not by him.

He looked up and down the street, studying the pedestrians on the sidewalk, then each car, each driver and passenger, watching for a face that did not belong, as Villiers had said of the two men in the Citroën had not belonged in Parc Monceau.

There were no breaks in the parade, no darting eyes or hands concealed in outsized pockets. He was being overly cautious; Neuilly-sur-Seine was not a trap for him. He moved away from the counter and started for the church.

He stopped, his feet suddenly clamped to the pavement. A priest was coming out of the church, a priest in a black suit, a starched white collar and a black hat that partially covered his face. He had seen him before. Not long ago, not in a forgotten past, but recently. Very recently. Weeks, days . . . hours, perhaps. Where was it? *Where?* He knew him! It was in the walk, in the tilt of his head, in the wide shoulders that seemed to glide in place above the fluid movement of his body. He was a man with a gun! Where *was* it?

Zurich? The Carillon du Lac? Two men breaking through the crowds, converging, brokering death. One wore gold-rimmed glasses; it was not he. That man was dead. Was it that other man in the Carillon du Lac? Or in the Guisan Quai? An animal, grunting, wild-eyed in rape. Was it he? Or someone else. A dark-coated man in the corridor at the Auberge du Coin where the lights had been shorted out, the spill from the staircase illuminating the trap. A reverse trap where that man had fired his weapon in darkness at shapes he thought were human. Was it *that* man?

Bourne did not know, he only knew that he had seen the priest before, but not as a priest. As a man with a gun.

The killer in the priestly dark suit reached the end of the stone path and turned right at the base of the concrete saint, his face briefly caught in the sunlight. Jason froze; the *skin*. The killer's skin was dark, not tanned by the sun, but by birth. A Latin skin, its hue tempered generations ago by ancestors living in or around the Mediterranean. Forebears who migrated across the globe . . . across the seas.

Bourne stood paralyzed by the shock of his own certainty. He was looking at Ilich Ramirez Sanchez.

Get Carlos. Trap Carlos. Cain is for Charlie and Delta is for Cain.

Jason tore at the front of his coat, his right hand grasping the handle of the gun in his belt. He started running on the pavement, colliding with the backs and chests of strollers, shouldering a sidewalk vendor out of his way, lurching past a beggar digging into a wire trash—— The *beggar!* The beggar's hand surged into his pocket; Bourne spun around in time to see the barrel of an automatic emerge from the threadbare coat, the sun's rays bouncing off the metal. The beggar had a gun! His gaunt hand raised it, weapon and eyes steady. Jason lunged into the street, careening off the side of a small car. He heard the spits of the bullets above him and around him, piercing the air with sickening finality. Screams, shrill and in pain, came from unseen people on the sidewalk. Bourne ducked between two automobiles and raced through the traffic to the other side of the street. The beggar was running away; an old man with eyes of steel was racing into the crowds, into oblivion.

Get Carlos. Trap Carlos. Cain is . . . !

Jason spun again and lurched again, propelling himself forward, throwing everything in his path out of his way, racing in the direction of the assassin. He stopped, breathless, confusion and anger welling in his chest, sharp bolts of pain returning to his temples. Where *was* he? Where was *Carlos!* And then he saw him; the killer had climbed behind the wheel of a large black sedan. Bourne ran back into the traffic, slamming hoods and trunks as he threaded his way insanely toward the assassin. Suddenly he was blocked by two cars that had collided. He spread his hands on a glistening chrome grille and leaped sideways over the impacted bumpers. He stopped again, his eyes searing with pain at what he saw, knowing it was pointless to go on. He was too late. The large black sedan had found a break in the traffic, and Ilich Ramirez Sanchez sped away.

Jason crossed back to the far pavement as the shrieking of police whistles turned heads everywhere. Pedestrians had been grazed or wounded or killed; a beggar with a gun had shot them.

Lavier! Bourne broke into a run again, back toward the Church of the Blessed Sacrament. He reached the stone path under the eye of the concrete saint and spun left, racing toward the arched, sculptured doors and the marble steps. He ran up and entered the Gothic church, facing racks of flickering candles, fused rays of colored light streaming down from the stained-glass windows high in the dark stone walls. He walked down the center aisle, staring at the worshipers, looking for streaked silver hair and a mask of a face laminated in white.

The Lavier woman was nowhere to be seen, yet she had not left; she was somewhere in the church. Jason turned, glancing up the aisle; there was a tall priest walking casually past the rack of candles. Bourne sidestepped his way through a cushioned row, emerged on the far right aisle and intercepted him.

"Excuse me, Father," he said. "I'm afraid I've lost someone."

"No one is lost in the house of God, sir," replied the cleric, smiling.

"She may not be lost in spirit, but if I don't find the rest of her, she'll be very upset. There's an emergency at her place of business. Have you been here long, Father?"

"I greet those of our flock who seek assistance, yes. I've been here for the better part of an hour."

"Two women came in a few minutes ago. One was extremely tall, quite striking, wearing a light-colored coat, and I think a dark kerchief over her hair. The other was an older lady, not as tall, and obviously not in good health. Did you by any chance see them?"

The priest nodded. "Yes. There was sorrow in the older woman's face, she was pale and grieving."

"Do you know where she went? I gather her younger friend left."

"A devoted friend, may I say. She escorted the poor dear to confession, helping her inside the booth. The cleansing of the soul gives us all strength during the desperate times."

"To confession?"

"Yes—the second booth from the right. She has a compassionate father confessor, I might add. A visiting priest from the archdiocese of Barcelona. A remarkable man, too; I'm sorry to say this is his last day. He returns to Spain . . ." The tall priest frowned. "Isn't that odd? A few moments ago I thought I saw Father Manuel leave. I imagine he was replaced for a while. No matter, the dear lady is in good hands."

"I'm sure of it," said Bourne. "Thank you, Father. I'll wait for her." Jason walked down the aisle toward the row of confessional booths, his eyes on the second, where a small strip of white fabric proclaimed occupancy; a soul was being cleansed. He sat down in the front row, then knelt forward, angling his head slowly around so he could see the rear of the church. The tall priest stood at the entrance, his attention on the disturbance in the street. Outside, sirens could be heard wailing in the distance, drawing closer.

Bourne got up and walked to the second booth. He parted the curtain and looked inside, seeing what he expected to see. Only the method had remained in question.

Jacqueline Lavier was dead, her body slumped forward, rolled to the side, supported by the prayer stall, her mask of a face upturned, her eyes wide, staring in death at the ceiling. Her coat was open, the cloth of her dress drenched in blood. The weapon was a long, thin, letter opener, plunged in above her left breast. Her fingers were curled around the handle, her lacquered nails the color of her blood.

At her feet was a purse—not the white purse she had clutched in her hands ten minutes earlier, but a fashionable

Yves St. Laurent, the precocious initials stamped on the fabric, an escutcheon of the *haute couture*. The reason for it was clear to Jason. Inside were papers identifying this tragic suicide, this overwrought woman so burdened with grief she took her own life while seeking absolution in the eyes of God. Carlos was thorough, brilliantly thorough.

Bourne closed the curtain and stepped away from the booth. From somewhere high in a tower, the bells of the morning Angelus rang splendidly.

The taxi wandered aimlessly through the streets of Neuilly-sur-Seine, Jason in the back seat, his mind racing.

It was pointless to wait, perhaps deadly to do so. Strategies changed as conditions changed, and they had taken a deadly turn. Jacqueline Lavier had been followed, her death inevitable but out of sequence. Too soon; she was still valuable. Then Bourne understood. She had not been killed because she had been disloyal to Carlos, rather because she had disobeyed him. She had gone to Parc Monceau—that was her indefensible error.

There was another known relay at Les Classiques, a gray-haired switchboard operator named Philippe d'Anjou, whose face evoked images of violence and darkness, and shattering flashes of light and sound. He had been in Bourne's past, of that Jason was certain, and because of that, the hunted had to be cautious; he could not know what that man meant to him. But he was a relay, and he, too, would be watched, as Lavier had been watched, additional bait for another trap, dispatch demanded when the trap closed.

Were these the only two? Were there others? An obscure, faceless clerk, perhaps, who was not a clerk at all but someone else? A supplier who spent hours in Saint-Honoré legitimately pursuing the cause of *haute couture*, but with another cause far more vital to him. Or her. Or the muscular designer, René Bergeron, whose movements were so quick and . . . *fluid.*

Bourne suddenly stiffened, his neck pressed back against the seat, a recent memory triggered. *Bergeron.* The darkly tanned skin, the wide shoulders accentuated by tightly rolled-up sleeves . . . shoulders that floated in place above a tapered waist, beneath which strong legs moved swiftly, like an animal's, a cat's.

Was it possible? Were the other conjectures merely phantoms, compounded fragments of familiar images he had convinced himself might be Carlos? Was the assassin—unknown to his relays—deep inside his own apparatus, controlling and shaping every move? Was it *Bergeron?*

He had to get to a telephone right away. Every minute he lost was a minute removed from the answer, and too many meant there would be no answer at all. But he could not make the call himself; the sequence of events had been too rapid, he had to hold back, store his own information.

"The first telephone booth you see, pull over," he said to the driver, who was still shaken by the chaos at the Church of the Blessed Sacrament.

"As you wish, monsieur. But if monsieur will please try to understand, it is past the time when I should report to the fleet garage. Way past the time."

"I understand."

"There's a telephone."

"Good. Pull over."

The red telephone booth, its quaint panes of glass glistening in the sunlight, looked like a large dollhouse from the outside and smelled of urine on the inside. Bourne dialed the Terrasse, inserted the coins and asked for room 420. Marie answered.

"What happened?"

"I haven't time to explain. I want you to call Les Classiques and ask for René Bergeron. D'Anjou will probably be on the switchboard; make up a name and tell him you've been trying to reach Bergeron on Lavier's private line for the past hour or so. Say it's urgent, you've got to talk to him."

"When he gets on, what do I say?"

"I don't think he will, but if he does, just hang up. And if d'Anjou comes on the line again, ask him when Bergeron's expected. I'll call you back in three minutes."

"Darling, are you all right?"

"I've had a profound religious experience. I'll tell you about it later."

Jason kept his eyes on his watch, the infinitesimal jumps of the thin, delicate sweep hand too agonizingly slow. He began his own personal countdown at thirty seconds, calculating the heartbeat that echoed in his throat as somewhere around two and a half per second. He started dialing at ten seconds, inserted the coins at four, and spoke to the Terrasse's switchboard at minus-five. Marie picked up the phone the instant it began to ring.

"What happened?" he asked. "I thought you might still be talking."

"It was a very short conversation. I think d'Anjou was wary. He may have a list of names of those who've been given the private number—I don't know. But he sounded withdrawn, hesitant."

"What did he say?"

"Monsieur Bergeron is on a fabric search in the Mediterranean. He left this morning and isn't expected back for several weeks."

"It's possible I may have just seen him several hundred miles from the Mediterranean."

"Where?"

"In church. If it *was* Bergeron, he gave absolution with the point of a very sharp instrument."

"What are you talking about?"

"Lavier's dead."

"Oh, my God! What are you going to do?"

"Talk to a man I think I knew. If he's got a brain in his head, he'll listen. He's marked for extinction."

—— 30 ——

"D'Anjou."

"Delta? I wondered when . . . I think I'd know your voice anywhere."

He had said it! The name had been spoken. The name that meant nothing to him, and yet somehow everything. D'Anjou knew. Philippe d'Anjou was part of the unremembered past. Delta. Cain is for Charlie and Delta is for Cain. Delta. Delta. Delta! He had known this man and this man had the answer! Alpha, Bravo, Cain, Delta, Echo, Foxtrot . . .

Medusa.

"Medusa," he said softly, repeating the name that was a silent scream in his ears.

"Paris is not Tam Quan, Delta. There are no debts between us any longer. Don't look for payment. We work for different employers now."

"Jacqueline Lavier's dead. Carlos killed her in Neuilly-sur-Seine less than thirty minutes ago."

"Don't even try. As of two hours ago Jacqueline was on her way out of France. She called me herself from Orly Airport. She's joining Bergeron—"

"On a fabric search in the Mediterranean?" interrupted Jason.

D'Anjou paused. "The woman on the line asking for René. I thought as much. It changes nothing. I spoke with her; she called from Orly."

"She was told to tell you that. Did she sound in control of herself?"

"She was upset, and no one knows why better than you. You've done a remarkable job down here, Delta. Or Cain. Or whatever you call yourself now. Of course she wasn't herself. It's why she's going away for a while."

"It's why she's dead. You're next."

"The last twenty-four hours were worthy of you. This isn't."

"She was followed; you're being followed. Watched every moment."

"If I am it's for my own protection."

"Then why is Lavier dead?"

"I don't believe she is."

"Would she commit suicide?"

"Never."

"Call the rectory at the Church of the Blessed Sacrament in Neuilly-sur-Seine. Ask about the woman who killed herself while taking confession. What have you got to lose? I'll call you back."

Bourne hung up and left the booth. He stepped off the curb, looking for a cab. The next call to Philippe d'Anjou would be made a minimum of ten blocks away. The man from Medusa would not be convinced easily, and until he was, Jason would not risk electronic scanners picking up even the general location of the call.

Delta? I think I'd know your voice anywhere. . . . Paris is not Tam Quan. Tam Quan . . . Tam Quan, Tam Quan! Cain is for Charlie and Delta is for Cain. Medusa!

Stop it! Do not think of things that . . . you cannot think about. Concentrate on what *is*. Now. *You*. Not what others say you are—not even what you may think you are. Only the now. And the now is a man who can give you answers.

We work for different employers. . . .

That was the key.

Tell me! For Christ's sake, tell me! Who is it? Who is my employer, d'Anjou?

A taxi swerved to a stop perilously close to his kneecaps.

[416]

Jason opened the door and climbed in. "Place Vendôme," he said, knowing it was near Saint-Honoré. It was imperative to be as close as possible to put in motion the strategy that was rapidly coming into focus. He had the advantage; it was a matter of using it for a dual purpose. D'Anjou had to be convinced that those following him were his executioners. But what those men could not know was that another would be following *them*.

The Vendôme was crowded as usual, the traffic wild as usual. Bourne saw a telephone booth on the corner and got out of the taxi. He went inside the booth and dialed Les Classiques; it had been fourteen minutes since he had called from Neuilly-sur-Seine.

"D'Anjou?"

"A woman took her own life while at confession, that's all I know."

"Come on, you wouldn't settle for that. Medusa wouldn't settle for that."

"Give me a moment to put the board on hold." The line went dead for roughly four seconds. D'Anjou returned. "A middle-aged woman with silver and white hair, expensive clothing, and a St. Laurent purse. I've just described ten thousand women in Paris. How do I know you didn't take one, kill her, make her the basis of this call?"

"Oh, sure. I carried her into the church like a pieta, blood dripping in the aisle from her open stigmata. Be reasonable, D'Anjou. Let's start with the obvious. The purse wasn't hers; she carried a white leather handbag. She'd hardly be likely to advertise a competing house."

"Lending credence to my belief. It was *not* Jacqueline Lavier."

"Lends more to mine. The papers in that purse identified her as someone else. The body will be claimed quickly; no one touches Les Classiques."

"Because you say so?"

"No. Because it's the method used by Carlos in five kills I can name." *He could. That was the frightening thing.* "A man is taken out, the police believing he's one person, the death an enigma, killers unknown. Then they find out he's someone else, by which time Carlos is in another country, another contract fulfilled. Lavier was a variation of that method, that's all."

"Words, Delta. You never said much, but when you did, the words were there."

"And if you were in Saint-Honoré three or four weeks from now—which you won't be—you'd see how it ends. A plane crash or a boat lost in the Mediterranean. Bodies charred beyond recognition or simply gone. The identities of the dead, however, clearly established. Lavier and Bergeron. But only one is really dead—Madame Lavier. Monsieur Bergeron is privileged—more than you ever knew. Bergeron is back in business. And as for you, you're a statistic in the Paris morgue."

"And you?"

"According to the plan I'm dead too. They expect to take me through you."

"Logical. We're both from Medusa, they know that—Carlos knows that. It's to be assumed you recognized me."

"And you me?"

D'Anjou paused. "Yes," he said. "As I told you, we work for different employers now."

"That's what I want to talk about."

"No talking, Delta. But for old times' sake—for what you did for us all in Tam Quan—take the advice of a Medusan. Get out of Paris or you're that dead man you just mentioned."

"I can't do that."

"You should. If I have the opportunity I'll pull the trigger myself and be well paid for it."

"Then I'll give you that opportunity."

"Forgive me if I find that ludicrous."

"You don't know what I want or how much I'm willing to risk to get it."

"Whatever you want you'll take risks for it. But the real danger will be your enemy's. I know you, Delta. And I must get back to the switchboard. I'd wish you good hunting but—"

It was the moment to use the only weapon he had left, the sole threat that might keep d'Anjou on the line. "Whom do you reach for instructions now that Parc Monceau is out?"

The tension was accentuated by d'Anjou's silence. When he replied, his voice was a whisper. "*What did you say?*"

"It's why she was killed, you know. Why you'll be killed, too. She went to Parc Monceau and she died for it. You've been to Parc Monceau and you'll die for it, too. Carlos can't afford you any longer; you simply know too much. Why should he jeopardize such an arrangement? He'll use

[418]

you to trap me, then kill you and set up another Les Classiques. As one Medusan to another, can you doubt it?"

The silence was longer now, more intense than before. It was apparent that the older man from Medusa was asking himself several hard questions. "What do you want from me? Except me. You should know hostages are meaningless. Yet you provoke me, astonish me with what you've learned. I'm no good to you dead or alive, so what is it you want?"

"Information. If you have it, I'll get out of Paris tonight and neither Carlos nor you will ever hear from me again."

"What information?"

"You'll lie if I ask for it now. I would. But when I see you, you'll tell me the truth."

"With a wire around my throat?"

"In the middle of a crowd?"

"A crowd? Daylight?"

"An hour from now. Outside the Louvre. Near the steps. At the taxi stand."

"The Louvre? Crowds? Information you think I have that will send you away? You can't reasonably expect me to discuss my employer."

"Not yours. Mine."

"Treadstone?"

He knew. Philippe d'Anjou had the answer. Remain calm. Don't let your anxiety show.

"Seventy-One," completed Jason. "Just a simple question and I'll disappear. And when you give me the answer—the truth—I'll give you something in exchange."

"What could I possibly want from you? Except you?"

"Information that may let you live. It's no guarantee, but believe me when I tell you, you won't live without it. *Parc Monceau*, d'Anjou."

Silence again. Bourne could picture the gray-haired former Medusan staring at his switchboard, the name of the wealthy Paris district echoing louder and louder in his mind. There was death from Parc Monceau and d'Anjou knew it as surely as he knew the dead woman in Neuilly-sur-Seine was Jacqueline Lavier.

"What might that information be?" asked d'Anjou.

"The identity of your employer. A name and sufficient proof to have sealed in an envelope and given to an attorney, to be held throughout your natural life. But if your life were to end unnaturally, even accidentally, he'd be instructed to open the envelope and reveal the contents. It's protection, d'Anjou."

"I see," said the Medusan softly. "But you say men watch me, follow me."

"Cover yourself," said Jason. "Tell them the truth. You've got a number to call, haven't you?"

"Yes, there's a number, a man." The older man's voice rose slightly in astonishment.

"Reach him, tell him exactly what I said . . . except for the exchange, of course. Say I contacted you, want a meeting with you. It's to be outside the Louvre in an hour. The truth."

"You're insane."

"I know what I'm doing."

"You usually did. You're creating your own trap, mounting your own execution."

"In which event you may be amply rewarded."

"Or executed myself, if what you say is so."

"Let's find out if it is. I'll make contact with you one way or another, take my word for it. They have my photograph; they'll know it when I do. Better a controlled situation than one in which there's no control at all."

"Now I hear Delta," said d'Anjou. "He doesn't create his own trap; he doesn't walk in front of a firing squad and ask for a blindfold."

"No, he doesn't," agreed Bourne. "You don't have a choice, d'Anjou. One hour. Outside the Louvre."

The success of any trap lies in its fundamental simplicity. The reverse trap by the nature of its single complication must be swift and simpler still.

The words came to him as he waited in the taxi in Saint-Honoré down the street from Les Classiques. He had asked the driver to take him around the block twice, an American tourist whose wife was shopping in the strip of *haute couture*. Sooner or later she would emerge from one of the stores and he would find her.

What he found was Carlos' surveillance. The rubber-capped antenna on the black sedan was both the proof and the danger signal. He would feel more secure if that radio transmitter were shorted out, but there was no way to do it. The alternative was misinformation. Sometime during the next forty-five minutes Jason would do his best to make sure the wrong message was sent over that radio. From his concealed position in the back seat, he studied the two men in the car across the way. If there was anything that set them apart from a hundred other men like them in Saint-Honoré, it was the fact that they did not talk.

Philippe d'Anjou walked out onto the pavement, a gray homburg covering his gray hair. His glances swept the street, telling Bourne that the former Medusan had covered himself. He had called a number; he had relayed his startling information; he knew there were men in a car prepared to follow him.

A taxi, apparently ordered by phone, pulled up to the curb. D'Anjou spoke to the driver and climbed inside. Across the street an antenna rose ominously out of its cradle; the hunt was on.

The sedan pulled out after d'Anjou's taxi; it was the confirmation Jason needed. He leaned forward and spoke to the driver. "I forgot," he said irritably. "She said it was the Louvre this morning, shopping this afternoon. Christ, I'm half an hour late! Take me to the Louvre, will you please?"

"*Mais oui, monsieur, Le Louvre.*"

Twice during the short ride to the monumental façade that overlooked the Seine, Jason's taxi passed the black sedan, only to be subsequently passed by it. The proximity gave Bourne the opportunity to see exactly what he needed to see. The man beside the driver in the sedan spoke repeatedly into the hand-held radio microphone. Carlos was making sure the trap had no loose spikes; others were closing in on the execution ground.

They came to the enormous entrance of the Louvre. "Get in line behind those other taxis," said Jason.

"But they wait for fares, monsieur. I have a fare; *you* are my fare. I will take you to the——"

"Just do as I say," said Bourne, dropping fifty francs over the seat.

The driver swerved into the line. The black sedan was twenty yards away on the right; the man on the radio had turned in the seat and was looking out the left rear window. Jason followed his gaze and saw what he thought he might see. Several hundred feet to the west in the huge square was a gray automobile, the car that had followed Jacqueline Lavier and Villiers' wife to the Church of the Blessed Sacrament and sped the latter away from Neuilly-sur-Seine after she had escorted Lavier to her final confession. Its antenna could be seen retracting down into its base. Over on the right, Carlos' soldier no longer held the microphone. The black sedan's antenna was also receding; contact had been made, visual sighting confirmed. Four men. These were Carlos' executioners.

Bourne concentrated on the crowds in front of the Louvre entrance, spotting the elegantly dressed d'Anjou instantly. He was pacing slowly, cautiously, back and forth by the large block of white granite that flanked the marble steps on the left.

Now. It was time to send the misinformation.

"Pull out of the line," ordered Jason.

"*What*, monsieur?"

"Two hundred francs if you do exactly what I tell you. Pull out and go to the front of the line, then make two left turns, heading back up the next aisle."

"I don't understand, monsieur!"

"You don't have to. Three hundred francs."

The driver swung right and proceeded to the head of the line, where he spun the wheel, sending the taxi to the left toward the row of parked cars. Bourne pulled the automatic from his belt, keeping it between his knees. He checked the silencer, twisting the cylinder taut.

"Where do you wish to go, monsieur?" asked the bewildered driver as they entered the aisle heading back toward the entrance to the Louvre.

"Slow down," said Jason. "That large gray car up ahead, the one pointing to the Seine exit. Do you see it?"

"But of course."

"Go around it slowly, to the right." Bourne slid over to the left side of the seat and rolled down the window, keeping his head and the weapon concealed. He would show both in a matter of seconds.

The taxi approached the sedan's trunk, the driver spinning the wheel again. They were parallel. Jason thrust his head and his gun into view. He aimed for the gray sedan's right rear window and fired, five spits coming one after another, shattering the glass, stunning the two men, who screamed at each other, lurching below the window frames to the floor of the front seat. But they had seen him. That was the misinformation.

"Get out of here!" yelled Bourne to the terrified driver, as he threw three hundred francs over the seat and wedged his soft felt hat into the well of the rear window. The taxi shot ahead toward the stone gates of the Louvre.

Now.

Jason slid back across the seat, opened the door and rolled out to the cobblestone pavement, shouting his last instructions to the driver. "If you want to stay alive, get out of here!"

The taxi exploded forward, engine gunning, driver screaming. Bourne dove between two parked cars, now hidden from the gray sedan, and got up slowly, peering between the windows. Carlos' men were quick, professional, losing no moment in the pursuit. They had the taxi in view, the cab no match for the powerful sedan, and in that taxi was the target. The man behind the wheel pulled the car into gear and raced ahead as his companion held the microphone, the antenna rising from its recess. Orders were being shouted to another sedan nearer the great stone steps. The speeding taxi swerved out into the street by the Seine, the large gray car directly behind it. As they passed within feet of Jason, the expressions on the two men's faces said it all. They had Cain in their sights, the trap had closed and they would earn their pay in a matter of minutes.

The reverse trap by the nature of its single complication must be swift and simpler still. . . .

A matter of minutes. . . . He had only a matter of moments if everything he believed was so. D'Anjou! The contact had played his role—his minor role—and was expendable—as Jacqueline Lavier had been expendable.

Bourne ran out from between the two cars toward the black sedan; it was no more than fifty yards ahead. He could see the two men; they were converging on Philippe d'Anjou, who was still pacing in front of the short flight of marble steps. One accurate shot from either man and d'Anjou would be dead, Treadstone Seventy-One gone with him. Jason ran faster, his hand inside his coat, gripping the heavy automatic.

Carlos' soldiers were only yards away, now hurrying themselves, the execution to be quick, the condemned man cut down before he understood what was happening.

"*Medusa!*" roared Bourne, not knowing why he shouted the name rather than d'Anjou's own. "Medusa—*Medusa!*"

D'Anjou's head snapped up, shock on his face. The driver of the black sedan had spun around, his weapon leveled at Jason, while his companion moved toward d'Anjou, his gun aimed at the former Medusan. Bourne dove to his right, the automatic extended, steadied by his left hand. He

[423]

fired in midair, his aim accurate; the man closing in on d'Anjou arched backward as his stiffened legs were caught in an instant of paralysis; he collapsed on the cobblestones. Two spits exploded over Jason's head, the bullets impacting into metal behind him. He rolled to his left, his gun again steady, directed at the second man. He pulled the trigger twice; the driver screamed, an eruption of blood spreading across his face as he fell.

Hysteria swept through the crowds. Men and women screamed, parents threw themselves over children, others ran up the steps through the great doors of the Louvre, as guards tried to get outside. Bourne got to his feet, looking for d'Anjou. The older man had lunged behind the block of white granite, his gaunt figure now crawling awkwardly in terror out of his sanctuary. Jason raced through the panicked crowd, shoving the automatic into his belt, separating the hysterical bodies that stood between himself and the man who could give him the answers. Treadstone. *Treadstone!*

He reached the gray-haired Medusan. "Get up!" he ordered. "Let's get out of here!"

"Delta! . . . It was Carlos' man! I know him, I've *used* him! He was going to kill me!"

"I know. Come on! Quickly! Others'll be coming back; they'll be looking for us. Come *on!*"

A patch of black fell across Bourne's eyes, at the corner of his eyes. He spun around, instinctively shoving d'Anjou down as four rapid shots came from a gun held by a dark figure standing by the line of taxis. Fragments of granite and marble exploded all around them. It was *him!* The wide, heavy shoulders that floated in space, the tapered waist outlined by a form-fitting black suit . . . the dark-skinned face encased in a white silk scarf below the narrow-brimmed black hat. Carlos!

Get Carlos! Trap Carlos! Cain is for Charlie and Delta is for Cain!

False!

Find Treadstone! Find a message; for a man! Find Jason Bourne!

He was going mad! Blurred images from the past converged with the terrible reality of the present, driving him insane. The doors of his mind opened and closed, crashing open, crashing shut; light streaming out one moment, darkness the next. The pain returned to his temples with sharp, jarring notes of deafening thunder. He started after the man in the black suit with the white silk scarf wrapped around his face. Then he saw the eyes and the barrel of the gun, three dark orbs zeroed in on him like black laser beams. Bergeron? . . . Was it Bergeron? *Was* it? Or Zurich . . . or . . . No time!

He feigned to his left, then dove to the right, out of the line of fire. Bullets splattered into stone, the screeches of richochets following each explosion. Jason spun under a stationary car; between the wheels he could see the figure in black racing away. The pain remained but the thunder stopped. He crawled out on the cobblestones, rose to his feet and ran back toward the steps of the Louvre.

What had he done? D'Anjou was gone! How had it happened? The reverse trap was no trap at all. His own strategy had been used against him, permitting the only man who could give him the answers to escape. He had followed Carlos' soldiers, but Carlos had followed *him!* Since Saint-Honoré. It was all for nothing; a sickening hollowness spread through him.

And then he heard the words, spoken from behind a nearby automobile. Philippe d'Anjou came cautiously into view.

"Tam Quan's never far away, it seems. Where shall we go, Delta? We can't stay here."

They sat inside a curtained booth in a crowded café on the rue Pilon, a back street that was hardly more than an alley in Montmartre. D'Anjou sipped his double brandy, his voice low, pensive.

"I shall return to Asia," he said. "To Singapore or Hong Kong or even the Seychelles, perhaps. France was never very good for me; now it's deadly."

"You may not have to," said Bourne, swallowing the whiskey, the warm liquid spreading quickly, inducing a brief, spatial calm. "I meant what I said. You tell me what I want to know. I'll give you—" He stopped, the doubts sweeping over him; no, he would say it. "I'll give you Carlos' identity."

"I'm not remotely interested," replied the former Medusan, watching Jason closely. "I'll tell you whatever I can. Why should I withhold anything? Obviously I won't go to the authorities, but if I have information that could help you take Carlos, the world would be a safer place for me, wouldn't it? Personally, however, I wish no involvement."

"You're not even curious?"

"Academically, perhaps, for your expression tells me I'll be shocked. So ask your questions and then astonish me."

"You'll be shocked."

Without warning d'Anjou said the name quietly. "Berge-ron?"

Jason did not move; speechless, he stared at the older man. D'Anjou continued.

"I've thought about it over and over again. Whenever we talk I look at him and wonder. Each time, however, I reject the idea."

"Why?" Bourne interrupted, refusing to acknowledge the Medusan's accuracy.

"Mind you, I'm not sure—I just feel it's wrong. Perhaps because I've learned more about Carlos from René Berge-ron than anyone else. He's obsessed by Carlos; he's worked for him for years, takes enormous pride in the confidence. My problem is that he talks *too* much about him."

"The ego speaking through the assumed second party?"

"It's possible, I suppose, but inconsistent with the extraordinary precautions Carlos takes, the literally impenetrable wall of secrecy he's built around himself. I'm not certain, of course, but I doubt it's Bergeron."

"You said the name. I didn't."

D'Anjou smiled. "You have nothing to be concerned about, Delta. Ask your questions."

"I thought it *was* Bergeron. I'm sorry."

"Don't be, for he may be. I told you, it doesn't matter to me. In a few days I'll be back in Asia, following the franc, or the dollar, or the yen. We Medusans were always resourceful, weren't we?"

Jason was not sure why, but the haggard face of André Villiers came to his mind's eye. He had promised himself to learn what he could for the old soldier. He would not get the opportunity again.

"Where does Villiers' wife fit in?"

D'Anjou's eyebrows arched. "Angélique? But of course—you said Parc Monceau, didn't you? How—"

"The details aren't important now."

"Certainly not to me."

"What about her?" pressed Bourne.

"Have you looked at her closely? The skin?"

"I've been close enough. She's tanned. Very tall and very tanned."

"She keeps her skin that way. The Riviera, the Greek Isles, Costa del Sol, Gstaad; she is never without a sun-drenched skin."

"It's very becoming."

"It's also a successful device. It covers what she is. For her there is no autumn or winter pallor, no lack of color in her face or arms or very long legs. The attractive hue of her skin is always there, because it would be there in any event. With or without Saint-Tropez or the Costa Brava or the Alps."

"What are you talking about?"

"Although the stunning Angélique Villiers is presumed to be Parisian, she's not. She's Hispanic. Venezuelan, to be precise."

"Sanchez," whispered Bourne. "Ilich Ramirez Sanchez."

"Yes. Among the very few who speak of such things, it is said she is Carlos' first cousin, his lover since the age of fourteen. It is rumored—among those very few people— that beyond himself, she is the only person on earth he cares about."

"And Villiers is the unwitting drone?"

"Words from Medusa, Delta?" D'Anjou nodded. "Yes, Villiers is the drone. Carlos' brilliantly conceived wire into many of the most sensitive departments of the French government, including the files on Carlos himself."

"Brilliantly conceived," said Jason, remembering. "Because it's unthinkable."

"Totally."

Bourne leaned forward, the interruption abrupt. "Tread-stone," he said, both hands gripping the glass in front of him. "Tell me about Treadstone Seventy-One."

"What can *I* tell *you?*"

"Everything they know. Everything Carlos knows."

"I don't think I'm capable of doing that. I hear things, piece things together, but except where Medusa's concerned, I'm hardly a consultant, much less a confidant."

It was all Jason could do to control himself, curb himself from asking about Medusa, about Delta and Tam Quan; the winds in the night sky and the darkness and the explosions of light that blinded him whenever he heard the words. He could not; certain things had to be assumed, his own loss passed over, no indication given. The priorities. Treadstone. Treadstone Seventy-One . . .

"What have you heard? What have you pieced together?"

"What I heard and what I pieced together were not always compatible. Still, obvious facts were apparent to me."

"Such as?"

"When I saw it was you, I knew. Delta had made a lucrative agreement with the Americans. Another lucrative agreement, a different kind than before, perhaps."

"Spell that out, please."

"Eleven years ago, the rumors out of Saigon were that the ice-cold Delta was the highest-paid Medusan of us all. Surely, you were the most capable *I* knew, so I assumed you drove a hard bargain. You must have driven an infinitely harder one to do what you're doing now."

"Which is? From what you've heard."

"What we know. It was confirmed in New York. The Monk confirmed it before he died, that much I was told. It was consistent with the pattern since the beginning."

Bourne held the glass, avoiding d'Anjou's eyes. The Monk. *The Monk. Do not ask. The Monk is dead, whoever and whatever he was. He is not pertinent now.* "I repeat," said Jason, "what is it they think they know I'm doing?"

"Come, Delta, *I'm* the one who's leaving. It's pointless to—"

"*Please,*" interrupted Bourne.

"Very well. You agreed to become Cain. The mythical killer with an unending list of contracts that never existed, each created out of whole cloth, given substance by all manner of reliable sources. Purpose. To challenge Carlos— 'eroding his stature at every turn' was the way Bergeron phrased it—to undercut his prices, spread the word of his deficiencies, your own superiority. In essence, to draw out Carlos and take him. This was your agreement with the Americans."

Rays of his own personal sunlight burst into the dark corners of Jason's mind. In the distance, doors were opening, but they were still too far away and opened only partially. But there was light where before there was only darkness.

"Then the Americans are—" Bourne did not finish the statement, hoping in brief torment that d'Anjou would finish it for him.

"Yes," said the Medusan. "Treadstone Seventy-One. The most controlled unit of American intelligence since the State Department's Consular Operations. Created by the same man who built Medusa. David Abbott."

"The Monk," said Jason softly, instinctively, another door in the distance partially open.

"Of course. Who else would he approach to play the role of Cain but the man from Medusa known as Delta? As I say, the instant I saw you, I knew it."

"A role—" Bourne stopped, the sunlight growing brighter, warm not blinding.

D'Anjou leaned forward. "It's here, of course, that what I heard and what I pieced together was incompatible. It was said that Jason Bourne accepted the assignment for reasons I knew were not true. I was there, they were not; they could not know."

"What did they say? What did you hear?"

"That you were an American intelligence officer, possibly military. Can you imagine? *You*. Delta! The man filled with contempt for so much, not the least of which was for most things American. I told Bergeron it was impossible, but I'm not sure he believed me."

"What did you tell him?"

"What I believed. What I still believe. It wasn't money— no amount of money could have made you do it—it had to be something else. I think you did it for the same reason so many others agreed to Medusa eleven years ago. To clean a slate somewhere, to be able to return to something you had before, that was barred to you. I don't know, of course, and I don't expect you to confirm it, but that's what I think."

"It's possible you're right," said Jason, holding his breath, the cool winds of release blowing into the mists. *It made sense. A message was sent. This could be it. Find the message. Find the sender. Treadstone!*

"Which leads us back," continued d'Anjou, "to the stories about Delta. Who was he? What was he? This educated, oddly quiet man who could transform himself into a lethal weapon in the jungles. Who stretched himself and others beyond endurance for no cause at all. We never understood."

"It was never required. Is there anything else you can tell me? Do they know the precise location of Treadstone?"

"Certainly. I learned it from Bergeron. A residence in

New York City, on East Seventy-first Street. Number 139. Isn't that correct?"

"Possibly . . . Anything else?"

"Only what you obviously know, the strategy of which I admit eludes me."

"Which is?"

"That the Americans think you turned. Better phrased, they want Carlos to believe they think you turned."

"Why?" *He was closer. It was here!*

"The story is a long period of silence coinciding with Cain's inactivity. Plus stolen funds, but mainly the silence."

That was it. The message. The silence. The months in Port Noir. The madness in Zurich, the insanity in Paris. No one could possibly know what had happened. He was being told to come in. To surface. You were right, Marie, my love, my dearest love. You were right from the beginning.

"Nothing else, then?" asked Bourne, trying to control the impatience in his voice, anxious now beyond any anxiety he had known to get back to Marie.

"It's all I know—but please understand, I was never told that much. I was brought in because of my knowledge of Medusa—and it was established that Cain was from Medusa—but I was never part of Carlos' inner circle."

"You were close enough. Thank you." Jason put several bills on the table and started to slide across the booth.

"There's one thing," said d'Anjou. "I'm not sure it's relevant at this point, but they know your name is not Jason Bourne."

"What?"

"March 25. Don't you remember, Delta? It's only two days from now, and the date's very important to Carlos. Word has been spread. He wants your corpse on the twenty-fifth. He wants to deliver it to the Americans on that day."

"What are you trying to say?"

"On March 25, 1968, Jason Bourne was executed at Tam Quan. You executed him."

31

She opened the door and for a moment he stood looking at her, seeing the large brown eyes that roamed his face, eyes that were afraid yet curious. She knew. Not the answer, but that there *was* an answer, and he had come back to tell her what it was. He walked into the room; she closed the door.

"It happened," she said.

"It happened." Bourne turned and reached for her. She came to him and they held each other, the silence of the embrace saying more than any spoken words. "You were right," he whispered finally, his lips against her soft hair. "There's a great deal I don't know—may never know—but you were right. I'm not Cain because there is no Cain, there never was. Not the Cain they talk about. He never existed. He's a myth invented to draw out Carlos. I'm that creation. A man from Medusa called Delta agreed to become a lie named Cain. I'm that man."

She pulled back, still holding him. " 'Cain is for Charlie . . .' " She said the words quietly.

" 'And Delta is for Cain,' " completed Jason. "You've heard me say it?"

Marie nodded. "Yes. One night in the room in Switzerland you shouted it in your sleep. You never mentioned Carlos; just Cain . . . Delta. I said something to you in the morning about it, but you didn't answer me. You just looked out the window."

"Because I didn't understand. I still don't, but I accept it. It explains so many things."

She nodded again. "The *provocateur*. The code words you use, the strange phrases, the perceptions. But why? Why *you*?"

" 'To clean a slate somewhere.' That's what he said."

"Who said?"

"D'Anjou."

"The man on the steps in Parc Monceau? The switchboard operator?"

"The man from Medusa. I knew him in Medusa."

"What did he say?"

Bourne told her. And as he did, he could see in her the relief he had felt in himself. There was a light in her eyes, and a muted throbbing in her neck, sheer joy bursting from her throat. It was almost as if she could barely wait for him to finish so she could hold him again.

"Jason!" she cried, taking his face in her hands. "Darling, my darling! My friend has come back to me! It's everything we knew, everything we felt!"

"Not quite everything," he said, touching her cheek. "I'm Jason to you, Bourne to me, because that's the name I was given, and have to use it because I don't have any other. But it's not mine."

"An invention?"

"No, he was real. They say I killed him in a place called Tam Quan."

She took her hands away from his face, sliding them to his shoulders, not letting him go. "There had to have been a reason."

"I hope so. I don't know. Maybe it's the slate I'm trying to clean."

"It doesn't matter," she said, releasing him. "It's in the past, over ten years ago. All that matters now is that you reach the man at Treadstone, because they're trying to reach you."

"D'Anjou said word was out that the Americans think I've turned. No word from me in over six months, millions taken out of Zurich. They must think I'm the most expensive miscalculation on record."

"You can explain what happened. You haven't knowingly broken your agreement; on the other hand, you can't go on. It's impossible. All the training you received means nothing to you. It's there only in fragments—images and phrases that you can't relate to anything. People you're supposed to know, you don't know. They're faces without names, without reasons for being where they are or what they are."

Bourne took off his coat and pulled the automatic from his belt. He studied the cylinder—the ugly, perforated extension of the barrel that guaranteed to reduce the decibel count of a gunshot to a spit. It sickened him. He walked to the bureau, put the weapon inside and pushed the drawer shut. He held on to the knobs for a moment, his eyes straying to the mirror, to the face in the glass that had no name.

"What do I say to them?" he asked. "This is Jason Bourne calling. Of course I know that's not my name because I killed a man named Jason Bourne, but it's the one you gave me. . . . I'm sorry, gentlemen, but something happened to me on the way to Marseilles. I lost something—nothing you can put a price on—just my memory. Now, I gather we've got an agreement, but I don't remember what it is, except for crazy phrases like 'Get Carlos!' and 'Trap Carlos!' and something about Delta being Cain and Cain is supposed to replace Charlie and Charlie is really Carlos. Things like that, which may lead you to think I do remember. You might even say to yourselves, 'We've got one prime bastard here. Let's put him away for a couple of decades in a very tight stockade. He not only took us, but worse, he could prove to be one hell of an embarrassment.' " Bourne turned from the mirror and looked at Marie. "I'm not kidding. What do I say?"

"The truth," she answered "They'll accept it. They've sent you a message; they're trying to reach you. As far as the six months is concerned, wire Washburn in Port Noir. He kept records—extensive, detailed records."

"He may not answer. We had our own agreement. For putting me back together he was to receive a fifth of Zurich, untraceable to him. I sent him a million American dollars."

"Do you think that would stop him from helping you?"

Jason paused. "He may not be able to help himself. He's got a problem; he's a drunk. Not a drinker. A drunk. The worst kind; he knows it and likes it. How long can he live with a million dollars? More to the point, how long do you think those waterfront pirates will let him live once they find out?"

"You can still prove you were there. You were ill, isolated. You weren't in contact with *anyone*."

"How can the men at Treadstone be sure? From their view I'm a walking encyclopedia of official secrets. I *had* to be to do what I've done. How can they be certain I haven't talked to the wrong people?"

"Tell them to send a team to Port Noir."

"It'll be greeted with blank stares and silence. I left that island in the middle of the night with half the waterfront after me with hooks. If anyone down there made any money out of Washburn, he'll see the connection and walk the other way."

"Jason, I don't know what you're driving at. You've got your answer, the answer you've been looking for since you woke up that morning in Port Noir. What more do you want?"

"I want to be careful, that's all," said Bourne abrasively. "I want to 'look before I leap' and make damn sure the 'stable door is shut' and 'Jack be nimble, Jack be quick, Jack jump over the candlestick—but for Christ's sake don't fall into the fire!' How's that for *remembering?*" He was shouting; he stopped.

Marie walked across the room and stood in front of him. "It's very good. But that's not it, is it? Being careful I mean."

Jason shook his head. "No, it isn't," he said. "With each step I've been afraid, afraid of the things I've learned. Now, at the end, I'm more frightened than ever. If I'm not Jason Bourne, who am I really? What have I left back there? Has that occurred to you?"

"In all its ramifications, my darling. In a way, I'm far more afraid than you. But I don't think that can stop us. I wish to God it could, but I know it can't."

The attaché at the American Embassy on the avenue Gabriel walked into the office of the First Secretary and closed the door. The man at the desk looked up.

"You're sure it's him?"

"I'm only sure he used the key words," said the attaché, crossing to the desk, a red-bordered index card in his hand.

"Here's the flag," he continued, handing the card to the First Secretary. "I've checked off the words he used, and if that flag's accurate, I'd say he's genuine."

The man behind the desk studied the card. "When did he use the name Treadstone?"

"Only after I convinced him that he wasn't going to talk with anyone in U. S. Intelligence unless he gave me a damn good reason. I think he thought it'd blow my mind when he said he was Jason Bourne. When I simply asked him what I could do for him, he seemed stuck, almost as if he might hang up on me."

"Didn't he say there was a flag out for him?"

"I was waiting for it but he never said it. According to that eight-word sketch—'Experienced field officer. Possible defection or enemy detention'—he could have just said the word 'flag' and we would have been in sync. He didn't."

"Then maybe he's not genuine."

"The rest fits, though. He *did* say D.C.'s been looking for him for more than six months. That was when he used the name Treadstone. He was from Treadstone; that's supposed to be the explosive. He also told me to relay the code words Delta, Cain and Medusa. The first two are on the flag, I checked them off. I don't know what Medusa means."

"I don't know what *any* of this means," said the First Secretary. "Except that my orders are to hightail it down to communications, clear all scrambler traffic to Langley and get a sterile patch to a spook named Conklin. Him I've heard of: a mean son of a bitch who got his foot blown off ten or twelve years ago in Nam. He pushes very strange buttons over at the Company. Also he survived the purges, which leads me to think he's one man they don't want roaming the streets looking for a job. Or a publisher."

"Who do you think this Bourne is?" asked the attaché. "I've never seen such a concentrated but formless hunt for a person in my whole eight years away from the States."

"Someone they want very badly." The First Secretary got up from the desk. "Thanks for this. I'll tell D.C. how well you handled it. What's the schedule? I don't suppose he gave you a telephone number."

"No way. He wanted to call back in fifteen minutes, but I played the harried bureaucrat. I told him to call me in an hour or so. That'd make it past five o'clock, so we could gain another hour or two by my being out to dinner."

"I don't know. We can't risk losing him. I'll let Conklin set up the game plan. He's the control on this. No one makes a move on Bourne unless it's authorized by him."

Alexander Conklin sat behind the desk in his white-walled office in Langley, Virginia, and listened to the embassy man in Paris. He was convinced; it *was* Delta. The reference to Medusa was the proof, for it was a name no one would know *but* Delta. The bastard! He was playing the stranded agent, his controls at the Treadstone telephone not responding to the proper code words—whatever they were—because the dead could not talk. He was using the omission to get himself off the meathook! The sheer nerve of the bastard was awesome. Bastard, *bastard!*

Kill the controls and use the kills to call off the hunt. Any kind of hunt. How many men had done it before, thought Alexander Conklin. He had. There had been a source-control in the hills of Huong Khe, a maniac issuing maniacal orders, certain death for a dozen teams of Medusans on a maniacal hunt. A young intelligence officer named Conklin had crept back into Base Camp Kilo with a North Vietnamese rifle, Russian caliber, and had fired two bullets into the head of a maniac. There had been grieving and harsher security measures put in force, but the hunt was called off.

There had been no fragments of glass found in the jungle paths of Base Camp Kilo, however. Fragments with fingerprints that irrefutably identified the sniper as an Occidental recruit from Medusa itself. There were such fragments found on Seventy-first Street, but the killer did not know it—Delta did not know it.

"At one point we seriously questioned whether he was genuine," said the embassy's First Secretary, rambling on as if to fill the abrupt silence from Washington. "An experienced field officer would have told the attaché to check for a flag, but the subject didn't."

"An oversight," replied Conklin, pulling his mind back to the brutal enigma that was Delta-Cain. "What are the arrangements?"

"Initially Bourne insisted on calling back in fifteen minutes, but I instructed lower-level to stall. For instance, we could use the dinner hour . . ." The embassy man was making sure a Company executive in Washington realized the perspicacity of his contributions. It would go on for the better part of a minute; Conklin had heard too many variations before.

Delta. Why had he turned? The madness must have eaten his head away, leaving only the instincts for survival. He had been around too long; he knew that sooner or later they would find him, kill him. There was never any alternative; he understood that from the moment he turned—or broke—or whatever it was. There was nowhere to hide any longer; he was a target all over the globe. He could never know who might step out of the shadows and bring his life to an end. It was something they all lived with, the single most persuasive argument against turning. So another solution had to be found: survival. The biblical Cain was the first to commit fratricide. Had the mythical name triggered the obscene decision, the strategy itself? Was it as simple as that? God knew it was the perfect solution. Kill them all, kill your brother.

Webb gone, the Monk gone, the Yachtsman and his wife . . . who could deny the instructions Delta received, since these four alone relayed instructions to him? He had removed the millions and distributed them as ordered. Blind recipients he had assumed were intrinsic to the Monk's strategy. Who was Delta to question the Monk? The creator of Medusa, the genius who had recruited and created him. Cain.

The perfect solution. To be utterly convincing, all that was required was the death of a brother, the proper grief to follow. The official judgment would be rendered. Carlos had infiltrated and broken Treadstone. The assassin had won, Treadstone abandoned. The *bastard!*

". . . so basically I felt the game plan would come from you." The First Secretary in Paris had finished. He was an ass, but Conklin needed him; one tune had to be heard while another was being played.

"You did the right thing," said a respectful executive in Langley. "I'll let our people over here know how well you handled it. You were absolutely right; we need time, but Bourne doesn't realize it. We can't tell him, either, which makes it tough. We're on sterile, so may I speak accordingly?"

"Of course."

"Bourne's under pressure. He's been . . . detained . . . for a long period of time. Am I clear?"

"The Soviets?"

"Right up to the Lubyanka. His run was made by means of a double-entry. Are you familiar with the term?"

"Yes, I am. Moscow thinks he's working for them now."

"That's what they think." Conklin paused. "And we're not sure. Crazy things happen in the Lubyanka."

The First Secretary whistled softly. "That's a basket. How are you going to make a determination?"

"With your help. But the classification priority is so high it's above embassy, even ambassadorial level. You're on the scene; you were reached. You can accept the condition or not, that's up to you. If you do, I think a commendation might come right out of the Oval Office."

Conklin could hear the slow intake of breath from Paris.

"I'll do whatever I can, of course. Name it."

"You already did. We want him stalled. When he calls back, talk to him yourself."

"Naturally," interrupted the embassy man.

"Tell him you relayed the codes. Tell him Washington is flying over an officer-of-record from Treadstone by military transport. Say D.C. wants him to keep out of sight and away from the embassy; every route is being watched. Then ask him if he wants protection, and if he does, find out where he wants to pick it up. But don't send anyone; when you talk to me again I'll have been in touch with someone over there. I'll give you a name then and an eye-spot you can give to him."

"Eye-spot?"

"Visual identification. Something or someone he can recognize."

"One of your men?"

"Yes, we think it's best that way. Beyond you, there's no point in involving the embassy. As a matter of fact, it's vital we don't, so whatever conversations you have shouldn't be logged."

"I can take care of that," said the First Secretary. "But how is the one conversation I'm going to have with him going to help you determine whether he's a double-entry?"

"Because it won't be one; it'll be closer to ten."

"Ten?"

"That's right. Your instructions to Bourne—from us through you—are that he's to check in on your phone every hour to confirm the fact that he's in safe territory. Until that last time, when you tell him the Treadstone officer has arrived in Paris and will meet with him."

"What will that accomplish?" asked the embassy man.

"He'll keep moving . . . if he's not ours. There are a half a dozen known deep-cover Soviet agents in Paris, all with tripped phones. If he's working with Moscow, the chances are he'll use at least one of them. We'll be watching. And if that's the way it turns out, I think you'll remember the time you spent all night at the embassy for the rest of your life. Presidential commendations have a way of raising a career man's grade level. Of course, you don't have too much higher to go . . ."

"There's higher, Mr. Conklin," interrupted the First Secretary.

The conversation was over; the embassy man would call back after hearing from Bourne. Conklin got up from the chair and limped across the room to a gray filing cabinet against the wall. He unlocked the top panel. Inside was a stapled folder containing a sealed envelope bearing the names and locations of men who could be called upon in emergencies. They had once been good men, loyal men, who for one reason or another could no longer be on a Washington payroll. In all cases it had been necessary to remove them from the official scene, relocate them with new identities—those fluent in other languages frequently given citizenship by cooperating foreign governments. They had simply disappeared.

They were the outcasts, men who had gone beyond the laws in the service of their country, who often killed in the interests of their country. But their country could not tolerate their official existence; their covers had been exposed, their actions made known. Still, they could be called upon. Monies were constantly funneled to accounts beyond official scrutiny, certain understandings intrinsic to the payments.

Conklin carried the envelope back to his desk and tore the marked tape from the flap; it would be resealed, remarked. There was a man in Paris, a dedicated man who had come up through the officer corps of Army Intelligence, a lieutenant colonel by the time he was thirty-five. He could be counted on; he understood national priorities. He had killed a left-wing cameraman in a village near Hu a dozen years ago.

Three minutes later he had the man on the line, the call unlogged, unrecorded. The former officer was given a name and a brief sketch of defection, including a covert trip to the United States during which the defector in question on special assignment had eliminated those controlling the strategy.

"A double-entry?" asked the man in Paris. "Moscow?"

"No, not the Soviets," replied Conklin, aware that if Delta requested protection, there would be conversations between the two men.

"It was a long-range deep cover to snare Carlos."

"The assassin?"

"That's right."

"You may *say* it's not Moscow, but you won't convince *me*. Carlos was trained in Novgorod and as far as I'm concerned he's still a dirty gun for the KGB."

"Perhaps. The details aren't for briefing, but suffice it to say we're convinced our man was bought off; he's made a few million and wants an unencumbered passport."

"So he took out the controls and the finger's pointed at Carlos, which doesn't mean a damn thing but give him another kill."

"That's it. We want to play it out, let him think he's home free. Best, we'd like an admission, whatever information we can get, which is why I'm on my way over. But it's definitely secondary to taking him out. Too many people in too many places were compromised to put him where he is. Can you help? There'll be a bonus."

"My pleasure. And keep the bonus, I hate fuckers like him. They blow whole networks."

"It's got to be airtight; he's one of the best. I'd suggest support, at least one."

"I've got a man from the Saint-Gervais worth five. He's for hire."

"Hire him. Here are the particulars. The control in Paris is an embassy blind; he knows nothing but he's in communication with Bourne and may request protection for him."

"I'll play it," said the former intelligence officer. "Go ahead."

"There's not much more for the moment. I'll take a jet out of Andrews. My ETA in Paris will be anywhere between eleven and twelve midnight your time. I want to see Bourne within an hour or so after that and be back here in

Washington by tomorrow. It's tight, but that's the way it's got to be."

"That's the way it'll be, then."

"The blind at the embassy is the First Secretary. His name is . . ."

Conklin gave the remaining specifics and the two men worked out basic ciphers for their initial contact in Paris. Code words that would tell the man from the Central Intelligence Agency whether or not any problems existed when they spoke. Conklin hung up. Everything was in motion exactly the way Delta would expect it to be in motion. The inheritors of Treadstone would go by the book, and the book was specific where collapsed strategies and strategists were concerned. They were to be dissolved, cut off, no official connection or acknowledgment permitted. Failed strategies and strategists were an embarrassment to Washington. And from its manipulative beginnings, Treadstone Seventy-One had used, abused and maneuvered every major unit in the United States Intelligence community and not a few foreign governments. Very long poles would be held when touching any survivors.

Delta knew all this, and because he himself had destroyed Treadstone, he would appreciate the precautions, anticipate them, be alarmed if they were not there. And when confronted he would react in false fury and artificial anguish over the violence that had taken place in Seventy-first Street. Alexander Conklin would listen with all his concentration, trying to discern a genuine note, or even the outlines of a reasonable explanation, but he knew he would hear neither. Irregular fragments of glass could not beam themselves across the Atlantic, only to be concealed beneath a heavy drape in a Manhattan brownstone, and fingerprints were more accurate proof of a man having been at a scene than any photograph. There was no way they could be doctored.

Conklin would give Delta the benefit of two minutes to say whatever came to his facile mind. He would listen, and then he would pull the trigger.

32

"Why are they doing it?" asked Jason, sitting down next to Marie in the packed café. He had made the fifth telephone call, five hours after having reached the embassy. "They want me to keep running. They're forcing me to run, and I don't know why."

"You're forcing yourself," said Marie. "You could have made the calls from the room."

"No, I couldn't. For some reason they want me to know that. Each time I call, that son of a bitch asks me where I am now, am I in 'safe territory'? Silly goddamn phrase, 'safe territory.' But he's saying something else. He's telling me that every contact must be made from a different location, so that no one outside *or* inside could trace me to a single phone, a single address. They don't want me in custody, but they want me on a string. They want me, but they're afraid of me; it doesn't make sense!"

"Isn't it possible you're imagining these things? No one said anything remotely like that."

"They didn't have to. It's in what they didn't say. Why didn't they just tell me to come right over to the embassy? Order me. No one could touch me there; it's U. S. territory. They didn't."

"The streets are being watched; you were told that."

"You know, I accepted that—blindly—until about thirty seconds ago when it struck me. By whom? *Who's* watching the streets?"

"Carlos, obviously. His men."

"You know that and I know that—at least we can assume it—but *they* don't know that. I may not know who the hell I am or where I came from, but I know what's happened to me during the past twenty-four hours. *They* don't."

"They could assume too, couldn't they? They might have spotted strange men in cars, or standing around too long, too obviously."

"Carlos is brighter than that. And there are lots of ways a specific vehicle could get quickly inside an embassy's gate. Marine contingents everywhere are trained for things like that."

"I believe you."

"But they didn't do that; they didn't even suggest it. Instead, they're stalling me, making me play games. Goddamn it, why?"

"You said it yourself, Jason. They haven't heard from you in six months. They're being very careful."

"Why *this* way? They get me inside those gates, they can do whatever they want. They control me. They can throw me a party or throw me into a cell. Instead, they don't want to touch me, but they don't want to lose me either."

"They're waiting for the man flying over from Washington."

"What better place to wait for him than in the embassy?" Bourne pushed back his chair. "Something's wrong. Let's get out of here."

It had taken Alexander Conklin, inheritor of Treadstone, exactly six hours and twelve minutes to cross the Atlantic. To go back he would take the first Concorde flight out of Paris in the morning, reach Dulles by 7:30 Washington time and be at Langley by 9:00. If anyone tried to phone him or asked where he had spent the night, an accommodating major from the Pentagon would supply a false answer. And a First Secretary at the embassy in Paris would be told that if he ever mentioned having had a single conversation with the man from Langley, he'd be descaled to the lowest attaché on the ladder and shipped to a new post in Tierra del Fuego. It was guaranteed.

Conklin went directly to a row of pay phones against the wall and called the embassy. The First Secretary was filled with a sense of accomplishment.

"Everything's according to schedule, Conklin," said the embassy man, the absence of the previously employed Mister a sign of equality. The Company executive was in Paris now, and turf was turf. "Bourne's edgy. During our last communication he repeatedly asked why he wasn't being told to come in."

"He did?" At first Conklin was surprised; then he understood. Delta was feigning the reactions of a man who knew nothing of the events on Seventy-first Street. If he had been told to come to the embassy, he would have bolted. He knew better; there could be no official connection. Treadstone was anathema, a discredited strategy, a major embarrassment. "Did you reiterate that the streets were being watched?"

"Naturally. Then he asked me who was watching them. Can you imagine?"

"I can. What did you say?"

"That he knew as well as I did, and all things considered I thought it was counterproductive to discuss such matters over the telephone."

"Very good."

"I rather thought so."

"What did he say to that? Did he settle for it?"

"In an odd way, yes. He said, 'I see.' That's all."

"Did he change his mind and ask for protection?"

"He's continued to refuse it. Even when I insisted." The First Secretary paused briefly. "He doesn't want to be watched, does he?" he said confidentially.

"No, he doesn't. When do you expect his next call?"

"In about fifteen minutes."

"Tell him the Treadstone officer has arrived." Conklin took the map from his pocket; it was folded to the area, the route marked in blue ink. "Say the rendezvous has been set for one-thirty on the road between Chevreuse and Rambouillet, seven miles south of Versailles at the Cimetière de Noblesse."

"One-thirty, road between Chevreuse and Rambouillet . . . the cemetery. Will he know how to get there?"

"He's been there before. If he says he's going by taxi, tell him to take the normal precautions and dismiss it."

"Won't that appear strange? To the driver, I mean. It's an odd hour for mourning."

"I said you're to 'tell him' that. Obviously he won't take a taxi."

"Obviously," said the First Secretary quickly, recovering by volunteering the unnecessary. "Since I haven't called your man here, shall I call him now and tell him you've arrived?"

"I'll take care of that. You've still got his number?"

"Yes, of course."

"Burn it," ordered Conklin. "Before it burns you. I'll call you back in twenty minutes."

A train thundered by in the lower level of the Métro, the vibrations felt throughout the platform. Bourne hung up the pay phone on the concrete wall and stared for a moment at the mouthpiece. Another door had partially opened somewhere in the distance of his mind, the light too far away, too dim to see inside. Still, there were images. On the road to Rambouillet . . . through an archway of iron latticework . . . a gently sloping hill with white marble. Crosses—large, larger, mausoleums . . . and statuary everywhere. Le Cimetière de Noblesse. A cemetery, but far more than a resting place for the dead. A drop, but even more than that. A place where conversations took place amid burials and the lowering of caskets. Two men dressed somberly as the crowds were dressed somberly, moving between the mourners until they met among the mourners and exchanged the words they had to say to each other.

There was a face, but it was blurred, out of focus; he saw only the eyes. And that unfocused face and those eyes had a name. David . . . Abbott. The Monk. The man he knew but did not know. Creator of Medusa and Cain.

Jason blinked several times and shook his head as if to shake the sudden mists away. He glanced over at Marie, who was fifteen feet to his left against the wall, supposedly scanning the crowds on the platform, watching for someone possibly watching him. She was not; she was looking at him herself, a frown of concern across her face. He nodded, reassuring her; it was not a bad moment for him. Instead, images had come to him. He had been to that cemetery; somehow he would know it. He walked toward Marie; she turned and fell in step beside him as they headed for the exit.

[445]

"He's here," said Bourne. "Treadstone's arrived. I'm to meet him near Rambouillet. At a cemetery."

"That's a ghoulish touch. Why a cemetery?"

"It's supposed to reassure me."

"Good God, how?"

"I've been there before. I've met people there . . . a man there. By naming it as the rendezvous—an unusual rendezvous—Treadstone's telling me he's genuine."

She took his arm as they climbed the steps toward the street. "I want to go with you."

"Sorry."

"You can't exclude me!"

"I have to, because I don't know what I'm going to find there. And if it's not what I expect, I'll want someone on my side."

"Darling, that doesn't make sense! I'm being hunted by the police. If they find me, they'll send me back to Zurich on the next plane; you said so yourself. What good would I be to you in Zurich?"

"Not you. Villiers. He trusts us, he trusts you. You can reach him if I'm not back by daybreak or haven't called explaining why. He can make a lot of noise, and God knows he's ready to. He's the one backup we've got, the only one. To be more specific, his wife is—through him."

Marie nodded, accepting his logic. "He's ready," she agreed. "How will you get to Rambouillet?"

"We have a car, remember? I'll take you to the hotel, then head over to the garage."

He stepped inside the elevator of the garage complex in Montmartre and pressed the button for the fourth floor. His mind was on a cemetery somewhere between Chevreuse and Rambouillet, on a road he had driven over but had no idea when or for what purpose.

Which was why he wanted to drive there now, not wait until his arrival corresponded more closely to the time of rendezvous. If the images that came to his mind were not completely distorted, it was an enormous cemetery. Where precisely within those acres of graves and statuary was the meeting ground? He would get there by one, leaving a half hour to walk up and down the paths looking for a pair of headlights or a signal. Other things would come to him.

The elevator door scraped open. The floor was three-quarters filled with cars, deserted otherwise. Jason tried to recall where he had parked the Renault; it was in a far corner, he remembered that, but was it on the right or the left? He started tentatively to the left; the elevator had been on his left when he had driven the car up several days ago. He stopped, logic abruptly orienting him. The elevator had been on his left when he had entered, not after he had parked the car; it had been diagonally to his right then. He turned, his movement rapid, his thoughts on a road between Chevreuse and Rambouillet.

Whether it was the sudden, unexpected reversal of direction or an inexperienced surveillance, Bourne neither knew nor cared to dwell upon. Whichever, the moment saved his life, of that he was certain. A man's head ducked below the hood of a car in the second aisle on his right; that man had been watching him. An experienced surveillance would have stood up, holding a ring of keys he had presumably picked up from the floor, or checked a windshield wiper, then walked away. The one thing he would not do was what this man did; risk being seen by ducking out of sight.

Jason maintained his pace, his thoughts concerned on this new development. Who was this man? How had he been found? And then both answers were so clear, so obvious he felt like a fool. The clerk at the Auberge du Coin.

Carlos had been thorough—as he was always thorough—every detail of failure examined. And one of those details was a clerk on duty during a failure. Such a man bore scrutiny, then questioning; it would not be difficult. The show of a knife or a gun would be more than sufficient. Information would pour from the night clerk's trembling lips, and Carlos' army ordered to spread throughout the city, each district divided into sectors, hunting for a specific black Renault. A painstaking search, but not impossible, made easier by the driver, who had not bothered to switch license plates. For how many unbroken hours had the garage been watched? How many men were there? Inside, outside? How soon would others arrive? Would Carlos arrive?

The questions were secondary. He had to get out. He could do without the car, perhaps, but the resulting dependency on unknown arrangements might cripple him; he needed transportation and he needed it now. No taxi would drive a stranger to a cemetery on the outskirts of Rambouillet at one o'clock in the morning, and it was no time to rely on the possibility of stealing a car in the streets.

He stopped, taking cigarettes and matches from his pockets; then, striking a match, he cupped his hands and angled his head to protect the flame. In the corner of his eye he could see a shadow—square-shaped, stocky; the man once more had lowered himself, now behind the trunk of a nearer automobile.

Jason dropped to a crouch, spun to his left and lunged out of the aisle between two adjacent cars, breaking his fall with the palms of his hands, the maneuver made in silence. He crawled around the rear wheels of the automobile on his right, arms and legs working rapidly, quietly, down the narrow alley of vehicles, a spider scurrying across a web. He was behind the man now; he crept forward toward the aisle and rose to his knees, inching his face along smooth metal, and peered beyond a headlight. The heavy-set man was in full view, standing erect. He was evidently bewildered, for he moved hesitantly closer toward the Renault, his body low again, squinting to see beyond the windshield. What he saw frightened him further; there was nothing, no one. He gasped, the audible intake of breath a prelude to running. He had been tricked; he knew it and was not about to wait around for the consequences—which told Bourne something else. The man had been briefed on the driver of the Renault, the danger explained. The man began to race toward the exit ramp.

Now. Jason sprang up and ran straight ahead across the aisle, between the cars to the second aisle, catching up with the running man, hurling himself at his back and throwing him to the concrete floor. He hammerlocked the man's thick neck, crashing the outsized skull into the pavement, the fingers of his left hand pressed into the man's eye sockets.

"You have exactly five seconds to tell me who's outside," he said in French, remembering the grimacing face of another Frenchman in an elevator in Zurich. There had been men outside then, men who wanted to kill him then, on the Bahnhofstrasse. "Tell me! *Now!*"

"A man, one man, that's all!"

Bourne relocked the neck, digging his fingers deeper into the eyes. "Where?"

"In a car," spat out the man. "Parked across the street. My God, you're choking me! You're blinding me!"

"Not yet. You'll know it when and if I do both. What kind of car?"

"Foreign. I don't know. Italian, I think. Or American. I don't *know*. Please! My eyes!"

"Color!"

"Dark! Green, blue, very dark. Oh my *God!*"

"You're Carlos' man, aren't you?"

"Who?"

Jason yanked again, pressed again. "You heard me—you're from Carlos!"

"I don't know any Carlos. We call a man; there is a number. That's all we do."

"Has he been called?" The man did not reply; Bourne dug his fingers deeper. "Tell me!"

"Yes. I *had* to."

"When?"

"A few minutes ago. The coin telephone on the second ramp. My God! I can't see."

"Yes, you can. Get up!" Jason released the man, pulling him to his feet. "Get over to the car. Quickly!" Bourne pushed the man back between the stationary automobiles to the Renault's aisle. The man turned, protesting, helpless. "You heard me. Hurry!" shouted Jason.

"I'm only earning a few francs."

"Now you can drive for them." Bourne shoved him again toward the Renault.

Moments later the small black automobile careened down an exit ramp toward a glass booth with a single attendant and the cash register. Jason was in the back seat, his gun pressed against the man's bruised neck. Bourne shoved a bill and his dated ticket out the window; the attendant took both.

"Drive!" said Bourne. "Do exactly what I told you to do!"

The man pressed the accelerator, and the Renault sped out through the exit. The man made a screeching U-turn in the street, coming to a sudden stop in front of a dark green Chevrolet. A car door opened behind them; running footsteps followed.

"*Jules? Que se passe-t-il? C'est toi qui conduis?*" A figure loomed in the open window.

Bourne raised his automatic, pointing the barrel at the man's face. "Take two steps back," he said in French. "No more, just two. And then stand still." He tapped the head of the man named Jules. "Get out. Slowly."

"We were only to follow you," protested Jules, stepping

[449]

out into the street. "Follow you and report your whereabouts."

"You'll do better than that," said Bourne, getting out of the Renault, taking his map of Paris with him. "You're going to drive me. For a while. Get in your car, both of you!"

Five miles outside of Paris, on the road to Chevreuse, the two men were ordered out of the car. It was a dark, poorly lighted, third-grade highway. There had been no stores, buildings, houses, or road phones for the past three miles.

"What was the number you were told to call?" demanded Jason. "Don't lie. You'd be in worse trouble."

Jules gave it to him. Bourne nodded and climbed into the seat behind the wheel of the Chevrolet.

The old man in the threadbare overcoat sat huddled in the shadows of the empty booth by the telephone. The small restaurant was closed, his presence there an accommodation made by a friend from the old days, the better days. He kept looking at the instrument on the wall, wondering when it would ring. It was only a question of time, and when it did he would in turn make a call and the better days would return permanently. He would be the one man in Paris who was the link to Carlos. It would be whispered among the other old men, and respect would be his again.

The high-pitched sound of the bell burst from the telephone, echoing off the walls of the deserted restaurant. The beggar climbed out of the booth and rushed to the phone, his chest pounding with anticipation. It was the signal. Cain was cornered! The days of patient waiting merely a preface to the fine life. He lifted the phone out of its curved recess.

"Yes?"

"It's Jules!" cried the breathless voice.

The old man's face turned ashen, the pounding in his chest growing so loud he could barely hear the terrible things being said. But he had heard enough.

He was a dead man.

White-hot explosions joined the vibrations that took hold of his body. There was no air, only white light and deafening eruptions surging up from his stomach to his head.

The beggar sank to the floor, the cord stretched taut, the

phone still in his hand. He stared up at the horrible instrument that carried the terrible words. What could he do? What in the name of God would he *do?*

Bourne walked down the path between the graves, forcing himself to let his mind fall free as Washburn had commanded a lifetime ago in Port Noir. If ever he had to be a sponge, it was now; the man from Treadstone had to understand. He was trying with all his concentration to make sense out of the unremembered, to find meaning in the images that came to him without warning. He had not broken whatever agreement they had; he had not turned, or run. . . . He was a cripple; it was as simple as that.

He had to find the man from Treadstone. Where inside those fenced acres of silence would he be? Where did he expect *him* to be? Jason had reached the cemetery well before one, the Chevrolet a faster car than the broken-down Renault. He had passed the gates, driven several hundred yards down the road, pulled off onto the shoulder and parked the car reasonably out of sight. On his way back to the gates it had started to rain. It was a cold rain, a March rain, but a quiet rain, little intrusions upon the silence.

He passed a cluster of graves within a plot bordered by a low iron railing, the centerpiece an alabaster cross rising eight feet out of the ground. He stood for a moment before it. Had he been here before? Was another door opening for him in the distance? Or was he trying too desperately to find one? And then it came to him. It was not this particular grouping of gravestones, not the tall alabaster cross, nor the low iron railing. It was the rain. *A sudden rain. Crowds of mourners gathered in black around a burial site, the snapping of umbrellas. And two men coming together, umbrellas touching, brief, quiet apologies muttered, as a long brown envelope exchanged hands, pocket to pocket, unnoticed by the mourners.*

There was something else. An image triggered by an image, feeding upon itself, seen only minutes ago. Rain cascading down white marble; not a cold, light rain, but a downpour, pounding against the wall of a glistening white surface . . . and columns . . . rows of columns on all sides, a miniature replica of an ancient treasure.

On the other side of the hill. Near the gates. A white mausoleum, someone's scaled-down version of the Parthenon. He had passed it less than five minutes before, looking at it but not seeing it. *That* was where the sudden rain had taken place, where two umbrellas had touched and an envelope been delivered. He squinted at the radium dial of his watch. It was fourteen minutes past one; he started running back up the path. He was still early; there was time left to see a car's headlights, or the striking of a match or . . .

The beam of a flashlight. It was there at the bottom of the hill and it was moving up and down, intermittently swinging back at the gates as though the holder were concerned that someone might appear. Bourne had an almost uncontrollable urge to race down between the rows of graves and statuary, shouting at the top of his voice. *I'm here! It's me. I understand your message. I've come back! I have so much to tell you . . . and there is so much you must tell me!*

But he did not shout and he did not run. Above all else, he had to show control, for what afflicted him was so uncontrollable. He had to appear completely lucid—sane within the boundaries of his memory. He began walking down the hill in the cold light rain, wishing his sense of urgency had allowed him to remember a flashlight.

The flashlight. Something was odd about the beam of light five hundred feet below. It was moving in short vertical strokes, as if in emphasis . . . as if the man holding it were speaking emphatically to another.

He was. Jason crouched, peering through the rain, his eyes struck by a sharp, darting reflection of light that shot out whenever the beam hit the object in front of it. He crept forward, his body close to the ground, covering practically a hundred feet in seconds, his gaze still on the beam and the strange reflection. He could see more clearly now; he stopped and concentrated. There were two men, one holding the flashlight, the other a short-barreled rifle, the thick steel of the gun known only too well to Bourne. At distances of up to thirty feet it could blow a man six feet into the air. It was a very odd weapon for an officer-of-record sent by Washington to have at his command.

The beam of light shot over to the side of the white mausoleum; the figure holding the rifle retreated quickly, slipping behind a column no more than twenty feet away from the man holding the flashlight.

Jason did not have to think; he knew what he had to do.

If there was an explanation for the deadly weapon, so be it, but it would not be used on him. Kneeling, he judged the distance and looked for points of sanctuary, both for concealment and protection. He started out, wiping the rain from his face, feeling the gun in his belt that he knew he could not use.

He scrambled from gravestone to gravestone, statue to statue, heading to his right, then angling gradually to his left until the semicircle was nearly complete. He was within fifteen feet of the mausoleum; the man with the murderous weapon was standing by the left corner column, under the short portico to avoid the rain. He was fondling his gun as though it were a sexual object, cracking the breach, unable to resist peering inside. He ran his palm over the inserted shells, the gesture obscene.

Now. Bourne crept out from behind the gravestone, hands and knees propelling him over the wet grass until he was within six feet of the man. He sprang up, a silent, lethal panther hurling dirt in front of him, one hand surging for the barrel of the rifle, the other for the man's head. He reached both, grabbed both, clasping the barrel in the fingers of his left hand, the man's hair in his right. The head snapped back, throat stretched, sound muted. He smashed the head into the white marble with such force that the expulsion of breath that followed signified a severe concussion. The man went limp, Jason supporting him against the wall, permitting the unconscious body to slip silently to the ground between the columns. He searched the man, removing a .357 Magnum automatic from a leather case sewn into his jacket, a razor-sharp scaling knife from a scabbard on his belt and a small .22 revolver from an ankle holster. Nothing remotely government issue; this was a hired killer, an arsenal on foot.

Break his fingers. The words came back to Bourne; they had been spoken by a man in gold-rimmed glasses in a large sedan racing out of the Steppdeckstrasse. There was reason behind the violence. Jason grabbed the man's right hand and bent the fingers back until he heard the cracks; he did the same with the left, the man's mouth blocked, Bourne's elbow jammed between the teeth. No sound emerged above the sound of the rain, and neither hand could be used for a weapon or as a weapon, the weapons themselves placed out of reach in the shadows.

Jason stood up and edged his face around the column.

The Treadstone officer now angled the light directly into the earth in front of him. It was the stationary signal, the beam a lost bird was to home into; it might be other things also—the next few minutes would tell. The man turned toward the gate, taking a tentative step as though he might have heard something, and for the first time Bourne saw the cane, observed the limp. The officer-of-record from Treadstone Seventy-One was a cripple . . . as he was a cripple.

Jason dashed back to the first gravestone, spun behind it and peered around the marble edge. The man from Treadstone still had his attention on the gates. Bourne glanced at his watch; it was 1:27. Time remained. He pushed himself away from the grave, hugging the ground until he was out of sight, then stood up and ran, retracing the arch back to the top of the hill. He stood for a moment, letting his breathing and his heartbeat resume a semblance of normalcy, then reached into his pocket for a book of matches. Protecting it from the rain, he tore off a match and struck it.

"Treadstone?" he said loud enough to be heard from below.

"Delta!"

Cain is for Charlie and Delta is for Cain. Why did the man from Treadstone use the name Delta rather than Cain? Delta was no part of Treadstone; he had disappeared with Medusa. Jason started down the hill, the cold rain whipping his face, his hand instinctively reaching beneath his jacket, pressing the automatic in his belt.

He walked onto the stretch of lawn in front of the white mausoleum. The man from Treadstone limped toward him, then stopped, raising his flashlight, the harsh beam causing Bourne to squint and turn his head away.

"It's been a long time," said the crippled officer, lowering the light. "The name's Conklin, in case you've forgotten."

"Thank you. I had. It's only one of the things."

"One of what things?"

"That I've forgotten."

"You remembered this place, though. I figured you would. I read Abbott's logs; it was here where you last met, last made a delivery. During a state burial for some minister or other, wasn't it?"

"I don't know. That's what we have to talk about first.

You haven't heard from me in over six months. There's an explanation."

"Really? Let's hear it."

"The simplest way to put it is that I was wounded, shot, the effects of the wounds causing a severe . . . dislocation. Disorientation is a better word, I guess."

"Sounds good. What does it mean?"

"I suffered a memory loss. Total. I spent months on an island in the Mediterranean—south of Marseilles—not knowing who I was or where I came from. There's a doctor, an Englishman named Washburn, who kept medical records. He can verify what I'm telling you."

"I'm sure he can," said Conklin, nodding. "And I'll bet those records are massive. Christ, you paid enough!"

"What do you mean?"

"We've got a record, too. A bank officer in Zurich who thought he was being tested by Treadstone transferred a million and a half Swiss francs to Marseilles for an untraceable collection. Thanks for giving us the name."

"That's part of what you have to understand. I didn't know. He'd saved my life, put me back together. I was damn near a corpse when I was brought to him."

"So you decided a million-odd dollars was a pretty fair ballpark figure, is that it? Courtesy of the Treadstone budget."

"I told you, I didn't *know*. Treadstone didn't exist for me; in many ways it still doesn't."

"I forgot. You lost your memory. What was the word? Disorientation?"

"Yes, but it's not strong enough. The word is amnesia."

"Let's stick to disorientation. Because it seems you oriented yourself straight into Zurich, right to the Gemeinschaft."

"There was a negative surgically implanted near my hip."

"There certainly was; you insisted on it. A few of us understood why. It's the best insurance you can have."

"I don't know what you're talking about. Can't you understand *that*?"

"Sure. You found the negative with only a number on it and right away you assumed the name of Jason Bourne."

"It didn't *happen* that way! Each day it seemed I learned something, one step at a time, one revelation at a time. A

[455]

hotel clerk called me Bourne; I didn't learn the name Jason until I went to the bank."

"Where you knew exactly what to do," interrupted Conklin. "No hesitation at all. In and out, four million gone."

"Washburn told me what to do!"

"Then a woman came along who just happened to be a financial whiz kid to tell you how to squirrel away the rest. And before that you took out Chernak in the Löwenstrasse and three men *we* didn't know but figured they sure as hell knew you. And here in Paris, another shot in a bank transfer truck. Another associate? You covered every track, every goddamned track. Until there was only one thing left to do. And you—you son of a bitch—you did it."

"Will you *listen* to me! Those men tried to kill me; they've been hunting me since Marseilles. Beyond that, I honestly *don't know* what you're talking about. Things come to me at times. Faces, streets, buildings; sometimes just images I can't place, but I know they mean something, only I can't relate to them. And names—there are names, but then no faces. Goddamn you—I'm an *amnesiac!* That's the truth!"

"One of those names wouldn't be Carlos, would it?"

"Yes, and you know it. That's the point; you know much more about it than *I* do. I can recite a thousand facts about Carlos, but I don't know *why*. I was told by a man who's halfway back to Asia by now I had an agreement with Treadstone. The man worked for Carlos. He said Carlos knows. That Carlos was closing in on me, that you put out the word that I'd turned. He couldn't understand the strategy, and I couldn't tell him. You thought I'd turned because you didn't hear from me, and I couldn't reach you because I didn't know who you were. I *still* don't know who you are!"

"Or the Monk, I suppose."

"Yes, yes . . . the Monk. His name was Abbott."

"Very good. And the Yachtsman? You remember the Yachtsman, don't you? And his wife?"

"Names. They're there, yes. No faces."

"Elliot Stevens?"

"Nothing."

"Or . . . Gordon Webb." Conklin said the name quietly.

"What?" Bourne felt the jolt in his chest, then a stinging,

[456]

searing pain that drove through his temples to his eyes. *His eyes were on fire! Fire! Explosions and darkness, high winds and pain. . . . Almanac to Delta! Abandon, abandon! You will respond as ordered. Abandon!* "Gordon . . ."

Jason heard his own voice, but it was far away in a far-away wind. He closed his eyes, the eyes that burned so, and tried to push the mists away. Then he opened his eyes and was not at all surprised to see Conklin's gun aimed at his head.

"I don't know how you did it, but you did. The only thing left to do and you did it. You got back to New York and blew them all away. You butchered them, you son of a bitch. I wish to Christ I could bring you back and see you strapped into an electric chair, but I can't, so I'll do the next best thing. I'll take you myself."

"I haven't been in New York for months. Before then, I don't know—but not in the last half-year."

"Liar! Why didn't you do it *really* right? Why didn't you time your goddamn stunt so you could get to the funerals? The Monk's was just the other day; you would have seen a lot of old friends. And your *brother's!* Jesus God Almighty! You could have escorted his wife down the aisle of the church. Maybe delivered the eulogy, that'd be the kicker. At least speak well of the brother you killed."

"Brother? . . . *Stop* it! For Christ's sake, stop it!"

"Why should I? Cain lives! We made him and he came to life!"

"I'm not *Cain*. He never *was!* I never was!"

"So you *do* know! Liar! *Bastard!*"

"Put that gun away. I'm telling you, put it down!"

"No chance. I swore to myself I'd give you two minutes because I wanted to hear what you'd come up with. Well, I've heard it and it smells. Who gave *you* the right? We all lose things; it goes with the job, and if you don't like the goddamned job you get out. If there's no accommodation you fade; that's what I thought you did, and I was willing to pass on you, to convince the others to *let* you fade! But no, you came back, and turned your gun on us."

"No! It's not true!"

"Tell that to the laboratory techs, who have eight fragments of glass that spell out two prints. Third and index fingers, right hand. You were there and you butchered five people. You—one of *them*—took out your guns—plural—and blew them away. Perfect setup. Discredited strategy.

Varied shells, multiple bullets, *infiltration*. Treadstone's aborted and you walk out free."

"No, you're wrong! It was Carlos. Not me, *Carlos*. If what you're saying took place on Seventy-first Street, it was him! He knows. They know. A residence on Seventy-first Street. Number 139. They know about it!"

Conklin nodded, his eyes clouded, the loathing in them seen in the dim light, through the rain. "So perfect," he said slowly. "The prime mover of the strategy blows it apart by making a deal with the target. What's your take besides the four million? Carlos give you immunity from his own particular brand of persecution? You two make a lovely couple."

"That's crazy!"

"And accurate," completed the man from Treadstone. "Only nine people alive knew that address before seven-thirty last Friday night. Three of them were killed, and we're the other four. If Carlos found it, there's only one person who could have told him. *You*."

"How *could* I? I didn't know it. I *don't* know it!"

"You just said it." Conklin's left hand gripped the cane; it was a prelude to firing, steadying a crippled foot.

"*Don't!*" shouted Bourne, knowing the plea was useless, spinning to his left as he shouted, his right foot lashing out at the wrist that held the gun. *Che-sah!* was the unknown word that was the silent scream in his head. Conklin fell back, firing wildly in the air, tripping over his cane. Jason spun around and down, now hammering his left foot at the weapon; it flew out of the hand that held it.

Conklin rolled on the ground, his eyes on the far columns of the mausoleum, expecting an explosion from the gun that would blow his attacker into the air. No! The man from Treadstone rolled again. Now to the right, his features in shock, his wild eyes focused on— There was someone else!

Bourne crouched, diving diagonally backward as four gunshots came in rapid succession, three screeching ricochets spinning off beyond sound. He rolled over and over and over, pulling the automatic from his belt. He saw the man in the rain; a silhouetted figure rising above a gravestone. He fired twice; the man collapsed.

Ten feet away Conklin was thrashing on the wet grass, both hands spreading frantically over the ground, feeling for the steel of a gun. Bourne sprang up and raced over; he

[458]

knelt beside the Treadstone man, one hand grabbing the wet hair, the other holding his automatic, its barrel pressed into Conklin's skull. From the far columns of the mausoleum came a prolonged, shattering scream. It grew steadily, eerily in volume, then stopped.

"That's your hired shotgun," said Jason, yanking Conklin's head to the side. "Treadstone's taken on some very strange employees. Who was the other man? What death row did you spring him from?"

"He was a better man than you ever were," replied Conklin, his voice strained, the rain glistening on his face, caught in the beam of the fallen flashlight six feet away on the ground. "They all are. They've all lost as much as you lost, but they never turned. We can count on them!"

"No matter what I say, you won't believe me. You don't *want* to believe me!"

"Because I know what you are—what you *did*. You just confirmed the whole damn thing. You can kill me, but they'll get you. You're the worst kind. You think you're special. You always did. I saw you after Phnom Penh—*everybody* lost out there, but that didn't count with you. It was only you, just *you!* Then in Medusa! No rules for Delta! The animal just wanted to kill. And that's the kind that turns. Well, I lost too, but I never turned. Go on! Kill me! Then you can go back to Carlos. But when I don't come back, they'll know. They'll come after you and they won't stop until they get you. Go on! Shoot!"

Conklin was shouting, but Bourne could hardly hear him. Instead he had heard two words and the jolts of pain hammered at his temples. *Phnom Penh! Phnom Penh. Death in the skies, from the skies. Death of the young and the very young. Screeching birds and screaming machines and the deathlike stench of the jungle . . . and a river. He was blinded again, on fire again.*

Beneath him the man from Treadstone had broken away. His crippled figure was crawling in panic, lunging, his hands surging through the wet grass. Jason blinked, trying to force his mind to come back to him. Then instantly he knew he had to point the automatic and fire. Conklin had found his gun and was raising it. But Bourne could not pull the trigger.

He dove to his right, rolling on the ground, scrambling toward the marble columns of the mausoleum. Conklin's gunshots were wild, the crippled man unable to steady his leg or his aim. Then the firing stopped and Jason got to his feet, his face against the smooth wet stone. He looked out, his automatic raised; he had to kill this man, for this man would kill him, kill Marie, link them both to Carlos.

Conklin was hobbling pathetically toward the gates, turning constantly, the gun extended, his destination a car outside in the road. Bourne raised his automatic, the crippled figure in his gunsight. A split half-second and it would be over, his enemy from Treadstone dead, hope found with that death, for there were reasonable men in Washington.

He could not do it; he could not pull the trigger. He lowered the gun, standing helpless by the marble column as Conklin climbed into his car.

The car. He had to get back to Paris. There was a way. It had been there all along. *She* had been there!

He rapped on the door, his mind racing, facts analyzed, absorbed and discarded as rapidly as they came to him, a strategy evolving. Marie recognized the knock; she opened the door.

"Dear God, look at you! What happened?"

"No time," he said, rushing toward the telephone across the room. "It was a trap. They're convinced I turned, sold out to Carlos."

"*What?*"

"They say I flew into New York last week, last Friday. That I killed five people . . . among them a brother." Jason closed his eyes briefly. "There was a brother—*is* a brother. I don't know, I can't think about it now."

"You never left Paris! You can prove it!"

"How? Eight, ten hours, that's all I'd need. And eight or ten hours unaccounted for is all *they* need now. Who's going to come forward?"

"I will. You've been with me."

"They think you're part of it," said Bourne, picking up the telephone and dialing. "The theft, the turning, Port Noir, the whole damn thing. They've locked you into me. Carlos engineered this down to the last fragment of a fingerprint. Christ! Did he put it together!"

"What are you doing? Whom are you calling?"

"Our backup, remember? The only one we've got. Villiers. Villiers' *wife.* She's the one. We're going to take her, break her, put her on a hundred racks if we have to. But

we won't have to; she won't fight because she can't win.
. . . Goddamn it, why doesn't he answer?"

"The private phone's in his office. It's three in the morning. He's probably—"

"He's on! General? Is that you?" Jason had to ask; the
voice on the line was oddly quiet, but not the quiet of interrupted sleep.

"Yes, it is I, my young friend. I apologize for the delay.
I've been upstairs with my wife."

"That's whom I'm calling about. We've got to move.
Now. Alert French Intelligence, Interpol and the American
Embassy but tell them not to interfere until I've seen her,
talked to her. We have to talk."

"I don't think so, Mr. Bourne. . . . Yes, I know your
name, my friend. As for your talking to my wife, however,
I'm afraid that's not possible. You see, I've killed her."

33

Jason stared at the hotel room wall, at the flock paper with the faded designs that spiraled into one another in meaningless contortions of worn fabric. "Why?" he said quietly into the phone. "I thought you understood."

"I tried, my friend," said Villiers, his voice beyond anger or sorrow. "The saints know I tried, but I could not help myself. I kept looking at her . . . seeing the son she did not bear behind her, killed by the pig animal that was her mentor. My whore was someone else's whore . . . the animal's whore. It could not be otherwise, and as I learned, it was not. I think she saw the outrage in my eyes, heaven knows it was there." The general paused, the memory painful now. "She not only saw the outrage, but the truth. She saw that I knew. What she was, what she had been during the years we'd spent together. At the end, I gave her the chance I told you I would give her."

"To kill you?"

"Yes. It wasn't difficult. Between our beds is a nightstand with a weapon in the drawer. She lay on her bed, Goya's Maja, splendid in her arrogance, dismissing me with her private thoughts, as I was consumed by my own. I opened the drawer for a book of matches and walked back to my chair and my pipe, leaving the drawer open, the handle of the gun very much in evidence.

"It was my silence, I imagine, and the fact that I could not take my eyes off her that forced her to acknowledge me, then concentrate on me. The tension between us had grown to the point where very little had to be said to burst the floodgates, and—God help me—I said it. I heard myself asking, 'Why did you do it?' Then the accusation became complete. I called her my whore, the whore that killed my son.

"She stared at me for several moments, her eyes breaking away once to glance at the open drawer and the gun . . . and the telephone. I stood up, the embers in my pipe glowing, loose . . . *chauffé au rouge*. She spun her legs off the bed, put both hands into that open drawer and took out the gun. I did not stop her, instead I had to hear the words from her own lips, hear my own indictment of myself as well as hers. What I heard will go to my grave with me, for there will be honor left by my person and the person of my son. We will not be scorned by those who've given less than us. Never."

"General . . ." Bourne shook his head, unable to think clearly, knowing he had to find the seconds in order to find his thoughts. "General, what happened? She gave you my name. How? You've got to tell me that. *Please*."

"Willingly. She said you were an insignificant gunman who wished to step into the shoes of a giant. That you were a thief out of Zurich, a man your own people disowned."

"Did she say who those people were?"

"If she did I didn't hear. I was blind, deaf, my rage uncontrolled. But you have nothing to fear from me. The chapter is closed, my life over with a telephone call."

"*No!*" Jason shouted. "Don't do that! Not now."

"I must."

"Please. Don't settle for Carlos' whore. Get Carlos! Trap Carlos!"

"Reaping scorn on my name by lying with that whore? Manipulated by the animal's slut?"

"Goddamn you—what about your *son*? Five sticks of dynamite on rue du Bac!"

"Leave him in peace. Leave me in peace. It's over."

"It's *not* over! Listen to me! Give a moment, that's all I ask." The images in Jason's mind raced furiously across his

[463]

eyes, clashing, supplanting one another. But these images had meaning. Purpose. He could feel Marie's hand on his arm, gripping him firmly, somehow anchoring his body to a mooring of reality. "Did anyone hear the gunshot?"

"There was no gunshot. The *coup de grâce* is misunderstood in these times. I prefer its original intent. To still the suffering of a wounded comrade or a respected enemy. It is not used for a whore."

"What do you mean? You said you killed her."

"I strangled her, forcing her eyes to look into mine as the breath went out of her body."

"She had your gun on you . . ."

"Ineffective when one's eyes are burning from the loose embers of a pipe. It's immaterial now; she might have won."

"She *did* win if you let it stop here! Can't you see that? Carlos wins! She broke you! And you didn't have the brains to do anything but choke her to death! You talk about *scorn?* You're buying it all; there's nothing left but scorn!"

"Why do you persist, Monsieur Bourne?" asked Villiers wearily. "I expect no charity from you, nor from anyone. Simply leave me alone. I accept what is. You accomplish nothing."

"I will if I can get you to listen to me! Get Carlos, trap Carlos! How many times do I have to say it? He's the one you want! He squares it all for you! And he's the one I need! Without him I'm dead. *We're* dead. For God's sake, *listen to me!*"

"I would like to help you, but there's no way I can. Or will, if you like."

"There is." The images came into focus. He knew where he was, where he was going. The meaning and the purpose came together. "Reverse the trap. Walk away from it untouched, with everything you've got in place."

"I don't understand. How is that possible?"

"You didn't kill your wife. *I* did!"

"*Jason!*" Marie screamed, clutching his arm.

"I know what I'm doing," said Bourne. "For the first time, I really know what I'm doing. It's funny, but I think I've known it from the beginning."

Parc Monceau was quiet, the street deserted, a few porch lights shimmering in the cold, mistlike rain, all the windows along the row of neat, expensive houses dark, except for the residence of André François Villiers, legend of Saint-Cyr and Normandy, member of France's National Assembly . . . wife killer. The front windows above and to the left of the porch glowed dimly. It was the bedroom wherein the master of the house had killed the mistress of the house, where a memory-ridden old soldier had choked the life out of an assassin's whore.

Villiers had agreed to nothing; he had been too stunned to answer. But Jason had driven home his theme, hammered the message with such repeated emphasis that the words had echoed over the telephone. Get Carlos! Don't settle for the killer's whore! Get the man who killed your son! The man who put five sticks of dynamite in a car on rue du Bac and took the last of the Villiers line. He's the one you want. Get him!

Get Carlos. Trap Carlos. Cain is for Charlie and Delta is for Cain. It was so clear to him. There was no other way. At the end, it was the beginning—as the beginning had been revealed to him. To survive he had to bring in the assassin; if he failed, he was a dead man. And there would be no life for Marie St. Jacques. She would be destroyed, imprisoned, perhaps killed, for an act of faith that became an act of love. Cain's mark was on her, embarrassment avoided with her removal. She was a vial of nitroglycerine balanced on a highwire in the center of an unknown ammunition depot. Use a net. Remove her. A bullet in the head neutralizes the explosives in her mind. She cannot be heard!

There was so much Villiers had to understand, and so little time to explain, the explanation itself limited both by a memory that did not exist and the current state of the old soldier's mind. A delicate balance had to be found in the telling, parameters established as to time and the general's immediate contributions. Jason understood; he was asking a man who held his honor above all things to lie to the world. For Villiers to do that, the objective had to be monumentally honorable.

Get Carlos!

There was a second, ground floor entrance to the general's home, to the right of the steps, beyond a gate, where deliveries were made to the downstairs kitchen. Villiers had agreed to leave the gate and the door unlatched. Bourne had not bothered to tell the old soldier that it did not matter; that he would get inside in any event, a degree of damage intrinsic to his strategy. But first there was the risk that Villiers' house was being watched, there being good reasons for Carlos to do so, and equally good reasons not to do so. All things considered, the assassin might decide to stay as far away from Angélique Villiers as possible, taking no chance that one of his men could be picked up, thus proving his connection, the Parc Monceau connection. On the other hand, the dead Angélique was his cousin and lover . . . *the only person on earth he cares about.* Philippe d'Anjou.

D'Anjou! Of course there'd be someone watching—or two or ten! If d'Anjou had gotten out of France, Carlos could assume the worst; if the man from Medusa had not, the assassin would know the worst. The colonial would be broken, every word exchanged with Cain revealed. Where? Where were Carlos' men? Strangely enough, thought Jason, if there was no one posted in Parc Monceau on this particular night, his entire strategy was worthless.

It was not; they were there. In a sedan—the same sedan that had raced through the gates of the Louvre twelve hours ago, the same two men—killers who were the backups of killers. The car was fifty feet down the street on the left-hand side, with a clear view of Villiers' house. But were those two men slumped down in the seat, their eyes awake and alert, all that were there? Bourne could not tell; automobiles lined the curbs on both sides of the street. He crouched in the shadows of the corner building, diagonally across from the two men in the stationary sedan. He knew what had to be done, but he was not sure how to do it. He needed a diversion, alarming enough to attract Carlos' soldiers, visible enough to flush out any others who might be concealed in the street or on a rooftop, or behind a darkened window.

Fire. Out of nowhere. Sudden, away from Villiers' house, yet close enough and startling enough to send vibrations throughout the quiet, deserted, tree-lined street. Vibrations . . . sirens; explosive . . . explosions. It could be done. It was merely a question of equipment.

Bourne crept back behind the corner building into the intersecting street and ran silently to the nearest doorway, where he stopped and removed his jacket and topcoat. Then he took off his shirt, ripping the cloth from collar to waist; he put both coats on again, pulling up the lapels, buttoning the topcoat, the shirt under his arm. He peered into the night rain, scanning the automobiles in the street. He needed gasoline, but this was Paris and most fuel tanks would be locked. Most, but not all; there had to be an unsecured top among the line of cars at the curb.

And then he saw what he wanted to see directly up ahead on the pavement, chained to an iron gate. It was a motorbike, larger than a street scooter, smaller than a cycle, its gas tank a metal bubble between handlebars and seat. The top would have a chain attached, but it was unlikely to have a lock. Eight liters of fuel was not forty; the risk of any theft had to be balanced against the proceeds, and two gallons of gas was hardly worth a 500 franc fine.

Jason approached the bike. He looked up and down the street; there was no one, no sounds other than the quiet spattering of the rain. He put his hand on the gas tank top and turned it; it unscrewed easily. Better yet, the opening was relatively wide, the gas level nearly full. He replaced the top; he was not yet ready to douse his shirt. Another piece of equipment was needed.

He found it at the next corner, by a sewer drain. A partially dislodged cobblestone, forced from its recess by a decade of careless drivers jumping the curb. He pried it loose by kicking his heel into the slice that separated it from its jagged wall. He picked it up along with a smaller fragment and started back toward the motorbike, the fragment in his pocket, the large brick in his hand. He tested its weight . . . tested his arm. It would do; both would do.

Three minutes later he pulled the drenched shirt slowly out of the gas tank, the fumes mingling with the rain, the residue of oil covering his hands. He wrapped the cloth around the cobblestone, twisting and crisscrossing the sleeves, tying them firmly together, holding his missile in place. He was ready.

He crept back to the edge of the building at the corner of Villiers' street. The two men in the sedan were still low in the front seat, their concentration still on Villiers' house. Behind the sedan were three other cars, a small Mercedes, a dark brown limousine and a Bentley. Directly across from Jason, beyond the Bentley, was a white stone building, its windows outlined in black enamel. An inside hallway light spilled over to the casement bay windows on either side of the staircase; the left was obviously a dining room; he could see chairs and a long table in the additional light of a rococo sideboard mirror. The windows of that dining room with their splendid view of the quaint, rich Parisian street would do.

Bourne reached into his pocket and pulled out the rock; it was barely one-fourth the size of the gas-drenched brick, but it would serve the purpose. He inched around the corner of the building, cocked his arm and threw the stone as far as he could above and beyond the sedan.

The crash echoed throughout the quiet street. It was followed by a series of cracks as the rock clattered across the hood of a car and dropped to the pavement. The two men in the sedan bolted up. The man next to the driver opened his door, his foot plunging down to the pavement, a gun in his hand. The driver lowered the window, then switched on the headlights. The beams shot forward, bouncing back in blinding reflection off the metal and the chrome of the automobile in front. It was a patently stupid act, serving only to point up the fear of the men stationed in Parc Monceau.

Now. Jason raced across the street, his attention on the two men, whose hands were covering their eyes, trying to see through the glare of the reflected light. He reached the trunk of the Bentley, the cobblestone brick under his arm, a matchbook in his left hand, a cluster of torn-off matches in his right. He crouched, struck the matches, lowered the brick to the ground, then picked it up by an extended sleeve. He held the burning matches beneath the gas-soaked cloth; it burst instantly into flame.

He rose quickly, swinging the brick by the sleeve, and dashed over the curb, hurling his missile toward the bulging framework of the casement window with all his strength, racing beyond the edge of the building as impact was made.

The crash of shattering glass was a sudden intrusion on the rain-soaked stillness of the street. Bourne raced to his left across the narrow avenue, then back toward Villiers' block, again finding the shadows he needed. The fire spread, fanned by the wind from the broken window, leaping up into the willowy backing of the drapes. Within thirty seconds the room was a flaming oven, the fire magnified by the huge sideboard mirror. Shouts erupted, windows lighted up nearby, then farther down the street. A minute passed and the chaos grew. The door of the flaming house was yanked open and figures appeared—an elderly man in a nightshirt, a woman in a negligée and one slipper—both in panic.

Other doors opened, other figures emerged, adjusting from sleep to chaos, some racing toward the fire-swept residence—a neighbor was in trouble. Jason ran diagonally across the intersection, one more running figure in the rapidly gathering crowd. He stopped where he had started only minutes before, by the edge of the corner building, and stood motionless, trying to spot Carlos' soldiers.

He had been right; the two men were not the only guards posted in Parc Monceau. There were four men now, huddling by the sedan, talking rapidly, quietly. No, five. Another walked swiftly up the pavement, joining the four.

He heard sirens. Growing louder, drawing nearer. The five men were alarmed. Decisions had to be made; they could not all remain where they were. Perhaps there were arrest records to consider.

Agreement. One man would stay—the fifth man. He nodded and walked rapidly across the street to Villiers' side. The others climbed into the sedan, and as a fire engine careened up the street, the sedan curved out of its parking place and sped past the red behemoth racing in the opposite direction.

One obstacle remained: the fifth man. Jason rounded the building, spotting him halfway between the corner and Villiers' house. It was now a question of timing and shock. Bourne broke into a loping run, similar to that used by the people heading toward the fire, his head angled back toward the corner, running partially backward, a figure melting into the surrounding pattern, only the direction in conflict. He passed the man; he had not been noticed—but he *would* be noticed if he continued to the downstairs gate of Villiers' house and opened it. The man was glancing back and forth, concerned, bewildered, perhaps frightened by the fact that now he was the only patrol in the street. He was standing in front of a low railing; another gate, another downstairs entrance to another expensive house in Parc Monceau.

Jason stopped, taking two rapid sidesteps toward the man, then pivoted, his balance on his left foot, his right lashing out at the fifth man's midsection, pummeling him backward over the iron rail. The man shouted as he fell down into the narrow concrete corridor. Bourne leaped over the railing, the knuckles of his right hand rigid, the heels of both feet pushed forward. He landed on the man's chest, the impact breaking the ribs beneath him, his knuckles smashing into the man's throat. Carlos' soldier went limp. He would regain consciousness long after some-one removed him to a hospital. Jason searched the man; there was a single gun strapped to his chest. Bourne took it out and put it into his topcoat pocket. He would give it to Villiers.

Villiers. The way was clear.

He climbed the staircase to the third floor. Halfway up the steps he could see a line of light at the bottom of the bedroom door; beyond that door was an old man who was his only hope. If ever in his life—remembered and unre-membered—he had to be convincing, it was now. And his conviction was real—there was no room for the chameleon now. Everything he believed was based on one fact. Carlos had to come after him. It was the truth. It was the trap.

He reached the landing and turned to his left toward the bedroom door. He paused for a moment, trying to dismiss the echo in his chest; it was growing louder, the pounding more rapid. *Part of the truth, not all of it.* No invention, simply omission.

An agreement . . . a contract . . . with a group of men—honorable men—who were after Carlos. That was all Villiers had to know; it was what he had to accept. He could not be told he was dealing with an amnesiac, for in that loss of memory might be found a man of dishonor. The legend of Saint-Cyr, Algeria and Normandy would not accept that; not now, here, at the end of his life.

Oh, God, the balance was tenuous! The line between be-lief and disbelief so thin . . . as thin as it was for the man-corpse whose name was not Jason Bourne.

He opened the door and stepped inside, into an old man's private hell. Outside, beyond draped windows, the sirens raged and the crowds shouted. Spectators in an un-seen arena, jeering the unknown, oblivious to its unfathom-able cause.

Jason closed the door and stood motionless. The large room was filled with shadows, the only light a bedside table lamp. His eyes greeted by a sight he wished he did not have to see. Villiers had dragged a high-backed desk chair across the room and was sitting on it at the foot of the bed, staring at the dead woman sprawled over the covers. Angélique Villiers' bronzed head was resting on the pillow, her eyes wide, bulging out of their sockets. Her throat was swollen, the flesh a reddish purple, the massive bruise having spread throughout her neck. Her body was still twisted, in contrast to the upright head, contorted in furious struggle, her long bare legs stretched out, her hips turned, the negligée torn, her breasts bursting out of the silk—even in death, sensual. There had been no attempt to conceal the whore.

The old soldier sat like a bewildered child, punished for an insignificant act, the meaningful crime having escaped his tormentor's reasoning, and perhaps his own. He pulled his eyes away from the dead woman and looked at Bourne.

"What happened outside?" he asked in a monotone.

"Men were watching your house. Carlos' men, five of them. I started a fire up the block; no one was hurt. All but one man left; I took him out."

"You're resourceful, Monsieur Bourne."

"I'm resourceful," agreed Jason. "But they'll be back. The fire'll be out and they'll come back; before then, if Carlos puts it together, and I think he will. If he does, he'll send someone in here. He won't come himself, of course, but one of his guns will be here. When that man finds you . . . and her . . . he'll kill you. Carlos loses her, but he still wins. He wins a second time; he's used you through her and at the end he kills you. He walks away and you're dead. People can draw whatever conclusions they like, but I don't think they'll be flattering."

"You're very precise. Assured of your judgment."

"I know what I'm talking about. I'd prefer not to say what I'm going to say, but there's no time for your feelings."

"I have none left. Say what you will."

"Your wife told you she was French, didn't she?"

"Yes. From the south. Her family was from Loures Barouse, near the Spanish border. She came to Paris years ago. Lived with an aunt. What of it?"

"Did you ever meet her family?"

"No."

"They didn't come up for your marriage?"

"All things considered, we thought it would be best not to ask them. The disparity of our ages would have disturbed them."

"What about the aunt here in Paris?"

[471]

"She died before I met Angélique. What's the point of all this?"

"Your wife wasn't French. I doubt there was even an aunt in Paris, and her family didn't come from Loures Barouse, although the Spanish border has a certain relevance. It could cover a lot, explain a lot."

"What do you mean?"

"She was Venezuelan. Carlos' first cousin, his lover since she was fourteen. They were a team, have been for years. I was told she was the only person on earth he cared about."

"A whore."

"An assassin's instrument. I wonder how many targets she set up. How many valuable men are dead because of her."

"I cannot kill her twice."

"You can use her. Use her death."

"The insanity you spoke of?"

"The only insanity is if you throw your life away. Carlos wins it all; he goes on using his gun . . . and sticks of dynamite . . . and you're one more statistic. Another kill added to a long list of distinguished corpses. *That's* insane."

"And you're the reasonable man? You assume the guilt for a crime you did not commit? For the death of a whore? Hunted for a killing that was not yours?"

"That's part of it. The essential part, actually."

"Don't talk to me of insanity, young man. I beg you, leave. What you've told me gives me the courage to face Almighty God. If ever a death was justified, it was hers by my hand. I will look into the eyes of Christ and swear it."

"You've written yourself out, then," said Jason, noticing for the first time the bulge of a weapon in the old man's jacket pocket.

"I will not stand trial, if that's what you mean."

"Oh, that's perfect, General! Carlos himself couldn't have come up with anything better. Not a wasted motion on his part; he doesn't even have to use his own gun. But those who count will know he did it; he caused it."

"Those who count will know nothing. *Une affaire de coeur . . . une grave maladie . . .* I am not concerned with the tongues of killers and thieves."

"And if I told the truth? Told why you killed her?"

"Who would listen? Even should you live to speak. I'm not a fool, Monsieur Bourne. You are running from more than Carlos. You are hunted by many, not just one. You as much as told me so. You would not tell me your name . . . for my own safety, you claimed. When and if this was over, you said, it was *I* who might not care to be seen with *you*. Those are not the words of a man in whom much trust is placed."

"You trusted me."

"I told you why," said Villiers, glancing away, staring at his dead wife. "It was in your eyes."

"The truth?"

"The truth."

"Then look at me now. The truth is still there. On that road to Nanterre, you told me you'd listen to what I had to say because I gave you your life. I'm trying to give it to you again. You can walk away free, untouched, go on standing for the things you say are important to you, were important to your son. You can win! . . . Don't mistake me, I'm not being noble. Your staying alive and doing what I ask is the only way I can stay alive, the only way I'll ever be free."

The old soldier looked up. "Why?"

"I told you I wanted Carlos because something was taken from me—something very necessary to my life, my sanity—and he was the cause of it. That's the truth—I believe it's the truth—but it's not the whole truth. There are other people involved, some decent, some not, and my agreement with them was to get Carlos, trap Carlos. They want what you want. But something happened that I can't explain—I won't try to explain—and those people think I betrayed them. They think I made a pact with Carlos, that I stole millions from them and killed others who were my links to them. They have men everywhere, and the orders are to execute me on sight. You were right: I'm running from more than Carlos. I'm hunted by men I don't know and can't see. For all the wrong reasons. I didn't do the things they say I did, but no one wants to listen. I have no pact with Carlos—you know I don't."

"I believe you. There's nothing to prevent me from making a call on your behalf. I owe you that."

"How? What are you going to say? 'The man known to me as Jason Bourne has no pact with Carlos. I know this because he exposed Carlos' mistress to me, and that woman was my wife, the wife I choked to death so as not to bring dishonor to my name. I'm about to call the Sûreté and confess my crime—although, of course, I won't tell them why I killed her. Or why I'm going to kill myself.' . . . Is that it, General? Is that what you're going to say?"

The old man stared silently at Bourne, the fundamental contradiction clear to him. "I cannot help you then."

"Good. Fine. Carlos wins it all. She wins. You lose. Your son loses. Go on—call the police, then put the barrel of the gun in your goddamn mouth and blow your goddamn head off! Go *on!* That's what you want! Take yourself out, lie down and *die!* You're not good for anything else anymore. You're a self-pitying old, *old man!* God knows you're no match for Carlos. No match for the man who placed five sticks of dynamite in rue du Bac and killed your son."

Villiers' hands shook; the trembling spread to his head. "Do not do this. I'm telling you, do not *do* this."

"Telling me? You mean you're giving me an order? The little old man with the big brass buttons is issuing a *command?* Well, forget it! I don't take orders from men like you! You're frauds! You're worse than all the people you attack; at least they have the stomachs to do what they say they're going to do! You *don't.* All you've got is wind. Words and wind and self-serving bromides. Lie down and *die,* old man! But don't give me an order!"

Villiers unclasped his hands and shot out of the chair, his racked body now trembling. "I told you. No more!"

"I'm not interested in what you tell me. I was right the first time I saw you. You belong to Carlos. You were his lackey alive and you'll be his lackey dead."

The old soldier's face grimaced in pain. He pulled out his gun, the gesture pathetic, the threat, however, real. "I've killed many men in my time. In my profession it was unavoidable, often disturbing. I don't want to kill you now, but I will if you disregard my wishes. Leave me. Leave this house."

"That's terrific. You must be wired into Carlos' head. You kill me, he sweeps the board!" Jason took a step forward, aware of the fact that it was the first movement he had made since entering the room. He saw Villiers' eyes widen; the gun shook, its oscillating shadow cast against the wall. A single half ounce of pressure and the hammer would plunge forward, bullet finding its mark. For in spite of madness of the moment, the hand that held that weapon had spent a lifetime gripping steel; it would be steady when the instant came. If it came. That was the risk Bourne had to take. Without Villiers, there was nothing; the old man had to understand. Jason suddenly shouted: "Go *on!* Fire. *Kill* me. Take your orders from Carlos! You're a soldier. You've got your orders. Carry them out."

The trembling in Villiers' hand increased, the knuckles white as the gun rose higher, its barrel now leveled at Bourne's head. And then Jason heard the whisper from an old man's throat.

" '*Vous êtes un soldat . . . arrêtez . . . arrêtez.*' "

"What?"

"I am a soldier. Someone said that to me recently, someone very dear to you." Villiers spoke quietly. "She shamed an old warrior into remembering who he was . . . who he had been. *'On dit que vous êtes un géant. Je le crois.'* She had the grace, the kindness to say that to me also. She had been told I was a giant, and she believed it. She was wrong—Almighty God, she was wrong—but I shall try." André Villiers lowered the gun; there was dignity in the submission. A soldier's dignity. A giant's. "What would you have me do?"

Jason breathed again. "Force Carlos into coming after me. But not here, not in Paris. Not even in France."

"Where then?"

Jason held his place. "Can you get me out of the country? I should tell you, I'm wanted. My name and description by now are on every immigration desk and border check in Europe."

"For the wrong reasons?"

"For the wrong reasons."

"I believe you. There are ways. The Conseiller Militaire has ways and will do as I ask."

"With an identity that's false? Without telling them why?"

"My word is enough. I've earned it."'

"Another question. That aide of yours you talked about. Do you trust him—*really* trust him?"

"With my life. Above all men."

"With another's life? One you correctly said was very dear to me?"

"Of course. Why? You'll travel alone?"

"I have to. She'd never let me go."

"You'll have to tell her something."

"I will. That I'm underground here in Paris, or Brussels, or Amsterdam. Cities where Carlos operates. But she has to get away; our car was found in Montmartre. Carlos' men are searching every street, every flat, every hotel. You're working with me now; your aide will take her into the country—she'll be safe there. I'll tell her that."

"I must ask the question now. What happens if you don't come back?"

Bourne tried to keep the plea out of his voice. "I'll have time on the plane. I'll write out everything that's happened, everything that I . . . remember. I'll send it to you and you make the decisions. With her. She called you a giant. Make the right decisions. Protect her."

" *Vous êtes un soldat . . . arrêtez.* ' You have my word She'll not be harmed."

"That's all I can ask."

Villiers threw the gun on the bed. It landed between the twisted bare legs of the dead woman; the old soldier coughed abruptly, contemptuously, his posture returning. "To practicalities, my young wolfpack," he said, authority coming back to him awkwardly, but with definition. "What's this strategy of yours?"

"To begin with, you're in a state of collapse, beyond shock. You're an automaton walking around in the dark, following instructions you can't understand but have to obey."

"Not very different from reality, would't you say?" interrupted Villiers. "Before a young man with truth in his eyes forced me to listen to him. But how is this perceived state brought about? And why?"

"All you know—all you remember—is that a man broke into your house during the fire and smashed his gun into your head; you fell unconscious. When you woke up you found your wife dead, strangled, a note by her body. It's what's in the note that's driven you out of your mind."

"What would that be?" asked the old soldier cautiously.

"The truth," said Jason. "The truth you can't ever permit anyone to know. What she was to Carlos, what he was to her. The killer who wrote the note left a telephone number, telling you that you could confirm what he's written. Once you were satisfied, you could destroy the note and report the murder any way you like. But for telling you the truth—for killing the whore who was so much a part of your son's death—he wants you to deliver a written message."

"To Carlos?"

"No. He'll send a relay."

"Thank God for that. I'm not sure I could go through with it, knowing it was him."

"The message will reach him."

"What is it?"

"I'll write it out for you; you can give it to the man he sends. It's got to be exact, both in what it says and what it doesn't say." Bourne looked over at the dead woman, at the swelling in her throat. "Do you have any alcohol?"

"A drink?"

"No. Rubbing alcohol. Perfume will do."

"I'm sure there's rubbing alcohol in the medicine cabinet."

"Would you mind getting it for me? Also a towel, please."

"What are you going to do?"

"Put my hands where your hands were. Just in case, although I don't think anyone will question you. While I'm doing that, call whomever you have to call to get me out. The timing's important. I have to be on my way before you call Carlos' relay, long before you call the police. They'd have the airports watched."

"I can delay until daybreak, I imagine. An old man's state of shock, as you put it. Not much longer than that. Where will you go?"

"New York. Can you do it? I have a passport identifying me as a man named George Washburn. It's a good job."

"Making mine far easier. You'll have diplomatic status. Pre-clearance on both sides of the Atlantic."

"As an Englishman? The passport's British."

"As a NATO accommodation. Conseiller channels; you are part of an Anglo-American team engaged in military negotiations. We favor your swift return to the United States for further instructions. It's not unusual, and sufficient to get you rapidly past both immigration points."

"Good. I've checked the schedules. There's a seven A.M. flight, Air France to Kennedy."

"You'll be on it." The old man paused; he had not finished. He stook a step toward Jason. "Why New York? What makes you so certain Carlos will follow you to New York?"

"Two questions with different answers," said Bourne. "I have to deliver him where he marked me for killing four

[477]

men and a woman I didn't know . . . one of those men very close to me, very much a part of me, I think."

"I don't understand you."

"I'm not sure I do, either. There's no time. It'll all be in what I write down for you on the plane. I have to prove *Carlos knew*. A building in New York. Where it all took place; they've got to understand. He *knew* about it. Trust me."

"I do. The second question, then. Why will he come after you?"

Jason looked again at the dead woman on the bed. "Instinct, maybe. I've killed the one person on earth he cares about. If she were someone else and Carlos killed her, I'd follow him across the world until I found him."

"He may be more practical. I think that was your point to me."

"There's something else," replied Jason, taking his eyes away from Angélique Villiers. "He has nothing to lose, everything to gain. No one knows what he looks like, but he knows me by sight. Still, he doesn't know my state of mind. He's cut me off, isolated me, turned me into someone I was never meant to be. Maybe he was too successful; maybe I'm mad, insane. God knows killing *her* was insane. My threats are irrational. How much more irrational am I? An irrational man, an insane man, is a panicked man. He can be taken out."

"Is your threat irrational? Can you be taken out?"

"I'm not sure. I only know I don't have a choice." *He did not. At the end it was as the beginning. Get Carlos. Trap Carlos. Cain is for Charlie and Delta is for Cain. The man and the myth were finally one, images and reality fused. There was no other way.*

Ten minutes had passed since he had called Marie, lied to Marie, and heard the quiet acceptance in her voice, knowing it meant she needed time to think. She had not believed him, but she believed *in* him; she, too, had no choice. And he could not ease her pain; there had been no time, there *was* no time. Everything was in motion now, Villiers was downstairs calling an emergency number at France's Conseiller Militaire, arranging for a man with a false passport to fly out of Paris with diplomatic status. In less than three hours a man would be over the Atlantic, approaching the anniversary of his own execution. It was the key; it was the trap. It was the last irrational act, insanity the order of that date.

Bourne stood by the desk; he put down the pen and studied the words he had written on a dead woman's stationery. They were the words a broken, bewildered old man was to repeat over the telephone to an unknown relay who would demand the paper and give it to Ilich Ramirez Sanchez.

I killed your bitch whore and I'll come back for you. There are seventy-one streets in the jungle. A jungle as dense as Tam Quan, but there was a path you missed, a vault in the cellars you did not know about—just as you never knew about me on the day of my execution eleven years ago. One other man knew and you killed him. It doesn't matter. In that vault are documents that will set me free. Did you think I'd become Cain without that final protection? Washington won't dare touch me! It seems right that on the date of Bourne's death, Cain picks up the papers that guarantee him a very long life. You marked Cain. Now I mark you. I'll come back and you can join the whore.

Delta

Jason dropped the note on the desk and walked over to the dead woman. The alcohol was dry, the swollen throat prepared. He bent down and spread his fingers, placing his hands where another's had been placed.

Madness.

34

Early light broke over the spires of the church in Levallois Perret in northwest Paris, the March morning cold, the night rain replaced by mist. A few old women, returning to their flats from all-night cleaning shifts in the city proper, trudged in and out of the bronze doors, holding railings and prayer books, devotions about to begin or finished with, precious sleep to follow before the drudgery of surviving the daylight hours. Along with the old women were shabbily dressed men—most also old, others pathetically young—holding overcoats together, seeking the warmth of the church, these clutching bottles in their pockets, precious oblivion extended, another day to survive.

One old man, however, did not float in the trancelike movements of the others. He was an old man in a hurry. There was reluctance—even fear, perhaps—in his lined, sallow face, but no hesitation in his progress up the steps and through the doors, past the flickering candles and down the far left aisle of the church. It was an odd hour for a worshiper to seek confession; nevertheless this old beggar went directly to the first booth, parted the curtain and slipped inside.

"Angelus Domini . . ."

"Did you *bring* it?" the whisper demanded, the priestly silhouette behind the curtain trembling with rage.

"Yes. He thrust it in my hand like a man in a stupor, weeping, telling me to get out. He's burned Cain's note to him and says he'll deny everything if a single word is ever mentioned." The old man shoved the pages of writing paper under the curtain.

"He used her stationery—" The assassin's whisper broke, a silhouetted hand brought to a silhouetted head, a muted cry of anguish now heard behind the curtain.

"I urge you to remember, Carlos," pleaded the beggar. "The messenger is not responsible for the news he bears. I could have refused to hear it, refused to bring it to you."

"How? *Why?* . . ."

"Lavier. He followed her to Parc Monceau, then both of them to the church. I saw him in Neuilly-sur-Seine when I was your point. I told you that."

"I know. But *why?* He could have used her in a hundred different ways! Against me! Why *this?*"

"It's in his note. He's gone mad. He was pushed too far, Carlos. It happens; I've seen it happen. A man on a double-entry, his source-controls taken out; he has no one to confirm his initial assignment. Both sides want his corpse. He's stretched to the point where he may not even know who he is any longer."

"He knows . . ." The whisper was drawn out in quiet fury. "By signing the name Delta, he's telling me he knows. We both know where it comes from, where *he* comes from."

The beggar paused. "If that's true, then he's still dangerous to you. He's right. Washington won't touch him. It may not want to acknowledge him, but it will call off its hangmen. It may even be forced to grant him a privilege or two in return for his silence."

"The papers he speaks of?" asked the assassin.

"Yes. In the old days—in Berlin, Prague, Vienna—they were called 'final payments.' Bourne uses 'final protection,' a minor variance. They were papers drawn up between a primary source-control and the infiltrator, to be used in the event the strategy collapsed, the primary killed, no other avenues open to the agent. It was not something you would have studied in Novgorod; the Soviets had no such accommodations. Soviet defectors, however, insisted upon them."

"They were incriminating, then?"

"They had to be to some degree. Generally in the area of who was manipulated. Embarrassment is always to be avoided; careers are destroyed by embarrassment. But then, I don't have to tell you that. You've used the technique brilliantly."

" 'Seventy-one streets in the jungle . . .' " said Carlos, reading from the paper in his hand, an icelike calm imposed on his whisper. " 'A jungle as dense as Tam Quan.' . . . This time the execution will take place as scheduled. Jason Bourne will not leave *this* Tam Quan alive. By any other name, Cain will be dead, and Delta will die for what he's done. Angélique—you have my word." The incantation stopped, the assassin's mind racing to the practical. "Did Villiers have any idea when Bourne left his house?"

"He didn't know. I told you, he was barely lucid, in as much a state of shock with his telephone call."

"It doesn't matter. The first flights to the United States began within the past hour. He'll be on one. I'll be in New York with him, and I won't miss this time. My knife will be waiting, its blade a razor. I'll peel his face away; the Americans will have their Cain without a face! Then they can give this Bourne, this Delta, whatever name they care to."

The blue-striped telephone rang on Alexander Conklin's desk. Its bell was quiet, the understated sound lending an eerie emphasis. The blue-striped telephone was Conklin's direct line to the computer rooms and data banks. There was no one in the office to take the call.

The Central Intelligence executive suddenly rushed limping through the door, unused to the cane provided him by G-2, SHAPE, Brussels, last night when he had commandeered a military transport to Andrews Field, Maryland. He threw the cane angrily across the room as he lurched for the phone. His eyes were bloodshot from lack of sleep, his breath short; the man responsible for the dissolution of Treadstone was exhausted. He had been in scrambler-communication with a dozen branches of clandestine operations—in Washington and overseas—trying to undo the insanity of the past twenty-four hours. He had spread every scrap of information he could cull from the files to every post in Europe, placed agents in the Paris-London-Amsterdam axis on alert. Bourne was alive and dangerous;

he had tried to kill his D.C control; he could be anywhere within ten hours of Paris. All airports and train stations were to be covered, all underground networks activated. Find him! *Kill him!*

"Yes?" Conklin braced himself against the desk and picked up the phone.

"This is Computer Dock 12," said the male voice efficiently. "We may have something. At least, State doesn't have any listing on it."

"*What,* for Christ's sake?"

"The name you gave us four hours ago. Washburn."

"What about it?"

"A George P. Washburn was pre-cleared out of Paris and into New York on an Air France flight this morning. Washburn's a fairly common name; he could be just a businessman with connections, but it was flagged on the readout, and since the status was NATO-diplomatic, we checked with State. They never heard of him. There's no one named Washburn involved with any ongoing NATO negotiations with the French government from any member nation."

"Then how the hell was he pre-cleared? Who gave him the diplomatic?"

"We checked back through Paris; it wasn't easy. Apparently it was an accommodation of the Conseiller Militaire. They're a quiet bunch."

"The Conseiller? Where do they get off clearing *our* people?"

"It doesn't have to be 'our' people or 'their' people; it can be anybody. Just a courtesy from the host country, and that was a French carrier. It's one way to get a decent seat on an overbooked plane. Incidentally, Washburn's passport wasn't even U.S. It was British."

There's a doctor, an Englishman named Washburn . . . It *was* him! It was Delta, and France's Conseiller had co-operated with him. But why New York? What was in New York for him? And who placed so high in Paris would accommodate Delta? What had he told them? Oh, Christ! How *much* had he told them?

"When did the flight get in?" asked Conklin.

"Ten thirty-seven this morning. A little over an hour ago."

"All right," said the man whose foot had been blow off in Medusa, as he slid painfully around the desk into his seat. "You've delivered, and now I want this scratched from the reels. Delete it. Everything you gave me. Is that clear?"

"Understood, sir. Deleted, sir."

Conklin hung up. New York. *New York?* Not Washington, but New York! There was nothing in New York any longer. Delta knew that. If he was after someone in Treadstone—if he was after *him*—he would have taken a flight directly to Dulles. What was in New York?

And why had Delta deliberately used the name Washburn? It was the same as telegraphing a strategy; he knew the name would be picked up sooner or later . . . Later . . . *After* he was inside the gates! Delta was telling whatever was left of Treadstone that he was dealing from strength. He was in a position to expose not only the Treadstone operation, but he could go God knows how much further. Whole networks he had used as Cain, listening posts and ersatz consulates that were no more than electronic espionage stations . . . even the bloody specter of Medusa. His connection inside the Conseiller was his proof to Treadstone how high up he had traveled. His signal that if he could reach within so rarefied a group of strategists, nothing could stop him. Goddamn it, stop him from *what?* What was the point? He had the millions; he could have faded!

Conklin shook his head, remembering. There had been a time when he would have let Delta fade; he had told him so twelve hours ago in a cemetery outside of Paris. A man could take only so much, and no one knew that better than Alexander Conklin, once among the finest covert field officers in the intelligence community. Only so much; the sanctimonious bromides about still being alive grew stale and bitter with time. It depended on what you were before, what you became with your deformity. Only so much . . . But Delta did *not* fade! He came back with insane statements, insane demands . . . crazy tactics no experienced intelligence officer would even contemplate. For no matter how much explosive information he possessed, no matter how high he penetrated, no sane man walked back into a minefield surrounded by his enemies. And all the blackmail in the world could not bring you back. . . .

No sane man. No *sane* man. Conklin sat slowly forward in his chair.

I'm not Cain. He never was. I never was! I wasn't in

New York. . . . It was Carlos. Not me, Carlos! If what you're saying took place on Seventy-first Street, it was him. He knows!

But Delta *had* been at the brownstone on Seventy-first Street. Prints—third and index fingers, right hand. And the method of transport was now explained: Air France, Conseiller cover . . . Fact: Carlos could not have known.

Things come to me . . . faces, streets, buildings. Images I can't place . . . I know a thousand facts about Carlos, but I don't know why!

Conklin closed his eyes. There was a phrase, a simple code phrase that had been used at the beginning of Treadstone. What was it? It came from Medusa . . . *Cain is for Charlie and Delta is for Cain.* That was it. Cain for *Carlos.* Delta-Bourne became the Cain that was the decoy for Carlos.

Conklin opened his eyes. Jason Bourne was to replace Ilich Ramirez Sanchez. That was the entire strategy of Treadstone Seventy-One. It was the keystone to the whole structure of deception, the parallax that would draw Carlos out of position into their sights.

Bourne. Jason Bourne. The totally unknown man, a name buried for over a decade, a piece of human debris left in a jungle. But he *had* existed; that, too, was part of the strategy.

Conklin separated the folders on his desk until he found the one he was looking for. It had no title, only an initial and two numbers followed by a black *X*, signifying that it was the only folder containing the origins of Treadstone.

T-71 X. The birth of Treadstone Seventy-One.

He opened it, almost afraid to see what he knew was there.

Date of execution. Tam Quan Sector. March 25 . . .

Conklin's eyes moved to the calendar on his desk.

March 24.

"Oh, my God," he whispered, reaching for the telephone.

Dr. Morris Panov walked through the double doors of the psychiatric ward on the third floor of Bethesda's Naval Annex and approached the nurses' counter. He smiled at the uniformed aide shuffling index cards under the stern gaze of the head floor nurse standing beside her. Apparently the young trainee had misplaced a patient's file—if not a patient—and her superior was not about to let it happen again.

"Don't let Annie's whip fool you," said Panov to the flustered girl. "Underneath those cold, inhuman eyes is a heart of sheer granite. Actually, she escaped from the fifth floor two weeks ago but we're all afraid to tell anybody."

The aide giggled; the nurse shook her head in exasperation. The phone rang on the desk behind the counter.

"Will you get that, please, dear," said Annie to the young girl. The aide nodded and retreated to the desk. The nurse turned to Panov. "Doctor Mo, how am I ever going to get anything through their heads with you around?"

"With love, dear Annie. With love. But don't lose your bicycle chains."

"You're incorrigible. Tell me, how's your patient in Five-A? I know you're worried about him."

"I'm still worried."

"I hear you stayed up all night."

"There was a three A.M. movie on television I wanted to see."

"Don't do it, Mo," said the matronly nurse. "You're too young to end up in there."

"And maybe too old to avoid it, Annie. But thanks."

Suddenly Panov and the nurse were aware that he was being paged, the wide-eyed trainee at the desk speaking into the microphone.

"Dr. Panov, please. Telephone for—"

"*I'm* Dr. Panov," said the psychiatrist in a *sotto voce* whisper to the girl. "We don't want anyone to know. Annie Donovan here's really my mother from Poland. Who is it?"

The trainee stared at Panov's ID card on his white coat; she blinked and replied. "A Mr. Alexander Conklin, sir."

"Oh?" Panov was startled. Alex Conklin had been a patient on and off for five years, until they both had agreed he'd adjusted as well as he was ever going to adjust—which was not a hell of a lot. There were so many, and so little they can do for them. Whatever Conklin wanted had to be relatively serious for him to call Bethesda and not the office. "Where can I take this, Annie?"

"Room One," said the nurse, pointing across the hall. "It's empty. I'll have the call transferred."

Panov walked toward the door, an uneasy feeling spreading through him.

"I need some very fast answers, Mo," said Conklin, his voice strained.

"I'm not very good at fast answers, Alex. Why not come in and see me this afternoon?"

"It's not me. It's someone else. Possibly."

"No games, please. I thought we'd gone beyond that."

"No games. This is a Four-Zero emergency, and I need help."

"Four-Zero? Call in one of your staff men. I've never requested that kind of clearance."

"I can't. That's how tight it is."

"Then you'd better whisper to God."

"Mo, *please!* I only have to confirm possibilities, the rest I can put together myself. And I don't have five seconds to waste. A man may be running around ready to blow away ghosts, anyone he thinks is a ghost. He's already killed very real, very important people and I'm not sure he knows it. Help me, help *him!*"

"If I can. Go ahead."

"A man is placed in a highly volatile, maximum stress situation for a long period of time, the entire period in deep cover. The cover itself is a decoy—very visible, very negative, constant pressure applied to maintain that visibility. The purpose is to draw out a target similar to the decoy by convincing the target that the decoy's a threat, forcing the target into the open. . . . Are you with me so far?"

"So far," said Panov. "You say there's been constant pressure on the decoy to maintain a negative, highly visible profile. What's been his environment?"

"As brutal as you can imagine."

"For how long a period of time?"

"Three years."

"Good God," said the psychiatrist. "No breaks?"

"None at all. Twenty-four hours a day, three hundred and sixty-five days a year. Three years. Someone not himself."

"When will you damn fools learn? Even prisoners in the worst camps could be themselves, talk to others who were themselves—" Panov stopped, catching his own words and Conklin's meaning. "That's your point, isn't it?"

"I'm not sure," answered the intelligence officer. "It's hazy, confusing, even contradictory. What I want to ask is this. Could such a man under these circumstances begin to . . . believe he's the decoy, assume the characteristics,

[487]

absorb the mocked dossier to the point where he believes it's him?"

"The answer to that's so obvious I'm surprised you ask it. Of course he could. Probably would. It's an unendurably prolonged performance that can't be sustained unless the belief becomes a part of his everyday reality. The actor never off the stage in a play that never ends. Day after day, night after night." The doctor stopped again, then continued carefully. "But that's not really your question, is it?"

"No," replied Conklin. "I go one step further. Beyond the decoy. I have to; it's the only thing that makes sense."

"Wait a minute," interrupted Panov sharply. "You'd better stop there, because I'm not confirming any blind diagnosis. Not for what you're leading up to. No way, Charlie. That's giving you a license I won't be responsible for—with or without a consulation fee."

" 'No way . . . *Charlie.*' Why did you say that, Mo?"

"What do you mean, why did I say it? It's a phrase. I hear it all the time. Kids in dirty blue jeans on the corner; hookers in my favorite saloons."

"How do you know what I'm leading up to?" said the CIA man.

"Because I had to read the books and you're not very subtle. You're about to describe a classic case of paranoid schizophrenia with multiple personalities. It's not just your man assuming the role of the *decoy*, but the decoy himself transferring *his* identity to the one he's after. The *target*. That's what you're driving at, Alex. You're telling me your man is three people: himself, decoy and target. And I repeat. No way, Charlie. I'm not confirming anything remotely like that without an extensive examination. That's giving you rights you can't have: three reasons for dispatch. No way!"

"I'm not asking you to confirm anything! I just want to know if it's *possible*. For Christ's sake, Mo, there's a lethally experienced man running around with a gun, killing people he claims he didn't know, but whom he worked with for three years. He denies being at a specific place at a specific time when his own fingerprints prove he was there. He says images come to him—faces he can't place, names he's heard but doesn't know from where. He claims he was never the decoy; it was never him! But it was! It *is!* Is it *possible?* That's all I want to know. Could the stress and time and the everyday pressures break him like this? Into three?"

Panov held his breath for a moment. "It's possible," he said softly. "If your facts are accurate, it's possible. That's all I'll say, because there are too many other possibilities."

"Thank you." Conklin paused. "A last question. Say there was a date—a month and a day—that was significant to the mocked dossier—the decoy's dossier."

"You'd have to be more specific."

"I will. It was the date when the man whose identity was taken for decoy was killed."

"Then obviously not part of the working dossier, but known to your man. Am I following you?"

"Yes, he knew it. Let's say he was there. Would he remember it?"

"Not as the decoy."

"But as one of the other two?"

"Assuming the target was also aware of it, or that he'd communicated it through his transference, yes."

"There's also a place where the strategy was conceived, where the decoy was created. If our man was in the vicinity of that place, and the date of death was close at hand, would he be drawn to it? Would it surface and become important to him?"

"It would if it was associated with the original place of death. Because the decoy was born there; it's possible. It would depend on who he was at the moment."

"Suppose he was the target?"

"And knew the location?"

"Yes, because another part of him had to."

"Then he'd be drawn to it. It would be a subconscious compulsion."

"Why?"

"To kill the decoy. He'd kill everything in sight, but the main objective would be the decoy. Himself."

Alexander Conklin replaced the phone, his nonexistent foot throbbing, his thoughts so convoluted he had to close his eyes again to find a consistent strain. He had been wrong in Paris . . . in a cemetery outside of Paris. He had wanted to kill a man for the wrong reasons, the right ones beyond his comprehensions. He *was* dealing with a madman. Someone whose afflictions were not explained in twenty years of training, but were understandable if one thought about the pains and the losses, the unending waves of violence . . . all ending in futility. No one knew anything really. Nothing made sense. A Carlos was trapped, killed today, and another would take his place. Why did we do it . . . David?

David. I say your name finally. We were friends once, David . . . Delta. I knew your wife and your children. We drank together and had a few dinners together in far-off posts in Asia. You were the best foreign service officer in the Orient and everyone knew it. You were going to be the key to the new policy, the one that was around the corner. And then it happened. Death from the skies in the Mekong. You turned, David. We all lost, but only one of us became Delta. In Medusa. I did not know you that well—drinks and a dinner or two do not a close companion make—but few of us become animals. You did, Delta.

And now you must die. Nobody can afford you any longer. None of us.

"Leave us, please," said General Villiers to his aide, as he sat down opposite Marie St. Jacques in the Montmartre café. The aide nodded and walked to a table ten feet away from the booth; he would leave but he was still on guard. The exhausted old soldier looked at Marie. "Why did you insist on my coming here? He wanted you out of Paris. I gave him my word."

"Out of Paris, out of the race," said Marie, touched by the sight of the old man's haggard face. "I'm sorry. I don't want to be another burden for you. I heard the reports on the radio."

"Insanity," said Villiers, picking up the brandy his aide had ordered for him. "Three hours with the police, living a terrible lie, condemning a man for a crime that was mine alone."

"The description was accurate, uncannily accurate. No one could miss him."

"He gave it to me himself. He sat in front of my wife's mirror and told me what to say, looking at his own face in the strangest manner. He said it was the only way. Carlos could only be convinced by my going to the police, creating a manhunt. He was right, of course."

"He was right," agreed Marie, "but he's not in Paris, or Brussels, or Amsterdam."

"I beg your pardon?"

"I want you to tell me where he's gone."

"He told you himself."

"He lied to me."

"How can you be certain?"

"Because I know when he tells me the truth. You see, we both listen for it."

"You both . . .? I'm afraid I don't understand."

"I didn't think you would; I was sure he hadn't told you. When he lied to me on the phone, saying the things he said so hesitantly, knowing I knew they were lies, I couldn't understand. I didn't piece it together until I heard the radio reports. Yours and another. That description . . . so complete, so total, even to the scar on his left temple. Then I knew. He wasn't going to stay in Paris, or within five hundred miles of Paris. He was going far away—where that description wouldn't mean very much—where Carlos could be led, delivered to the people Jason had his agreement with. Am I right?"

Villiers put down the glass. "I've given my word. You're to be taken to safety in the country. I don't understand the things you're saying."

"Then I'll try to be clearer," said Marie, leaning forward. "There was another report on the radio, one you obviously didn't hear because you were with the police or in seclusion. Two men were found shot to death in a cemetery near Rambouillet this morning. One was a known killer from Saint-Gervais. The other was identified as a former American Intelligence officer living in Paris, a highly controversial man who killed a journalist in Vietnam and was given the choice of retiring from the army or facing a court-martial."

"Are you saying the incidents are related?" asked the old man.

"Jason was instructed by the American Embassy to go to that cemetery last night to meet with a man flying over from Washington."

"*Washington?*"

"Yes. His agreement was with a small group of men from American Intelligence. They tried to kill him last night; they think they have to kill him."

"Good God, why?"

"Because they can't trust him. They don't know what he's done or where he's been for a long period of time and he can't tell them." Marie paused, closing her eyes briefly.

"He doesn't know who he is. He doesn't know who *they* are; and the man from Washington hired other men to kill him last night. That man wouldn't listen; they think he's betrayed them, stolen millions from them, killed men he's never heard of. He hasn't. But he doesn't have any clear answers, either. He's a man with only fragments of a memory, each fragment condemning him. He's a near total amnesiac."

Villiers' lined face was locked in astonishment, his eyes pained in recollection. " 'For all the wrong reasons . . .' He said that to me. 'They have men everywhere . . . the orders are to execute me on sight. I'm hunted by men I don't know and can't see. For all the wrong reasons.' "

"For *all* the wrong reasons," emphasized Marie, reaching across the narrow table and touching the old man's arm. "And they do have men everywhere, men ordered to kill him on sight. Wherever he goes, they'll be waiting."

"How will they know where he's gone?"

"He'll tell them. It's part of his strategy. And when he does, they'll kill him. He's walking into his own trap."

For several moments Villiers was silent, his guilt overwhelming. Finally he spoke in a whisper. "Almighty God, what have I done?"

"What you thought was right. What he convinced you was right. You can't blame yourself. Or him, really."

"He said he was going to write out everything that had happened to him, everything that they remembered . . . How painful that statement must have been for him! I can't wait for that letter, mademoiselle. We can't wait. I must know everything you can tell me. Now."

"What can you do?"

"Go to the American Embassy. To the ambassador. Now. *Everything.*"

Marie St. Jacques withdrew her hand slowly as she leaned back in the booth, her dark red hair against the banquette. Her eyes were far away, clouded with the mist of tears. "He told me his life began for him on a small island in the Mediterranean called Ile de Port Noir. . . ."

The secretary of state walked angrily into the office of the director of Consular Operations, the department's section dealing with clandestine activities. He strode across the room to the desk of the astonished director, who rose at the sight of this powerful man, his expression a mixture of shock and bewilderment.

"Mr. Secretary? . . . I didn't receive any message from your office, sir. I would have come upstairs right away."

The secretary of state slapped a yellow legal pad down on the director's desk. On the top page was a column of six names written with the broad strokes of a felt-tipped pen.

BOURNE
DELTA
MEDUSA
CAIN
CARLOS
TREADSTONE

"What is this?" asked the secretary. "What the hell *is* this?"

The director of Cons-Op leaned over the desk. "I don't know, sir. They're names, of course. A code for the alphabet—the letter D—and a reference to Medusa; that's still classified, but I've heard of it. And I suppose the 'Carlos' refers to the assassin; I wish we knew more about him. But I've never heard of 'Bourne' or 'Cain' or 'Treadstone.' "

"Then come up to my office and listen to a tape of a telephone conversation that I've just had with Paris and you'll learn all about them!" exploded the secretary of state. "There are extraordinary things on that tape, including killings in Ottawa and Paris, and some very strange dealings our First Secretary in the Montaigne had with a CIA man. There's also outright lying to the authorities of foreign governments, to our *own* intelligence units, and to the European newspapers—with neither the knowledge nor the consent of the Department of State! There's been a global deception that's spread misinformation throughout more countries than I want to think about. We're flying over, under a deep-diplomatic, a Canadian woman—an economist for the government in Ottawa who's wanted for murder in Zurich. We're being *forced* to grant asylum to a fugitive, to subvert the laws—because if that woman's telling the truth, we've got our ass in a sling! I want to know what's been going on. Cancel everything on your calendar—and I mean *everything*. You're spending the rest of the day and all night if you have to digging this damn thing out of the ground. There's a man walking around who doesn't know who he is, but with more classified information in his head than ten intelligence computers!"

It was past midnight when the exhausted director of Consular Operations made the connection; he had nearly missed it. The First Secretary at the embassy in Paris, under threat of instant dismissal, had given him Alexander Conklin's name. But Conklin was nowhere to be found. He had returned to Washington on a military jet out of Brussels in the morning, but had signed out of Langley at 1:22 in the afternoon, leaving no telephone number—not even an emergency number—where he could be reached. And from what the director had learned about Conklin, that omission was extraordinary. The CIA man was what was commonly referred to as a shark-killer; he directed individual strategies throughout the world where defection and treason were suspected. There were too many men in too many stations who might need his approval or disapproval at any given moment. It was not logical he would sever that cord for twelve hours. What was also unusual was the fact that his telephone logs had been scratched; there were none for the past two days—and the Central Intelligence Agency had very specific regulations concerning those logs. Traceable accountability was the new order of the new regime. However, the director of Cons-Op had learned one fact: Conklin had been attached to Medusa.

Using the threat of State Department retaliation, the director had requested a closed circuit readout of Conklin's logs for the past five weeks. Reluctantly, the Agency beamed them over and the director had sat in front of a screen for two hours, instructing the operators at Langley to keep the tape repeating until he told them to stop.

Eighty-six logicals had been called, the word Treadstone mentioned; none had responded. Then the director went back to the possibles; there was an army man he had not considered because of his well-known antipathy to the CIA. But Conklin had telephoned him twice during the space of twelve minutes a week ago. The director called his sources at the Pentagon and found what he was looking for: Medusa.

Brigadier General Irwin Arthur Crawford, current ranking officer in charge of Army Intelligence data banks, former commander, Saigon, attached to covert operations—still classified. *Medusa.*

The director picked up the conference room phone; it bypassed the switchboard. He dialed the brigadier's home in Fairfax, and on the fourth ring, Crawford answered. The State Department man identified himself and asked if the general cared to return a call to State and be put through for verification.

"Why would I want to do that?"

"It concerns a matter that comes under the heading of Treadstone."

"I'll call you back."

He did so in eighteen seconds, and within the next two minutes the director had delivered the outlines of State's information.

"There's nothing there we don't know about," said the brigadier. "There's been a control committee on this from the beginning, the Oval Office given a preliminary summation within a week of the inauguration. Our objective warranted the procedures, you may be assured of that."

"I'm willing to be convinced," replied the man from State. "Is this related to that business in New York a week ago? Elliot Stevens—that Major Webb and David Abbott? Where the circumstances were, shall we say, considerably altered?"

"You were aware of the alterations?"

"I'm the head of Cons-Op, General."

"Yes, you would be . . . Stevens wasn't married; the rest understood. Robbery and homicide were preferable. The answer is affirmative."

"I see . . . Your man Bourne flew into New York yesterday morning."

"I know. We know—that is Conklin and myself. We're the inheritors."

"You've been in touch with Conklin?"

"I last spoke to him around one o'clock in the afternoon. Unlogged. He insisted on it, frankly."

"He's checked out of Langley. There's no number where he can be reached."

"I know that, too. Don't try. With all due respect, tell the Secretary to back away. You back away. Don't get involved."

"We *are* involved, General. We're flying over the Canadian woman by diplomatic."

"For God's sake, why?"

"We were forced to; she forced us to."

"Then keep her in isolation. You've *got* to! She's *our* resolve, we'll be responsible."

"I think you'd better explain."

"We're dealing with an *insane* man. A multiple schizophrenic. He's a walking firing squad; he could kill a dozen innocent people with one outburst, one explosion in his own head, and he wouldn't know why."

"How do you know?"

"Because he's already killed. That massacre in New York—it was *him*. He killed Stevens, the Monk, Webb—above all, Webb—and two others you never heard of. We understand now. He *wasn't* responsible, but that can't change anything. Leave him to us. To Conklin."

"Bourne?"

"Yes. We have proof. Prints. They were confirmed by the Bureau. It was him."

"Your man would leave prints?"

"He did."

"He couldn't have," said the man from State finally.

"What?"

"Tell me, where did you come up with the conclusion of insanity? This multiple schizophrenia or whatever the hell you call it."

"Conklin spoke to a psychiatrist—one of the best—an authority on stress-breakdowns. Alex described the history—and it was brutal. The doctor confirmed our suspicions, Conklin's suspicions."

"He *confirmed* them?" asked the director, stunned.

"Yes."

"Based on what Conklin said? On what he *thought* he knew?"

"There's no other explanation. Leave him to us. He's our problem."

"You're a damn fool, General. You should have stuck to your data banks or maybe more primitive artillery."

"I resent that."

"Resent it all you like. If you've done what I think you've done, you may not have anything left but resentment."

"Explain that," said Crawford harshly.

"You're not dealing with a madman, or with insanity, or with any goddamned multiple schizophrenia—which I doubt you know any more about than I do. You're dealing with an *amnesiac*, a man who's been trying for months to find out who he is and where he comes from. And from a telephone tape we've got over here, we gather he tried to tell you—tried to tell Conklin, but Conklin wouldn't listen. None of you would *listen* . . . You sent a man out in deep cover for three years—three *years*—to pull in Carlos, and when the strategy broke, you assumed the worst."

"Amnesia? . . . No, you're wrong! I spoke to Conklin; he *did* listen. You don't understand; we both knew—"

"I don't want to hear his name!" broke in the director of Consular Operations.

The general paused. "We both knew . . . Bourne . . . years ago. I think you know from where; you read the name off to me. He was the strangest man I ever met, as close to being paranoid as anyone in that outfit. He undertook missions—risks—no sane man would accept. Yet he never asked for anything. He was filled with so much hate."

"And that made him a candidate for a psychiatric ward ten years later?"

"Seven years," corrected Crawford. "I tried to prevent his selection in Treadstone. But the Monk said he was the best. I couldn't argue with that, not in terms of expertise. But I made my objections known. He was psychologically a borderline case; we knew why. I was proven right. I stand on that."

"You're not going to stand on anything, General. You're going to fall right on your iron ass. Because the Monk was right. Your man *is* the best, with or without a memory. He's bringing in Carlos, delivering him right to your goddamn front door. That is, he's bringing him in unless you kill Bourne first." Crawford's low, sharp intake of breath was precisely what the director was afraid he might hear. He continued. "You can't reach Conklin, can you?" he asked.

"No."

"He's gone under, hasn't he? Made his own arrangements, payments funneled through third and fourth parties unknown to each other, the source untraceable, all connections to the Agency and Treadstone obliterated. And by now there are photographs in the hands of men Conklin doesn't know, wouldn't recognize if they held him up. Don't talk to me about firing squads. Yours is in place, but

[497]

you can't see it—you don't know where it is. But it's prepared—a half a dozen rifles ready to fire when the condemned man comes into view. Am I reading the scenario?"

"You don't expect me to answer that," said Crawford.

"You don't have to. This is Consular Operations; I've been there before. But you were right about one thing. This *is* your problem; it's right back in your court. We're not going to be touched by you. That's my recommendation to the Secretary. The State Department can't afford to know who you are. Consider this call unlogged."

"Understood."

"I'm sorry," said the director, meaning it, hearing the futility in the general's voice. "It all blows up sometimes."

"Yes. We learned that in Medusa. What are you going to do with the girl?"

"We don't even know what we're going to do with you yet."

"That's easy. Eisenhower at the summit: 'What U-Twos?' We'll go along; no preliminary summation. Nothing. We can get the girl off the Zurich books."

"We'll tell her. It may help. We'll be making apologies all over the place; with her we'll try for a very substantial settlement."

"Are you *sure?*" interrupted Crawford.

"About the settlement?"

"No. The amnesia. Are you positive?"

"I've listened to that tape at least twenty times, heard her voice. I've never been so sure of anything in my life. Incidentally, she got in several hours ago. She's at the Pierre Hotel under guard. We'll bring her down to Washington in the morning after we figure out what we're going to do."

"Wait a minute!" The general's voice rose. "Not tomorrow! She's here . . . ? Can you get me clearance to see her?"

"Don't dig that grave of yours any deeper, General. The fewer names she knows, the better. She was with Bourne when he was calling the embassy; she's aware of the First Secretary, probably Conklin by now. He may have to take the fall himself. Stay out of it."

"You just told me to *play* it out."

"Not this way. You're a decent man; so am I. We're professionals."

"You don't understand! We have photographs, yes, but

they may be useless. They're three years old, and Bourne's changed, changed drastically. It's why Conklin's on the scene—where I don't know—but he's there. He's the only one who's seen him, but it was night, raining. She may be our only chance. She's been with him—living with him for weeks. She *knows* him. It's possible that she'd recognize him before anyone else."

"I don't understand."

"I'll spell it out. Among Bourne's many, many talents is the ability to change his appearance, melt into a crowd or a field or a cluster of trees—be where you can't see him. If what you say is so, he wouldn't remember, but we used to have a word for him in Medusa. His men used to call him . . . a chameleon."

"That's your Cain, General."

"It was our Delta. There was no one like him. And that's why the girl can help. Now. Clear me! Let me see her, talk to her."

"By clearing you, we acknowledge you. I don't think we can do that."

"For God's sake, you just said we were decent men! Are we? We can save his life! Maybe. If she's with me and we find him, we can get him out of there!"

"*There?* Are you telling me you know exactly where he's going to be?"

"Yes."

"How?"

"Because he wouldn't go anywhere else."

"And the time span?" asked the incredulous director of Consular Operations. "You know *when* he's going to be there?"

"Yes. Today. It's the date of his own execution."

— 35 —

Rock music blared from the transistor radio with tin-like vibrations as the long-haired driver of the Yellow Cab slapped his hand against the rim of the steering wheel and jolted his jaw with the beat. The taxi edged east on Seventy-first Street, locked into the line of cars that began at the exit on the East River Drive. Tempers flared as engines roared in place and cars lurched forward only to slam to sudden stops, inches away from bumpers in front. It was 8:45 in the morning, New York's rush hour traffic as usual a contradiction in terms.

Bourne wedged himself into the corner of the back seat and stared at the tree-lined street beneath the rim of his hat and through the dark lenses of his sunglasses. He had *been* there; it was all indelible. He had walked the pavements, seen the doorways and the storefronts and the walls covered with ivy—so out of place in the city, yet so right for this street. He had glanced up before and had noticed the roof gardens, relating them to a gracious garden several blocks away toward the park, beyond a pair of elegant French doors at the far end of a large . . . complicated . . . room. That room was inside a tall, narrow building of brown, jagged stone, with a column of wide, lead-paned windows rising four stories above the pavement. Windows made of thick glass that refracted light both inside and out in subtle flashes of purple and blue. Antique glass, perhaps, ornamental glass . . . bulletproof glass. A brownstone residence with a set of thick outside steps. They were odd steps, unusual steps, each level crisscrossed with black ridges that protruded above the surface, protecting the descender from the elements. Shoes going down would not slip on ice or snow . . . and the weight of anyone climbing up would trigger electronic devices inside.

Jason knew that house, knew they were coming closer to it. The echo in his chest accelerated and became louder as they entered the block. He would see it any moment, and as he held his wrist, he knew why Parc Monceau had struck such chords in his mind's eye. That small part of Paris was so much like this short stretch of the Upper East Side. Except for an isolated intrusion of an unkempt stoop or an ill-conceived whitewashed façade, they could be identical blocks.

He thought of André Villiers. He had written down everything he could remember since a memory had been given him in the pages of a notebook hastily purchased at Charles de Gaulle Airport. From the first moment when a living, bullet-ridden man had opened his eyes in a humid, dingy room on Ile de Port Noir through the frightening revelations of Marseilles, Zurich and Paris—especially Paris, where the specter of an assassin's mantle had fallen over his shoulders, the expertise of a killer proven to be his. By any standards, it was a confession, as damning in what it could not explain as in what it described. But it was the truth as he knew the truth, infinitely more exculpatory after his death than before it. In the hands of André Villiers it would be used well; the right decisions would be made for Marie St. Jacques. That knowledge gave him the freedom he needed now. He had sealed the pages in an envelope and mailed it to Parc Monceau from Kennedy Airport. By the time it reached Paris he would be alive or he would be dead; he would kill Carlos or Carlos would kill him. Somewhere on that street—so like a street thousands of miles away—a man whose shoulders floated rigidly above a tapered waist would come after him. It was the only thing he was absolutely sure of; he would do the same. Somewhere on that street . . .

[501]

There it was! It was *there*, the morning sun bouncing off the black enameled door and the shiny brass hardware, penetrating the thick, lead-paned windows that rose like a wide column of glistening, purplish blue, emphasizing the ornamental splendor of the glass, but not its resistance to the impacts of high-powered rifles and heavy-calibered automatic weapons. He was *here*, and for reasons—emotions—he could not define, his eyes began to tear and there was a swelling in his throat. He had the incredible feeling that he had come back to a place that was as much a part of him as his body or what was left of his mind. Not a home; there was no comfort, no serenity found in looking at that elegant East Side residence. But there was something else—an overpowering sensation of—*return*. He was back at the beginning, *the* beginning, at both departure and creation, black night and bursting dawn. Something was happening to him; he gripped his wrist harder, desperately trying to control the almost uncontrollable impulse to jump out of the taxi and race across the street to that monstrous, silent structure of jagged stone and deep blue glass. He wanted to leap up the steps and hammer his fist against the heavy black door.

Let me in! I am here! You must let me in! Can't you understand?

I AM INSIDE!

Images welled up in front of his eyes; jarring sounds assaulted his ears. A jolting, throbbing pain kept exploding at his temples. He was inside a dark room—*that* room—staring at a screen, at other, inner images that kept flashing on and off in rapid, blinding succession.

Who is he? Quickly. You're too late! You're a dead man. Where is this street? What does it mean to you? Whom did you meet there? What? Good. Keep it simple; say as little as possible. Here's a list: eight names. Which are contacts? Quickly! Here's another. Methods of matching kills. Which are yours? . . . No, no, no! Delta might do that, not Cain! You are not Delta, you are not you! You are Cain. You are a man named Bourne. Jason Bourne! You slipped back. Try again. Concentrate! Obliterate everything else. Wipe away the past. It does not exist for you. You are only what you are here, became here!

Oh, God. Marie had said it.

Maybe you just know what you've been told. . . . Over and over and over again. Until there was nothing else. . . .

Things you've been told . . . but you can't relive . . . because they're not you.

The sweat rolled down his face, stinging his eyes, as he dug his fingers into his wrist, trying to push the pain and the sounds and the flashes of light out of his mind. He had written Carlos that he was coming back for hidden documents that were his . . . "final protection." At that time, the phrase had struck him as weak; he had nearly crossed it out, wanting a stronger reason for flying to New York. Yet instinct had told him to let it stand; it was a part of his past . . . somehow. Now he understood. His identity was inside that house. His *identity*. And whether Carlos came after him or not, he had to find it. He *had* to!

It was suddenly insane! He shook his head violently back and forth trying to suppress the compulsion, to still the screams that were all around him—screams that were his screams, his voice. *Forget Carlos. Forget the trap. Get inside that house! It was there; it was the beginning!*

Stop it!

The irony was macabre. There was no final protection in that house, only a final explanation for himself. And it was meaningless without Carlos. Those who hunted him knew it and disregarded it; they wanted him dead because of it. But he was so close . . . he had to find it. It was there.

Bourne glanced up; the long-haired driver was watching him in the rearview mirror. "Migraine," said Jason curtly. "Drive around the block. To this block again. I'm early for my appointment. I'll tell you where to let me off."

"It's your wallet, mister."

The brownstone was behind them now, passed quickly in a sudden, brief break in the traffic. Bourne swung around in the seat and looked at it through the rear window. The seizure was receding, the sights and sound of personal panic fading; only the pain remained, but it too would diminish, he knew that. It had been an extraordinary few minutes. Priorities had become twisted; compulsion had replaced reason, the pull of the unknown had been so strong that for a moment or two he had nearly lost control. He could not let it happen again; the trap itself was everything. He had to see that house again; he had to study it again. He had all day to work, to refine his strategy, his tactics for the night, but a second, calmer appraisal was in order now. Others would come during the day, closer appraisals. The chameleon in him would be put to work.

Sixteen minutes later it was obvious that whatever he intended to study no longer mattered. Suddenly, everything was different, everything had changed. The line of traffic in the block was slower, another hazard added to the street. A moving van had parked in front of the brownstone; men in coveralls stood smoking cigarettes and drinking coffee, putting off that moment when work was to commence. The heavy black door was open and a man in a green jacket, the moving company's emblem above the left pocket, stood in the foyer, a clipboard in his hand. Treadstone was being dismantled! In a few hours it could be gutted, a shell! It couldn't be! They had to stop!

Jason leaned forward, money in his hand, the pain gone from his head; all was movement now. He had to reach Conklin in Washington. Not later—not when the chess pieces were in place—but right now! Conklin had to tell them to stop! His entire strategy was based on darkness . . . always darkness. The beam of a flashlight shooting out of first one alleyway, then another, then against dark walls and up to darkened windows. Orchestrated properly, swiftly, darting from one position to another. An assassin would be drawn to a stone building at night. At *night*. It would happen at night! Not now! He got out.

"Hey, mister!" yelled the driver through the open window.

Jason bent down. "What is it?"

"I just wanted to say thanks. This makes my—"

A *spit*. Over his shoulder! Followed by a cough that was the start of a scream. Bourne stared at the driver, at the stream of blood that had erupted over the man's left ear. The man was dead, killed by a bullet meant for his fare, fired from a window somewhere in that street.

Jason dropped to the ground, then sprang to his left spinning toward the curb. Two more spits came in rapid succession, the first imbedded in the side of the taxi, the second exploding the asphalt. It was unbelievable! He was marked before the hunt had begun! Carlos was *there*. In position! He or one of his men had taken the high ground, a window or a rooftop from which the entire street could be observed. Yet the possibility of indiscriminate death caused by a killer in a window or on a rooftop was crazy; the police would come, the street blocked off, even a reverse trap aborted. And Carlos was *not* crazy! It did not make sense. Nor did Bourne have the time to speculate; he had to get out of the trap . . . the reverse trap. *He had to get to that phone*. Carlos was here! At the doors of Treadstone! He had brought him back. He had actually brought him back! It was his proof!

He got to his feet and began running, weaving in and out of the groups of pedestrians. He reached the corner and turned right—the booth was twenty feet away, but it was also a target. He could not use it.

Across the street was a delicatessen, a small rectangular sign above the door: TELEPHONE. He stepped off the curb and started running again, dodging the lurching automobiles. One of them might do the job Carlos had reserved for himself. That irony, too, was macabre.

"The Central Intelligence Agency, sir, is fundamentally a fact-finding organization," said the man on the line condescendingly. "The sort of activities you describe are the rarest part of our work, and frankly blown out of proportion by films and misinformed writers."

"Goddamn it, *listen* to me!" said Jason, cupping the mouthpiece in the crowded delicatessen. "Just tell me where Conklin is. It's an emergency!"

"His office already told you, sir. Mr. Conklin left yesterday afternoon and is expected back at the end of the week. Since you say you know Mr. Conklin, you're aware of his service-related injury. He often goes for physical therapy—"

"Will you *stop* it! I saw him in Paris—outside of Paris—two nights ago. He flew over from Washington to meet me."

"As to that," interrupted the man in Langley, "when you were transferred to this office, we'd already checked. There's no record of Mr. Conklin having left the country in over a year."

"Then it's buried! He was there! You're looking for codes," said Bourne desperately. "I don't have them. But someone working with Conklin will recognize the words. Medusa, Delta, Cain . . . Treadstone! Someone *has* to!"

"No one does. You were told that."

"By someone who doesn't. There are those who do. Believe me!"

"I'm sorry. I really—"

"Don't hang up!" There was another way; one he did not care to use, but there was nothing else. "Five or six minutes ago, I got out of a taxi on Seventy-first Street. I was spotted and someone tried to take me out."

"Take . . . you out?"

"Yes. The driver spoke to me and I bent down to listen. That movement saved my life, but the driver's dead, a bullet in his skull. That's the truth, and I know you have ways of checking. There are probably half a dozen police cars on the scene by now. Check it out. That's the strongest advice I can give you."

There was a brief silence from Washington. "Since you asked for Mr. Conklin—at least used his name—I'll follow this up. Where can I reach you?"

"I'll stay on. This call's on an international credit card. French issue, name of Chamford."

"Chamford? You said—"

"*Please.*"

"I'll be back."

The waiting was intolerable, made worse by a stern Hassid glaring at him, fingering coins in one hand, a roll in another, and crumbs in his stringy, unkempt beard. A minute later the man in Langley was on the line, anger replacing compromise.

"I think this conversation has come to an end, Mr. Bourne or Chamford, or whatever you call yourself. The New York police were reached; there's no such incident as you described on Seventy-first Street. And you were right. We do have ways of checking. I advise you that there are laws about such calls as this, strict penalties involved. Good day, sir."

There was a click; the line went dead. Bourne stared at the dial in disbelief. For months the men in Washington had searched for him, wanted to kill him for the silence they could not understand. Now, when he presented himself—presented them with the sole objective of his three-year agreement—he was dismissed. They still would not listen! But that man *had* listened. And he had come back on the line denying a death that had taken place only minutes ago. It could not be . . . it was *insane*. It had *happened*.

Jason put the phone back on the hook, tempted to bolt from the crowded delicatessen. Instead, he walked calmly toward the door, excusing himself through the rows of people lined up at the counter, his eyes on the glass front, scanning the crowds on the sidewalk. Outside, he removed his topcoat, carrying it over his arm, and replaced the sunglasses with his tortoise-shells. Minor alterations, but he would not be where he was going long enough for them to be a major mistake. He hurried across the intersection toward Seventy-first Street.

At the far corner he fell in with a group of pedestrians waiting for the light. He turned his head to the left, his chin pressed down into his collarbone. The traffic was moving but the taxi was gone. It had been removed from the scene with surgical precision, a diseased, ugly organ cut from the body, the vital functions in normal process. It showed the precision of a master assassin, who knew precisely when to go in swiftly with a knife.

Bourne turned quickly, reversing his direction, and began walking south. He had to find a store; he had to change his outer skin. The chameleon could not wait.

Marie St. Jacques was angry as she held her place across the room from Brigadier General Irwin Arthur Crawford in the suite at the Pierre Hotel. "You wouldn't listen!" she accused. "None of you would listen. Have you any idea what you've *done* to him?"

"All too well," replied the officer, the apology in his acknowledgment, not his voice. "I can only repeat what I've told you. We didn't know what to listen *for*. The differences between the appearance and the reality were beyond our understanding, obviously beyond his own. And if beyond his, why not ours?"

"He's been trying to reconcile the appearance and reality, as you call it, for seven months! And all you could do was send out men to kill him! He tried to *tell* you. What kind of people *are* you?"

"Flawed, Miss St. Jacques. Flawed but decent, I think. It's why I'm here. The time span's begun and I want to save him if I can, if *we* can."

"God, you make me sick!" Marie stopped, she shook her head and continued softly. "I'll do whatever you ask, you know that. Can you reach this Conklin?"

"I'm sure I can. I'll stand on the steps of that house until he has no choice *but* to reach me. He may not be our concern, however."

"Carlos?"

"Perhaps others."

"What do you mean?"

"I'll explain on the way. Our main concern now—our *only* concern now—is to reach Delta."

"Jason?"

"Yes. The man you call Jason Bourne."

"And he's been one of you from the beginning," said Marie. "There were no slates to clean, no payments or pardons bargained for?"

"None. You'll be told everything in time, but this is *not* the time. I've made arrangements for you to be in an unmarked government car diagonally across from the house. We have binoculars for you; you know him better than anyone now. Perhaps you'll spot him. I pray to God you do."

Marie went quickly to the closet and got her coat. "He said to me one night that he was a chameleon . . ."

"He remembered?" interrupted Crawford.

"Remembered what?"

"Nothing. He had a talent for moving in and out of difficult situations without being seen. That's all I meant."

"Wait a minute." Marie approached the army man, her eyes suddenly riveted on his again. "You say we have to reach Jason, but there's a better way. Let him come to us. To *me*. Put me on the steps of that house. He'll see *me*, get word to me!"

"Giving whoever's out there two targets?"

"You don't know your own man, General. I said 'get word to me.' He'll send someone, pay a man or a woman on the street to give me a message. I know him. He'll do it. It's the surest way."

"I can't permit it."

"Why not? You've done everything else stupidly! Blindly! Do one thing intelligently!"

"I can't. It might even solve problems you're not aware of, but I can't do it."

"Give me a reason."

"If Delta's right, if Carlos has come after him and is in the street, the risk is too great. Carlos knows you from photographs. He'll kill you."

"I'm willing to take that risk."

"I'm not. I'd like to think I'm speaking for my government when I say that."

"I don't think you are, frankly."

"Leave it to others. May we go, please?"

[508]

"General Service Administration," intoned a disinterested switchboard operator.

"Mr. J. Petrocelli, please," said Alexander Conklin, his voice tense, his fingers wiping the sweat from his forehead as he stood by the window, the telephone in his hand. "Quickly, please!"

"Everybody's in a hurry—" The words were shorted out, replaced by the hum of a ring.

"Petrocelli, Reclamation Invoice Division."

"What are you people *doing?*" exploded the CIA man, the shock calculated, a weapon.

The pause was brief. "Right now, listening to some nut ask a stupid question."

"Well, listen further. My name's Conklin, Central Intelligence Agency, Four-Zero clearance. You *do* know what that means?"

"I haven't understood anything you people've said in the past ten years."

"You'd better understand this. It took me damn near an hour, but I just reached the dispatcher for a moving company up here in New York. He said he had an invoice signed by you to remove all the furniture from a brownstone on Seventy-first Street—139, to be exact."

"Yeah, I remember that one. What about it?"

"Who gave you the order? That's *our* territory. We removed our equipment last week, but we did not—repeat, did *not*—request any further activity."

"Just hold it," said the bureaucrat. "I saw that invoice. I mean, I read it before I signed it; you guys make me curious. The order came directly from Langley on a priority sheet."

"*Who* in Langley?"

"Give me a moment and I'll tell you. I've got a copy in my out file; it's here on my desk." The crackling of paper could be heard on the line. It stopped and Petrocelli returned. "Here it is, Conklin. Take up your beef with your own people in Administrative Controls."

"They didn't know what they were doing. Cancel the order. Call up the moving company and tell them to clear out! Now!"

"Blow smoke, spook."

"What?"

"Get a written priority requisition on my desk before

three o'clock this afternoon, and it may—just may—get processed tomorrow. Then we'll put everything back."

"Put everything *back?*"

"That's right. You tell us to take it out, we take it out. You tell us to put it back, we put it back. We have methods and procedures to follow just like you."

"That equipment—everything—was on loan! It wasn't—*isn't*—an Agency operation."

"Then why are you calling me? What have you got to do with it?"

"I don't have time to explain. Just get those people out of there. Call New York and get them out! Those are Four-Zero orders."

"Make them a hundred and four and you can still blow smoke. Look, Conklin, we both know you can get what you want if I get what I need. Do it right. Make it legitimate."

"I can't involve the Agency!"

"You're not going to involve me, either."

"Those people have got to get out! I'm telling you—" Conklin stopped, his eyes on the brownstone below and across the street, his thoughts suddenly paralyzed. A tall man in a black overcoat had walked up the concrete steps; he turned and stood motionless in front of the open door. It was *Crawford*. What was he doing? What was he doing *here?* He had lost his senses; he was out of his mind! He was a stationary target; he could break the trap!

"Conklin? Conklin . . . ?" The voice floated up out of the phone as the CIA man hung up.

Conklin turned to a stocky man six feet away at an adjacent window. In the man's large hand was a rifle, a telescopic sight secured to the barrel. Alex did not know the man's name and he did not want to know it; he had paid enough not to be burdened.

"Do you see that man down there in the black overcoat standing by the door?" he asked.

"I see him. He's not the one we're looking for. He's too old."

"Get over there and tell him there's a cripple across the street who wants to see him."

Bourne walked out of the used clothing store on Third Avenue, pausing in front of the filthy glass window to appraise what he saw. It would do; everything was coordinated. The black wool knit hat covered his head to the middle of his forehead; the wrinkled, patched army field jacket was several sizes too large; the red-checked flannel shirt, the wide-bulging khaki trousers and the heavy work shoes with the thick rubber soles and huge rounded toes were all of a piece. He only had to find a walk to match the clothing. The walk of a strong, slow-witted man whose body had begun to show the effects of a lifetime of physical strain, whose mind accepted the daily inevitability of hard labor, reward found with a six-pack at the end of the drudgery.

He would find that walk; he had used it before. Somewhere. But before he searched his imagination, there was a phone call to make; he saw a telephone booth up the block, a mangled directory hanging from a chain beneath the metal shelf. He started walking, his legs automatically more rigid, his feet pressing weight on the pavement, his arms heavy in their sockets, the fingers of his hands slightly spaced, curved from years of abuse. A set, dull expression on his face would come later. Not now.

"Belkins Moving and Storage," announced an operator somewhere in the Bronx.

"My name is Johnson," said Jason impatiently but kindly. "I'm afraid I have a problem, and I hope you might be able to help me."

"I'll try, sir. What is it?"

"I was on my way over to a friend's house on Seventy-first Street—a friend who died recently, I'm sorry to say— to pick up something I'd lent him. When I got there, your van was in front of the house. It's most embarrassing, but I think your men may remove my property. Is there someone I might speak to?"

"That would be a dispatcher, sir."

"Might I have his name, please?"

"What?"

"His name."

"Sure. Murray. Murray Schumach. I'll connect you."

Two clicks preceded a long hum over the line.

"Schumach."

"Mr. Schumach?"

"That's right."

Bourne repeated his embarrassing tale. "Of course, I can easily obtain a letter from my attorney, but the item in question has little or no value—"

"What is it?"

"A fishing rod. Not an expensive one, but with an old-fashioned casting reel, the kind that doesn't get tangled every five minutes."

"Yeah, I know what you mean. I fish out of Sheepshead Bay. They don't make them reels like they used to. I think it's the alloys."

"I think you're right, Mr. Schumach. I know exactly in which closet he kept it."

"Oh, what the hell—a fishing rod. Go up and see a guy named Dugan, he's the supervisor on the job. Tell him I said you could have it, but you'll have to sign for it. If he gives you static, tell him to go outside and call me; the phone's disconnected down there."

"A Mr. Dugan. Thank you very much, Mr. Schumach."

"Christ, that place is a ballbreaker today!"

"I beg your pardon?"

"Nothing. Some whacko called telling us to get out of there. And the job's firm, cash guaranteed. Can you believe it?"

Carlos. Jason could believe it.

"It's difficult, Mr. Schumach."

"Good fishing," said the Belkins man.

Bourne walked west on Seventieth Street to Lexington Avenue. Three blocks south he found what he was looking for: an army-navy surplus store. He went inside.

Eight minutes later he came out carrying four brown, padded blankets and six wide canvas straps with metal buckles. In the pockets of his field jacket were two ordinary road flares. They had been there on the counter looking like something they were not, triggering images beyond memory, back to a moment of time when there had been meaning and purpose. And anger. He slung the equipment over his left shoulder and trudged up toward Seventy-first Street. The chameleon was heading into the jungle, a jungle as dense as the unremembered Tam Quan.

It was 10:48 when he reached the corner of the tree-lined block that held the secrets of Treadstone Seventy-One. He was going back to the beginning—his beginning —and the fear that he felt was not the fear of physical harm. He was prepared for that, every sinew taut, every muscle ready; his knees and feet, hands and elbows weapons, his eyes trip-wire alarms that would send signals to those weapons. His fear was far more profound. He was about to enter the place of his birth and he was terrified at what he might find there—remember there.

Stop it! The trap is everything. Cain is for Charlie and Delta is for Cain!

The traffic had diminished considerably, the rush hour over, the street in the doldrums of midmorning quiescence. Pedestrians strolled now, they did not hasten; automobiles swung leisurely around the moving van, angry horns replaced by brief grimaces of irritation. Jason crossed with the light to the Treadstone side; the tall, narrow structure of brown, jagged stone and thick blue glass was fifty yards down the block. Blankets and straps in place, an already weary, slow-witted laborer walked behind a well-dressed couple toward it.

He reached the concrete steps as two muscular men, one black, one white, were carrying a covered harp out the door. Bourne stopped and called out, his words halting, his dialect coarse.

"Hey! Where's Doogan?"

"Where the hell d'you t'ink?" replied the white, angling his head around. "Sittin' in a fuckin' chair."

"He ain't gonna lift nothin' heavier than that clipboard, man," added the black. "He's an *executive*, ain't that right, Joey?"

"He's a crumbball, is what he is. Watcha' got there?"

"Schumach sent me," said Jason. "He wanted another man down here and figured you needed this stuff. Told me to bring it."

"Murray the menace!" laughed the black. "You new, man? I ain't seen you before. You come from shape-up?"

"Yeah."

"Take that shit up to the executive," grunted Joey, starting down the steps. "He can *allocate* it, how about that, Pete? *Allocate*—you like it?"

"I love it, Joey. You a regular dictionary."

Bourne walked up the reddish brown steps past the descending movers to the door. He stepped inside and saw the winding staircase on the right, and the long narrow corridor in front of him that led to another door thirty feet away. He had climbed those steps a thousand times, walked up and down that corridor thousands more. He had come back, and an overpowering sense of dread swept through him. He started down the dark, narrow corridor; he could see shafts of sunlight bursting through a pair of

French doors in the distance. He was approaching the room where Cain was born. *That* room. He gripped the straps on his shoulder and tried to stop the trembling.

Marie leaned forward in the back seat of the armor-plated government sedan, the binoculars in place. Something had happened; she was not sure what it was, but she could guess. A short, stocky man had passed by the steps of the brownstone a few minutes ago, slowing his pace as he approached the general, obviously saying something to him. The man had then continued down the block and seconds later Crawford had followed him.

Conklin had been found.

It was a small step if what the general said was true. Hired gunmen, unknown to their employer, he unknown to them. Hired to kill a man . . . for all the wrong reasons! Oh, God, she loathed them all! Mindless, stupid men. Playing with the lives of other men, knowing so little, thinking they knew so much.

They had not listened! They never listened until it was too late, and then only with stern forbearance and strong reminders of what might have been—had things been as they were perceived to be, which they were not. The corruption came from blindness, the lies from obstinacy and embarrassment. Do not embarrass the powerful; the napalm said it all.

Marie focused the binoculars. A Belkins man was approaching the steps, blankets and straps over his shoulder, walking behind an elderly couple, obviously residents of the block out for a stroll. The man in the field jacket and the black knit hat stopped; he began talking to two other movers carrying a triangular-shaped object out the door.

What was it? There was something . . . something odd. She could not see the man's face; it was hidden from view, but there was something about the neck, the angle of the head . . . what was it? The man started up the steps, a blunt man, weary of his day before it had begun . . . a slovenly man. Marie removed the binoculars; she was too anxious, too ready to see things that were not there.

Oh, God, my love, my Jason. Where are you? Come to me. Let me find you. Do not leave me for these blind, mindless men. Do not let them take you from me.

Where was Crawford? He had promised to keep her informed of every move, everything. She had been blunt. She did not trust him, any of them; she did not trust their intelligence, that word spelled with a lower-case *i*. He had promised . . . where *was* he?

She spoke to the driver. "Will you put down the window, please. It's stifling in here."

"Sorry, miss," replied the civilian-clothed army man. "I'll turn on the air conditioning for you, though."

The windows and doors were controlled by buttons only the driver could reach. She was in a glass and metal tomb in a sun-drenched, tree-lined street.

"I don't believe a word of it!" said Conklin, limping angrily across the room back to the window. He leaned against the sill, looking out, his left hand pulled up to his face, his teeth against the knuckle of his index finger. "Not a goddamned word!"

"You don't want to believe it, Alex," countered Crawford. "The solution is so much easier. It's in place, and so much simpler."

"You didn't hear that tape. You didn't hear Villiers!"

"I've heard the woman; she's all I have to hear. She said we didn't listen . . . you didn't listen."

"Then she's lying!" Awkwardly Conklin spun around. "Christ, of course she's lying! Why wouldn't she? She's his woman. She'll do anything to get him off the meathook."

"You're wrong and you know it. The fact that he's here proves you're wrong, proves I was wrong to accept what you said."

Conklin was breathing heavily, his right hand trembling as he gripped his cane. "Maybe . . . maybe we, maybe . . ." He did not finish; instead he looked at Crawford helplessly.

"We ought to let the solution stand?" asked the officer quietly. "You're tired, Alex. You haven't slept for several days; you're exhausted. I don't think I heard that."

"No." The CIA man shook his head, his eyes closed, his face reflecting his disgust. "No, you didn't hear it and I didn't say it. I just wish I knew where the hell to begin."

"I do," said Crawford, going to the door and opening it. "Come in, please."

The stocky man walked in, his eyes darting to the rifle leaning against the wall. He looked at the two men, appraisal in his expression. "What is it?"

"The exercise has been called off," Crawford said. "I think you must have gathered that."

"What exercise? I was hired to protect him." The gunman looked at Alex. "You mean you don't need protection anymore, sir?"

"You know exactly what we mean," broke in Conklin. "All signals are off, all stipulations."

"What stipulations? I don't know about any stipulations. The terms of my employment are very clear. I'm protecting you, sir."

"Good, fine," said Crawford. "Now what we have to know is who else out there is protecting him."

"Who else where?"

"Outside this room, this apartment. In other rooms, on the street, in cars, perhaps. We have to *know*."

The stocky man walked over to the rifle and picked it up. "I'm afraid you gentlemen have misunderstood. I was hired on an individual basis. If others were employed, I'm not aware of them."

"You *do* know them!" shouted Conklin. "Who *are* they? *Where* are they?"

"I haven't any idea . . . sir." The courteous gunman held the rifle in his right arm, the barrel angled down toward the floor. He raised it perhaps two inches, no more than that, the movement barely perceptible. "If my services are no longer required, I'll be leaving."

"Can you *reach* them?" interrupted the brigadier. "We'll pay generously."

"I've already been paid generously, sir. It would be wrong to accept money for a service I can't perform. And pointless for this to continue."

"A man's life is at stake out there!" shouted Conklin.

"So's mine," said the gunman, walking to the door, the weapon raised higher. "Goodbye, gentlemen." He let himself out.

"*Jesus!*" roared Alex, swinging back to the window, his cane clattering against a radiator. "What do we *do?*"

"To start with, get rid of that moving company. I don't know what part it played in your strategy, but it's only a complication now."

"I can't. I tried. I didn't have anything to do with it. Agency Controls picked up our sheets when we had the equipment taken out. They saw that a store was being closed up and told GSA to get us the hell out of there."

"With all deliberate speed," said Crawford, nodding. "The Monk covered that equipment by signature; his statement absolves the Agency. It's in his files."

"That'd be fine if we had twenty-four hours. We don't even know if we've got twenty-four minutes."

"We'll still need it. There'll be a Senate inquiry. Closed, I hope. . . . Rope off the street."

"What?"

"You heard me—rope off the street! Call in the police, tell them to rope everything off!"

"Through the Agency? This is domestic."

"Then *I* will. Through the Pentagon, from the Joint Chiefs, if I have to. We're standing around making excuses, when it's right in front of our eyes! Clear the street, rope it off, bring in a truck with a public address system. Put *her* in it, put her on a *microphone!* Let her say anything she likes, let her scream her head off. She was right. He'll come to *her!*"

"Do you know what you're saying?" asked Conklin. "There'll be questions. Newspapers, television, radio. Everything will be exposed. Publicly."

"I'm aware of that," said the brigadier. "I'm also aware that she'll do it for us if this goes down. She may do it anyway, no matter what happens, but I'd rather try to save a man I didn't like, didn't approve of. But I respected him once, and I think I respect him more now."

"What about another man? If Carlos is really out there, you're opening the gates for him. You're handing him his escape."

"We didn't create Carlos. We created Cain and we abused him. We took his mind and his memory. We owe him. Go down and get the woman. I'll use the phone."

Bourne walked into the large library with the sunlight streaming through the wide, elegant french doors at the far end of the room. Beyond the panes of glass were the high walls of the garden . . . all around him objects too painful to look at; he knew them and did not know them. They were fragments of dreams—but solid, to be touched, to be felt, to be used—not ephemeral at all. A long hatch table where whiskey was poured, leather armchairs where men sat and talked, bookshelves that housed books and other things—concealed things—that appeared with the touch of buttons. It was a room where a myth was born, a myth that had raced through Southeast Asia and exploded in Europe.

He saw the long, tubular bulge in the ceiling and the darkness came, followed by flashes of light and images on a screen and voices shouting in his ears.

Who is he? Quick. You're too late! You're a dead man! Where is this street? What does it mean to you? Whom did you meet there? . . . Methods of kills. Which are yours? No! . . . You are not Delta, you are not you! . . . You are only what you are here, became here!

"Hey! Who the hell are *you?*" The question was shouted by a large, red-faced man seated in an armchair by the door, a clipboard on his knees. Jason had walked right past him.

"You Doogan?" Bourne asked.

"Yeah."

"Schumach sent me. Said you needed another man."

"What for? I got five already, and this fuckin' place has hallways so tight you can't hardly get through 'em. They're climbing asses now."

"I don't know. Schumach sent me, that's all I know. He told me to bring this stuff." Bourne let the blankets and the straps fall to the floor.

"Murray sends new junk? I mean, that's new."

"I don't—"

"I know, I *know!* Schumach sent you. Ask Schumach."

"You can't. He said to tell you he was heading out to Sheepshead. Be back this afternoon."

"Oh, that's great! He goes fishing and leaves me with the shit. . . . You're new. You a crumbball from the shape-up?"

"Yeah."

"That Murray's a beaut. All I need's another crumbball. Two wiseass stiffs and now four crumbballs."

"You want me to start in here? I can start in here."

"No, asshole! Crumbballs start at the top, you ain't heard? It's further away, *capisce?*"

"Yeah, I *capisce.*" Jason bent down for the blankets and the straps.

"Leave that junk here—you don't need it. Get upstairs, top floor, and start with the single wood units. As heavy as you can carry, and don't give me no union bullshit."

Bourne circled the landing on the second floor and climbed the narrow staircase to the third, as if drawn by a magnetic force beyond his understanding. He was being pulled to another room high up in the brownstone, a room that held both the comfort of solitude and the frustration of loneliness. The landing above was dark, no lights on, no sunlight bursting through windows anywhere. He reached the top and stood for a moment in silence. Which room was it? There were three doors, two on the left side of the hallway, one on the right. He started walking slowly toward the second door on the left, barely seen in the shadows. That was it; it was where thoughts came in the darkness . . . memories that haunted him, pained him. Sunlight and the stench of the river and the jungle . . . screaming machines in the sky, screaming down from the sky. *Oh, God, it hurt!*

He put his hand on the knob, twisted it and opened the door. Darkness, but not complete. There was a small window at the far end of the room, a black shade pulled down, covering it, but not completely. He could see a thin line of sunlight, so narrow it barely broke through, where the shade met the sill. He walked toward it, toward that thin, tiny shaft of sunlight.

A scratch! A scratch in the darkness! He spun, terrified at the tricks being played on his mind. But it was not a trick! There was a diamondlike flash in the air, light bouncing off steel.

A knife was slashing up at his face.

"I would willingly see you die for what you've done," said Marie, staring at Conklin. "And that realization revolts me."

"Then there's nothing I can say to you," replied the CIA man, limping across the room toward the general. "Other decisions could have been made—by him and by you."

"Could they? Where was he to start? When that man tried to kill him in Marseilles? In the rue Sarrasin? When they hunted him in Zurich? When they shot at him in Paris? And all the while he didn't know why. What was he to do?"

"Come out! Goddamn it, come out!"

"He did. And when he did, you tried to kill him."

"You were there! You were with him. You had a memory."

"Assuming I knew whom to go to, would you have listened to me?"

Conklin returned her gaze. "I don't know," he answered,

breaking the contact between them and turning to Crawford. "What's happening?"

"Washington's calling me back within ten minutes."

"But what's *happening?*"

"I'm not sure you want to hear it. Federal encroachment on state and municipal law-enforcement statutes. Clearances have to be obtained."

"Jesus!"

"Look!" The army man suddenly bent down to the window. "The truck's leaving."

"Someone got through," said Conklin.

"Who?"

"I'll find out." The CIA man limped to the phone; there were scraps of paper on the table, telephone numbers written hastily. He selected one and dialed. "Give me Schumach . . . please . . . Schumach? This is Conklin, Central Intelligence. Who gave you the word?"

The dispatcher's voice on the line could be heard halfway across the room. "What word? Get off my back! We're on that job and we're going to finish it! Frankly I think you're a whacko—"

Conklin slammed down the phone. "Christ . . . oh, *Christ!*" His hand trembled as he gripped the instrument. He picked it up and dialed again, his eyes on another scrap of paper. "Petrocelli. Reclamations," he commanded. "Petrocelli? Conklin again."

"You faded out. What happened?"

"No time. Level with me. That priority invoice from Agency Controls. Who signed it?"

"What do you mean, who signed it? The top cat who always signs them. McGivern."

Conklin's face turned white. "That's what I was afraid of," he whispered, as he lowered the phone. He turned to Crawford, his head quivering as he spoke. "The order to GSA was signed by a man who retired two weeks ago."

"Carlos . . ."

"Oh, God!" screamed Marie. "The man carrying the blankets, the straps! The way he held his head, his neck. Angled to the right. It was him! When his head hurts, he favors the right. It was Jason! He went *inside.*"

Alexander Conklin turned back to the window, his eyes focused on the black enameled door across the way. It was closed.

The hand! The skin . . . the dark eyes in the thin shaft of light. *Carlos!*

Bourne whipped his head back as the razorlike edge of the blade sliced the flesh under his chin, the eruption of blood streaming across the hand that held the knife. He lashed his right foot out, catching his unseen attacker in the kneecap, then pivoted and plunged his left heel into the man's groin. Carlos spun, and again the blade came out of the darkness, now surging toward him, the line of assault directly at his stomach. Jason sprang back off the ground, crossing his wrists, slashing downward, blocking the dark arm that was an extension of the handle. He twisted his fingers inward, yanking his hands together, vicing the forearm beneath his blood-soaked neck and wrenched the arm diagonally up. The knife creased the cloth of his field jacket and once above his chest. Bourne spiraled the arm downward, twisting the wrist now in his grip, crashing his shoulder into the assassin's body, yanking again as Carlos plunged sideways off balance, his arm pulled half out of its socket.

Jason heard the clatter of the knife on the floor. He lurched toward the sound, at the same time reaching into his belt for his gun. It caught on the cloth; he rolled on the floor, but not quickly enough. The steel toe of a shoe crashed into the side of his head—his temple—and shock waves bolted through him. He rolled again, faster, faster, until he smashed into the wall; coiling upward on his knee, trying to focus through the weaving, obscure shadows in the near total darkness. The flesh of a hand was caught in the thin line of light from the window; he lunged at it, his own hands now claws, his arms battering rams. He gripped the hand, snapping it back, breaking the wrist. A scream filled the room.

A scream and the hollow, lethal cough of a gunshot. An icelike incision had been made in Bourne's upper left chest, the bullet lodged somewhere near his shoulder blade. In agony, he crouched and sprang again, pummeling the killer with a gun into the wall above a sharp-edged piece of furniture. Carlos lunged away as two more muted shots were fired wildly. Jason dove to his left, freeing his gun, leveling it at the sounds in the darkness. He fired, the explosion deafening, useless. He heard the door crash shut; the killer had raced out into the hallway.

Trying to fill his lungs with air, Bourne crawled toward

the door. As he reached it, instinct commanded him to stay at the side and smash his fist into the wood at the bottom. What followed was the core of a terrifying nightmare. There was a short burst of automatic gunfire as the paneled wood splintered, fragments flying across the room. The instant it stopped, Jason raised his own weapon and fired diagonally through the door; the burst was repeated. Bourne spun away, pressing his back against the wall; the eruption stopped and he fired again. There were now two men inches from each other, wanting above all to kill each other. *Cain is for Charlie and Delta is for Cain. Get Carlos. Trap Carlos. Kill Carlos!*

And then they were not inches from each other. Jason heard racing footsteps, then the sounds of a railing being broken as a figure lurched down the staircase. Carlos was racing below; the pig-animal wanted support; he was hurt. Bourne wiped the blood from his face, from his throat, and moved in front of what was left of the door. He pulled it open and stepped out into the narrow corridor, his gun leveled in front of him. Painfully he made his way toward the top of the dark staircase. Suddenly he heard shouts below.

"What the hell *you doin'* man? Pete! *Pete!*"

Two metallic coughs filled the air.

"Joey! *Joey!*"

A single spit was heard; bodies crashed to a floor somewhere below.

"Jesus! *Jesus*, Mother of—!"

Two metallic coughs again, followed by a guttural cry of death. A third man was killed.

What had that third man said? *Two wiseass stiffs and now four crumbballs.* The moving van was a Carlos operation! The assassin had brought two soldiers with him—the first three crumbballs from the shape-up. Three men with weapons, and he was one with a single gun. Cornered on the top floor of the brownstone. Still Carlos was inside. *Inside.* If he could get out, it would be Carlos who was cornered! If he could get out. *Out!*

There was a window at the front end of the hallway, obscured by a black shade. Jason veered toward it, stumbling, holding his neck, creasing his shoulder so to blunt the pain in his chest. He ripped the shade from its spindle; the window was small, the glass here, too, thick, prismatic blocks of purple and blue light shooting through it. It was

[522]

unbreakable, the frame riveted in place; there was no way he could smash a single pane. And then his eyes were drawn below to Seventy-first Street. The moving van was gone! Someone had to have driven it away . . . one of Carlos' soldiers! That left two. *Two* men, not three. And he was on the high ground; there were always advantages on the high ground.

Grimacing, bent partially over, Bourne made his way to the first door on the left; it was parallel to the top of the staircase. He opened it and stepped inside. From what he could see it was an ordinary bedroom: lamps, heavy furniture, pictures on the walls. He grabbed the nearest lamp, ripped the cord from the wall and carried it out to the railing. He raised it above his head and hurled it down, stepping back as metal and glass crashed below. There was another burst of gunfire, the bullets shredding the ceiling, cutting a path in the plaster. Jason screamed, letting the scream fade into a cry, the cry into a prolonged desperate wail, and then silence. He edged his way to the rear of the railing. He waited. Silence.

It happened. He could hear the slow, cautious footsteps; the killer had been on the second floor landing. The footsteps came closer, became louder; a faint shadow appeared on the dark wall. *Now.* Bourne sprang out of his recess and fired four shots in rapid succession at the figure on the staircase; a line of bullet holes and eruptions of blood appeared diagonally across the man's collar. The killer spun, roaring in anger and pain as his neck arched back and his body plummeted down the steps until it was still, sprawled faceup across the bottom three steps. In his hands was a deadly automatic field machine gun with a rod and brace for a stock.

Now. Jason ran over to the top of the staircase and raced down, holding the railing, trying to keep whatever was left of his balance. He could not waste a moment; he might not find another. If he was going to reach the second floor it was now, in the immediate aftermath of the soldier's death. And as he leaped over the dead body, Bourne knew it was a soldier; it was not Carlos. The man was tall and his skin was white, very white, his features Nordic or northern European, in no way Latin.

Jason ran into the hallway of the second floor, seeking the shadows, hugging the wall. He stopped, listening. There was a sharp scrape in the distance, brief scratch from below. He knew what he had to do now. The assassin was on the first floor. And the sound had not been deliberate; it had not been loud enough or prolonged enough to signify a trap. Carlos was injured—a smashed kneecap or a broken wrist could disorient him to the point where he might collide with a piece of furniture or brush against a wall with a weapon in his hand, briefly losing his balance as Bourne was losing his. It was what he needed to know.

Jason dropped to a crouch and crept back to the staircase, to the dead body sprawled across the steps. He had to pause for a moment; he was losing strength, too much blood. He tried to squeeze the flesh at the top of his throat and press the wound in his chest—anything to stem the bleeding. It was futile; to stay alive he had to get out of the brownstone, away from the place where Cain was born. Jason Bourne . . . there was no humor in the word association. He found his breath again, reached out and pried the automatic weapon from the dead man's hands. He was ready.

He was dying and he was ready. *Get Carlos. Trap Carlos . . . Kill Carlos!* He could not get out; he knew that. Time was not on his side. The blood would drain out of him before it happened. The end was the beginning: Cain was for Carlos and Delta was for Cain. Only one agonizing question remained: who was Delta? It did not matter. It was behind him now; soon there would be darkness, not violent but peaceful . . . freedom from that question.

And with his death Marie would be free, his love would be free. Decent men would see to it, led by a decent man in Paris whose son had been killed on rue du Bac, whose life had been destroyed by an assassin's whore. Within the next few minutes, thought Jason, silently checking the clip in the automatic weapon, he would fulfill his promise to that man, carry out the agreement he had with men he did not know. By doing both, the proof was his. Jason Bourne had died once on this day; he would die again but would take Carlos out with him. He was ready.

He lowered himself to a prone position and crept hands over elbows toward the top of the staircase. He could smell the blood beneath him, the sweet, bland odor penetrating his nostrils, informing him of a practicality. Time *was* running out. He reached the top step, pulling his legs under him, digging into his pocket for one of the road flares he had purchased at the army-navy store on Lexington Avenue. He knew now why he had felt the compulsion to buy them. He was back in the unremembered Tam Quan, forgotten except for brilliant, blinding flashes of light. The flares had reminded him of that fragment of memory; they would light up a jungle now.

He uncoiled the waxed fuse from the small round recess in the flare head, brought it to his teeth and bit through the cord, shortening the fuse to less than an inch. He reached into his other pocket and took out a plastic lighter; he pressed it against the flare, gripping both in his left hand. Then he angled the rod and the brace of the weapon into his right shoulder, shoving the curved strip of metal into the cloth of his blood-soaked field jacket; it was secure. He stretched out his legs and, snakelike, started down the final flight of steps, head below, feet above, his back scraping the wall.

He reached the midpoint of the staircase. Silence, darkness, all the lights had been extinguished . . . Lights? *Light?* Where were the rays of sunlight he had seen in that hallway only minutes ago? They had streamed through a pair of french doors at the far end of the room—that room—beyond the corridor, but he could see only darkness now. The door had been shut; the door beneath him, the only other door in that hallway, was also closed, marked by a thin shaft of light at the bottom. Carlos was making him choose. Behind which door? Or was the assassin using a better strategy? Was he in the darkness of the narrow hallway itself?

Bourne felt a stabbing jolt of pain in his shoulder blade, then an eruption of blood that drenched the flannel shirt beneath his field jacket. Another warning: there was very little time.

He braced himself against the wall, the weapon leveled at the thin posts of the railing, aimed down into the darkness of the corridor. *Now!* He pulled the trigger. The staccato explosions tore the posts apart as the railing fell, the bullets shattering the walls and the door beneath him. He released the trigger, slipping his hand under the scalding barrel, grabbing the plastic lighter with his right hand, the flare in his left. He spun the flint; the wick took fire and he put it to the short fuse. He pulled his hand back to the weapon and squeezed the trigger again, blowing away everything below. A glass chandelier crashed to a floor somewhere; singing whines of ricochets filled the darkness.

And then—*light!* Blinding light as the flare ignited, firing the jungle, lighting up the trees and the walls, the hidden paths and the mahogany corridors. The stench of death and the jungle was everywhere, and he was there.

Almanac to Delta. Almanac to Delta. Abandon, abandon!

Never. Not now. Not at the end. Cain is for Carlos and Delta is for Cain. Trap Carlos. Kill Carlos!

Bourne rose to his feet, his back pressed against the wall, the flare in his left hand, the exploding weapon in his right. He plunged down into the carpeted underbrush, kicking the door in front of him open, shattering silver frames and trophies that flew off tables and shelves into the air. Into the trees. He stopped; there was no one in that quiet, soundproof, elegant room. No one in the jungle path.

He spun around and lurched back into the hallway, puncturing the walls with a prolonged burst of gunfire. No one.

The door at the end of the narrow, dark corridor. Beyond was the room where Cain was born. Where Cain would die, but not alone.

He held his fire, shifting the flare to his right hand beneath the weapon, reaching into his pocket for the second flare. He pulled it out, and again uncoiled the fuse and brought it to his teeth, severing the cord, now millimeters from its point of contact with the gelatinous incendiary. He shoved the first flare to it; the explosion of light was so bright it pained his eyes. Awkwardly, he held both flares in his left hand and, squinting, his legs and arms losing the battle for balance, approached the door.

It was open, the narrow crack extending from top to bottom on the lock side. The assassin was accommodating, but as he looked at that door, Jason instinctively knew one thing about it that Carlos did not know. It was a part of his past, a part of the room where Cain was born. He reached down with his right hand, bracing the weapon between his forearm and his hip, and gripped the knob.

Now. He shoved the door open six inches and hurled the flares inside. A long staccato burst from a Sten gun echoed throughout the room, throughout the entire house, a thousand dead sounds forming a running chord beneath, as sprays of bullets imbedded in a lead shield backed by a steel plate in the door.

The firing stopped, a final clip expended. *Now.* Bourne

whipped his hand back to the trigger, crashed his shoulder into the door and lunged inside, firing in circles as he rolled on the floor, swinging his legs counterclockwise. Gunshots were returned wildly as Jason honed his weapon toward the source. A roar of fury burst from blindness across the room; it accompanied Bourne's realization that the drapes had been drawn, blocking out the sunlight from the french doors. Then why was there so much light . . . magnified light beyond the sizzling blindness of the flares? It was overpowering, causing explosions in his head, sharp bolts of agony at his temples.

The *screen!* The huge screen was pulled down from its bulging recess in the ceiling, drawn taut to the floor, the wide expanse of glistening silver a white-hot shield of ice-cold fire. He plunged behind the large hatch table to the protection of a copper dry bar; he rose and jammed the trigger back, in another burst—a final burst. The last clip had run out. He hurled the weapon by its rod-stock across the room at the figure in white overalls and a white silk scarf that had fallen below his face.

The *face!* He knew it! He had seen it before! Where . . . where? Was it Marseilles? Yes . . . no! Zurich? Paris? Yes *and* no! Then it struck him at that instant in the blinding, vibrating light, that the face across the room was known to many, not just him. But from where? *Where?* As so much else, he knew it and did not know it. But he *did* know it! It was only the name he could not find!

He spiraled back off his feet, behind the heavy copper dry bar. Gunshots came, two . . . three, the second bullet tearing the flesh of his left forearm. He pulled his automatic from his belt; he had three shots left. One of them had to find its mark—Carlos. There was a debt to pay in Paris, and a contract to fulfill, his love far safer with the assassin's death. He took the plastic lighter from his pocket, ignited it and held it beneath a bar rag suspended from a hook. The cloth caught fire; he grabbed it and threw it to his right, as he dove to his left. Carlos fired at the flaming rag, as Bourne spun to his knees, leveling his gun, pulling the trigger twice.

The figure buckled but did not fall. Instead, he crouched, then sprang like a white panther diagonally forward, his hands outstretched. What was he *doing?* Then Jason knew. The assassin gripped the edge of the huge silver screen, ripping it from its metal bracket in the ceiling, pulling it downward with all his weight and strength.

It floated down above Bourne, filling his vision, blocking everything else from his mind. He screamed as the shimmering silver descended over him, suddenly more frightened of it than of Carlos or of any other human being on the earth. It terrified him, infuriated him, splitting his mind in fragments; images flashed across his eyes and angry voices shouted in his ears. He aimed his gun and fired at the terrible shroud. As he slashed his hand against it wildly, pushing the rough silver cloth away, he understood. He had fired his last shot, his *last*. As a legend named Cain, Carlos knew by sight and by sound every weapon on earth; he had counted the gunshots.

The assassin loomed above him, the automatic in his hand aimed at Jason's head. "Your execution, Delta. On the day scheduled. For everything you've done."

Bourne arched his back, rolling furiously to his right; at least he would die in motion! Gunshots filled the shimmering room, hot needles slicing across his neck, piercing his legs, cutting up to his waist. Roll, *roll!*

Suddenly the gunshots stopped, and in the distance he could hear repeated sounds of hammering, the smashing of wood and steel, growing louder, more insistent. There was a final deafening crash from the dark corridor outside the library, followed by men shouting, running, and beyond them somewhere in the unseen, outside world, the insistent whine of sirens.

"In here! He's in *here!*" screamed Carlos.

It was insane! The assassin was directing the invaders directly toward him, *to* him! Reason was madness, nothing on earth made sense!

The door was crashed open by a tall man in a black overcoat; someone was with him, but Jason could not see. The mists were filling his eyes, shapes and sounds becoming obscured, blurred. He was rolling in space. Away . . . away.

But then he saw the one thing he did not want to see. Rigid shoulders that floated above a tapered waist raced out of the room and down the dimly lit corridor. *Carlos.* His screams had sprung the trap open! He had *reversed* it! In the chaos he had trapped the stalkers. He was *escaping!*

"Carlos . . ." Bourne knew he could not be heard; what emerged from his bleeding throat was a whisper. He tried again, forcing the sound from his stomach. "It's *him*. It's . . . *Carlos!*"

There was confusion, commands shouted futilely, orders swallowed in consternation. And then a figure came into focus. A man was limping toward him, a cripple who had tried to kill him in a cemetery outside of Paris. There was nothing left! Jason lurched, crawling toward the sizzling, blinding flare. He grabbed it and held it as though it were a weapon, aiming it at the killer with a cane.

"Come on! Come *on!* Closer, you bastard! I'll burn your eyes out! You think you'll kill me, you *won't!* I'll kill you! I'll burn your eyes!"

"You don't understand," said the trembling voice of the limping killer. "It's me, Delta. It's Conklin. I was wrong."

The flare singed his hands, his eyes! . . . *Madness. The explosions were all around him now, blinding, deafening, punctuated by ear-splitting screeches from the jungle that erupted with each detonation.*

The jungle! Tam Quan! The wet, hot stench was everywhere, but they had reached it! The base camp was theirs!

An explosion to his left; he could see it! High above the ground, suspended between two trees, the spikes of a bamboo cage. The figure inside was moving. He was alive! Get to him, reach him!

A cry came from his right. Breathing, coughing in the smoke, a man was limping toward the dense underbrush, a rifle in his hand. It was him, the blond hair caught in the light, a foot broken from a parachute jump. The bastard! A piece of filth who had trained with them, studied the maps with them, flown north with them . . . all the time springing a trap on them! A traitor with a radio who told the enemy exactly where to look in that impenetrable jungle that was Tam Quan.

It was Bourne! Jason Bourne. Traitor, garbage!

Get him! Don't let him reach others! Kill him! Kill Jason Bourne! He is your enemy! Fire!

He did not fall! The head that had been blown apart was still there. Coming toward him! What was happening? Madness. Tam Quan . . .

"Come with us," said the limping figure, walking out of the jungle into what remained of an elegant room. *That* room. "We're not your enemies. Come with us."

"Get *away* from me!" Bourne lunged again, now back to the fallen screen. It was his sanctuary, his shroud of death,

[529]

the blanket thrown over a man at birth, a lining for his coffin. "You are my enemy! I'll take you all! I don't care, it doesn't matter! Can't you understand!? I'm *Delta!* Cain is for Charlie and Delta is for Cain! What more do you want from me? I was and I *was* not! I am and I *am* not! Bastards, *bastards!* Come on! Closer!"

Another voice was heard, a deeper voice, calmer, less insistent. "Get her. Bring her in."

Somewhere in the distance the sirens reached a crescendo, and then they stopped. Darkness came and the waves carried Jason up to the night sky, only to hurl him down again, crashing him into an abyss of watery violence. He was entering an eternity of weightless . . . memory. An explosion filled the night sky now, a fiery diadem rose above black waters. And then he heard the words, spoken from the clouds, filling the earth.

"Jason, my love. My only love. Take my hand. Hold it. Tightly, Jason. Tightly, my darling."

Peace came with the darkness.

EPILOGUE

Brigadier General Crawford put the file folder down on the couch beside him. "I don't need this," he said to Marie St. Jacques, who sat across from him in a straightback chair. "I've gone over it and over it, trying to find out where we missed."

"You presumed where no one should," said the only other person in the hotel suite. He was Dr. Morris Panov, psychiatrist; he stood by the window, the morning sun streaming in, putting his expressionless face in shadow. "I allowed you to presume, and I'll live with it for the rest of my life."

"It's nearly two weeks now," said Marie impatiently. "I'd like specifics. I think I'm entitled to them."

"You are. It was an insanity called clearance."

"Insanity," agreed Panov.

"Protection, also," added Crawford. "I subscribe to that part. It has to continue for a very long time."

"Protection?" Marie frowned.

"We'll get to it," said the general, glancing at Panov. "From everyone's point of view, it's vital. I trust we all accept that."

"Please! Jason—who is he?"

"His name is David Webb. He was a career foreign service officer, a specialist in Far Eastern affairs, until his separation from the government five years ago."

"Separation?"

"Resignation by mutual agreement. His work in Medusa precluded any sustained career in the State Department. 'Delta' was infamous and too many knew he was Webb. Such men are rarely welcome at the diplomatic conference tables. I'm not sure they should be. Visceral wounds are reopened too easily with their presence."

"He was everything they say? In Medusa?"

"Yes. I was there. He was everything they say."

"It's hard to believe," said Marie.

"He'd lost something very special to him and couldn't come to grips with it. He could only strike out."

"What was that?"

"His family. His wife was a Thai; they had two children, a boy and a girl. He was stationed in Phnom Penh, his house on the outskirts, near the Mekong River. One Sunday afternoon while his wife and children were down at their dock, a stray aircraft circled and dove, dropping two bombs and strafing the area. By the time he reached the river the dock was blown away, his wife and children floating in the water, their bodies riddled."

"Oh, God," whispered Marie. "Whom did the plane belong to?"

"It was never identified. Hanoi disclaimed it; Saigon said it wasn't ours. Remember, Cambodia was neutral; no one wanted to be responsible. Webb had to strike out; he headed for Saigon and trained for Medusa. He brought a specialist's intellect to a very brutal operation. He became Delta."

"Was that when he met d'Anjou?"

"Later on, yes. Delta was notorious by then. North Vietnamese Intelligence had put an extraordinary price on his head, and it's no secret that among our own people a number hoped they'd succeed. Then Hanoi found out that Webb's younger brother was an army officer in Saigon, and having studied Delta—knowing the brothers were close—decided to mount a trap; they had nothing to lose. They kidnapped Lieutenant Gordon Webb and took him north, sending back a Cong informant with word that he was being held in the Tam Quan sector. Delta bit; along with the informer—a double agent—he formed a team of Medusans who knew the area and picked a night when no aircraft should have left the ground to fly north. D'Anjou was in the unit. So was another man Webb didn't know about; a white man who'd been bought by Hanoi, an expert in communications who could assemble the electronic components of a high-frequency radio in the dark. Which is exactly what he did, betraying the unit's position. Webb broke through the trap and found his brother. He also found the double agent and the white man. The Vietnamese escaped in the jungle; the white man didn't. Delta executed him on the spot."

"And that man?" Marie's eyes were riveted on Crawford.

"Jason Bourne. A Medusan from Sydney, Australia; a runner of guns, narcotics and slaves throughout all Southeast Asia; a violent man with a criminal record who was nevertheless highly effective—if the price were high enough. It was in Medusa's interests to bury the circumstances of his death; he became an MIA from a specialized unit. Years later, when Treadstone was being formed and Webb called back, it was Webb himself who took the name of Bourne. It fit the requirements of authenticity, traceability. He took the name of the man who'd betrayed him, the man he had killed in Tam Quan."

"Where was he when he was called back for Treadstone?" asked Marie. "What was he doing?"

"Teaching in a small college in New Hampshire. Living an isolated life, some said destructive. For him." Crawford picked up the file folder. "Those are the essential facts, Miss St. Jacques. Other areas will be covered by Dr. Panov, who's made it clear that my presence is not required. There is, however, one remaining detail which must be thoroughly understood. It's a direct order from the White House."

"The protection," said Marie, her words a statement.

"Yes. Wherever he goes, regardless of the identity he assumes or the success of his cover, he'll be guarded around the clock. For as long as it takes—even if it never happens."

"Please explain that."

"He's the only man alive who's ever seen Carlos. *As* Carlos. He knows his identity, but it's locked away in his mind, part of an unremembered past. We understand from what he says that Carlos is someone known to many people—a visible figure in a government somewhere, or in the media, or international banking or society. It fits with a prevalent theory. The point is one day that identity may come into focus for Webb. We realize you've had several discussions with Dr. Panov. I believe he'll confirm what I've said."

Marie turned to the psychiatrist. "Is it true, Mo?"

"It's possible," said Panov.

Crawford left and Marie poured coffee for the two of them. Panov went to the couch where the brigadier had been sitting.

"It's still warm," he said, smiling. "Crawford was sweating right down to his famous backsides. He has every right to, they all do."

"What's going to happen?"

"Nothing. Absolutely nothing until I tell them they can go ahead. And that may not be for months, a couple of years for all I know. Not until he's ready."

"For what?"

"The questions. And photographs—volumes of them. They're compiling a photographic encyclopedia based on the loose description he gave them. Don't get me wrong; one day he'll have to begin. He'll want to; we'll all want him to. Carlos has to be caught, and it's not my intention to blackmail them into doing nothing. Too many people have given too much; *he's* given too much. But right now he comes first. His head comes first."

"That's what I mean. What's going to happen to him?"

Panov put down his coffee. "I'm not sure yet. I've too much respect for the human mind to deal you chicken soup psychology; there's too damn much of it floating around in the wrong hands. I've been in on all the conferences—I insisted upon that—and I've talked to the other shrinks and the neurosurgeons. It's true we can go in with a knife and reach the storm centers, reduce the anxieties, bring a kind of peace to him. Even bring him back to what he was, perhaps. But it's not the kind of peace he wants . . . and there's a far more dangerous risk. We might wipe away too much, take away the things he has found—will *continue* to find. With care. With time."

"Time?"

"I believe it, yes. Because the pattern's been established. There's growth, the pain of recognition and the excitement of discovery. Does that tell you something?"

[534]

Marie looked into Panov's dark, weary eyes; there was a light in them. "All of us," she said.

"That's right. In a way, he's a functioning microcosm of us all. I mean, we're all trying to find out who the hell we are, aren't we?"

Marie went to the front window in the cottage on the waterfront, with the rising dunes behind it, the fenced-off grounds surrounding it. And guards. Every fifty feet a man with a gun. She could see him several hundred yards down the beach; he was scaling shells over the water, watching them bounce across the waves that gently lapped into the shore. The weeks had been good to him, for him. His body was scarred but whole again, firm again. The nightmares were still there, and moments of anguish kept coming back during the daylight hours, but somehow it was all less terrifying. He was beginning to cope; he was beginning to laugh again. Panov had been right. Things were happening to him; images were becoming clearer, meaning found where there had been no meaning before.

Something had happened *now!* Oh, *God*, what *was* it? He had thrown himself into the water and was thrashing around, shouting. Then, suddenly, he sprang out, leaping over the waves onto the beach. In the distance, by the barbed-wire fence, a guard spun around, a rifle whipped up under an arm, a hand-held radio pulled from a belt.

He began racing across the wet sand toward the house, his body lurching, swaying, his feet digging furiously into the soft surface, sending up sprays of water and sand behind him. *What was it?*

Marie froze, prepared for the moment they knew might come one day, prepared for the sound of gunfire.

He burst through the door, chest heaving, gasping for breath. He stared at her, his eyes as clear as she had ever seen them. He spoke softly, so softly she could barely hear him. But she did hear him.

"My name is David . . ."

She walked slowly toward him.

"Hello, David," she said.

LUDLUM
ON
LUDLUM

Few writers have skyrocketed to popularity with the speed of Robert Ludlum, with each succeeding thriller becoming a bigger bestseller. The key to his success may lie in John Leonard's comment in *The New York Times,* "Mr. Ludlum stuffs more surprises into his novels than any other six-pack of thriller writers combined."

Some people claim Ludlum has secret sources for information found in his stories. In one, an early book, a key theme was CIA involvement in domestic surveillance. At that time the subject shocked many people. Later, of course, this fact proved to be correct. Other people suspect Ludlum was an agent himself during the years prior to his career as a novelist. Not true. For close to twenty years he was in show business—as an actor, producer, and as the "voice" of dozens of television commercials for products ranging from Tiparillos to Tuna Helper.

During his "voice" period, Ludlum's wife crowned him "King of the Toilet Bowls." As he tells it, "there was this product called Plunge. All I had to do was read three words: Plunge works fast. In spite of my off-hand delivery, they used my three words in over one hundred different commercials. The money from this put one of my children through two years of college."

Although none of Ludlum's novels draws on his show business background for subject matter, they all reflect techniques he learned in the theater. Ludlum says, "the theater man knows that he must involve the audience. He understands structure more than anyone else—the logical evolving of one event into another event without losing the audience's attention. Because if you lose their interest, you're closing Saturday night."

Ludlum admits, "I write primarily as an entertainer. But I find that whether you're writing comically or dramatically, you write from a point of view of something that disturbs or outrages you. And that's what I do. I admit to being outraged—mostly by the abuse of power by the fanatics. The extremes bother me, right or left." Yet he adds, "I disapprove of violence, that's why I show pain for what it is. When my characters get hit, they hurt. They don't jump back into action like John Wayne."

All of this—and more—can be found in the published work of Robert Ludlum. Since his first novel, *THE SCARLATTI INHERITANCE,* he has amassed an enviable record of success: *THE OSTERMAN WEEKEND, THE MATLOCK PAPERS, THE RHINEMANN EXCHANGE, THE GEMINI CONTENDERS;* more recently, *THE CHANCELLOR MANUSCRIPT, THE HOLCROFT COVENANT, THE MATARESE CIRCLE* and *THE BOURNE IDENTITY.*

BOOKS AROUND THE WORLD

For your reading pleasure Bantam Books has the following international bestsellers available in local English language bookstores:

THE DOGS OF WAR by Frederick Forsyth

PASSAGES by Gail Sheehy

SLEEPING MURDER by Agatha Christie

FUTURE SHOCK by Alvin Toffler

RAISE THE TITANTIC by Clive Cussler

THE NEW SPANISH-ENGLISH, ENGLISH-SPANISH DICTIONARY by Edwin Williams

THE OLD MAN AND THE SEA by Ernest Hemingway

STORM WARNING by Jack Higgins

TRINITY by Leon Uris

LIFE AFTER LIFE by Raymond A. Moody

THE CHANCELLOR MANUSCRIPT by Robert Ludlum

THE HONOURABLE SCHOOLBOY by John Le Carré

JAWS 2 by Hank Searles

THE BOOK OF LISTS by D. Wallechinsky, I. & A. Wallace

GUINNESS BOOK OF WORLD RECORDS by N. McWhirter

DELTA OF VENUS by Anaïs Nin

If you are unable to obtain these Bantam books, fill out the form below and mail it to us with a self-addressed envelope. We will return it to you with the name and address of the nearest place where you can buy, or obtain information about, Bantam books.

The above books are not available in the Britis' Commonwealth.